ARCHITECTURE THROUGH THE AGES

ARCHITECTURE THROUGH THE AGES

BY *Talbot Hamlin* PROFESSOR OF ARCHITECTURE, COLUMBIA UNIVERSITY. FELLOW, AMERICAN INSTITUTE OF ARCHITECTS

To study something of great age until one grows familiar with it and almost to live in its time, is not merely to satisfy a curiosity or to establish aimless truths: it is rather to fulfill a function whose appetite has always rendered History a necessity. By the recovery of the Past, stuff and being are added to us; our lives, which, lived in the present only, are a film or surface, take on body—are lifted into one dimension more.

—HILAIRE BELLOC, *"The Old Road."*

G·P·PUTNAM'S SONS   NEW YORK

Sixth Impression of Revised Edition

TO JESSICA, MY WIFE

whose intelligent, painstaking, and devoted assistance

has made the preparation of this book a pleasure

and rendered its publication possible

Designed by Robert Josephy

INTRODUCTION

IN THE thirteen years since the first edition of *Architecture Through the Ages* appeared there have been striking developments not only in architectural design but also in historical knowledge.

During this period a second world war of unprecedented destructiveness has swept over the globe; its sequels are still with us in a deep schism between great numbers of peoples—a schism that almost for the first time since the Reformation has produced an effective barrier against the free intercourse of peoples and the free exchange of knowledge and cultural achievement. In addition, the war has left a heritage of economic difficulty and confusion which hampers the creation of a humane environment and necessarily funnels all too large a proportion of national expenditures into those engines of war which all countries euphemistically call defense measures. And it has left in its wake, as well, tasks of urban reconstruction almost insoluble.

Yet the effect of the war has not been altogether negative. The world-wide economic stringency has forced a new examination of ways of economical building, with a consequent revolutionary development of new kinds of steel and concrete construction. It has forced the consideration of architectural uses of new materials and a new attack on the problems of planning. It has shown with increased clarity the need of large-scale city, regional, and national planning and has added impulse to the already existing trends toward the decentralization of industry and of urban populations. And, if on the one hand it has produced a nostalgia for the quieter earlier times, on the other hand it has acted as a great divider between "past" and "present," so that people as a whole have been more willing to look at the new with sympathy and to adopt it with understanding. Manifestly these results have not been uniformly true of all the countries of the Western world, but in one country or another they may all be seen working as creative impulses.

Moreover, during this period the aims of architecture in the broad sense became gradually clearer. It was more and more realized not only that the creation of an adequate architectural environment for the post-war world could not result from the blanket adoption of any single a priori theory or style, but also that in it as a whole there must be as a basis a broad understanding of the rich diversity of individuals and of cultures. All of this has suggested a complete rewriting of the final chapter of the present book and an attempt to illustrate some, at least, of the varied answers modern architects have made to this basic problem.

In architectural history, too, there have been impressive developments. Widely distributed archaeological effort has brought a flood of new evidence, necessitating occasional drastic reassessments; in some fields interpretations of even widely known facts have radically changed. Any adequate architectural history, therefore, must change with the new facts, must alter its critical comment in the light of the new interpretations. Thus, with growing factual knowledge on the one hand and continual shifts of interpretation and of emphasis on the other, no history can remain a purely static statement; our histories reveal us to ourselves just as they reveal to us the forces that helped make us what we are. Architectural history is particularly revealing in this respect—for architects can build only what their clients permit them to build—and, as evaluations of past cultures shift, evaluations of their architectures will shift too. In the text of this newly revised edition an attempt has been made to indicate at least some of the recently discovered facts and to take account of at least the major changes of interpretation.

These major changes have occurred especially in four general fields: ancient classic architecture; the architecture of the Early Christian and Byzantine periods; the architecture of the early and middle nineteenth century; and so-called modern architecture. Typical of the new discoveries in the first field, with regard to Greece, are the almost complete excavation of the Athenian agora and further discoveries of pre-Hellenic work in Grecian lands; in the broad field of Roman building, further excavation of Ostia has revealed a kind of freely designed architecture so different from the usual stereotype "Roman architecture" as to make a new history of the entire Roman development drastically necessary. In the Early Christian and Byzantine fields, such discoveries as that of the little church of Castelseprio have given rise to fundamental revisions in the dating of many monuments and in the concept of the persistence of "classic" ideas and forms into the Middle Ages. In the field of nineteenth-century architecture there has been a flood of valuable research, especially in England and the United States. Changes in the last field, "modern" architecture, as already noted are indicated in the new final chapter; for the others, revisions in the text have been made to bring out at least the salient points.

The post-war period has also produced a flood of valuable publications describing these new discoveries and illuminating these new evaluations and interpretations. Much of this writing still exists in periodicals only, and for any complete and detailed study recourse must again and again be had to learned and art periodicals not too often or too widely available. But there have been numbers of important books as well; a selection is listed below:

Blake, Marion Elizabeth, *Ancient Roman Construction in Italy ... to Augustus* (Washington: Carnegie Institution, 1947). A pioneer work classifying and dating Roman building materials and techniques.

Braun, Hugh, *An Introduction to English Medieval Architecture* (London: Faber & Faber [c1951]). A modern interpretation of English Gothic.

Cresswell, Keppel Archibald Cameron, *The Muslim Architecture of Egypt* (Oxford: Clarendon Press, 1952—). An authoritative and carefully documented primary source in an important field.

Dinsmoor, William Bell, *The Architecture of Ancient Greece ...* revised and enlarged edition (London and New York: Batsford, 1950). A magnificent and scholarly summation of present-day knowledge, based on meticulous research and close personal acquaintance with the monuments.

Giedion, Sigfried, *Mechanization Takes Command* (New York: Oxford University Press, 1948). An important historical study of the impact of industry on human beings and its results in design.

Gloag, John, and Derek Bridgwater, *A History of Cast Iron in Architecture* (London: G. Allen Unwin [c1948]). A first attempt at a complete study of its field, devoted chiefly, however, to British developments.

Hautecoeur, Louis, *Histoire de l'architecture classique en France*, Vols. I-IV (Paris: Picard, 1943-52). A lavishly factual compendium, well illustrated and thoroughly documented.

Kaufmann, Emil, *Three Revolutionary Architects: Boullée, Ledoux, and Lequeu* (Philadelphia: American Philosophical Society, 1952). A new interpretation of the rationalist, poetic, and classic-revival manifestations of architecture in a period of change.

Lavedan, Pierre, *Histoire de l'urbanisme,* three vols. (Paris: Laurens, 1926-52). A valuable contribution to the field of city planning, exploring several new approaches.

Morrison, Hugh Sinclair, *Early American Architecture ...* (New York: Oxford University Press, 1952). The best and the only comprehensive history of American Colonial architecture, remarkably complete and authoritative.

Salzman, Louis Francis, *Building in England, down to 1540 ...* (Oxford: Clarendon Press, 1952). An interesting history of the development of English construction techniques.

Smith, Earl Baldwin, *The Dome; a Study in the History of Ideas* (Princeton: Princeton University Press, 1950). A history from the standpoint of symbolism, largely neglecting technical aspects.

Summerson, John N., *Georgian London* (London: Pleiades Books, 1945; New York: Scribner's, 1946). The best local architectural history yet written, broad in scope and fascinating in its implications.

Swift, Emerson H., *Roman Sources of Christian Art* (New York: Columbia University Press, 1951). An important and original study aimed at showing the great contributions made by Roman architecture and art to later developments.

Wittkower, Rudolf, *Architectural Principles in the Age of Humanism* (London: Warburg Institute, University of London, 1949). Renaissance architecture evaluated from the symbolic viewpoint as an expression of the harmony of the universe.

Wüsten, Ernst, *Die Architektur des Manierismus in England* (Leipzig: Seemann [1951]). A fresh consideration of a little-treated subject—the vivid architecture of late Tudor and Jacobean times.

Zevi, Bruno, *Storia dell'architettura moderna* ([Torino:] Einaudi, 1950). A pioneer attempt at a comprehensive history of the modern movement in architecture, with special emphasis on the "organic architecture" concept.

For help in the preparation of this revised edition I must express my indebtedness to many from whose advice and conversation I have gathered much of value. Especially I wish to thank Dean Leopold Arnaud and Professors William Bell Dinsmoor, Julius Held, Marion Lawrence, Meyer Schapiro, Emerson Swift, and James Van Derpool of Columbia University, Professor Turpin Bannister of the University of Illinois, Dr. Richard Ettinghausen, editor of *Ars Islamica,* Dr. Emil Kaufmann, Mr. Eric Mendelsohn, Dr. Myron Bement Smith, and Mr. Frank Lloyd Wright. I must also express my gratitude for unfailing assistance to Dr. Adolf Placzek and the staffs of the Avery Library and the Ware Library of Columbia University, to the staffs of the Library of Congress and the Museum of Modern Art, and to the American Swedish News Exchange and the British Information Services. And I wish to note here my deep appreciation of the editorial advice (in addition to revision of the earlier index) and much other assistance from my wife, Jessica Hamlin.

TALBOT HAMLIN

Columbia University

CONTENTS

ILLUSTRATIONS

*All photographs not otherwise credited are from the collections of the
Avery and Ware Libraries of Columbia University.*

Following page 28

Following page 268

Following page 652

TEXT FIGURES

FOREWORD

TO ATTEMPT a listing of all the scholars to whom I am indebted for so much that has gone into this book would be to set myself an impossible task. It would mean discovering and analyzing all the sources of whatever knowledge may have entered these pages. Any writer of a generalized history naturally draws upon the varied reading and study of years, whether casual or purposeful; and to pick out from this mosaic these particular pieces which are most necessary to form its peculiar color and pattern is only perhaps to destroy the pattern itself. Yet, beyond those books and those special helpers I am listing below, because their contribution was definite and direct, it seems only just to add as well the names of a few books, especially those dealing with the background material which is outside of my own specialized interests, on which I have drawn heavily and to the inspiration of which I owe so much. It is particularly necessary, I believe, in a work of this nature on architecture; for if architecture is part and parcel of living—as closely bound up with it and as integral a part of it both as expression and as inspiration as is, for instance, religion—then the so-called background material must have a part as important as, or perhaps even greater than, that which belongs to the technical architectural works themselves. A listing of a few of these works not only serves to set down my gratitude to them but also should form an introduction to a vast store of fascinating material into which it might pay the interested reader of this book to delve further. Of course the most valuable sources for the life of a period must be the works produced in that period—not merely the famous literary masterpieces but, frequently even more enlightening, some of the less known or less read yet still available works, such as Baldassare Castiglione's *Il Cortegiano,* or, for an earlier period, some of the minor poets of the classic era and the satirists like Lucian or Petronius. Nevertheless, the secondary, interpretive works have their own importance, especially in those fields where the original source material is scarcer in amount or more difficult to obtain—fields such as the early Middle Ages—or, on the other hand, those in which the amount of available material is unwieldy through its size, as in the case of the Nineteenth Century.

These background historical works, then, are especially the following, all available in English: First of all, Oswald Spengler's *Decline of the West,* translated by Charles Francis Atkinson, New York, A. A. Knopf, 1934, a monumental attempt to give form to the whole flux of human endeavor, often biased and incorrect but stimulating, exciting, and full of many passages of acute insight; it is particularly interesting because of its correlation of art and civilization. The second is a somewhat similar attempt, more detailed and intensive, to apply the same method to a more limited period, that which we know as the Renaissance and Baroque; it is Egon Friedell's *A Cultural History of the Modern Age, the Crisis of the European Soul from the Black Death to the World War,* translated by Charles Francis Atkinson, 3 vols., New York, A. A. Knopf, 1930-32. For the earlier periods in Europe I have been especially interested in and affected by Alfons Dopsch's *The Economic and Social Foundations of European Civilization,* London, Kegan Paul, Trench, Trubner, 1937, a careful study of the persistence of Roman influence in medieval culture— a subject still deeply controversial. For the other side of this question, which attempts to minimize the contributions of Rome, Henri Pirenne's *Medieval Cities,* translated by Frank D. Halsey, Princeton University Press, 1925, is an excellent summary.

Helen Waddell's *The Wandering Scholars,* New York, Henry Holt & Co., 7th Edition Revised, 1934, covers the same ground from the point of view of poetry and writing generally. It is an admirable introduction to the medieval mind and to one little-remembered side of early medieval life. Important also is all the monumental work of G. G. Coulton, especially his *Art and the Reformation,* now tragically and unbelievably out of print, Oxford, B. Blackwell, 1928. Many of his more detailed studies have been excellently digested and recreated in his superb book, *Medieval Panorama, the English Scene from Conquest to Reformation,* New York, The Macmillan Company, Cambridge, England, The University Press, 1938. Other illuminating works on the origins of religious architecture in medieval Europe are Sartell Prentice's *The Heritage of the Cathedral,* New York, William Morrow, 1936, and *The Voices of the Cathedral,* New York, William Morrow, 1938.

Jakob Burckhardt's *The Civilization of the Renaissance in Italy,* translated by S. G. C. Middlemore, Vienna, The Phaidon Press, London,

G. Allen & Unwin, Ltd., 1937, is an invaluable introduction to Renaissance ways of feeling. It should, of course, be complemented by contemporary works, especially the captivating *Memoirs* of Benvenuto Cellini and Vasari's *The Lives of the Painters, Sculptors, and Architects,* both of which are obtainable in several good translations.

For the more modern periods, and especially for the impact of science and invention upon human life, Lewis Mumford's *Technics and Civilization,* New York, Harcourt, Brace & Co., 1934, is an indispensable contribution. The same author's *The Culture of Cities,* New York, Harcourt, Brace & Co., 1938, applies the conclusions of the earlier book more especially to the problems of city creation and forms a salutary criticism and analysis of much in city life that is today taken for granted. Gilbert Seldes's *The Stammering Century,* New York, The John Day Company, 1928, a book too little known, is important as showing the other side of nineteenth-century development—the side one might label both spiritual and idealistic. It reveals the dreams, often fantastic enough, of the early nineteenth century, as Mumford attempts to reveal its deeds. Especially interesting is the article on Noyes, which shows but one example of many of the Utopian concepts of the period that had important architectural effects.

For the problem of architecture today, in addition to the works which will be mentioned later, the following should prove valuable: Le Corbusier's *Towards a New Architecture,* translated from the thirteenth French edition by Frederick Etchells, New York, Payson & Clarke, Ltd., n. d., the first popular trumpet blast of propaganda for the new style; Sheldon Cheney's *The New World Architecture,* New York, Longmans, Green and Company, 1930; Henry-Russell Hitchcock Jr.'s *Modern Architecture, Romanticism and Reintegration,* New York, Payson and Clarke, 1929, the best attempt thus far at a critical history of the building of our own time; Bruno Taut's *Modern Architecture,* London, The Studio, 1929, a sane presentation of the ideals of architecture today; N. Pevsner's *The Pioneers of the Modern Movement, from William Morris to Walter Gropius,* London, Faber and Faber, n. d., interesting for its historical sidelights; Curt Behrendt's *Modern Building, its Nature, Problems and Forms,* New York, Harcourt, Brace and Co., 1937; and two books by Frank Lloyd Wright—the Princeton lectures published under the title *Modern Architecture,* Princeton, N. J., Princeton University Press, 1931, and *An Autobiography,* London, New York, Toronto, Longmans, Green and Company, 1932.

I owe special gratitude to many people who have helped in the completion of this book: First, to the staffs of the Avery, Fine Arts, and Ware Libraries of Columbia University for unending assistance in many ways, and to the Ware Library for the use of many photographs from its collection; to Dean Leopold Arnaud and the staff of the School of Architecture of Columbia University for continued co-operation, and to its students in my courses whose reports and questions have brought new lights on many matters. I wish here to set down my appreciation of the help received from Professor Kenneth Conant of Harvard University for assistance in obtaining illustrations, and to The Fogg Museum of Art, at Harvard, for permission to use some of its photographs. I must also thank Mr. John Coolidge for the photographs of New England industrial villages; Mr. Carl Feiss, city planner and architect of Washington, D.C., for the loan of many photographs of Spain and Mexico; Professor I. Carrington Goodrich, Columbia University, for translating Chinese references; Professor Henry-Russell Hitchcock Jr., of the Smith College Museum, Northampton, Mass., for photographs of nineteenth-century America; Mr. Italo William Ricciuti for photographs of New Orleans; Mr. Myron Bement Smith, at the Library of Congress, Washington, for his kindness in allowing me to use three of his superb copyrighted photographs of Persian architecture; Dr. Ryusaku Tsunoda, of Columbia University, for assistance in choosing Japanese illustrations; the late Sir Raymond Unwin, for permission to use his plan of a garden city and satellite towns; and Professor Everard Upjohn, Columbia University, for permission to reproduce the original preliminary rendering of Trinity Church made by his great-grandfather, Richard Upjohn.

Also I wish to acknowledge my deep indebtedness to many museums and learned societies, especially to the American Geographical Society for permission to reproduce the photograph of Chan Chan; to the photograph department of The Metropolitan Museum of Art and to the Museum itself for permission to use many photographs; to The Museum of the American Indian, Heye Foundation, for photographs of Indian dwellings; to Mr. John McAndrew and the architectural department of The Museum of Modern Art for the use of many photographs of recent buildings; and to the Museum of the University of Pennsylvania for permission to reproduce the restoration of the shrine at Ur.

To illustrate any work of this nature one must pillage the published work of the past and the present unmercifully. Many of the works from which illustrations have been chosen are old and no longer covered by copyright, but it would seem ungrateful to pass them over without notice; for my debt to their authors and publishers is great, though many are centuries gone, and to set down here their names seems only their just due. These works include:

Count Melchior de Vogüé: *Syrie centrale, Architecture civile et religieuse,* Paris, Noblet and Baudry, 1865. E. Viollet-le-Duc: *Dictionaire raisonné de l'architecture française du XIme. au XVIme. siècles,* Paris, Morel, 1861-1875. P. Letarouilly: *Édifices de Rome moderne,* Paris, Lamoureux, 1840. J. Fergusson: *A History of Indian and Eastern Architecture,* London, John Murray, 1899. J. Marot: *Le magnifique chasteau de Richelieu,* Paris, 16—. F. Cuvilliés: *École d'architecture bavaroise,* Paris and Munich, *circa* 1770. J. C. Krafft and Thiollet: *Choix des plus jolies maisons de Paris et des environs,* Paris, Morel, *circa* 1835. Sieur de Neufforge: *Recueil élémentaire d'architecture,* Paris, 1767-68. *The Works in Architecture of Robert and James Adam,* London, 1773-1822. C. Percier and P. L. Fontaine: *Recueil de décorations interieures,* Paris, 1801. C. F. Schinkel: *Sammlung architektonischer Entwürfe,* Berlin, 1840. J. Soane: *Designs for Public and Private Buildings,* London, Priestley and Weale, 1826. Asher Benjamin: *The American Builder's Companion; or, A New System of Architecture,* Boston, 1806. M. Lafever: *The Modern Builders' Guide,* New York, Sleight, Collins, and Hannay, 1833. G. Robins: *Catalogue of the Classic Contents of Strawberry Hill, Collected by Horace Walpole,* London, 1842. Richard Upjohn: *Upjohn's Rural Architecture,* New York, G. P. Putnam, 1852. C. Vaux: *Villas and Cottages,* New York, Harper and Brothers, 1864. Robert Owen: A broadside of 1817.

The list of works of more recent date which I have used is long. For convenience I have arranged it in accordance with the order in which the material appears. First of all, I am grateful to Hilaire Belloc and Constable & Co., London, for permission to use the quotation from *The Old Road* on my title page. I am also indebted to the following authors and publishers:

For figure 1, to Leo Frobenius and Oskar Beck, Munich, for two illustrations in *Das unbekannte Afrika,* 1923.

For figure 3, to Chapman and Hall, Ltd., London, for two illustrations from G. Perrot and C. Chipiez: *A History of Art in Sardinia and Judaea, Syria and Asia Minor,* 1890.

For figure 4, to Hans Reinerth and the Curt Kabitsch Verlag, Leipzig, for an illustration from Hans Reinerth: *Haus und Hof in nordischen Raum,* 1937.

For figure 5, to E. Baldwin Smith and the Appleton-Century Company, New York, for illustrations from E. Baldwin Smith: *Egyptian Architecture as Cultural Expression,* 1938.

For figure 6, to Chapman and Hall, Ltd., London, for an illustration from Perrot and Chipiez: *A History of Art in Ancient Egypt,* 1887.

For figure 7, to Longmans, Green and Company, London, for an illustration from F. M. Simpson: *A History of Architectural Development,* Vol. I, 1905.

For figure 8, to A. E. Richardson and H. C. Corfiato and the English Universities Press, London, for an illustration from Richardson and Corfiato: *The Art of Architecture,* 1938.

For figures 9 and 10, to Seton Lloyd and Peter Davies, Ltd., London, for an illustration from Lloyd: *Mesopotamia, Excavations on Sumerian Sites,* 1936.

For figure 11, to O. Puchstein and the J. C. Hinrichs Verlag, Leipzig, for an illustration from Puchstein: *Boghasköi, die Bauwerke,* 1912.

For figure 12, to W. Andrae and the J. C. Hinrichs Verlag, Leipzig, for an illustration from Andrae: *Das wiederstandene Assur,* 1938.

For figure 13, to Longmans, Green and Company, London, for an illustration from F. M. Simpson: *A History of Architectural Development,* Vol. I, 1905.

For figure 14, to John Murray, London, for an illustration from J. Fergusson: *Rude Stone Monuments,* 1872.

For figure 15, to Sir Arthur Evans and The Macmillan Company, London, for an illustration from Evans: *The Palace of Minos . . . at Knossos,* Vol. II, Part 2, 1928.

For figures 16, 17, 18, to Alfred Knopf, New York, and George Routledge and Sons, London, for illustrations from G. Glotz: *The Aegean Civilization,* 1925.

For figure 19, to D. S. Robertson and the Cambridge University Press, for an illustration from Robertson: *A Handbook of Greek and Roman Architecture,* 1929.

For figure 20, to Hachette & Cie., Paris, for an illustration from Perrot and Chipiez: *Histoire de l'art dans l'antiquité,* Tome VI, 1894.

For figures 21 and 23, to The Museum of the American Indian, Heye Foundation, New York, for the photographs from which the drawings were made.

For figure 22, to Professor Ralph Linton and the *American Anthropologist,* for an illustration from Vol. 21, 1919.

For figure 24, to the author and publishers of G. O. Totten: *Maya Architecture,* Washington, 1926, for the Catherwood drawings published there.

For figure 27, to Longmans, Green and Company, London, for an illustration from F. M. Simpson: *A History of Architectural Development,* Vol. I, 1905.

For figures 28 and 29, to M. Schede and Walter de Gruyter, Berlin and Leipzig, for illustrations from Schede: *Die Ruinen von Priene,* 1934.

For figure 31, to the Archæological Institute of America, Cambridge, Mass., for an illustration from F. H. Bacon: *Investigations at Assos,* 1902.

For figure 32, to D. M. Robinson and J. W. Graham and the Johns Hopkins Press, Baltimore, and to M. Schede and Walter de Gruyter, Berlin and Leipzig, for illustrations from Robinson and Graham: *Excavations at Olynthus,* Part 8, *the Hellenic House;* and from Schede: *Die Ruinen von Priene,* 1934.

For figure 33, to J. Durm and Diehl, Darmstadt, for an illustration from Durm: *Die Baukunst der Etrusker und Römer,* Vol. II, Part 2 of the *Handbuch der Architektur,* 1905.

For figure 34, to The Macmillan Company, New York and London, for an illustration from A. Mau, translated by F. W. Kelsey: *Pompeii, its Life and Art,* 1902.

For figure 35, to G. Calza and Hoepli, Milan, for an illustration from Calza in *Monumenti Antichi,* the Reale Accademia dei Lincei, Vol. 23, 1916.

For figure 37, to the Houghton Mifflin Company, Boston, for an illustration from R. Lanciani: *Ancient Rome in the Light of Recent Excavations,* 1889.

For figure 38, to C. Weichardt and K. F. Koehler, Leipzig, for an illustration from Weichardt: *Pompeii vor der Zerstoerung.*

For figure 39, to Sir Bannister Fletcher, Charles Scribner's Sons, New York, and B. T. Batsford, Ltd., London, for an illustration from Fletcher: *A History of Architecture on the Comparative Method,* 1929.

For figure 40, to R. de Maeyer, de Sikkel, Antwerp, and M. Nijhoff, The Hague, for two illustrations from de Maeyer: *Romeinsche Villa's in België,* 1937.

For figure 41, to D. Krencker and Zschietzschmann and the Archäologisches Institut des Deutschen Reiches, Berlin, for an illustration from Krencker and Zschietszschmann: *Römische Tempel in Syrien,* Vol. 5 of the *Denkmäler antiker Architektur.*

For figure 42, to The Macmillan Company, New York and London, for an illustration from R. Sturgis: *European Architecture,* 1896.

For figures 43 and 44, to M. S. Briggs and the Clarendon Press, Oxford, for three illustrations from Briggs: *Muhammadan Architecture in Egypt and Syria,* 1924.

For figure 45, to H. Saladin and Alphonse Picard, Paris, for the plan by Coste, reproduced from Saladin: *L'Architecture,* Vol. 2 of the *Manuel d'art musulman,* 1907.

For figure 46, to the Architectural Book Publishing Company, New York, for the drawing by B. G. Goodhue, from Goodhue: *A Book of Architectural and Decorative Drawings,* 1924.

For figures 48 and 50, to Baumgärtner, Leipzig, for four illustrations from K. G. Stephani: *Der älteste Deutsche Wohnbau und seine Einrichtung,* 1902-03.

For figure 50 to K. Schuchhardt and the Akademische Verlags Gesellschaft Athenion, Potsdam, for an illustration from Schuchhardt: *Die Burg im Wandel der Weltgeschichte,* 1931.

For figure 52, to Charles Scribner's Sons, New York, for an illustration from my *Enjoyment of Architecture,* 1920.

For figure 53, to Longmans, Green and Company, London, for two illustrations from F. M. Simpson: *A History of Architectural Development,* Vol. I, 1905.

For figure 54, to E. Lundberg and the Akademisk Avhandlung Stockholm, for an illustration from Lundberg: *Herremannens Bostad,* 1935.

For figures 58, 61, 65, 66, 70, to Longmans, Green and Company, London, for illustrations from F. M. Simpson: *A History of Architectural Development,* Vol. II, 1913.

For figure 59, to Mrs. Francis Bond, Humphrey Milford, and the Oxford University Press for an illustration from F. Bond: *Introduction to English Church Architecture,* 1913.

For figures 67 and 68, to Mrs. Francis Bond and B. T. Batsford, Ltd., London, for illustrations from F. Bond: *Gothic Architecture in England,* 1905.

For figure 69, to B. T. Batsford, Ltd., London, for two illustrations from T. Garner and A. Stratton: *The Domestic Architecture of England during the Tudor Period,* 1911.

For figures 72, 73, 74, part of 75, 77, 78, to Longmans, Green and Company, London, for illustrations from F. M. Simpson: *A History of Architectural Development,* Vol. III, 1911.

For figure 75 (part), to Charles Scribner's Sons, New York, and B. T. Batsford, Ltd., London, for an illustration from W. J. Anderson: *The Architecture of the Renaissance in Italy,* 5th Edition revised by Arthur Stratton, 1927.

For figure 79, to the Appleton-Century Company, New York, for two illustrations from A. D. F. Hamlin: *A History of Ornament, Renaissance and Modern*, 1923.

For figure 80, to B. T. Batsford, Ltd., London, for an illustration from T. Garner and A. Stratton: *The Domestic Architecture of England during the Tudor Period*, 1911.

For figure 81, to B. T. Batsford, Ltd., London, for an illustration from J. A. Gotch: *Early Renaissance Architecture in England*, 1914.

For figure 82, to Sidney R. Jones, C. Holme, and The Studio, London, for a drawing by Sidney R. Jones from Holme: *Old English Country Cottages*, 1906.

For figure 83, to Methuen, London, for an illustration from J. A. Gotch: *Old English Houses*, 1925.

For figures 84 and 85, to Mrs. Mildred Stapley Byne and G. P. Putnam's Sons, New York, for illustrations from A. Byne and M. Stapley: *Spanish Architecture of the Sixteenth Century*, 1917.

For figure 88 (part), to the Society for Research in Chinese Architecture, late of Peking, for an illustration from its *Bulletin*, Vol. IV, 1934.

For figures 91, 92, 96, 97, 98, to Longmans, Green and Company, London, for illustrations from F. M. Simpson: *A History of Architectural Development*, Vol. III, 1911.

For figure 93, to M. S. Briggs and Ernest Benn (for T. Fisher Unwin), for an illustration from Briggs: *Baroque Architecture*, 1913.

For figure 95, to W. H. Ward, Charles Scribner's Sons, New York, and B. T. Batsford, Ltd., London, for an illustration from Ward: *The Architecture of the Renaissance in France*, 1926.

For figure 100, to B. T. Batsford, Ltd., London, and Charles Scribner's Sons, New York, for illustrations from J. Belcher and M. Macartney: *Later Renaissance Architecture in England*, 1911.

For figures 104 and 105, to J. F. Kelly and the Yale University Press, New Haven, for illustrations from Kelly: *Early Domestic Architecture of Connecticut*, 1924.

For figure 116, to Sir Raymond Unwin, for his drawing of a garden city

For figure 117, to Schroll, Vienna, for an illustration from O. Wagner: *Einige Skizzen, Projekte, und ausgeführte Bauwerke*, 1892-1922.

I am also grateful to many individuals and publishers for material used in the half-tone plates, as follows:

Plate 1, the Irish stone hut, an illustration from Ake Campbell: *Notes on the Irish House*, II, in *Folk-Liv*, published by the Bokforlags Aktiebolaget Thule, Stockholm, 1938, No. 2.

Plate 2, the Sakkara interior, from Jean-Phillipe Lauer: *Fouilles à Saqqarah, La Pyramid à degrés, L'architecture*, Vol. II, Cairo, Services des antiquités, Imprimerie de l'Institut français d'archéologie orientale, 1936.

Plate 5, the columnar hall at Uruk, from E. Heinrich: *Schilf und Lehm*, Berlin, Verlag für Kunstwissenschaft, 1934; the shrine portal at Ur, from H. R. Hall and C. L. Woolley: *Ur Excavations*, Vol. I, *Al-'Ubaid*, Oxford University Press, 1927, courtesy of the Museum of the University of Pennsylvania; the palace of Sargon, Khorsabad, from V. Place: *Ninive et l'Assyrie*, Paris, Imprimerie Nationale, 1867-70; the Apadana at Susa, from M. Dieulafoy: *L'acropole de Suse*, Paris, Hachette, 1892.

Plate 6, the temple at Hal Tarxien, from L. M. Ugolini: *Malta, origini della civiltá Mediterranea*, Rome, Libreria dello Stato, 1934; the detail from Hal Tarxien, from Sir Themistocles Zammit: *Pre-Historic Malta*, London, Humphrey Milford and the Oxford University Press, 1930; the restoration of the Palace at Knossos, from Sir Arthur Evans: *The Palace of Minos . . . at Knossos*, Vol. II, Part 2, London, The Macmillan Company, 1928.

Plate 7, the Temple of the Warriors, Chichen Itza, from a photograph courtesy of the Carnegie Institution.

Plate 8, the air-view of Chan Chan, from a photograph by Shippee-Johnson Expeditions, courtesy of the photographers and the American Geographical Society; the general view of Machu Picchu, from a copyright photograph by Hiram Bingham, leader of the Peruvian Expeditions under the auspices of Yale University and the National Geographic Society, courtesy of Hiram Bingham and the National Geographic Society.

Plate 9, the temple at Paestum, from a photograph by Ernest Nash; the Parthenon model, from The Metropolitan Museum of Art, New York.

Plate 10, the Paestum interior, from a photograph by Ernest Nash; the Parthenon model interior, from The Metropolitan Museum of Art; the Erechtheum, from a photograph by, and courtesy of, Dean Leopold Arnaud.

Plate 11, both models from The Metropolitan Museum of Art.

Plate 12, the Artemesium at Magnesia, from F. Krischen: *Die Griechische Stadt*, Berlin, Gebrüder Mann, 1938.

Plates 13, 14, 15, all photographs by Ernest Nash.

Page 167, the Temple of Fortuna Virilis and the Porta Maggiore, Rome, from photographs by Ernest Nash.

Plate 21, the mosque, the bazaar, and the mihrab from the Djouma Mosque, all at Isfahan, from copyrighted photographs by, and courtesy of, Myron Bement Smith.

Plate 24, the interior of Santa Maria de Naranco, from a photograph courtesy of Professor Kenneth Conant and The Fogg Museum of Art, Harvard University.

Plate 34, the model of Nuremberg, from The Metropolitan Museum of Art.

Plate 38, the interior of Palma de Mallorca, courtesy of Carl Feiss, Columbia University.

Plate 47, the Pierre Lescot wing of the Louvre, from a photograph courtesy of The Metropolitan Museum of Art.

Plate 48, the plate reproduced, from Wendel Dietterlin: *Architecturae Liber Tertius, De Ionica*, Nuremberg, 1598.

Plate 50, the interior of Crewe Hall, from J. Nash: *The Mansions of England in the Olden Time*, London, 1839-49; the interior of Thame Park, from Garner and Stratton: *The Domestic Architecture of England during the Tudor Period*, London, B. T. Batsford, Ltd., 1911.

Plate 52, the window *reja* from the House of Pilate and the three views of the Escorial, courtesy of Carl Feiss.

Plate 53, the temple at Khajuraho and the eastern gopuram of the Temple at Trichinopoly, from photographs courtesy of The Metropolitan Museum of Art.

Plate 55, the four Japanese examples, courtesy of Dr. Ryusaku Tsunoda, of Columbia University; the Shinto shrine, from S. Masuyama: *Early Japanese Shinto Shrines and Buddhist Temples*, Tokyo, 1936; the Phoenix Hall, Uji, *ibid;* the interior, from the Shokin-tei Katsura detached palace, *Complete Photographs of the Detached Palace in Kyoto.* . . . Kawakami Kunimoto, for the Society for Studies of Ancient Architecture and Gardens, Tokyo, 1930.

Plate 56, the façade of the church of Santi Marcelli, from De Rossi: *Insignum Romae Templorum Prospectus.* . . ., Rome, 1684.

Plate 57, the Karlskirche, Vienna, from a photograph courtesy of The Metropolitan Museum of Art.

Plate 60, the interior of St. Paul's, London, from a photograph, courtesy of The Metropolitan Museum of Art; the Greenwich Hospital view and Trinity

Chapel, Oxford, from Belcher and Macartney: *Later Renaissance Architecture in England,* London, B. T. Batsford, 1911.

Plate 61, the oval salon of the Hôtel Soubise and the bedroom from Venice in The Metropolitan Museum of Art, courtesy of the Museum.

Plate 62, all photographs courtesy of Carl Feiss.

Plate 63, the House in the Close, Salisbury, from Belcher and Macartney: *Later Renaissance Architecture in England,* London, B. T. Batsford, Ltd., 1911; the view of the ruin, Kew Gardens, from G. L. Le Rouge: *Jardins anglo-chinois, détails de nouveaux jardins à la mode,* Paris, 1776-85; the elevation of Kedleston, from J. Paine: *Plans, Elevations and Sections of Noblemen and Gentlemen's Houses . . .,* London, 1783; the view of Red Lion Square, from J. Kip: *Brittannia Illustrata,* London, 1727.

Plate 65, from G. B. Piranesi, *Prigioni,* Rome, 17—.

Plate 66, the interior of Lord Derby's house and the furniture detail, from *The Works in Architecture of Robert and James Adam,* London, 1773-1822; the frontispiece, from G. B. Piranesi: *Le Antichitá Romane,* Rome, 1756.

Plate 67, the detail from Tepotzotlan, courtesy of Carl Feiss.

Plate 68, the photograph of the Ward house, courtesy of The Essex Institute, Salem, Mass.

Plate 71, the Ledoux plate, from *L'architecture de C. N. Ledoux,* Paris, Lenoir, 1840, a partial reprint of C. N. Ledoux: *Architecture considérée sous le rapport de l'art, des moeurs, et de la législation,* Paris, 1804.

Plate 73, the Gandy plate, from J. Gandy: *The Rural Architect,* London, Harding, 1806; the Derby Railroad Station, from an Ackermann aquatint of about 1835 in the Parsons Collection of Railway Prints, Columbia University.

Plate 75, the interior of the Tredwell house, courtesy of the Historic Landmark Society, New York, the owner; the Louisiana plantation photograph, "Three Oaks," from I. W. Ricciuti: *New Orleans and its Environs, the Domestic Architecture, 1727-1870,* New York, William Helburn, 1938.

Plate 76, the illustrations of Fonthill Abbey, from J. B. Nichols: *Historical Notices of Fonthill Abbey,* London, Nichols, 1836; the Pugin plate, from A. W. Pugin: *Contrasts . . .,* London, 1836.

Plate 77, the rendering of Trinity Church, New York, courtesy of Professor Everard Upjohn.

Plate 80, the Newport villa, "The Breakers," courtesy of Professor Henry-Russell Hitchcock, Jr.

Plate 81, the view of the Marshall Field Store, courtesy of Professor Henry-Russell Hitchcock, Jr.

Plate 82, the two views of early housing, from photographs by, and courtesy of, John Coolidge.

Plate 83, the interior of the projected Franz Josef Museum, Vienna, from O. Wagner: *Einige Skizzen, Projekte, und ausgeführte Bauwerke,* Vienna, Schroll, 1892-1922.

Plate 84, the housing in Berlin and Frankfurt, from photographs by, and courtesy of, Carl Feiss.

Plate 85, the photograph of the Nebraska Capitol, courtesy of Mayers, Murray, and Phillip, architects, New York.

Plate 88, the interior of the Johnson Wax Company, Racine, from Pictures, Inc., New York; the two views of "Falling Water," from photographs by, and courtesy of, John McAndrew, and courtesy of The Museum of Modern Art, New York.

All other photographs on Plates 84 to 88, courtesy The Museum of Modern Art; also the Pampulha Chapel on Plate 90.

Plate 89, Lever House, courtesy Lever Brothers.

Plate 90, Museum of Public Works, Paris, from *Construction Moderne.*

Plate 91, model of B'nai Amoona Synagogue, St. Louis, courtesy Eric Mendelsohn.

Plate 92, Town Square model and Trinity Congregational Church, as well as the Susan Lawrence School on Plate 93, all in the Lansbury Neighborhood, London, courtesy British Information Services; Istituto Vital-Brazil, courtesy *Progressive Architecture* and Alvaro Vital-Brazil.

Plate 93, public school at Stockholm, courtesy American Swedish News Exchange; Administration Building, Florida Southern College, courtesy Florida Southern College.

Plate 95, Union High School, Exeter, Calif., courtesy Ernest J. Kump.

Plate 96, Library, University of Mexico, courtesy Hon. Carlos Lazo, Minister of Education and Public Works, and University of Mexico.

TALBOT HAMLIN

New York
June, 1953

BOOK I

Introductory

Chapter 1

PRIMITIVE ARCHITECTURE

THE building instinct is not limited to human beings; it extends over large numbers of species and types of living organisms. Even if we omit those animals which create their own dwellings from secretions made by themselves, like the shellfish or the spider, the field of animal builders is still vast. A few fish build nestlike structures of weed; almost all birds construct nests of sticks and twigs and vegetable fibers; ants build elaborate excavated communal dwellings, with different chambers set apart for different uses, and cut straight roads through grass or underbrush for ease of travel between anthill and food supplies. Any number of the smaller mammals excavate homes for themselves, which vary from the single cylindrical chamber of the woodchuck to the elaborate passages and chambers of moles and prairie dogs. Beavers construct dams and houses with trees and branches they have cut down; sometimes their instinctive skill in choosing sites and in using materials seems uncanny. And chimpanzees and gorillas, among the highest of the apes, build rough shelters of leaves and branches for their families. The ability to erect adequate shelters against weather and enemies may be, in fact, the specific element which controls the survival of some species in the relentless struggle of evolutionary life.

Sometimes, too, these shelters are of considerable engineering complexity. The hanging nests of the orioles are well known, with their strong, closely woven textures. The projecting nests of clay of various members of the swift family bring in the principles of cantilevering, or bracketing, and the cohesive strength of the clay itself. Some spiders' and beetles' burrows use little pellets of dirt or sand in a way analogous to vaulting. There is great variety in building materials, too, with each material used for its own special function—long fibers of hair or thread or grasses for tensile strength in hanging nests, clay or a special saliva as a mortar to give cohesion, feathers or hair or thistledown to give a soft and comfortable interior lining.

Not only is the building instinct highly developed and widespread in the animal world, but also there are many evidences of a sense or an emotion which approaches the aesthetic. Crows collect bright objects as though there were in them some value entirely apart from their possible usefulness. Birds' songs, though they are often part of the courting and mating procedure, seem at times merely a sort of activity for its own sake, or merely to give auditory pleasure to the mate and the performer. Many animals—insects, birds, and mammals—seem to have courting dances. And when dogs bay the moon it is sometimes with voices quite different from the ordinary bark or the hunting cry. The moonlight seems to make them restless; they lift up their voices, apparently to relieve their feelings; is not this almost a beginning of lyric song?

If, then, there is this beginning both of structural ability and of aesthetic feeling in the lower animal world, we may, I believe, be quite justified in thinking that even in primitive man, who biologically was such an advance over the lower forms, the same two instincts existed. Very slowly, as man took advantage little by little of the possibilities inherent in his brain and his senses, we may imagine these two instincts developing and becoming more conscious, until they blended in varying degrees with almost all of his activities, especially with his family life, the making of his utensils, and his religion. Thus we find even among paleolithic man special skills at representation highly developed; and, though we may say that the primary purpose of the magnificent cave paintings of Altamira or the Dordogne was not artistic but magical, and that these early men drew animals so accurately because they wished, by drawing them, to assert and to increase their power over them, nevertheless in the drawings themselves there is evident a delight in line and form, a pleasure in creating with their hands, that is essentially similar to the artist's delight today. The same is true of the early statues of the universal Mother Deities which have come down to us from those early days between 20,000 and 50,000 years ago. In them artistic creation is even more obvious than in the cave paintings. These statues, like the so-called "Venus of Willendorf," are no mere representations of women. The early sculptor has obviously changed "reality"; he has emphasized those elements of the figure which are symbolic of those attributes he wished to express, and he has slighted the others; the statue is no longer mere woman, but motherhood, creation incarnate. And something of the same power of abstraction seems to have guided his hand in developing the bold rounded surfaces of the whole; there is in them some hint of a love of forms for their own sake.

Similarly, with utensils, primitive man seems not to have remained permanently satisfied with their mere utility; he sought from an early date to impress "form" upon them; he shaped his pots so that they felt pleasant to the touch and were good to look at. Then perhaps he scratched lines on the surface; pure "decoration" had begun. During the neolithic age—when men had learned to polish stone, domesticate animals, and carry on a developed agriculture—this decorating instinct was almost universal.

It is the integration of the constructing instinct and the creative or expressive art instinct which gave rise to what we call architecture. Just as man had come to desire beautiful pots and other utensils, so he came to desire beautiful shelters. His standards of beauty have varied enormously through the centuries, and his means of achieving beauty have changed as much, but always the desire to give some sort of "form," some kind of attractive or decent consistency, to all the structures he needed to shelter himself and his gods has existed, except in the lowest and most primitive stages of savagery, which we may accept perhaps as decadent stages, rather than mere survivals of primitivism. It is the history of these shelters men have built for themselves and for their gods, these protections against the weather and against hostile men or animals, which is the true history of architecture.

Seen thus, the history of architecture becomes much more than a procession of those crystallized related forms we call "styles." Instead, it becomes almost a history of ways of life, a chronicle of the rise and development and decadence of building techniques, and an expression—all the more complete for being unconscious—of what men thought of life and death, of each other, and of their gods. For, if building forms are sensitive to changes in building materials—the house of wood will always be different from the house of stone—and to differences in the way in which buildings are put together, they are equally sensitive to changes in religious or social ideals. Some civilizations are essentially temple or tomb builders, like Egypt; some are chiefly creators of vast structures for general public use, like the Romans; some are known especially for their palaces, like the Baroque European powers of the seventeenth and eighteenth centuries. In differences like these may be read the record of the great controlling thoughts of each culture—its ideals, the things in human life for which it particularly sought.

In the course of this long development of ten millennia and more, mankind has developed several important building types, and several contrasting methods of construction, which are so universally found that brief descriptions of them are necessary.

Man's first building efforts were probably directed at individual huts or houses. Paleolithic man seems to have been chiefly a cave dweller, at least in Europe. But it seems more than likely that in the course of the long paleolithic period—perhaps 20,000 years—he must also have learned to construct rough huts, covered with leaves or skins. Simple they must have been, for his roughly chipped stone tools were of the simplest. They probably consisted merely in leaning a group of light sticks together to form a crude cone, and perhaps tying them, or weaving them together with vines or reeds; on this framework skins or a thatch of leaves could be hung. In this elementary tepee-like structure lay the origin of the round hut, the first of the great building types.

The round hut is found widely distributed in Europe, Asia, Africa, and the Americas. It exists in two chief forms: those built of a framework of sticks or timbers covered with hides or a thatch of leaves, and those built of piled stones more or less crudely shaped. Both are occasionally built partly underground, becoming what are known as round pit dwellings. The crudest of them make little or no differentiation between walls and roof, like the tepees, which are conical, or the beehive stone houses of western Ireland, which curve gradually from vertical sides below to an almost flat top, like a hemisphere.

The development of the vertical wall was nevertheless inevitable. Though

1. TYPICAL AFRICAN ROUND HUTS. *Left:* TEMPLE IN TUMANA, SUDAN. *Right:* INTERIOR OF A HUT IN THE FARO VALLEY, ADAMAUA. (Frobenius: *Das unbekannte Afrika.*)

he might have to stoop to enter—the doors of most primitive round huts are very low—even primitive man liked to stand up within his house, and the convenience and added spaciousness given by vertical walls was too great to be neglected. Hence arose the habit of starting the hut with vertical walls, which, in the timber dwellings, could be closed with mud plaster on a crude lathing of twigs or withes, or in the stone dwellings made by setting the first courses, or horizontal rows of stones, vertically over each other, or by using unusually large stones at the base, set on edge. This wall treatment meant that it was necessary to build the roof separately from the walls, and so led to all sorts of fruitful experiments in building methods.

Although the round hut was essentially a primitive house form, it persisted into times and cultures of a relatively high state of development, as in Africa, where chiefs' palaces may even today consist of a great agglomeration of circular hut units, some of great size, and many with mud-plaster walls lavishly decorated with bold painted patterns of marked decorative effectiveness. Similarly, in many parts of the neolithic and bronze-age Mediterranean world, round huts were built in connected groups, each forming a complex dwelling, as in early Greece and Crete; or a number would be regularly arranged in a rectangular pattern, such as we see in the ruins of the neolithic towns of Citania and Vianna do Castelio in Portugal.

Although many of the Greek and Cretan examples were built of wood and sun-dried, unbaked brick, the same form was also sometimes built of stones. In the round stone huts, the covering was contrived by setting each row of stones a little inward from the row below, so that little by little a conical shape developed, until the hole at the top was so small that it could either be capped by a single stone, or else left open to carry off the smoke from the hearth fire within. Such stone huts have been built in many parts of the world; they are especially characteristic of a band running through the Mediterranean islands, across Spain and Portugal, and up the Atlantic coast to the British Isles; even today one finds such dwellings occasionally still in use in the western islands of Ireland.

As skill in stone building increased, and stones were more and more carefully shaped, this type was made more usable by building vertical walls below, and gradually curving the inner faces in, to give the type known as the beehive hut, a form long preserved in the Greek and Italian areas. In this stone hut and beehive building, there is as yet no realization of the arch principle. The stones are flat; laid in horizontal courses, they owe their stability merely to the fact that the portion of the stone which projected was less in weight than the portion supported by the stones below.

Combinations of stone walls with roofs of timber covered with earth or turf are also common in primitive building. These show their origin in the round hut because they usually are round-ended, but the additional freedom gained in the use of timber roofing led the builders, in their search for roomy interiors, to make one dimension much longer than the other, creating ovals, or rectangles with curved ends. Such houses are occasionally still in use in some of the Scottish islands, where they are known as "black houses," because of their dark, windowless, smoke-begrimed interiors. The tradition of this kind of building is of long duration in those regions; for stone building of somewhat similar type has gone on there for over 2000 years, and the village of Skara Brae, in the Orkneys, excavated a few years ago, dates undoubtedly to Pictish times somewhere near the beginning of the Christian era.

Skara Brae is a close-built community of seven or eight stone houses, connected with a winding walk or "street." The house walls are built of the thin slabs of stone which can be so easily split from the stratified rock of the island, laid horizontally with a beautiful precision. The entrance doors are small and low; one has to stoop or crawl to enter. Within, the floor is paved with flat stones; a hearth, surrounded by a raised border to keep the ashes from spreading, occupies the approximate center, and often there are boxes or chests of stone sunk beneath the floor and once covered with floor slabs. The furniture, all of stone, is remarkably varied. Beds are usually placed in the corners, and consist of an area bordered by slabs of stone set on edge to form a box-type bedstead, within which resilient branches, twigs, and hay or straw could be placed to give both warmth and comfort. Dressers, of one or two shelves of thin stone slabs set horizontally, supported by vertical stones, are common, and often cupboards and storage spaces are contrived in the thickness of the wall. These ancient huts, like the modern "black houses," were probably roofed with turf, and must have been as dark as their present-day descendants; but in construction, in finish and beauty of technique, they are much more advanced than the modern work, and one feels, studying them, that the inhabitants of the ancient Skara Brae houses lived in more comfort, with greater cleanliness achieved at less effort, than the Scottish island peasants of, say, the eighteenth century. For architectural forms and methods can degenerate just as easily as they can progress.

In heavily timbered countries, the rectangular house became the standard type of dwelling at an early date. This was only natural, for tree trunks are generally straight and—if they are laid horizontal at the base of a wall, to form its foundation or to edge the floor—will form inevitably a house with straight sides. Rectangular shapes, moreover, are generally more usable than round or oval areas; furniture, such as beds or benches, can be more easily adapted to them. Thus, in central and northern Europe, as in large parts of eastern Asia, the rectangular hut was, and is, the rule; and even in stone and brick building areas, such as Mesopotamia and Egypt, the vastly increased convenience of the rectangular plan—particularly when several units or rooms had to be joined together in a single building—made it well-nigh universal.

The typical timber rectangular hut was built in three different ways. In one, vertical logs of similar size, sometimes split so that one face is flat, are driven into the ground vertically, set close together to form walls; this is often called "stockade" construction. In another, the logs are placed horizontally upon each other, with the corners notched together in various ways; this is the true log-cabin construction. If the timber is squared into planks, the Swiss châlet type of building results. By far the most common type of timber building, however, is the framed type of structure, in which posts are set vertically, at some distance from each other, the tops joined by horizontal timbers, and the wall areas between the posts filled with a screen designed merely to shut out the weather and to protect the inhabitants, but not as a support. The material and thickness of this screen varies according to the climate and the available materials; woven mattings, a thatch or mat of reeds, and the skins of animals were all used, especially in warm southern climates. In the north, and in Europe generally, the filling usually consisted of a lathing of intertwined twigs and branches or reeds, coated heavily on both sides with mud plaster. Usually the posts remained exposed, and the building type that we term "half-timber" arose—of posts of wood, with light-colored flat wall areas between. As building techniques developed and man's knowledge of materials increased, the mud plaster gave way to gypsum plaster, to lime and cement stuccoes, and even in some cases to brick; but the principle remained the same—the posts did the supporting, and the walls between, whatever their material, were only protecting screens.

Roof types varied widely, too. In warm, dry countries, the simplest method was to place tree trunks horizontally as beams spanning from wall to wall, supported occasionally by intermediate posts where the spans were long. On these would be placed a cross layer of reeds or smaller sticks, and the whole would be covered with earth or clay, beaten down to form a strong mass. The top was sometimes, in more developed civilizations, painted or cemented to render it more waterproof. Some of the earliest Greek temples may have had flat roofs of this type, and they are the normal roof coverings of houses in western central Asia, in parts of Syria, and in Egypt, even to the present day. More highly developed types can be seen in the Pueblo villages of the southwestern United States and in Central India.

In climates where rain is greater in amount, and more constant, such flat roofs are useless; some roofing must be used which discharges the water more rapidly. Hence, the characteristic roofs of rainy countries—central and northern Europe, eastern and southeastern Asia, the Malay country, and the islands of the Pacific, for instance—are sloped roofs. These were usually made by resting on the walls pairs of sloped beams, called rafters, which met in the center, at the ridge; these pairs would be set close enough together to support boards or smaller beams across them, which in turn could be covered with a thatch of straw, reeds, or leaves to keep out the water. As building technique developed, other materials besides thatch for roofing were used—wood shingles, flat stones or slates, or baked clay tiles.

Mankind came to learn, too, that different slopes fitted different climates. In southern, sunny climates, where there is, nevertheless, considerable rain, the low slope was the rule, and gave rise to the classic temple pediment. In damp countries, with much rain and some but not a great deal of snow, high steep roofs, like those of the German towns, were general. In windy, snowy, northern climates, a roof of comparatively low and gentle slope was used, for people came to realize that a heavy layer of snow on a roof made houses much warmer, while the gentle slope allowed water from the melting snow to trickle off gradually. Thus, in Scandinavia, in parts of Japan, and in the Alps, the characteristic roof slope is gentle and roofs are comparatively low, with broadly spreading eaves.

Besides the round and simple rectangular types of house, a third type grew up in sunny southern areas—the house built around a court, with its rooms opening off the court rather than towards the outside. This type is common in Mediterranean, western Asiatic, and Chinese areas, and allows the desirable combination of privacy and protection with pleasant outdoor living.

Religious buildings fall into four different categories. The first type results from the conception of the temple as a House of God—that is, the god's actual or symbolic residence. Among peoples where this conception rules, the temple tends to follow house designs, with the cult statue or symbol replacing the human inhabitant. The classic Greek and Roman temples are of this type, and the elaborate temples of Egypt are but a development of the same idea; Chinese and Japanese temples were originally based on it also

The second category may be generically referred to as the High Place—that is, an area set apart for the worship of a nature god (frequently a sky or sun god) and so arranged that the worshiper is brought into close communion with the deity. Hills and mountains were natural locations for such areas; where they were lacking, the sects erected artificial hills of earth or brick or stone to raise the worshipers from the plain to higher and purer air. Such were the *ziggurats,* the artificial pyramidal temple mounds of Mesopotamia, and the great pyramids of Maya, Toltec, and Aztec Mexico. In many cases suggestions of the first category appear in connection with the second, and shrines are built on the summits of these pyramids.

The third type is that of the tomblike shrine over the body or a relic of a saint or a deity. Since early man, in many parts of the world, erected a pile of earth over a king's or hero's body to form a tumulus, it is natural that the same tumulus form was taken over, regularized, and built in all sorts of symbolic shapes to memorialize a god or a saint. The *stupas* or *topes* of Buddhist Asia are characteristic examples of this type of religious building. Owing to its solid, hill-like shape, there is occasional confusion between this type of structure and that of the High Place, but the origins of the two types are different and their purposes dissimilar.

The last type of religious building, and in some ways the most advanced, is the meeting place. Here the dominance is given not to the god but to the worshipers. Classic "mystery" religions, like the mysteries of Eleusis or the cult of Mithra, developed religious buildings of this type, wherein the faithful could meet to take part in a ritual service or observe a ritual drama. The Jewish synagogue was primarily a meetinghouse, and the prayer hall has an important place in many Chinese and Japanese temples. It was natural that early Christianity should adopt the same idea and for its early churches take over and modify the basilica—the great public courtroom and meeting hall of the Roman world.

As life developed, and as religious ideas became more complex and building techniques advanced, the lines of demarcation between these original categories became vague and ill-defined. Ideas from one of them would be borrowed for the fuller development of another, so that many great religious structures have elements from all four. Moreover, the combination of residential quarters for priests, or specially dedicated persons, with the purely religious buildings led to the development of complex groups like the monasteries of China or of Europe. Yet the elements of which these later, complex structures are composed can usually be traced back to one of the four great original classes of religious buildings.

In all the long struggle to develop these various types of building, mankind fought against one powerful enemy—gravity. Everything left to itself tends to fall to the ground; yet since man was building, above all else, shelters—that is, protected hollow spaces large enough for living or worshiping or meeting, as the case might be, which should be protected from rain and cold—the method of support of the sheltering elements above this hollow space became one of his chief architectural difficulties, and the various solutions of the problem gave rise to many of the most characteristic architectural forms.

In a sense, then, all building becomes a struggle between the force of gravity pulling things down, and the strength of materials and the way they are used holding them up. To build any shelter whatsoever brings in this constant battle—so much so in fact that, to some, architecture has seemed above all an art and a science dealing with gravity and materials. Schopenhauer founded his entire architectural aesthetics on this idea. To him architecture is beautiful because it expresses dramatically, yet impersonally, this constant fight, the sense of emotional tension, resulting from the conflict of the force of gravity with the strength of the buildings man has built.

Four chief basic principles have been discovered, in the course of the long development of building, by means of which sheltered space below and the openings in the walls that surround it can both be covered over safely with roofs or floors, or with upper walls. These are usually termed: Post-and-Lintel construction, Corbel or Cantilever construction, Arch and Vault construction, and Truss construction.

Post-and-lintel construction consists merely in laying a horizontal beam across the space between two supports. In some cases the supports are continuous and the type of construction might better be called wall-and-lintel construction, the lintel in each case being merely a horizontal beam which does the supporting. Post-and-lintel construction gives rise normally to simple rectangular shapes, and is characteristic of much primitive construction, as well as the more highly developed types of Egypt, Crete, and classic Greece. It is also the basic system used in most modern steel and concrete framed structures as well as in much modern wood building, and anyone who has watched a crane swing a horizontal girder into position between two steel columns can realize both its simplicity and its possible strength.

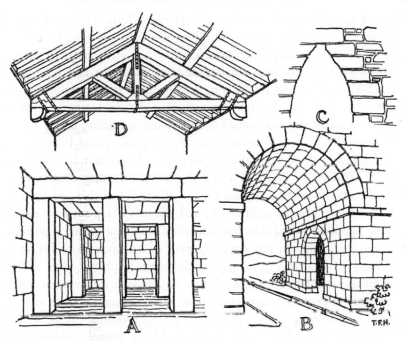

2. FOUR TYPICAL BUILDING METHODS. (Drawn by the author.) A. POST-AND-LINTEL. B. ARCH AND VAULT. C. CORBEL OR CANTILEVER. D. TRUSS.

The corbel or cantilever is merely a bracket member, with one end built into a wall, or held in a fixed position by some other means, the outer projecting end being used to carry weights of some kind upon it—balconies, or even roof members. Thus, the round stone beehive hut is an excellent example of corbeled construction. In stone, corbeled construction requires extremely heavy walls and an excessive amount of material, but with the great strength of modern steel and reinforced concrete it has been possible to utilize again the principle of the cantilever or the corbel to produce interesting and highly developed structures. Accordingly, many large steel bridges are of the cantilever type, and in considerable modern industrial and commercial work, and occasionally even in houses, in order to get the greatest unbroken window spaces the supporting columns are set well in from the outside walls; the parts of the floors outside the columns and all the exterior walls in this case are held up by another development of the same cantilever principle.

The origin of the arch and the vault is lost in the tantalizing fog that hangs over so much of primitive architecture. We only know that it was apparently in Mesopotamia, a land of brick building, that the arch and the vault first came into widespread use, and there fully developed examples existed as early as the fourth millennium B.C. It is probable that the discovery of the arch principle occurred more or less accidentally in the effort to build corbeled roofs with smaller and smaller units and less and less weight. Because this effort finally produced unstable ceilings, which began to collapse inward, the builders may have supported them temporarily in place with some kind of wooden framework. The inward-falling bricks or stones would naturally tend to develop generally radiating joints between them, and the builder would naturally fill the space between with units which gradually changed in direction from the inward-slanting courses on one side to the inward-slanting courses on the other. When this had been completed, the whole became rigid again, and the temporary supports could be removed. Mankind would thus have developed his first arched construction, for the arch is, roughly, any covering over of an open space below with small units of material, generally wedge-shaped, placed with radiating joints. Since, owing to its wedge shape, no single brick or stone can fall inward without pushing others out, the whole will remain stable as long as its base is kept from spreading. A vault is merely a continuous piece of arch construction over a relatively large depth, like a tunnel; custom usually reserves the term "arch" for a covering over of an opening in a single wall.

Generally speaking, in the effort to get all of the elements of an arch of the same size and shape, the arch and vault generally have a semicircular form, but this is by no means universal, and forms other than the semicircle can be used without disturbing the underlying structural laws. Thus, arches with a completely flat underside, or *intrados,* are possible, provided the joints in the stones of which they are made radiate, and such flat arches have frequently been used to cover over very large doors or similar openings where a flat top was desired.

Because of their very nature, all arches and vaults exert on their supports not only a downward weight but also a sidewise thrust. Gravity is always pulling each wedge-shaped unit or *voussoir* downward and inward; and, since the only way in which this is possible is by an enlargement of the opening, the thrust of the arch outward is always at work. In a sense, this thrust is merely the development on a larger scale of the same forces which make it impossible to build an ordinary card house on an absolutely smooth, glazed surface; unless the bottoms of the cards are held from spreading, the house will collapse. Even when mortar of exceptional strength is used, or the building material is of concrete so that the whole arch or vault is homogeneous, nevertheless the same forces are working. All materials are elastic to some degree; and, since there is no way in which a vaulted structure can fall except by widening its span, the elasticity of even the most homogeneous vault still allows powerful thrusts at its base. One of the great things which made the building of vaulted edifices difficult was this matter of providing resistance to the sidewise thrusts, and various means of achieving this have given rise to many beautiful and characteristic architectural elements.

Trussed construction grew naturally from the use of the pointed roof. Geometrically, the triangle is always a rigid form—that is, none of its angles can be altered without altering the length of its sides;—and builders found at an early period that, if the walls of a house were well tied together by beams at their top, the slanting rafters supported on those walls would hold their position unchanged. Since any triangle is rigid, combinations of triangles are also rigid; and, if the space to be spanned or the roof to be built is too large for the strength of single timbers or beams, still, by arranging the material to form a series of triangles, spans of almost any size can be safely bridged. Despite the simplicity of this general theory, the problems of finding out exactly what forces are at work in each of the members of the truss is a complicated one, dependent upon comparatively recent types of mathematical and geometrical analysis, so that the early trusses are seldom scientific in design. Even the implications of the basic principle were often little understood, and some building cultures seem to have had no knowledge whatsoever of the truss principle. Early Greek architecture, for example, depends upon simple post-and-lintel types of building even in the construction of gabled roofs; and one of the chief characteristics of Chinese and Japanese architecture is the extreme and unnecessary elaboration of the construction of its great sloping roofs, because of a dependence on post-and-lintel thinking and an apparently complete ignorance of the truss principle. Modern mathematical analysis and the definite knowledge of the strengths of all types of material, both in compression and in tension, have enabled modern truss designs to be developed to a great degree of perfection and elegance, and have allowed us to build roofs over vast areas, as in great auditoria, armories, convention halls, and so on, which without the truss would be impossible.

With these four great building principles, mankind has set out to defy gravity and to construct those shelters, protected from weather and from hostile elements and forces, which he needed. As his civilization developed, so his wants increased. This space which man thus enclosed to form his shelters was eventually seen to be not one thing but many things. Living space was different in quality from worshiping space, and that in turn from meeting space or working space; but, essentially, the quality of enclosed space remains perhaps the primary quality in all architecture, and its exterior expression generates the exterior appearance of buildings just as its interior arrangement determines their beauty within and their efficiency. With these four building methods and the growing complexity of man's wants, all of architecture has developed and become not merely a matter of use, but a matter of beauty, of emotional and intellectual satisfaction, complementing and in a way even adding to the usefulness itself. Convenience, construction, beauty—these are the three great elements in architecture which Vitruvius enunciated, and these are still the elements the interrelation of which produces all the buildings we create today and all those which mankind has brought forth from the beginning of civilization until now.

Chapter 2

THE FIVE GREAT BUILDING
CULTURES

DURING the long struggle into civilization, humanity passed through many stages which are generally parallel the world over, though they occur at vastly different dates in different places. The long ages of paleolithic or rough stone-age life, when man was a hunter and food gatherer alone, without knowledge of pottery or agriculture, yielded gradually to neolithic culture. The neolithic period, the new stone age, saw mankind not only able to polish as well as to chip his stone tools, but also able at last to make and burn pottery, to master at least the first techniques of agriculture, and, because of this new command over his food, to settle into permanent villages and there learn to construct real houses.

The discovery of copper and, later, of bronze and the ability to work them brought to mankind tools and weapons of such enormously greater efficiency than the old stone and wooden axes, knives, and clubs that revolutionary changes in human living were inevitable, and with his new metal tools man was finally enabled to carve and cut and finish his building materials with an accuracy before unknown. Later still, the ability to work iron brought revolution again, for the iron tools and weapons far surpassed those of copper or bronze, and the iron-wielding peoples arose naturally to military command and eventually to cultural supremacy. In a sense we are still living in the iron age, but how future archaeologists two millennia from now may class us is of course a question; and, just as within the long period of the iron age they will be able to pick out and to classify various levels of development and to assign to each its local origin and its history, so in each of the other ages archaeologists have found it possible with increasing accuracy to pattern out the past development.

Although humanity seems generally to have passed through these stages of increasing command over its environment in much the same order all over the world, nevertheless the periods at which one stage of culture yielded to another varied greatly from place to place. The world was never uniform, and peoples were under extraordinarily different environmental conditions; climate, topography, floods, pestilence, war, all have affected the speed of mankind's cultural progress; and, just as today there are vast areas in Australia and Africa, for instance, in which the population is still in the bronze age and in some cases even in the stone age, save for occasional imported objects, so at all times in the past there have been backward peoples and peoples more advanced, and the words describing these periods are never date or time expressions unless limited by definite geographical areas. Nor must these cultural terms be confused with racial concepts. The more archaeologists learn of the peoples and the products of those distant eras, the more they have come to realize that such earlier simplifications as the terms commonly used to describe the races of mankind have little archaeological meaning. Long-headed peoples and short-headed peoples are found all over Europe at an early date, and, although the natural inertia of tribal life tends to make the products of one tribe uniform over relatively long periods, it is also true that similar materials, similar conditions, and similar functions may produce the same forms in places thousands of miles and hundreds of years apart.

The parentage of the forms of utensils, and even of their ornament, is therefore a much more complicated problem than would appear on the surface, for decorative as well as purely utilitarian shapes arise from many sources, and the same ornamental form may have not one but many reasons for being—imitation of nature, imitation of the forms of neighboring peoples, the desire to decorate a space of a given shape and kind, the ease with which the form can be carved or painted, the influence of the material from which it is made. All sorts of decorative and structural techniques give rise naturally to their own particular convenient and natural shapes; and the fact that the fret is found in Greek, in Chinese, and in American Indian ornament is obviously no evidence of mutual borrowing between them or even the most distant mutual influence, but only of the fact that the fret is a natural development of the straight lines that arise in weaving, whether of basketry or of cloth, and that, once its beauty was discovered, it was applied to other materials besides those involving the technique which gave rise to it.

Archaeologists have learned, too, that there was much more interchange in commerce during primitive periods than was believed a few decades ago. Stone axes are found, in the great stone tombs and *dolmens* of western France, the shape of which is not based on stone techniques but is a direct imitation of bronze axes made in the islands of the Aegean. Amber from the Baltic found its way at an early period to the Mediterranean world, and seal types from the Indus valley have been dug up in Mesopotamian sites. It would seem as though the peoples of the world had always been, as the Gilbert and Sullivan song says, "either a little radical, or else a little conservative," and that the radical peoples seeking for change were eager to borrow forms from their neighbors and invent new forms for themselves, while the conservative peoples remained more static.

Thus the art forms of the early world indicate much interchange of ideas as well as of goods between one part of the civilized world and another; and the final results for any one people at any one time are the effect of the balance between the conservative element, which tends to crystallize and stabilize, and the radical element, which tends toward imitation of the "foreign" and toward experiment and discovery. This should lead to a general skepticism about too obvious and too definite dogmas concerning artistic derivatives. The desire to classify and to systematize is a natural part of the human knowledge search, but it gives rise to the temptation to oversimplify. In the art world especially it has produced a school of critical historians who seek to find behind each artistic manifestation, whether it be building or painting, ornament or sculpture, a definite series of influences which explain it completely. This is clearly absurd; it reduces the artist or the architect to the position of being a mere adding machine, automatically adding influence to influence and automatically producing an inevitable result. This is an entire misapprehension of the artistic process and denies to the artist the creative imagination which is his greatest distinguishing quality.

Still, general trends can be traced, and different peoples working at their own problems have produced different manifestations which we call *styles*. Seen thus, style is a term used to define a whole body of work with certain common characteristics, produced by people living under a common culture. Changes in style will occur, then, when for some reason—commercial, military, religious, or purely psychological—the culture which produces the style has, itself, changed, bringing with that change new ideals of what is right, fitting, and beautiful.

In the long ages since the ice sheets of the last glacial age slowly retreated, to be followed hesitatingly by paleolithic men in their search for food, five chief centers of building skill, giving rise to architecture of notable beauty, have developed. It was only with the coming of neolithic civilization that the building art became an essential part of human life, for it was only with command over agriculture—a command gained in the neolithic period—that mankind found it possible to form permanent settlements. By this period in human evolution, differentiations between the various stocks of mankind then in the world had already developed. Man had learned that certain areas in the world were more fitted for human living than others, and the building cultures naturally grew up in those areas which were most favorable to life—not too hot or too cold, with soil of sufficient fertility, if possible also with available wood, stone, and other minerals. The five areas giving rise to the five great building cultures may be called, roughly: First, the central Asian area, especially what is now Armenia, Persia, Iraq, eastern Syria, and the Tigro-Euphrates valley, with extensions southward into the Indus valley and the Punjab in India; second, the Mediterranean basin, including Egypt, North Africa, the Mediterranean Islands, the Syrian and Asia Minor shores, Italy and Greece, and especially Crete and the islands of the Aegean, with extensions westward across Spain and Portugal, and spottily up the Atlantic coast to the British Isles; third, central and northern Europe, particularly along the Danube valley, with extensions eastward to the Black Sea and north and west through Scandinavia; fourth, eastern Asia, notably China and Japan; and, fifth, the Americas, especially Central America, the northwestern parts of South America, and the southern portions of North America. Although these all are definite and distinct culture areas, the actual work in each in historical times may have been much influenced by the work of other areas. The exchanges between the first and the second areas—central Asia and the Mediterranean basin—and between the second and third—the Mediterranean basin and central Europe—were especially important.

The central Asian area had almost all the requirements necessary to produce an early and vivid culture. The Tigro-Euphrates valley was immensely fertile; minerals of many kinds abounded in the mountains to the north and the east; and a climate perhaps somewhat better then than it is today made agriculture productive and profitable. Into this central region came peoples from Arabia to the south, from Armenia and Persia to the north and east, from Syria to the west. These peoples somewhere had hit upon the secret of the smelting of copper, so that they were no longer dependent upon stone or wood tools. Another river valley further south, the valley of the Indus, saw the rise of a similar civilization, perhaps produced by similar peoples; and, whatever the kinship between their makers may have been, the civilizations themselves were almost entirely parallel in building methods and decorative motifs. That commerce between them existed is proved by the discovery in Ur of beads and seals obviously of Indian manufacture. The gradual burying of the remains of earlier times by repeated flooding of the land with the silting from river floods not only has preserved for us a great many of the buildings and the manufactures of periods as early as the fourth millennium and perhaps even the fifth millennium B.C., but has enabled the relative chronology of different phases of this culture to be carefully determined with an exactitude not often possible elsewhere.

In the remains we find the unmistakable evidences of the climate and the materials at hand. The buildings, as we should expect from a people living in an alluvial valley, are at first round huts of mud plaster on a lathing of woven river reeds (a method of building which is still in use in the area), and later, as skill developed, of mud or adobe bricks, with an occasional use of burned bricks. Stone is rare though not unknown; it evidently was brought in by water from the Persian Gulf or else brought down from the eastern hills.

This culture developed at an early date almost all of the methods characteristic of brick building—the thick wall, brick and tile paving, burned-brick or colored faïence facings, the arch and vault,—and although many different governments ruled over the region successively, and invaders of various hereditary strains came into it from different directions at different times, the buildings which it produced remained surprisingly consistent over a period of more than 2500 years.

The Mediterranean basin, with its comparatively mild climate, its extremely varied coast lines, and its wealth of good building stone and marble, was bound to produce a building culture of an entirely different sort. Essentially, this was a stone culture; and even during purely neolithic times, which here lasted perhaps up to *circa* 2500 B.C., over a thousand years later than in Mesopotamia, stone buildings of great size, intricately and beautifully planned, were already erected. Such are the cave temples and the constructed temples of Malta, where not only is there a beautiful use of great stones carefully finished to form vast rooms, but also the beginnings of carved decorative ornament by the use of spiral patterns on altars and tablets.

In the islands of the Aegean, building development was also extremely rapid; and the fact that copper and bronze came early into use in this part of the Mediterranean, probably introduced from the East, gave to the building culture of this section a quality even more advanced than that of Malta, and finally developed into the grandeur of the Cretan buildings, which will be covered later.

Further west, Sardinia and the Iberian Peninsula show indications of skill in stone-age building, in which the round house of beehive type is the characteristic architectural form. In Sardinia especially, this was carried out on a scale elsewhere unapproached, and each village seems to have had its central castle, with a great cone-shaped interior room surrounded by enor-

3. EXTERIOR AND INTERIOR OF SARDINIAN NOURAGHI. *Left,* AT ORTU. *Right,* AT ZURI. (Perrot and Chipiez: *Histoire de l'art dans l'antiquité.* Tome IV.)

mously heavy walls that sometimes rise to a height of fifty or sixty feet, forming large cone-shaped towers. Within the thickness of the walls, other rooms and corridors were contrived, all, like the central room, roofed over by corbeled vaults.

In Portugal, the village system was different though still highly organic. Each village consisted of a generally rectangular area enclosed by stone walls and containing round stone houses, sometimes formed into groups, with the single houses and the groups separated from each other by streets and courts carefully paved with flat stones. Examples are Vianna do Castelio and Citania. Some reminiscences of this same kind of round stone building seem to have been carried north, by traders or sailors, to the British Isles, and the beehive-type stone hut is still found in large numbers on the western coast of Ireland.

But the earliest and greatest of the cultures which grew up around the Mediterranean and which may be related in its lost origin to these other evidences of skillful stone building was the civilization which flourished in the Nile valley at a period as early as, or perhaps even earlier than, that of the Mesopotamian civilization. Here, as in Mesopotamia, one finds a locality admirably fitted for intensive agriculture. Unlike Mesopotamia, however, the Egyptian valley was narrow and surrounded on each side by mountains and cliffs containing excellent building stones of various types, especially sandstones and granites. Moreover, this section was protected from primitive invaders by its geographical location, so that discoveries, once made, could be developed to a high degree of perfection without danger of interruption. These conditions enabled the culture to flower with extraordinary rapidity, but in addition gave it, after its maturity, a strangely static quality that kept its general building types constant for almost three millennia.

The third great center of building development lies in central and northern Europe, where along the banks of the Danube and the Swiss lakes there grew up in stone-age times a civilization of hunters and agriculturists, whose great building material, instead of the clay of Mesopotamia or the stone of the Mediterranean, was timber. At Vinca, on the Danube, on the lakes of Geneva and Neufchâtel, in the moorlands of eastern Prussia and of Poland, are evidences that, even in these areas so far from the great so-called classic centers of the Mediterranean world and the western Orient, mankind at an early period had developed no little skill in building. At Vinca the houses are generally rectangular, with interior hearths and special ovens. The holes left by the posts of their walls show them to have been of typical framed construction. The walls were of mud plaster on withe or reed lathing, and where the fires which destroyed the houses has baked these walls hard one may see that the interiors of many of the house walls were elaborately decorated by scratched patterns of zigzags and other simple geometrical forms.

The lake villages of Switzerland and the moor villages of Poland were perhaps decoratively more crude, but structurally they showed considerable knowledge, in the way great platforms, supported on piles, were built of simple tree trunks, and by the way in which the houses were framed on this platform, each with its clay floor and raised hearth. The preservation of many of these timbers, because of their underwater position, has enabled archaeologists to reconstruct the original appearance of some at least of these houses. They were capped with high-pitched roofs covered with thatch and ending in steep triangular gables. The walls were either framed, as in the Vinca example, or else built of horizontal logs laid one on the other, with each end sharpened to fit into a groove cut into the vertical posts which held the whole firm and furnished the real support.

In Poland, the houses were built in long lines on a solid mat or floor of felled timber, with straight streets between the rows, the whole giving perhaps more the appearance of a barracks than of a modern village.

4. RESTORED MOOR VILLAGE OF AICHBÜHL. (H. Reinerth: *Haus und Hof in nordischen Raum.*)

It is in such German sites as Aichbühl that the origin of many modern European village layouts can be seen, for here a group of houses stretches rather informally along on either side of the street. The houses themselves are characteristic timber-framed houses with mud-plaster walls and high-pitched thatched roofs. They have central hearths, and some at least served as stable and home dwelling in one large unbroken interior space, thus setting a tradition which gives rise to the enormous rectangular farmhouses that dot the countryside in many sections of modern Germany. In some of these early houses of north Europe, an open porch roofed over by a continuation of the house gable distinguishes the front and gives a place for outdoor living as well as a sheltered entrance. This type of rectangular house with a porch in front, a traditional northern type, is by many people considered the origin of the Greek *megaron,* and thus is deemed to have given rise to a long history of building progress which culminated at last in the Parthenon.

The fourth principal building culture of the primitive world was that of eastern Asia, which arose in China and spread from there both north into Mongolia, Korea, and Japan, and south into Indo-China and Malaya. Little has yet been discovered of very primitive building in this area; yet the extremely high development of the building art which is obvious in the earliest buildings known argues a long history of gradual development still to be traced.

The great characteristic of this eastern Asiatic building culture is its combined use of masonry and timber, of stone and brick and wood, with each material used for specific purposes in line with its qualities. Thus, foundation platforms and sometimes the lower stages of buildings will be of masonry, whereas the superstructure is entirely of wood, and even where masonry is used in the superstructure it is chiefly used merely as a screen built between and around the wooden columns which hold up the great roof. Like the peoples of western and central Asia, the eastern Asiatics seem to have known the principle of the vault from a very early period, perhaps borrowing it from their western neighbors, or perhaps developing it inde · pendently.

The fifth center is that of the Americas, especially of the brick and stone builders of Central America, Peru, Mexico, and our own Southwest. Here, too, as in the case of eastern Asia, much of the earlier history is still unknown, but the extreme elaboration of technique and the magnificence of conception evident in the monuments of even the earliest Mayan Empire, which goes back to before the Christian era, indicate long centuries of previous development. Similarly, the great stone structures of pre-Inca Peru, with their marvelously worked stone walls and restrained and effective decorative sculpture—a contrast to Mayan exuberance,—are an unanswered archaeological puzzle. It is nevertheless obvious that here in America, as in Mesopotamia, or Egypt, or northern Europe, or the Atlantic shores of the British Isles, man, faced with the need of shelter for himself and for his gods, and confronted with natural building materials of various kinds, started at an extremely early period in his development to create buildings and to work out the structural problems they entailed, along lines suggested to him by the materials with which he worked and by the conditions of the climate in which he built.

These, then, may be taken as the five great centers in which building types were worked out almost independently of each other, at least in the earlier stages of their development. Later, as facilities for travel grew greater and the scope of commerce broadened, as man's wants ceased to be satisfactorily fulfilled by the things immediately around him, all sorts of interrelations of influence between these various centers occurred. Indian seals and beads in Mesopotamia, idols carved from Baltic amber in Crete, Cretan pottery in Egyptian tombs, Cretan tools discovered in Brittany, the Dorians in Greece decorating the developed megaron with ornaments taken from Syria and Egypt—these all show how important, even at a very early date, was this exchange of ideas between various peoples of the world.

One other quality may be seen through even the briefest comparative study of the works of these different centers: the fact that, in all, development of the building arts led inevitably along three different but related ways toward three different but related ideals—the way of utility, toward the ideal of perfect adjustment of ways and means to pleasant living; the way of construction, toward the ideal of a structure that should combine economy, efficient use of materials, and permanence; and the way of beauty, toward the ideal of creating an environment for life or worship that should be, intellectually, satisfying to man's eternal longing for pattern and form, and that should be at the same time emotionally rich. It is the search for these three ideals along these three different lines which produces the changes that distinguish one building style from another, and it is these changes in expression which together form the body of the history of architecture.

BOOK II

The Early Architecture
of the Western World

RECTANGULAR THATCHED HUT, STATE OF VERA CRUZ, MEXICO.

STONE HUT, INISHMORE, ARAN ISLANDS, IRELAND. (*Folk-Liv.*)

TRULLI, ALBEROBELLO, ITALY. (Alinari.)

Plate 1

ABU SIMBEL, ROCK-CUT TEMPLE OF RAMESSES THE GREAT.

SAKKARA, TOMB TEMPLE; COLONNADED HALL. (Lauer: Saqqarah.)

KARNAK. TEMPLE OF THOTHMES; TWO TYPES OF COLUMNS.

Plate 2

CHICHEN ITZA, TEMPLE OF THE WARRIORS. (Carnegie Institution.)

LABNA, THE ARCH, SHOWING CORBELED CONSTRUCTION AND STONE MOSAIC.

CHICHEN ITZA; GENERAL VIEW.

CHICHEN ITZA, CIRCULAR TEMPLE (CARACOL).

ZUNI PUEBLO; MODEL. (Museum of the American Indian, Heye Foundation.)

CHICHEN ITZA; CHARACTERISTIC FAÇADE SHOWING STYLIZED MASKS. (Brehme.)

Plate 7

TEOTIHUACAN, PYRAMID OF THE SUN; GENERAL VIEW.

TEOTIHUACAN, TEMPLE OF QUETZALCOATL DETAIL.

XOCHICALCO, TEMPLE; DETAIL SHOWING FEATHERED SERPENT.

MITLA, THE PALACE; INTERIOR OF COURT. (Brehme.)

CHAN CHAN, CHIMU PALACE AND CIT RUINS; AIR VIEW. (Shippee-Johnson Expediti and American Geographical Society.)

MACHU PICCHU; GENERAL VIEW SHOWING TYPICAL INCA MASONRY; TEMPLES IN THE C TER, HOUSES AND PALACES TO LEFT AND RIGHT. (Hiram Bingham, National Geographic Society, University Press.)

Plate 8

Chapter 3

EGYPTIAN ARCHITECTURE

EVERY year the waters of the Nile, fed by torrential seasonal rains in the distant hinterland of Africa, rise from twenty to thirty feet and spread out over the narrow alluvial valley below the Second Cataract. The fertile ground left by earlier floods drinks the water eagerly, and a new layer of rich soil is left by the flood as it recedes. For over 3000 years the rise of this annual inundation has been recorded, for upon it depended the productivity, almost the life itself, of this desert-held valley. A "good" flood meant bumper yields of crops; a "bad," one that rose less than twenty feet, might mean near-starvation. The river made the country—it almost was the country.

In the long valley which this great river cut for itself between its Second Cataract and the Mediterranean—a distance of about 700 miles, but with a width of only between two and ten miles until the Mediterranean delta is reached—there grew up through the unrecorded millennia of prehistory one of the great neolithic civilizations of the world. The Egyptians who produced this culture were apparently a mixed race, with elements of Nilotic dark-skinned types, types related to the Semites (the Arabs and the Syrians), and elements derived from the early white race which ringed the shores of the Mediterranean Sea and inhabited its islands. By about 4000 B.C., this energetic people had become acquainted with the use of copper and gold, and had become organized, village-dwelling, agricultural people, busily engaged in developing the building and the decorative arts; yet the stone-age basis of much of their civilization went on for another two millennia, and all through the greatest period of Egyptian art beautifully made stone knives and other tools preserved its memory.

The early Egyptians lived in shelters built of river reeds, bound together to give strength and plastered with river mud. These dwellings were either round and conical like the houses of many of the upper-river tribes today, or else rectangular in plan with curved arched tops. In order to provide spaces for outdoor living which were sheltered from the sun, often these huts would be preceded by a columned portico, the columns consisting of those tied-together bunches of reeds which formed such an important part of much Egyptian building and gave rise to many of the later forms which were perpetuated in stone. Sometime in this dim prehistoric period the making of adobe bricks from the river mud was developed, and these mud bricks became an essential part of all of the later architecture.

There are evidences that Egypt in these early millennia was much more wooded than it is today, and palm, sycamore, and acacia wood was used with increasing freedom and skill. Later, fir, pine, and cedar came into use, imported from Syria. It is probable, too, that from the same Asiatic source came the first Egyptian knowledge of the metals.

In this predynastic era, the elements of Egyptian religion and Egyptian decorative forms were alike developed. Egyptian religion was based primarily on a cult of the dead, coupled with a mythology coming from two sources: the first an African leaning toward the deification of animals and probably related to totemism as a tribal matter, and the second a quite advanced type of anthropomorphic theology which came—like the evergreens and the metals—from Syria. The cult of the dead had an enormous influence on Egyptian architecture. The idea of immortality as somehow connected with the preservation of the dead man's body led from the earliest periods to attempts—first by means of various embalming methods, and later by careful study of the architecture of sepulchral buildings—to preserve the corpse indefinitely. It was this search for permanence which led, little by little, to the replacing of temporary materials with those more permanent, and so eventually to the stone architecture of the great Egyptian monuments which have persisted so long, perhaps the most impressive evidences ever built of man's desire to transcend the temporal limitations of his own life.

Even the decorative forms which the Egyptians used frequently had a close relationship with this same desire for permanence. The carved or painted representation of a person or an action took on a reality that was the direct result of this feeling; the desire to perpetuate life led early to a kind of realism in decorative work, an effort to show mankind at work and at play and worship, which developed an extraordinary skill in Egyptian artists and gave to us priceless information on Egyptian life.

The blend of the other two religious ideas—the African animal worship and the later anthropomorphism—led to the series of animal- and bird-headed but otherwise human gods which played such a large part in

Egyptian temple carvings and produced in the artist a sense of the fantastic and the imaginative to counterbalance the other, realistic, approach.

All of these architectural and decorative beginnings achieved definitive expression only when the separated though related tribes of the valley were at last united into one organized whole—that is, only when the dynastic history of Egypt began. Estimates of the relative chronology of early Egyptian dynastic history vary enormously, but the general consensus of the best opinion today is that the first dynasty began about 3200 B.C., when a chief of the Hawk tribe of upper Egypt, King Min, first united the country. Egyptian history is usually divided into a series of periods—the Old Kingdom, including the first to the tenth dynasties, which lasted from *circa* 3200 to *circa* 2160 B.C.; the Middle Kingdom, covering the eleventh and twelfth dynasties, from 2160 to *circa* 1680 B.C.; the Hyksos period, during which Egypt was under the control of foreign rulers from Asia, from 1680 to *circa* 1580 B.C., including the thirteenth to the seventeenth dynasties; and the New Empire, extending from the eighteenth to the twenty-second dynasties, from 1580 to *circa* 1100 B.C. This was followed by another period of 500 years of foreign domination by Libyans and Assyrians, and this in turn by a brief renaissance usually known as the Saitic period, comprising the twenty-sixth dynasty and lasting from 663 to 525 B.C., when the kingdom was overwhelmed by the Persian Conquest. Another renaissance and a new period of prosperity and great building arose under the Ptolemies, who reigned after the death of Alexander the Great.

With the greater security and efficiency given by the unified government of the kingdom, the arts and crafts made tremendous strides, and already in the third dynasty the great pyramid and tomb temple of King Zoser in Sakkara, designed by the architect Imhotep, shows an exquisite artistic feeling combined with a perfection in the use of stone which was not to be surpassed for many centuries. The Egyptians honored many of their architects, who became respected court officials, frequently of great wealth, but for Imhotep they reserved the honor of deification, probably as the first great user of stone for monumental buildings. The fourth dynasty saw the building of the great pyramids of Gizeh.

The Old Kingdom buildings are primarily sepulchral. Even the temples which have lasted are usually those attached to tombs. Other temples were apparently, if we can judge from carved representations, still the traditional reed and mud-plaster edifices of primitive tribes. Yet it was in the Old Kingdom period that many of the stone forms of later Egyptian architecture took form, and it is a significant fact that most of these, as we shall see, owed large parts of their design to origins developed with reeds and mud.

The Middle Kingdom saw a new freedom in the use of these stone forms and the development of others. It witnessed as well the beginnings of a monumental religious architecture, but it was not until the New Empire period that the great temple forms of Egypt, with their tremendous courts and columned halls, became common. With the fall of the New Empire the creative development of Egyptian architecture almost ceased, and the later periods of building under the Saitic restoration and the Ptolemies were in large measure mere attempts to recapture the greatness of earlier work in buildings usually smaller in scale. Their only advance is in the additional clarity and simplicity of their plans, a certain definiteness of outlook in design, that may perhaps be credited to the growing influence of Greek and later of Roman ideals.

The Nile made Egypt, and the conditions of the Nile valley determined Egyptian building materials. Reeds and mud must always have been the most available, and doubtless conditioned the design of the greater part of the domestic, country architecture of the nation throughout its history. Increasing technical skill led to a greater refinement of form. Posts were made by binding papyrus stalks together. Beams might be either of bound papyrus stalks like the posts, or else of palm trunks. The ordinary one-story structure had a framework of these posts and beams, with a wall between formed of a matting of single stalks woven together, which could be plastered—both outside and in—with mud plaster. Roofs were formed by resting other mats of reeds on the beams and covering the whole with mud. The weight of the mud would force the projecting ends of the wall matting out into a projecting curve. Since the country is nearly rainless and often hot, a flat roof has great usefulness as additional living space, and therefore this type of roof rapidly superseded the earlier curved hut roofs; and even in little one-story houses a stair to the roof became an essential part of the design.

In the form of adobe brick, the river mud was a material very generally employed. Used at first only for tombs, city or town walls, and similar monumental works, little by little it began to take the place of the wattle-and-daub construction for houses. Since these mud bricks were somewhat compressible and never of very great strength, the early Egyptians studied carefully ways in which walls of them could be built so as to avoid the danger of cracks and to guarantee their strength. Often they would be built in sections, each section built with its brick laid in concave beds, with the joints curving up both at the ends and at the sides. Between these curved sections, other horizontal sections were placed, so that cracks which did occur would occur at definite places where they could be easily repaired. Moreover, because the weight of these walls was tremendous and their strength slight, in order to reduce both weight and material almost all of the brick walls were built with inclined faces, the walls being narrower at the top than at the bottom, where greater strength was necessary; and this batter- ing or sloping of the walls became almost a universal feature in all later Egyptian architecture.

Another characteristic brick form developed by the Egyptians was the vault. Whether a knowledge of the arch principle was borrowed from the peoples of western Asia or developed independently will perhaps never be known; but, whatever the source may have been, the Egyptians were well acquainted with the principle and used vaults frequently, in tombs— especially of the Middle Kingdom—and in drains, and occasionally vaults were used to cover rows of storage rooms, as in the Ramesseum, the mortuary temple which Rameses the Great, of the nineteenth dynasty, built for himself in Thebes. Nevertheless, though vaulting was known and used as a struc- tural element, it never became a controlling factor in either planning or exterior design. Curved ceilings occur frequently, but usually the curves are cut on a single surface of stone, evidently with the idea of symbolizing the curved reed roofs of primitive huts and houses rather than the forms of masonry vaults.

The native woods of Egypt are usually not obtainable in large straight pieces; and Egyptian carpentry, even when working on the large sizes available in the imported woods, developed in the effort to put together many small pieces to give a large single form. Thus the earliest type of wooden house, usually called the *serekh* house, was made of a series of small vertical boards placed overlapping, alternate ones behind the others, and sewn together with leather thongs. This gave a series of recessed vertical panels running from top to bottom, and openings were formed merely by omitting a certain number of the vertical planks; this allowed ample ventila- tion. The openings in almost all of the earlier structures were hung with matting woven in rich geometrical patterns; this was rolled up to open and let down to close the door or the window. Even in these early times, in the primitive mud-and-reed or wooden buildings, considerable color bril- liance was achieved by these vivid hangings, and the habit of using color so developed led early to the painting of the wood and plaster in bright colors.

The sides of the Nile valley are almost all of high cliffs or precipitous hills of rock left when the river, in the course of the ages, cut its way down through the desert plateau of northern Africa. There was thus easily available an unlimited reservoir of building stone—sandstones, limestones, and granites. Nevertheless, stone came into Egyptian architecture comparatively late, and in almost all of its later development shows the influence of forms which are not primarily stone forms, but rather the interpretation in the new and permanent material of the shapes and details developed in the earlier wood, reed, and mud buildings. Despite this limitation, the Egyptians used the stone magnificently. They soon learned its strength, its permanence, its beauty of surface. They became expert in quarrying the hardest stones with simple and primitive means. They developed an extraordinary technique in the handling of enormous single blocks, building great banks of earth of gentle slope up which the blocks could be drawn, to be dropped gently into their final position by digging away the earth. Though apparently ignorant of the principle of the tackle, they understood the lever thoroughly and developed a rocker system of raising stones. The stone would be placed on a cradle with curved lower runners; with levers one end could easily be rocked up and a wedge placed under it, the stone would then be rocked in the reverse way and a wedge placed under the other end, and so little by little the whole could be raised to almost any desired height.

The dynastic stone architecture of Egypt demanded two things—almost unlimited labor power, and careful organization. The buildings were apparently designed ahead of time in almost all their details, and the individual stones cut and roughly finished to size at the quarry itself. Labor power was furnished largely by slaves captured in war and by the forced labor of peasants, for whom whole towns would be built at the site of a great project. The king, as a god as well as a human autocrat, had absolute power to command the amount of labor necessary. Yet, in general, the treatment of these workmen was fairly good, their wages adequate, and the existence of strikes even in those early days proves that they were in no way mere slave automatons.

The necessary organization was furnished by the diligent cultivation of good architects and skilled craftsmen; such perfection of execution, such grandeur of design, and such beauty in decorative adornment could only have been produced where the artist and the craftsman were honored members of society.

The great stone architecture of Egypt sprang into sudden and almost completely mature life, like Athena from the head of Zeus, in the third dynasty, with the magnificent tomb group designed by the architect Imhotep for King Zoser. Here, within a vast enclosing wall, rose an enormous stepped pyramid, surrounded by a most ingeniously arranged series of narrow courts and columned halls. The columns are all fluted or reeded, evidently recalling in stone the typical primitive reed supports of earlier buildings; but they are handled with the most consummate grace and perfection of detail. In the large halls the columns are simple, with only plain square capitals and bases, and alternate pairs of columns are connected with stone walls, as though the architect were still skeptical of the strength of his material. One of the courts is bordered by a row of ten so-called chapels, great solid structures the fronts of which have delicately curved tops apparently supported on the most slender of engaged columns, tapering and reeded, and capped with conventionalized heads of the goddess Hathor. The general impression given by these chapels, though graceful and delicate, is that of a representation in stone of a light construction of reeds and plaster. This same tentative quality distinguishes the whole group, and the amount of stone in its thick walls and its great solid masses would seem almost to indicate a desire on the part of the builders to imitate the solidity of native rock itself rather than to express the walls and columns and roofs of a true stone building. However, from the purely aesthetic standpoint, the delicacy, the refinement, of every detail is amazing, and the quality we see in much of this Sakkara temple is almost that restraint which we associate with modern architecture. Zoser's successor, Sanakht, started a tomb-temple near by, using similar forms and details, but it was never completed.

The great pyramids and temples of the fourth dynasty show an entirely different approach. In these, austere simple rectangular blocks of granite serve alike as piers and beams. The decoration consisted entirely of surface painting. The plans of the pyramid temples are as simple as the architectural treatment. Superficially they seem more primitive than Zoser's building, but actually from the structural point of view they are more advanced, because their use of pier and beam and of wall and slab shows at last a definite realization of the structural possibilities of stone. More and more, through the latter part of the Old Kingdom and all of the Middle Kingdom, to the coming of the Hyksos, this knowledge of the structural possibilities of stone increased. The fifth dynasty saw the development of the palm-leaf column. By the twelfth dynasty, lotus-bud and papyrus-stalk columns were also in common use, as well as a fluted or polygonal column similar to that which Zoser had used, and all the typical Egyptian cornice treatments and other characteristic details had reached almost final development. However, through all of this period, stone building was re served almost entirely for sepulchral uses, and stone temples even of the advanced and highly cultivated Middle Kingdom are always mortuary or tomb temples. It was not until the New Empire, after the Hyksos had come and gone, that the building of great stone temples for the direct worship of the gods began to be common, and it was perhaps only because this New Empire was more completely militarized and systematized and its Pharaohs were more absolute monarchs, working with a serf agriculture and with a plenitude of slaves that resulted from aggressive foreign conquests, that these colossal structures which still stand so impressively on both banks of the Nile—especially at the site of ancient Thebes—were possible.

Almost every form in Egyptian stone architecture is an attempt to symbolize or to represent earlier and more primitive types of reed-and-mud building. Thus, nearly all Egyptian stone walls are battered, recalling the battered sides of the old mud-brick structures. At projecting corners of walls and those great gate towers we call pylons, there is always a projecting round molding or bead running up the edge, painted with circular lines along it and a spiral as of a binding cord around. This is not a type of decoration which would occur naturally to a stone mason; it is merely a stone interpretation of the bundle of reeds which was the corner post of Egyptian huts. The characteristic cornice which crowns the stone walls is similarly based on other than stone prototypes. A projecting round element exactly like the corner bead runs across the top of the wall, recalling the horizontal beam made of a bundle of reeds; and above this sweeps out, in a single concave curve, the projecting cornice form. This *cavetto* cornice is always decorated with vertical scallops or scales, which without doubt recall the tops of the reed lathing of the primitive wattle-and-daub construction, pressed out into a curve by the weight of the mud roof.

The columns themselves show the same kind of development from similar reed origins. The earlier columns are either fluted or reeded like those of Sakkara, or else scalloped in plan, thus representing even more vividly posts formed of papyrus stalks bound together. As the papyrus stalks taper, so the columns taper; and the capitals represent either the flowers of papyrus opening out to form a kind of bell shape, or else the buds of the unopened plant. Later, lotus forms begin to replace the papyrus forms, and the lotus-bud column becomes one of the most general types in New Empire work. Manifestly the lotus was never used to make posts, for its stems are as weak and sinuous as those of its American cousin the water lily; but the lotus as the great symbol of the Nile had tremendous religious significance, and—once the old structural origin of the column form had been forgotten— the replacing of the papyrus by this more magical flower was natural, especially as no great basic change in general outline was necessary. The palm-leaf and palm-trunk type of column also obviously symbolizes the early use of palm wood for supporting posts; and the Egyptian architect, in order to make this even more clear, gave to the single cylindrical trunk of the tree, when it was represented in stone, a capital of spreading palm leaves.

As the centuries went on, it is easy to see how this earlier origin of the Egyptian stone forms was no longer remembered, and, although the basic outlines remained as a crystallized body of architectural tradition which held true for almost two millennia, nevertheless stone was more and more seen as stone, columns tended more and more to be simple cylindrical stone supports, but the basic types of battered wall with reeded edges, of cavetto cornice, and of column capital either of the bud or open-flower type remained unchanged.

Such a stone architecture created vast surfaces, and on these the Egyptians lavished a wealth of decorative carving and painting. The idea of structural elements as primarily structural elements, to be emphasized because of the work they do, is almost always secondary to the idea of a building as a succession of flat surfaces of wall and curved surfaces of column to be covered with a wonderfully rich all-over patterning. This is another example of the derivative quality of Egyptian stone architecture, for the type of decoration used was that which resulted either from painting the plain plaster surfaces of house or palace or else from carving plain stone walls of excavated rock-cut tombs. None the less, it is a decoration of extraordinary power and vitality, compounded not only of inscriptions in hieroglyphics—perhaps the most decorative "lettering" ever developed by man—in which the history of the building, the glories of the king who built it, and religious rituals are all perpetuated, but also of magnificent representations of gods and men, scenes of worship, historical events, triumphs, battles, or hunting scenes and pictures of palace life. The earliest of these decorative stone carvings, the tomb carvings of the Old Empire, show an exquisite balance of realism and convention. Even the usual convention of the figure, by which the head, hips, and feet are always in profile, whereas the shoulders are in front elevation and the torso usually in a somewhat distorted three-quarter view, seems natural in this early work, and the vividness of gesture is extraordinary. As time went on, the treatment tended to grow less naturalistic and more conventional; yet imagination always controlled the basic design, and above all there was a remarkable sense of scale. In the developed work of the New Empire, small and large figures are used at will. Size is often considered a purely symbolic matter; but this very fact enables the observer to build up the total size of the composition in a way impossible in the ranked realistic miniatures of the earlier work. It is this rich yet usually only delicately relieved carving—the effect of which was heightened by brilliant coloring—that alone makes it possible for the tremendous buildings of Karnak and Luxor, with their broad surfaces and simple shapes, to appear of the colossal size they really are.

The building types of Egypt may be divided into three great classes: tombs, domestic buildings and palaces, and temples. Throughout the history of ancient Egypt, the tomb necessarily played an enormous part, for all of Egyptian religion was in some way tied up with the mystery of death, and the search for permanence already noted led to lavish expenditure for tomb buildings.

The *mastaba* was the characteristic tomb of the noble in the Old Kingdom, as the pyramid was of the Pharaoh. Essentially it consists of a mass of stone, flat-topped and with inclined sides, containing one or more funeral chapels and rooms for sacrifice, worship, and votive offerings. There is in it always a false door as though to lead to the funeral chamber itself, but the burial is in a chamber cut out of the living rock many feet below and reached by a vertical shaft as well as by an inclined shaft through which the coffin is placed, the upper part of the inclined shaft usually filled up to hide it. To gain additional security, this inclined shaft was also cut off by a series of vertically sliding stone doors, let down from the ground level in grooves prepared for them ahead of time. These burials have fared somewhat better than pyramid graves. Architecturally, the most significant part of the mastaba is the above-ground structure, which again and again obviously recalls house types of the time. Especially on the interiors of the chambers we find the painted representations of matting, hangings, and wood-paneled walls, and even the ceilings will be decorated like those of the simple houses. Much of what we know of primitive Egyptian wood and reed domestic architecture has come from representations within the mastabas as well as from the mastaba forms themselves.

The pyramid was developed from the mastaba type by projecting its sloping sides upward until they met in a point, or else by building on the flat top of the mastaba a pyramidal form of slightly less steep slope. This origin is indicated by the existence of stepped pyramids, which were formed by a central core—the original mastaba with its sides projected upward—surrounded by two or three additional layers with parallel sloping walls but flat tops, forming a series of steps up to the final point. This type of construction is particularly evident in the great stepped pyramid of Sakkara, and it has been surmised that all the great pyramids were constructed in essentially a similar manner, with the exception that when the steps were completed they were filled in to give the smooth pyramidal shape. The fact that the slopes of the wall portions of the stepped pyramids are much steeper than the slopes of the unbroken pyramids gives color to this idea.

In the Old Kingdom, tombs are either of the pyramid or mastaba type, the pyramid being usually reserved for royal burials. The pyramid is essentially an artificial mound and perhaps recalls the very general primitive tumulus burials, though there is little evidence of these in Egypt itself. The burial chamber is either within the pyramid itself, as in the great pyramid of Cheops, or else carved in the living rock beneath it. The choice of the pyramidal form for these structures undoubtedly reflects a realization of the tremendous static quality which the pyramid as a form possesses, both actually and aesthetically. Some of the pyramids are built of brick, like that at Meydum and the smaller pyramids of undistinguished Pharaohs of later periods at Abusir and elsewhere. Yet in general the search for the most permanent material led to the choice of stone, and the amount of cut stone in one of the great pyramids reaches almost astronomical proportions. Only legions of laborers working for years could bring such a structure to completion, and the passionate search for personal immortality that characterizes so much of Egyptian thought has few more moving expressions than the fact that Pharaoh after Pharaoh seems to have devoted almost all his wealth through almost all his reign to the construction of his own tomb. This movement reached its climax in the great pyramid of Gizeh—the Pyramid of Khufu, of the fourth dynasty, a vast, solid mountain of stone some 756 feet on the side and rising originally to a height of 482 feet. Deep within it lies the burial chamber, approached by a long sloping gallery. Above the chamber, to prevent its granite ceiling from being crushed by the weight upon it, is a series of open spaces, each roofed by its own granite slabs and topped at the last by a primitive two-part vault of two great slabs leaned inclined against each other so as to distribute the weight above them on either side. By means of stone gates and sliding doors which sank into place and blocked the entrance, it was hoped to make this chamber, surrounded by so many hundreds of thousands of tons of stone, absolutely inviolate; yet it is an ironic fact that not a single one of the pyramid tombs has been discovered which was not long ago broken into and robbed!

Many attempts have been made to explain the orientation and design of the great pyramid in mystical and astronomical terms; but beyond the general fact that Egyptian structures, like most of the important buildings of the ancient world, were designed with orientations conditioned on simple natural phenomena like the rising of the sun on some special day or the direction of some important star, little that is irrefutable and definite has been discovered.

In the Middle Kingdom the tendency was away from constructed tombs toward tombs cut deep into the sides of the cliffs that bordered the Nile valley. Usually these had columnar porches in front, leading into a hall behind, with its roof usually supported on columns. This formed the worship or public part of the tomb, but as in the case of the mastaba the real burial was usually many feet below. It is from the twelfth-dynasty tombs of Beni Hassan, with their fluted proto-Doric columns in front and their lotus-bud columns within, that much of our knowledge of this intermediate stage of Egyptian architecture is derived. In the New Empire, still another stage was reached. Experience had shown that all the earlier tombs had been susceptible of robbery and defilement, and the search for permanence forced less obvious burials. The result was the great rock-cut tombs of the New Empire, with no such elaborate porches as those of the earlier period, but rather with an entrance concealed as far as possible and plans labyrinthine, full of false turnings and empty chambers, as though by concealing rather than by displaying the burial the greed of tomb thieves could be defeated. To take the place of the earlier mastaba halls or rock-cut caves, the Pharaohs of this time built, in addition to their tombs, large funerary temples in the plain, where all the funeral rites could be carried on as before, and on an even larger and more magnificent scale, without danger of revealing where the body itself was laid.

The early one-room reed or wattle-and-daub huts were succeeded by houses of wood, at least for the better-class homes. These were built of vertical boards sewn together in the way described earlier. However, the rectangular house of mud brick must have made its appearance at an early date in Egyptian history, and all through the course of the Middle Kingdom and the New Empire the mud-brick house or palace became the rule for town dwellings and at least the larger country houses. It is probable that the reed hut continued in use also among the lower classes of the population. Nevertheless, the town which was built by the heretic Pharaoh Ikhnaton to house the craftsmen who were employed in building his new city at Tel el Amarna was a town of close-built masonry-walled houses, arranged in a strict checkerboard patterning and opening on narrow streets or alleys. Each house consisted of a small court, a large central living room, and two or three other rooms, one of which probably served as kitchen and one as workshop; each house had a stair which led up to the flat roof.

This basic arrangement persisted as the foundation for the smaller Egyptian house plans through the greater part of Egyptian history, and many small models in terra-cotta or in wood, which were buried in the tombs to furnish a home for the dead, remain to show us the type. Sometimes the courtyard is planted with trees, sometimes the house is in two stories, frequently an open colonnaded porch separates the living rooms from the courtyard and gives an opportunity for outdoor living in the shade.

In the larger houses, the central living room was increased in size and usually had its ceiling and roof some feet above the remainder of the house, to allow clerestory openings through which light and air could penetrate. In these larger houses this higher roof was almost always supported by four or even more wooden columns; and such a room, with its brightly painted posts, its blue ceiling, its matting curtains which regulated the light and air coming in from the clerestory windows, its masonry divan or bench along one side covered with gay textiles and cushions, must have been a pleasant living space, cool and clear and colorful, warm in cold weather and cool in the heat of summer. From this central living room or receiving room, the descendants of which are found in many oriental houses to the present time, the smaller rooms—bedrooms, service rooms, storage spaces— opened out. Often a colonnaded porch shielded the door, and additional privacy was given by the long narrow vestibule through which the visitor was required to enter.

In the city houses of Tel el Amarna and elsewhere there was always an enclosed court before the house entrance, and cooking was often done in the open air in such a space; but in the country villas, where the construction was usually lighter and often of wood, the rectangular block of the house was set free within extensive parks and gardens, the whole surrounded by a solid exterior wall. The importance given to the garden of the courtyards and the house surroundings was characteristic. Since much of the building was on land almost desert except when irrigated, imported soil and elaborate systems of pools and irrigation ditches were common; just because of its rarity water occupied an important place in the decorative

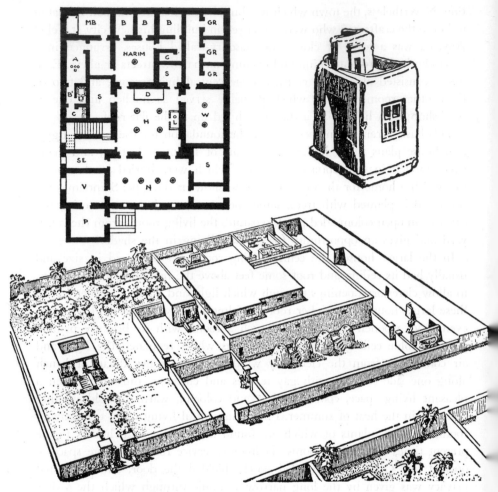

5. EGYPTIAN HOUSE AT TEL EL AMARNA, RESTORED, AND AN ANCIENT EGYPTIAN HOUSE MODEL. (Baldwin Smith: *Egyptian Architecture as Cultural Expression.*)

P. PORCH
V. VESTIBULE
H. GREAT HALL
D. DAIS OR COUCH

B. BEDROOM
MB. CHIEF BEDROOM
GR. GRANARY
B'. BATH

scheme, and in the great palace at Tel el Amarna a large part of one side of the garden was occupied by a charming water-garden pavilion, with a series of T-shaped basins under a column-supported roof.

In the better-class houses the pavements were often of a special hard plaster, gaily painted with flowers and plants and with birds and fishes, as though the wealthy Egyptian were always trying to bring outside nature and especially the beauties of his own garden into the house itself; even where the house walls have perished and the wooden columns long since rotted away, these colorful pavements still remain to bring before us the luxury of the houses they once adorned.

Even the largest palaces were essentially mere enlarged examples of the basic house type already described. Instead of the central room of four columns, the great hall might have as many as thirty-six, but the general idea was the same. Size was given by more reduplication of similar parts; that is, a large house might contain, not one columned living room, but four or five—one, the largest, for the master, one for a harem, one for guests, another for retainers or service, and so on. This is an extremely important fact, because the later Egyptian temples as the House of God were mere adaptations of this original domestic plan.

For the lighter structures, which must have played such an important part in Egyptian life and have formed such a large element in the Egyptian landscape, we are forced to depend upon painted representations. Fortunately, owing to the Egyptian cult of the dead and the desire to surround the coffin with symbolic portrayals of all of the happiest and loveliest phases of human life, such representations are plentiful, and by a comparative study one can pick out easily the salient components of the Egyptian country houses. Egypt was largely agricultural; and, since money as a medium of exchange hardly existed until the Ptolemaic and Roman times, wealth consisted largely in the products of fields and pastures and fishponds. Thus, storerooms became of vast importance, and every house—especially every country house of any pretension—had a large area given over to granaries and warehouses, which often formed one side of the entire compound.

The house itself would stand in the middle of the compound, surrounded by a carefully planted grove of trees, set in formal lines and avenues and often surrounding in the middle a large artificial pool, to serve alike as fishpond and as a source from which the gardens could be watered. The house would often be in two stories, with wooden posts, walls of plaster gaily painted, and large window spaces in which rolled matting screens

6. TYPICAL EGYPTIAN VILLA; RESTORED VIEW BASED ON ANCIENT WALL
PAINTINGS. (Perrot and Chipiez. Tome I.)

served as curtains. On the flat roof there would often be tents or temporary
shelters of wooden posts and hanging awnings.

Within, the house might have its central room of the normal columned
type running the full height, although occasionally interior courts existed,
making the house almost similar in plan to the Pompeiian house. Bright
blues and reds and yellows were everywhere, and the total effect must have
been cheerful and summerlike and charming, a fit decoration for the garden
which surrounded it. The garden itself, besides the groves of trees, would
contain flower beds and little summerhouses, and life outdoors seems to have
been more important than life within.

From the tomb reliefs we gain a vivid idea, almost as though from a
"documentary movie," of the lines of farmer-tenants driving the trains of

donkeys loaded with the produce of their fields. We can see the scribes measuring off and recording the rent paid as the grain was dumped into the storerooms. We can see the slaves lifting the precious water from the Nile by means of great wooden counterweighted sweeps like the old New England well sweeps. We can see the master of the house hunting ducks in the reeds along the Nile or sitting on his housetop in the cool of the evening; and we can see, too, feasts where the dancing girls whirl to the thrumming of harps in front of the merrymakers.

With the coming of the militarized might of the New Empire, something of a change went over Egyptian life. As the king assumed more and more power, the old landed nobility were replaced by court officials and imperial favorites, and the peasantry sank into virtual serfdom. Something of the insouciance of the earlier Egyptian life died. A new and more formalized, and perhaps more materialistic, luxury came in to take its place; and this story, too, we can read in the tomb paintings.

Until the New Empire, all of the great temples had been mortuary temples, and the distinction between tomb and temple had been but vaguely made. Yet from the beginning the idea that the temple was the House of God can be noted, and various early kingdom tomb temples have the colonnaded porch and the columned hall which we have seen as an integral part of the large Egyptian house. The climax of grandeur in the earlier temples was reached in the great tomb temple which was built by Mentuhotep III, of the twelfth dynasty, at Deir el Bahri. In this, a central pyramid was surrounded on all four sides by a wide colonnaded hall, and the columned front was approached by a series of terraces cut into the cliff or filled against retaining walls as necessary. The whole had a magnificence of axial monumental effect which was a new note in Egyptian architecture, and the court gateway was approached from the river by a long straight avenue of sphinxes, which have now disappeared.

In the eighteenth dynasty, Queen Hatshepset, a glorious woman who was the wife of three Pharaohs in turn—Tuthmosis I, II, and III,—built herself, at Deir el Bahri, a great tomb temple, obviously accepting many ideas from the earlier adjoining monument but carrying the entire scheme to a much greater perfection of architectonic complexity. Her architect, Senmut, realized that the pyramid forms and the long straight lines of colonnade and terrace were fundamentally inharmonious. Moreover, the pyramid type of tomb had gone out of fashion. He therefore designed a series of courtyards on successively raised terraces, the front of each terrace wall decorated with a long, continuous colonnade, which led up with ever-increasing grandeur and richness to the simple colonnaded court which was the climax of the whole, behind which was the mortuary chapel. Each terrace was approached from the one below by a great stone ramp with solid railings; and from the river the view of these consecutive tiers of colonnades, so firmly and beautifully composed, shows one of the great conceptions of Egyptian architecture and gives a hint of the new architectural feeling that was to characterize the New Empire.

From this it was but a step to the great temples which the later Pharaohs built on the river plains of Thebes, which still stand as the superb ruins of Karnak, Luxor, and Medinet Abu. Here the rulers of the eighteenth, nineteenth, and twentieth dynasties built a series of tremendous temples, which were an expression of their attempt to make Thebes the dominant religious center of the empire, as well as an expression of their own grandeur and power as sovereigns. The original impetus to this building may have come from large mortuary temples which these rulers built, far from their own hidden tombs in the hinterland cliffs. The Ramesseum is a characteristic example, noteworthy for the complex rows of storage rooms, all carefully vaulted in brick, which surround the shrine portion of the temple. Even more interesting, and much better preserved, is the Temple of Seti I at Abydos. This is remarkable for its seven chapels at the back of the great hall, through one of which, sacred to Osiris, a whole new series of shrines and halls dedicated to that god is entered.

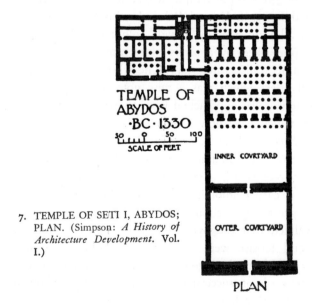

TEMPLE OF
ABYDOS
·BC·1330
SCALE OF FEET

INNER COURTYARD

OUTER COURTYARD

PLAN

7. TEMPLE OF SETI I, ABYDOS; PLAN. (Simpson: *A History of Architecture Development*. Vol. I.)

These temple structures generally consisted of a colonnaded hall, approached by a colonnaded porch and opening at the rear into a chapel or a series of chapels, the whole surrounded by a complex group of storerooms to hold the royal treasure as well as the votive offerings. The only new element in the scheme was the much enlarged forecourt, which preceded the building proper and was entered by an impressive monumental gateway flanked by two great pylons. The pylon type of entrance, built at first of mud brick, had been used for 1000 years. The high forms were given scale by masts carrying banners ranked along the fronts, and later by the addition also of obelisks, the vertical forms of which gave excellent accent to the wide surfaces behind.

All the later temples of the gods were merely more highly developed expressions of this same theme. All are approached through pylon entrances, which led into a court. Opposite the entrance a colonnade ran across the building, in some examples continuing down the sides of the court as well; and from the porch so formed a great columnar hall was entered. Behind this hall, repeated chapel or shrine rooms of growing sacredness and smaller size were placed, all laid out on the main axis, so that the impression of reducing size and fainter and fainter light, combined with richer and richer decoration, must have had an extraordinary emotional power. The Holy of Holies, the final shrine, was usually a simple room of solid stone walls, with a central basis on which the sacred figure of the god was placed. If the god was Ra, the sun god, the statue was replaced by a sacred boat, which signified the passage of the sun across the sky. Around this group of central elements was a labyrinth of smaller rooms, containing all of the paraphernalia needed in the rites and including certain larger columned halls either as parts of priests' residences or to symbolize the larger rooms of normal houses.

The variations in this normal scheme were many. Generally speaking, each succeeding sovereign tried to outdo his predecessor in the grandeur and the size of the elements of which the whole was built. Thus the early simple columned hall, which recalled the house reception room, grew into the great hypostyle hall. That at Karnak is a vast enclosure, 160 feet deep and over 300 feet wide. The three central aisles are supported by enormous columns some 60 feet high, carrying a roof that is over 70 feet above the ground. These central columns bear spreading bell-shaped capitals of papyrus-flower type. The lower portions on each side have, each of them, 59 columns of papyrus-bud type, and the space between the higher roof and the lower roof is occupied by large clerestory windows with stone gratings through which the center of the whole was dimly lighted. In this case, as in a few other temples, the front of the hall, instead of being a porch, is formed by a pair of great pylons like those at the entrance.

Many of the temples had two or three forecourts, and some of the plans are of extraordinary complexity because later Pharaohs added to and altered the works of their predecessors relentlessly. The spirit of such great structures as those of Karnak and Luxor seems one of almost unbridled megalomania. It was the smaller temples, such as those at Medinet Abu, which

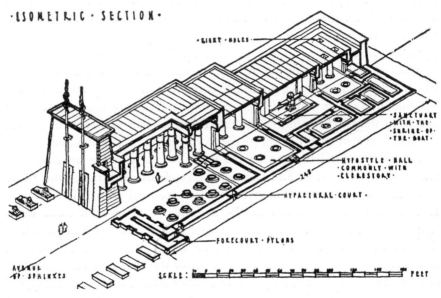

8. TEMPLE OF KHONS, KARNAK; CUTAWAY ISOMETRIC VIEW. (Richardson and Corfiato: *The Art of Architecture*.)

were perhaps more deeply effective; but in its prime almost any one of them must have been a building of overwhelming emotional power. The rich color and the changing surface of the reliefs which covered almost every surface both of column and wall, the deep light percolating down from the dim clerestory windows above on the enormous forms of the great columns, the long perspectives of column after column stretching back into the gloom—all of this must have been a most moving contrast to the brilliance of the Egyptian sun outside; and, when one left the great spaces of these columned halls to enter the more sacred shrines behind, the growing darkness and the growing silence, the sense of wall after wall between one and the outside world, could not fail to produce an amazing sensation of awe if not of terror. Yet, complicated and huge as these structures are, their ancestry is clear. The *hypostyle* hall, as these great many-columned temple halls are called, is the old house reception room; the colonnaded courtyard is the old house porch; and the little shrine is the small house bedroom.

Another special type of New Empire temple can be seen in the great rock-cut shrines at Abu Simbel, where an attempt was made to carve the whole of a simple temple—columned hall, shrines, side chambers, and so on—out of the living rock of the river cliffs. The most remarkable quality in the greater of the two temples is the treatment of the front, where the door is flanked on each side by two enormous *colossi*—seated figures sixty feet high—which for three millennia have gazed out over the valley in their strange and magical dignity almost unchanged.

With the disintegration of Egyptian power which followed the fall of the New Empire, Egyptian architecture, too, seems to have almost died, and little but minor building was done for six centuries. Libyans from the desert and Assyrians from Asia successively dominated the whole of the Nile valley. Egypt went on, but it was an Egypt poverty-struck, looking backward, and dependent for its public and its religious buildings at least upon the work of its ancestors. Only when the rule of the Ptolemies which followed the Alexandrine Empire, and later still the rule of the Romans, had brought back to the valley a new peace and a new prosperity did Egyptian architects again attempt buildings of great size. The extraordinary thing is that in these later structures, although there are evidences, obvious to the specialists, of foreign and of classic influence, nevertheless in general the old forms and the typical old plans are preserved almost unmodified.

The series of magnificent temples built during this period gives evidence of the vitality of the Egyptian tradition. They do not possess the colossal size of the New Empire work, but they have other virtues which almost counterbalance this loss. The plans are usually simpler, and the progression from court through hypostyle hall to shrine more direct, more carefully expressed. There is greater symmetry, a more careful study of the relative heights and proportions; and in such a temple as that at Edfu there is a sense of simple directness of design, of perfect interrelation of parts, which is sometimes missing in the larger, more complex work of the earlier time. In part, this effect may be due to the fact that Edfu still exists in almost perfect preservation, with its stone roof in large measure intact; so that it is Edfu, more than any of the other earlier temples, which gives one today the impression of that growing awe, that powerful emotional excitement, for which the Egyptian temple designer was always working.

Differences between this and the earlier work are largely matters of detail. The sculpture is less skillfully composed, a little bit more mechanical in execution, and the scale less magnificently handled; something of the old simplicity has perished. There is a greater variety in the capital forms also; and, instead of the old conical bud forms and the bell-shaped papyrus-flower forms of the earlier period, all sorts of complicated types of lotus-bud and lotus-flower capital occur. At times it seems almost as though a distant memory of the Corinthian column were present, so complicated are the projecting flower forms. The palm-leaf capital, which had been developed in the fifth dynasty and largely forgotten during the intermediate period, again comes into common use; and in some buildings several types of capital are used in the same composition, as in the front of the hypostyle hall at Edfu. This same temple shows another characteristic late form—the low screen wall built between the columns in such a way as to allow large open spaces above to light the hall behind, and combined with these screen walls a monumental doorway, somewhat greater in height, placed between the two central columns.

Another form which came into great use was the Hathor-headed column, in which the shaft is surmounted by a cubical block carved like a little shrine, and topped by four colossal heads looking out in different directions. It is a heavy form and overcomplicated for its supporting function, and it is characteristic of a loss of a sense of delicacy in detail which is typical of the later-period work. On the island of Philae, at the First Cataract, is a large group of temples, all of the late period, which show the imaginative and playful quality, the basic simplicity of conception, and occasionally the coarseness and heavy-handed detail which distinguish the Ptolemaic work.

At Denderah, a Temple of Hathor built as late as the time of Augustus shows the persistence of the Egyptian traditions. In Alexandria and the delta region generally, where classic settlement was greatest, there is much more evidence of Greek forms; and a cemetery recently excavated there shows pure Greek Doric capitals in some portions, and yet elsewhere, almost in the same composition, the typical cavetto cornice and battered walls of Egyptian tradition.

Quite outside this common tradition of Egyptian temple design lie a few exceptional examples in which there is some kind of approximation to the idea of the High Place as opposed to the House of God. This, naturally enough, occurs in temples to the sun god Aten. One of the earliest existing temples built to a god, and not connected with a tomb, is that which Ne-User-Re, the fifth-dynasty Pharaoh, built at Abusir, to Aten. It consists of a single court surrounded by a thick wall and containing a sacrificial altar; behind rose a high platform topped by a low obelisk of tremendous width, which was the symbol of Aten. This example apparently remained almost unique for nearly 1000 years, until the heretic King Ikhnaton or Akhenaten, who is also sometimes known as Amenophis IV or Amenhotep, built his new City of the Sun at Tel el Amarna. Since all the temple structures were of sun-dried brick, their remains are fragmentary; nevertheless, on the basis of their ruins and certain careful representations in tomb paintings it is possible to reconstruct Ikhnaton's sun temple. Like the earlier example at Abusir, it is chiefly open to the sky, without columnar halls or dark shrines. Columns are only used in porches and for purely decorative purposes. In essence the temple consisted of a series of open courts with pylons between, courts filled with row after row of offering tables, each with its own sacrificial altar. Trees and planting played a great part in the design as a whole, and the aim obviously was to make nature as great an element in the composition as possible; the architecture was minimized.

Nevertheless, even this simple and stunning conception remained childless. Ikhnaton's successors declared him heretical, ruthlessly destroyed the whole of Tel el Amarna, and even attempted to erase his name from all existing inscriptions.

There is much controversy as to the direct influence of Egyptian architecture on other and later developments. In some ways it seems a unique and isolated phenomenon, as unique as the valley which gave it birth. Born in the earliest days of Egyptian history, it continued well into Roman times, and seems only at last to have died when the last traditions of ancient Egyptian life passed away with the coming of Christianity. No other nation attempted such colossal structures of cut stone, depending entirely on the post-and-lintel type of construction. No other nation built such tombs or conceived the temple in quite the same way. In its basic controlling forms, therefore, Egyptian architecture died without descendants.

However, many of the decorative forms used in the ornamentation of Egyptian structures had an enormous and widespread influence. It used to be believed that even the Greek Doric column was based on the simple polygonal or fluted Egyptian piers, which were therefore called proto-Doric. Now, however, we know better; the Greek Doric was an independent characteristic development, as we shall see. But there is no denying the fact that the Persians adopted the cavetto cornice to cap the doors and windows of their palaces at Persepolis, and many other minor details can be found in modified forms in the later architecture of all western Asia. Specifically, Egyptian ways of using spiral forms to make a square all-over pattern are found reproduced in the decorative work of the Aegean islands in pre-Hellenic times, and there is much evidence of the borrowing of decorative elements by the Cretans, and some of a reverse borrowing by the Egyptians from Crete.

The lotus flower, which as a symbol of the Nile the Egyptians used so frequently as the basis for painted patterns, became one of the great original sources of all Western decorative art. It was taken over and modified by the Assyrians and by the Phoenicians and Hebrews of the Syrian coast, and the "knops and flowers" which the Bible tells us were so frequently used in the decoration of Solomon's Temple were neither more nor less than the well-known Egyptian lotus-flower and lotus-bud border pattern.

From Syria the modified lotus and lotus-bud forms were carried to Cyprus, Crete, and the Aegean islands, where they became a fertile source of endless modifications that gave rise eventually to all of the rich anthemion patterns that decorate the Greek vases and Greek friezes. From Greece the form traveled to Etruria and Rome, and from them it came down through the centuries. Wherever the progeny of the Greek anthemion can be traced, there too the parentage of Egypt is sure.

Historically, Egyptian architecture is important, because it shows what finished and beautiful results can be achieved by endless patience, almost unlimited man power, and great care. The Egyptian house was admirably suited to its climate, gay in color, generally well planned for its uses, and a pleasant place to live. The great Egyptian tombs of the earlier period, like the pyramids, command our respect even today because of the sublime faith that made them necessary and possible. The Egyptian temples are important, because in them, perhaps for the first time, a tremendous yet unified conception of a complex plan of many different elements for different uses was all integrated into one monumental whole, every part of which had a definite aesthetic relationship to every other part. But, above all else, Egyptian architecture can teach us the quality of scale, a quality by means of which big things appear big and small things small, a quality dependent on every bit of decoration and its relation to the form it decorates. It is not mere size alone which has made the buildings and ruins of the Nile valley a thing of wonder to mankind from the time of the Greeks down to the present day; it is, rather, the fact that they look their size, and for this the skill of the Egyptian architect is alone responsible.

Chapter 4

THE EARLY ARCHITECTURE
OF WESTERN ASIA

THE wide flat alluvial plains of the Tigro-Euphrates River made ideal fields for the neolithic farmers, and from a period possibly as early as the end of the fifth millennium B.C. they had formed flourishing villages, especially in the swampy delta where the river poured into the Persian Gulf at a point far up the valley from the present mouth. There, wherever deep excavations have been made, traces of their life are found—round clay hut floors, occasional remains of the hut walls themselves, and especially a great deal of exquisitely made, richly decorated pottery. These peoples had some knowledge of copper, and their wares show a nice sense of shape and of ornament. From the present name of the site where this decorated pottery was first excavated, the long period which had produced it is usually called the Al 'Ubaid Period. Although the ceramics show an advanced technique, architecture seems to have remained in a primitive hut-building state for many centuries. It is interesting to note that many of the poor inhabitants of the region today still live in precisely the same kind of wattle-and-daub shelters which their ancestors inhabited 6000 years ago.

This late neolithic and early copper-age culture, of which the Al 'Ubaid finds are but one trace, existed over large areas of western and central Asia. Almost identical pots and urns were found in the high Persian table-lands at Susa, and there are even traces of the same kind of early civilization far east into Turkestan.

The history of these earliest times is still largely a puzzle. The "King Lists" which have been translated are filled in the earliest eras with mytho logical figures who later became gods or demigods and who lived, many of them, the same unbelievably long lives that one finds set forth in the genealogies in the earlier chapters of Genesis. The general picture is that of many widely separated and politically independent villages or towns up and down the fertile "Valley of the Two Rivers," sometimes at war with each other but generally at peace, carrying on a busy agricultural life that developed at an early period an extensive commerce requiring accounts and the development of a written language.

It is in Ur that the history of the early Mesopotamian valley can most clearly be seen. The excavations show evidence of great floods which apparently wiped out the Al 'Ubaid civilization. The people who followed the flood made pottery which, though more carefully turned, was much cruder and less beautiful in its decoration and its shapes; yet these new people seem to have had one ability that the earlier people had lacked— the ability to organize large building enterprises and to make the most of their limited building materials. It is in this period that true history begins to emerge from the mists of ancient myth; and from the time of the first dynasty at Ur, probably about 3200 B.C., the general developments, both historical and architectural, can be definitely traced.

Even then these early dynasties of the valley ruled but small districts, and each chief town—Ur, Erech or Warka, Kish, and so on—had its own king, who was sometimes able to impose his rule on the neighboring towns and sometimes in turn was under the domination of some other kingdom he had previously ruled. Occasionally new elements seem to have come down, to exert a temporary overlordship and then to be absorbed into the population; especially troublesome were the Elamites, who made periodical raids into the rich valley from the more barren Persian highlands to the east. It was not until nearly 1000 years had passed that the whole valley finally came under one power, that of King Sargon of Akkad, who ruled the valley from a center further up the river near Babylon.

During the second millennium B.C. the valley was again troubled by invaders, this time from the north, from the rocky hills of Armenia, as the Hittites—a people we now know to have spoken a language related to Greek and Latin,—perhaps pushed out of their own country by the disturbances that arose from the Dorian migration and its predecessors, fell upon their neighbors in the fertile valleys south and established a Hittite Empire that swept from the Tigris to the Mediterranean and from the borders of Egypt north to the Black Sea.

This Hittite power, in turn, disintegrated, and the dominion of the valley passed to other inhabitants along the northern reaches of the river, the Assyrians, who fell heir to the Hittite conquests and like them ruled from Persia to the Mediterranean coast. Later still, this military empire itself disintegrated and Babylon reasserted its importance, with the new Babylonian Empire rising to heights of luxury before unknown. It was this new empire which held the Jews in captivity "by the waters of Babylon," only to be liberated when the Persian Empire in its new-found strength overwhelmed the valley and Belshazzar saw the writing on the wall.

The extraordinary thing about the architecture of the Tigro-Euphrates valley is the fact that, despite all these invasions by peoples speaking different languages and of different racial make-up, the architectural development was so consistent and its results everywhere so similar. Only two of the many conquests had definite architectural effects—the Hittite supremacy, which brought into the valley a new kind of decorative carving and a new delight in the decorative use of the forms of beasts; and the Persian, which finally put an end to the old type of building and developed over almost all of western Asia an eclectic civilization with elements borrowed from here, there, and everywhere.

The building materials of the greater part of the valley were limited. Mud brick, reeds, and clay plaster played by far the greatest part. Timber was scarce and of poor quality until, under the later empires, wood could be imported down the river from Asia Minor. Stone from the highlands of Persia, or rafted down from Armenia, was used only occasionally, chiefly for foundations and, in the later periods, in Assyria, for the decorative wainscoting on the lower parts of palace rooms. Owing to the scarcity and expense of fuel, the use of burned bricks was rare; yet a people as skilled in pottery making as the inhabitants of this valley always were could not but realize the remarkable permanence and hardness of burned clay. When burned clay brick was used, it was chiefly as a facing for the important parts of buildings, and was often decorated with color patterns baked on it. It was, in fact, a kind of faïence or colored terra-cotta rather than simple brick. The masses of the walls behind the facing were always of the sun-dried mud brick. Since this was fragile and eventually would wash away under continued rain, the outer surfaces were often protected by coats of plaster, or else, especially in the earlier days of the third millennium B.C., by a facing formed of nails or cones of baked clay driven into the surface, point first, close together so that their colored heads, exposed on the outside, could be used to form interesting mosaic patterns.

It was the comparative difficulty of obtaining good timber which led to two typical elements in Mesopotamian architecture—the long narrow room, and the vault. The first of these was well-nigh universal. Whether temple or palace or house, and whether in the early dynasties at Ur or the later Babylonian Empire, the Mesopotamian building almost always consisted of a group of narrow rooms, separated by enormously thick mud-brick walls and usually grouped around an open court. The roofs, usually covered with beaten clay and plaster, supported on a matting which rested on tree-trunk beams bridging the narrow spans, were always flat and often protected at the outer edges by a parapet of stepped brickwork, forming a kind of stepped battlement.

The second great feature, the arch or the vault, was in the earlier periods reserved for minor work. Vaulted brick graves have been found at Ur in the predynastic era at least as early as the fourth millennium b.c., and the vaulted drain is a common element in almost all Mesopotamian sites. Gateways and the larger doors were also often vaulted or arched, but the question of whether vaults were used over the long palace and temple halls is still unanswered. The evidence would seem to point to the fact that, in some cases at least, these great halls were roofed with vaults. It is significant that the Parthians and Sassanian Persians, who dominated the valley after the fall of the Alexandrine Empire and who fought and later overcame the Romans along their eastern boundaries, made of the vault the greatest and most magnificent feature which their architecture knew. It was the tremendous vaults of the Sassanian palaces which inspired the ingenious vaulting experiments of Mohammedan Persia and so came indirectly to affect the medieval architecture of the Western world. It seems almost impossible that these Sassanian vaults were without local predecessors. The probability is therefore strong that the vaulted hall was already a well-known type of structure in Mesopotamia before the Assyrian Empire fell.

The exterior aspect of all of these mud-brick structures was severe and simple. No cornices broke the height from ground to parapet. Openings were scarce along the narrow streets of the typical Mesopotamian town, for all the houses turned inward on their own courts and even temples had but single portals to the outside world. Nevertheless, there was no poverty in this simplicity; interest of form was given by occasional projecting towers or buttresses, by successive breaks where the house and street lines did not quite agree, by paneling the walls with long, narrow, vertical recesses or by reeding them into a series of vertical convex projections. Sometimes in palaces and temples columns were used; especially famous is the great columnar hall, with its eight-feet-thick columns, found in the palace of Warka, the Biblical Erech.

And there was color, produced by painting the plaster wall coverings, by the geometrical patterns of the terra-cotta cone heads used for the facings of palaces and temples, and later, in the Assyrian period, by gorgeous colored faïence friezes—rows of animals, magnificently modeled, and bands of rosettes or modified lotus flowers. In rare cases, even in the earliest work, copper animals in long friezes sometimes occurred, and the shrine which crowned the earliest ziggurat of Ur had an elaborate porch, with mosaicked columns bearing a stone lintel carved with a flying eagle flanked by heraldic stags, and walls banded with successive friezes of beasts and birds in repoussé copper, in stone, and in faïence mosaic.

Of the interior appearance we are less sure, though we know that plaster walls were often painted and, in the Assyrian period at least, frescoed with scenes of battle and the hunt or ritual pictures of the gods and goddesses. We may imagine color given by an abundance of patterned textiles and of mattings, and by furniture often brilliant with enamel and mosaic panels, many examples of which have been found in the royal tombs. In these long, narrow, dim halls there was much glint of gold and of jewels, and the gold dishes and cups that have come from the tombs, like the jewelry and the headdresses found there as well, give evidence of a luxurious, gorgeously colored, elaborately costumed kind of life to which the simple forms of the architecture were an admirable foil.

More and more we are learning, too, of the sculptural wealth which adorned these early houses and temples—sculpture both in terra-cotta and in stone brought down from the mountains. Especially renowned is the highly sophisticated, stylized, and simplified realism of the portrait work done at the time of King Gudea in the third dynasty of Ur.

The building types of this early Mesopotamian culture consisted only of houses and temples, burials being always underground, often under the house floors themselves, although buried vaulted chambers often protected the corpse. The houses usually comprised four or five narrow rooms grouped around an inner court. The entrance was generally through a vestibule so arranged with doors in different corners of the room that the passer-by was prevented from looking through into the courtyard. The courtyard itself was often paved with square burned tiles, and occasionally one of the smaller rooms, obviously designed for bathroom use, would be similarly paved and furnished with a drain. The hearth for cooking was often in the court, as in some of the Egyptian houses; only in larger palaces were separate cooking quarters supplied.

The palace was merely an enlarged house, or sometimes a reduplicated house—that is, instead of the single court there would often be three or more: a court for the lord and his official life, a court with an especially guarded and tortuous entrance for a harem, a court manifestly for service use with kitchens and servants' rooms around, and sometimes a temple or shrine court as well. However, even in these large palaces, though the courts might be impressive in size, the individual rooms remained the long, narrow, dark chambers of the smaller house, and it was apparently not until Assyrian times that greater halls were built. The palace of the Second Babylonian Empire, at Babylon, perhaps of the seventh century B.C., possessed one colossal hall, probably vaulted originally, which perhaps served as a prototype for the great vaulted audience halls of later Parthian and Sassanian palaces.

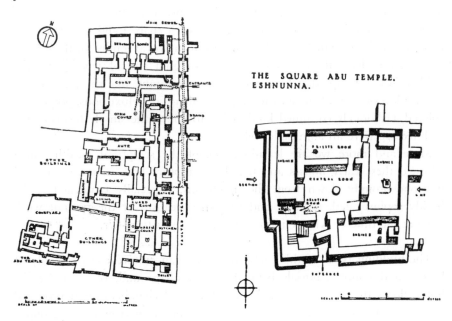

9. THE AKKADIAN PALACE AND ABU TEMPLE, TELL ASMAR; RESTORED PLANS.
(Lloyd: *Mesopotamia, Excavations at Sumerian Sites.*)

Religious buildings were of two types: the first an elaboration of the High Place; the second merely the developed House of God, often built in connection with the first, but frequently also existing by itself. The Mesopotamian High Place was a tremendous artificial hill of brick, square or rectangular in plan, with steeply battered sides and an open platform at the top. Such a structure is called a *ziggurat,* and excavations have shown that ziggurats have existed in these valley towns from predynastic times. Because of its sheer bulk it is almost impossible to destroy such a building completely, and as a result later rulers frequently merely enlarged older ziggurats, surrounding them with new walls and raising them to new and greater altitudes, thus, often unwittingly, preserving for us priceless evidences of the earlier work. Sometimes the ziggurat was a single truncated pyramid, approached by a long ramp or a flight of steps, but in later and more highly sophisticated times the earlier, simpler form was often replaced by an elaborate stepped pyramid.

Of these buildings, the one at Babylon was the most famous—a great eight-staged pyramid, with a spiral ramp leading around it continuously from bottom to top, and with each step painted a different color and symbolizing a different planet. This final structure, described by Herodotus, was only the last stage of a structure which had been famous for at least 1000

GIMILSIN TEMPLE AND GOVERNORS PALACE.

ESHNUNNA.

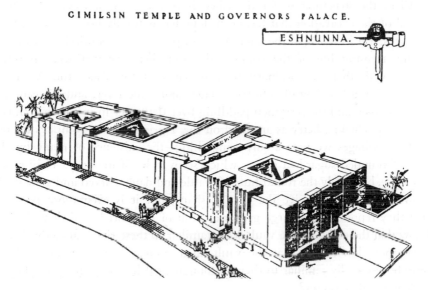

10. GOVERNOR'S PALACE AND GIMILSIN TEMPLE; RESTORED BIRD'S-EYE VIEW. (Lloyd.)

years, and which has gone down the ages, through its Biblical notoriety, as the Tower of Babel.

When this Mesopotamian civilization was at its height in any one of its successive phases, these great stepped towers and flat-topped pyramids, rising high from every town and sometimes from every royal palace as well, must have formed a striking feature of the landscape; and even today, after two millennia of wind and rain erosion and human destruction, the low hills that dot the Mesopotamian valley are almost all of them merely the ruined debris of ziggurats and towns.

The other type of temple was obviously the House of God, in plan almost identical with the larger examples of the simpler one-court type of dwelling, and only distinguished from them by the additional regularity of the building, the greater richness of the ornament, the existence of an altar and votive offerings within the walls, and the fact that one of the halls, usually on the side opposite the entrance, opened to the court by a wide doorway and contained a pedestal for the cult statue. Although in the temples the approach from street to court was more direct than in most of the houses, the old tradition of avoiding straight axes still existed, as shown by the fact that the entrance was rarely in the center of the front and that the sanctuary was never on a straight line with the entrance door.

All of the structures so far described have been city or town buildings, for all of the excavation that has been done has naturally been on town and city sites. Yet in reliefs of the later Assyrian period there is priceless evidence of the teeming life of the countryside, and there we can see, carefully carved with that extraordinary realism which distinguishes the Assyrian reliefs, view after view of country villages along the river, and we can see the fishermen and the ferrymen paddling over the water in just such circular boats of pitched basketry as are used on the Tigris and the Euphrates today. In these villages we note a surprising thing—the existence of many buildings of rounded sugar-loaf shape, which seem to be of masonry. They may, of course, be merely the round huts of wattle-and-daub, curved and smoothed with mud plaster to give the domed shape, but it is even more possible that they represent very large granaries built of mud brick and domed. We know that the arch and the vault were familiar to these river-valley dwellers; what more likely than that the vault on a circular plan—the dome—may have been equally familiar to them, although used here only for these lowly and practical purposes?

THE INDUS VALLEY

The great western Asia culture area, of which Mesopotamia is a part, had important early architectural parallels as far south and east as the Indus valley, in India, where excavations show a building culture going back to the very beginning of the third millennium B.C., which had many resemblances to, as well as marked differences from, the Mesopotamian work. So similar are certain pictographic inscriptions, as well as the spirit of some of the earliest sculpture, that many authorities feel that both cultures were descended from the same beginnings, located perhaps on the high plateau of Elam.

Both cultures created closely built, congested cities; both used brick to the

almost total exclusion of other materials, at least for urban and monumental structures; both developed house types consisting of long narrow
rooms around a court; and both made much of water supply and careful
drainage. In both cultures, bathing was an important function of life, and
almost every house of any pretensions had one of its rooms arranged as a
bathroom. The Indus River sites, of which Harappa and especially Mohenjo-
Daro are the most important, reveal, however, a building skill in some ways
more advanced than that in contemporary Mesopotamia. Practically all of
the construction is in burned brick; as a result, walls were much thinner
and building lines more accurate. In the Indian cities, crude or unbaked
brick was used only for platforms. It was perhaps the greater strength of
the Indian burned brick which allowed constructions of greater height than
were common further north, and highly developed stairs occurring in almost
every house thus far excavated indicate that the two-or-more-story building
was the rule. It is significant of the high technical level reached by these
builders that in many cases drainpipes of terra-cotta were built into the
walls, obviously to take the outflow of upper-floor bathrooms and privies.

Yet in some ways these Indus River cities are less advanced than the
Sumerian. The building is almost all of a strictly practical or utilitarian type.
There is little of that search for exterior richness which produced the
architectural sculpture, the inlaid friezes, and the faïence cone-mosaics which
gave color and life to so many Mesopotamian buildings. Instead, there is in
Mohenjo-Daro a monotonous, accurate rectangularity of forms, with almost
no indication whatsoever of any architectural ornament except a few fragments of gratings that originally filled the small high window openings,
and in a few cases in the better buildings of wall recesses of almost Babylonian type. Furthermore, there is as yet no evidence that the Indus valley
builders were aware of the principle of the arch. Everywhere that masonry
openings have been preserved, they are of the simple corbeled type, and
even the great drains have the same primitive corbeled coverings.

But this stark, undecorated quality of building was not an expression of
a lack of artistic feeling. The Mohenjo-Daro seals, tablets, and votive offerings
are magnificent pieces of careful, stylized, yet creative design, and the few
examples of sculpture in the round that have been preserved all show a
highly developed sense of form and a freedom that somehow seems more
related to the later decorative work of India than to the contemporary
work of the Mesopotamian valley.

The existence of seals and beads of Indus valley manufacture at several

Sumerian sites is evidence of commercial contact, if not close cultural connection, between these two civilizations. The remarkable thing seems to be that, whereas the one went on to develop and to live, in varying guise, almost up to the Christian era, the other, after perhaps 500 years of brilliant activity, seems to have been suddenly, about 2500 B.C., cut off and utterly killed, so that the archaeologists of India have up to this time found nothing to connect it with the later and different developments that came in India after the so-called Aryan immigration.

THE HITTITES

In the second millennium B.C., the highlands of eastern Asia Minor formed the site of a rapidly growing, aggressive military empire—the Hittite Empire. The Hittite language was descended from the same parent stock as Greek and Latin, to both of which it has many resemblances; and the Hittites themselves seem to have been a mixed people, partly invaders from the north and the west, partly indigenous peoples in the Asia Minor mountains. Historical records tell of various stocks which later coalesced, and the language itself exists in the records in many dialects. The present-day Armenians would seem to be very largely descendants of these Hittite peoples.

The problem of the exact derivation of the Hittite skill in building and in sculpture, and its relation to earlier Mesopotamian cultures, is still unsolved. It is significant that at Tell Halaf, a city where one of the largest tributaries of the Euphrates descends into the plain from the Kurdish mountains, an interesting group of buildings has been excavated, which have been tentatively dated as early as the second half of the third millennium B.C. At Tell Halaf the city gate shows definite Hittite characteristics, and, just as in the later Hittite buildings of Boghaz Keui, Carchemish, and Sindjirli, the lower parts of the walls of the palace are decorated with a carved stone frieze of animals, gods, and rulers, which stylistically has a close relationship to the Hittite work. At the main gate to the palace-temple, in Tell Halaf, the frieze ends on each side in a strange mythical beast, a distant ancestor of the later winged bulls of Assyrian gateways. The most unusual feature at Tell Halaf is the entrance porch of the great palace-temple. This porch formed a loggia recessed between bastion towers, and the roof over it was held up by three supports each consisting of a colossal figure—god, goddess, and king—standing on the back of a lion. This strange front, which has been reconstructed complete in the Berlin Museum, is a unique feature in western Asian architecture. Perhaps further excavation in the hills around Mardin and Van to the north will make its historical position more clear.

Pressing down from the mountains into the river valleys and along the Syrian coasts, the Hittite power soon gained control over almost the entire Mesopotamian valley and large areas of Syria. At the same time, the military prowess of the New Empire of Egypt was at its height, so that for almost two centuries, from 1500 to 1300 B.C., nearly all of western Asia was under the military control either of the Hittite Empire to the north or of Egypt to the south. The culture of both peoples was bound to affect all subsequent building in the region.

11. ENTRANCE GATE, BOGHAZ KEUI. (Puchstein: *Boghasköi, die Bauwerke.*)

Hittite architecture was primarily and originally a stone building architecture, achieving its greatest results in magnificent fortifications and huge royal palaces. Like early Greek architecture, it made much use of sun-dried brick for upper walls of domestic structures, but it depended for its characteristic elements upon stone. The capital, Boghaz Keui, was a large town, with temples, palaces, and elaborately fortified walls. Especially interesting are the city gates, which were usually double—an inner and an outer gate,— flanked by towers, and covered over with tall, narrow, elliptical arches. Around the base of the gates, not only at Boghaz Keui but elsewhere, as at Sindjirli, ran a frieze of carved animals, gods, and men. The same type of decoration is used around the base of palace walls and is especially highly developed at palace entrances; and this sculpture, in its bold plastic values, in its intense interest in muscle structure, and in the details of costume and ritual, has a quality quite different both from the stylized realism of Egypt and the heavy placidity of the earlier Sumerian work. It is all dynamic, emotional, and vivid; no matter how crude the workmanship may be, these soldiers in their tall helmets, these priests and rulers in their long cloaks, these parading animals seem somehow real and give the impression that the sculptor who carved them was definitely moved by what he saw.

Another quality which distinguishes Hittite architecture is its common use of columns. Colonnades frequently border courts, and columns are used to help support the roofs of wide chambers. The columns, usually made of wood, have almost all perished, but elaborate stone bases remain. Often these are of cushion shape, sometimes decorated with rough, scalloped moldings, and occasionally given added richness by being placed upon the backs of animals. This elaborate development of the stone base for high wooden columns has a vast importance historically. On the one hand, to the west, it undoubtedly influenced the Ionian Greeks of Asia Minor in their development of the complex base used with the Ionic order (see pp. 120, 121). On the other hand, to the south and east, it made the use of columns more frequent in the regions of Iraq and Mesopotamia, and eventually led to the development of the high, richly carved stone bases of later Persian architecture.

Yet, despite these achievements, despite the magnificence and perfection of its military architecture and the broad extent of its political power, the Hittite Empire, except through its sculpture and its columns, affected but little the general type of building throughout the district under its control. The characteristic Mesopotamian house still continued to be built, and the ziggurats still rose alongside temples and palaces.

ASSYRIAN ARCHITECTURE

Like all military empires which become too broadly extended, the Hittite Empire eventually disintegrated and fell, almost of its own weight. Successive rebellions within the Mesopotamian valley undermined its power, restoring little by little political independence to the valley towns. The final crash came with the revolt of Assyria at the northern end of the region and the rapid rise of the Assyrian Empire, which from the ninth almost to the sixth century B.C. controlled an area as large as the Hittites had controlled, and even threatened the power of the Pharaohs in Egypt as well.

The Assyrians were, in a sense, a border people, belonging half to the northern Asian highlands and half to the river valley. Centered as they were at the region where the Tigris and Euphrates leave the mountains of eastern Armenia to enter their long leisurely course across the plain, the Assyrians were ideally placed to take advantage both of the clay of the river valley and the stone of the hills to the north. Assyrian architecture adopted the house and palace and temple forms of earlier Mesopotamia, but carried them to new heights of complexity in plan and perfection in execution; and to this basic tradition they added a new luxury of decoration.

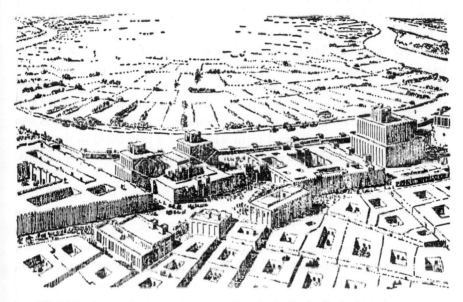

12. TEMPLE AND PALACE, ASSUR; RESTORED VIEW. (Andrae: *Das wiederstandene Assur.*)

This, too, was based on a double source. It descends on the one hand from the dynamic sculpture of the Hittites, and on the other from the glazed terracotta of the valley.

The typical Assyrian palace was a vast structure of many courts surrounded by the long narrow halls we have come to know so well. It was set almost always on a high artificial platform of unbaked brick, to raise it above the valley floods. Its courts were approached through vast gates, in which the influence of earlier Hittite architecture may often be seen—gates flanked by towers, topped by stepped battlements, and the gates themselves crowned by vaults. Around the lower part of these entrances another Hittite element was to be seen—the frieze of beasts carved in stone,—and although the upper walls were of unbaked brick they were always lined at important entrances and in important halls with wainscots from six to ten feet high, of carved slabs of alabaster. On each side of the gate itself stood a great carved stone, man-headed, winged bull, and these gateway guardians have a power of imaginative design which well expresses the arrogant military character of the Assyrian monarchs. These Assyrian buildings are distinguished from the earlier structures not only by their guardian bulls and their wainscots of carved stone, but also by the frequent use of friezes of the richest and most beautifully colored enamel-baked brick, in which, on a field usually of rich green, there strides forward a long procession of lions and legendary beasts, bordered frequently at the top by a band of rosettes or of lotus ornaments in which the Egyptian parentage is obvious. Similar bands of rosettes ran around the arch over the gate and decorated the edges of the stepped battlements, so that the whole palace exterior had not only, because of its great arches and battlemented towers, a richness and a decorativeness of architectural form which was a new thing in the valley, but also a new lavishness of carved, modeled, and brilliantly colored decoration.

It is from the alabaster wainscots of the palace halls that we can gain much of our knowledge of the details of these buildings, for the Assyrian artist was essentially a realist and loved to present the buildings which he showed with as much accuracy in detail as he used in the costumes of the kings and the accouterments of the army. Here we can see the king out hunting and the anguished lion, arrow-pierced, crawling off dragging his paralyzed hind legs after him; here we can see the Assyrian army swarming up the battlements of the besieged town, or crossing the river on inflated skins; and here we can see the little column-decorated windows which gave light to the vast halls of these enormous palaces. The great centers of Assur, of Nineveh, of Til Barsip all tell the same story, all reveal forms essentially similar. The last of these is remarkable because in its ruins there were preserved not only the usual Assyrian motifs, but also a series of elaborate wall paintings showing that the same verve, the same dynamic quality, the same realism went into the upper wall decorations of these palaces as distinguished the carved and modeled wainscots below.

Nevertheless, the basic Mesopotamian forms—the long narrow rooms grouped around courts, the heavy little-broken walls, the great stepped pyramids of the ziggurats—continued in use all through this period.

THE NEW BABYLONIAN EMPIRE

When Assyria in its turn fell, the power passed to the city of Babylon, and there, in the two centuries which remained until the whole country was conquered by the Persians, all of these Mesopotamian motifs, coupled with all of the Assyrian additions, were welded together into a new fusion and brought to an even higher pitch of technical perfection, which made sixth-century-B.C. Babylon one of the greatest and certainly one of the most remarkable cities of its time. The Hittite and the Assyrian military genius were united in the construction of its great inner and outer walls, with their vast towers and their river gates. The old ziggurat was refaced and reconstructed to form the great eight-stage pyramid which Herodotus describes, and the "hanging gardens," supported on a vast series of arched substructures, set a new note in royal luxury and extravagance. A tremendous series of vaulted chambers, supported by vast walls and piers, still remain, which may have once been the substructures of these famous gardens, and close by are the ruins of a great royal palace, surrounded by a quarter containing the houses of the courtiers. The main court of this palace leads to a colossal throne room some 55 feet wide and over 160 feet long, which from the thickness of its walls originally must have been vaulted. Here perhaps is the very hall where Belshazzar's Feast took place, on the same night when Babylon was betrayed into the hands of Cyrus and a new era began.

SYRIA, PHOENICIA, AND PALESTINE

Along the eastern coast of the Mediterranean there stretched one of the most disputed and fought-over areas of all western Asia. Inhabited originally by pastoral, nomadic tribes, its position made of it, almost against the will of its inhabitants, a great commercial and trading center, a place where all the influences from north and south, from east and west, were bound to meet. Under the dominance now of Egypt, and now of the Hittites, then of the Assyrians and the Babylonians, its architecture reveals the confused influences behind it. In general, it may be divided into three sections. Syria, to the north, was most directly under the influence of the Mesopotamian valley, and later of the Hittites; later still, it became extensively Hellenized, and eventually developed into a prosperous Roman province, famous for its wealth and its classic cultivation.

Phoenicia, a narrow coastwise strip possessed of two good harbors, developed almost inevitably as the great commercial, seafaring power of the early Mediterranean world; almost halfway between the Hittites and the

Egyptians, it suffered perhaps less from their struggles than the countries both to the north and the south of it; and, never apparently eager for military conquest or broad political power, it went on its own mercantile and industrial seafaring way for many centuries, carrying the wares of Egypt and Greece and of all western Asia to hundreds of towns and ports all over the Mediterranean, and perhaps even further—to the shores of Britain itself.

Phoenician sites have been but little excavated; yet enough is known to reveal that they were skillful builders in cut stone and in wood at an early period, building moles and docks for their harbors, and temples and shrines as well. The ruined examples which have come down to us all show a strange mixture of Egyptian and Asiatic influences. The Biblical accounts of the building of Solomon's Temple contain ample evidence of the building skill of the Phoenicians. It is they who seem to have furnished all of the timber and much of the skilled labor which went into that building as well as into Solomon's Palace, and the decorations which the Bible so clearly describes are obviously of the same confused mixture of Assyrian and Egyptian elements which we find in all the Phoenician buildings and decorative work. Even the type of the temple itself seems to have the same mixed parentage. In some ways it partakes of the early Mesopotamian High Place. The high-pyloned entrance is Egyptian, and even the division of the temple proper into outer space and Holy of Holies has its Egyptian analogies. But the building method, using large amounts of wood and linings of repoussé metal, is as definitely Asiatic, and the ornaments which are so accurately described are the debased, modified lotus ornaments of Assyria. The two great free-standing columns which stood outside the entrance have their counterparts in an existing ancient model of a Phoenician shrine; undoubtedly they are distant descendants of originally phallic symbols.

Even more definitely Egyptian is the type of Solomon's Palace. One of his wives was an Egyptian princess, and it may have been her influence which led to the many-columned halls with their high roofs held up by a forest of wooden posts that are the chief feature of this royal residence. And the plan of the palace of Ikhnaton at Tel el Amarna has much in common with Solomon's buildings in Jerusalem. But, if the plan of this palace is Egyptian, its decoration, like that of the temple, is purely Asiatic, and the fact that wood played such a vital part in its construction throughout is probably the reason why so little work of this period remains extant in either Phoenicia or Palestine.

Excavations since the First World War are bringing us a much clearer knowledge of the development of architecture in Palestine. Especially at Samaria, Megiddo, and Jericho, we are learning of the successive eras in building, that show these towns continuously inhabited for two millennia. Sun-baked brick played a large part in the domestic work, although stone was lavishly used for city walls and foundations. The High Place type of temple, with a sacrificial altar as its chief feature, is common. It is significant also that all Palestine sites have yielded a large number of decorative objects of Egyptian manufacture, and that many of these towns were for several hundred years more military outposts of the Egyptian Empire than independent entities. The architectural importance of these areas is therefore largely secondary. Phoenicia was important as the great distributor of goods; Palestine, as the home of the first great monotheistic religion.

PERSIA

The story of the rapid growth of the Persian Empire after the two related tribes of Medes and Persians had coalesced is one of the extraordinary phenomena of history. Perhaps it merely is evidence that the long course of three millennia of Mesopotamian culture had resulted at the end only in a weak and decadent people, to whom the addition of this new blood from the north and the east came as a necessary rejuvenation. Architecturally at least, the new power brought a tradition entirely different from the native tradition of the Mesopotamian plains—a tradition of highland building, of square huts, often of mud plaster, with flat roofs held up by wooden columns, and of temples formed of raised platforms on which was the altar where the sacred fire burned. The courtyard idea, so prevalent both in the domestic and the religious architecture of earlier western Asia, did not exist. With these simple and primitive traditions, the new empire found itself soon in close contact with the works of two of the greatest ancient building cultures, Egyptian and Assyrian, and also gifted with almost unbelievable wealth and power. The result was a sudden flowering, as brief as it was sudden, of a vivid, daring, experimental architecture, which borrowed its decorative details wholesale from its neighbors and predecessors, but developed its building types in plan and in structure on the basis of its own native usages.

Of its smaller works we know little. Persian houses were probably the old square huts, with their tree-trunk columns and beams, such as are still built in the Persian mountains. For religion, the new empire continued to construct its raised altars; but in Susa at least, the Shushan of the Bible, a temple has been discovered in which the holy fire burned in an enclosed Holy of Holies, a square room with four columns fronted by an open court. Even here certain foreign ideas taken from Mesopotamian or even Egyptian shrines are perhaps to be seen. The royal tombs were generally cut in the face of a cliff; and the great series of them at Nakht-i-Rustam, with their rock-cut façades imitating palace fronts, tell us much of what we know of the roofs and upper portions of the Persian palace buildings. One great free-standing tomb remains at Pasargadae. This is often called the Tomb of Cyrus, and with very probable accuracy. It consists of a single, simple, large, shrine-shaped sarcophagus, with a low-pitched gabled roof, standing on a series of great stone steps. Originally a wall surrounded this, and along one side ran a columned hall. The whole has a large simplicity of scale which is most impressive even today.

But the greatest and most characteristic of these ancient Persian buildings were the palaces, of which those at Susa and at Persepolis have been carefully excavated. The earliest of these date from not before 600 B.C., the latest of them hardly after 450. Slightly over a century covers this climax period of Persian building. The characteristic Persian palace consisted of a great square hall, with its roof supported by a large number of tall slim columns, equally spaced. The hall usually had an open, columned porch at back and front. Minor rooms were at the sides. The whole was high, delicate, and graceful—in marked contrast to the blocky heaviness of Mesopotamian work. The walls were of sun-dried brick; but all door and window frames were of stone, and, though the brick has long since vanished, the stone foundations and the still standing door frames allow their easy restoration. At Persepolis a whole group of such palaces stands, on a great stone-faced monumental platform; and, since there is little evidence in these columnar buildings themselves of the large amount of necessary service and dwelling area, it is probable that these halls served merely as reception rooms or ceremonial halls, and that the actual living quarters—at least of the courtiers —were in mud and wood houses of the old type, grouped around and behind them. The whole concept of these high, airy halls, with their slender columns, has marked resemblances to some of the palaces of Isfahan which Persians nearly 2000 years later still built and enjoyed.

The stone columns are the most individual portions of these edifices. Often of extraordinary slenderness, sometimes as much as fifteen diameters high, they bear witness to their wooden ancestry; nevertheless their fluting and their tall graceful bases are expressive of stone and stone alone. It is more than possible that the fluting and the high bases were both borrowed from the early Greek work of Asia Minor, with which the Persians came into contact very near the beginning of the expansion of their empire. The capitals carried by these columns consisted of a crosspiece of stone— a sort of bracket block—the outer ends of which were carved with the heads and foreparts of horses or bulls, and sometimes between this crosspiece and the shaft proper a reversed bell-shaped form, carved with scalloped leaves, and a queer aggregation of vertical scrolls, is found. The whole combination of bell and scroll and beasts was illogical and fantastic, but, high in the air under the shadowed beams of the flat roof, the effect must have been extraordinarily rich and imaginative. Some authorities find Greek influence in the scrolls and bell portion of this capital, but the crosspiece with its carved animals is essentially Persian and merely a decorative expression of the old wooden crotched posts so frequently used in the early simple houses. Strangely enough, the main girders or crossbeams did not rest on the heads of the animals or run parallel to this crosspiece, but rather at right angles, supported on a depression carved midway between the two heads.

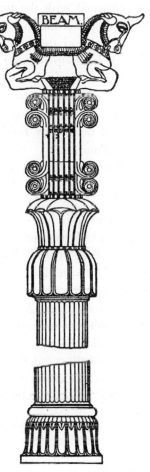

13. PERSIAN COLUMN FROM PERSEPOLIS, RESTORED. (Simpson. Vol. I.)

The shameless eclecticism of Persian architecture is nowhere better seen than in the luxurious decorations with which walls and gates, windows and door frames, were all embellished. At Persepolis, for instance, a frieze of very Assyrian-looking soldiers flanks the monumental entrance stairway. At the top the way leads through a great *propylaea* or porch, the walls of which have the winged guardian bulls with human heads that we have already seen in Assyrian palaces. In Persepolis, however, their scale is raised far above any of the Assyrian examples; the great bodies and the tremendous heads rise twenty feet into the air, and the whole has that colossal effect which somehow fitted the military character of the Persian court. At Susa, friezes of Assyrian lions in enameled brick, made in exactly the Assyrian fashion, run around the base of the palace, and everywhere there are endless repetitions of Assyrian stepped battlements. Once the palaces are reached, the Egyptian influence becomes apparent, for all the doors and windows are crowned with the typical Egyptian cornice with projecting bead and a simple projecting quarter-round cavetto molding.

The roofs of these buildings were flat, the great girders were banded as though built up of several timbers, and the crossbeams projected beyond them to hold up the overhanging roof. This portion, too, would seem to indicate a borrowing from the architecture of western Asia Minor—from the Lycians, whose developed wooden construction is preserved for us in a series of beautifully finished rock-cut tombs, and from the Greeks of the Asia Minor coast.

All of this Persian work is, then, exciting, luxurious, richly detailed, but it is in great part derivative and its structural elements are simple and set; there is in it little evidence of development or growth. It was a style somehow entirely expressive of the thoughtless, well-organized, military power which ancient Persia was; but, just as the Persian Empire seems to have been controlled by no real idealism save that of power-lust, by no great plans save those of temporary military or political expedience, and to have brought to the world little except the accidental values of a new shifting and stirring of the Asiatic populations, just so Persian architecture, despite its magnificent scale, despite its rich, luxuriant ornament, despite its many-columned halls with their sixty-foot bull-crowned columns, seems somehow fundamentally sterile—and, after the Persian Empire had fallen before the armies of Alexander the Great, Persian architecture of this older type disappeared as completely as though it had never been.

Chapter 5

THE MEDITERRANEAN
AND THE AEGEAN

AROUND the Mediterranean shores, neolithic man developed a dynamic, advanced culture. In Spain, the Balearic Isles, Sardinia, Sicily, and Malta, remains of huts and houses, of tombs and fortresses, show that by the fourth millennium B.C., at least, late stone-age man had created not only a social system of some complexity, but also a personal life of considerable richness. Pottery, decorated with geometric incised lines or with simple colored patterns, and sculptured statuettes of mother deities show artistic ideals as well as craft skill. Evidently these Mediterranean peoples were of a type not to be satisfied with the accomplishments of their past or present, but shared with their neolithic equals of central Asia, the Danube valley, and the Nile regions that combination of imagination with self-criticism, of energy with discipline, which enables a people to progress.

Especially remarkable were the great stone temples which the neolithic builders erected in Malta, particularly those at Mnaidra, Hal Tarxien, and Hagiar Kim. In them we have an evidence of extraordinary building skill. The temples, for in Hal Tarxien there are several of them combined into a single great complex, are fronted with a great segmental recessed façade of huge blocks. In the center is the entrance, at the ends strange shrines which have been interpreted as divination chapels. The entrance, the jambs and threshold of which were of carefully squared, smoothly finished single blocks, led into a central area or court, approximately square, with a great apse at each side. From the central area one entered a similar, smaller group—a central area with side apses—and from that, sometimes, a third, still smaller and apparently more holy. Around these larger elements were grouped smaller rooms and shrines—one, at least, obviously an oracle, so arranged that the voice of a hidden priest reached the worshiper in concealed ways, as though from the great stones of the walls themselves. Could this be a symbolic representation of cave oracles of an earlier day? Might it be that such oracles as the later Greek oracle of Delphi went back thousands of years to neolithic or even paleolithic times?

These Malta temples are superb examples of the most careful megalithic building. The stones of which they are built are meticulously finished and fitted. There is true architectural sense in the careful, axial planning—the way space leads to space, with a final climax;—there is apparent a real sense of proportion in the carefully built niche shrines and their attendant altars and benches. And these temples were not only well built, but well decorated and richly furnished as well. In Hal Tarxien there are the remains of an

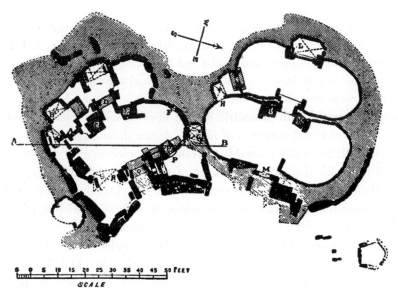

14. NEOLITHIC TEMPLE AT MNAIDRA, MALTA; PLAN. (Fergusson: *Rude Stone Monuments.*)

over-life-sized, seated statue of the great mother goddess who was apparently worshiped there. Stone panels and altar frontals are carved with connected spirals, exquisitely finished; in a great excavated cave tomb or temple not far away, Hal Salfieni, similar spirals are painted on the ceiling of one of the rooms. One important panel at Hal Tarxien represents a procession of sacrificial animals.

Large quantities of pottery and of votive offerings have been found in these temples—bowls and urns, statuettes, beads. The pottery is lavishly decorated, some of it in polychrome. The statuettes of heavy, thick-thighed women and the phallic objects show that the cult was a fertility cult; these strange figures represent what may have been the great parent deity of the

Mediterranean world who later appeared as Aphrodite in Greece, as Astarte in Syria, as Isis in Egypt, and their heavy, crouching, obese, exaggerated forms the real precursors of the exquisite grace of the Aphrodite of Cnidus or of Melos. . . .

The Malta temples were eventually deserted. Sand and earth filled them up, little by little. Then, perhaps 1000 years—more or less—later, new peoples came to them, threw down some of the stones, leveled off the sites and used them as cemeteries in which to bury their cinerary urns. For the new people were early bronze-age people, who knew and used copper, and burned their dead instead of burying them as the neolithic people had done. The urns and votive and burial offerings of these newer peoples were cruder than the ware of a millennium earlier; these later people were at the beginning of a new cultural era, while the neolithic temple builders had been the most cultivated, the most advanced, perhaps the last exponents of the stone age that was doomed by the advent of metal.

These buildings and this culture arouse a flood of important questions, the answers to which, alas, lie still in the field of speculation. What is their actual date? Who were the builders? What is the relationship between these structures and the more highly developed and better known work of Egypt and of Crete and pre-Hellenic Greece? Obviously there are close ties between Malta and Sicily, southern Italy, Sardinia, the Balearic Isles, the Spanish peninsula. But of what form was this tie—racial? linguistic? How far east can the influence of this culture be traced? And here we get into the most perplexing question of all. For in the island of Crete there existed, at an early date, a civilization of an even higher level of development. Was this Cretan culture merely a further and higher and later development of the Mediterranean culture of neolithic Malta? Or was Malta merely a provincial copy of Crete? There are arguments both ways. To Sir Arthur Evans, the great student of Cretan culture, the similarity in decorative forms between neolithic Malta and copper-age Crete is merely an example of cultural borrowing from the advanced Cretan peoples by peoples much more primitive. The spirals on Maltese temples are, for him, copies of the spirals on Cretan pottery—evidences of expanding Cretan commerce.

Nevertheless, there are serious difficulties with the theory. The Cretan spiral-decorated pottery is of bronze-age date. Examples of Cretan pottery have been discovered in Egypt, in Sicily, in Syria, in Italy; its distribution was obviously wide. Cretan bronze and copper weapons were also widely distributed, and influenced local designs in many far-separated localities. Copper and bronze were in early use in Italy. Yet the culture that built the Maltese temples was entirely a neolithic, stone-age culture. In the extraordinarily rich lower-level deposits in the temples and in the cave of Hal Salfieni there is not a trace of copper or copper-age influence. In Hal Tarxien, the bronze-age deposits and pottery are separated from the stone-age deposits by over a yard of soil; in all probability nearly a millennium separated them. Furthermore, in the neolithic deposits of Malta not a single piece of Cretan pottery has been found. Pottery is almost impossible to destroy. If the Maltese builders used Cretan ware for patterns to copy in stone, where is the Cretan ware? And why did they not copy it in pottery, which they made so well themselves?

If all this is so, it seems at least a possibility that the Malta temples predate the bronze-age culture of Crete; perhaps the very peoples who built these remarkable structures deserted the island of Malta because of pestilence or some natural catastrophe, and went to other lands—Crete among them— to furnish their own quota of skill and hereditary patterns and symbolisms to the culture that flowered there so luxuriantly after copper and bronze had come into use.

All this, of course, brings up the question, who were the Cretans of that early time? Where did they come from? Some would have it that they came from the Nile valley; some that they were members of the supposititious "Mediterranean race," who settled the island in neolithic times. Some consider the possibility of an origin in Asia Minor, or further east still. And some recent students have even visioned the possibility that the Cretans came originally from the west, perhaps from Spain, perhaps via Malta itself. What we are fairly sure of is that they did not settle Crete until the neolithic period, and that they spoke a language not only totally different from that of classic Greece, but also not even of Indo-European stock. Nor was it Semitic. Like the Etruscan language, that of Crete also is still a closed book, though we have its written records and know some of its probable words which have persisted in classical Greek.

With the coming of the use of metals, whether discovered independently or borrowed from the peoples of Asia, the Cretans developed a civilization of great complexity and refinement, and a culture which spread widely through the Aegean islands, into the mainland of Greece, and even to Asia Minor and the Syrian shores. From about 2500 to 1200 B.C. (the dates are approximate and may vary a century or two) this culture—called, in its Cretan expressions, Minoan; in its expressions on the Greek islands, Cycladic; and in its expressions on the mainland of Greece, Mycenaean and Helladic—was the great creative culture of the Western world, rivaling in its artistic productions the work of Egypt and Mesopotamia, with which it was coeval. It was a culture profoundly different from the civilizations of Asia and Africa; already there is in it a quality which seems, by contrast, almost European. It was a marine civilization, owing much to ships and shipping. It was a nature-loving, life-loving culture, with none of that preoccupation with death, and little of that cult of the dead, which distinguished Egypt. Its religion was simpler and more primitive, and at the same time perhaps more human and anthropomorphic, than those of the Nile or the Euphrates. Accordingly, it is primarily a palace-building and town-building civilization, loving gay colors and bright pictures, making use of realistic natural forms in its ornament, and often decoratively preoccupied with the flora and fauna of the sea—seaweeds, shells, fishes, flying fish, the octopus.

The products of Cretan art were usually divided into three great classes, according to their age—Early, Middle, and Late Minoan, corresponding generally to the primitive, climax, and decadent phases of the culture. Each of these three classes is also divided generally into three subgroups, according to date; and somewhat similar periods are differentiated for the Cycladic, Mycenaean, and Helladic phases, though the dates, naturally, vary. The Early Minoan period was for the most part a time of gradual governmental development, the subordination of small local chiefs to more highly organized feudal powers, and the gradual improvement of building methods and of pottery making to suit a growing luxury and refinement of life. Bronze was being made and was superseding copper, and trade was growing rapidly. Closer and closer commercial ties with Egypt were being forged, and Cretan wares were more and more widely distributed.

The Middle Minoan period was the period of the great palaces of Knossos and Phaistos, of large towns of two- and three-story houses, of blossoming trade, of exquisitely refined and lavishly decorated pottery, of delicate statuettes and rich frescoes. The period was one of local wars, too, probably between the local lords; palaces were burned and rebuilt in the struggle; gradually the power of the house of Knossos—the family of the legendary Minos—became supreme. Meanwhile, the Cretan culture was spreading rapidly in Greece, modifying profoundly the original local types. This period lasted from about 2000 to 1600 B.C.; and it was during these centuries that tribes from the north—the Achaeans of Homer, perhaps, the earliest Indo-European settlers of the area—began to press into the Balkan peninsula, into Greece, and down along the shores of Asia Minor. They seem to have settled with the native tribes they found there, assuming a military overlordship. The troubles that resulted from this migration are spoken of in Egyptian inscriptions. As the new people became adjusted to their new homes, they gradually adopted the arts and the crafts of the locality, and came more and more under the cultural domination of Crete.

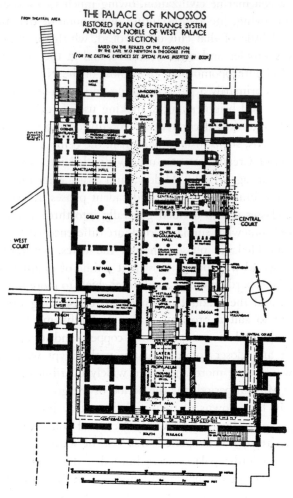

15. THE PALACE, KNOSSOS; PLAN OF THE *PIANO NOBILE*, RESTORED. (Evans: *The Palace of Minos*. Vol. II.)

The Late Minoan period began with a time of great affluence. The palaces were rebuilt with more complexity and elegance. Vase decoration became freer, more naturalistic, more rococo. On the mainland, the "Achaean" chieftains were erecting their own palaces, with plans quite different from those of Crete, yet decorated with paintings and ornament entirely in the

Cretan manner, perhaps executed by Cretan artists. As the Achaeans grew more powerful and began to spread widely over the Aegean sea, at first equaling, then surpassing, their Cretan teachers in marine skill, the Cretan power lapsed, Cretan building skill declined. At first the Achaean chiefs had been tributary to Knossos. The legend of Theseus and the Minotaur, with its annual tribute of youths and maidens to be given to the Minotaur— that is, probably, to serve as bullfighters and bull-victims in the Cretan sacred games,—is probably based on fact; the liberation of Athens from the paying of tribute symbolized the growing power of the mainland lords. All the palaces of Crete were destroyed at about the same period, possibly by earthquake and fire, about 1400 B.C. Crete never recovered from that catastrophe; after that period it was under the domination of Greece, ruled by Achaean rulers, as appears in the Homeric poems.

For the last period, then, the center of gravity shifted north. Mycenae, Tiryns, Argos, all towns on the Peloponnesus in Greece, are the great names, and for two or three centuries they enjoyed a period of great prosperity and military power. They continued to develop the Cretan painting types, the Cretan ornament; but their life was different—more military, more energetic, perhaps; less luxurious and commercial—and the buildings they built expressed that difference. Theirs is the culture Homer describes in the *Iliad* and the *Odyssey,* and the Homeric palace is a Mycenaean or Achaean palace; their ambitions and struggles were the basis of the Trojan War.

Around the end of this period—some say about 1200 B.C., some say about 1000—new bands of marauders and conquerors swept down from the north, bringing a quick and terrible end to the Aegean culture. The Dorian migration, like the barbarian invasions 1500 years later, overwhelmed an existing culture; but, like them, with ideas and inspirations from the very culture it destroyed, it was eventually to create a new and higher civilization, the Hellenic life of classical Greece.

Aegean building materials were simple: stone, sun-dried brick, wood, and plaster. Walls in the smaller houses were of rough, small stones, with much mortar, or of sun-dried brick on stone foundations; carefully cut or finished stone was reserved for door frames or house corners. Often the rough walls were tied together and strengthened with wooden beams and ties, and the whole was plastered over, outside and in. Only in the palaces and tombs is carefully cut *ashlar* stonework used—that is, masonry of regularly cut, rectangular stones laid in continuous horizontal courses. Many of the buildings, even the small town houses. were of two or three stories. Floors had wooden beams of large size, the sockets for which can sometimes be seen in the masonry which remains, and roofs seem to have been generally flat. Large rooms often had pillars or columns to support the span. If of stone, the pillars were square; if of wood, round, and often tapering downward. These wood columns were set on stone bases and carried large, awkward capitals, sometimes of stone, with a broad spreading convex molding, or *echinus* (so-called from its resemblance in general shape to the sea urchin; Greek, *echinos*), and a square block or plinth above. These columns are shown in many wall paintings and other representations. Occasionally single columns, like that between the lions on the Lion Gate at Mycenae, were used as sacred objects, perhaps with phallic significance. In the palaces and temples these columns were freely used in porches, courts, and colonnades.

One characteristic feature of Aegean architecture is its free use of wooden beams to support heavy stone walls. When the palaces burned and the beams gave way, the masonry above crashed to the ground, but sometimes, although fallen, it preserved its original shape; this has allowed, at Knossos, the restoration and reconstruction of at least part of the upper floors.

In general, the Aegeans' structural sense was elementary. They used what structural elements and methods were necessary in a purely pragmatic and often hit-or-miss method. They covered up crudities of conception or execution with plaster or a lining of gypsum slabs; it was on these linings that they lavished their care, smoothing and painting the plaster, or fitting the gypsum slabs with exquisite perfection. Only in the *tholoi* or "beehive" tombs, in the palace structures of Middle and Late Minoan times, and in occasional mainland fortifications do we find large-scale stone masonry exposed and built with perfect integrity.

The fortifications, particularly of the mainland towns and of Troy, are well planned and impressive. Gates are designed so that entrance is always around corners or bends, never straight, in order that attackers could always be flanked. The sixth city at Troy—undoubtedly the Homeric city—had large defense towers as well, to buttress the walls. The Troy walls are built of excellent coursed masonry, almost like ashlar, as though there the influence of the fine craftsmanship of Crete had been strong; those of Tiryns and Mycenae, and generally on the Greek mainland, are of great polygonal stones, rather rough, giving an appearance both stronger and more crude than the Trojan fortifications.

A noteworthy feature of the Mycenae walls is the famous Lion Gate. Over the gateway proper, above the stone crosspiece or lintel, there was left a triangular opening formed by corbeling inward the heavy masonry of the walls on either side, so that none of the real wall weight was carried by the lintel. In this triangular opening a carved slab was set, bearing on its outer face a representation of a central column of Cretan type flanked by two powerfully carved lions. It is one of the few examples of large-scale stone sculpture which has been preserved from those times.

The whole picture which these fortified cities of Greece and Ilion suggest reveals the real cultural gulf that separates them from the peaceful, luxurious cities of Crete. Visiting Tiryns or Mycenae or Troy, seeing the bastioned, towered walls of the Trojan hill or the great megalithic ramparts of Mycenae, or strolling through the palace courts and halls of Tiryns, once resplendent with metal and wall painting, one is at once in the world of the *Iliad* and the *Odyssey;* one can imagine the rough camp of the Greeks on the Trojan plains, and the futile assaults against the high walls; one can readily reconstruct the rich palaces of military chieftains like Menelaus or Odysseus. When the Mycenae graves were opened, and their treasure of gold cups and masks, gold plaques and buttons, and weapons with gold and ivory hilts and exquisitely inlaid blades all brought to light, the Homeric descriptions of the rich gear of the Greek warriors suddenly took on new reality. Homer, to be sure, wrote his verses perhaps four centuries after the event, in the dark ages that followed the Dorian migration; but the legends and tales he collected and recreated had preserved over all that time pictures remarkably exact of that older, richer, turbulent "Achaean" time....

The Cretans in their highest period—Middle Minoan and Late Minoan I and II—had been essentially builders of towns and palaces. With them fortifications had been incidental only; their work is the work of people confident of an untroubled present and future. Some walls in Knossos are thicker than mere strength demands, as though to form a sort of "keep" or stronghold where palace treasures could be safe against marauders or rioters. The towns sometimes had weak enclosure walls; of real fortification there was none. The Cretan empire, founded on manufacture and sea-borne trade, felt secure enough.

The towns were almost always aggregations of small houses around a chieftain's palace. Narrow streets and alleys—their average width not over six or seven feet, and often paved with stone—show that wheeled vehicles were little, if at all, used except for ritual and court purposes. Beyond the most elementary connection of the streets to certain roads outside the town, and general rough rectangular patterning which results from the close building of rectangular houses, there is little evidence of conscious town planning. The Gournia alleys wind like the streets of colonial Boston. But Gournia does have a large open area or plaza in front of the palace; this probably served alike as market and forum, and perhaps also as bull ring. And other towns were somewhat similarly arranged.

The individual houses, though small, are far from being the primitive hut. The greater number have at least four or five rooms to a floor. Some undoubtedly had upper stories, and much of the foundation work left was originally a basement, entered through holes in the floor above. Occasionally one finds evidence of rooms grouped around a court, and probably some of the "rooms" shown in the plans were light-wells like those in the palaces.

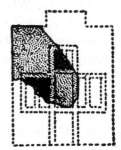

16. FAÏENCE PLAQUES SHOWING TOWN HOUSES. FROM PHAESTOS. (Glotz: *The Aegean Civilization.*)

In some of the larger houses the chief living room was large enough to require interior columns or posts. A series of faïence tiles from Knossos shows these house exteriors. The beams which strengthened the masonry walls are exposed, and give a sort of half-timber effect. Windows are large, and often divided into smaller units by vertical wooden posts—*mullions*—and horizontal transoms. Often the flat roofs are crowned by a smaller building, or cupola, and the whole effect is extraordinarily modern. Evidently the small merchants and craftsmen who lived in these houses lived comfortably and well, and sometimes—from the vessels and other finds discovered in the ruins—luxuriously as well, surrounded by gaily painted plaster walls, richly decorated pottery plates and cups and urns, and a little private chapel with figurines and tiny "horns of consecration."

The palaces of Crete—Phaistos, Gournia, Knossos—are all basically similar in plan, though they differ in size and details. In all, there is a large, open area in front or at the side of the palace; it is as much a public square as a part of the palace, and it is usually so arranged as to provide, on a hillside slope, a series of wide steps or benches obviously designed as seating spaces for the spectators at some performance. The palace proper is a vast combination of rooms around its own court; it is usually extremely complicated in plan, arranged on different layers connected by monumental stairs, and divided into several quite distinct areas. In Knossos, the purposes of the various portions can be fairly well identified—storage of palace goods and treasure, service space, a ritual throne-room area, and two separated residence quarters. The complexity of the plan is reflected in the Greek legend of the Labyrinth, just as the Cretan love for bullfighting—perhaps ritualistic —is reflected in the legend of the Minotaur.

The extraordinary thing about all the palaces is the richness of the furniture and decoration, the love of light, airy effects as evidenced by the light-wells which illuminate the large rooms through wide windows or a series of doors occupying the entire side of the room, the fact that almost all the large rooms are entered through large antechambers and vestibules, and the elaborate, well-designed systems of drainage and water supply. Even primitive water closets are found, and the whole has a sense of luxurious comfort that was not to be equaled again till the days of the Roman Empire. Occasional rooms once thought to be baths, sunk below the level of the rest and approached by steps, are now recognized as areas devoted to ritual, for no method of draining them is present. Real bathrooms did, however, exist.

The fragments of wall paintings which have been preserved show the colorful richness these palaces must have once possessed. But they do more than that, for they give us priceless pictures of the life of the time. In them we can see the court ladies and their friends, with low-cut bodices, slim waists, and flounced skirts, crowding together to watch a game, or grouped on an upper colonnaded loggia to take advantage of the outdoor cool, and one long panel shows them sitting on cushions talking gaily together; in another place a parade of tall, slim, tanned young men stride along bearing great vases of tribute or offering; elsewhere one sees the actual bull games, with young men and women leaping and somersaulting over the charging animals. Could it be that these youths and maidens were unwilling performers, victims rather than athletes, as the Theseus legend suggests? Certainly the frescoes suggest games rather than sacrifices, and yet some representations show people trampled beneath the bulls' feet. Some have even suggested that the Spanish bullfights of today are distantly descended from an old, preclassic bull cult that spread all over the Mediterranean basin, and that when the excited crowds in the bull rings of Seville or Mexico watch the brightly costumed toreadors and matadors and the doomed, charging bulls they are merely the modern representatives of a custom that took its original, different form in the palace at Knossos, before the crowd of court ladies we can see in the fresco there today.

The frescoes are not limited to palace and bullfight scenes. The Cretans were a nature-loving people, fully appreciative of natural beauty. One fa-

17. FLYING FISH FRESCO. FROM PHYLAKOPI. (Glotz.)

mous fresco, from Hagia Triada, shows a cat gingerly stepping through garden flowers, stalking a bird; another, from Phylakopi, shows dolphins leaping through the waves; and another fragment from the same house had flying fishes soaring over the water. Knossos has a frieze of nautilus shells, their saillike tentacles spread into spirals. On vases the crocus appears, and on the urns of the "palace style," *circa* 1500 B.C., the whole fauna of the seashore is drawn upon for designs.

Ornamental patterns are found, too, especially spirals, rosettes, and half-rosettes separated by a vertical panel. The spiral ornaments have often a considerable resemblance to Egyptian spiral patterns from tomb ceilings, and direct Egyptian influence may be seen here and there in lotus flowers and other minor motifs. Evidently the commerce between Crete and Egypt was large, the contacts between the two areas close, and many Cretans must have traveled to Egypt on the little ships which carried the wares of each to the other. Yet the Cretans always modified these borrowed forms, and made them wholly their own.

We know less of Cretan temples than of palaces; there were fewer of them, and they were smaller in size. They were chiefly of the open shrine type—a little area surrounded by a wall, with, inside, a sacred tree and a shrine of two columns on a pedestal, which carried as well the "horns of consecration," a great pair of stylized bull horns set vertically. Caves and gorges were sacred, too; many such Cretan sites yield large numbers of ex-voto offerings—little figurines, and especially miniature representations of the sacred double ax. A male god, known to the later Greeks as Velchanos, was worshiped, and the Cretan mother-goddess or Aphrodite, with whose cult both doves, as in later Greek mythology, and snakes were intimately connected, was the female deity. Minor deities or powers, sometimes animal-headed—especially deer-headed,—and gryphons and other legendary beasts are shown on the seal rings, but their exact significance is still unknown. The throne at Knossos is flanked by frescoes of two large wingless monsters. Worship seems largely to have been on the one hand a private matter of household and palace shrines, and on the other a matter of nature rites in the outdoor air, like the harvest festival carved on the famous "Harvester Vase," cut in steatite and found at Hagia Triada.

The tombs are better known from a multitude of examples. They are of four chief kinds: cist graves, pit graves, chamber tombs, and beehive tombs or *tholoi*. The cist grave is merely a burial lined with stone slabs, often well cut and carefully fitted to form a sort of stone coffin. The pit graves are shafts cut vertically downward through the rock; often a smaller pit at the bottom was covered with a stone slab to protect the burial, before the shaft was filled; sometimes a little chamber opens off the side of the shaft at the bottom. The large chamber tombs and tholoi were evidently either the tombs of chieftains, or sometimes the burial places for whole families. The best chamber tombs consist of a rectangular chamber cut in the side of a hill or cliff and approached by a long passage, or *dromos*, which leads down to the chamber door. The doorway was sealed with stone masonry after the burial was made. In the greatest of them, at Isopata, the cut—chamber, forehall, and dromos—was lined with beautifully finished ashlar masonry, and the roof was evidently of stone, too, contrived by corbeling out each course over the one below and curving the inner surface to form a pointed corbeled vault.

In the tholos a similar method of roofing was used, but the chamber was circular instead of rectangular; the effect was that of a pointed dome. Tholoi built of rough rather than finished stone—probably recalling the occasional primitive circular huts—were frequent in western Crete at an early date, but later they seem to have gone out of fashion on the island itself, only to

18. THRONE ROOM OF THE PALACE AT KNOSSOS, PARTLY RESTORED. (Glotz.)

reappear with greater splendor on the Greek mainland, as at Mycenae and Orchomenos.

These mainland people of the fifteenth to the thirteenth century B.C. had different burial customs, too, and sometimes cremated their heroes instead of burying them. In general their tombs are more architectural; at Mycenae, in addition to the great tholoi, the so-called "Treasury of Atreus" and that "of Clytemnestra," which were famous monuments even in classic days 2000 years ago, there was, at the foot of the acropolis, a carefully built paved circle, surrounded by a low stone wall, beneath which was a group of several pit graves, which excavators found full of a rich treasure of exquisite weapons and jewelry and thin gold repoussé masks which had once covered the heads of the wrapped bodies.

But it is the mainland tholoi which are the chief masterpieces of this pre-Greek sepulchral architecture. In the "Treasury of Atreus," the circle of the interior is forty-five feet across, and the beautifully worked stone corbeled dome rises to the same height above; originally it was decorated with rows of bronze rosettes. After it was built it was covered above with earth; it was approached by a dromos like an underground hillside tomb, and the main entrance was decorated with engaged columns, carved with finely patterned spirals, and delicately tapering downward, with a rich

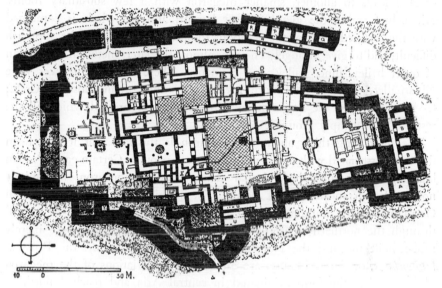

19. PLAN OF THE PALACE, TIRYNS. (Robertson: *A Handbook of Greek and Roman Architecture.*) F. PALACE FORECOURT. K. GATEWAY. L. COURT. M. MEN'S MEGARON. q. WOMEN'S MEGARON.

carved triangular slab filling an opening over the door lintel, like that of the "Lion Gate." The great tholos at Orchomenos has even more beautiful masonry, and is distinguished by the lavishly carved ceiling over the burial chamber which opened off the tholos proper at one side. This carving—an all-over pattern of interlocking spirals—reproduces almost exactly the painted patterns of tomb chambers along the distant Nile, and is eloquent evidence of the close relation of Egypt and Greece in that period—*circa* 1400 B.C.

The greatest differences between the preclassic architecture of Crete and that of mainland Greece lie in the palaces. The essential and dominating element of the royal dwellings of Mycenae and Tiryns and Troy is a large central room with a floor hearth in the middle, approached through a vestibule and a porch; the whole combination is termed a "megaron." Porch, vestibule, and hall are all equally wide, so that the side walls of all three are continuous; the two or three columns of the porch are set between the walls, in a way which the classic writers term *"in antis."* In the large megara there are four columns at the corners of the central hearth, as though to support an upper clerestory to let out the fire smoke. In Tiryns, the best preserved of these palaces, the great megaron fronts on a colonnaded court, entered through a monumental porch or gateway. From the court a narrow passage leads to another, smaller megaron with a few subsidiary rooms, evidently forming the *gynakeion,* or harem; and the whole is combined with the fortified walls of the acropolis in such a way as to make approach difficult, and to give, strangely enough, almost the later, medieval castle plan of outer bailey, inner bailey, and residence. These mainland palaces were all smaller, simpler, and more formally planned than those of Crete; the dominance of the megaron constituted a center around which all the rest could be simply grouped.

The interesting thing about the megaron is the fact that it is a form distinctly associated with northern and western peoples. Certain early Persian buildings, to be sure, show similar shapes; but the megaron is definitely not a Mediterranean type of house. The prehistoric houses of northern Germany and of Scandinavia, and more modern examples still in use all through the northern sector of Europe and even into Russia, are merely timber-built megara; the Norwegian *stuga,* the Saxon *hof,* the Prussian *laubenhaus,* or porched-house, are all essentially variations of the megaron idea. Whether the form originated in central Asia and reached northern Europe via Russia, and Greece via the Balkans and Thessaly, or whether, as others claim, it was a timber form born in Scandinavia and the Baltic lands, is still uncertain; perhaps the first hypothesis is at present the more commonly accepted.

Nevertheless, despite the basic plan differences between Cretan and Mycenaean palaces, their decoration was the same. In Tiryns and Mycenae the walls were painted with the same naturalistic gaiety as in Knossos; flying fish and the nautilus showed the same love of the sea, and the same slim-waisted women in rich costumes with the same bronzed, short-aproned men were shown hunting, bearing offerings, or enjoying the spectacles of court life. The wooden columns were like the Cretan, tapering downward, with heavy bulging capitals; and Cretan decorative ideas governed all the house furnishings, pottery, metalwork, and jewelry. Either the Achaean lords were using Cretan craftsmen (or perhaps the pre-Achaean "Pelasgian" natives who were their racial and cultural cousins) or else they were apt pupils indeed.

It is the life in these megaron palaces which Homer shows—Odysseus shooting deadly arrows at the suitors as they banqueted in the megaron; Circe welcoming her guests to just such a house; in the land of the Phaeacians, Odysseus entertained by Alcinous in a home which is merely

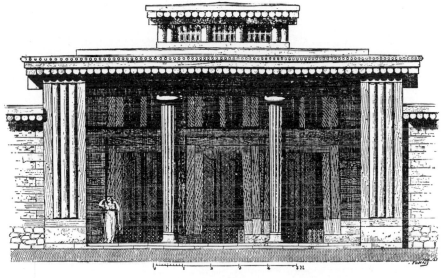

20. FRONT OF THE PALACE AT TIRYNS, RESTORED. (Perrot and Chipiez. Tome VI.)

a sort of fairy-tale version of the palace of Tiryns. The Achaean world was a different, a more turbulent, world than the old Cretan world. Perhaps in its chieftains' wars, of which the Trojan War legend is the most important relic, lay the cause of its own decadence. For certainly decadence did set in, all over the Aegean world, and the wares and buildings of both the last Minoan and the last Mycenaean periods are but crude and awkward caricatures of their predecessors. It was over this last decadent culture that the Dorian migration swept down, sometime between 1200 and 1000 B.C., to bring to this whole Aegean world the death of one of the world's great early cultures. Perhaps the death it brought was deserved, was as much the result of internal disintegration as of external force.

The Pre-Columbian Architecture
of America

Interlude A

THE PRE-COLUMBIAN ARCHITECTURE
OF AMERICA

WHEN the European explorers—from Spain and Portugal, from England and Italy, from France and Holland—gradually discovered the American continent, the New World they found was a world almost as varied in culture as their own. Although the jungle areas of the Amazon and the bitter, barren country around the Straits of Magellan were inhabited by peoples of the most primitive type, the Indians of America as a whole were far from savage. The Spaniards sailing along the coasts of Yucatan in the early sixteenth century were amazed at the magnificent buildings they discerned from the shore; what they saw was but an indication of the high types of civilization that some of the American peoples had already developed.

The Americas of those days were filled with varying types of people speaking different languages, perhaps the result of separate emigrations from Asia many millennia before. Scattering little by little over first North and later South America from their original entrance in Alaska, they had gradually coalesced into separate groups developing separate types of culture fitted to the land in which they lived. Thus, the hunters tended to remain nomadic, and for that reason developed buildings of only the simplest type, of which the well-known tepee of the plains Indians was the best example; those, on the other hand, who had developed a primitive agriculture tended to settle where soil was good and climate propitious, and there to develop villages and a closer kind of social organization. As time went on, some of the agricultural civilizations became apt as masonry builders, and architecture of highly advanced types was created.

Even among the forest-dwelling or primitively agricultural people of the eastern half of the United States the building instinct was far from dormant. Most of the Indians along the Atlantic coast lived in villages, often surrounded by a stockade; the houses were usually rectangular with round tops, and consisted of a simple framework of light wooden branches covered with skins of animals or occasionally with thatch. In some tribes communal dwellings were in use—the long houses of the Iroquois are especially well known. These were merely enlarged versions of the individual house. About 18 to 20 feet wide, they were from 60 to 100 feet long, and the log-and-branch framework would be divided by the chief supports into separate bays, one for each family.

Nor were other types of building unknown; for example, we find mound building a general feature of Indian sites all through the Ohio and Mississippi valley, and in a belt extending eastward through Alabama and Georgia to Florida and the Atlantic. These mounds were large earthworks,

21. A: TYPICAL TEPEE OF THE PLAINS INDIANS, CROW TRIBE; SHOWING THUN-DER-BIRD DECORATION. B: TYPICAL REED-MAT AND BIRCH-BARK WIGWAM OF THE FOREST INDIANS, CHIPPEWA TRIBE. (Drawn by the author from photographs, courtesy of the Museum of the American Indian, Heye Foundation.)

built for three different purposes: sepulchral, like some of the great tumuli of Europe and Asia; for fortifications, as village walls or forts built at important strategic fords or hill passes; and religious. The religious mounds often take animal form; the great Serpent Mound of Ohio is perhaps the most notable example, but mounds in the form of deer, mountain lions, and eagles also exist. In some cases the mounds may be strengthened or even bordered by rough stone walls, showing that masonry was slowly coming into use. The general opinion seems to be that mound building had almost ceased in the northeastern part of America perhaps 300 or 400 years before the coming of the white men. The builders, though obviously Indians, like the later inhabitants of the same areas, may have been of slightly different strain and been forced by more warlike tribes to flee to other centers, or may perhaps have been eliminated by disease.

Among these mounds there are many of a geometrical, pyramidal shape. These pyramid mounds usually have a flat area on the top; and in some cases, we know, wooden temple shrines crowned the tiny plateau. This was true in some of those described by early visitors to Florida and Georgia, and it is probable that the same kind of temple was widely distributed over large parts of North America. It is an excellent example of the simplest form of the High Place type of temple building.

Along the Northern Pacific coasts the Indians developed a wooden archi-

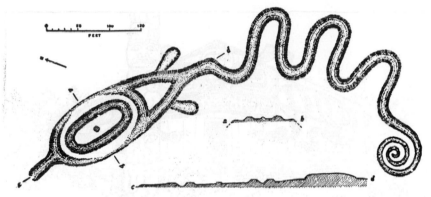

22. PLAN OF THE SERPENT MOUND, ADAMS COUNTY, OHIO. (*The American Anthropologist*, 1919.)

tecture of a character quite different from that further east. Using only stone and bone tools, they were nevertheless able to cut down large trees and to shape them into planks. From the planks, set endwise in the ground, they constructed large houses with low-pitched roofs, the fronts of which were often decorated with gigantic conventionalized masks and animal forms in brilliant paint. Sometimes these houses were built on the hillside, so that part was below the surface of the ground to give greater warmth in winter; and semi-underground or pit dwellings of various kinds were at one time widely used over much of the plains area as well as along parts of the Pacific coast. This western coastal culture has lasted on almost to the present day; and when the Indians began to use iron, traded to them by white settlers or visitors, it was only to carry further their skill in wood building and wooden sculpture. The great totem poles, for instance, which are such a characteristic element in these coast villages, were never made until the nineteenth century, when iron tools had become common; prior to that the difficulty of working with stone tools had limited the sculpture to smaller objects. Nothing could explain more simply the immediate sensitiveness of architecture and decoration to changes in tools and work methods.

Masonry building flourished in only three regions. The first is that generally arid portion of the southwestern United States comprising parts of New Mexico, Arizona, Texas, Utah, and Colorado. Here timber was more difficult to obtain. Stone was commonly available, and the system of irrigated agriculture which had been developed necessitated settlements of the most permanent type. The second great section consisted of the southern half of Mexico and the northern portions of Central America; and the third

23. ALASKAN PAINTED WOODEN HOUSE AND TOTEM POLE, CAPE FOX, ALASKA; TLINGIT CULTURE. (Drawn by the author from photographs, courtesy of the Museum of the American Indian, Heye Foundation.)

was the western slope of the Andes and the Pacific coastal plain of the northern half of South America.

The first of these three areas saw a long period of continual progress from primitive tribes known as the *Basket Makers,* perhaps 1300 years ago, through periods when the beginnings of masonry building may be seen in the walling up of cavern mouths to form half-artificial cave dwellings, up to the full development of the Pueblo villages sometime in the fifteenth or sixteenth century. It was legends of these hilltop towns, passed through many intermediate Indian tribes, which set Coronado on his amazing trip from Mexico in search of the Seven Cities, a trip which took him in the early 1540's as far north as Kansas.

The essential nature of these towns was based on their close communal arrangement. They were placed on heights or in narrow river gorges for ease of defense; and the one-room houses of which they consisted were built close to each other, forming one continuous building, often around an open square where the ritualistic dances took place and the tribal councils were held. The houses were built with rather rough walls of small stones laid in clay, and often plastered outside and in with clay and sometimes lime as well. Flat-roofed, their only entrance was from above; and the roof hatch, through which a roof ladder led down to the floor, served also to admit light and air and to take away the cooking smoke. As the population of the villages grew and little by little the hilltop filled, the only remaining place for addition was upward; new houses, accordingly, would be built above the old, tier on tier, until heights of several stories were frequently reached, stepped back to give a terrace at each floor. The upper-level houses would have their doors leading out on the roofs of those below, so that only the bottom tier would eventually be entered from above. Later still, after contact with the Spanish settlers had begun, the builders of the villages began to add doors and window openings in the European fashion.

Two further types of construction came into use at some time during this period. One was a kind of rough concrete of clay and pebbles, poured between forms of wickerwork and pounded hard, so that, when the wickerwork was removed, walls of the desired width and height were left, of this *terre pisée* (beaten earth). Such work, like the rough masonry, was usually plastered to give it a smooth finish. The other type was that which is now called *adobe*, and consisted merely of forming bricks of any desired size, of clay mixed with some kind of binding material—plant fibers, straw, moss, or what not—and then left in the sun to dry until they became perfectly hard. Adobe was, however, little used in the Pueblo country until after the Spanish invaders introduced the idea from Mexico. The roofs of these buildings were usually made of logs set horizontally and covered with brush or smaller branches; on this, clay or beaten earth was placed and tamped down until it formed a firm and impervious layer. Oftentimes the ends of the beam logs projected beyond the wall, and this series of projecting members with their insistent shadows gave a pleasant decorative finish at the top of the house walls. The flat roofs were enormously useful; in pleasant weather the family life could be carried on there rather than in the dark and stuffy interior beneath, and when the ritual dancers circulated in the open square of the town the roofs furnished excellent points of vantage.

For religious architecture these Southwest Indians depended on the *kiva,* a circular underground room, its walls lined with stone, its roofs formed of tree trunks placed horizontally as in the case of the houses. Here were kept the sacred symbols of the tribe; here too, at times, were stored surplus foods in case of droughts or siege; and sometimes also these kivas were used as a sort of clubhouse by the young braves of the town. They are perhaps memories of distant periods when remote ancestors had lived in caves or pit dwellings beneath the ground's surface; for it is a frequent rule that primitive dwelling types are long perpetuated in the temples of the gods, just as primitive folkways persist for generations embalmed in religious ritual.

The architecture of early Central America and Mexico was of a quite different, more highly developed nature. Here one comes for the first time in America upon the ideas of large-scale, conscious planning and of design in which the aesthetic element played as large a part as the practical. Exactly what primitive stages lay behind the developed work of the Early Mayan Empire is as puzzling and unsolved a question as that of the ultimate sources of Egyptian art. Since evidences of wooden technique represented in stone are obvious in much of the early work, it is probable that long centuries of highly advanced wooden building preceded the magnificent masonry structures we know.

The Early Mayan Empire—if such a loose federation of tribes with similar cults can be termed an empire—began the artistic and architectural career which has made it famous sometime around the beginning of the Christian era, and during the first six centuries of that era created an extraordinary galaxy of ritual buildings in a region stretching from the southwestern corner of Mexico through Guatemala into Honduras, and constructed in the middle of the forests a series of colossal "cities"—Copan, Palenque, Tikal, and Quirigua. What remains to us in these centers is chiefly religious in origin—a series of great artificial pyramids, stone-faced, with temple shrines on their summits; and also a number of lower buildings with many chambers around a central court, which may have been the residences of the priests or the palaces of the rulers. The pyramids are almost always stepped, forming a series of terraces with steeply sloping sides, and a steep stair runs up the center of one side from the bottom to the top. Along the stairs and frequently on the terrace walls as well, there is a rich decoration in sculpture, where gods and men are presented with extraordinary skill and, in the earlier work at least, often with an accuratelv observed realism. The stone shrines were long narrow rooms with immensely thick walls, roofed over by corbeling the courses of stone one over the other until an opening remained that was narrow enough to be covered by a single slab. To hold this corbeling in place a heavy mass of masonry would usually be piled upon it, and crowning all would be a rich openwork cresting or *roof comb*, as it is generally termed. The amount of labor necessary to produce these imposing groups bears witness to a large and disciplined population; yet the dwellings, save for the occasional "palace" or "monastery" groups, have completely disappeared, and it seems likely

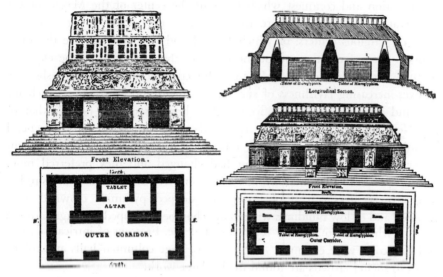

24. TWO MAYA TEMPLES AT PALENQUE; PLANS AND SECTIONS. *Left:* SO-CALLED TEMPLE OF THE CROSS. *Right:* SO-CALLED TEMPLE OF THE INSCRIPTIONS. (Drawings by Catherwood, in G. O. Totten: *Maya Architecture*.)

that all through the period of great Mayan architecture the ordinary people lived in the slightest kind of thatched branch-framed huts, like those in which their descendants reside today.

The work of the Early Mayan Empire is distinguished by its superb general planning, so that each monument in the group bears a definite relationship to all the others; by a general simplicity of surface; and by carefully placed, elaborate sculpture, often of great naturalistic charm. Only in the roof combs and the stair decorations is to be found the beginning of that amazing sense of conventionalization and symbolization which made of the later Mayan, Toltec, and Aztec gods such intricate and terrible effigies, obscure yet fascinating in their complex imagery. Copan is particularly remarkable for the subtle way in which the smaller pyramids enframe a great open square, above which rises the chief temple tier on tier, and for the way the lower temple terrace is carried around beyond the pyramid proper as a frame for the open square—perhaps to serve as a sort of grandstand overlooking one side of the sacred area. The residential buildings are universally more simple. Some remains show that their interior walls were carefully plastered and richly frescoed.

Sometime during the seventh and eighth centuries this earlier Mayan Empire collapsed and its cities were deserted; and chronicles tell of a period of migration and conquest which brought the center of the Mayan power northward into Yucatan, there to establish a new, even larger group of cities or religious centers, of which Uxmal and Chichen Itza are the most famous. Here, from the end of the tenth to the beginning of the eleventh century, a new flowering of Mayan architecture occurred, distinguished by an ever-increasing lavishness of surface treatment and a growing search for size and almost brutal magnificence. The builders of this period—that of the New Mayan Empire, as it is called—were less interested in general planning than those of the earlier empire had been; or, perhaps we might better say, their ideals of planning had changed and they preferred more picturesque and less formal layouts. Yet essentially the structures are similar. The great centers consist of groups of stepped pyramids crowned with temples, and of low buildings with many chambers grouped in ranges around a court, which are manifestly for residential use. Frescoes of intricate design and rich color were common. At times, too, large columnar halls and colonnades to shelter crowds are found in this later work.

Later still, around the beginning of the thirteenth century, other tribes with a different language, pressing down from the north, overcame the Mayan Empire. This new group of peoples, called Toltecs, brought to Yucatan their own architectural ideas and their own ways of life and religion, introducing great ball games, which made necessary the vast ball courts of Chichen Itza and Uxmal, and introducing too the cruel human sacrifices of the north. But their coming also brought new life to the decadent Mayans; and the last work in these Yucatan centers, built under the combined Mayan and Toltec influence and lasting down well into the fifteenth century, was decoratively its most skillful—as it was its most abstract—period, and gave rise to buildings which in their gorgeousness of color, their over-all richness of light-and-shade patterning, their great scale, and their complex plans were equal if not superior to the earlier work.

Further north in the valley of Mexico lived other tribes also possessed of great building skill and, like the Mayans, pyramid builders. The Toltecs were the most accomplished of these; and, even after the inroads and conquests of their victorious cousins the Aztecs had destroyed their political power, they still remained as honorable citizens especially famous for their ability in the building and decorative crafts, and Aztec architecture was largely produced by Toltec craftsmen and infused with Toltec ideals. The Toltecs developed no such extraordinary stone buildings as did the Mayans to the south, but raised impressive stepped pyramids of even greater size and richer decoration. The famous group of pyramids at Teotihuacan is perhaps their most remarkable achievement. Especially common in their work was the decorative use of the serpent—the plumed serpent, the symbol of their supreme god, Quetzalcoatl. Here was a deity perhaps worshiped over large areas in Mexico and Central America; for the supreme Mayan deity, Kukulcan, came also to be symbolized as a plumed serpent, and in fact the two names in their respective languages have precisely the same significance.

The Toltecs were followed by the Aztecs, who had scarcely more than consolidated their power when, in turn, they were overthrown by the Spanish conquest. It was Aztec Mexico which Cortes conquered, and Aztec palaces and temples at which his men felt such awe and admiration. Yet of the Aztec architectural work scarcely any still remains. Obviously it was deeply under Toltec influence, and probably largely executed by Toltec builders. It manifestly made more of its domestic buildings than did that of the Mayans, for the Mexico City which Cortes captured was a close-built town, regularly planned, with straight streets, and tied to the mainland by stone-lined causeways and bridges across the marshes and lake which surrounded it. These houses, like some of the buildings of the Mayans, were groups of rooms around a court. They were usually built of rough stone or rubble, plastered with a stucco so beautifully polished that it shone like silver. They had flat roofs and decorative battlements or parapets. It is possible that the influence of these Aztec dwellings went far in modifying the Spanish tradition to produce the typical Spanish-Colonial Mexican house.

Of the exact relationships of these cultures to each other and to others in North and South America, and of their buildings to those of other tribes in this large Mexican area, little is yet definitely known, for scientific archaeological study of this area is still in its infancy. At Mitla there is, for instance, a "palace" consisting of a series of long narrow halls, superbly built and decorated with rich geometric patterns in a kind of projecting stone mosaic, that is completely unlike any other structure known elsewhere.

Perhaps the closest similarities to its ornament can be found in early buildings far away on the Pacific coast in Peru. Similarly, in the later Mayan work itself there seem to be strains taken from many different sources still difficult to trace.

In all of this work erected by Mayan, Toltec, or Aztec builders there is one conspicuous quality—an apparent lack of understanding of the real structural nature of stone. Despite fourteen centuries of use of stone as a building material, they always seem to have regarded it as a surface decoration. Bonding in the masonry—that is, the arranging of the stones in such a way that the whole mass shall work as one—is often absent altogether, the stone consisting merely of a series of independent layers. The halting and tentative corbeled "vaults" over the narrow halls have already been mentioned. Often the Mexican builder used timber as a lintel when stone would have served, and the rotting out of these lintels has ruined monument after monument.

But, if the Mexican Indian was timid in his structural use of stone, he was brilliantly facile in his decorative embellishment, especially when it is realized that he had only stone tools to use in its carving. Projecting moldings were carried in horizontal bands around the pyramid sides; great conventionalized masks, their essentially human quality often concealed under a maze of rather geometric symbolic ornament, were often placed over doors or as the central feature of a roof comb; animals, especially the tapir and puma, occur again and again, sometimes conventionalized so that their original source is obscured and the attribution only possible because intermediate and more naturalistic phases of the same kind of decoration are known. In the later work, after Toltec influence was paramount, tremendous serpent forms were used as borders and stair railings, and often bright color added to the splendor of the whole effect.

The decorative genius revealed in this Mexican ornament has seldom been equaled. Its designers had an amazing command over the inevitable placing of light and shade so as to give an impressive unity to the extraordinary complexity of detail with which the forms were swathed. Every motif leads strongly to another, and there is an infallible sense of right placing of accents to create climax. This complexity was necessary in an art based on the most elaborate hieratic symbolisms. In the frequent colossal face patterns, for instance, the detailed elements like eyes or mouth or hair might each become an intricate organism of other smaller heads or serpents and birds; yet beneath the whole implicated network there is always the strongest artistic geometry. This complex and conventional art is nevertheless immensely expressive and emotional. One cannot help feeling, before it, the underlying gracious dignity of the early Mayan civilization, and, by contrast, in the Aztec work, the expression of a terrible and oppressive sense of sadistic horror. Could it be that underneath this terror, as its cause, lay a nation-wide neurosis which made the Mexican altars run with the blood of human sacrifices by the thousands, until the whole end of life and government seemed only death? And could it be that this neurosis, this strange aberration, was the real reason for the latent weakness of Mexico, so that the entire flourishing empire fell before Cortes with unbelievable rapidity?

But it was in the western valleys of the Andes and the Pacific coast adjacent that the greatest civilization of pre-conquest America arose. There, under the influence of fertile ground easily irrigated by the streams flowing from the eternal snows of the Andes, in a dry invigorating air, two cultures developed at about the same time the Early Mayan Empire came into being. One was the coastal culture of Chimu to the north and Nazca further south. The other, a highland culture, had its center around Lake Titicaca, 13,000 feet above sea level; it is called after the name of its chief ruined city, Tiahuanaco. Both cultures, highland and coastal, were accomplished weavers from an early period.

The Chimu culture was gracious, peaceful, artistic, delighting in naturalistic presentations in pottery and paint, and cultivating great skill in adobe and *terre pisée* construction. Like the Indians further north, the coastal Indians were great pyramid builders and set the fashion, followed more or less throughout later Peru, of placing their temples on high artificial terraces if not actual pyramids. Houses were simple single-room shelters with steep roofs covered with thatch, and towns or even cities of considerable size grew up at the climax period of the culture about 600 A.D. The most remarkable examples are the palace buildings of Chan Chan, the earlier parts having stuccoed adobe walls, frescoed; the later portions, built likewise of adobe, have rich geometrical patterns in relief in the stucco. Beyond the palace groups, the city of Chan Chan spread over a large area; its impressive ruins show its formal, rectangular planning, its straight streets, its reservoirs, and its parks and gardens and fields. Outstanding also is the great fortification at Parmunca, built in many terraces, with corner bastions of polygonal shapes almost recalling the star-shaped fortifications of the European seventeenth century.

The highland culture, like the lowland, existed in two basic forms, usually called Tiahuanaco I and II. Owing to its location among rocky, precipitous mountains, it became of necessity a stone-cutting and stone-building culture. In the early period, when the great city of Tiahuanaco first took form, the building was comparatively rough, with carefully cut stones at intervals and the rougher stonework piled between them; but the conceptions of plan and basic effect were always large-scaled and grand. The greater part of Tiahuanaco edifices, the ruins of which have been famous from the time of the Incas down, date chiefly from the later, Tiahuanaco II, type of culture. In this, an extraordinary skill in stone-cutting had already developed. Especially remarkable were the great portals cut out of enormous single blocks of stone (through which the sacred enclosures were entered) and the terrace and fortification walls built of the most carefully fitted polygonal stones, cut with painstaking care so as to key together and give unity to the whole wall. Sculptured decoration was occasionally found on portals. In it the earlier naturalistic approach had already been smothered under an elaborate symbolic conventionalization, which is evidenced not only by the reliefs of the great portal at Tiahuanaco but also by the pottery design and the beautiful textiles which remain from that period. Tiahuanaco has been too much ruined and the ruins too little studied to justify any complete reconstruction, or even to decide the purposes of many of its vast structures. Essentially, it seems to be a group of religious buildings, chiefly large open raised areas, surrounded by walls and occasionally by colonnades, and entered through monumental steps and portals. As in the case of the Mayan cities, there is nothing which can be definitely recognized as palace or even house building, and it is likely that at this period—say, between 600 and 900 A.D.—people still lived in comparatively simple and perishable huts.

Both coastal and highland cultures seem to have fallen into a decline about the tenth century, a decadence which well paved the way for the development of a new power. That power came from the Incas, apparently one of the highland tribes, from the hills near Cuzco, who came down into the plain and gradually, through military prowess and extraordinary organizational skill, built up a great centralized empire with its capital at Cuzco. This was about the beginning of the twelfth century; and little by little the successive rulers or emperors of the Inca dynasty enlarged their boundaries until, at the time of the Spanish conquest in 1530, the Incas ruled over a large region including all of Peru, large parts of Ecuador, and smaller portions of Bolivia, the Argentine, and Chile.

The secret of the success of the Incas was as much careful internal organization as it was military power, and this organization demanded in turn enormous amounts of construction. Roads were built which bound the whole vast area together, crossing streams on primitive suspension bridges and winding in great hairpin curves over the steepest and most forbidding mountain passes. Canals brought water for irrigation from great distances, and distributed it carefully to hundreds of little gardens. In order to get greater space for agriculture, an older Indian system of building terraced fields on the hillsides was much further developed, until there was hardly a slope with a good aspect anywhere in the empire which was not tiered with its narrow flourishing gardens held up by stone walls. The land system, like that of many other American Indian cultures, was based essentially on village ownership, and land was distributed according to the needs of the family.

Great fortifications, temples, and palaces were also built by the Incas, with growing skill and growing restraint and grandeur of plan. At first, like most of the highland Indians of their time, they had constructed only rough stone walls, cemented together with clay. Later, after the conquest of Tiahuanaco, their builders learned the Tiahuanaco lesson of carefully finished stone masonry; and, following a few attempts to build the elaborate keyed polygonal walls of the earlier culture, they worked out a new system of their own, using stones of more or less similar sizes, with beautifully polished surfaces, laid in long and gently waving courses. The Inca constructions were as much for residence as for worship; and, since wooden furniture was almost entirely absent from the Inca houses, ingenious methods were devised for furnishing storage space by means of numerous deep niches in the thick walls. These niches became one of the chief distinguishing characteristics of all Inca building. The Inca roofs were universally steep-pitched and thatched; even the great temples like the Temple of the Sun at Cuzco, the exterior walls of which now hold up the monastery of St. Dominic, were roofed with thatch. The thatch, according to the old chronicles, was so beautifully laid and so even that the effect was as monumental as though it had been made of more permanent materials. There was little or no carving in any of these Inca structures; they depended for their superb effect upon the magnificent quality of their masonry and their great scale and simplicity, and for interior richness on the amazing wealth of gold and silver—especially of gold —which was used in plates and bands and repoussé reliefs to decorate them. An old Spanish manuscript still preserves for us a view of the altar wall of the Palace of the Sun. The high-pitched gable is indicated unmistakably, and it shows the great wall beneath covered with a complex series of golden reliefs symbolizing the earth, the stars, and man and woman. The climax was a huge oval shield of gold hung high in the center and representing the creative might and brilliance of the sun. It was flanked on either side by two smaller golden circular images, one the sun and the other the moon. The square altar below seems itself to have been covered with a sheathing of square plates of gold. The city of Cuzco follows in its street plan the essential divisions of the old Inca town; and the walls of palaces, of the old imperial university, and of the convent of the chosen women who acted as priestesses of the sun still are there, carrying above them the walls of the modern Cuzco residences and churches.

The most completely preserved examples of pure Inca architecture are, however, not at Cuzco but rather at Machu Picchu, where the houses with their niched walls and their sharp gables still remain, again and again, in almost perfect preservation, brilliantly ranged tier on tier on the precipitous slopes of a hill, with steep stair streets leading up between to the summit, the sacred area, the precinct of the sun, where the sun's temple was, and the *inti-huatana* (the ritual sundial) with marks carefully scored in the stone where the shadow of the gnomon falls on June 21 and December 21, thus marking the passage of the year.

All of this carefully organized empire fell before the Spanish with shocking rapidity. Its very careful centralization of power aided in the process; for, once the Spaniards had command of the person of the emperor, in a sense they commanded the empire itself. And, just as they killed the emperor, so they killed the Inca culture; the carefully irrigated, terraced fields dropped into disuse, the population declined, barbarism reasserted its sway. The Spaniards were only interested in gold and Christianity, and their headlong search for the precious metal—which had owed its value in Peru only to the fact that it symbolized the sun and was a pretty material for decoration—led to the insensate and unnecessary destruction of all that was best in both ancient Peruvian architecture and ancient Peruvian life. Even today it is said the population of Peru is hardly half of what it was when the Spanish grandees took it over.

The existence of these high cultures of Mexico and Peru has been a source of amazement to the European world ever since the Spaniards discovered them toward the beginning of the sixteenth century, and they have remained in many ways puzzles ever since. They have given rise to the most extravagant fancies and legends, from an early theory that these Indians were the descendants of the lost tribes of Israel and their culture therefore fundamentally Biblical and Jewish, through all the speculations as to a lost continent of Atlantis, down to other theories of direct colonization from Buddhist Asia. That some contact with the Asian continent may have occurred through seagoing junks blown out of their course by storms is not perhaps unlikely; but the claims for direct Buddhist influence in the cross-legged figures that sometimes decorate Mayan buildings, or reminiscences of Asia in the elephantlike forms sometimes found, seem hardly plausible. The elephant myth has been dispelled by further study, which shows that the elephantlike forms are merely decorative developments from the quite American tapir. Yet these civilizations still lend themselves to the making of myths. Not so many years ago, a professor claimed to have proved by dint of astronomical calculations that the ruins of Tiahuanaco were between 10,000 and 14,000 years old, and that it was therefore the oldest city in the world. Careful comparative archaeology seems to have demonstrated, however, that these buildings date chiefly from the second Tiahuanaco period between 600 and 900 A.D. A more recent theory has been popularized by the Norwegian anthropologist, Thor Heyerdahl—the idea that the culture of the Polynesian islands of the Pacific may owe much to pre-Inca Peruvians, who, floating west on balsa rafts, came eventually to these distant islands and brought with them the sweet potato, other plants, and many elements to be traced in Polynesian myths today. The possibility of such voyages he confirmed by making one, but the theory is not yet universally accepted.

Perhaps the real lesson to be learned is in the variety of cultures which the Europeans found on the American continent. It is the lesson that human beings in building are controlled by the needs of the kind of life they live and the kind of locality and climate in which they are placed; and that, although hunting and nomadic civilizations generally produce few buildings, those cultures founded on the more permanent basis of agriculture, particularly when they enjoy the general internal peace which is given by efficient governmental organization, will naturally progress to more and more elaborate, more and more beautiful, more and more skillful types of building. America may also show, I believe, that in all of these manifold expressions of the building sense there is almost always evident not only the desire to erect adequate shelters and to memorialize dead heroes or symbolize gods and natural forces, but also the wish to do these things with a certain pattern and form, a certain search for that quality which we call beauty.

BOOK III

Ancient Classic Architecture

R, SHRINE PORTAL; RESTORATION. (Hall and Woolley: *Excavations*).

BABYLON, ISHTAR GATE, RECONSTRUCTED IN THE BERLIN MUSEUM.

SA, COLUMNAR HALL (APADANA) OF ARTAXERXES; RESTORED MODEL, LOUVRE MUSEUM. eulafoy: *L'acropole de Suse*.)

RSABAD, PALACE OF SARGON. (Place: .)

URUK (WARKA), COLUMNAR HALL: RESTORATION. (Heinrich: *Schilf und Lehm*.)

Plate 5

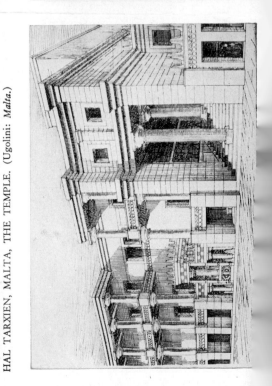

HAL TARXIEN, MALTA, TEMPLE; DETAIL. (Zammit: *Prehistoric Malta.*)

HAL TARXIEN, MALTA, THE TEMPLE. (Ugolini: *Malta.*)

Plate 6.

KARNAK, TEMPLE OF KHONS; EXTERIOR
SHOWING PYLONS.

KARNAK, TEMPLE OF KHONS; THE COURT,
WITH PAPYRUS-BUD COLUMNS.

KARNAK, HYPOSTYLE HALL, SHOWING
CLERESTORY WINDOW.

KARNAK, HYPOSTYLE HALL; AN AISLE.

Plate 3

EDFU, PTOLEMAIC TEMPLE; ENTRANCE FRONT.

EDFU, PTOLEMAIC TEMPLE; VIEW IN COURT, LOOKING TOWARDS THE HYPO-
STYLE HALL.

Plate 4

Chapter 6

THE ARCHITECTURE OF ANCIENT
HISTORIC GREECE

INTO the luxurious Aegean world there came, over a period of several centuries prior to 1000 B.C., wave on wave of new peoples from the north. At
first they seemed to have come in slowly, percolating little by little, tribe by
tribe, settling villages in waste places, and finally by mere force of population
becoming the dominant leaders of much of mainland Greece and parts of
Asia Minor. These newcomers, at the beginning, by the gradualness of their
coming, were enabled thoroughly to absorb the culture of the Cretan and
Aegean world, and to modify it to suit their own needs. It was they who,
about 1400 B.C., were the builders of the cities of Mycenae and Troy. It was
their chiefs who were the heroes of the Troy legends. It was their culture
which we can study in the Homeric poems.

Under the influx of these new peoples, the Cretan civilization gradually
decayed and its power diminished; and the disturbances caused by these
changes set up movements of peoples which finally beat upon the gates of
Egypt itself, and the Egyptian inscriptions tell us of the restlessness and
the wandering beyond the seas. Finally, about 1000 B.C., the greatest influx of
all took place, that mass migration a part of which even Greek legend remembered as the coming of the Dorians. Where the earlier migrations had
been peaceful, this seems on the contrary to have been chiefly military, and,
whereas the earlier immigrants were enabled largely to absorb and re-use the
culture which they found, thus producing the Mycenaean culture, the
Dorians seem largely either to have neglected it or destroyed it; only little by
little did they come to adopt here and there a feature of the earlier cultures,
and from these few borrowings and their own traditions, controlled and disciplined by an extraordinary demand for perfection, they developed an architecture which ranks among the greatest plastic creations of all time.

There is much dispute as to who the historic Greeks—the Dorians and
the Ionians, and the waves of immigrants who had preceded them—really
were, and from where they came. It is enough to know that they came speak-

III

ing a language which belongs to the Aryan linguistic group, that many were blond—witness Homer's "fair-haired Achaeans,"—and that they brought with them into this new Mediterranean world a building culture founded essentially upon timber. These new invaders did not exterminate their predecessors. There was evidently a great deal of gradual absorption and intermarriage. They became a hereditary caste, using perhaps the craft skills of the earlier inhabitants. It is significant, for instance, that many Greek words dealing with the arts and crafts, and especially with ships and navigation, seem to have roots entirely non-Aryan—roots which were recognized even by ancient Greek writers as imbedded in the ancient Cretan pre-Greek language.

Gradually the invaders adopted many of the religious ideas of the earlier peoples. Their own gods had been nature gods, natural forces in human form, and especially a sky god, Zeus. The innumerable legends that grew up telling of the amours of Zeus with all sorts of local nymphs and even human women are but fanciful ways of expressing the gradual adoption and modification of earlier and local myths. Similarly, there was everywhere an attempt to merge the mythologies of the invading race with those current in the lands to which it came. Thus, throughout the early Mediterranean, there is evidence of widespread worship of a great mother goddess, of whom the dove and the serpent were attributes; at times she becomes the new Greek Aphrodite, goddess of love and procreation, while in other parts of the Greek world the same original goddess is absorbed into the idea of Artemis, chaste goddess of the hunt.

The latest migration seems to have had two chief strains, closely related but still separate—one branch settling first central Greece and later the Asia Minor coast, the other staying chiefly in Greece and the islands nearest to it. The former were called Ionians and the latter Dorians, and each created its own characteristic building traditions, summed up in the Doric and Ionic orders.

The early history of this new Greek architecture produced by the invaders is as confused as the development of their mythology. Built of timber and unbaked brick, most of what they constructed during those early centuries has perished; only here and there foundation remains enable us to reconstruct the dwellings and the temples where they lived and worshiped. In these few remains of the ninth and tenth centuries B.C., one has already evidence of two different ideas—primarily the long, narrow rectangular house, and the circular hut.

As we have seen, buildings of circular shape were current in many parts of the prehistoric Mediterranean world, and were often used as houses in the early Cretan civilization. On the other hand, we know that timber-building peoples of even neolithic times all through central Europe were building long, narrow, high-roofed houses framed of timber, roofed in thatch, and with walls covered with mud plaster. We also know that the developed palace and house building of the Cretan world had been entirely rectangular in plan, so that it is impossible to say either that all round huts were of the new barbarians or that the rectangular plans represented the barbarian adaptation of the developed Cretan ideas. If we may speculate on the remains, we may say with a fair chance of accuracy that the new invaders, who talked an Aryan language that later grew into Greek, probably were builders of the typical rectangular one-roomed house of the north, and that they found a people living partly in round huts and partly in complex rectangular houses. From these people they seem to have borrowed both forms, although their traditional interest was in the rectangular house, and by combining certain Cretan ideas with their own traditions they rapidly developed the hall with central hearth, with its roof carried by wooden posts, which we know as the Homeric *megaron*. We may also surmise that, just as many neolithic houses had porches or porticoes supported on rough tree trunks in front of the doors, so these half-barbaric invaders would tend to build porches of a similar type in front of their megara.

To religious architecture of this old Greek world the new invaders brought a new idea, that of the religious structure as the House of God—the actual physical home of the deity. Cretan temples had been mere shrines or sacred areas. The new Greeks wanted an actual enclosed and roofed building; since the temple was the house of god, what more logical than to base its structure on the megaron where the chief of the tribe lived? Sometimes, as in the foundation of an old temple at Thermon, which may go back to the tenth century, the megaron had one end in a rough oval like an apse, but the foundations show a porch in front. It is significant, however, that a century or two later a new temple was built, of the long, narrow rectangular shape, with the roof held up by a row of posts down the center and a colonnade around the whole. Similarly at Sparta there exists the foundation of a temple of perhaps even earlier date which shows a rectangular room with a central row of posts. It is characteristic of the similarity between the temple and the chief's hall that, on the acropolis at Selinus in Sicily, the foundations of a megaron have been found which may have been the house either of a chief or of a god; there is no way of distinguishing.

We may, then, form some kind of a picture of a Greek town a century after the Dorian migration. In the center would rise the house of the chief, with walls of unburned brick and a roof either gabled and thatched or else flat and covered with turf. In front of it would be a porch made by continuing out the side walls beyond the end wall, with one or two posts between. Inside the door would be a long narrow hall of almost Norse type, with a central hearth in the middle of the floor and either one or two rows of posts holding up the roof above. Behind, a door might admit to a smaller squarish room, the private bedroom of the lord—the *thalamos* or "bridal chamber." Close to this would be grouped two or three minor buildings, the houses for the servants and the women of the household, the spinning room, and so on; and these all might be set together within a stockade. Round about would be grouped the houses or huts of the town—some perhaps rectangular, of the megaron form; some round and covered with conical roofs, perhaps the homes of the original autochthonous inhabitants, preserving their old method of building in a cruder form. These would be grouped around a rough open space, the origin of the later Greek *agora* or market place; and close to this on the other side would rise another megaron, the temple of the presiding deity of the town, distinguished from the chief's house by the altar in front of it, by the crude votive offerings that stood around the altar and by the temple door, and perhaps also by a colonnade porch on all four sides of the building. Out of this crude beginning, duplicated hundreds of times on the mainland of Greece and so far as materials would permit in the Greek islands, grew the glory of later Greek architecture.

Many reasons lie behind the extraordinary development of the next 500 years. The Greek world that was slowly taking form through the merging of the new and the old populations had the double advantage of an extraordinary elasticity in political make-up and yet a common language and mythology. The Greeks were Hellenes, sons of the mythical Hellen, but they were also Athenians, Spartans, Olympians, Ionians; and the continuing rivalry symbolized in the Olympic Games, which were held once every four years, was a tremendous stimulus to intellectual and artistic progress. Moreover, the people were adventurous and experimental. Early they began to found colonies, in Sicily, in southern Italy, in southern France, even on the shores of the Black Sea; and these colonies, though recognizing some bond with the city from which their founders came, nevertheless enjoyed an autonomous freedom. Slave labor also contributed. But the slaves were not the brutalized chattels of some later systems but rather merely the lowest order of society, with recognized rights.

Their country stood at the crossroads of the east and of the west, of the north and of the south. Strong influences from the older cultures of Asia and of Egypt beat continually at their doors, and the Phoenician sailors brought constantly to their harbors the goods of Syria, of Mesopotamia, and of the Nile. The Hellenes themselves soon became excellent sailors and traders on their own account, so that travel became comparatively easy, and all the advances made in one Greek city were known almost at once all over the Hellenic world.

Yet there was more behind this development than the mere physical nature of the country and its commercial opportunities. There was, in addition, a spirit of continual inquiry into everything, a spirit that seems almost to approach what we know today as the scientific attitude. The Greek was always questioning, demanding answers from nature and from himself and his own works. He was never satisfied with the merely conventional. Though he respected his ancestors, he never believed that what was good enough for them was good enough for him, so that there was no opportunity for that progress-destroying crystallization of culture that kept all Egypt so much the same for well-nigh 2000 years.

And in addition to this self-questioning, this continuous curiosity, which is behind the origin of so much Greek philosophy and Greek science, there was still another quality, the ability to synthesize and to speculate, the ability to create beautiful patterns out of the knowledge which had been gained. The Hellene seems to have had an innate aesthetic sensitiveness of a different character from any that had gone before, a sensitiveness to rhythms, to music, and to plastic form, which in its own special sureness and emotional serenity found its final and perfect expression alike in Greek tragedy, Greek sculpture, and Greek architecture. Furthermore, the Greek insisted that this artistic culture should somehow be generalized and be at the command of all, so that the greatest works were public or religious. The extraordinarily high level of even the most modest Greek pottery in shape and in painted decoration reveals how universal this love of beautiful things and the ability to produce them must have been.

With such a character and such a location, the Hellene could not long remain satisfied with the crude villages and towns he had first constructed. He began by adopting the rather bulbous convex capital forms of Cretan and Mycenaean art, and by studying ways in which the wooden beams carried by the posts could be made more beautiful. First he laid upon his posts, and supported on the broad *abacus* or square-top member of the capital, single straight beams running from post to post, carefully squared, sometimes covered with a slightly projecting board laid horizontally to even any in-equalities. On this he placed smaller crossbeams running from colonnade to wall, to support the ceiling. The ends of these were brought out to the edge of the beam below, and sometimes a little beyond, and were held in place by wooden pegs driven up through their lower ends. One crossbeam would be placed over each column; if the distance between the columns were large, intermediate beams would also be used. On top of these crossbeams, another beam or board would be placed running the length of the building, to act as a *roof plate*, to support the slanting roof rafters. These rafters would project out to form eaves, and on them the roof tiles, which the Greek had already begun to manufacture, were placed. On the underside of the roof beams, at the eaves, other boards might be placed, to make the whole more solid; these, too, would be held in place by wooden pegs. The open-ings which were left between the crossbeams, the lower beam or architrave, and the roof-plate beam or lowest element in the cornice could then be filled with thin boards or terra-cotta slabs and the whole brightly painted with decorative patterns. This is the beginning of the Doric entablature.

A little later, as the Grecian skill in making terra-cotta increased, perhaps

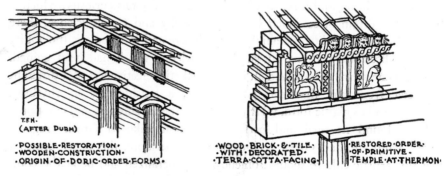

T.F.H.
(AFTER DURM)

·POSSIBLE·RESTORATION·
·WOODEN·CONSTRUCTION·
·ORIGIN·OF·DORIC·ORDER·FORMS·

·WOOD·BRICK·&·TILE·
·WITH·DECORATED·
·TERRA·COTTA·FACING·

·RESTORED·ORDER·
·OF·PRIMITIVE·
·TEMPLE·AT·THERMON·

25. *Left:* PROBABLE TYPE OF WOODEN CONSTRUCTION FROM WHICH THE DORIC ORDER EVOLVED. *Right:* RESTORATION OF PRIMITIVE TERRA-COTTA-SHEATHED ENTABLATURE FROM THERMON. (Drawn by the author from various sources.)

in the eighth and seventh centuries B.C., in order to protect the most exposed parts of the wood from rot, the front edge of the eaves cornice would be sheathed in richly decorated terra-cotta. Then the ends of the lowest roof tiles could be turned up and made into decorative palmlike forms. A gutter could be contrived in the terra-cotta cornice, from which the water was discharged through the open mouths of lions' heads or through little spouts.

In the meanwhile, the column and its capital were becoming more refined. Most of the Cretan columns, as we have seen, tapered with the small end down, although there are indications that there was an occasional use of columns with the small end up. It was not long before the Greeks realized the greater grace of the latter system, and it is probable that the larger number of the early wooden columns tapered in this way. One wooden column still remained in the old Temple of Hera at Olympia when Pausanias visited it in the second century A.D. All the others had gradually been replaced by stone, and even today in the ruins we can see these columns, the differing shapes and details (and even the differing materials) of which show the difference in the times when they were set in place, one by one replacing the old wood posts as they rotted.

The Cretan capital soon suffered modification, as the simplifying genius of the Greeks worked upon it, clarifying its lines and making it ever more graceful. The square abacus and the projecting, convex, cushionlike form known as the *echinus* were brought close together, so that the echinus seemed to support the abacus more powerfully. The joint between the echinus and the shaft was studied with care, and many experiments in different treatments were made before the final perfect shape was arrived at.

A revolutionary change in all of this building was caused by the substitution of stone for wood in all the important structural members. For temples this change seems to have been fairly universal about 600 B.C. The permanence and monumentality of stone as opposed to wood were too obvious for a cultivated people to neglect; yet the Greeks, originally and traditionally timber-builders, were cautious to the extreme in their use of the new material. They seem to have had little real knowledge of the very great bearing strength of good stone or marble; and, though Greek architecture reveals a continual development toward more and more slender proportions, in no case did the weight supported justify from any mechanical point of view the size of the columns used to hold it. In the earlier work, stone columns are enormously thick, usually only about four or four and a half diameters high, and sometimes set so close together that the space between them is less than the diameter of the column.

But, if stone is comparatively strong for posts, it is comparatively weak for beams, and the substitution of stone for wood in entablatures brought with it difficult problems. By the time the change had been made, the Greek was so attached to the forms developed in his wooden architecture that he sought only to reproduce them in stone. Thus the bottom beam became the *architrave;* the board above it the projecting member known as the *taenia;* the ends of the crossbeams became the *triglyphs;* and the spaces between them the sculptured stone *metopes*. Even the forms of the wooden pegs which had held the whole together were retained as the *guttae* ("drops") which decorated the bottom of the taenia under the triglyphs and the underside of the cornice. Since the roof beams remained of wood, the cornice was the last element to be changed from wood to stone; and many of the early stone temples, although the architrave and frieze were of stone, retained a wooden cornice completely sheathed in painted terra-cotta. At last, however, even the cornice was made of the more permanent material, and by the time of Pericles, in the middle of the fifth century B.C., the Greek passion for stone and marble was so great that practically all of the largest temples had their roofs completely of marble tile, although supported still on wooden beams.

Since the architrave beam was basically a weak spot in the construction, carrying as it did all the weight above, the early Greeks gave the column capitals a large projection, in an effort to cut down the unsupported spans of the beams. One early capital, perhaps of the seventh century, from Tiryns, has an abacus width two and one-third times as great as the upper diameter of the column, and all the earlier temples have capitals which project enormously. As the Greeks learned more about the strength of their materials—stone and marble—they began to be more daring in the spans they designed. They tied the blocks together with bronze keys and occasionally even built iron bars into the entablature, as in the Athenian Propylaea, to gain more strength. Not only were columns more widely spaced, but the abacus projection was reduced, and the line of the echinus beneath it grew ever more graceful and refined.

The best of the earlier stone temples are to be found in the Greek colonies of Sicily and south Italy. There, in the seventh century B.C., an age of despotic rule and of powerful and driving leaders, the great increase in the accumulation of wealth naturally gave rise to great building activity. Great temples rose in Syracuse, in Selinus, and in Paestum during the first seventy-five years of the sixth century B.C. All are completely of stone, with at least the architrave and frieze of stone; but in one at least, Temple "C" at Selinus, the cornice was still covered with terra-cotta. In Paestum, the Temple of Demeter, besides having an unusual and experimental plan, has a cornice and pediment treatment entirely different from the ordinary, for, instead of having the cornice run through horizontally under the pediment and then a repeated sloping cornice at the pediment sides, it has no horizontal cornice at the pediment ends at all, and the whole cornice just runs up the slope following the line of the roof behind.

In Paestum, too, a temple, usually called the Basilica, still preserves the old system of a central colonnade, which had been abandoned elsewhere for at least a century. The Temple of Zeus at Agrigentum was of extraordinary size (173 by 361 feet) and unique construction due to the fact that, owing to its enormous scale and to the fear which the Greeks had of the great spans of unsupported beams, a whole wall was carried up between the columns, making what should have been the exterior colonnade a covered passage, perhaps lighted by openings in the upper part. Another temple of great interest was begun at Segesta, in Sicily, during the first half of the fifth century B.C., and never finished, so that in its present condition it contains priceless evidence of the way in which the Doric temples were built. Thus, projecting bosses were left on the stones, around which rope slings could be placed to hoist the stones in place. When the stone was placed, the boss was tooled away. Flutes were carefully started only at the bottom and at the very top of the shaft, and the fluting in between was worked after the column had been set in place. Furthermore, the colonnade, with its entablature and pediments, was built first. In Segesta they never got around to building the walls of the enclosed cella at all. In these temples we can see, too, the beginning of great architectural sculpture, and in the magnificent placing of the temples at Selinus realize the Greek genius for taking advantage of beautiful sites and arranging their buildings with an eye to cumulative effect.

Almost the only early temple with extensive remains preserved in their original form, on the Greek mainland, is the Temple of Apollo at Corinth, dating perhaps from the middle of the sixth century B.C. Elsewhere, rebuildings—as in the Temple of Hera at Olympia—or the preservation of the traditional older temples which were built largely of wood and unburned brick, and have therefore perished, made almost unnecessary the construction of any new primitive Doric work.

In almost all of these primitive temples we can see a continual striving for grace and beauty, a continually growing effort to systematize and regularize the architectural elements. We find a continually growing relative lightness of proportion; columns are more slender, the earlier columns being hardly four diameters high, whereas the later ones are five and six, and in the culmination of the style seven. The entablature, which in some of the earlier examples is a third the height of the columns, is gradually reduced to about a quarter. The metopes, which in some of the earlier work varied in size according to the spacing of the columns, were made all square, so that the columns at the corner were drawn closer to their neighbors than elsewhere in the composition in order to bring a triglyph on the corner of the frieze.

Column capitals were also enormously refined during the sixth century. The early examples have a tremendous spread and an echinus profile in a broad and bulbous curve, beneath which there is often a decorated hollow running around the top of the shaft and carved with leaves or ornament. This broke the whole composition too much into two parts, and little by little this hollow beneath disappeared and was replaced by a series of little projecting fillets at the bottom of the echinus, which just served, as it were, to bind together the flutes of the shaft below and connect them with the echinus above. As the projection of the abacus decreased, the curve of the echinus tended to become flatter and more vertical in feeling, approaching almost to the conical, but always with a slight convex curve to remove any possibility of a feeling of stiffness.

Similarly with the decoration; the earlier crude terra-cotta forms were replaced by much more refined painted patterns, and the metopes by carved stone sculpture. The pediments, too, were seen to be admirable places for sculptured groups. An early example dug up from the debris of the Persian destruction of the Athenian Acropolis in 480 B.C., and thus prior to that date, shows a strange marine monster, crudely carved, with twining tails which filled the triangular corners of the pediment. Yet, once the application of sculpture to the Doric architecture had begun, the way was open to the development of the final triumphs of the Parthenon.

In the meanwhile, the Ionic Greeks in Asia Minor were working out their type of architecture, applying to their own conditions and to the influences which surrounded them the same kind of experimental invention. At that time, Asia Minor was heavily wooded and timber-building was universal. A building system different from that of the European north was in vogue, to produce the flat roofs which the Asiatics had always loved. Vertical posts were widely spaced, and to cover these wide spacings beams built up of two or three, or even four, members one over the other were used; since the joints between these pieces could not be permanently concealed, they were expressed by making each beam slightly wider than the one below it. On these beams were laid small crossbeams close together, which sometimes took the form of mere round tree trunks. These supported in turn a layer of boards or of reeds, which carried a roof of beaten earth or of cement.

The type of main beam used was not a scientific use of the material, and, in order to prevent these beams from sagging and to reduce their span, horizontal bracket beams were set on top of the posts and underneath the girders. Much of this early type of Asiatic timbering we can see reproduced in rock-cut tombs which still exist in the southern Asia Minor kingdoms.

The problem that confronted the Ionic Greeks was the gradual refinement of this system. The first great step which they made was an attempt to unify the sense of connection between the post and the bracket beam above it, by carving on the bracket beam two spirals, growing apparently out of the post and spreading out on each side. This development may have been suggested to them by decorative ornament produced by the Semitic races of Syria, but they gave it their own particular grace of curve. In Cyprus, such a form had been applied to square piers; in Asia Minor circular posts were used, and the temple of Neandria, perhaps dating from the beginning of the seventh century B.C., shows a developed example of this early Ionic capital, with its crude, overheavy, tremendously spreading double-spiraled capital. Bases were an essential part of these posts or columns from the beginning, and here again the Ionic groups borrowed from their Asian precursors, who had customarily kept their wooden posts from rotting by raising them on high molded bases of stone. To give grace to these bases and prevent them from seeming overheavy, the Greeks molded them with hollow rings running round them, so that the light and shade make, as it were, a series of dark collars at the bottom.

When stone was substituted for wooden posts, the base and the capital were retained; and, moreover, the extreme slenderness of proportion of the wooden post was as far as possible carried over into the new material, so that Ionic columns are always slimmer and more delicate in proportion than the Doric. Like the Doric, they were usually fluted to emphasize their vertical lines.

But the capital was still essentially unbeautiful. The lines of the spiral seemed to spring too suddenly out of the shaft, and therefore the Greeks added at the top of the shaft, and before the spirals began, a convex round molding and sometimes a sort of bell-shaped form carved with leaves. This gave a transition but it broke up the unity, and little by little the moldings at the top of the shaft and the scroll forms tended to coalesce. A great step in advance was made sometime early in the sixth century B.C., when the lines of the two spirals, instead of being continued down vertically into the middle of the shaft, were joined by a horizontal or slightly downward-waving line across the top, thereby not only uniting them into one form but also expressing more clearly the projecting bracket type.

The first highly developed example of this Ionic order which we know is that of the great temple at Ephesus, built by the famous King Croesus between 560 and 546 B.C. Of colossal size, this temple had, strangely enough,

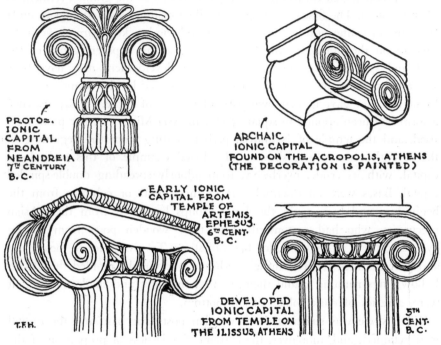

PROTO⁼.
IONIC
CAPITAL
FROM
NEANDREIA
7ᵀᴴ CENTURY
B. C.

ARCHAIC
IONIC CAPITAL
FOUND ON THE ACROPOLIS, ATHENS
(THE DECORATION IS PAINTED)

EARLY IONIC
CAPITAL FROM
TEMPLE OF
ARTEMIS,
EPHESUS.
6ᵀᴴ CENT.
B. C.

T.F.H.

DEVELOPED
IONIC CAPITAL
FROM TEMPLE ON
THE ILISSUS, ATHENS

5ᵀᴴ
CENT.
B. C.

26. EARLY AND DEVELOPED IONIC CAPITALS. (Drawn by the author.)

nine columns across the rear portico and only eight across the front, so that the central intercolumniation of the front opposite the entrance was extraordinarily wide. The long slender columns were raised still higher by being placed on high sculptured drums; and the broad, spreading capitals, at least twice as wide as they were deep, had the fully developed scrolls, with the convex molding below—a sort of echinus—carved with egg and dart, which are found in the later developed examples.

Just as the wooden post and bracket grew into the Ionic column, with its base and spiraled cap, so the wooden beam system grew into the Ionic entablature—the group of wooden beams being replaced by a stone architrave with projecting bands one over the other, recalling the increased width of its wooden prototype, and the little crossbeams becoming the *dentils* or little projecting square blocks that ornament so many classical cornices. At first there was no frieze; later in Greece, and later still even in Asia Minor, the influence of the Doric order and the love for spaces to carry sculpture led to the placing of a frieze between the architrave and the cornice.

Asia Minor was the great battleground of Persian and Greek influence during the years when the Persian Empire was gradually spreading to the west, so that Greek work in Asia Minor is almost entirely limited to very early work of the sixth and seventh centuries B.C., and to very late work which corresponded with the rise and oriental dominance of the Empire of Alexander the Great.

In both Ionic and Doric development, a number of common trends which show the Hellenic background are evident. The first is the gradual change from wood construction to stone, and yet the preservation in the stone of elements taken directly from the wooden prototypes. Such, as we have seen, are the triglyphs, the guttae, the banded architraves, and the dentils. In a sense, this may argue a certain lack of sensitiveness to building materials. Yet the Greeks had a marvelous intuitive sense for the expression of structure; that is, the creation of forms which should give the impression of being light, easily supported, and strong. The Greek architect was always striving to outdo those who had preceded him, but at the same time he seems never to have attempted violently revolutionary innovations. It was as if, looking upon the work of his father or grandfather, he had said, "This element is beautiful, but it can be made more beautiful; it is graceful, it makes pleasant light and shade, but I will make it a little bit more graceful, I will see that the light and shade on it are a little more perfectly distributed." Thus there is not only in Greek work a continual progress, but also a certain standardization of generic types, giving rise to the development of "orders" of architecture—that is, standard arrangements of the column, with its capital, shaft, and base, and the entablature, the beam-and-eaves system which the columns carry, consisting generally of architrave, frieze, and cornice.

The second of these great common trends is a general attitude toward architectural ornament. The Greeks apparently had little native tradition of decoration when they first came down into the Mediterranean world. They borrowed forms from everyone with whom they came in contact. In that sense, they were perfectly and unashamedly eclectic. From the Cretans they took the convex form which they reworked into the Doric capital; from the Asiatics they borrowed the banded architrave, the dentil systems, and the bracketed post which evolved into the Ionic; from the Egyptians and the peoples of the Syrian coasts they borrowed lotus and palmette forms which they reworked into their own inimitable anthemions and carved molding decorations. Still, if their borrowing was wide, what they did with the forms they borrowed was their own unique contribution; each one was changed, recombined with other elements, made more delicate, more refined, or stronger as the case might be, until the final decorations achieved a perfection of rhythmic curved line which has seldom been equaled. Developed Greek ornament is seldom naturalistic. It is typical of the clear Greek thinking that, where naturalism was desired, sculpture and perhaps figure painting were used; but, where mere decoration was appropriate, the Greeks used motifs which, whatever their origin might have been, were essentially abstract. Many of these are founded on modifications of the Egyptian lotus, formed into those graceful spreading palmlike units called *anthemions* and connected together by various kinds of S-scroll. Rosettes, frets, rhythmical scale patterns (which became the egg-and-dart), branching scrolls, and bands of anthemions—these form the basis of much Greek ornament. Later, in the fifth century B.C., the acanthus leaf was adopted; but it is characteristic of the Greek desire for abstract ornament that, in Greek work, acanthus motifs were as rigidly conventionalized as was the lotus. The earlier Greek ornament was almost always painted, whether on terra-cotta or on marble. When, in the richer work of the fifth and fourth centuries B.C., the carving of ornament came into vogue, its old linear, painted character was preserved in the rather flat, line-sharp quality of the relief.

The culmination of all of this magnificent development took place in a tragically brief space of time. The Persian wars occupied the Greeks to the exclusion of almost everything else from 492 B.C., just when the Doric style was beginning to reach its full flowering, up to almost the middle of the century. In 480 the Persians captured and burned Athens, and destroyed the buildings of the Acropolis to their foundations. In 431 B.C. began the disastrous Peloponnesian War, the result of foolish and unnecessary rivalries between Athens and Sparta. The great era of Greek architecture lies only in the fifty years between, when, under the influence of Pericles and as an expression of gratitude at the liberation from the threat of Persia, temple after temple, each more gorgeous and more perfect than the one before, rose all over the Greek mainland, to reach a final climax in the Athenian Parthenon, designed by the architects Iktinos and Kallikrates and built between 447 and 438 B.C., and the Erechtheum, probably by Mnesikles, begun just before the beginning of the Peloponnesian War and never entirely completed. Yet, in this short half-century and less, all the developments toward grace and perfection which had gone before went on with almost redoubled speed. The earliest building which shows the marks of the finished style is the little Treasury of the Athenians at Delphi, begun as early as 500. Twenty years later, the Temple of Zeus at Olympia, by Libon, showed

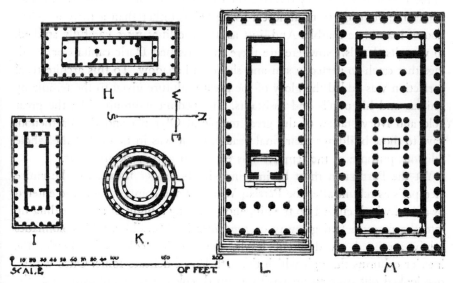

27. TYPICAL GREEK TEMPLE PLANS. (F. M. Simpson. Vol. I.) H. TEMPLE OF APOLLO AT BASSAE. I. SO-CALLED TEMPLE OF THESEUS, ATHENS. K. *THOLOS*, OR CIRCULAR TEMPLE, EPIDAURUS. L. PSEUDO-DIPTERAL TEMPLE AT SELINUS. M. PARTHENON, ATHENS.

a great advance over the colonial work in the greater refinement of its moldings, the greater perfection of its proportions, and the beauty and fitness of its architectural sculpture.

The Temple of Apollo at Phigalia first showed the genius of Iktinos; and the originality of its interior, with unusual Ionic columns and a central column which has one of the first Corinthian capitals, is expressive of the new time. In the Parthenon, Iktinos went one step further in the search for perfection, by curving the greater number of the structural lines in the building; and the peculiar fascination which even its ruins have exerted on centuries of observers is at least in part due to the feeling of life given by these subtle curves. Thus, the horizontal steps on which the columns rest and the entablature which they carry are both curved upward slightly in the center, as though the floor of the temple were part of an enormous sphere. Similarly, the columns are all inclined inward to give a feeling of serene strength, but the inclination is so slight that it has been calculated that the lines of their axes if continued would only meet at a point about two and a half miles above the center of the edifice. The same kind of curvilinear refinements are found in several of the great Greek buildings, but it is only in the Parthenon that they received their final and complete statement, which makes the building seem almost a living being rather than a mere aggregation of inanimate marble. And, just as its basic lines were carefully studied, so were its details. Nowhere are there more refined Doric capitals or moldings that catch so perfectly sun and shade and shadow. To this architectural perfection was added the glory of the great sculpture given to the temple by Phidias and his pupils and assistants. The pediment groups, like the great gold and ivory statues of the great temple at Olympia and the Parthenon, gave to those buildings their final beauty, for it was in them that the whole religious purpose of the temples was expressed and made manifest.

Yet the Parthenon must be imagined in its proper frame, for the entire Acropolis as rebuilt after the Persian War was one composition. One entered by a road which curved up the hill, and finally by a flight of stairs leading up into the monumental gateway or *propylaea* by Mnesikles, with colonnades subtly arranged on different levels, the exterior colonnades Doric, the interior columns through which the path led of delicate Ionic. Once within, one looked out over an area with a superb colossal statue of Athena as the nearest and most important element. Behind it on the right, seen in perspective so that all of its beauties might appear, continued the Parthenon; to the left, a little further away, the interesting mass of the L-shaped Erechtheum, with its two Ionic porticoes and its Porch of the Maidens. All of this view was most subtly contrived to bring out the buildings themselves, the great statue, the altar, and the votive offerings around; but without doubt it was also designed with a clear realization of the magnificent effect of the broad spreading view beyond—the land with its sharp mountains and hills at one side, and off to the other the clear horizon of the island-dotted Aegean.

The whole development of this crowning phase of Greek architecture can best be seen in the sacred precincts of Olympia, Delphi, and Eleusis; for, whatever the political separations and rivalries of the Greek cities, all the Hellenic world was represented in them—they formed, as it were, its cultural centers, its symbols of Hellenic as opposed to political unity. In them, too, we can see another quality of the Greek genius which is too little considered—their ability to place buildings together in ways not formal or rectangular, but with a free grouping suggested by the use and the site, in such a way as to magnify the beauty of all.

To gain some idea of what Greek architecture really meant to the Greeks themselves, we should go in imagination to one of these cult centers. Instead of the cold marble ruins we see today, cold even when they are as perfectly preserved as the temple in Athens known as the Theseum, we should find buildings brilliant with color applied knowingly to salient portions. We should find the temple itself surrounded with pedestals carrying votive offerings, bronze tripods, vases, statues. At one side might be treasuries, rows of little buildings, each the product of a separate city where the gifts made to the god by that city would be preserved. We should find the whole embowered in trees and shrubs, for the Greeks in their way were extremely sensitive to natural beauty. Everywhere would be variety, everywhere sculpture of an extraordinarily high level of execution; and yet the whole would be arranged, not in a confusion, but in an order all the more effective because of its subtle informality.

We should also have to visit the town agora, to find the same kind of subtle, informal richness. Around, the old wooden market halls would have been replaced with stone colonnades, *stoa,* some of which took the place of a modern museum, so beautifully decorated were they with mural paintings and sculpture. We should find them frequently, as at Assos, placed on the brink of a hill where the view is most picturesque. From them we could enter the official buildings—the council chambers and the prytania, with their simple, almost primitive dignity.

We should also have to go to the theater and see those splendid sweeping curves of marble seats filled with an intent crowd, listening to the choruses of Aeschylus or Sophocles, as the dancers performed around the altar in the center of the *orchestra,* and behind them, in front of the simplest of stage buildings, the actors, dignified and impersonal, spoke their immortal lines. For the Greek theater is another type of civic building a knowledge of which is necessary for any complete understanding of Greek life. Some form of religious pageantry seems to have been a part of Greek life from the earliest times, and even in pre-Hellenic Crete one side of the court of the great palace at Knossos was arranged with a tier of steps stretching almost its entire length, obviously intended to receive a crowd of spectators for some such game or pageant. In Hellenic times, the theater grew gradually from bases originally entirely religious, a combination of song and ritual dance around an altar to a presiding deity, usually Dionysus. Though the earliest performances may have been entirely lyric, little by little stories telling sacred myths and legends were added, often in narrative form, with choruses and dances coming in at proper intervals. As these performances became more formalized, the altar would be placed in the middle of a circular area, if possible surrounded by a rising bank of earth on which the spectators could sit. Later still, stone seats would line the embankment, following the curve of the circle, and the foundations of the later theater were laid. Meanwhile, the narrative form of storytelling gradually gave away to the

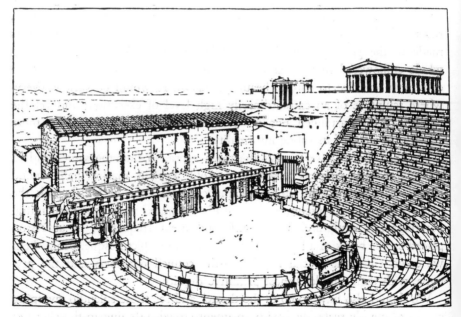

28. THEATER AT PRIENE, RESTORED. (Schede: *Die Ruinen von Priene.*)

dramatic, but throughout the history of Greek drama the influence of the older form was to be seen in the way in which many important elements of the action of any play would be narrated by observers, rather than acted out as in a modern play. By the fifth century, Greek tragedy had achieved its final classic form, and the works of Aeschylus and Sophocles show what enormous emotional power the somewhat stylized presentation of a great legend could possess.

By the same date, the architectural form of the theater had also become settled. It consisted, first, of a circular orchestra with an altar in the center, surrounded by curving rows of seats of slightly more than semicircular plan. The site chosen was always on the side of a hill, where, by excavation and filling, the conical shape required by the curving seats could be easily achieved. Behind the orchestra rose a low building, evidently of the greatest simplicity, which served as a background for the action and contained the actors' dressing rooms. Open passages led into the orchestra on either side in front of the stage building, thus making impressive processional entries possible. The lowest row of seats closest to orchestra and stage was usually reserved for priests and town dignitaries, who frequently were seated in exquisitely carved marble chairs instead of on the continuous stepped benches used elsewhere. The spectators' portion was divided by one or two passages leading around the curve, from which the sloping steps to the banks of seats were entered. Sometimes, if the hillside permitted, the curve was perfectly regular, but sometimes irregularities in a site were reflected in the irregular plan of the seating.

Theater sizes were great. Greek dramatic design did not require the unitary perspective which the modern play demands. The exact perspective relation of actor, background, and chorus was not important. Circular seating allowed enormous crowds to be comfortably arranged at the least possible distance from the actors, and therefore theaters seating several thousand people, and yet having every auditor within vocal range of the stage, were possible.

At the end of the fifth century B.C. the theater became more and more humanized, and satirical comedies came to rival the tragedies in popularity as they did in literary merit. With this added humanism the individual actors achieved a greater importance, and the whole problem of illusion began to enter in. As this happened, the raised stage made its appearance, in order to give the actors a more commanding position; and the background to the stage grew larger and larger, usually containing several wide openings in which painted scenery could be placed.

The great theaters of Epidaurus, of Aizani, of Delphi, and of Athens show the full development of this process, and in their concentric rings of rising seats and the perfect circle of the orchestra floor below there is a beauty and a dignity which is remarkable. Sometimes it would seem almost as though sites with striking, wide views had been chosen partly on account of those views, as if somehow the magnificent sweeps of landscape over and beyond the stage were deemed aids to the dignity and the poetry of the plays.

The Greek theater was never personal in the modern sense; tragic and comic masks veiled the personality of the actor. Prior to the Hellenistic period, everything was done to enhance the generic, almost the unreal, quality of the drama, as though inevitably the passions and desires of mankind and the inevitability of fate were more emphasized by this impersonal, one might almost say cosmic, treatment. It is only with a thorough realization of this deep effect that one can reach a proper understanding of the great simple lines, the tremendous size and large distances, of the Greek theater.

One quality, above all, seems to have characterized these Greek cities—the large area and great lavishness of their public and religious structures. Houses were simple, four or five rooms grouped around a court, arranged

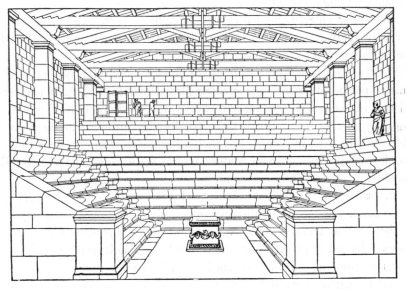

29. COUNCIL CHAMBER AT PRIENE, RESTORED. (Schede.)

to make the most of the sun and to shut off the cold winds. Simply painted plaster walls with only occasional decoration, infrequent mosaic floors, colonnaded porches on one or two sides of the court and very rarely all around—these were the only architectural adornments, though the furnishings and the utensils, if we are to judge by the enormous quantity of beautiful painted pottery remaining, were ample in amount and exquisite in the refinement of their design. The money in the town did not go to building palaces; it went to erecting buildings for public and communal usage—the agora or market place, often with halls or covered markets around; the schools or *gymnasia;* the *bouleterion* or council hall; and the *prytanium* or official town center, which still often preserved very primitive types of curved plan; and theaters and stadia. Building was the great thing into which the wealth of the time flowed, and even the tyrants like Croesus could think of little better to do with their wealth than to build temples, so that the amount of great building in the Grecian cities was tremendously high in proportion to the actual population; and, however ill-gotten the wealth that gave birth to these great building projects, its benefits flowed inevitably in the end to all of the citizens. Perhaps in this is an architectural reflection of the fact that, politically, the republic—either oligarchic or democratic—seemed almost the normal form of government for the ancient Greeks, and the tyrannies were mere interludes.

Priene, in Asia Minor, is the town which has been best preserved and most studied. Though a century later than the Periclean period, the qualities it shows must have been the qualities of all the cities of the Hellenic world. In it we find that choice of dramatic and lovely site that has already been noted. We find a great agora with colonnades around, decorated with a large amount of statuary, the whole carefully designed to separate the traffic portion from the rest. There is a council hall with stepped seats, a prytanium, a gymnasium, a terrace promenade by the city wall overlooking a wide valley view, a theater, and several temples, one of which was an Ionic building of great size and superb magnificence. All of this grandeur, this beauty of buildings and spaces arranged for popular use, was supported by a city which can never have had more than 500 comparatively small houses—that is, a city with a population of between 3000 and 5000.

That, perhaps, is the great lesson of Greek architecture; it retained its vitality, it progressed, because it was designed not for private but for public and religious use, and because every bit of it was under the constant scrutiny of a population brought up to be sensitive to it, to criticize it, and to be proud of it.

·TOWER·OF·THE·WINDS·
·ATHENS·

·THOLOS·AT·EPIDAURUS·

·CHORAGIC·MONUMENT·
·OF·LYSIKRATES·
·ATHENS ·330·B.C.·

30. THREE GREEK CORINTHIAN CAPITALS. (Drawn by the author.)

Chapter 7

HELLENISTIC ARCHITECTURE

WHATEVER may have been the political results of the career of Alexander the Great, its cultural impact was tremendous. Alexander's campaigns brought, it is true, Greek life and Greek influence into all the Near East, from Armenia to the Punjab, from Persia to Egypt; but, even more, it brought into Greek life a new knowledge of oriental culture and a new desire for oriental luxury. Moreover, it established the leadership of the Greek cities of Asia Minor. Freed at last from Persian rule, they were able to take advantage of their superb positions as the great connecting units between the East and the West. Wealth flowed to them; and, though the usual democratic governments which Alexander had set up in them soon yielded to individual despotisms, nevertheless these rulers were many of them men of vision and energy, and under their rule Pergamon, Miletus, and Ephesus rose to new heights of prosperity and power. It is the architecture of these cities, from the middle of the fourth century B.C. down to their final capitulation to the Roman power, which is generally called Hellenistic architecture.

From its very nature, Hellenistic culture was bound to represent a new fusion of elements from Europe and from Asia. The purely Greek tradition of the Doric and Ionic orders had tended perhaps, in the later fourth century B.C., to become crystallized and sterile, working for greater and greater refinement, which could only lead to eventual decay. The new forces, by suddenly injecting new ideals of civic design, broke up the old rigid forms and gave birth to a new kind of architecture, still basically Greek but none the less characterized by conceptions and details quite different from the older work. Naturally this process affected not only the work of those cities on the Asian shore, where first it came to bloom, but also the entire Hellenic world. Whatever the political rivalries between the Greek cities, whatever the form of Grecian governments, never had the unity of the Hellenic world been destroyed. In the days of the Peloponnesian War this ideal may have tottered, and that long, futile struggle between Athens and Sparta must have seemed to threaten all of Hellenic culture. The empire of Alexander at first served to bring new life into the old Panhellenic conceptions, and so to bring to all the Hellenic world the new, freer forms. Thus, Hellenistic architecture is to be found in the later buildings of Olympia; on the Greek islands, at Delos and Mitylene; at Pergamon, Priene, Miletus, and Ephesus, in Asia; at Alexandria, in Egypt; and even in the far-away Greek colonies of southern Italy and Sicily. So distributed over almost all the Mediterranean world, Hellenistic architecture had an even greater influence upon later peoples and cultures than did that of continental Greece itself. It was through Hellenistic architecture that the Romans learned something of the Greek ideals and the Greek forms.

All Greek culture was ready for the change. The old impersonal ideals of perfection, which had given rise alike to the Greek Doric order and the austerity of the tragedies of Aeschylus, made demands upon humanity that the Greek world was unable to fulfill. Its rigidity, its relentless impersonality, could only seem cold and lifeless when once the secret of its greatness had been missed. With the drama of Euripides, in which the tragedy seems no longer a thing almost cosmic, a sort of twilight of the gods, but becomes instead a tragedy of a single individual, an all-too-human soul, the old concepts were doomed. The Platonic dialogues pointed the way to the new kind of life and of thought, for in them philosophical truth is expressed and developed by means of the dramatic clash of differing, highly individualized personalities, as though for the first time truth was conceived as a distillation of individual thinking rather than as an impersonal absolute. Platonic thought was characteristic of the new age, too, because in it we find the beginnings of a mysticism which is essentially oriental in tone, and which in certain dialogues seems almost to approach the doctrines of India seen through Western eyes.

Precisely the same thing happened in Hellenistic architecture—the old rigid classifications, the old absolutes, yielded to experimentalism and personal invention. It is that which makes it so difficult to set fixed categories for Hellenistic architectural forms.

Yet the spirit is unmistakable. There is a new sense of grandeur in city planning, a new luxury in city decoration. There is tremendous variety in the details of the Doric and Ionic orders, and the early tentative experiments toward a new order with a bell-shaped capital surrounded by leaves, which had been made in the fifth century B.C., blossomed magnificently into the developed Corinthian capital, with its lavish panoply of acanthus leaves and the graceful scrolls which rise to support the corners of the abacus. There is an almost complete freedom in the use of all the orders; Doric entablatures are even found with Ionic columns, as in the great portico which surrounded the Temple of Athena at Pergamon. There is a new love for colossal scale, reaching its climax in such an enormous structure as the Didymaion—the Temple of Apollo Didymaios at Miletus—where the old modest cella of the Greek temple has become a huge open court, much too wide to be roofed over by any techniques which the Greeks knew, and with an elaborate shrine, almost a second temple, at the end. And everywhere there was a search for the dramatically exciting in detail and sculptural decoration, so that moldings were carved with rich leafage, panels with boldly projecting, freely composed ornament; and carved friezes, for temple and tomb alike, tended to give up the old rhythmical yet serene repose, such as we see in the Parthenon frieze, in favor of scenes of intense and almost frenzied struggle. It is characteristic that the great Altar of Zeus at Pergamon, built by Eumenes in 180 B.C., was surrounded by a colonnade on the high basement of which was carved, in full and powerful relief, the Battle of the Giants and the Gods. Its magnificent fragments are instinct with a kind of dynamic vitality that was not to be equaled again until the greatest work of the Italian Baroque.

Even the basic conception of the temple changed. Religion itself was affected by the mystery cults of Asia; and, instead of the popular outdoor processions and simple rituals of the earlier time, more and more extremely conventionalized hieratic types of ritual came into play, which demanded an initiated priesthood and larger and larger temple interiors. Only in the great traditional centers of Greek religious life, like Olympia, Delos, and Delphi, were the old forms preserved, and the new architecture was expressed in them only by the building of ever more formal and lavish minor buildings.

It became customary also, again following Asian precedent, to surround the temple with a wall pierced by a monumental gate, and in that way place it in a closed court surrounded by colonnades. In the great temple at Aizani, in Phrygia, there are even two entirely separate surrounding colonnades and walls, so that an outer court completely surrounds the inner court, and that in turn completely surrounds the temple proper. Such a conception as this necessarily gives rise to an entirely different type of architectural effect from that presented by the old informal and picturesque temple precincts of fifth-century-B.C. Greece. It has an axio-symmetrical monumentality of effect, which seems to have been the element that most deeply affected the Roman architecture to come.

Nowhere did this new ideal of monumental grandeur have more influence than in the civic buildings which had always constituted such an important part of the Greek town, and almost everywhere we find the old simple agora, colonnades, and shops replaced by an elaborate colonnade or *stoa,* sometimes in two stories and frequently of great width, with a central row of columns, not only to give a more formal and definite outline to the old free market

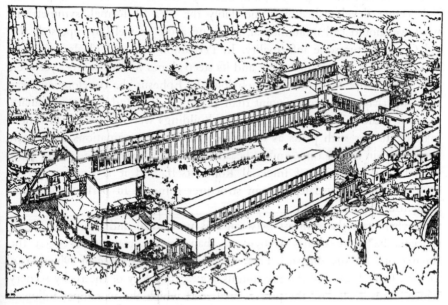

31. THE AGORA AT ASSOS, RESTORED BIRD'S-EYE VIEW. (Bacon: *Investigations at Assos.*)

place, but also to create along its edges a row of buildings of the greatest impressiveness. At Corinth the agora was almost entirely rebuilt, until it came to have the aspect more of a Roman forum than of the old town center; at Athens the great Stoa of Attalus formed a splendid front along one side; and at Assos the superb high plateau which served as agora was given a rich architectural investiture of terrace walls and a lovely two-storied market hall and promenade.

This development reached its zenith in a number of the cities of Asia, where a series of powerful military tyrants held sway and poured the wealth from the loot of their wars into city beautification. In these Hellenistic

Asian cities like Pergamon, Ephesus, Miletus, and Antioch, the old agora itself could not be made into a public space of sufficient magnificence to suit the taste of the time. Into the center of the city, besides the agora, were massed a tremendous and connecting series of temple courtyards, great altars, libraries, *palaestrae*—combined schools and gymnasiums,—theaters, and concert halls. Their number was manifestly too great to be grouped around any one square, and accordingly new public places or piazzas, connected with each other and with the agora by great gateways or monumental streets, became the rule; and little by little, as this kind of impressive civic center developed, almost inevitably the idea of formal, symmetrical, what we should call monumental, planning arose as well, to supersede the old Greek picturesque informality. In Pergamon the two ideals exist side by side, and its mountainous site and its steep slopes forced variety; yet even here the attempt to regularize is obvious. In Ephesus the development was carried perhaps to a greater point than anywhere else, and the extraordinary series of great squares and lavish public buildings were all formal in a new manner. It was such plans as this which fired the imaginations of Roman conquerors in a later time, and so became indirectly responsible for the great formal civic buildings of imperial Rome itself, and it is significant that even at Ephesus the later Roman structures came to fit perfectly into the Hellenistic frame.

Nowhere can the contrast between this new ideal and the older Greek concepts be more clearly recognized than in the contrast between the squares of Ephesus and such great sacred precincts as those of Olympia or Delphi. In Delphi itself the precipitous slopes, the glory of the rocky scenery which controls all, and the processional road which the worshiper followed carried him up from terrace to terrace, by paths dictated by the mountain shape itself. Below him and around stretched the sweeping view over the Gulf of Corinth. On either side, where a shoulder of rock permitted, terrace walls supported shrines and votive offerings, and along the ascending path as he approached the temple he passed the row of city treasuries, each different from the next but harmonized by the general simplicity of the Greek forms. By these he came at last to the main terrace where the temple stood, its serene Doric forms a dramatic contrast to the mountain slopes behind, that rose above the cave where the oracles were given. At one side, the theater filled a natural hollow, and, however great the play, it must have been difficult indeed to keep one's eyes from wandering to the beauty of the view beyond.

In Olympia, though the site was flat, it was nature again—and groves of pine and olive—which gave character and point to the whole. Although, as befits the location, the planning was generally more rectangular and the parts more closely integrated, nevertheless there was no applied or artificial formality. As at Delphi, there was a street or row of treasuries. Instead of the Delphic theater, there was a long low stadium where the Olympic Games were held. The two great Temples of Zeus and of Hera, with their altars, stood freely in a large open area, around which were grouped, with pleasant informality and yet in accordance with a perfectly natural arrangement, the *bouleterion* or council house, the official priest's residence, a palaestra, and all the minor buildings which such a great religious center demanded. Everywhere there was the contrast of green foliage and white or painted marble, of the varied and changing views of buildings and of landscape. The old Greek gods had been nature gods, and in almost all the primitive Greek sites like Delphi or Olympia it is nature itself which somehow seems to be and to remain the dominant thing, despite the wealth of beautiful buildings and the lavish display of sculpture and votive offerings.

In Ephesus, on the other hand, it is the human being which dominates, not nature. The gods are no longer the old Greek gods; though their names are the same, their worship has been modified alike by literary humanism and Asiatic mysticism. They are urban gods, and the beauty of Ephesus is the carefully calculated, conscious beauty of a highly complex and highly sophisticated urban civilization exulting in its command over natural difficulties and its ability to create with purely man-made objects a new kind of ordered glory.

But such a complex life as this requires more buildings than temples and public squares; it is only natural that in the Alexandrine period there was a tremendous development of both domestic architecture and the architecture of such utilitarian elements as dockyards, harbor works, and warehouses. It is in Olynthus and Priene that we find the best examples of the earlier house, and in Delos of the later.

Recent excavations at Olynthus, in northern Greece, have laid bare the foundations of a town which was burned by Philip of Macedon, 348 B.C. It shows us Greek houses of the later Hellenic period. They are, as one would expect, simple, without ostentation, built generally around a court, with a colonnade usually on one side of the court only. This colonnade gives onto a long, wide corridor, extending almost entirely across the house and undoubtedly used as a sort of outdoor living room; from it the chief rooms, usually three—a main bedroom, a living room, and a kitchen,—could be entered. The minor rooms were on the other sides of the court. These houses were built of mud brick on stone foundations, and, though bases and capitals of the court colonnade have been found, the total absence of shafts leads to the conclusion that all of the posts were of wood. Frequently, stairs show the presence of a second story. Terra-cotta bathtubs are often found, in a room opening from the kitchen, but sanitary arrangements seem to have been of the crudest and most primitive types. Walls were painted in plain colors, with occasionally a ruling off as though to imitate the joints of masonry,

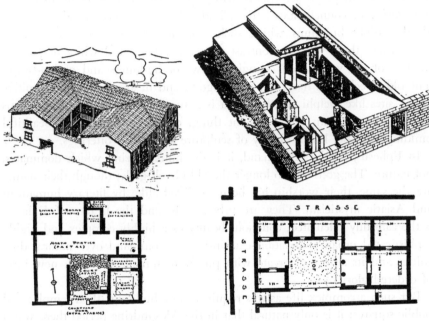

32. TYPICAL GREEK HOUSES, FROM OLYNTHUS (*left*) AND PRIENE (*right*); PLANS AND RESTORED VIEWS. (Olynthus—Robinson and Graham: *Excavations at Olynthus.* Priene—Schede.)

and there was some use of different-colored bands. Richness, however, is sometimes given to these houses by pebble mosaic floors in the principal rooms. The whole picture is one of a rather primitive kind of ample comfort but of little luxury.

In Priene, the houses show a slightly different tradition, owing to the fact that the main room is often entered from the court through its own special vestibule, as in the old Mycenaean megaron. The houses are built of stone and around a court, but the general impression is that of a kind of simplicity quite similar to that of Olynthus, and the Priene houses are as a rule even smaller than those of the Greek mainland town.

The houses of Delos, which date generally from a period two centuries later—the second half of the second century B.C.,—though still essentially Greek in architectural detail, reveal the changes that Hellenistic life had brought. The court colonnades in Delos usually extend all around the court, with an open garden space in the center like the peristyles of the Pompeian houses, and the columns are now almost always of marble. Mosaic floors of exquisite delicacy show the new ideal of personal luxury that had become common. Rooms are larger, wall decoration is more elaborate, and the whole impression is of a new search for rich, almost monumental house forms to enframe the new kind of sumptuous and nearly oriental mode of living.

Remains of the great harbor works which the Hellenistic peoples erected dot almost all the harbors of the Aegean Sea. The new city of Rhodes, founded at the very end of the fifth century B.C., was laid out according to a regular and careful plan prepared by the architect Hippodamos. Its great moles still remain, in part, and at the harbor side was raised the great colossal statue of Apollo—the Colossus of Rhodes, 105 feet high. Erected by Chares, of Lindos, in the middle of the third century B.C., it was characteristic of the Hellenistic ideals of lavish city beautification. After it had stood for fifty-six years, an earthquake brought an end to it in 224 B.C., but its tremendous fragments remained by the harbor for seven centuries, and it is said that 900 camels were required to carry them away when they became Saracen loot.

The Pharos, or lighthouse, at Alexandria, a tower 100 feet square and 400 feet high, is equally typical of the Hellenistic love of size, but it also expresses a keen realization of the necessities which arose from a developed commerce, and is but one of many such lighthouse towers built during the period at important harbors or upon important capes.

Even in Attica the new sea commerce had its effects, and the old harbor works of the Athenian seaport Piraeus, which had been designed originally by Hippodamos, the town planner of Rhodes, no longer sufficed. A long-existing inscription not only records the building of new warehouses and arsenal buildings in the third century B.C., but also contains a complete specification for their construction. This tells us of the strength and permanence of the work, and reveals too that even these purely utilitarian structures were still detailed with all the care and composed with all the beauty that were characteristic Greek traits.

Hellenistic architecture was doubly important. Its freedom, the lyrical grace of its decoration, the dramatic and individualistic power of its sculpture, broke down the old hard and fixed categories; yet, basically, it was an architecture still Greek in ideals, still working with the Greek orders, though modifying them where it wished, still devoted to the Greek search for beauty and perfection even in the most utilitarian things. But Hellenistic architecture was not only Greek; it was also, and perhaps pre-eminently, cosmopolitan. It brought Greece to the Orient and to Egypt, but it also brought to the Greek Mediterranean world new oriental ideals of magnificence and civic grandeur. But the Hellenistic architects had another gift of vast importance to the world ahead. This was the ability to make magnificent formal plans, in which each element—each temple, colonnade, open space, and avenue—played its foreordained part in one integrated and symphonic whole. The earlier Greeks had created superb building groups, yet one feels them to be at least partly the result of historical or topographic accident; not until Hellenistic or even Roman times did the public squares of Athens and Corinth achieve their final consummation. It was the Hellenistic architects who, in Ephesus, in Pergamon, in Alexandria, as in houses and temples everywhere, discovered or developed the ability to integrate the many parts of a complicated program into one ordered whole. All these elements Hellenistic architects spread over all of the eastern Mediterranean; and, when the Roman power grew gradually to include this entire area, it was this new blend of Greek and oriental art that we call Hellenistic which so impressed the Romans, and thus came to be one of the chief influences behind the development of Roman architecture.

Chapter 8

ROMAN ARCHITECTURE

WHEN Virgil, in *The Aeneid,* gave such superb form to the tale of how Aeneas, escaping from the capture of Troy, came at last to Italy and became, at least symbolically, the first Roman, he was merely giving expression to an old tradition that somehow the culture of Italy came from sources further east. The early history of Italy, like that of Greece, gives us a confused picture of invaders from the north coming down into the fertile south, to conquer, to dominate, and, at last, to assimilate and amalgamate with other indigenous peoples who were perhaps racially related to the Sardinians, the early inhabitants of the Iberian peninsula, Crete, the Greek islands, and the north shore of Africa. The Etruscans, who were the first of the local powers in Italy to develop a highly civilized culture of their own, may perhaps have come from a source shared in common by some of the Asia Minor peoples—a source, as some would have it, in central or western Europe, or, according to others, in central Asia.

As in Greece, too, these invaders from the north came not in one but in many waves or groups; and little by little, linguistically at least, it was strains not too unlike those which made up the Dorian migration that came to dominate the peninsula.

If the actual racial origin of the Etruscans is still a matter of doubt, since their language has not as yet been deciphered, the source of their culture is clear; it was a creation by a brilliant people, on the basis of techniques and artistic forms taken, in many cases almost bodily, from early Greece, from Phoenicia, perhaps from Anatolia, and from Egypt. Quick-minded, facile in learning, remarkably adept with their hands, out of this confused amalgam they created an art and an architecture brilliantly alive and definitely their own, notwithstanding its foreign sources. The extraordinary breadth of commerce through the Mediterranean world, in even pre-historic days, is being more and more revealed to us, as the artifacts of those early days are studied. Cretan copper and bronze objects are found occasionally even in Brittany; the amber from the Baltic was used by peoples as far distant from its source as the Sumerians and the Egyptians; but nowhere did a people make such creative use of the opportunities which this commerce offered as did the Etruscans in the four centuries from 700 to 300 B.C.

To the painting and sculptural skill of the Greeks, and to the palmettes and decorative forms which they borrowed from the peoples of the Near East, the Etruscans added their own great skill as metalworkers, as builders, and as engineers; so that the Etruscan tombs are far different things from those of the peoples to the east, and Etruscan buildings differ from those of Greece. Everything which they touched they modified, in tune with their own energetic, passionate, and sometimes apparently humorous character; and the skill with which they developed simple arched structures—city gates and bridges—was a prophecy of the still greater engineering ability which the Romans were to possess.

Etruscan buildings fall into four chief classes: city walls, fortifications, and bridges; dwellings; tombs; and temples. The masonry is excellent, often of large-sized stones, beautifully cut. In many city walls the influence of the Greek work in southern Italy is obvious, but the arch is normally used to cover over large openings. Etruscan dwelling types are known to us from tombs and cinerary urns. Essentially they were the rectangular hut of the north; round huts like those of Greece or the Mediterranean countries were more rare. The center of the hut was the kitchen and living room, with its hearth fire and a hole in the roof through which the smoke escaped. Later, when growing luxury forced a functional differentiation and the kitchen became a separate room, the central hall was still called the *atrium,* from the Latin word for "black," because of the smoke from the kitchen fire that had once discolored it. The hole in the roof, no longer a chimney, became a means of collecting water, and beneath it, instead of the early hearth, was a pool that drained into the house cistern; naturally the roof that had formerly sloped away from the central hole was now changed to slope toward it. Thus, the original hall-type house became essentially a court-type house, but it seems probable that through all the ancient period the two types of house—the single block and the court type—were current together, in Italy.

It is from the tombs that we come to know the Etruscans best. Sometimes cut out of the solid rock, sometimes built of large stones, they seem usually to reflect the house types of the people who built them; and the paintings on their walls and the furniture with which they were garnished alike afford us a picture, not only of the great artistic skill of the makers and of the eclectic quality of the ornament, but also of the whole spirit of Etruscan life. Characteristically, their mythology bore a definite relationship to that of Greece; but the detailed differences were tremendous, and all through it one gets a haunting sense of the mysticism surrounding the idea of death and the dead, and an occasional feeling of the grotesque, which is quite foreign to Greek thought; again and again one is reminded of that feeling for nature, that intense and troubled reaction to the cruelty of nature as well as its beauty, which found such poignant expression in the Roman-esque carvings of western Europe 1500 years later. It is this spirit which creates the unique quality in the tomb paintings of feast and festival, the technique and drawing of which are so reminiscent of early Greek vase painting. It is the same spirit which shows in the beaten bronze reliefs of sphinx and warrior and god which decorated their gorgeous chariots, and which shines through the life-size terra-cotta figures that have come down to us, with their staring eyes and all the body tensed in muscular strain. It is this same feeling for dramatic power, this same sensitiveness to nature, which in a later and more poised manner lies behind much Roman decora-tive carving, just as surely as it shows in the Virgil *Eclogues* or the country poems of the *Priapeia.*

The Etruscan temples, like those of early Greece, were largely built of wood, but they preserved even more closely than did the Greek the signs of their origin in the old porched hall or megaron. They were always built on a high platform, with broad steps leading up; and the colonnade, instead of surrounding them on all sides, remained usually an entrance porch at the front only, or occasionally at the front and sides. The building proper, the *cella,* always tended to be nearly square in plan, as the house atrium was square; in some cases it was divided by two interior walls into three different chapels or shrines. The front porch generally was four columns across in width, but often projected to a depth as great as the total depth of the cella, so that two or three columns along each side were necessary. The beams and roofs of true Etruscan work were always of wood—although the later Etruscans, like the Greeks, came to substitute stone for the columns. This preservation of the wooden beam led to much wider spacing of the columns than the Greeks were used to, and so gave to the Etruscan temple an aspect totally different, no matter how much of Greek influence might be found in the details. The roof eaves projected widely, and the whole complex of crossbeam and roof beam was in the developed temples sheathed in terra-cotta.

33. RESTORATION OF THE CORNER OF AN ETRUSCAN TEMPLE, SHOWING
WOODEN CONSTRUCTION AND TERRA-COTTA SHEATHING. (Durm: *Die
Baukunst der Etrusker und Römer. Handbuch der Architektur.*)

It is from these terra-cotta housings that we can in some measure regain
the form of the Etruscan temples, for naturally the wood has entirely disappeared. It is possible that this system of terra-cotta sheathing of wooden
members was taken over from the primitive Greek temples. Certainly many
of the forms with which the terra-cotta was decorated—leaf moldings, eggs
and darts, acanthus scrolls, and so on—were borrowed directly from Greek
precedent; and the Etruscan capital which crowned the columns had obvious
relationships to the Greek Doric capital, or perhaps rather to some common
origin in the Mediterranean world which gave rise to both. Nevertheless,
the Etruscans seldom copied directly the forms of the Greek Doric, and the
general preservation of the widespreading eaves and the broad spacing of
the columns was continued throughout the course of Etruscan history.

Confronted with the arch, the Etruscan architects faced a problem which the Greeks disregarded. Manifestly the arch fitted but poorly into the general scheme of the classic orders, and even the Etruscans seem never to have quite reached a perfect solution; yet what they did was of great importance. To conceal the difficult joint between the outer edges of the wedge-shaped stones of the arch and the general horizontal stonework of the rest of the wall, in later work they often used a projecting molding running concentrically around the arch. Since this stuck out from the face of the wall, it had to be supported at the level where the arch began—that is, at the *spring.* Therefore, projecting moldings, running horizontally, often marked out the spring line. These moldings are called *imposts,* and together with the molding around the arch, called an *archivolt,* began to give architectural and visual expression to the structural fact. Sometimes boldly projecting sculpture was also used in connection with arches, as in the famous Etruscan gate at Perugia.

It is not for their architectural detail that the Etruscans were important. In almost every case this is eclectic, if not strictly derivative. Tomb piers have capitals with the palmette and modified lotus of early Syria; molding profiles often resemble the ordinary Greek moldings except that they are usually heavier, with stronger and more powerful contours; and everywhere one finds the scrolls and the palmettes of Greek vase painting. What makes Etruscan architecture distinctive is its creative approach to structural problems, its development of the arch and that continuous arch we call a vault, and its basic spirit by which something new and human could be created out of so many and such various elements.

The Etruscans were essentially a town-dwelling people; and again and again the hill towns of present-day Italy, with their crowded buildings and their masonry walls rising sheer from the cliffs, continue the sites of old Etruscan towns as they must in some measure still preserve something of their aspect.

The process by which Rome, a little pastoral town on the Tiber, gradually asserted its sway and achieved a domination over all the Italian peninsula is one of the almost unexplainable mysteries of history. Generally speaking, it seems to have been the victory of organization over disorganization; of a new thriving and vital people over powers already in the first stage of decadence. Perhaps it was merely the fact that the growing population of Italy, the closer and closer contact between Italy and the rest of the Mediterranean world, the continually increasing commerce, made centralized organization necessary, and that Rome alone was prepared to give that:

but, if the characteristics of the conquest of Italy itself were remarkable, the results of the conquest were still more significant, and even before Rome became a world power the qualities which were to make that world power supreme for four centuries were already foreshadowed by the happenings in Italy. The Roman conquest had its military side, of course; yet this was in every case subsidiary, and the concept of the totality of the Roman Imperium grew as fast as its geographical borders spread. From the beginning the Romans adopted the theory, in fact if not in words, that the Roman Empire was the sum of many and various parts, and that part of its strength lay in the preservation and assimilation of those parts. Accordingly, the Etruscan became a Roman, but at the same time Rome itself became partly Etruscan, and in a later period the benefits of Roman citizenship might be held by peoples of Egypt, of Anatolia, of Gaul; and "Roman" became the name of the whole, not because a few inhabitants of the city of Rome and their descendants were military despots over many helpless peoples, but because the native of North Africa or Spain felt himself just as Roman as legendary Romulus himself.

This ability to assimilate differing peoples and cultures had extraordinary architectural results. Instead of attempting to force their own crude country building upon their neighbors, the Romans became eager students of what their neighbors had produced, and they seem to have had from an early period not only the old Etruscan engineering ability, but also much of the Etruscan skill in adopting, adapting, and fitting for their own uses all sorts of motifs taken from all sorts of sources. Great organizers and constructors, they were also great absorbers and digesters of other cultures.

Naturally the hegemony of Italy brought Rome, at an early date, into the closest touch with the Greek colonies of southern Italy and Sicily, and later with Greece itself. It was perhaps this geographical accident, that Rome was nearer south Italy and Sicily than Etruria had been, which gave added importance in Roman work to Greek architectural details, and led to the foolish but oft-repeated accusation that the Romans were mere architectural thieves, dressing themselves in other people's stolen raiment which they wore but ill. As we shall see, this is a manifest misunderstanding of the Roman ideals and the Roman achievement, exactly as silly as it would be to call the English language a compound of bad French and bad German.

What little we know of the earliest Roman architecture seems to prove that in many ways it was closely allied in form and construction to the more highly developed Etruscan work to the north, as though there were some cultural similarities despite the chasm of linguistic difference. It was only well on in republican history, when the Roman conquest had been sufficiently wide and sufficiently secure to allow an assimilation from many sources, that the real qualities of Roman work appeared; yet it is noteworthy that in later republican buildings certain characteristics are already well developed—the ability to build skillfully with either cut stone or brick, skill in using the arch and simple vault forms, but, even more, a desire for magnificent spatial effects and a general sense of dignified power in design. These are well shown in such a great plan as that of the Temple of Fortune at Praeneste (Palestrina), where the temple itself, on the summit of a hill, is approached by a superb series of terraces, stairs, and vaulted halls; and in the dignified simplicity of the arcaded front of the *Tabularium* —the Hall of Records—which rose on the side of the Capitoline Hill at one end of the Roman Forum. Evident also, in such buildings as the two earlier baths in Pompeii—the Baths of the Forum and the Stabian Baths,—is a love for large vaulted interiors in public buildings and a remarkable skill in their practical and yet charming arrangement. It is significant that the secret of the effect of much of this work lies in the broad, simple surfaces of plain wall, varied by arched openings and niches, with the simplest possible moldings, and with much of the plane surface richly decorated with painting and stucco work. The whole history of Roman architecture is that of the gradual growth of these basic ideas.

The full development of Roman architecture came only after the foundation of the Empire. As such it was primarily not the architecture of a single city, nor even of the peninsula of Italy, but the architecture of a world civilization growing up under the fostering and beneficent influence of the Pax Romana. It was the architecture of an empire the foundations of which were laid upon tolerance, assimilation, and organization, and supported by a widespread commerce which brought prosperity alike to the provinces and to Rome itself. It was an architecture of utility, but of utility seen always as the opportunity for aesthetic effect. It was an architecture always greater in its plans and its general conceptions than in its details. Naturally it was an architecture susceptible of almost infinite variation according to the needs of climate, of local materials, and of local culture. In it may be found Greek elements, Etruscan elements, Syrian elements; but all are fused and used in a new way, which we can only call Roman. Since it is an architecture of utility and organization, the building materials at hand played an important part in it, and the methods in which they were used gave rise to some of its essential qualities.

The chief Roman building materials were brick, concrete, stone, and wood. From the time of the late Republic on, brick and concrete were favored, since by the use of these materials it was possible to build more quickly, more easily, and more cheaply. Yet where there was no scarcity of stone, as in North Africa, Syria, and parts of France, the Roman architects used this with equal facility, changing and modifying both their detail and their plans to suit the new material. Wood was much used for bridges, for roofs, for floors in some of the minor buildings, and obviously for much country work; but for the most part the Romans preferred other materials as more permanent and more fireproof. The Roman bricks were usually one or two feet square, and from an inch to an inch and a half thick, and were used not only to build entire walls but also, cut diagonally in two and with the diagonal side laid as the front of the wall so that the corners projected back into the wall, as facing for walls of rubble or concrete. Bricks were also used for building arches and vaults. The Roman discovery of the fact that walls of great strength could be cheaply built of a mixture of sand, small stones, and a hydraulic cement largely of volcanic materials—in other words, of a material essentially like modern concrete—made possible extraordinary constructions which could have been achieved in no other way. This was cast in wooden forms, as modern concrete work is built, and was also used in all sorts of most interesting ways in combination with facings of brick or small stones. Nowhere does the Roman genius in the use of building materials show more clearly than in this handling of stone, brick, and concrete in the same building, with each material used where it best performed its work.

The development of vault and arch construction in cut stone, brick, and concrete was perhaps the Roman architect's greatest contribution to the evolution of the building art. Etruscan vaults seem to have been limited to bridges, drains, and gates, and in the earlier period Rome went little further. In the last years of the Republic, however, the architects began to experiment not only with the barrel or tunnel vault, which they started to use over rooms of large size, but also with the dome and simple intersecting or groined vault. If two vaults of the same size and rising from the same height are built at right angles to each other over a single square area, they will naturally intersect in elliptical curves placed diagonally across the squares; these curves are called the groins and separate the vault surfaces running in the two directions. Since the vaults end at the sides of the square in semicircles, it is possible to make a large arched opening on all the sides of the square, and the whole roof is then supported only on four piers at the corners. The freedom which this gave to the arrangement of spaces in the building was enormous, but the difficulties were great also. As we have seen, vaults always exert a sidewise thrust (see pp. 14, 15), and piers which may be sufficiently large to carry the weight of the vault are not necessarily strong under sidewise pressure—they may need additional buttressing to prevent the thrust of the vault from overturning them. The genius of the Roman architects can nowhere be better seen than in the way they took this difficulty and made it an opportunity, by so arranging necessary buttresses that they became essential elements in the entire arrangement of the building, adding both to its utility and to its beauty.

Another form of vault, which came early into use and is found in the Tabularium built by Sulla in 80 B.C., is the cloister vault, which in a sense is the reverse of the groined vault. It, too, is based on the intersection of two vaults at right angles; but, instead of their being so arranged as to give an arch on each face, they rise to a high center from a level spring on all four faces to form a sort of square dome. Little by little, however, the use of the cloistered vault yielded to the groined vault, because of the Roman wish for large openings.

The dome is merely a hemispherical vault, built in rings of stone or brick, with the joints between the rings radiating from the center, and the joints of each ring also necessarily radiating as well. Thus, the completion of each ring makes a self-supporting unit, because, owing to the wedge shape of the elements of which it is combined, no one of them can collapse inward; it is this quality which enabled the Romans to build domes like that of the Pantheon, with its great "eye" or circular opening in the center. Like all vaults, the dome also exerts great outward pressure at its base. This pressure the Romans usually buttressed merely by making the supporting walls tremendously thick. However, realizing that this thickness was not needed for support, but only for its crosswise strength, they frequently cut out from these thick walls recesses and niches to lighten its weight without reducing its strength, thereby producing all sorts of interesting interior effects such as we see today in the Pantheon.

But, if the Romans were skillful in adapting the vault form to many various uses, they were equally skillful in the actual techniques of its construction. Since any arch or vault needs to be supported from below until its final completion, when it becomes self-supporting, the construction of great vaults usually necessitates a tremendous and costly building of these temporary supports, which are called *centerings*. By subdividing the vault into sections which could be built separately, the amount of centering needed was vastly decreased; and therefore the ribbing of the vault not only defined its forms and acted as a kind of network to give it strength, but also made its construction much easier and less expensive. If the vault were of concrete, layers of light tiles might be laid flatwise directly on the centering, which was designed to carry their weight only. When this tile lining was complete, it formed, itself, an arch of sufficient strength to carry the concrete which was then laid over it to form the final vault thickness. These are but a few of the many ingenious devices created by the Romans in the effort to systematize and regularize constructive methods, and thereby make possible the vast constructions which the Romans erected all over the then-known Western world.

Yet mere constructive ability was not enough. It might help to build those great aqueducts which furnished all the Roman cities with ample water, to bridge rivers, and to cover warehouses, but if it did no more than that the Roman was still unsatisfied. Out of this engineering necessity, he must, by careful design and beautiful proportion, produce beauty as well as use, and the secret of Roman organization is as much aesthetic as it is practical.

It is this combination of use, structure, and beauty which makes utilitarian engineering become architecture; and in Roman life the architect played an important and dignified role. We are fortunate in possessing the ten books on architecture written by Marcus Vitruvius Pollio sometime during the reign of Augustus; and, though they have little in them about the great Roman vaulted structures which were the glory of the later Empire, they are nevertheless a mine of information about the Roman attitude toward architecture and the professional position which the architect held. His chapters concerning the education of the architect and the architect's professional duties and responsibilities are almost as applicable today as they were nearly 2000 years ago, and it is interesting to see that to Vitruvius architecture has always the triple essence mentioned above—constructive strength, practical utility, and aesthetic effect, or, as Sir Henry Wotton quaintly worded it, "commodity, firmness, and delight."

As an architecture of a great, highly organized, and complicated world civilization, Roman architecture necessarily developed a differentiation of building types greater than any which had preceded it. The simplest class consists of the dwellings; yet it is significant that even here the growing differentiation of different types of person and different types of private life led to many different types of dwelling. The city or town house, where space allowed, generally consisted of a combination of the old traditional Italian atrium, with certain ideas taken from the late Greek houses of the Hellenistic world, such as the colonnaded court. Besides the city and town house, country houses for the summer living of the wealthy and farmhouses constituted well-differentiated types. In the great cities, where a congestion almost modern began to exert a continually growing influence on building types, the individual house had given way even in early imperial times to the communal dwelling or apartment house, except for the residences of the very rich.

Commerce and industry also produced several building types—shops, markets, shopping centers or bazaars, exchanges, warehouses, and harbor works. The old Greek agora and the traditional Roman forum, the primitive market places where all commerce went on, were manifestly insufficient not only for the developed retail trade a great city demands, but also for the exigencies of large-scale wholesale commerce. Thus, two or perhaps three quite different markets opened off the forum at Pompeii, and in Rome whole areas were given over to different kinds of trade. Individual shops grew common, often with residences above, but sometimes combined in large buildings which form a true shopping center. Warehouses were obviously necessary for the storage of goods, and were sometimes given great architectural dignity; and harbor works included not only the building of rough breakwaters and piers, but also the elaborate architectural treatment of the embankment of the river at Rome and such monumental combinations of dock and mole, warehouse and lighthouse, as distinguished the great harbor of Rome at Ostia.

Education, too, demanded its own architectural forms; and, though schools as we know them seem not to have existed—elementary education being largely a private matter, with teachers holding their classes in their own homes or in the public colonnades of the forum,—nevertheless the omnipresent existence of large libraries open to the public, the furnishing of many lecture halls around the great baths, shows the fact that the literacy of the Roman civilization was widespread and the necessity for adult as well as child education fully realized.

The buildings for public recreation form some of the most characteristic of Roman monuments. Theaters and amphitheaters were scattered far and wide over the Roman world, and their remains today give evidence of the care applied to their design and the wealth expended in their execution. Typical also are the great Roman public baths, the halls of which offered such congenial opportunities to the Roman architect. The luxury and complexity of these great buildings, with their surrounding gardens for exercise and rest, are extraordinary; and when we discover them in Trier, far to the north, in Timgad and Leptis Magna to the south, in Paris to the west, and in the towns of distant Syria to the east, we may begin to have some idea of the breadth and the scope of the Roman architectural concepts, as well as of the benefits which the Pax Romana brought even to the lowliest citizens.

It is in the religious buildings, and especially in the great temples, that Rome went furthest in borrowing and using forms originally Greek, and it is the Roman temple more than anything else which has caused the common accusation against the Romans as bad copyists. However, the aims of Greek and Roman religious architecture were essentially different, and to the Roman the court or the forum around the temple, with its colonnades and its monumental entrance, was as important as the temple building itself. Moreover, the Roman never completely abandoned the old Etruscan or Italic temple conceptions; if he failed to produce the refinement of the Parthenon, if he substituted for the restraint of the Greek form the luxury of the Corinthian order, if he raised the scale of his great buildings far above that which the Greeks would have considered proper, he nevertheless achieved a type of monumental grandeur which was unique. To the Roman the temples were much more than religious buildings to contain a cult statue; they were, even more, civic monuments, often consciously used as art museums, and containing in their precincts public libraries.

It was, in fact, in the great civic structures of Roman cities that the Roman ideal can perhaps best be read. The old Italic forum became merely the center of a great nexus of public structures, just as in the Hellenistic world the Greek agora blossomed into the grandeur of the public buildings at Ephesus. Porticoes for public promenade, often surrounding gardens used as public parks, were frequent, and many of the earlier wealthy families of Rome, like the Rockefellers today, left private gardens to the city to become public recreation grounds. Everywhere in the Roman city was the plash of water, for if there was one thing which the Romans seem to have demanded above all it was an adequate water supply, and the great aqueducts of Seville or of Constantinople reveal the fact that this passion was not limited to the city of Rome itself.

In fact, to the Roman of the imperial period, the city was apparently conceived as a work of art, to be consciously designed and deliberately changed where necessary, for the purpose of constructing an impressive, a convenient, and a beautiful surrounding for the lives of its citizens.

Characteristic of this desire for the convenient and beautiful organization of the city are the Roman garrisons and camps. Here if anywhere one might have expected mere utilitarianism; yet how much more was achieved in them the ruins themselves tell us. Founded originally on an old Italic conception of town design, these camps had usually two chief intersecting streets, with the rest of the areas divided into careful rectangular blocks. The old primitive idea seen in the type of neolithic settlement called the *terra mare* is preserved in these Roman camps almost intact, and shows how deeply seated in tradition and history the Roman search for regularized monumentality must have been. At Neuss, near Düsseldorf, the foundations of the great Roman garrison of Novaesium reveal streets arcaded or colonnaded for their entire length, barrack buildings laid out with an almost scientific convenience for pleasant ventilation, large storehouses, a great bath building, an officers' school, and a monumental *praetorium* around a colonnaded court, which served not only as residence for the commander but as a sort of provincial capitol. Though only foundations were preserved, the excavations revealed sufficient of the rich architectural details to show that this military garrison on the German frontier was a place where soldiers could live in health and a place which must have had a definite, if highly ordered and monotonous, beauty.

Nothing is more expressive of the Roman ideals than Roman domestic architecture. According to Vitruvius, each room should be planned for its specific use, with just exactly the correct orientation to gain sun and warmth, or coolness, as the case might be, to give the proper views, and to have the simplest connections to other rooms with which it was related. In large houses this differentiation went so far as to provide for different living and dining rooms for summer and winter. The construction is described with a similar care; the various types of masonry wall and the devices used for protection against damp or cold are carefully set forth.

In arrangement, the house which Vitruvius describes is the private house of the earlier Roman period, such as we know it from the excavated portions of Pompeii—a house that results from the addition of the Greek colonnaded court or peristyle to the earlier Italian central hall or atrium house, though the atrium has now become less a hall than another court. In general, the more public rooms surround the atrium, and the peristyle—frequently richly gardened—has become the center of family life. Bedrooms are usually small

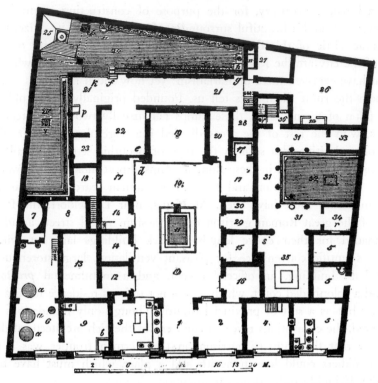

34. SO-CALLED HOUSE OF SALLUST, POMPEII; PLAN. (Mau: *Pompeii, Its Life and Art.*)

1. VESTIBULE
2. SHOP
3. DRINKING SHOP
    (2 and 3 opened into the main house when it was changed from a private house to an inn)
6. BAKERY
7. OVEN

10. ATRIUM
14. BEDROOMS
17. ALAE
19. TABLINUM (reception room)
21. COLONNADED PORCH
22. DINING ROOM
24. GARDEN

25. OUTDOOR DINING ROOM
26. SERVICE COURT
27, 36. KITCHENS
31. COLONNADE
32. GARDEN
33, 34. BEDROOMS
35. DINING ROOM AND LIVING ROOM

and often lighted only by their doorways, the only large rooms being the *tablinum* or official reception room, which was placed in the middle of the back of the atrium and usually had a large window opening on the peristyle, and the dining hall or *triclinium*. Often, even in modest houses, outdoor dining in summer was provided for by building a small triclinium under an arbor in the court or garden. In these outdoor triclinia the couches are masonry benches around three sides of an open space in which the table rises. Careful excavation in Pompeii has allowed us to regain not only the plans of garden beds and the garden paths of these modest house courts, but also through a study of the carbonized roots a knowledge of the actual plants which grew there, so that court after court today has been replanted with the old shrubs; and a visitor to such a house as that of the Vetii in Pompeii sees now, in its combination of flowering shrub, green foliage, and white marble or bronze statuettes and fountain figures, much of the urbane and gracious loveliness with which the cultivated Romans of the early Empire liked to surround themselves.

Such a house as this requires a large land area, and as the urban population grew such areas were no longer available except for the houses of the very wealthy. The result was a gradual change in living ways, which resembles surprisingly the development in many modern cities. It can be seen already under way in Pompeii, where house after house shows evidences that some time before the final catastrophe it had been divided up into separate apartments. Gone was the old amplitude of large courts and great rooms; instead, the growing congestion forced the subdivision of large rooms and even the enclosure of some courts.

The larger houses of the earlier type had almost always included a suite of bathrooms for the warm, cold, and steam baths the Romans so loved. As city congestion grew, public baths of greater and greater size and luxury began to be built in ever-increasing numbers, so that the later houses are frequently without any bathing facilities, the dependence being upon the large and magnificent public conveniences. Yet sanitation was seldom forgotten. Water was piped to individual houses in almost all the larger Roman communities, and sewer systems were adequate and highly developed, so that every house was furnished with its own private toilets, its own water supply and drainage connected to the city system.

Along with this change from the larger, many-courtyarded houses to more modest abodes of smaller area went a general change in the architectural type, which can be well seen in a comparison of the smaller houses of Herculaneum with those of Pompeii. The new type, which we might almost call the characteristically Roman type, is in a sense a return to earlier Italian forms. In general, the colonnaded court disappears. In towns like Herculaneum and Ostia, except in the largest houses and in public buildings, columns hardly exist, and where garden courts occur they are often surrounded either by simple rectangular piers, sometimes with flower boxes or dwarf walls between, or by continuous walls pierced with large window openings to light the rooms behind. In a sense, this new type of house, with few or no columns, has a strangely modern look about it. The scale is usually more that of the modern residence; and, although the grace of the earlier Hellenistic colonnade has disappeared, it is replaced by a new kind of charm based on a greater intimacy and the beautiful contrast of foliage and simple wall surface. This movement seems to have occurred at about the beginning of the second half of the first century, for in Vitruvius there is little mention of it, whereas by the time of the destruction of Pompeii and Herculaneum, in 79 A.D., it was well advanced.

The Romans were great lovers of rural living and country scenes, and whenever they could afford it nad country places in addition to their town residences. Moreover, throughout the length and breadth of the Roman Empire there were thousands of families, many of considerable wealth, who lived entirely a country life on great estates—who lived as some of the English "country families" do today. These Roman country houses, grouped all together under the generic name of *villas*, were of widely differing types, which show the extraordinary practical adaptability of Roman architecture to different conditions and different climates. At one end of the scale were the enormous country palaces of the emperors and the great estate owners. The Villa of Hadrian at Tivoli was almost a city in itself, with exquisite colonnaded courts, great walled gardens, magnificent terraces overlooking superb views, two large sets of bathing establishments almost of public bath scale, and grounds decorated with fountains, temples, and statues, all so varied in character that one could find walks and views to fit every possible mood.

Numerous remains of great villas in North Africa and Europe show building groupings of an almost comparable scope, though naturally of less magnificence; and the way in which the practical needs of a great agricultural establishment and all the amenities of luxurious and gracious living are combined is a remarkable evidence of Roman planning skill. A frequent type has a long colonnade, facing south and if possible overlooking a view, backed by a narrow band of rooms—the chief reception, dining, and living rooms— and terminated at the end by two wings, one of which usually contains the more private residential portions, while the other holds a large suite of bath chambers. In the northern countries, not only the bathrooms are heated, but practically all of the important living rooms. The heating was provided for by raising the floor on a forest of small masonry posts; a furnace discharged its smoke and heat directly into this under-floor area; and hollow vertical tiles in the walls conducted the smoke and heat upward, finally discharging it above the roof. Thus, both floor and walls became heating surfaces, and the result perhaps the first highly developed central heating system in history. In these villas, much the same kind of development was going on that had occurred in the city houses—that is, a trend away from the columnar architecture of the Greeks, more and more toward an architecture of simple walls and large and ample window areas.

Pliny the Younger has left us two letters which describe vividly two of his country houses. One, at Laurentinum, on the sea shore, is of the more urban courtyard type; the other, in the hills at Tusculum, is of the long narrow type described above. It is significant in both that the views, the beauty of the natural surroundings, the gardens with their pleasant places both for winter and summer, and the close relationship of the building to its surroundings are stressed even more than the details of the architecture.

35. A STREET IN OSTIA, RESTORED. (Calza in *Monumenti Antichi.* 1916.)

The final development of the growing congestion of the Roman town was naturally the apartment house or tenement of many stories; and stringent legislation governing the heights of buildings, which was enacted by the Roman emperors, shows the ever-increasing seriousness of the problems such buildings presented. Buildings of four stories were common; six-, seven-, or eight-story buildings seem to have been occasionally used; and a picture of imperial Rome would show us large areas filled with apartment houses running up sixty or seventy feet into the air, with large windows and many balconies—would show us, in fact, a picture not unlike that of some cities of the present day.

These apartment houses were often built in long narrow blocks called *insulae,* usually two rooms deep, with stairs at intervals leading from top to bottom. At times arcades occurred on one side of the blocks, furnishing passages from which the individual rooms could be entered; at other times, the apartments would be entered directly from the stair landings. The congestion possible in such crowded rooms may be imagined, and the only thing which saved Rome from disaster and pestilence was the remarkably complete sanitary system and the great areas of public open space, which brought light and air into the crowded towns. In some cases the arrangements were less convenient than those furnished by these two-room-deep insulae. A shop building and apartment house uncovered on the slope of the Capitoline Hill was six stories high. The apartments consisted of three rooms each, arranged across the building. The corridor which gave access to the apartments ran at the back, against the Capitoline cliff, and must have been always dark and gloomy. Only the outer room of each apartment had exterior light; the other two merely had borrowed light.

It used to be imagined that the poor alone lived in these Roman apartment houses, and that they were common only perhaps in Rome, Alexandria, and one or two of the other largest cities of the Empire. The excavations at Ostia, however, show that some of the smaller towns as well were chiefly apartment-house towns, and that even the well-to-do lived in apartments apparently by preference. Characteristic are the luxurious duplex apartments in the Casa dei Dipinti in Ostia, where the living room and dining room were two full floors in height, while the bedrooms were but one. These two high rooms were connected by a broad passage, from which the smaller rooms opened, and the big rooms and the passage alike looked out onto a large gardened area through windows relatively as big as those in any modern building. These windows were closed in the poorer houses by wooden shutters, and sometimes by frames covered with oiled cloth or thin velum; but glass was used extensively in the more expensive buildings, and the use of thin sheets of mica or gypsum, often transparent enough to see through, was extensive. Many fragments of this were discovered in the course of the excavations at Ostia. Not only did these buildings have ample light and air through these enormous window areas, but they were also often provided with projecting balconies for outdoor sitting. Pipes still existing in the walls show that water and drains were both carried up to the upper floors of at least the better-class apartments, and one can imagine a present-day family moving into one of these suites and living a normal life with almost no change of habits or attitude.

One quality which surprises any careful student of the remains at Ostia or at Herculaneum, or who runs through the thousands of pieces of Roman sculpture found in France and Germany, must be the extremely high level of Roman middle-class taste expressed in them. In even the simplest houses at Herculaneum, the furniture, the lamp stands, the wall decorations, the utensils are lovely in form and often exquisite in execution. The amount of furniture was small; bedrooms seem universally to have possessed only

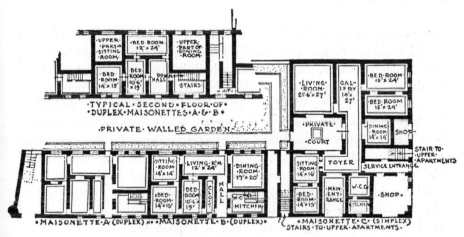

36. A HIGH-CLASS ROMAN APARTMENT HOUSE OF 127 A.D.; THE CASA DEI DIPINTI, OSTIA; PLAN. (Drawn by the author.)

a bed, a tall lamp stand, and a little table often of marble; yet, if we are to judge by the examples found, all three would be works of extreme refinement and excellent design. It is significant, too, that a grocer's house in Herculaneum—with his store in front still remarkably preserved with all its old store fittings, even to wine amphorae in a rack at the side and a great jar of beans on the counter,—although a small house, has some of the most exquisite wall paintings in all the town thus far unearthed.

The Romans, as soldiers, as administrators, as businessmen, traveled widely and naturally required inns and hotels. Most of the inns seem to have been simple and crude, like Italian country inns today; but, at Ostia at least, a large hotel and public bath combined in one structure—perhaps designed for the sea captains and traders who gathered there from all over the Mediterranean world—shows that on occasion more elaborate buildings were to be found. In this case, a square court, surrounded by an arcade, is bordered by two floors of sleeping rooms, the second floor opening out on a balcony. The whole is simple in finish, but more than adequate in design and size. At the rear opens a large and luxurious bathing establishment, where the tired sea captain could forget the storms in the delights of a warm bath, in rooms gay with colored marbles, lavish mosaics, and rich wall paintings. As he took off his clothes or dressed again in the dressing room, he could read ribald sayings attributed apocryphally to famous philosophers, whose caricatures were boldly sketched on the walls above. Thus there was humor as well as luxury in Rome.

As manufacturers and traders, the Romans needed large areas of commercial building. Shops were usually ample rooms opening out onto the street through wide arches, often with a built-in counter below the arch, so that the shopper stayed outside on the sidewalk, leaving the interior free for storage or manufacture. Wooden shutters closed the shops at night. Often the shop was combined with a mezzanine, which had its own window above the shop arch and was used either as a residence for the shopkeeper or for additional storage space. Sometimes, as in the case especially of drinking shops, the counter would be built of colored marbles, setting a tradition which seems to have persisted unbroken down to the modern soda fountain; one example in Ostia shows the luxurious splendor of marble fitment, including a little range of stepped shelves for the display of goods or cups, which these saloons sometimes achieved. Herculaneum furnishes us with the best-preserved example of a shop of more pedestrian type, in the grocer's shop referred to above, where all its wooden shelving and racks were sufficiently well preserved to warrant a complete restoration; so that today, 1800 years later, one may almost imagine the grocer in his white apron tipping up the amphora to fill a customer's pitcher with the desired wine, or dipping out the beans or dried peas from the jar on the counter, or turning back to the boxes on the shelves behind to fetch the spices for the customer's shopping basket.

In Rome itself, the concentration of commercial enterprise led early to setting certain areas apart for specific types of trade. For example, there was a quarter near the Forum on the Sacra Via renowned for its jewelry shops; another street famed for its book publishing and its copyists; a spice market; and so on. The entire area at one side of the Forum of Trajan was made into a shopping center and bazaar, and its brick buildings rising up the hillside, tier on tier, form one of the most impressive bits of ancient Rome still preserved. In general, this center consists of a series of shops and mez-zanines opening off streets or terraces which commanded lovely views over the imperial fora; but on one of the higher levels a large, well-lighted, vaulted hall served almost the purpose of a modern "arcade," with shops opening off it probably reserved for more perishable or more luxurious merchandise.

In addition to the individual shops, public markets, often sumptuously fitted up, bordered the fora of the Roman towns. One side of the Pompeiian forum is almost entirely occupied with three such buildings, which have tentatively been identified as markets for fish, for meat, and for vegetables. These usually took the form of an open courtyard where the merchants' booths could be set up, sometimes with a central shrine or covered area. The high development of commerce in the Roman Empire is shown by the great Merchants' Exchange at Ostia, a vast court with the Temple of Ceres—the goddess of grain—in the center, and with a colonnade around, from which opened the booths of the businessmen. In front of each booth, set in the colonnade floor, a mosaic gave the name of the dealer or trader embodied in a decorative pattern of ships, fish, or harbor scenes. Ropemakers, sail-makers, boat builders—all are represented, and in addition offices for the guilds or corporations of traders and shipmasters from towns bordering the Mediterranean all the way from Syria to Spain. Here orders were given, cargoes assigned; here the Spaniard could meet the Syrian and the Egyptian, have dealings with the Roman; here undoubtedly was one of the great nerve centers by means of which food and luxuries from all over the Mediterranean world and beyond came for the provisioning of Rome and the satisfying of its growing thirst for the exotic.

Warehouses, too, were necessary for the storage of goods of all kinds. Large areas of waterside Rome were apparently lined with them, so that boats coming up the Tiber from Ostia and berthed alongside a series of magnificent stone quays, of which large remains exist, could discharge directly into ample warehouses—usually ranges of simple vaulted rooms opening on an arcade or onto a long narrow court. Ostia also has similar *horrea*, and the general refinement of detail, the excellence of construction, and the occasional richness of doorway show that, to the Roman at least, these practical necessities might be made just as much an opportunity for architectural decency, if not monumental beauty, as the trader's house itself.

The vast sea-borne trade of the Roman Empire made elaborate dock and harbor works inevitable. In these the Romans followed the lead of the Hellenistic world, repeating again and again on a smaller scale the general forms of the *pharos* or lighthouse at Alexandria, but carrying even further than the Hellenistic designers the careful, practical, and yet monumental treatment of mole, pier, and dock building. At Portus, close to Ostia, first Claudius, then Trajan, built enormous enclosed artificial harbors, protected by ample breakwaters and lined with rows of well-designed warehouses, broken here and there by temples and administrative buildings. The skill of the engineers in so constructing these as to break the sea, and yet not

37. ROMAN RELIEF SHOWING THE CLAUDIAN HARBOR OF PORTUS. (Lanciani: *Ancient Rome in the Light of Recent Excavations.*)

permit gradual silting up or the formation of bars, was great, as is shown especially by the remains at Pozzuoli on the Bay of Naples, where the breakwater, instead of being solid, is arched to allow the current to sweep through, and the harbor is lined by a mole with two sets of arches—the piers of the inner set being set opposite the openings of the outer set, in order to break the force of beating waves. Nowhere can the extraordinary complexity, the "modern" character, of the Roman commercial world be more clearly seen than in these superb harbor works and the great grain ships that sailed between them.

It is the religious buildings of Rome which have been the chief cause of the fashionable indictment of Roman architecture as a mere bad copy of the Greek. Yet, even in the case of temples, a little examination will show that this accusation is much exaggerated. Normally the Roman temple was a development of the Etruscan temple, and to this origin it remained true in customarily having a high *podium,* with the temple proper raised above it and approached by a broad flight of steps, and in the fact that the colonnade was primarily an entrance porch; only in the most exceptional cases was the colonnade carried around the sides as in the normal Greek temple. At once this differing composition demanded a different treatment from that which the Greeks gave to their shrines; and many of the differences between Greek and Roman work, such as the higher pediment usually used in the Roman examples, are due to the different proportions which the Italian scheme developed.

But manifestly the influence of the Hellenic world on Roman temple design was great. Situated as Rome was between Etruria and the Greek colonies to the south, it could hardly have been otherwise. At the end of the Republic, when Roman power was being extended over the entire eastern Mediterranean, the great temples of Hellenistic Asia Minor impressed the Romans tremendously by their very size and lavishness. It is noteworthy that, of all the temples of Greece proper, the one which had the most direct influence on Rome was the huge Corinthian Temple of Zeus at Athens, a temple already Hellenistic in its vast size and the richness of its Corinthian order. The problem of the Roman architect then became that of adjusting the older Italic forms, a simple chamber fronted by a deep porch, to the new magnificence which they were so quickly learning from the Hellenistic cities. This was done by replacing the earlier wooden construction of the Etruscan temple with masonry, a change which forced, of course, a closer relative spacing of the columns and a redesigning of the entablature to fit the new material. As a result, entablatures following in their main lines those of the Greek orders were almost universally used.

With the closer spacing of the columns it became more customary to run the colonnade down the sides, at least, of the cella; and, since the Romans found the added effect of these columnar flanks pleasant, they sometimes simulated such side colonnades by placing engaged columns against the cella walls even where no side colonnade existed, producing that type of temple which is technically called *pseudo-peripteral,* as we can see it today in the little Temple of Fortuna Virilis in Rome and the Maison Carrée at Nîmes.

The cella itself always retained something of the earlier Etruscan character, and was both wider and relatively shorter than in most Greek examples. In some cases, in fact, as in the Temple of Concord in the Roman Forum, the desire for a wide cella was so great that the porch and the main entrance were placed on the long side of the temple instead of on the short side, thus forming a sort of T-shaped plan. The interiors of these temples were generally even more different from the Greek than were the exteriors. The Romans loved large, simple enclosed spaces, and therefore tended to produce temple interiors stretching unbroken from wall to wall, though sometimes with purely decorative columns placed along the sides, and roofed either with great wooden trusses and a flat ceiling or, in the more magnificent examples, with barrel vaults; and the cult statue was sometimes given enhanced and climax importance by being placed in a great niche or apse at the end.

One element of the Hellenistic temples profoundly affected Roman practice—the custom of placing temples within rectangular colonnaded courts;—and, except where the temple fronted directly on a forum or public square of some type, it was usually placed within such an enclosure even when the sizes were comparatively small. This at once gave rise to a formal composition of entirely different character from the informal Greek *temenos*, and led, as the difference in plan type had led, to a different emphasis in the architectural treatment—a more dramatic forcing of the central axis, a greater insistence on height in relation to width, and a richness of comparatively small-scale carved decoration, designed to be seen from the relatively narrow spaces of the enclosure. What remains of the old idea of the pure Greek temple, then, is only the use of the "orders"—the Doric, Ionic, and Corinthian—all much modified from Greek precedent by the new demands put upon them, and also perhaps the general treatment of the pediment with its sculpture. Beyond that, the entire conception is merely an elaboration of earlier and native temple types combined with a desire for grandeur, learned perhaps from the Hellenistic world.

These temples were used not only for religious ceremonies, but, even more than those of Greece, for museums as well; and, in addition to the votive offerings which decorated the courtyards and the temples themselves, they frequently contained a great wealth of statuary presented to them by emperors or wealthy people and placed there, not primarily for religious reasons, but merely because there they could receive the best public display.

Throughout the Empire, Roman religion was beginning to take on a more and more purely formal and symbolic character, as the new religions from the East—Judaism, Christianity, Mithraism, and the worship of Isis—became gradually more popular. The temples of the older gods continued

in use, though largely as symbols only, symbols of Roman unity, but practically they became largely mere museums, places for picturesque public
pageantry, and public promenades. Thus the Portico of Octavia, built as
a lavish public covered promenade around an ample public park or garden,
contained temples which gave it, as it were, some kind of traditional reason
for being; and thus all of the later imperial fora of Rome itself had temples
as essential parts of their design. What the later temples lost in simple and

38. TEMPLE OF APOLLO, POMPEII, RESTORED. (Weichardt: *Pompeii vor der
Zerstoerung.*)

reverent religious meaning they gained in increasing size and magnificence.
Many of them were dedicated to emperors, for emperor worship was the
great unifying emotional force of the Empire; and the refusal to perform
sacrifices to the emperor—one of the chief reasons for the persecutions of
Christians—was considered in a sense a kind of national treason. Characteristic of the later temples is the great double temple of Venus and Rome, built
by Hadrian, a vast structure with two cellas back to back, each with an
enormous domed niche, with a porch all around, the columns of which
rose to a height of almost sixty feet. This structure was set within a rectangular courtyard, colonnaded itself with columns of more modest scale, so that
the bulk of the central building rose high above the enclosing wall.

Other types of Roman temples differed even more strongly from the Greek standards. A tradition of round temples, probably based on primitive round huts, existed from an early period. The Temple of Vesta, where the symbolic city fire was kept continuously alight, seems to have been always round in form; and as its light is symbolic of an earlier day reaching far back into the dim past, when fire was rare and difficult to produce, so its basic round plan may go back to a similar antiquity. These round temples were early surrounded by colonnades and roofed with conical roofs of low slope; the resultant shape was graceful and had a quality of charm which the rectangular temples lacked. Three remarkable examples exist in Rome itself—the old Temple of Vesta in the Roman Forum, a round temple sometimes called the Temple of Hercules, and another round temple recently uncovered in the Area Argentina, probably a Temple of Hercules Custos. Still another, dating perhaps from the time of Sulla, gloriously crowns a cliff in the village of Tivoli, and the delicacy of its molding profiles and the originality of its exquisite capitals are eloquent evidence of the Roman genius for creative modifications of earlier prototypes.

The greatest of the round temples was that enormous rotunda which Hadrian built on the site of an earlier building of Agrippa's—the temple we know today as the Pantheon, which still stands, in almost perfect preservation, to reveal not only Roman genius for construction, in roofing this 140-foot circle so simply with one great dome, but also Roman skill in treating a tremendous interior in such a way as to emphasize both its vastness and its unity. Approached by a deep porch, once covered with a bronze vaulted ceiling supported on great bronze girders and trusses, the entrance doorway, twenty feet wide and forty high, with its original bronze doors and transom-screen, leads the visitor at once into the great enclosed space. The thick walls required to support the thrust of the dome are lightened by eight great niches, one containing the doorway, the others altars to the major deities, and each separated from the central area by a screen of columns. Smaller shrines decorate the walls between, and all the wall surface up to the entablature which runs over the columns is sheathed in rich marbles laid in beautiful decorative geometric shapes. Above the entablature runs a frieze once decorated with a continuous row of small pilasters, instead of the awkward Renaissance false windows and panels which now occupy the area. Above this the perfect hemisphere of the dome sweeps upward, its curve emphasized by deep coffers, to a central *oculus* or opening thirty feet in diameter that lights the whole. The magnificent quality of the resultant simple vertical light, which seems to bathe the whole interior so evenly and yet to emphasize so forcefully the shadowed recesses of the shrines and the niches, is something no photograph or drawing can reproduce. The whole shows how brilliantly the Roman architects conceived and realized that quality which we moderns call *space*. It is this quality of spaciousness, this sense of enormous areas and great heights, well lighted and nevertheless closed in from the weather and the surroundings, which is perhaps the most unique of all Roman architectural qualities. It is this which none of the previous architectures had ever approached or perhaps even dreamed of; and it is this quality which, working through Byzantine and Romanesque architecture, set all design on a new search for interior architectural beauty.

Another quality which the Roman temples show is that called *scale*—that is, the correct adjustment of parts of a building, and their correct decoration, in such a way that a building shall appear its true desired size. A small temple and a large temple can never be similar in treatment, even when the order used is the same. Generally speaking, the smaller the columns, the wider relatively to their height they may be spaced; and the entire system of carved detail will naturally be different on an order twenty feet high and one which rises to sixty feet, for the eye will be able to see in the smaller example all sorts of delicate details which, if used merely magnified on the larger example, would be woefully coarse. A comparison, for instance, of the details of the little round temple at Tivoli and those of the sixty-foot order of the colossal Temple of Castor and Pollux in the Roman Forum will show the delicate and refined intimacy, if one may use such a word here, of the Tivoli example, and the lavish and deeply carved ornament of the other. Raised to the scale of the Castor and Pollux order, the Tivoli detail would become brutal and overwhelming; reduced to the smaller scale, the prodigal complexity of the large order would be overelaborate and finicking. It is perhaps because of the freedom in detail offered by the Corinthian order that the Romans preferred it. This quality of a true feeling for scale runs through all of the best Roman architecture, from small houses up to the most enormous and monumental constructions.

The Romans seem to have produced few specialized building types for educational purposes. Nevertheless, the average of literacy within the Roman Empire was extremely high, approaching modern American standards. Schools for children were held in fora, in porticoes and colonnades, and in private houses. Thus, paintings in Pompeii show elementary-school scenes going on in the forum colonnade; and *graffiti*—that is, scratched inscriptions—on the walls and piers of the Forum of Julius Caesar in Rome show without a doubt that a school was held there, and that much of the chief teaching was through the pages of Virgil's *Aeneid,* lines from which are scratched on the wall in childish characters.

Although there is little which can be called truly school or college archi-tecture, the literary wants of the adult were amply provided for, and public libraries were common elements of Roman towns. Rome itself had several; one was later made over into the church of Santa Maria Antiqua, and even today one may see the colonnaded court which served as the reading room, and the hall within, surrounded by niches, which held the bookcases where the rolls were kept. The Forum of Trajan had twin library rooms across a small court from each other, one devoted to Greek and one to Latin literature. The two best-preserved examples, however, are in far-off provincial cities, one in Ephesus and one in Timgad in North Africa. In both, the architectural treatment is lavish and the scale large. In the Ephesus example the book storage probably was on two levels, with a balcony around the room giving access to the upper tiers. The Timgad example, like that on the forum in Rome, had a colonnaded reading court in front; in both of these, the readers may have had direct access to the books. In Ephesus, on the other hand, librarians must have handed the rolls to the readers, for the reading area in the whole center of the hall is dropped several feet below the podium on which the bookcases rested; this podium was wide enough to contain the bookcases and to allow the librarian to pass in front of them.

Of buildings for higher education, as we know it, there is no trace. Lecture halls existed in connection with the public baths and perhaps else-where, but the famous professors seem usually to have had their students come to their own houses, or else, in exceptional cases, they served as tutors in the houses of the wealthy young people.

The Roman theater was manifestly based on the Greek, though changes both in dramatic form and structural methods gave it a quite different ex-pression. What early Etruscan or Italic theaters may have been we do not know, but from the very beginning the Roman plays themselves were more human, sometimes more humorous, much more dependent on individual action and individual gesture—in a word, more realistic—than the Greek. We know of various types of comedy and satire; and the classic Roman comedies like those of Plautus date from a period two centuries before the Empire, when Roman architecture was still in a crude and transitional state. We know, too, that the earliest theaters in Rome were of wood, and it was not until nearly the end of the Republic that the building of permanent structures of stone was considered. The old Greek idea of the hillside site was seldom if ever adopted; the Roman wished his theater, whenever possible, right in the middle of his city. Yet the Greek idea of the general curved concentric seats in rising tiers was too practical to be abandoned, and the Roman architect was therefore forced to develop ways of holding up these tiers of seats.

Since the Roman plays were essentially human plays of realistic action, there was no need of the orchestra for a dancing chorus and an altar, and therefore the area at the bottom of the curved seats was itself given over to seating, and the "orchestra seats" became in Rome, as they are still today, the most distinguished positions. Since there was no need of an orchestra, there was similarly less need for the great processional entrances on each side of the stage, and with these omitted the old Greek method of using more than a half-circle for the seats became both unnecessary and illogical. Now the action was entirely on the stage, and the best seats were those which faced it; therefore Roman theaters always adopted the semicircle as the basis of their plan.

Because the plays had a naturalistic aim, the problem of stage background began to play a much greater part in the whole than it had done in Greece, and accordingly the Roman stage tends to have a high wall at the back, completely shutting out anything beyond, projecting elements at the side taking the place of the modern wings, and sometimes even a roof covering the stage portion. The back wall became a place for exuberant architectural display, usually with two tiers of columns over each other, a most intricate and lavish adornment of pediments, curved and straight, and richly carved entablatures, which were a decoration pure and simple against the great structural wall. To give at least symbolically the idea of naturalistic environment, a certain amount of painted scenery was used, and the idea of the stage curtain was introduced. In Roman theaters the curtain was lifted from below to close off the stage, and dropped to open it; the wide crack in the floor and the stone bases for the machinery to work it are still clearly evident in the front of the stage of the theater in Pompeii. Painted scenery usually took the form of a series of triangular prisms of considerable height, erected at the sides of the stage and so arranged that they could be turned. These were so planned that when they were turned at a certain angle their edges almost touched. Each side of the prism could be painted with its section of a different scene, so that by merely turning the prisms three different sets could be produced.

If the stage element of the Roman theater, with its great height and its rich architectural adornment, was a different thing from the Greek, the audience portion was even more so. For the support of this half cone of masonry seats, high above the ground, produced difficult and complicated structural questions, and moreover the problem of getting several thousand people from the streets to their seats conveniently and in an orderly manner made the careful study of stairs and exits a prime necessity. The general system adopted was to support the seats on a series of walls radiating out from the center, and to connect the various wedge-shaped sections so developed, at least on the outside face, by a continuous vaulted passage running around the whole semicircle, so that stairs could be conveniently arranged in the spaces between the radiating walls; and, in order to make entrance and exit simple and to distribute the crowds easily, the outside circumferential corridor frequently would be in two stories. To give ample entrances and exits on the ground floor and to light the whole great area under the seats on both floors, the outer corridors were opened to the air by a continuous series of open arches. In order to buttress the outward thrust of the vaults of the corridors, the outer piers were thickened by applying engaged columns or projecting square buttresses to their outer sides. These in turn carried entablatures running continuously around the building, thus giving restful horizontal lines as well as expressing the various floor levels of the building corridors.

Within the rectangles formed by these columns or buttresses and the entablature were the open arches leading in, and so was developed one of the most characteristic Roman architectural features, the so-called Roman arcade—that is, a succession of arches with engaged columns or pilasters on the piers between them, carrying entablatures which run continuously over the arch tops. Sometimes, to tie the arches into the rectangular composition, horizontal impost moldings occur at the arch springs, and the key blocks of the arches are projected and carved. This arrangement has been much criticized as illogical; yet, when the buttressing function of the projecting columns or pilasters is realized, and when the problem which the designers faced in theater and amphitheater design is understood, the logical quality of this treatment, at least in this use, may be easily appreciated. The magnificent arcades of the Theater of Marcellus in Rome, curving so majestically and simply round the curve of the semicircular theater, still stand to attest the unmistakable grandeur which the Roman theaters possessed.

The stage elements have suffered much more from the passage of time. The great walls of the theaters at Orange, in France, at Aspendus, in Asia Minor, and elsewhere still stand at their original height, although completely stripped of their early rich architectural decoration, but many details of the typical architectural ornament have been preserved in a much ruined condition. The columns of the stage of the Theater of Taormina, in Sicily, are among the most picturesque of Roman ruins anywhere.

As Roman imperial life progressed, the popularity of the theater was seriously threatened by the growing passion for athletic games and chariot races; hence the growing importance of the amphitheater and the hippodrome or circus. The amphitheater is a characteristic Italian and essentially a Roman building, designed for gladiatorial combats, fights between wild beasts, and battles between wild beasts and gladiators. Since such spectacles needed no background, it was logical to place the spectators all around; and from an early date such structures, roughly elliptical in shape, were built, of wood, in Roman towns. In the last century B.C., these wooden structures began to be replaced little by little by permanent buildings of stone, with the seats supported and the entrances and exits arranged much as has already been described for theaters. Sometimes, in the smaller and more primitive towns, the amount of stone required was vastly reduced by excavating the arena area considerably below the surface of the surrounding ground, and using the material to bank up around to receive the higher seats. Such was the basic construction of the existing amphitheater of Pompeii, and such seem to have been most of the provincial amphitheaters like that at Silchester, in England.

From the purely aesthetic point of view, the amphitheater, both inside and out, because of its absolute continuity of curve, had a power and a unity which the semicircular theater could never quite achieve, and it is no accident that the great Flavian Amphitheater built by Vespasian and Titus on the site of part of Nero's fantastic palace, the Golden House, has remained for centuries perhaps the most famous Roman ruin in all the Empire. The Colosseum, as it is called, is 615 feet long and 510 feet wide, with an arena 281 by 177 feet. Present estimates are that it seated about 50,000 people. Naturally, few of the provincial amphitheaters attained anything like this size; yet even in comparatively small towns they were important and monumental edifices, designed to seat, it would seem, almost the entire population of the town.

These Roman amphitheaters are impressive not only because of their tremendous mass, their long lines of Roman arcade marching around the building, and their tier on tier of stone seats, but also because of the elaborate arrangements often found beneath the arena floor to house the cages of wild beasts and to allow their sudden and dramatic introduction into the arena. Thus, the floor of the amphitheater at Pozzuoli consists of a large number of traps, one set completely ringing the outer edge of the arena, others distributed in the more central parts, while down the main axis runs a long narrow opening, originally covered by a movable wooden floor. The Colosseum had a similarly elaborate system of underground passages and cells. In every case an outer wall separated the arena proper from the lowest seats, just as is found today in the Spanish bull rings. The interior aspect of one of these may best be seen in the sections of the ranked seats of the amphitheater at Verona, where the entrances and exits, closely spaced, are perfectly preserved. The Colosseum at Rome has been used as a quarry for ten centuries, but large sections of it still stand in such perfect preservation that its entire system of corridors running around the building and of entrance stairs can be easily seen.

The great circuses or hippodromes of Rome were as grand in scale, though entirely different in plan. Long narrow areas, straight at the two sides and curved at one end, formed the basis of the plan. At the end opposite the closed semicircular curve were placed the stalls from which the chariots were released at the beginning of a race; and down the center, though not exactly parallel to the axis, but so designed as to equalize the chances of all the chariots, was built a dividing line, the *spina,* with curved stone uprights at each end to mark its termination and the turning point of the racecourse. Around this racing area rose the seats, straight along the long sides and curving around the semicircular. These were often held up by a structural system similar to that used in the theaters and amphitheaters, although, because there were not generally as many tiers from top to bottom as in the shorter amphitheaters, the structural parts were not so large. Sometimes, as in the Circus Maximus in Rome, a triumphal arch marked the center of the curve and broke the continuity of the whole.

In some ways the most typical of all of the Roman buildings for public recreation were the public baths, which rose in all the towns of the Roman Empire from the Tigris to the Atlantic and from the Sahara to the Rhine. Bathing as an art and a pleasure as well as a necessity has been a common phenomenon of life in the eastern Mediterranean through at least three millennia. The palaces of Crete had elaborate bathing equipment, many of the Greek palaestrae were furnished with baths, and Greek vase paintings occasionally show bathers enjoying the jets of water pouring out on them from spouts above. In the Hellenistic period, the elaboration of bathing went on apace, and certain buildings with round rooms—which seem to have been

PAESTUM, SO-CALLED TEMPLE OF POSEIDON. (Ernest Nash.)

ATHENS, THE PARTHENON; RESTORED MODEL. (Metropolitan Museum of Art.)

Plate 9

PAESTUM, TEMPLE OF POSEIDON; INTERIOR.
(Ernest Nash.)

ATHENS, THE PARTHENON; INTERIOR (
RESTORED MODEL. (Metropolitan Museum
Art.)

ATHENS, THE ERECHTHEUM. (Leopold Arnaud.)

Plate 10

OLYMPIA, THE SACRED AREA; RESTORED MODEL. (Metropolitan Museum of Art.)

DELPHI, PART OF THE SACRED AREA; RESTORED MODEL. (Metropolitan Museum of Art.)

Plate 11

MAGNESIA, GREAT TEMPLE OF ARTEMIS. (Krischen: *Die Griechische Stadt.*)

PERGAMON, GREAT ALTAR OF ZEUS; AS RECONSTRUCTED IN THE BERLIN MUSEUM.

Plate 12

POMPEII, HOUSE OF THE SILVER WEDDING;
ATRIUM, PERISTYLE BEYOND. (Ernest
Nash.)

POMPEII, HOUSE OF THE VETII; PERISTYLE.
(Ernest Nash.)

SEASIDE VILLAS; ROMAN PAINTING, HOUSE
OF LUCRETIUS FRONTO, POMPEII. (Ernest
Nash.)

POMPEII, HOUSE OF L. TIBURTINUS, SHOW-
ING CHARACTERISTIC WALL DECORATION.
(Ernest Nash.)

POMPEII, HOUSE OF L. TIBURTINUS; GARDEN
PAVILION AND FOUNTAIN. (Ernest Nash.)

Plate 13

ROME, SHOPPING CENTER (MERCATO TRAIANI), FORUM OF TRAJAN.
(Ernest Nash.)

ROME, VIA BIBERATICA; STREET THROUGH THE SHOPPING CENTER.
(Ernest Nash.)

ROME, MERCATO TRAIANI; ARCADE. (Alinari.)

Plate 14

OME, THE SENATE (CURIA). (Ernest Nash.)

OSTIA, A WAREHOUSE (HORREA); COURT. (Ernest Nash.)

TIA, A STREET, VIA DI DIANA, SHOWING OPS, BALCONIES, AND SIMPLE BRICK AR- ITECTURE. (Ernest Nash.)

OSTIA, A WAREHOUSE; DECORATIVE BRICK ENTRANCE. (Ernest Nash.)

Plate 15

ROME, BASILICA OF MAXENTIUS & CONSTANTINE. (E. Nash.)

ROME, IONIC TEMPLE OF FORTUNA VIRILIS. (Ernest Nash.)

ROME, PORTA MAGGIORE; IN THE FOREGROUND A TOMB.

LOOKING FROM LOUNGE.

Plate 16

ORANGE, THE THEATER; INTERIOR.

ROME, THE PANTHEON; DETAIL.

ROME, THE PANTHEON; INTERIOR, GENERAL VIEW.

ORANGE, THE THEATER; THE STAGE WALL.

Plate 17

SAINTES, TRIUMPHAL ARCH.

NÎMES, MAISON CARRÉE; EXTERIOR.

Plate 18

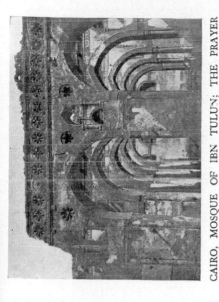

CAIRO, MOSQUE OF IBN TULUN; THE PRAYER HALL.

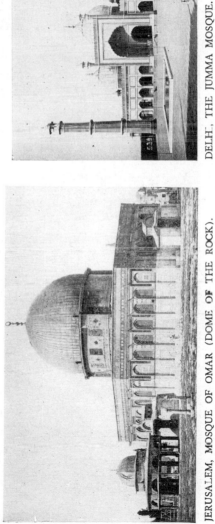

DELHI, THE JUMMA MOSQUE.

MSCHATTA, THE PALACE; EXTERIOR WALL.

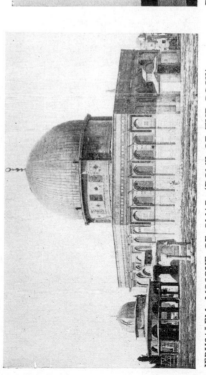

JERUSALEM, MOSQUE OF OMAR (DOME OF THE ROCK).

Plate 19

GRANADA, THE ALHAMBRA; COURT OF THE MYRTLES.

GRANADA, THE ALHAMBRA; COLONNADE OF THE COURT OF THE LIONS.

CORDOVA, THE MOSQUE; INTERIOR OF THE PRAYER HALL.

Plate 20

ISFAHAN, MADRASA MADAR-I-SHAH; THE ...AN. (Copyright, Myron Bement Smith.)

ISFAHAN, THE KAISARIYYAH BAZAAR. (Copyright, Myron Bement Smith.)

...IAN, MIHRAB IN THE DJOUMA ...UE. (Copyright, Myron Bement)

AGRA, THE TAJ MAHAL; TOMB OF MUMTAZ MAHAL.

Plate 21

DELHI, THE PALACE; DIWAN-I-KHASS.

CONSTANTINOPLE, MOSQUE OF SULEIMAN; INTERIOR. Sinan, architect.

CONSTANTINOPLE, MOSQUE OF SHAH ZADÉ; EXTERIOR.

Plate 22

OME, STA. MARIA IN COSMEDIN; EXTERIOR.
Alinari.)

ROME, STA. MARIA IN COSMEDIN; INTERIOR.
(Alinari.)

STA. MARIA IN TRASTEVERE; INTERIOR SHOWING CHARACTERISTIC RE-USE OF ANCIENT
LS AND MOSAIC APSE.

Plate 23

RAVENNA, SO-CALLED PALACE OF THEO-
DORIC; ENTRANCE.

OVIEDO, VISIGOTHIC PALACE, NOW TF
CHURCH OF STA. MARIA DE NARANCO; I
TERIOR. (Courtesy Professor Kenneth Conant.)

POITIERS, MEROVINGIAN BAPTISTRY OF ST.
JEAN; INTERIOR.

POITIERS, MEROVINGIAN BAPTISTRY OF
JEAN; EXTERIOR.

Plate 24

used for hot baths—foreshadow the later developments which the Roman Empire was to make.

The earlier Roman baths were simple, usually consisting merely of a group of two or three rooms for the proper cold and hot temperatures required by the Roman bathing technique, often incorporated as an essential part of private houses; but, by the middle of the first century B.C., Pompeii had at least two public baths, in which the evolution of this earlier scheme had gone much further. In these, a dressing room with cubicles for the bathers' clothes was added; the rooms were made large enough for use by considerable numbers of people at the same time, and were richly decorated with mural paintings and plaster reliefs. Moreover, in addition to the bathrooms themselves, there was a colonnaded court for outdoor exercise, an elaborate public toilet, and in the Stabian Baths a large outdoor swimming pool. In both of these Pompeiian examples there are two sets of bathrooms, one larger and richer than the other; the smaller set was undoubtedly designed for women.

Even at this early date the arrangements for heating the rooms and furnishing hot water were already remarkably complete. Separate service entrances and courts gave access to the furnace, from which flues led to the under-floor spaces and wall flues, which have been described before. This whole system was called a *hypocaust*. The same service area also contained an elaborate water heater, with three storage tanks so arranged that water for the cold, the warm, and the hot baths was always available. The piping arrangements of these heaters show at least an elementary knowledge of the theory of water circulation through temperature change.

The bath suites themselves consisted of a dressing room or *apodyterium;* a *tepidarium* or warm bath, which was usually the largest room and served as a sort of lounge; the *frigidarium,* or cold bath, in the earlier examples usually a round room containing a large round stepped basin; and the hot bath, or *calidarium,* often made with an apse end to contain a shallow basin of almost boiling hot water. All later baths, however gorgeous in architectural treatment, are merely developments of this system of rooms.

The earlier Pompeiian baths are casual in plan and without definite exterior architectural effect; undoubtedly the last century of Pompeii found them old-fashioned, for at the time of the destruction of the city a vast new group was under construction, in which the same elements appear, but arranged with conscious attention to monumental symmetry and richness of exterior design, and, most revolutionary of all, furnished with the large windows which were more and more coming into use.

Under the Empire, public bathing had become such a passion that the public bath added to its functions those of a modern club or even a lyceum. They were preferably set in sizable gardens, with ample space for both quiet strolling and violent exercise. The old tepidarium was magnified into a vast central lounge. Small rooms containing separate baths for more private use were added, and often the whole was surrounded by a group of rooms for lectures, poetry readings, or group meetings. As emperor succeeded emperor, from the time of Titus onward, each seems to have tried to outdo the other in the size, magnificence, and luxury of the bath building which he presented to the city, until the climax was reached in the great Baths of Diocletian, the ruins of which stretch over so many blocks near the present railway station, and the central hall of which still remains as the church of Sta. Maria degli Angeli, refurbished and decorated by Michelangelo, while its vast exedra at one side of the garden is recalled by the great curves of the Piazza dell' Esedra which is built on its foundations.

Nor were these large and splendid buildings limited to the city of Rome itself. In the gardens of the Cluny Museum, in Paris, the great vaulted halls are parts of the baths built there by Maxentius. Still further north, at Trier, colossal remains still exist of a magnificent bath structure which rivaled in elaborateness some of those of Rome itself. In North Africa, both Timgad and Leptis Magna had thermae which, though smaller, were equally luxurious, as lavish in their decoration, and designed with as sure a sense of straightforward architectural form.

Certain great changes of form differentiate these later imperial baths from the earlier type we have seen in Pompeii. Instead of the small round frigidarium, there is usually a huge rectangular swimming pool, sometimes covered by a great flat ceiling. Instead of the simple dressing room there is frequently a whole suite of rooms, often doubled, one set at each of two side entrances; in the Baths of Caracalla these were on two floors. One entrance, with its suite of dressing rooms, may have been for women and the other for men, for during the greater part of the imperial period mixed bathing was the rule. Instead of the earlier simple calidarium there was often an enormous room, with very thick walls and considerable height; in the Baths of Caracalla, perhaps the most famous of all Roman baths, this took the form of a vast domed rotunda, which almost rivaled the Pantheon itself. In such an establishment the Roman could spend almost the entire day meeting friends, talking, listening to the latest literature or the latest gossip, attending lectures by the most famous rhetoricians, playing games or running races, and finally climaxing the whole with an actual bath proc-

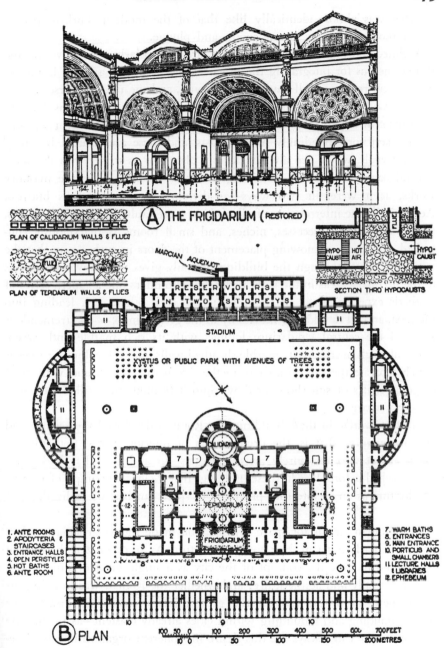

39. BATHS OF CARACALLA, ROME; PLAN AND VIEW OF FRIGIDARIUM, RESTORED.
(Fletcher: *A History of Architecture on the Comparative Method.*)

ess that was almost identically like that of the modern Turkish bath—warm room, cleansing, steam room, and plunge.

Architecturally these vast structures are particularly expressive of the Roman genius for integrating the practical, the necessary, and the beautiful. Their great rooms are all vaulted in masonry, and the use of intersecting or groined vaults allows large window areas high up in the wall, thus flooding even the central part of these buildings with light. Naturally, such enormous vaults exert correspondingly huge thrusts, and these are abutted by cross-buttress walls, which are always cleverly placed so as to serve as the most natural partitions between adjoining rooms or recesses. Thus the masonry works, as it were, in two ways—as dividing partition and as buttress. Aesthetically the interrelation of all of these great vaults, clerestory windows, arched and vaulted recesses, niches, and small rooms is marvelously controlled, with a most knowing placement of the doors in such a way that the natural progress through the building not only gives one convenient access to the necessary areas in the right order, but also offers one a superb series of aesthetic experiences, all of them related to each other, each leading into the next, and all developing inevitably to the great climax of the tremendous space of the central tepidarium lounge, with its rich marble and sweeping vault high overhead, its marble-sheathed walls, and the columnar screens which separate the central area from the side bath recesses, and with great diagonal shafts of sun shooting down into it through the grilled clerestory windows above.

In other words, in these buildings the Romans developed the science and art of *planning*—that is, the organization of interior spaces, not only for practical but also for purely artistic reasons—to a degree that had never been reached before. It is in these buildings that the great triumph of Roman architecture as an architecture primarily of space can best be realized.

This Roman genius for space organization made them particularly adept and particularly eager in their civic architecture. As an organizer, the Roman was bound to have the concept of the city as a single great organic whole, both practically and aesthetically; and whether the Roman was building his cities anew—as in the case of the great military colony of Timgad—or merely building and rebuilding within cities already existent—as in the case of Rome—one can always see this desire for coherent organization, for integration of many elements into one great composition. Great areas of Rome were made and remade; slums were wiped out and replaced with fora and monuments; and, if Nero took over large areas of the most valuable land in Rome to create the Golden House and its surrounding park, his successors with equal temerity tore down what he had built and gave it back to the citizens in the form of the Colosseum, great baths, and additional open spaces. One has only to look at a plan of the Roman fora to realize that each, although a unit in itself, has a spatial relationship to those next it; so that the citizen of, say, the time of Trajan, strolling from the Roman Forum into that of Nerva, then into the Forum of Augustus, and from that in turn into the great area of the Forum of Trajan, with its tremendous colonnaded basilica across the end, was having an experience similar in kind to that of the man who walked through the great rooms of the Roman baths.

When to this series of imperial fora we add the superb temples with their surrounding courts that crowned the Capitoline Hill, so brilliantly and picturesquely fronted by the simple arcades of the Tabularium, and the group of imperial residences on the Palatine Hill, part of which at least were more for public use than for residence, some idea of the magnificence of the Roman conceptions of civic art may be gained. If to this central group one adds the vast areas of garden porticoes, the great bridges which spanned the Tiber, and the elaborate embankment works which confined its swift waters, one perhaps may wonder at the amount of absolutely free and public civic beauty and open space the Roman citizen had for his enjoyment. He might sleep in a slum five flights up, but almost all of his leisure hours could be spent, if he wished, in public places of a beauty, a variety, and a grandeur that few other civilizations have ever equaled.

Chapter 9

PROVINCIAL AND LATER ROMAN
ARCHITECTURE

THE extraordinary adaptability of the Romans is reflected in the wide variations between the buildings which they built in one part of the Empire and those constructed in another. At its height, its climate range was greater than that even of the modern United States, covering the tropical river valleys of Asia and the Nile, the deserts and shores of North Africa, the moderate climate of the Mediterranean coasts, the rains and the cold of central Europe, the fogs and Atlantic storms of the British Isles. And, as the climate varied from place to place, so did the available building materials. Though Roman architecture in Italy was dependent on brick and concrete made from volcanic *pozzolana,* pozzolana cement was unavailable in large sections of the Roman Empire, and brick clays were not to be found in other large areas. Naturally architectural forms could not help revealing both difference in climate and difference in materials; the Roman house in Britain or on the banks of the Rhine was a different thing from the Roman house in Africa or Syria. And the imagination and logicality in Roman design is clear in these differences. It was this quality of being designed always in terms of site, climate, and material which enabled Roman architecture to endure for three centuries and to leave behind it an influence that has modified or formed almost all the building of the Western world, until the nineteenth century and the coming of iron changed the whole building conception.

In the heavily forested northern European provinces the Roman builders made generous use of the wood which was such a natural material there. Walls, wherever possible, they liked to build of stone or brick, but the columns of Italy were frequently replaced by wooden posts in northern buildings. The villas were designed with the most careful reference to orientation; usually a colonnade or piazza stretched along the south side of the house, and large window areas were used to catch the utmost sun. Occasionally hardened nuggets of once-melted glass found in the ruins of

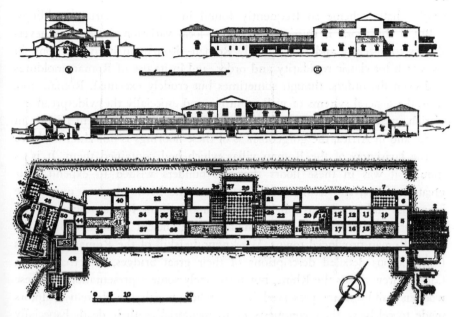

40. ROMAN VILLA AT BASSE WAVRE, BELGIUM; PLAN AND RESTORED ELEVA-
TION. THE SMALL SPOTS FILLING MANY ROOMS SHOW THE BRICK PILLARS
OF THE HYPOCAUST WHICH HEATED THE VILLA. (De Maeyer: *Romeinsche Villa's
in België*.)

1. COLONNADE
2. LARGE LIVING ROOM
5, 6, 7, 10-15. PRIVATE LIVING ROOMS
25, 26, 27. GREAT HALL

31-40. RESIDENTIAL ROOMS
8, 9, 18, 23, 24, 33, 41. OPEN COURTS
44-50. BATHS

villas that had burned show that some at least of these windows had been
glazed with glass. Heating was arranged by typical Roman hypocaust
methods, often in the more northern villas built under all the living quarters.
Just as the Romans liked masonry walls, so wherever possible they used
tiled roofs; but remains in England and northern France, as well as carved
representations, show that on occasion wood shingles, flat stones set like
slate, and even thatch were all employed. These great provincial Roman
estates usually contained not only the house itself, sometimes built with a forecourt, but also a large group of farm buildings, often set in another enclosure,
and at least in some cases, as we know from the villa at Anthée in Belgium, a
formally arranged group or village of workshops and tenants' houses.

It is interesting to see how, occasionally, even the earlier typically "barbarian" types of building influenced Roman building, and some of the simpler structures were merely somewhat Romanized versions of the great

single "hall" scheme so frequently found in earlier barbarian buildings.

But if this work is thus susceptible to local variation, it remains nevertheless consistently and recognizably Roman—Roman in its proportions, in its search for classic regularity and order, and in its use of Roman moldings and even the orders, though sometimes but crudely executed. Roman, too, were the general systems of wall painting, and especially the widespread use of rich, even magnificent, mosaic floors; and, alike in England, in France, in Syria, and in Africa, the gorgeousness of these floorings is our chief evidence of the lavishness of the Roman villas which had contained them. It is as though it was in these floors that the builders wished to expend their greatest efforts, and skilled mosaicists from the Mediterranean must have been busy and prosperous inhabitants of almost all the Roman towns.

Naturally there are but few remains of the ancient wooden architecture of the Roman provincial towns. We know the skill of the Roman architects from various detailed descriptions of their great bridges, like that which Caesar threw across the Rhine, but fortunately some representations of these wooden buildings are preserved in the reliefs which the Roman sculptors made to celebrate their conquests or to memorialize their dead. Especially interesting is a view of a provincial Roman town on the banks of the Danube shown on the Column of Trajan, in which we can see not only the wooden "blockhouses" of the fortifications, but also, clearly carved, wood-braced houses within the walls, and, most extraordinary of all, a large wooden amphitheater with its construction of great compound posts, horizontal girders, and diagonal braces most clearly indicated.

The temples of Roman Gaul and Germany were as different from those of Italy as were the houses, and show clearly the superb Roman talent for synthesizing their own culture and their own religion with those of other peoples. Thus the characteristic northern temple was a square building, often of almost tower type, with a lower colonnade, and frequently with wooden posts surrounding it on all four sides. This in turn was set within a precinct or court, generally square but sometimes circular, and the whole is obviously merely a Romanized expression of much more primitive shrine types. Examples of temples of this type are common in many parts of France and in Germany.

The best-known Roman town in England, that at Silchester, shows a large area enclosed within the rectangular walls and a plan manifestly based originally on the Roman camp. In the center was a forum, bordered as usual by the commanding officer's house and the government center, temples, and a market. The rest of the site was covered with private houses, in general widely spaced so that each must have had a large garden area—sometimes almost a little farm. There was also an amphitheater, in this case formed by excavating a conical area in generally flat land and using the excavated material to raise the surrounding banks.

The life which was lived in these Roman provincial towns was a busy, essentially peaceful existence based on agriculture, commerce, and manufacture. Many phases of it have been preserved to us with almost photographic accuracy on the Roman tomb carvings which are numerous through France and Germany. Here we can see the family party sitting around the supper table, in chairs more like Windsor chairs than those we know from Pompeii. We can see the lady of the house in a luxurious wicker armchair. We watch the shopkeeper pointing up to the stores of goods on his shelves with an inquiring glance at the customer. We see the boys at school, and in one we can even see the librarian reaching for the roll on the shelf in his library. In general this provincial sculpture, like much of the provincial ornament, is crude in execution, and the Roman acanthus leaf has suffered many strange changes; yet the spirit behind the whole is essentially the spirit of cultivated Rome; and the changes are significant, because so many of them reveal a search for a freedom in decorative treatment that gives definite promise of the Romanesque forms which were to come in the same countries a few centuries later.

In south France—Provence and Savoy—the picture is essentially different. Here the Roman provinces were in a region much of which had been settled by the Greeks centuries earlier—areas already enjoying a high degree of civilized and essentially classic culture. Moreover, instead of the forests, the river valleys, and the meadows of the north, one has the stony mountains and the great fertility which characterizes the Riviera. Here, the Roman buildings are of stone and the ornament of a delicacy and finish rivaling, if not exceeding, that of Roman itself. The perfection of the detail and the beauty of the forms of the Maison Carrée at Nîmes, with its delicate yet lavish Corinthian order, have made it deservedly one of the most famous classic temples.

The use of stone as the chief building material caused changes both in construction and in ornament. The Nymphaeum at Nîmes—sometimes called the Temple of Diana—has a semicircular stone vault which is a remarkable adaptation of design to material. It consists of a series of stone arches or ribs, each of which could be built separately with the same centering. On their outer sides are rested stone slabs, bridging from one to the next, which could be placed without any centering at all. Under each rib, at the sides, there is a column, set close to the wall, which gives actual and apparent support, and the whole has a richly rhythmical effect that is essentially the result of its brilliant construction.

The hardness of the stone led to a general simplification and flattening of decorative detail, and a general economy in its use, but with the greatest free imagination in placing. Especially characteristic is the use of small orders—either engaged columns or pilasters—as mere decorative frames around a large and simple arch.

North Africa was one of the wealthiest and most prosperous of the Roman provinces. With a climate quite different from the aridity that rules today, it was extremely productive, and the wealth which flowed into it gave rise to Roman cities of unusual splendor. Two of these, Timgad and Leptis Magna, have been excavated with some completeness; and, although both were cities of no especial fame, founded modestly enough as veterans' colonies, they had both by the end of the third century come to have a magnificence of architectural adornment out of all proportion to their size. Timgad, regularly planned on a rectangular basis, contains a large colonnaded forum, various marvelous temples, one of the most beautiful of Roman public libraries, and two bath groups of almost Roman size. The houses are all built around colonnaded courts, and the general impression is that of a city of both wealth and charm. Leptis Magna is especially famous for its magnificent thermae.

In both of these, as in other North African towns, the monumental architecture is purely of stone, although wood must have been used as the roofing and floor material for most of the houses, vaults being reserved for thermae and temples. The North African stonework is larger and grander than that of south France. There is in it all a certain bravura and daring which perhaps expresses the character of the inhabitants; sometimes there is about it a hint of the overostentatious, the *nouveau-riche*. The lavishness of the North African mosaic floors is famous. Chiefly of the third and fourth century, they are more naturalistic than in most other parts of the Roman Empire—full of views of buildings and even complete landscapes of rivers with their shores, the roaming animals, and all sorts of people doing all sorts of things. As decorations they are probably inferior to the more formalized patterns frequent elsewhere; yet, like the stone architecture itself, they have a certain verve which is delightful.

In Syria and the shores bordering the eastern Mediterranean generally, the purely stone architecture of the Romans produced perhaps its most successful, as well as its most colossal, achievements. In this region stone was the natural material not only for walls, columns, and vaults, but even in some cases for floors and roofs as well, owing to the lack of suitable building timber. Here, too, the old Hellenistic ideas of grandeur still persisted undimmed, and to them the Roman Empire with its building skill and its wealth brought merely new means of producing regal magnificence. The temple group at Baalbec (the ancient Heliopolis) was a combination of great courts, a tremendous propylaea, and enormous temples, so lavish and so huge, and yet essentially so disciplined and powerfully designed, that it may well be regarded as one of the climax productions of the Roman genius. Begun by Hadrian, this group represents what might be called the Baroque period in Roman architecture. The walls are almost everywhere decorated with niches between the great pilasters or columns which rise from ground to top; and each niche, often crowned with a shell top, is bordered in turn by its own pair of columns or pilasters and capped by a pointed or curved pediment, sometimes broken in true Baroque fashion. The scale is superb, and the temple itself and the exedras which project from the surrounding court were all vaulted in solid cut stone, carved with the richest of ornamented coffers. There seems, in fact, a kind of megalomania over the entire conception, which would be repellent were not the basic elements so thoroughly integrated—a megalomania which extended even to the size of the individual stones, for the foundation of the temple contains three great stones, the largest of which is nearly sixty feet long.

Yet, though this group was unique in its colossal size, the same ideals of monumental grandeur show in almost all the Roman work so widely scattered through the Syrian countries. Colonnades decorated the entire length of the important streets of many towns. Temples were preceded by profusely decorated courts, and approached by imposing flights of steps. The town of Gerasa, with its main street colonnaded from end to end, interrupted by impressive gateways and pylons at the main street intersections, and opening at one end into a large oval colonnaded forum, is characteristic. In Syria generally, during this period, the orders were used with essential correctness; yet changes in minor details from the standards of Italy are obvious. The oriental conception of decoration as a matter of surface ornament is everywhere apparent; and, instead of the full and varied relief of the best ornament of Rome, one has, again and again, complex lacelike patterns of leafage at small scale, with all the raised portions coming out to a plane and the background deeply cut away to give black shadows.

As the third and fourth centuries went on, this Syrian tendency toward change from Roman ideals became greater and greater. Band after band of intricate carving cuts across the earlier clear surfaces of the true classic forms. Molding profiles become flatter, in order to carry their surface decoration. Sometimes in the work of the fourth century the place of earlier

41. ROMAN TEMPLE AT NIHA, SYRIA; INTERIOR, RESTORED. (Krencker and Zschietzschmann: *Römische Temple in Syrien.*)

projecting moldings is taken by a series of incised bands, hardly breaking the surface of the wall. Even the capital itself changes, often becoming flatter in contour, with the leaves more closely forced against the central bell and sometimes all curling slightly out in the same direction as though blown by the wind.

The basic conceptions were different, too. Even such temples as those of Baalbec, while on the outside resembling the pedimented, colonnaded temples of the classic world to the west, within have quite a different aspect. The influence of the oriental mystery religions is upon them. The idea of the Holy of Holies, of sacred and mysterious and unapproachable places, is well developed. Almost all have elaborate colonnaded shrines at the end of the cella, raised on a high pedestal above the floor; and beneath them there is frequently an elaborate system of stairs and crypts and hidden entrances, which suggest the use of mysterious voices coming from unseen sources as an essential part of the ritual.

The lack of wood in part of this region caused many structural innovations, in the effort to roof over secular buildings, and later the early churches, with stone. Instead of the continuous or intersecting vaults of the Western world, the Roman architects here began to use widely spaced low piers, carrying wide low arches. On the arches little pieces of wall were built, until the whole was raised to a level bed to receive long stone slabs running from wall to wall, with which the entire area could be closed. Naturally these wide low arches gave rise to proportions totally different from those of the West, and the whole membering of these stone edifices, so different from the great masses of concrete in the Roman thermae, proves the inventiveness and the logic of the Roman constructors. These elements were aesthetically of enormous importance, for from this modified work there stemmed the tradition which finally blossomed in Byzantine architecture.

As the Roman Empire pushed more and more deeply into the East, this orientalizing modification naturally increased as well, and in the garrison town of Dura Europos, on the very borders of the Roman Empire, one finds buildings so different both from the Roman work elsewhere and from the purely oriental work which preceded it and followed it as to warrant almost a separate and distinct classification. Further excavation of other sites in similar locations would probably reveal much more of this free orientalized classic; and, just as the Syrian work influenced the Byzantine, so this influenced the early work of the Mohammedan conquerors.

It was natural, as Roman power pressed north and west to the Atlantic and the forests beyond the Rhine, and south and east to the Sahara Desert and the Tigro-Euphrates valley, that influences from all these varied lands should pour into Rome itself and profoundly affect its character. Indeed, it was the very strength of the Roman Empire that this was so, for this was the chief basis of that tolerance, that synthesizing adaptability, which made the Pax Romana a fact as well as a theory. If the Roman was at home at

Trier or Silchester or Timgad or Gerasa, so also, before many generations had passed, the Briton, the German, the African, and the Syrian were equally at home in Rome. Roman architecture of the later Empire felt this influence and reflected this fact as clearly as did Roman religion and Roman government.

Especially strong was the influence of the Orient. Judaism, Christianity, and the cult of Mithra all came from the East; all were popular in Rome from the first century on. Oriental luxury gradually replaced Greek restraint and Italian austerity in architecture as in life, and from the middle of the second century refinement of detail yielded to a mania of endless repetition. The Roman decorative ideal had altered, and, although occasional carving of the time of Constantine shows the earlier verve and spirit, the greater part is coarsened and crude in execution. Characteristically, in the Arch of Constantine there are two completely different types of work used together, with little apparent realization of their incompatibility: reliefs taken from earlier buildings and full of the old delicacy, and others done at the time, which are crude by contrast although marked with a new dramatic stylization.

This deterioration of carved detail was compensated for by a new grasp of the importance of color, a new skill in the use of sheets of colored marbles for wall sheathing, and the new developments in the art of mosaic which more and more came to be used on walls, preparing the way for the later glories of Byzantine mosaic that were to come. The best of the Italian mosaics of this type are those which so richly decorate the vaults of the fifth-century Tomb of Galla Placidia and the Baptistry of the Arians at Ravenna —works still full of purely classic details.

And the development of creative forms continued. Houses of the third century in Ostia are quite different from earlier ones; often C- or L-shaped, on deep narrow lots, they are built around a court or garden at one side. Sometimes, too, they have windows of two or three grouped arched lights, separated by columns which carry the arches on bolster-type capitals of unconventional design, quite like early Romanesque work.

Nor did the change in decorative skills entail any loss in structural inventiveness, for the engineering ability went on to create ever lighter vaults and more varied and ingenious structural designs all through the fourth century. The ten-sided Nymphaeum of the Licinian Gardens, sometimes called the Temple of Minerva Medica, from the end of the third century or the beginning of the fourth, shows an extraordinary skill in sustaining a masonry dome on the slimmest of supports, which are separated by wide-spreading niches, and the whole is lighted by large windows. Under

Diocletian, in the early fourth century, there was built a great bath, the Thermae of Diocletian, even grander and more skillful in its construction than the Baths of Caracalla. The Basilica of Constantine, the ruins of which still dominate all the space between the Colosseum and the Forum, is equally brilliant; and the Palace of Diocletian at Spalatro, of which more will be said later, shows a bold invention, both aesthetically—in its colonnaded court, in which the columns carry arches instead of a horizontal entablature—and structurally, that is typical of the new period.

It was largely a mere accident that the early churches built by Constantine and his followers show none of this engineering skill. The sudden necessity of building large churches as a sort of public recognition of the formal Christianizing of the Roman Empire made speed and structural inexpressiveness an essential quality in their design. Furthermore, the basilica type, which was adopted as that most fitting for the new worship, was not one to require elaborate structural experiments. Essentially, the basilica consisted of a rectangular hall separated into three aisles by two rows of columns. The central part, or nave, was carried up above the roofs of the side aisles in order that clerestory windows above the side-aisle roofs might flood it with light. At one end of the nave was a large apse, replacing the pagan Roman *bema,* the raised area satisfactory when the basilica was used as a law court. The roofs of both side aisles and nave were of simple wood trusses, so that the only vaulting necessary was the half dome over the apse; and the general lightness of the structure made the simplest and most rapid construction easy.

Thus the basilica church, which because of its sacred character carried on the Roman tradition into the Middle Ages, was a building which by its very nature incorporated within itself almost nothing of the Roman structural genius. This is perhaps one reason why the architects of the early Middle Ages made such slight use of the magnificent precedents set in the Roman baths and the greater Roman temples, and when they wished to vault their churches had to restudy the problem from the beginning.

But, if the basilicas were unimportant structurally, they were most important both decoratively and because of their general layout; and the Early Christian architecture, which is of course merely one phase of later Roman architecture, is of primary interest as the foundation of almost all later church design. The early basilicas achieved their effect through their long rows of gorgeous marble columns, the parade of arches which these supported, the lavish color decoration by marble, mosaic, and paint, and the furniture which early ritual made necessary. The walls, wherever possible, were sheathed on the inside with marble slabs. The pavement was also of rich marble slabs, and later of a special kind of mosaic formed of marble cut into comparatively large pieces and so arranged as to develop interesting geometric patternings. Above the marble wainscot, the walls would be painted with scenes of religious interest, often revealing traces of earlier pagan traditions. Around the apse the clergy were seated on marble benches, and in the center was a throne for the bishop. In front of the apse was placed the altar, covered in later times by a *baldachino* supported on four columns; and before this, and leading up to it, was the chancel for the priest, so-called from the *cancellae,* or screens, which surrounded it. This choir screen consisted, in early churches, of a simple railing of solid marble

42. BASILICA OF SAN CLEMENTE, ROME, SHOWING CHARACTERISTIC EARLY CHRISTIAN CHOIR ENCLOSURE AND CHANCEL. (Sturgis: *European Architecture.*)

some four feet high, with a rich cap and some decoration by inserts of colored marble or by paneling; and on each side of it rose a pulpit or *lectern*.

Over this general scheme the orientalized decorative sense of the later Roman Empire played with the greatest extravagance. Mosaics decorated the apse vault and sometimes, in the greater churches, the triumphal arch which fronted the apse and the walls of the clerestory, as well. In the search for grandeur, the side aisles were sometimes doubled and a *transept* or cross-hall placed in front of the apse, with its own triumphal arch separating it from the nave. At the front of the basilica there was always an enclosed *narthex* or porch, in which the catechumens or those preparing for reception into the church could be received, although they were prevented from access to the church proper; and outside of this, in turn, was a colonnaded court or *atrium,* with a fountain for ablutions in the center. In the earliest churches the apse was at the western end, and the priest officiated on the apse side of the altar—that is, the side away from the congregation. This enabled him to face east to the rising sun. In the sixth and seventh centuries a general change in ritual occurred, by which the priest officiated at the altar on the side nearest the congregation. Accordingly, in order that he might still face the east, the apse was placed at the eastern end of the church; this became later the established and canonical position. The change is well expressed in the basilica of St. Lorenzo Outside the Walls in Rome, where to an older basilica with a western apse a later basilica with the apse to the east was added in the thirteenth century.

In that way the early church began gradually to take form in the fourth and fifth centuries; and such great structures as the old St. Peter's, St. John Lateran, Sta. Maria Maggiore, and St. Paul's Outside the Walls, in sheer magnificence of decoration, as in their great size and the long perspective of their naves, rivaled the pagan structures.

The same necessity for speed in building, which seems to have somewhat controlled their design, also gave rise to another significant thing—the fact that many of their columns, capitals, and ornamental work generally were taken from older pagan buildings which had fallen either into disuse or, because of the change of religion, into actual disgrace. This habit increased as the centuries went on, as the importance of the city of Rome itself gradually yielded to that of other centers, and as poverty succeeded wealth and ignorance replaced knowledge, until many of the basilicas of the period from the sixth to the tenth centuries seem almost mere awkward picture puzzles of details of different sizes and different types put together as best they could be. Yet the importance of the early Christian basilicas canno, be overestimated. Rome as a pilgrimage center for all the Western world exerted enormous importance long after its economic, commercial, and governmental role had been played. In these Roman basilicas we already find almost all the essential distinguishing marks of the Christian church building as a type—the nave and side aisles, the apse and transept, the clerestory lighting, the glorified altar, the separated choir;—and so through these churches the influence of later Roman architecture went marching on down the centuries.

The Architecture of Islam

Interlude B

THE ARCHITECTURE OF ISLAM

THE Mohammedan Conquest is one of the most unexplainable stories in all history. Out from Arabia, there suddenly came, in the seventh century, a new militant emotional religion, which swept the Near East like a conflagration, gathered fire from fire, and gave a new point and purpose to all the smoldering fanaticisms of the Near-Eastern peoples. The Hegira, Mohammed's fateful trip from Mecca to Medina, took place in 622, and from that year the whole Moslem world takes its dates. Within twenty years the Moslems had gained complete control of Trans-Jordania and Syria; they had overthrown the power of Sassanian Persia and overwhelmed the weak Byzantine government of Egypt. Before fifty years had passed, large parts of North Africa were under their sway, and the end of a century from the time of Mohammed's death found them supreme even in Spain. Before this cataclysm of military conquest and this flood of religious excitement, the power of the Eastern Byzantine Empire fell away and the last glimmering remnants of the Roman cultural world crumbled to nothing.

The Mohammedans never formed a nation. They represented a religion and a culture; they were Syrians, Persians, Egyptians, Moroccans, as the case might be; and, though at least in the beginning there was a strong Arabian strain in the leaders, little by little the actual political power fell increasingly into the hands of the indigenous peoples. This was both the strength and the weakness of the Moslem movement—its strength because it raised the whole problem above any matters of national interest, its weakness because it led inevitably to the formation of many different and frequently hostile powers. Architecturally, this double quality is especially obvious; the religious unity changed all religious building types, and created certain common ways both of planning and of decorating the new buildings. Similarly, the national differences within the Moslem world show in the vital variations which exist in the Moslem architecture of different regions.

The central problem of Moslem architecture was design of the mosque, and to understand it something of the religious nature of Mohammedanism must be understood. Mohammedanism originally was a salvation religion, an attempt to purify the existing Arabian beliefs, which had apparently been founded on a strange mixture of Christian, Jewish, and pagan elements, and to return to a clearer, a simpler, and a more living conception of the oneness of God and the necessity for personal and congregational worship. At first it was probably an antiritualistic religion, rebelling against the semi-pagan symbols which had been currently accepted; only later, like all religions, it built up its own ritualism, its own systems of specially educated clergy.

Founded essentially on the old Jewish Ten Commandments, it aimed to take the second of these with a much more strict literalness than had been the custom, and thus to strip from the worship building—the mosque—any representations or symbols which could ever be considered in the slightest degree idolatrous. The only symbol which was permitted was an indication, in one wall of the mosque, of the direction of Mecca, toward which good Mohammedans were supposed to face when they prayed. This generally took the form of a niche recessed in the wall, called the *mihrab*. Then a hall was necessary, large enough to contain all the people served by the mosque, and so arranged that they could stand in long lines facing the mihrab. Thus, colonnaded halls were developed as the simplest solution to this problem, often with flat roofs, and frequently with the long dimension parallel to the mihrab wall. Since the reading of the sacred book (the Koran) and sermons played an important part in the Moslem service, a pulpit, the *mimbar* or *mimber,* was an indispensable element. It usually flanked the mihrab and often consisted of a small raised platform, approached from in front by a long steep flight of stairs, and with some sort of canopy or sounding board above it, usually shaped like a tall pyramidal spire. In front of the prayer hall there was frequently an open court, surrounded by colonnades or arcades and containing in the center a fountain of running water, where the faithful could perform the ritual ablutions before the service. Since Mohammed had decreed a certain number of prayer periods during each day, a *minaret* or tower became a necessary part of the mosque; from this the muezzin could call the people to prayer by singing the sacred words in a strange, weird chant in all directions over the camp or the city. All of these elements took the most varied forms in different parts of the world under Moslem control, but the general conception held true throughout.

Certain decorative qualities also became common. The religious com

mandment against idolatry played a continuously greater role in Mohammedan ornament as time went on. It was interpreted in different ways in
different parts of the Moslem world. The Persians always remained more
free in their use of animals and figures in decoration than did other Moslem
peoples, and Moslems of the earlier times much freer than those of later
eras; but everywhere the commandment was followed in the mosques. This
turned the Moslem decorative genius away from representation into abstract
paths, and elaborate geometrical interlaces, coupled with a decorative use

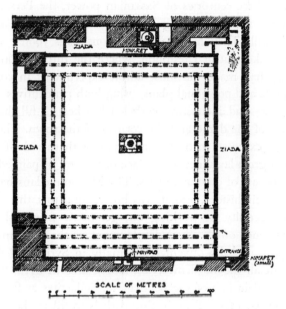

SCALE OF METRES

43. MOSQUE OF IBN TULUN, CAIRO; PLAN. (Briggs: *Muhammadan Architecture in
Egypt and Syria.*)

of lettering by means of which sacred texts could be magnificently displayed, became flourishing elements in Moslem decoration. At first, foliated
ornament, even ornament handled quite naturalistically in the old classic
manner, was accepted without question; but later, either because of growing
strictness in interpreting the laws, or because of the general trend toward
the abstract which the law had set up, even foliage was admitted grudgingly
—and then only if much conventionalized.

When the Mohammedans started on their career of conquest, they had
little if any artistic tradition behind them. Almost everywhere in the Moslem
world, they were in the position of comparatively untutored builders in lands
where native building traditions were strong, and where impressive native

monuments of Byzantine, Early Christian, Sassanian, or Roman type already existed. Naturally they borrowed wholesale; not only did they use again and again capitals and columns and bits of architectural detail taken piece-meal from Roman structures, but they had no hesitation whatsoever in using the skills of Byzantine craftsmen and of Persian masons in building and decorating their new structures.

In all of this borrowing, perhaps that which played the most revolutionary, if not the most important, part was the borrowing from Sassanian Persia. All through the three centuries of Sassanian power, the Persians had gone on experimenting with and using all kinds of vaults with an advancing ingenuity and skill. They had built enormous halls roofed with oval or parabolic vaults like that at Ctesiphon, where the throne room was eighty feet wide. They had made the most adroit experiments in combining the dome with square and polygonal plans, using both pendentives and diagonal arches—squinches—and interesting corbeled brackets to fill the corners be-tween the circle of the dome and the corners of the room. These buildings had been chiefly executed in brick, and along with this skillful brick con-struction went a great lavishness of surface ornament, in painted or modeled plaster, and some use of decorative tiles. The Mohammedans had conquered Persia early in their history, and it was but natural that this skill in brick vaulting, this ingenuity in working out geometric forms, should have a tremendous influence on the final development of the Mohammedan style. The pointed arch, probably invented originally in Syria, was developed to a high degree in all the Moslem styles, and it was in Syria that stalactite work first occurred in lieu of the pendentive. Stalactites at first were struc-tural elements—rows of small projecting corbels to fill in the upper corners of a square room to the circle required for a dome. But later stalactites were purely decorative—often of plaster or even, in Persia, of mirrored glass—and applied or hung to the actual hidden construction.

The Byzantine borrowings are naturally heaviest in Syria, Egypt, and Turkey. From the Eastern Empire the Mohammedans learned the Byzan-tine type of dome on pendentives, the continuous arcade, and much of that intricate kind of surface ornament to which they gave their own interpre-tation. Byzantine Greek craftsmen decorated the mihrab of the mosque at Cordova, and the mosaics on the inside of the "Dome of the Rock" in Jeru-salem—one of the most sacred of all mosques—are purely Byzantine in design, color, and workmanship. In Damascus the great mosque, built about A.D. 720, used so many Early Christian forms and followed the basilican

scheme so closely that for years there was much discussion as to whether
the work itself was actually Christian or Moslem. The mosque arcades
within have mosaicked decorations of lovely and freely drawn landscapes and
buildings in which the Greek hand is unmistakable.

From the Romans the Moslems took the acanthus-leaf decoration and the
idea of the Corinthian capital. Many mosques, like those at Kairouan and
Cordova, used actual ancient Corinthian capitals; and later Moslem capitals
were often based on the Corinthian scheme in general pattern, although the
tendency toward abstraction gradually removed all remaining signs of realism from the carving of the leaves. The same thing happened to the Roman

·DIAGRAM· SHOWING·   ·FROM·THE·   ·DOORWAY· FROM·
·ELEMENTARY·FORMS·   ·PORCH·OF·A·SCHOOL·   ·MOSQUE·KHAN·ASAD PASHA·
·OF·STALACTITES·   ·AT·JERUSALEM·   ·AT· DAMASCUS·
                        REDRAWN· FROM· BRIGGS·

44. TYPICAL STALACTITE FORMS, AND TWO APPLICATIONS. (Drawn by the author,
the two examples from Briggs.)

acanthus leaf; at first used in ways extraordinarily classic and profuse, as in
the ornament on the front of the palace at Mschatta in Trans-Jordania—a
building of the seventh century, quite Roman in its plan, as it was in much
of its detail,—the acanthus leaf gradually became more and more angular,
more and more simple in surface, and more and more involved in elaborate
geometric interlaces, until the almost purely abstract leafage which is to be
found in the Alhambra was developed.

Thus, out of many sources, the various local styles of Moslem architecture
arose.

One of the earliest of Moslem styles appeared in parts of Syria, in Trans-
Jordania, and in what is now Iraq; it influenced deeply much of the Moslem
building in Egypt, North Africa, and even far-away Spain. The great
Abbasid mosque of Samara, now in ruins, was typical of the early mosque

type. The prayer hall consisted of long aisles between piers supporting a flat roof. The minaret is of the heavy, primitive type, almost like a miniature Assyrian ziggurat, with a stair running around from ground to top spirally. There is a brick wall around the whole, with round towers at the corners, as though for fortification. Very similar to this is the mosque of Ibn Tulun in Cairo, A.D. 879. Here there are arcades of pointed arches, supported on rectangular piers with delicate colonnettes on the corners, and there is a simply ordered surface decoration of intricate, almost Byzantine type, which runs around the arches and across the top of the piers. In Palestine and Damascus the influence of Christian church types is much stronger. Occasionally the early Mohammedan mosque builders even rebuilt on old Early Christian foundations, and frequently re-used much of the earlier Roman and Early Christian detail; this was the case with the famous El Aksa mosque (A.D. 688) in Jerusalem. Only in the Dome of the Rock (the so-called Mosque of Omar) was a new type essayed; yet this, with its dominant central dome, was as close a modification of the Byzantine domed polygonal churches as El Aksa was of the basilica type.

Recent excavations in various parts of Syria and Iraq have unearthed more and more evidence of the earliest Mohammedan buildings, and their eclectic nature is increasingly apparent. Several palaces are among these ruins. In them the influence of the great courts and the rich bathing establishments of Roman work is plain, but there is also manifest much direct borrowing from Persia, so that sometimes it is almost a matter of doubt whether the building is a Sassanian or a Moslem construction. Literary evidences describe the court life of the Umayyads and the Abbasids down to the time of Harun Al-Rashid as of the utmost luxury, conducted in buildings of sumptuous splendor. Of all this early secular work little enough remains. We may recognize, however, in the descriptions the natural Mohammedan love for rich surface ornament, for bright color, and for gardens. We may imagine these palaces simple brick constructions, perhaps somewhat Roman in plan, with several colonnaded courts, with a few large vaulted halls, and owing their lavishness of effect to wall paintings, to intricate modeled plasterwork, and to an extravagant use of those magnificent textiles which the Mohammedans have always loved. Typical is the early palace of Qusair Amra in Trans-Jordania, built probably in the first half of the eighth century, which is richly painted with charming frescoes of almost purely pagan classic type, in which the nude is used freely and there are many references both to classic myth and to Byzantine rulers. Its lavish yet delicate decoration is characteristic of the luxury of the Abbasid court. And we may imagine these buildings set in walled gardens, the design of which combined something of the formality of ancient Rome with that of early Persia, with the free plash of fountains everywhere and with water, so rare and so valued in these flat and arid lands, carried through the garden in marble-lined canals.

Later, the whole architecture of this part of the world was deeply affected by the Turkish conquests, and the new Turkish power sweeping in from the north and east gave a new direction toward monumentality in Moslem building. The Turks had learned the Byzantine lesson better than any of their coreligionists, and more and more the low dome on pendentives typical of Constantinople began to make its appearance in the mosques of this region. Much of Mohammedan Cairo owes its present appearance to this later Turkish influence in Moslem design; and the tombs of the Mamelukes and such later mosques as that of Kaid Bey, however different in their ornament, are essentially Turkish in their conception.

Many of the more primitive types of Moslem architecture were perpetuated for a long time in North Africa, which seems to have long preserved the cultural impress of the Umayyads—the original dynasty of the Arabian caliphs—despite changing rulers and dynastic feuds. Thus the mosque at Kairouan is one of the oldest, if not the oldest, of the mosques still in good preservation and use. Traditionally founded as early as A.D. 670, it was rebuilt in its present state during the ninth century. It has the usual pillared hall and arcaded court, but the tendency toward an emphasis on symbolic and ritual features has already in the rebuilding produced changes in the original absolute simplicity. The cross-aisle of the hall nearest the mihrab wall is higher than the others, and a similar higher aisle extends at right angles from the mihrab to the court; where they intersect, the area directly in front of the mihrab is enlarged and covered with a dome, as though to emphasize the special sacredness of this spot. In a bay adjacent to this crossing is the enclosed space where the prince worshiped—called, in the Moorish work of North Africa and Spain, the *maksura*.

Another early example of a highly developed mosque of the same kind is that at Cordova, in Spain; but here the development shows that special local variations have already occurred, setting apart the Moorish work from other work in Moslem countries. There is a kind of phantasy about the handling of the structural members which is a new thing—a delight in using complicated forms of arches, cusped and of horseshoe shape, in order to get a sufficient height in the hall and at the same time to use comparatively low columns. The arches are raised tier on tier above each other, giving a bewildering complexity to the upper portions of the building. A love of color appears in arches of alternate voussoirs of light marble and dark brick. In the maksura the dome is especially rich and complicated, supported on ingeniously intersected arches which cut down the total span and serve, like pendentives, to give an approximately circular support for the dome over the square below. The mihrab itself is surrounded by a field of rich mosaic of Byzantine type; in that at least the older fashions remained strong. The building shows two other interesting Moorish developments: one an extraordinary complexity of skillful carpentry in the wooden ceilings, the other the development of intricate plaster surface ornament in which leaf arabesques and geometric forms and Arabic lettering are welded together into a closely organized pattern.

Still another specifically Moorish building element almost universal in North Africa and Spain is the Moorish minaret. This always takes the form of a square tower of considerable height, with its sides often profusely patterned in paneled brickwork; it carries a smaller, more open stage, usually crowned with a dome. It was from the area at the top of the square portion that the muezzin sang the call to prayer. These towers are famous for their beauty of proportion, and have influenced deeply many types of Renaissance tower built centuries later. The suggestion has been made that these Moorish minarets, in turn, had been influenced by the sign of the great ancient *pharos* or lighthouse in Alexandria. The famous Giralda tower in Seville is a characteristic example of the type, although its recessed upper stages are Christian and Renaissance additions.

The Moorish designers produced perhaps the loveliest of all Moslem houses. In their courtyard plans there is possibly a reminiscence of Roman houses and villas, but in the richness of decoration in modeled stucco relief, in black-and-white arcading, and in those elaborate geometric ceilings which the Spanish called *artesonados* they are unique. One special feature is the importance of fountains and of water in their design, so that the trickle or plash of fountain and the freshness of running water are almost constantly at hand to give relief from burning sun and dry, desert-blown winds. During the later years of the Moslem occupation of Spain, this Moorish architecture reached its highest point in complex delicacy; and the Alhambra at Granada, a royal palace completed during the fourteenth century, reveals that special combination of intricate, refined surface ornament, of light supports, of plaster arabesques, of cusped arches, of large cool halls—wainscoted below in geometrical patterns of glazed tile and above in polychromed plaster relief, and crowned with lavish wooden ceilings in which combinations of stalactite forms and geometrical interlaces give a sense of strangely light and airy complexity,—of sunny gardened courts and cool shadowed rooms, which is the essence of the later Moorish house. In plan it is ingenious yet organ-ized. Especially characteristic is the way in which the water from central fountains is led by marble-lined channels into all the important rooms, as well as the elaborate development of a set of bath chambers of almost Roman luxury. The art of the Alhambra is a brilliant art, but already there are signs of decadence within it. It is overjeweled, overornamented. Only the delicacy of the motifs keeps it from vulgarity. Some of the larger houses and palaces of Morocco and Algiers, or of Tunis, are perhaps even better, because of their greater restraint.

Moorish architecture played an important part in building history; its influence, alike in craftsmanship and in the formation of basic aesthetic tastes, was powerful in Spain long after the capture of Granada by Ferdi-nand and Isabella. Its emphasis on the decoration of doors, its use of tiles, and its love of surface richness are dominant all through Renaissance and Baroque Spain, and came with the Spaniards to the Western Hemisphere; even today, in Mexico or Peru, the trace of Moorish tastes and Moorish ways may still at times be read.

The Sassanian builders of Persia had been brilliant designers and daring constructors; so that it is not strange to find over all the Moslem work in Persia a spirit of grandeur and a definite architectonic kind of composition often lacking in other Moslem work. Little Persian work prior to the Mongol conquest exists except in fragments. It shows simplicity of scheme and detail, and even the earliest Mongol work, like the Tomb of Timur, is basically simple. But from the fourteenth century on there was an amazing efflores-cence of building skill, in both planning and decoration. All the possible changes were rung on the pointed arch, the dome, and the stalactites. A love of complication led to the support of domes on interlacing arches and the hiding of construction with an extraordinary lavishness of decorative ribs and hung stalactite work. Even elaborate ribbed vaults, apparently structu-ral, are often only decorative embellishments, although Persian skill in build-ing all kinds of vaulting with little centering was—and continues—great. Earlier theories that Persian intersecting and ribbed vaults influenced Gothic construction are no longer tenable, for we now know the Persian examples are from one to four centuries later than Gothic cathedrals.

The Persians had been indubitably great builders in brick, and it was as a brick architecture that Mohammedan building in Persia evolved. The region had been notable not only for plain brick but for all sorts of other highly developed ceramics, like the polychrome wall tiles of Babylonian buildings. Apparently this art had never died, and under the Moslem builders it received a new, vivid advancement. New kinds of lustrous and metallic glazes were invented, new types of composition in which the geometry of the Moslem tradition was united with the naturalism of

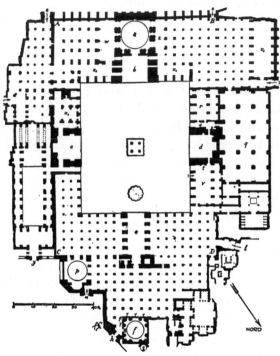

45. GREAT MOSQUE, ISFAHAN; PLAN. (*Ars Islamica.*) A, DOMED HALL WITH MIHRAB. B, C, D, E, IWANS. F, SELDJUK DOMED HALL. V, WINTER HALL.

Sassanian design. The Persians never accepted so completely as other Moslems the idea that representations of animals or plants or even people was a violation of the second commandment. Lovely flower forms were the basis of exquisite tiles, as they were of Persian textile patterns, and murals of scenes of palace life or of hunting often decorated the interiors of the secular buildings.

But it was in architectural form rather than in decoration that the greatest quality of the Persian building genius emerged—a sense of monumental composition, of great open planning, of creative structure. Even the basic mosque idea became changed. The Persian search for monumental forms led them to substitute for the plain pillared hall a great vaulted, open-front room called the *liwan* (Arabic *iwan*), and the façade of this was made by a single wide arch frequently framed between two slender minarets. The principal forms were simple, as befitted the building material, brick; over the wide surfaces achieved by this simplicity was a rich surface decoration either in mosaic brick or, still more characteristic, in glazed tile. The gorgeous blues, blue-greens, yellows, and pearl whites of this tile gave to the later Persian buildings a polychrome radiance almost unequaled. Typical, too, of the Persian building skill was the love of the domed form, and domes became more and more the salient feature of the mosques, so that the characteristic later composition was a domed hall fronted by a great arched porch that was flanked by two minarets, which also enframed the dome. From the thirteenth century onward the dome was treated with greater and greater freedom. Usually a high drum supported an exterior dome above the interior ceiling dome, and the exterior dome came to take all kinds of shapes. Almost always pointed at the top, it swelled out near the bottom to a width greater than that of its supporting drum, and then contracted to the drum width in a continuous curve, giving a sort of onion shape to the silhouette. Often timber braces and ties were built in to give it stability.

Since mosques were often connected with educational centers, a kind of university building was developed—the *medresa*. In this a large square arcaded court was accented by three great liwans in the centers of three of its sides; the center of the fourth side would be a monumental gateway. The contrast between the high liwan façades with their great arches and the lower arcaded court wings gave superb scale to these structures, and gave also a kind of architectonic power too little found in some of the other Moslem buildings. These medresas affected much of the later work in Egypt, North Africa, and India.

The same qualities of great scale and powerful general composition can be seen in the city planning and public works which the Persian Empire undertook—especially bridges and open squares. Particularly impressive is the great square of Isfahan, with the ranked public buildings and mosques around it.

In the later Persian Empire another type of work received great attention —the building of palaces and palace pavilions of the lightest and most delicate type, in wood, ornamented with a rich polychrome painting. A beautiful example is the pavilion, known as the *Palace of the Forty Columns*, in the palace at Isfahan.

Moslem work in India shows the astounding ability of Moslem culture to assimilate and use the native forms current in the areas conquered. Mohammedan work in India is of course dominantly under Persian influences, as it was the Persians who, from the eleventh century on, began winning more and more of the peninsula for the new religion. Nevertheless, Indian work could never be mistaken for Persian; especially in the earlier examples of the thirteenth and fourteenth centuries it is Indian forms of column and

46. THE TELEGRAPHER'S HOUSE, SHIRAZ. (Drawing by the late Bertram G. Goodhue; from *A Book of Architectural and Decorative Drawings*.)

beam, Indian corbeled and bracketed domes and ceilings, Indian ornamental motifs which give character to the buildings. Even later, in Mogul times in the sixteenth and seventeenth centuries, though the Persian domes and minarets and pointed arches had now become common, they were decorated with a lavishness of pierced marble, of inlay, and of carved foliated ornament in which the Indian taste was supreme.

Perhaps the climate and the landscape affected the conquerors. At any rate, there grew up in their work an expression of a delight in sensuous beauty, a kind of languorous luxury, quite unlike any Mohammedan work elsewhere. Perhaps, too, Indian philosophy had its influence; surely, in the almost endless profusion of jeweled workmanship there is a touch of the

feeling of activity for its own sake rather than for the sake of the end involved. The palaces of Delhi, of Agra, of Fatehpur Sikri, of Lahore, and of
Udaipur are perhaps the nearest approach to the true fairy-tale palace the
world has ever known, the most complete embodiments of an almost universal human dream. These vast combinations of courts and halls, passages
and gardens, prodigal bathing establishments and private rooms, each one
decorated as though it were almost the only thing in the universe to which
all mankind's efforts at designed elaboration had been directed, have an
astonishing character of emotional beauty.

In the palaces there are always two great halls: one, the larger, the
diwan-i-aum, for public audiences; the other, the *diwan-i-khass,* for more
private receptions. These are usually open arcaded halls without walls,
beautiful in proportion and detail, and on them is showered the rarest work
of inlayer and carver. In the difference between these effulgent structures
and the slim, discreet pavilions of the Persian palaces can be readily seen
the differences between buildings erected by the same or similar courts
in the two different countries. Of the detail forms which these buildings
take it need only be said that in them, although the pointed Persian arch
remains an almost constant feature, the details of carving and of cornice,
and especially the bays and loggias which decorate the great exterior walls,
have roots purely in the Hindu rather than in the Mohammedan tradition.
The curved roofs, the composition by means of repeated horizontal lines,
the rounded projections—these are all notes purely indigenous.

In the mosques the influence of Moslem Persia is stronger. Certain of
the earlier mosques, to be sure—as in the case of the ruined mosque in Old
Delhi with its marvelous reeded minaret, the Kutub Minar, and the old
mosque at Ajmir,—use the molded columns and the bracketed domes of
Hindu architecture, but later the pointed arch and the constructive dome of
Persia became universal. Persian, as well, was the composition on the gateways of some of the great mosques, with their liwan-arched fronts flanked
by minarets and carrying a dome. But the Indian architects were never
content merely to copy the Persian forms; they were continually searching
for new kinds of expression for the colonnaded prayer halls and the arcaded
courts. Characteristic was the Kalburgah mosque, a vast rectangular construction of many columns forming arcaded aisles in both directions, with
a domed maksoura at the mihrab three aisles wide in both directions, and a
wider narthex arcade running around three sides and accented by domes
at the corners. Other typical examples are the great mosque at Bijapur, of
the sixteenth century, with its superb entrance gateway; and the beautiful

mosque at Delhi, with its three domes, its simple niched entrance, its flower-like shrines and minaret details.

The two climax buildings of Mogul architecture in India are both tombs. The first is the tomb of Mahmud in Bijapur, known as Gol Gunbaz, built in 1626-56. A vast square building, 135 feet across inside its thick walls, it is crowned by a dome the apex of which is 198 feet above the floor. The dome is supported on a system of intersecting arches rising from eight points in the interior and forming two intersecting squares. The exterior is as grand

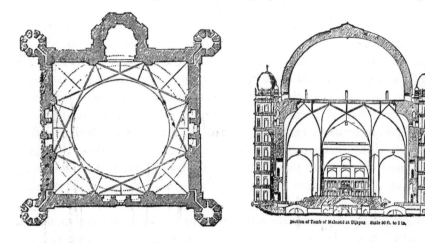

Section of Tomb of Mahmud at Bijapur   Scale 50 ft. to 1 in.

47. TOMB OF MAHMUD, BIJAPUR; PLAN AND SECTION. (Fergusson: *A History of Indian and Eastern Architecture.*)

in its simple mass as the conception is daring; the quiet surfaces of its four walls are given magnificent scale by the tiered towers at the corners, the intricate pierced work of the windows and doors in the center of each side, and the rich arcaded cornice which crowns the square portion.

The other building is of course the Taj Mahal, completed in A.D. 1650, perhaps the most exquisite sepulchral structure in the world, erected by the emperor, Shah Jehan, to memorialize his love for his favorite wife, Mumtaz Mahal. The Taj Mahal has to a superlative degree that combination of basic simplicity of conception with interesting complexity of detail which is a part of all of the best Indian architecture. The purity of its white marble dome on a square base, the rhythms of its minarets, its niched entrances, and its wall panels, and the delicate color radiance of the elaborate inlays of colored marbles and semiprecious stones which pattern it are all sensitively related to each other and form a moving evidence of a singularly percep-tive love of the beautiful. Nowhere else perhaps has detail as lavish as this, or as fine as the pierced marble screen which surrounds the cenotaphs within, been used to enhance so perfectly a basic scheme so clear and pure. The extraordinary difference between the Taj Mahal and the tomb of Mahmud, each in its way supreme, is a striking proof of the imagination and sensitiveness of the architects of Moslem India.

Mohammedanism penetrated even into China, and colonies of Chinese in many parts of that great country still worship in their own mosques. In these the influence of Chinese temple forms and of Chinese detail is completely dominant; only the pointed arch over the mihrab, an occasional dome, and the Arabic letters formed into arabesques to decorate it show the influence of the Moslem cultural centers so far away to the west. Elsewhere, in these mosques, the courtyard forms, the bracketed eaves, and the curved roofs are all essentially Chinese.

The history of the successive waves of Turkish invaders into the Near-Eastern world is complicated. Converted early in their aggressive career to the Moslem faith, the Turks brought to Moslem culture a new kind of energy, and gave to all of their artistic productions a quality fundamentally their own. Coming from the East, their first contacts with Moslem art had been in Persia; and, just as Persian and Arabic words became incorporated in the Turkish language, so the pointed arch of Persia, the stalactite ornaments of the Moslem Near East, and Persian ceramics became alike vital influences in Turkish architecture.

Yet, as they pressed more and more deeply into Asia Minor, finally sweeping up and around the shores of the Black Sea, crossing the Hellespont, establishing their power widely in the Balkans, and overwhelming at last the final, weak, decadent Eastern Empire, it was Byzantine architecture which became their greatest inspiration. In various Asiatic buildings of the thirteenth and fourteenth centuries, the Turkish style is already well developed. The mosques tend to become simple domed rooms, sometimes with colonnaded side aisles, and the domes are on pendentives in the Armenian and Byzantine manner. Cut stone is used a great deal, delicately molded, and characteristic column capitals based on the stalactite motif rather than on foliage become the rule. The entrance doors were sharply accented; they were often placed in tall niches enframed in a great pointed arch, so that the entrance motif extended the whole height of the wall. The mosques are usually fronted with square arcades, each bay of which carries its own little dome on pendentives; and these successive little domes, covered with lead, form an interesting prelude to the great lead-covered dome over the mosque proper. The Turkish minaret too achieved its own special character. The Persian minarets had been slender cylindrical towers, capped with a dome-covered, arcaded pinnacle, around which was the corbeled balcony for the muezzin. From the Persians the Turks took the slim cylindrical pattern; but, instead of the domelike pinnacle, they substituted a high conical roof of wood, and often had two or more galleries in the total height.

After the conquest of Constantinople, not only was the Byzantine influence much increased by the conquerors' admiration of the glorious churches of Constantinople, but architects of Greek family began to come to the fore, and the greatest of all, Sinān, the architect of Suleiman the Magnificent, was Greek. Under this new flood of Byzantine enthusiasm Turkish architecture became more than ever an architecture of domes. Baths, bazaars, and mosques all used domes to roof every possible space. In fact, the Turks took the Byzantine version of elaborate buildings covered with domes, in which the outer, exposed surface is merely the lead-covered exterior of the interior dome, and carried it to a perfection of development far beyond any which the Byzantines had accomplished. They abandoned entirely the later Byzantine types of church, with small domes and high drums, in favor of concentrating on the great simplicities of Santa Sophia. Everywhere the walls are so arranged as to leave the elaborate roofing vaults exposed to view, and these in turn are designed with an admirable sense of their relation to each other and to the whole dome; so that the developed Turkish mosque of the sixteenth or seventeenth century has a composition in which the walls play an almost subsidiary part, and act merely as a pedestal above which spring the half domes, big and little, leading the eye inevitably to the big swelling curve of the great central dome. The tremendous mass of the mosque is prepared for by the walls and little domes of the court, and emphasized by the superb slim height of the white minarets, often in pairs, sometimes at the four corners—in the mosque of Ahmed in Constantinople there are six. Even in the smaller mosques, the same effect is sought in plainer ways, and the functional simplicity of some of the later examples is striking. Typical is the eighteenth-century mosque called the *Nuri Osmanieh*—"the lantern of Osman"—where the mosque consists of a single square room covered by a single dome on pendentives. The round-topped walls of the four sides are pierced with many windows; the swelling curves of the vault rise naturally and easily from the corner piers.

On the interior of the mosques the Byzantine influence is less clear; here, as in much of the decorative detail, it is the Persian precedent which has controlled. The mihrab niches are often set in great rectangular panels covered with glazed tile from Anatolian kilns, with rich patterns of leaves and flowers; and their characteristic blue-greens, yellows, whites, and little touches of red give a lively sparkle. Sometimes whole mosque walls are so covered. But at times this search for surface brilliance of Persian type has led to the expedient of painting arabesques over vast areas of white plaster in dome and ceiling and upper wall—arabesques frequently as crude in execution as they are coarse in design. Nevertheless, generally speaking, the search for interior effect pointed always toward a greater and greater simplicity, a larger scale, a clarifying of detail; and such a hall as that of the Suleimanieh mosque in Constantinople is magnificent in its clear composition, its lovely sense of wide spaces so vividly covered, and in the touches of richness and color given by the tiled mihrab, the marble columns, and the lustrous jeweled windows of colored glass set into plaster frames.

From the end of the seventeenth century on, European influence began to creep into Turkish work with growing strength. French Rococo ideas affected the decorative carving of almost all the eighteenth-century work, giving swirling lines of foliage and C-scrolls neither all European nor yet all of the East, but largely subduing the old dependence on Persian decorative forms. Later still, in the nineteenth century, when Turkey was seeking to become a Western power, all the baggage of nineteenth-century eclecticism was taken over and had added to it a new kind of orientalized eclecticism from the forms of the Mohammedan East. This weird mixture is especially well shown in the great palaces which later sultans built along the Bosphorus, like Beylerbey and Dolma Baghtche, where the exteriors are rich with pilaster and entablature and encrusted with a wilderness of Rococo ornament, and the interiors vary from vulgar imitations of nineteenth-century European palace halls to fantastic recreations of oriental types, Persian and Turkish, that sometimes achieve almost the dreamlike character of the Mogul work in India.

The Turks developed another interesting type of architecture besides that seen in the mosques and the palaces. Turkish baths were made into elaborate and beautifully planned combinations of domed chambers, simple yet graceful and in the larger examples monumental, and lovely because of their perfect fitness for their function. Bazaars and *khans*, or caravanserais—vast courts surrounded with arcades to furnish shelter for both the men and the beasts of the traveling caravans of merchants,—all were designed with a basic sense of monumental planning and of dignified if simple decoration. Town fountains, too, became a field for elaborate decoration, as they had in medieval Europe. Often the fountains are grouped around a square cistern, and the whole space is covered by a widespreading roof, often domed in the center and lavishly decorated in carving and color.

The Turkish houses also have distinction. Generally the upper stories are of frame, while the ground floor is of stone. The upper floors have many projecting bays and broad eaves to shelter the numerous windows beneath. The whole is simple, direct, functional, and remarkable for the tremendous area of glass in the long strings of windows which light the chief halls.

Thus, Moslem culture expressed itself in a different guise for each of the great national or racial groups which adopted it. To them all it brought the inspiration of a new way of thinking about life, and new problems. To them all it allowed almost complete freedom in using this new inspiration and solving these new problems in their own way, based on their own special past and their own special skills. This is perhaps the reason for the tremendous vitality which characterized Mohammedan building, and for the new life that it brought to decadent and dying forms of architecture. Just as Mohammedan science and Mohammedan medicine preserved, improved, and finally passed on to the Western world many of the writings and much of the knowledge of the ancient world, so Mohammedan architecture was important both because of its own superb solutions of many of the great building problems, and because it became the great mediating force between the buildings of the Eastern world and the West, as well as one of the great inspirations and sources behind much of the building development of the Gothic period and the Renaissance.

BOOK IV

Medieval Architecture

Chapter 10

THE DECAY OF ROME, AND ITS
CONQUERORS AS BUILDERS

AUSONIUS, living in Bordeaux at the end of the fourth century, knew nothing of the great changes that were going on around him. This Roman gentleman and poet sings of the waters of the Moselle in liquid words, hauntingly lovely, and, Christian though he was, his verse is full of the old pagan sensual freedom. He sings the delights of a love all too promiscuous, with a vividness almost Catullan. So the wealthy young Roman of the same period, walking through the Forum and seeing the columned façades of the temples and the arcades of the basilicas, could have had little realization that all the things he saw were doomed. The gorgeousness and the lavish grandeur of the new churches that Constantine had built, the glittering splendors of the Lateran Palace, the magnificent size and dignity of the basilica which Constantine had so recently completed on the Sacra Via all of these would seem to indicate for the future only a continued growth in building skill and resplendent luxury. His own clothes and those of his companions had a new richness in color and design almost barbaric. If they talked of politics or of the Empire, it was probably of the new ascendance of Milan rather than of any happenings on the distant frontiers. The fall of Rome was a long process, and few of those who lived during it realized it as a fact.

In its own greatness lay the germs of Rome's decay. Rome gave the world organization, only to develop at last a system so complex, so unwieldy, that it began to crumble with its own weight. Too many possibilities for the misuse of power lay in the hands of provincial governors, so that the later emperors, from the Antonines onward, were forced to take more and more power into their own hands, until the final absolutism of the Empire of Constantine. Yet even this absolutism had its weakness; no one individual, no matter how good his intentions, could control the wide-flung agencies beneath him—and the intentions of many of these later despots could hardly be called good

Rome had created vast wealth in the Mediterranean world, only to find this wealth itself a burden, as it became more and more concentrated in the hands of a few families. The senators, the emperors, and the imperial officers all too often saw their power only as a means of increasing their fortunes, and little by little creative wealth was sucked from the countryside into the great cities, there to become largely sterile or to be expended only in noncreative luxuries. Rome became a civilization which, instead of creating capital, lived on its capital—and more and more on its capital alone. The great ships that bore the grain from all the ports of the Mediterranean, and poured it into the waiting warehouses of Ostia, carried back little that was a worthy exchange. Land itself became increasingly a monopoly of the wealthy classes, and the old native yeoman landowners, who had been the strength of Rome and its provinces, tended to fall into the position of mere tenant farmers, almost serfs, with little feeling of responsibility toward their land. Moreover, with the growing concentration of wealth in the great cities, people as well as wealth streamed into them, leaving hopeless farms for the free if wasteful life of the Roman proletariat.

The great novel of Petronius not only shows the beginnings of a realistic fiction, but also leads us into the devious back streets of Rome and the provincial towns, streets teeming with a picaresque population living largely by its wits and the combined generosity of wealthy show-offs and of the state. This was as early as the time of Nero, and, as later this mass of nonproductive humanity increased in all the towns by leaps and bounds, disaster became inevitable. Of course, Petronius does not give the entire picture; for, if he describes a city of rogues, the existing buildings show as well a city of hard-working, industrious bourgeoisie, of manufacturers and businessmen. As we have seen, the more crowded the city became, the greater was the problem of its sanitation; the more the country emptied, the more the irrigation ditches became clogged or broken. Farm land changed gradually into waste or swamp, and the ubiquitous mosquito found ideal breeding places throughout the Roman campagna. Malaria waxed mightily, until the whole low country around Rome gained the evil reputation as a breeder of fevers and weakness which it was to hold for 1500 years.

It was in this period of the growing decline of Roman life—a decline amid continually increasing luxury and even of growing building skill—that movements of nomadic tribes to the north and east of the Roman boundaries gathered momentum. Some historians have claimed that it was the building of the Chinese Wall, which prevented the Mongols from finding their normal outlet to the south, that set the movement going, and so

the creation of this enormous monument 6000 miles away became perhaps
the indirect reason for at least the military debacle of the Roman Empire.
The barbarians had been troublers of the peace of the Mediterranean world
for centuries. The Roman system, by civilizing them and within its boundaries making them an integral part of itself, had for nearly three centuries
put an end to this menace; yet strains outside the boundaries were bound
to be reflected within, and the period of the "people's wanderings" shows
the result of the gradual decay of the earlier Roman imaginative efficiency.

The fall of Rome was no sudden catastrophe. It was a gradual cultural
change that spread over at least 200 years. It began with a financial depression; it ended with almost universal anarchy. The Roman, of the later
Empire at least, had no feeling of the "barbarians" as a class being enemies
of the "Romans" as a class. He was probably at least a quarter barbarian
himself; many of his rulers had been entirely barbarian. To him the word
meant very much the same as "foreigner" would to us. By entering the
army and later becoming a colonist in an agricultural settlement, the barbarian became a Roman. By the time of Constantine the army was almost
entirely "barbarian," and many of the most important positions in Rome and
in the provinces were held by men with barbarian names and origins. In
the fifth century a bishop complains that fashions and customs in Rome
itself had been almost completely changed, that trousers were worn and
long sleeves were common, that those who set the fashions and held the
power were no longer men of the old tradition, but men but recently foreigners, barbarians.

Just as Rome became barbarianized in this new sense, so the barbarians
themselves became Romanized, and every military camp on the frontier
became a center to which all the farmers and cattle raisers flocked, from
regions even many miles away. Returning to their thatched timber villages
they carried with them Roman money, Roman pottery and metalwork.
When, with the spread of the Roman boundary, or because of those shifts
of population which were a growing element in the life of the time, the
barbarians found themselves at last within the Empire and at least in part
Roman, they did their utmost to build as the Romans built and to live as
the Romans lived. Naturally the buildings they copied were not the great
monumental structures of Rome itself, nor even of Trier, that gorgeous
capital of the Three Roads, where the great baths and the wealthy palaces
rivaled even those of Rome, although almost on the very edge of the
German forests. It was the modest buildings of camp, of country village,
and of great provincial estate which these new Romans lived among, and it

was to these they turned for inspiration in their buildings. Thus, around the Roman camps and the cities of Gaul and of Germany, there grew up villages in which the half-timber and thatched roofs of the older barbarian tradition mingled with the simple brick or stone walls and low tiled roofs, the quiet courtyards and the painted rooms, which they borrowed from the Romans.

By the end of the fourth century this fusion was in many parts of the Empire well-nigh complete, and it is impossible from the existing remains to distinguish the buildings of the barbarians from the buildings of the Romans. Thus the great villas of England and of Belgium preserved some of the forms and the general arrangement of the earlier, more strictly "Roman" type, the originals of which can be seen in the wall paintings of Pompeii and Herculaneum—but their roofs were sometimes thatched instead of tiled; their walls were simple; square piers frequently took the place of columns; moldings were scarce or crude; more and more, semi-circular arches replaced the earlier square lintels of windows and doors; and arcades began to take the place of colonnades.

But, to develop marked differences from older work, new conditions are needed; and these new conditions came with the military campaigns and the mass migrations of the so-called barbarian invasions which followed the disintegration of the Roman power. Here again the story is not of sudden and absolute disaster, of complete destruction of a whole countryside or a whole nation. However terrible, however destructive the military ideals of a tribe might be, however great the loot taken from villa and town and church, however many villas and villages went up in columns of smoke, much remained. Goths and Franks, Vandals and Lombards poured across France and Austria and even into Italy and Spain; the Huns carved a swath of desolation across the face of the Empire. Yet the actual numbers of these people were relatively small, the actual path of desolation of each migration comparatively narrow; and more and more, as time went on, these tribes from across the border intermarried with the Roman inhabitants who were there before them, and took over their legal customs, their church, and their architecture. Some of them, like the Franks, even boasted of their Roman ways. Undoubtedly they employed Roman as well as barbarian craftsmen, and the churches which Gregory of Tours describes as built in France during the fifth and sixth centuries—richly painted with Biblical scenes, brilliant with mosaic, variegated marbles, and many columns—are in style not the churches of a barbaric people but provincial versions of the early Christian churches of Rome.

One thing which these barbarians did not bring with them was stability. Accustomed to a generation of looting, the chieftains became passionately greedy for wealth and power, and wealth and power they sought with a relentless cruelty and a crude arrogance which only the accounts of eye-witnesses render credible. Brothers tortured brothers, mothers killed sons, and sons their mothers, throughout that terrible period of Merovingian France, until, as the pages of Bishop Gregory show, even the clergy themselves became hardened to the terrors. Through it all, Roman culture struggled to preserve its life, largely by means of the semi-independence of the towns and the bishops, and fortification became more and more a need of even the smallest village. Similarly the great Roman estate system, which was rapidly developing into the feudal system of later ages, contributed to the confusion and to the necessity for fortification.

In the meantime another great change was taking place—the gradual substitution of wood for stone in the smaller buildings, the gradual disintegration and final eclipse of the old Roman masonry skills, and in their place the development of new skills in the use of the chisel and saw and plane. The timber building had many advantages; it could be rapidly built, and if it was destroyed—in one of those gangsters' battles or gangsters' raids which took the place of government—it was no great matter. Furthermore, since it seems obvious that the population of many portions of the Roman Empire had decreased markedly in the fifth century, despite the addition of the invading barbarians, much land previously pasture and field went back into forest, and wood was a cheap and easy material to obtain.

Fortified towns had areas rigorously limited by their walls, and timber buildings suggest height rather than breadth. Thus the two elements—the mad, anarchic fighting of the time, and development of skill in wood building—combined to produce a new type of city dwelling, the tower house; that is, the house of one or at most two rooms to a floor, within a simple rectangular outline, and two or three stories high. These houses, moreover, were themselves easier to defend than the old spread-out type of house, and the manuscripts of the Merovingian and Carolingian periods are full of representations of them. Often they had a ground floor of stone and an upper floor of half-timber stuccoed over, with a low tiled roof of almost Roman pitch. Within, the narrow quarters made necessary a different kind of life from that in the old Roman houses. The ground floor was usually semipublic, a sort of guardroom, which could be used as an audience chamber or a banquet hall; the upper rooms were the private residence of the owner, frequently extraordinarily rich with hangings of embroidered and richly worked cloth, the furniture simple, but replete with an amazing display of silver, gold, and bronze utensils. Windows often took the form of a series of small arches, the carpenter sometimes copying stone forms in wood just as the stoneworker occasionally reproduced forms originally developed in timber, as in the gatehouse at Lorsch. Fortunatus has a poem describing Chilperic's house, built along the wall at Metz, from the upper windows of which as he sat at dinner he could watch the fishermen in their boats on the river below.

48. EARLY MEDIEVAL REPRESENTATIONS OF TOWER HOUSES. *Left* and *center:* FROM THE EGBERT CODEX. *Right:* FROM THE RELIQUARY OF HENRY I OF GERMANY. (Stephani: *Der älteste Deutsche Wohnbau.*)

Occasionally these tower houses were of stone, and one or two still stand, much altered, like the Frankenturm, in Trier. For the most part, however, they have all perished, and what we know of them we must learn from poems, letters, and manuscript illuminations.

Of course the chieftains and kings had greater houses than these, and especially tried to continue in them some of the amenities of the great imperial villas. Like the Roman villas, these country palaces of the Frankish nobles had great banqueting rooms, luxurious baths, colonnades or porticoes with square piers, and gay, decorative gardens. Since the nobles had early adopted Christianity, their houses all contained chapels or churches; and the right to establish private chapels was one of the moot points of the feudal struggle. Remains of two of these palaces, of somewhat later date, still exist—

those which Charlemagne built at Ingelheim and at Aachen. Both are groups
of vast extent, enclosing large church areas, courts, cloisters and quarters
for the clergy, a basilica or throne room, in addition to the residence itself.
Both, too, are probably better built and better planned than those which
had preceded them, for Charlemagne, feeling himself the heir of the old
Roman Empire, made it a point to cultivate the building arts, as he made
it a point to cultivate Latin and literature. To his court came architects
and craftsmen from all over the old Roman world, and especially from the
Eastern Roman Empire, so that a great influx of Byzantine influence for

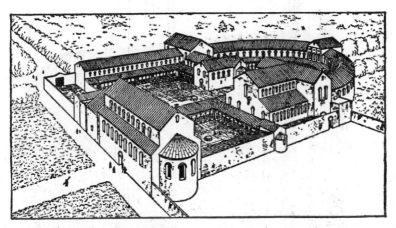

49. CAROLINGIAN PFALZ (PALACE) AT INGELHEIM, RESTORED. (Schuchhardt: *Die
Burg im Wandel der Weltgeschichte.*)

the first time began to modify the combined Roman and barbarian forms
of the work of the two centuries that had gone before.

A third type of building, the church, received a new impetus under
Charlemagne. The fifth- and early-sixth-century churches, as we know from
Gregory of Tours, had been merely imitations, more or less close, of the
early Roman churches of Rome itself, and buildings at least superficially
resplendent. The little local churches, however, could never equal these,
and more and more during this Frankish period we may imagine, rising
in the villages, little churches of timber, perhaps not unlike some of those
still to be found in Norway. We can see, even where masonry was used,
that the barbarian masons had lost the cunning of their Roman predecessors,
and built but poorly, with small stones, with little carving, and with what
there was crude and based as much on barbarian metal and wood work
as on the old classic orders. The churches which Charlemagne erected, how-

ever, were different in feeling. He strove always for strength and dignity, and for as much decorative richness as he had means available for. The octagonal church at Aachen is as much Byzantine as it is Western, but it is well built and its simple ornament well carved. The gatehouse of the monastery of Lorsch, with its rich polychrome masonry and its effective delicate carving, which seems a charming caricature of Roman work, gives some hint of the richness which must have been common in Carolingian

50. MONASTERY GATEWAY AT LORSCH. 9TH CENTURY. (Stephani.)

centers; and the Carolingian basilicas of Werden, Fulda, and Germigny des Prés have, in their simplicity, something of a magnificent dignity and proportions which are strong and beautiful.

None of these Carolingian buildings are any longer in the Roman tradition. The old Roman work had already been left three centuries behind, and three centuries of brawling, gold-grabbing chieftains had killed forever the old Roman decorative skills. Charlemagne, consciously or not, realized this, and in his own work built upon the facilities he had, borrowing from what was, yet building for his time and not attempting to resurrect a past, however beautiful, which was irrevocably dead. Yet it is significant perhaps that the earliest surviving manuscript of Vitruvius in the British Museum dates from a time only shortly after Charlemagne's reign.

One other development of these three centuries was a new type of country village and small town. Here it is that the old northern background of the invading barbarians most clearly found expression. The period, though building a transient architecture of little technical skill, was a period of great richness in many of the allied arts, especially in metalwork, jewelry, and the shaping of gold and silver. Gorgeous luxury in personal adornments was the rule, and, to make these, obviously a skilled trade was necessary; to distribute them, a more highly developed commerce than that which we usually associate with the time. So we may imagine growing up, not only around the villas and palaces of king and noble, but also in particularly favored fertile valleys and along new trade routes, villages of farmers and metalworkers, millers and businessmen. Usually stretched along a road, with houses separated by appreciable distances, these country villages had an aspect different both from the closely grouped huts of northern Germany and the close-built Latin town. The houses, save in the far south, were probably simple rectangles with high-pitched roofs, thatched or shingled. Within, under the one roof, was the living space, with its floor hearth— the smoke rising into the rafters to seep out where it might,—and also the stabling for cattle, horses, and pigs, or the forges and benches of the metal-workers, or the looms of the cloth weavers. In such a village an open space for meetings and for markets developed naturally in some part convenient to the river or the road. Another open space grew up around the church door and served probably as the administrative or governmental center. These villagers were frequently dependent upon and paid rentals to an overlord or a monastery; yet even at this early date, before the final crys-tallizations of the feudal system, the seeds of the medieval city and the medieval free town were already sown.

Thus the old traditional picture of the fall of Rome and a savage and barbaric dark-age period when civilization died has come little by little to be modified. Archaeology and historical research are more and more showing with what an almost wistful longing these new Romans from beyond the borders attempted to preserve the Roman culture. They have shown how inevitably the gradual changes came, through depopulation, through the old barbaric traditions of art and metalwork, and through 150 years of Mero-vingian anarchy. It was a violent, a cruel, a grasping world, but a world of vivid colors, of inordinate personal luxury for the rich—a world of gold and silver treasure arrogantly displayed. It was a world that gave rise to legends later coalescing into such epics as the *Nibelungenlied* and the *Song of Roland;* but it was an age, too, that had its own Latin poets and historians, an age whose rulers boasted of their Roman culture and their Christianity. For such an age of contradiction and confusion, its tentative architecture of crude stone and highly finished wood, of palace and church and thatched farm, was the perfect expression.

When the Goths came into the Roman Empire, they split into two portions—one branch, the Ostrogoths, settled in Italy; and one, the Visigoths, in Spain. Ostrogothic architecture is centered chiefly around Ravenna, which had been also the center of Byzantine power in Italy. Naturally, the Ostrogothic architecture is almost entirely Byzantine in type, and, save in minor decorative features, its buildings are almost indistinguishable from other Byzantine work of the time. Thus the churches of San Apollinare Nuovo and of San Vitale are usually studied as Byzantine monuments; and even the palace of the great Theodoric himself, the chief gatehouse of which still stands, would hardly be out of place in Constantinople or on the Dalmatian coast. In minor decorative work, however, there is evidence in a few pulpits, friezes, altars, and capitals of its characteristic barbarian motifs—one a circle decorated with star-shaped rays, obviously based on the chip carving of an early wooden technique; and the other the angular interlace, quite different in spirit from the more suave interlaces of Constantinople.

The Visigoths in Spain produced an architecture more creative. Here too the conquering barbarians evidently made large use of the Romanized Spanish natives for their decorative work, and developed both an imagination in planning buildings and a skill in building them of stone which, outside of the Eastern Empire, were unique in their time. The Palace Throne Room, built about 800 A.D. by King Ramiro I, now the Church of Santa Maria de Naranco, has twisted columns, ribbed barrel vaults, twin-arched windows, and rich carved ornament. The same skill and the same richness can be seen in any one of several of these early Visigothic churches which still stand, such as San Cristo de la Luz in Toledo, or San Juan Bautista at Baños. Other important churches are San Miguel de Escalada and San Miguel de Lino at Oviedo. In some of these a great use is made of a new structural form, the horseshoe arch, which seems to have been invented by the Visigoths and which, taken over by the Moors later, was to have such an important place in Moorish design. In all of them there is great richness of carved stone ornament. Capitals are usually based on the Roman Corinthian, although modified both in proportion and in detail; and there is great use of the carved roundels and the interlaces mentioned before, which were in Spain developed to an excellence that other barbarian builders never equaled. It is interesting that these Visigoths, for whom the Franks had the greatest contempt, as a people who refused to fight or fought badly, far outstripped their northern detractors in building skill.

Visigothic architecture is of special importance during this period, because of its profound effect upon the later Romanesque architecture of France and Spain.

The Lombards, who superseded the Ostrogoths in Italy and gave their name to the province occupying the Po valley, were less skillful builders and, prior to their conquest by Charlemagne, produced little of marked significance. Parts of San Stefano at Bologna and San Pietro at Toscanella are theirs and show confused influences from Rome, from Byzantine work, and from their own northern background. The churches of Santa Maria in Valle at Cividale (eighth century) and of Santa Maria at Pomposa (sixth century) are their most polished monuments. The tiny basilica at Castelseprio (probably eighth century), discovered after the Second World War, is distinguished by its tri-lobe eastern end and its remarkable mural paintings, full of classic feeling and possibly painted by a Byzantine artist. The Lombard rulers had a high regard for building and gave special legal advantages to the much discussed builders' guild, the Comacini; yet the work produced was small in amount and generally crude. There is some polychrome brickwork, there are crude capitals which caricature Roman originals, and there are several altar canopies, pulpits, and chancel railings with rich surface ornament based partly on Byzantine precedent and partly on the interlaces, the grotesque animals, and the carved roundels of their northern tradition.

This very lack of real building skill in the old ways led the Lombard builders to interesting experiments in building in new ways, with stepped arches and similar forms, which were later to have important consequences. However, it was only after the fall of the Lombard power, and under other and foreign governments, that the Lombard builders were to carry this experimentalism to a point where in arch and vault building it became one of the great fructifying sources of medieval architecture.

It was perhaps because the Franks inhabited the most Romanized of the provinces, boasted of their Roman culture, and as far as possible used old

Roman buildings, that their own attempts at developing a new architecture were so sterile. Little of it remains. A church crypt here and there exists—like that at Jouare, with its stone walls laid in geometric patterns,—but they show little creative thought and less decorative skill. The best of the buildings, the Baptistry of St. Jean at Poitiers, is almost Roman in its plan and structure, but the all-pervading barbarian love of decorative surface richness has given it an exterior dress of geometric patterns in stone and brick that has great delicacy. Of the larger churches and houses we know little, but from manuscript illuminations we can judge of the importance which rich hangings and polychrome surface decoration held in their interior aspect. It was only when Charlemagne had succeeded in uniting the Franks and establishing his empire far beyond the original Frankish borders that there was a definite change for the better. To Charlemagne architecture was as much one of the fine arts as literature, and to both he gave his enthusiastic protection and support. Remnants of Carolingian work are widely spread over France, parts of Germany, and northern Italy. The best of it has been already described.

Chapter 11

BYZANTINE ARCHITECTURE

FOR two centuries prior to the Fall of Rome the influence of the eastern part of the empire had been growing stronger, as the rich provinces of Asia Minor and Syria gained an increasing importance in Roman economic life, and as the mystic oriental religions were becoming more and more popular throughout the Roman Empire. In architecture, too, the same stories of growing Eastern influence can be read. Up to the time of Hadrian it was the Romans who were the teachers of the Syrians, but the great importance of the Asiatic centers even at that time is shown by the magnificence of the imperial structures of Baalbec, Palmyra, and Antioch.

Yet, as we have seen, Roman architecture was always susceptible to local influences, in decoration, in the use of building materials, and even, as the temples of Palmyra show, in basic plan conceptions—for the temples at Palmyra preserve the secret chambers and elaborate sanctuaries of Eastern rather than of classic religion. Even in Hadrian's buildings in Baalbec, decorative forms are modified by the oriental love of surface ornament, and the clear pattern of the classic structural members tends to be hidden under a veil of almost lacelike surface carving.

Moreover, the necessity of using a hard stone as almost the only building material produced enormous changes, especially in the smaller buildings; and from the fourth century on till the Mohammedan Conquest in the seventh, when the area was almost depopulated, the towns of Syria developed an architecture of their own, based on stone and surface decoration, which differed more and more from the work of the West. This Syrian architecture uses stone not only for walls and columns, but also for floors, for roofs, and even sometimes for doors. The stone is usually laid without mortar in as large blocks as could conveniently be handled; and the house types, which usually consist of a band of rooms, in two or even three stories, fronted by open colonnades connecting them, were unique in their perfect fitness for the climate and the material. The hardness of the stone gradually forced many changes in the heritage of Roman classic detail. Moldings became flatter, projections were decreased, columns tended to be shorter and more stumpy, and incised ornament—in the form of bands of shallow moldings or close-ranged leaves under a beveled cornice— became a controlling element. Even the Corinthian capital itself suffered all sorts of inventive modifications; its leaves were flattened and more closely ranged, with deep drill holes separating them and many incised lines replacing the old full roundness, and sometimes the ends of the leaves

51. CHARACTERISTIC SYRIAN BUILDING, A 5TH-CENTURY VILLA AT EL-RABAH, RESTORED. (De Vogüé: *Syrie centrale.*)

were bent to one side as though blown by the wind. The shape of the capital as a whole changed, too, and became simpler and more geometric.

The continually growing skill of these Syrian masons made them, at least in the fourth century, the teachers of Rome itself, where the old decorative skill had tended to be forgotten and where, during the third century, mere ostentatious richness had come to take its place. Thus, when Diocletian built his great palace in Dalmatia, across the Adriatic from Italy—a palace which gave its name Spalatro (or Split) to the town that grew up within it,—the decorative forms of the rich carving show again and again, if not the actual handiwork of Syrian artisans, at least a strong influence from the flatter, heavier, Syrian forms. The arch plays a more important role in later Roman architecture than in earlier work, and in the great forecourt of the palace the colonnade, instead of carrying a flat entablature, carries a series of arches. In this, as in the decoration, Diocletian's building was prophetic of many developments to come, although its plan was based on the typical Roman camp and the great halls of its residential portion were planned and vaulted in the Roman manner.

When Constantine the Great moved the capital of the Roman Empire from Rome to Constantinople, in 330, he was merely expressing politically this turning toward the East which had been such a marked feature in the past century of Roman life. The city which he founded there, on a site ideal from the military point of view, as it was attractive in climate and beautiful in location—with its seven hills washed on three sides by clear salt water and its magnificent views of the Asian hills across the Bosphorus, —not only became the center of an empire which lasted more than 1000 years, until the Turkish Conquest of 1453, but also became the center from which a new culture and a new art which we call Byzantine radiated in all directions.

The Eastern Roman Empire, which, after the final decay of the western Roman power in the fifth century, became the wealthiest and most powerful political force of its time, was in many ways a totally different structure from the earlier Roman government. The gradual growth of centralized power begun under the later Roman emperors culminated at last, in the court of Constantinople, in a hard-and-fast despotism founded on a large, specialized, and highly trained bureaucracy, which was regulated in accordance with a fixed caste system. All trades and employment became hereditary; and, if this rigid specialization of work was ill-fitted to the development of flexible progress, it did frequently result in extreme technical proficiency. At the bottom of the hierarchy were the slaves, and only slightly above them the agricultural serfs; then came tradesmen in an ascending scale, until at the top there was a small body of wealthy landholders and high government officials, together with a tremendous number of people associated with the church—monks, and priests, and bishops.

Because of its very rigidity, this system was particularly subject to riot and revolution, for violence offered the only method of change. The great cities of the Eastern Empire were almost continually turbulent, and more and more to them flocked the discontented and the rebellious, as well as the successful and the famous. Thus Constantinople was at its height a city of extraordinary contrasts, of amazing wealth and luxury in its imperial court and its churches, and of poverty and upheaval beneath—the whole held in some kind of precarious order by an elaborate military organization and overwhelming military forces. Public games in the Hippodrome gave amusement to the proletariat and the nobles alike, and the factional conflicts between the two chief organizations of chariot racers, the Blues and the Greens, often reached the pitch of battle and murder, and offered a fertile field for the development of the theological controversies that periodically racked the empire.

Into this city flowed the silks and the spices and the pottery of the East, to be exchanged for the gold of Western treasuries, and from its busy shops a stream of exquisite goods poured out—carved ivories, illuminated manuscripts, jewelry and jeweled metalwork—to find its way across the Balkans and the Adriatic to Italy, or by the Varangian Route all across Russia to the Baltic and the Atlantic. To its magnificent harbor came ships from all the Mediterranean world and from the Black Sea; they lay hull to hull along the shore of the Golden Horn, and the sailors' voices echoed along the water front in many strange languages, Slav and Semitic, Romance and Teutonic. Through Constantinople passed pilgrims from France and England and Germany, bound for the Holy Land, to return to their homes with tales of the wealth and the comforts of Constantinople, of its paved streets, its colonnaded fora, and the legendary luxury of its imperial court. It is hardly strange that Charlemagne, planning to build his palace chapel in Aachen, should turn to Constantinople for help, and with the aid of Greek architects build the most Byzantine structure of the West; nor is it strange that four centuries later the Fourth Crusade, overcome alike by envy of the city's riches and disgust at the rapacity of its shipowners, should turn aside temporarily from their holy quest to besiege and capture it, and establish a dynasty of Norman rulers there which lasted sixty years.

Constantinople already in the sixth century was incomparably the most luxurious city in Europe. In its streets the traveler saw a continuous pageant. The crowds of ordinary folk, in costumes still not unlike those of classic times, would suddenly be parted, and through the open lane would come the Imperial Guards, with purple cloaks and gilded, plumed helmets, and behind them perhaps the Emperor himself borne on an ivory litter, surrounded by courtiers all swathed in heavy cloaks and long-sleeved coats stiff with embroidery and glittering with jewels, so that their very humanity seemed hidden, almost forgotten, under the gorgeous artificiality—the easy grace of the old classic drapery replaced by the hard, concealing lines of the new rich fashions. There would be priests and bishops, too, for the church stood high in the court; and their long robes and heavy vestments would be as heavy and as brilliant with color and gems as those of the courtiers themselves. The procession would all be unbelievably lavish, under the warm sky and against the blue background of the Sea of Marmora at the end of the street; but it would all be distant and aloof from the city crowd, too, and relentlessly cruel and brutal if need or caprice indicated; woe to the commoner who was slow in clearing the way, who was not quick enough to retreat to the house walls as the guard charged by....

Yet, despite all this, the emperors themselves contrived somehow to preserve the old Roman tradition of great buildings, both religious and temporal, and the Byzantine architecture which they there developed became one of the great, significant styles of Western architecture. Naturally its roots are double, in Rome and in the East. Roman architecture had been, as we have seen, pre-eminently an architecture of interior space, open and magnificent, surrounded by richly decorated walls. This ideal was preserved by the Byzantine builders, although with a continuous and growing modification. But, if it was the Roman ideal of space which generated the basic plan, it was Eastern ideals which governed the decoration. The greatest modification of the Roman space concepts came from the development of the dome; and the greatest contribution of the Byzantine architects to architecture was the final perfect and simple solution of the problem of putting a dome over a square or polygonal edifice by the use of those spherical triangles we call pendentives.

The Romans seem to have known the pendentive as a geometric or decorative form, although in the West they made no use of it structurally. In the East, however, the form seems to have been used from an early date. The earliest example we know is in Gerasa, in Palestine, and probably dates from the second century; yet this remained seemingly an isolated case, and it was not until the Byzantine period and under the Eastern Empire that the enormous structural possibilities of the pendentive were appreciated.

The difficulty which the Romans found in placing a dome over a square or polygonal room was that, if the dome was made of the same diameter as the width of the room, it would not reach the corners—and the dome had to be supported somehow over these corners. The secret of the final solution of this problem lay merely in making the dome base large enough to fill these corners completely—that is, to make the diameter of the dome the diagonal of the room rather than the width of the room. The result was a spherical surface cut off where it intersected the planes of the walls in semicircular curves, and exactly meeting the corners of the room at the base of the dome. Such a covering for a room is called a pendentive dome.* Later, by building these domical surfaces only up to the crown of the supporting arches, a horizontal circle was produced, on which a complete and separate dome could be constructed as though on a circular wall; and it is this combination of forms which made possible the magnificent open interiors of Santa Sophia in Constantinople and St. Mark's in Venice.

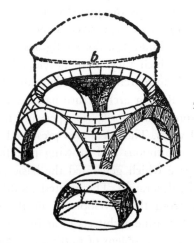

52. DIAGRAM SHOWING THE PENDENTIVE. (T. F. Hamlin: *The Enjoyment of Architecture.*)

Another basic problem which confronted the Byzantine builders was how to carry on comparatively small columns the thick arches required by heavy walls. The old classic entablature above the regular column capital had tended to disappear; yet some way of increasing the size of the column to the size of the masonry it carried was still necessary. With their love of splayed forms, the Byzantines developed a square beveled block, sometimes called a *pulvino* or impost block, the bottom of which was much smaller than the top. Its sides could be elaborately decorated with surface carving, and it was a simple and logical shape to place on the top of the column capital. Later still, it came gradually to replace the capital, and instead of being square at the bottom was made circular, so that the new capital had a continuously changing surface, from the circular bottom on top of the shaft up to a square of much larger size above, which supported

---

* To understand the form of a pendentive, it is only necessary to place half an orange with its flat side down on a plate and cut equal portions vertically off the sides. What is left of the original hemisphere is called a pendentive dome. Each vertical cut will be in the shape of a semicircle. Sometimes these semicircles were built as independent arches to support the upper spherical surface of the dome. If the top of the orange is cut off horizontally at the height of the top of these semicircles, the triangular pieces still left will be exactly the shape of pendentives. This new circle can be made the base for a new complete dome, or a vertical cylinder can be built upon it to support another dome higher up.

the arches directly. This shape could then be carved with surface ornament of leaves or interlacing of any desired intricacy; and, to give this carving greater brilliance, often the stone beneath the surface was deeply cut away, so that sometimes the entire outside face of the capital was quite separate from the solid block behind, and the result had a sparkle and a vividness which was extraordinary.

But the love of surface decoration did not stop with carved capitals and bands, for the Byzantines, like the Romans, loved color almost as much as form. Accordingly, the old Roman methods of sheathing the interiors of buildings with slabs of colored marble were carried to new heights of complexity and richness; and glass mosaic, which the Romans also had used, became, in a new and more highly developed form, the great method of interior decoration of the upper parts of walls and the undersides of all vaults.

These developments reached almost their highest form in one of the earliest of the developed Byzantine monuments, the great church, designed by Anthemius of Tralles, which Justinian built in Constantinople in honor of the Holy Wisdom—Santa Sophia—begun in A.D. 532. From its marble floor to the gold mosaic of the dome, its interior sings with color and light. Its plan conception of concentrated loads on large transverse buttress piers is Roman, suggested probably by the Basilica of Maxentius. The scheme—a central dome buttressed by half domes at the ends—allows the entire interior to break upon one as a unit the moment one enters. Amply lighted by many windows under the arches on the sides and by a ring of windows in the base of the dome, the whole becomes almost space itself; and the change in color from the sober marbles below to the richly patterned, gold-background vaults adds to this sense of lightness and space.

At first the ornament in the vaults was undoubtedly chiefly abstract, with crosses to give it symbolic meaning and with many ornaments obviously borrowed from textile patterns. Later, probably in the tenth century, after the iconoclastic controversy had ended and religious images were again permitted in churches, magnificent figure pieces were inserted in the gold background, saints between the windows of the side walls, and a colossal Virgin and Christ Enthroned over the apse. Little by little, these are today emerging from the coat of plaster which has covered them almost ever since the Turkish Conquest.

If the interior of Santa Sophia is one of the greatest interiors of the world, its exterior gives the impression of being little considered. Size gives it grandeur, and the frank expression on the exterior of its domed forms, covered with lead, has that inevitable power which any frank expression of structure must give; yet the details are crude and there is little or no decoration to relieve its somewhat chaotic exterior forms. The entire artistic emphasis was within; it may even be that the exterior was left so starkly plain in the conscious effort to give a dramatic climax to the splendor inside.

In many ways the eight centuries between Santa Sophia and the Fall of Constantinople to the Turks produced little in architecture to compare with

SANTA SOPHIA, CONSTANTINOPLE.

53. SANTA SOPHIA, CONSTANTINOPLE; PLAN AND SECTION. (Simpson. Vol. I.)

it. Churches continued to be built—the number of churches in the city was enormous;—but the later churches were mainly small parish churches or monastery chapels of the most modest dimensions. Their domes (for almost all of them follow their great predecessor in being domed churches) are often no larger than twenty feet in span. One has the impression again and again of being in the presence of a dainty miniature. In the effort to light these churches, a circular wall (called a drum), pierced by arched windows, was built over the pendentives and under the tiny dome, and this use of the drum is universal in the later buildings. Often the domes were so small and the drums so high that the impression is almost that of towers; and sometimes the tops of the drum are scalloped over each arch so that the outline becomes very rich, and the outside roof takes an almost melon-shaped, lobed form.

Yet what these later churches lost in size and grandeur they tended to make up in exterior elaboration, and the walls are often richly banded with brick and stone and decorated with recessed, vertical, arch-headed panels. Brick cornices, too, came to play an important part in their design, with the most interesting shapes caused by projecting bricks cornerwise and building out little brick brackets. Within, these churches preserved largely the same kind of decoration as in Santa Sophia—marble slabs below and mosaics above, although occasionally mural painting took the place of the mosaics;—and the type of elongated, rather stiffly drawn figure which was so fitting to the conventions of mosaic decoration, so strong and architectural in its simplifications, gradually crystallized into a series of fixed conventions which exerted a tremendous influence on the manuscript illumination and the mural painting of Italy, Russia, and the entire western Mediterranean.

Of the gorgeous palaces built for the luxurious court of Constantinople disappointingly little is known. There are numerous vaulted halls with lavishly decorated balconies and windows in a small palace overlooking the Sea of Marmora; there is a three-storied hall, called Tekfour Serai, which may be the guardroom and banquet hall of the great Blachernae Palace on the landward walls; and recent excavations are little by little uncovering some of the imperial palace near Santa Sophia and showing, through the magnificence of its mosaic pavements, not only the richness which must have characterized the whole, but also a much stronger persistence of classic feeling in its decoration than is found in the church work.

Tekfour Serai is remarkable in its many resemblances to such western Romanesque palaces as that at Goslar. There is an open loggia beneath, which once fronted on a court, and above that vast rectangular halls which once had timber floors and ceilings and large, regularly spaced, arched windows. Undoubtedly, beneath the crowded Turkish houses of present-day Istanbul and the gardens and fairylike kiosks of the Turkish Palace of the Seraglio, much more still remains which someday we may know.

Yet, though domestic remains are rare in Constantinople, we are fortunate in possessing a deserted Byzantine town—Mistra—which preserves for us much of the later domestic architecture of the Byzantine Empire, as Pompeii and Herculaneum show us that of the earlier Roman Empire. There, only three miles away from ancient Sparta, above the valley, climbing a precipitous slope, street after street of unroofed buildings remain. From Mistra we learn that, in Greece at least, the Byzantine houses were generally rectangular, of two or three stories, with large window areas and many corbeled balconies, to give even in the crowded town some opportunity for outdoor living. Floors were usually of timber, and the timber and tiled roofs retained the old classic pediment and roof slope. There is little architectural ornament within, and the richness in these interiors, as in the Merovingian and Carolingian, must have come largely from hangings and furniture. In general aspect, the ruins of Mistra look not unlike a hill town of Italy or southern France; perhaps the original inspiration behind them all may have been the multistory buildings of the late Roman Empire.

Monasteries were another characteristic product of Byzantine life, for the very luxury and corruption of the Constantinople court forced more and more thinking people into the reaction of asceticism. The monasteries of the Eastern Empire are therefore fundamentally different from those of the West, where the ideal was that of carrying on a full life within the monastic framework. In the East the monasteries, when they are not in important places of pilgrimage like the great group at Kalat Siman in Syria, were on the most inaccessible cliffs and promontories. To many the approach is only by means of chairs or baskets hoisted up by pulleys. Once arrived at the top, the visitor finds small arcaded courts of the simplest construction, stuccoed white; the only decoration lies in the marvelous icons and occasional magnificent mural paintings of the small domed chapels, in the old manuscripts which each monastery preserves, and in the gorgeous, wide-sweeping views over blue sea or gray-green valley and distant mountain. The constricted sites usually leave little opportunity for monumental general planning, and the courts and blocks of monks' cells and halls are built where shelves in the mountainside allow. Immured in these high-hung retreats, with rare visits from the outside world, these monks were and still are removed from the world indeed. Several beautiful examples line the hills near Mistra, but the most famous group lies high above the Aegean on the inaccessible cliff of Mt. Athos.

Of the radiations of the Byzantine style, the most important were into Dalmatia and across the Adriatic into Italy. Large portions of Italy—the Exarchate of Ravenna—were under the domination of the Eastern Empire from the sixth to the eighth century. Later, Byzantine ideals governed much of the architecture of Venice until the coming of the Gothic influence in the thirteenth century, and even after that the Byzantine love of marble sheathing, of mosaic, and of intricate lacelike surface ornament profoundly affected all the buildings of Venice until well into the Renaissance.

In Ravenna, the great Byzantine monument is the church of San Vitale, almost contemporary with Santa Sophia in Constantinople, and distinguished by carved capitals of unusually intricate design, by the high dome over the octagon which forms the main body of the church, and by the magnificent mosaics which decorate the vault and the upper walls. In these and in the mosaics of the church of San Apollinare Nuovo, Byzantine mosaic reached its apogee, and the balance between conventional decorative quality and naturalistic representation is perfect.

Occasionally in Ravenna, and more often in Venice, influences from the barbarian world to the north and west give some of the carving a quite different character from the work in Constantinople. Grotesque beasts, borrowed from the work of the Goths and the Lombards, sometimes decorate carved panels, and the interlace, so loved by the barbarian metal-workers, comes to play a larger and larger part in the decoration. More-over, the conditions of all buildings in Venice were so different from those in Constantinople that great differences in the buildings themselves were bound to occur.

When refugees, fleeing from the barbarian invasions, settled among a few lowly fisherfolk on some sandy islands in the salt marshes near the head of the Adriatic, they little dreamed that they were founding one of the great maritime cities of the world. Each invasion brought a few more to these islands; the greatest number came to seek refuge from the Lombards in 568. The islands they settled were almost impregnable; as dangers on the main-land increased, the inhabitants moved gradually to islands and sandbars further out in the lagoon; finally, to escape the armies of the Frankish empire under Pippin, they settled the group, far out, which came to be the Venice of history.

Situated as it was at the head of the Adriatic Sea, just where important trade routes across Italy met the shore, Venice was ideally placed to become a great port. Across the Adriatic lay the Dalmatian provinces of the Eastern Empire; south of them the Gulf of Corinth led deep into Greece; around Greece the way lay clear to Constantinople and the busy harbors of Asia Minor. So placed, and with such a history, Venice was bound to feel itself more a part of the Byzantine Empire than of western Europe; and during the ninth and tenth centuries, while Venice grew from a fishing village to be Queen of the Adriatic, and Venetian life and culture were taking form, it was Byzantine power which was supreme, and Byzantine art which directed the building and the decoration of the growing city.

Eleventh-century Venice had become not only the Queen of the Adriatic, but the supreme maritime power throughout the entire eastern Mediterranean, the great gateway between the East and the West. Venetian ships brought ivories and silks from Constantinople, and marbles from Greece, and this traffic brought gold to Venetian coffers until its riches were second only to those of Constantinople itself; it was this wealth which built St. Mark's and all the palaces, big and little, that rose along the curving canals.

It was the island position of Venice which controlled its growth. If Venetian wealth came from the sea, Venice would express that fact by bringing the sea deep into its midst, by weaving salt water through between its buildings; the little islands might grow, but always they were kept separate islands, with the lagoon, as it were, disciplined into the canals. Everywhere boats could go; every building could be approached directly by water. The great galleons could lie alongside the palaces of their owners; beyond, the canal was always busy with the flat lighters bringing food or fuel from the mainland, or with the long, slim, flat-bottomed, gaily colored rowboats that were to develop into the gondolas of later history.

The church of St. Mark's in Venice has a plan based on Justinian's church of the Holy Apostles in Constantinople, which no longer stands. Begun in the tenth and dedicated in the eleventh century, St. Mark's continued to receive its decorative enrichment for centuries afterward; and its fanciful and exquisite exterior is, as it were, a Gothic frosting, climaxed by the onion domes of the fourteenth century, built high over the spherical domes beneath. Yet, once within the doors, the impression of large space, of simple marble surfaces, and of gorgeous but somber color is Byzantine pure and simple; and, though the dome mosaics may be of the seventeenth century, the glint of gold in their background yields the true Byzantine splendor, and the mosaics of the narthex or vestibule which surrounds three sides of the nave (though later in date than the Ravenna examples by almost six centuries) retain all the compositional strength and decorative fitness of the earlier work. Because St. Mark's still preserves its choir screen, its pulpit and lecterns, and much of its chancel furniture, we can perhaps gain from it a better conception of what the Byzantine was meant to be than from Santa Sophia itself, where all similar work was removed at the Turkish Conquest.

In Venice, too, numbers of Byzantine houses still remain, to show how early the Venetian type of house was developed. All are basically rectangular in plan, with a great central hall running through from front to back, and smaller rooms at each side. An almost continuous band of tall, round-

CONSTANTINOPLE, STA. SOPHIA; INTERIOR
SHOWING BYZANTINE SPACE AND SURFACE
RICHNESS.

RAVENNA, SAN VITALE; INTERIOR SHOW-
ING BYZANTINE CAPITALS AND IMPOST
BLOCKS, WITH MOSAIC BEYOND.

VENICE, ST. MARK'S; INTERIOR SHOWING BYZANTINE MOSAIC VAULTS, MARBLE WALL
SHEATHING, AND CHANCEL SCREEN.

Plate 25

CONSTANTINOPLE, TEKFOUR SERAI; A RUINED BYZANTINE PALACE HALL.

VENICE, FONDACHO DEI TURCHI, RESTORED; A CHARACTERISTIC VENETIAN
BYZANTINE PALACE.

Plate 26

CONSTANTINOPLE, STA. SOPHIA; AN EARLY
BYZANTINE EXTERIOR.

ATI, ARMENIAN MONASTERY OF ST.
HOLAS.

ATHENS, CHURCH OF ST. THEODORE; CHAR-
ACTERISTIC DEVELOPED BYZANTINE EXTE-
RIOR.

MOSCOW, THE KREMLIN, THE WEDDING
CHURCH.

OW, ST. BASIL'S CHURCH.

Plate 27

CLUNY, ROMANESQUE HOUSE.

MONASTERY OF ST. MARTIN DE CANIGÓ. (Courtesy Professor

GOSLAR, GERMAN ROMANESQUE PALACE. 11th AND 12th CENTURIES.

Plate 28

BEAULIEU, MONASTERY DOOR. 12th-CENTURY ROMANESQUE PORTAL SCULPTURES, BUR-
GUNDIAN SCHOOL.

CHARTRES CATHEDRAL, WEST DOOR; THE CLIMAX OF ROMANESQUE ARCHITECTURAL
SCULPTURE.

Plate 29

CLERMONT-FERRAND, NOTRE DAME DU
PORT; BARREL-VAULTED INTERIOR.

PERIGUEUX, ST. FRONT; CHARACTERISTI[C]
DOMICAL INTERIOR OF AQUITANIA.

PARAY-LE-MONIAL, MONASTERY CHURCH;
CHOIR.

MONREALE CATHEDRAL; INTERIOR SHOW[ING]
MOSAIC.

Plate 30

LE PUY EN VELAY, CATHEDRAL; IN-
TERIOR WITH ROMANESQUE POINTED
ARCHES.

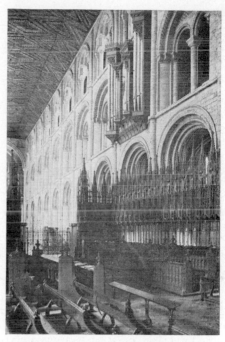

PETERBOROUGH CATHEDRAL; CHAR-
ACTERISTIC NORMAN INTERIOR.

DURHAM CATHEDRAL; INTERIOR
SHOWING DEVELOPED ROMANESQUE
VAULT.

CAEN, ABBAYE AUX DAMES; PRIMITIVE
SIX-PART RIBBED VAULT.

Plate 31

CLERMONT-FERRAND, NOTRE DAME DU PORT; EXTERIOR OF APSE SHOWING RADIATING CHAPELS AND PRIMITIVE BUTTRESSES.

COMO, SAN ABBONDIO; CHARACTER LOMBARD CAMPANILES, BUTTRESS S1 AND CORNICES.

MILAN, SAN AMBROGIO; EARLY LOMBARD RIBBED VAULT.

FLORENCE, SAN MINIATO, INTERIOR; ACTERISTIC TUSCAN ROMANESQUE CHROMY.

Plate 32

arched windows lets floods of light into the front and rear of the hall, with narrower windows, more closely spaced, lighting the small end rooms. On the ground floor an arcade of doors replaced the banded window above, and sometimes the ground-floor arches were much wider than the upper ones; so that, whereas on the ground floor there might be five arches leading into the central hall, on the floor above, the upper room, though of the same width as that below, would have seven or nine arched windows. The capitals are usually of simple Byzantine type, though the typical Italian love for naturalistic form as well as the stronger influence of the ancient Roman types caused subtle modifications. This type of house remained in plan the fundamental type all through the Gothic and most of the Renaissance period; and, in fact, such a house as the Ca d'Oro, despite its rich tracery and its cusped Gothic arches, preserves the old Byzantine tradition of flat walls, of polychrome decoration, and even of basic plan arrangement. Similarly, the little church of Santa Maria dei Miracoli, of the late fifteenth century, in spite of its lavish Renaissance ornament, has in its marble-sheathed walls and its inlays of richly colored porphyry and serpentine an effect that would never have been possible had not the Byzantine tradition been so firmly established in Venice six centuries earlier.

Another extremely important local school of Byzantine architecture sprang up in Armenia, to reach a brilliant climax in the eleventh-century churches of Ani, and then to disappear suddenly under the waves of the Turkish invasion. The Armenian work is especially interesting because it is all built of cut stone like the Syrian, and not of brick like most of the Constantinople buildings. The whole Byzantine system of marble sheathing and gold-ground mosaic therefore was impossible, and the Armenian architect in his search for decorative effect was forced to a great exuberance in carved ornament. The churches are frequently square, with a cross-shaped higher nave and transepts set within the square, a stone dome at the crossing, and smaller domes at the corners. The proportions are almost always high and narrow, and the exteriors carefully designed and handsomely decorated with little arched cornices, enormous arch forms, and occasional friezes of animals.

This style seems to have had an especial influence on the architecture of Russia and the northern Balkans, and it is possible that some of the Armenian architects and stone cutters, fleeing before the Turkish hordes, sailed across the Black Sea and up the Danube. The confusion of tongues in the Balkan states in the Middle Ages was extraordinary, as Germans, Greeks, Latins, and Slavs fought for dominance or survival, and it was naturally only after these turbulent years of migration had drawn to a close that much monumental architecture became possible. It was hardly surprising that these Avars and Bulgars, Magyars and Croats, newly Christianized, should turn for inspiration in their church building to that Christian power which was nearest—that is, to Constantinople—and that the Byzantine type of domed church came to be the standard model on which the local variations were made. Exaggerations of the height which characterized late Byzantine churches were the rule, and the vertical wall paneling which had decorated portions of the later Constantinople churches here stretched itself over the entire edifice from ground to roof. Occasionally, exterior mural painting added to the bizarre richness of these high, narrow-windowed, paneled exteriors, so that the final result in the work of Rumania or northern Bulgaria of the fourteenth and fifteenth centuries had a character quite different from the Constantinople work on which it had been originally modeled. Moreover, counterinfluences were at work—the old barbarian tradition of timber-building, and in the later periods influences from western Europe coming with trade down the Danube and bringing in strange caricatures of Gothic forms. The stumpy molded columns that are sometimes used, with their broad, spreading capitals, seem more fitted to wood than to stone; and occasional early wooden churches remain, which show the wooden forms which the stone work so ineptly copied. Thus, it was less the details of Byzantine work than the basic idea of the domed church which these peoples developed, and the further one gets from the center at Constantinople the more this becomes true.

During the early Middle Ages, the Varangian trade route from the Black Sea to the west brought an enormous river of goods from Constantinople, continually flowing north through the Black Sea and the Crimea, and then by the Russian rivers across Russia to the far-away Baltic and the West. Largely, this trade was under Norse auspices, and it is an interesting speculation to wonder how much the earliest Russian architecture is due to the Scandinavian rulers, to the Slavic population over whom they ruled, and to the Byzantine influence from the south. Naturally, the earliest churches are the most Byzantine. Thus, the oldest church in Kiev, begun in 991, is almost purely Byzantine, with its three apses and a square plan; and the church of the Holy Virgin, 1165, near Vladimir, with its high, scalloped, polygonal façade, its decorative arcades and crude carving, and its high dome drum, seems a mixture of influences from Armenia, from Constantinople, and from the Balkans.

Sometime in the eleventh or twelfth century the Russians began to cover the masonry domes with elaborate onion-shaped cupolas, apparently developing the form independently, although the shape parallels some Persian types. These onion domes grew more bulbous as time went on and were repeated on little pinnacles and towers, until in the seventeenth century they became well-nigh universal marks of Russian buildings. They survived the influx of Renaissance ideas in the sixteenth century and in the seventeenth gave rise to the fantastic elaborateness of such churches as St. Basil, at Moscow. In these later churches, too, rows of little arched forms, like inverted scales, surround the dome drums and form crestings and cornices.

Gradually the exterior and interior became completely independent of one another, until there resulted designs basically dual—the Byzantine influence on the exterior almost hidden under forms either borrowed from western Europe or developed as a sort of native Russian Baroque, the interiors still basically Byzantine in their simple vaulted structure and their rich hieratic and conservative mural paintings that filled them with mystery.

A remarkable feature of Russian building was the development, in forested regions, of an effective and original architecture in wood. This was based on piling logs, sometimes squared, one upon another as in log cabins or Swiss chalets. Not only houses but even large churches were built in this way, especially in the Archangel region; the logs were sometimes corbeled inward to form high vaults or tall towers. The decoration was also of wood; posts were often hewn into bulbous baluster-like shapes, and simulated arches of cut-out boards connected them, recalling the distant masonry origin of the style.

Chapter 12

ROMANESQUE ARCHITECTURE

FOUR factors profoundly affected the development of building during the period broadly covered by the tenth, eleventh, and twelfth centuries—the feudal system of social and governmental organization; the monastic system, which led to the gathering together into protected and peaceful communities of selected groups of scholars, book copyists, and men skilled in the arts and crafts; the growing religious veneration of sacred relics, which led untold numbers to set out on pilgrimages and thereby gain the broadening effects of travel; and the enormous development of commerce, particularly toward the close of the period, which distributed over all the European lands objects of use and luxury made in distant parts.

The feudal system was a logical outgrowth of two ideas: the great landed estates of the provincial Romans, and the Germanic system under which military leaders surrounded themselves with a "companionship" (*comitatus*) of younger or less powerful men, who received support and advancement in return for their military service. This combination of such divers influences from the old Roman Empire and the primitive north is characteristic of the gradual process by which, during the long period from the Fall of Rome to the twelfth century, modern Europe gradually began to take form by the fusion of many peoples and many ideas—a fusion to which the Frankish Empire, the Goths of Italy and of Spain, the Greco-Romans of the Eastern Empire, the Latins of France and Italy, the German agricultural and pastoral tribes of the north and the west, and the Viking pirates from Scandinavia all contributed.

In essence, the feudal system remained a military and agricultural arrangement. To the liege lord the vassal nobles owed military service, of an amount proportionate to the size of their individual holdings; from him they received a guaranty of peaceful occupation of the lands which had been granted to them. Under the vassals were the agricultural laborers who farmed the vassals' land. To their lords, in turn, these laborers owned not only a certain amount of military service, but also a stated number of days of agricultural service and some proportion of the yield of their own land; as their share in the arrangement they received the right to enjoy their land for life and to pass it on to their children, but not to sell it or otherwise alienate it.

Early European agriculture was founded on either the two- or the three-field system, according to which the usable land of each single manorial holding would be divided into four parts: one reserved for common pasturage for the tenants' animals, and three assigned to agricultural use; one of these three fields would be left fallow each year in rotation, the other two would be planted with different crops—perhaps spring crops in one and fall crops in the other,—and the use of all three would rotate annually so that the land would not be impoverished by too intensive use. Within each field the tenants' holdings were in long, narrow strips—the strips of each farmer frequently widely separated from each other;—and, since over the generations each tenant willed his property to his children or grandchildren, the system of land holding became extraordinarily confused. In addition to the three fields, there would be another area, perhaps similarly divided, which was reserved for the lord of the manor, and which was worked by the tenants with the labor dues that were part of the rent they paid for the land. Neither the tenant nor his children were allowed theoretically to leave the land without permission from their lord; and, although if the land were good they might achieve considerable wealth through the sale of their surplus, they remained serfs bound to the soil and in many ways subject to the autocratic will of the landlord.

As the system grew more and more complicated, each immediate manor holder or landlord would owe service to a superior lord, this lord in turn might owe service to another, and so on through an ascending hierarchical scale to the ultimate lord from whom all of the grants were theoretically held, who might be either a great duke or, later, the king—who was deemed to hold his power and position by direct delegation from the Almighty. Owing to marriages and the right of inheritance, feudal loyalties eventually became extremely mixed and homage from the same manor might come to be claimed by two hostile superior nobles. The great example of this inevitable confusion is of course the Hundred Years' War between the kings of England and France, with regard to their lordship not only over Normandy but over all western France. Thus, at the beginning, the system, by its primitive and simple directness, tended toward stability and the efficient exploitation of the land, but toward the end of its dominance it led to struggle, rivalry, and war, and to the devastation of the lands it was designed to protect.

The monastic system was, in a sense, the religious parallel of the feudal system. It was also a rather fortuitous result of three entirely different elements in the religious life of the Middle Ages—the ideal of asceticism and withdrawal from the world, the missionary ideal, and the fact that through gift and bequest the church had become a great landowner. In the East, as we have seen, the ascetic ideal remained dominant, but in the West it was the other two factors which came to control the system. Groups of missionaries in distant and primitive parts of Europe would be almost forced to band together for protection and create thereby a definite centralized community. What more logical than to apply this same community idea to the vast land holdings which the church had accumulated, and, in order to assure their profitable development, to establish in each a community of monks to take a place similar to that of the feudal lord? These communities filled an insistent cultural need, for entrance into them furnished almost the only outlet to those dissatisfied with the bickering, the crudity, and the hard-and-fast castes of the feudal system.

Thus, during the darkest ages, there flowed into the monasteries a continual stream of the best minds and the most imaginative personalities of the era, and the monasteries became not only the feudal lords of large territories farmed by tenants precisely as the feudal manors were farmed, but also the guardians of learning and of skill in agriculture and the arts and crafts. These monasteries were organized in great orders, and monks in the same order were sent from one of its monasteries to another as need occurred, so that the particular skills developed in one center tended to be spread with great rapidity over the entire face of Europe. This accounts for many similarities in the art and architecture of the period in places as far apart as England and Italy.

The function of the monasteries was therefore both secular and religious; and, because of their wealth, life in the monasteries and the ideals of the orders became increasingly obsessed with the secular field of organization and profit-making. Religious rebellions against this growing worldliness occurred spasmodically throughout the whole period, and order after order was founded with the idea of protesting against the temporal interests of earlier orders and returning to the ascetic ideals that had dominated the earliest monks. Even this movement had its architectural reflections, for the angry protest of St. Bernard of Clairvaux against the overornamented richness and the grotesque carvings that were common in monastery buildings led to a new attempt to produce simple buildings with their effect dependent on structural rather than decorative elements, and in that way was one of the factors that went into the creation of new forms which resulted in Gothic architecture. Since the monasteries had become guardians of skill in the arts and crafts, and the great employers of even those laymen who had such skills, it is natural to find that much Romanesque architecture is essentially a monastic architecture, and that the greater number of Romanesque churches were originally monastic churches.

The feudal system was, as we have observed, essentially agricultural and military, and feudal building was therefore dominantly the building of castles and of agricultural villages. The castle had its root in the great Roman villas on the one hand and in the single great halls of the barbarian military leaders on the other—great halls in which the retainers ate and slept, with a dais at the end reserved for the leader and his family. These great halls, built of timber, high-roofed, with a central hearth, and with few if any windows, such as we read of in Beowulf and see in restorations in the Swedish islands, remained the central feature of much Romanesque castle design.

At first the castles would consist merely of such a great hall, with another smaller similar hall (called a "bower") where the lord's family had its private residence, a chapel, and whatever barns were necessary—all surrounded by a wooden stockade within a moat. Later, the builders borrowed the Roman villa idea of connecting all of these elements into one rambling structure, sometimes built around a court. Later still, as building skill increased and settled residence became more common, stone began to replace the old timber stockades and halls, and at once the entire character of the castle suffered a change.

With the growth of feuds and warfare between neighboring rival feudal lords, the military strength of the castle became of prime importance in the design. Travel by pilgrimage had brought many into contact with the elaborate fortifications of the Near East, and toward the end of the period the Crusades furnished a dangerous but fruitful laboratory for castle design. Towers at the corners and the gateways, to flank the walls between, became universal; the old carved richness of timber yielded to the heavy simplicity of stone; and, since the arch is the simplest way to cover wide stone openings, the use of the arch for doors and windows was quite general. Yet the old idea of the great hall as the central feature of the castle remained, and Oakham Hall in England—with its little windows, its low stone walls, and its high roof supported on interior arcades almost like those of a church—shows perfectly the twelfth-century English type.

Nevertheless, military science was advancing too, and the old confused, almost riotous battles gave way to disciplined attack—and, where it was a matter of the capture of a castle, to the siege. Siege warfare led to the subdivision of the castle into independent elements, if possible so designed that the capture of any one would not necessarily endanger the rest; and this idea, in turn, led to the keep or donjon, the last and most strongly fortified center of the whole, designed so that theoretically it became itself an independent fortress. Since height of position in those days gave enormous military advantage, the keep tended to become towerlike in shape, and in its development the precedent of the old tower houses of Merovingian times played an important part. Hence, the fully developed Romanesque keep was often called a tower, like the Tower of London; and, as we can see it in a twelfth-century development in Hedingham Castle, it would consist of several great halls one over the other, the bottom one perhaps used as a guardroom, the one above as the old castle great hall, and the top as the private residence. Privacy, so far as it existed, was given by cabinets or passages built in the thickness of the great walls, particularly on the upper floors, and by the deep window embrasures often built with stone seats, curtained off from the hall.

This gradual evolution made the study of new ways of heating inevitable, for in a building of more than one story the old central hearth became well-nigh impossible. It is therefore during this period that the fireplace, with a great hood over it and a smoke chamber running up above the roof as a real chimney, makes its appearance. Sometimes in the more primitive examples the smoke is merely led diagonally out through a hole in the side of the wall, without any vertical chimney at all. This centralization of the fire, and the removal of the smoke from a room quickly and efficiently, revolutionized all secular design.

Still, even with this new heating convenience, life in the castle was bound to be rough, uncomfortable (in our eyes), and without individual privacy. Luxury chiefly consisted in overeating and heavy drinking, punctuated by periodical frenzied physical exertion in war, tournaments, and the hunt. But there was a kind of barbaric splendor to these interiors. Chests, ironbound and carved, lined the walls, and frequently cushions made them comfortable as seats. Great beds were surrounded with gorgeous curtains, and every room of any pretension would boast a standing cabinet, carved and painted, and sometimes a carved chair or throne. Stools which could be used either as tables or seats were common, and in the more luxurious castles hangings of embroidered or printed cloth concealed the crude stone. Sometimes the walls would be painted with scenes of the tournament, of war, or of love. If additional privacy became necessary, as for instance when one lord made a ceremonial visit with his entire suite to another, hangings from temporary posts and curtain rods would divide the great hall into separate sections known as tents or *pavillons*. None the less, generally speaking, life in the

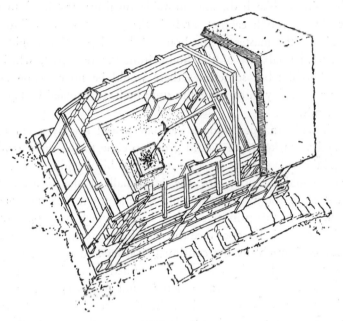

54. TYPICAL EARLY SCANDINAVIAN FARMHOUSE OR STUGA; CUTAWAY VIEW TO SHOW INTERIOR. (Lundberg: *Herremannens Bostad*.)

castles remained conservative. The great advances in comfort and luxury came from another section of the population, as we shall see.

The agricultural system of the feudal era naturally gave rise to village rather than individual farm buildings, and the villages grew up along the roads and paths in rather helter-skelter fashion. In the north the influence of the old Germanic villages was dominant; and, since the same type of house—a long rectangle used both for animals and for the family, with a high-pitched, thatched roof—is found in excavated villages of the fourth century or earlier, and again almost unchanged in houses built as late as the seventeenth century, we may be sure that the type remained in constant use throughout the intervening ages.

These houses would generally be set with their gable ends to the street and would be built of a timber framing, more or less beautifully constructed, with the spaces between the timbers filled with mud plaster on a lathing of woven reeds or withes. There would be no windows except in the latter part of the period, when small square or rectangular windows, closed with wooden shutters or "glazed" with oiled parchment or oiled linen, would be used. The one room inside would generally have a central hearth, built-in boxlike beds, and movable furniture restricted to a table, a few benches, a rough cabinet, and—if the peasant were well-to-do—one carved chair for the master of the house. A board partition might separate this front, residential part of the house from the rear part, which served as barn and stable; but sometimes there would be no partition at all, as we can see even today in some of the stone-built, turf-roofed cottages of the Scottish islands.

A church with an open square in front would occupy a commanding position, and a market place would grow up close to the main road, or by the shore if the village were on a stream. Of public buildings in the beginning there would be none, for the great hall of the lord's castle, the bishop's palace, or the monastery would serve as town hall and courthouse. The first change in this primitive village layout, which had apparently been common in Germanic Europe since the neolithic era, came with the necessity for fortification brought by the continual rivalries and wars of neighboring feudal lords. Once the village area was confined by stockades—or later by stone walls—a more regular arrangement became necessary and the buildings were built closer and closer together. But the essential character remained largely unchanged until growing trade gave a new direction to the growth; and even today there are hundreds of villages, still chiefly agricultural, in England, in central Germany, and in parts of France, which have preserved their old straggling character. In the Mediterranean countries the tradition of urban living of the old Roman Empire still remained strong; and even little villages in south France, like the hill towns in central and southern Italy, have a pre-eminently urban appearance, with the little cottages built close together, of masonry, covered with the low-pitched tile roofs that remained constantly in use in the south from Roman times to the present day.

The second great architectural type of community was of course the monastery; and, because of the traveling of the monks from one center to another, as well as because of the rules of the various orders, a surprising uniformity is present. There still exists, in the Benedictine monastery of St.

Gall, a famous plan on parchment showing a monastery layout of the ninth century. No one knows whether it is the plan of an actual group or some monk's ideal arrangement, but it is interesting as showing the tremendous complexity of the community there set down. The largest building is the monastery church. Closely grouped around it are the living quarters for the monks, the abbot's house, the guesthouse, a hospital, shops, a brewery, a wine cellar, and all the barns and stables necessary for a prosperous agricultural community.

As time went on and the size of monastic holdings increased, decentralization of many of these elements inevitably set in, but certain features remained constant. These were, briefly, an arcaded court or cloister, usually set into the corner between the nave and transept of the cross-shaped church, and bordered on the two other sides by a chapter house or place for official meetings of the governing body; a refectory, a long narrow hall where all the monks ate together, with a raised pulpit from which a selected brother could read to them; and a dormitory or *dortoir,* another long narrow hall, sometimes on an upper floor, in which the monks slept. There would also sometimes be a library. Outside of the main group, but often connected with it, would be subsidiary buildings containing the abbot's residence, sleeping and eating places for guests and visitors, a hospital or infirmary, and occasionally shops for the manufacture of ecclesiastical ornaments, or rooms where the copying of books could go on. Oftentimes the abbot's house and the guesthouse would have cloisters of their own, so that the term cloister became almost synonymous with monastery.

The cooking for such a large community demanded special buildings, and it is characteristic of the greater amenity of monastery living, as compared with secular, that the culinary arts seem to have been as assiduously cultivated as the other, less carnal, crafts. Luxurious living was a criticism often levied against the monasteries; its architectural expression is to be found in such grand kitchen buildings as the twelfth-century kitchen of Fontevrault Abbey in France. These great monastic kitchens were often almost circular, with a ring of great separate fireplaces, each with its own chimney, surrounding a central, ventilated, open work space; and their elaborate construction and design is typical of the ingenuity of the monastic architects.

To build a group of buildings of such complex character and large size required not only the development of a skillful building technique to erect the large churches, the arcaded cloisters, and the high and ample halls required for dormitory and refectory use, but also demanded the development of an accomplished architectural skill in the economical, convenient, and beautiful arrangement of these elements. The problem was manifestly more complex than that of the castle except from the point of view of military strength, and it is not strange therefore to find that the architecture of monasteries during this period is the most competent and highly developed that existed, and that during their long history through these 300 years there was a constant advance in beauty, luxury, and convenience; it is not

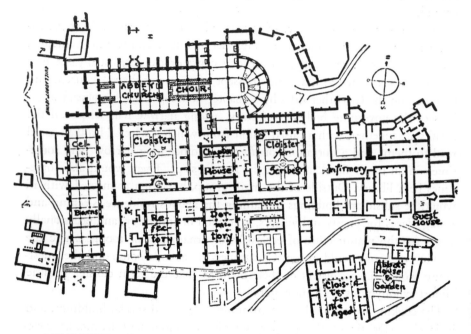

55. MONASTERY OF CLAIRVAUX; PLAN. (Viollet-le-Duc: *Dictionnaire raisonné de l'architecture française.*)

strange that extensive remains, or even completed groups, have lasted to the present, while secular buildings, often badly designed and crudely built, have been replaced or have vanished to dust. The larger monasteries were frequently rebuilt in Gothic and Renaissance times, but good examples of the smaller Romanesque monasteries which still retain their original aspect are those of St. Martin at Canigó in the Pyrenees, and of Fontfroide in Burgundy. Two interesting larger monasteries, both, however, of transitional early Gothic type, are the Cistercian monasteries at Poblet in Spain and Alcobaça in Portugal; the latter almost duplicates the plan of the mother house at Clairvaux.

The monastery became, in fact, an abode often of sumptuousness as well as of piety. Wandering poets and clerics brought to it tales of strange places, the interest of new ideas, and the beauty of new songs; in its shops the manuscript writer produced those magnificent manuscripts which, especially in the Dark Ages, were the most highly evolved and lavishly executed of art works; and within his secure walls of carefully cut stone and warmed by excellently built fireplaces—common here while they were still rare in the outside world—the monk had a protection against the weather unmatched elsewhere. Moreover, through the gifts of pilgrims, of lords, and of kings, the monasteries became treasure houses of all sorts of metalwork and textiles of the greatest beauty. The altars were hung with silk and velvet brocade, sometimes woven in far-off Syria or the Byzantine Empire; and they were decked with reliquaries of gilded bronze or of silver and gold, enriched with brilliant enamels and studded with roughly polished precious and semi-precious jewels.

In the monasteries glass came early into use for windows, and the art of the making of stained glass for the church received its earliest development. Mural painting added to the gorgeousness in St. Ceneri; and in St. Savin we can today see walls lined below with diaper patterns or paintings of hung tracery, and above the great Biblical stories and the holy legends of the time painted with breadth and power. This mural art was not realistic; the size of the figures might be conditioned either by their supposed relative importance or by the decorative demands of the composition. There is in it something of the architectural quality to be found in the Byzantine mosaics of the East; yet it is an art singularly alive, which, despite its origins in manuscript illumination and in the Eastern mosaic, rapidly achieved a character admirably suited to its position on the walls or the ceilings of these great monastic churches.

The stonecarver, too, was busy. The capitals of the cloister columns were rich with leafage often distantly based on the old Roman work, and with the imaginative grotesque animals so beloved by the north. There are even strange occasional reflections of pagan legend; centaurs and mermaids and nymphs peek sometimes shyly from between the leaves. In fact, the monastic sculptor seems to have allowed the freest possible play to his fancy, with results frequently scarcely religious in their implication, though perhaps he could find for them some orthodox explanation in current legends or in the strange symbolisms dear to the heart of the early church writers.

The sculptor's chief effort was of course applied to the monastic church itself and especially to its great door, through which the laity could come and fill the nave, although the choir was reserved for the monks. Here, in these entrances, was the great opportunity to impress upon the folk who came, who doubtless could not read, the chief lessons which the church had to give, the chief truths which it inculcated; so we find the central door the scene of carvings of the greatest of the church conceptions of those days—the Last Judgment, Christ in Glory, or the Virgin Enthroned with Christ on her knee. The chief figures would often be within a sort of oval form, pointed at its ends, called a *vesica* or *mandorla;* around might be the symbols of the Four Evangelists—the winged man, the winged ox, the winged lion, and the eagle—and on the minor portions all sorts of Bible stories—the Creation, the Expulsion from Paradise, Daniel in the Lions' Den, or the great Christmas cycle from the New Testament such as the Nativity, the Adoration of the Three Kings, the Flight into Egypt.

All of this richness would be displayed with amazing decorative skill, within the actual structural requirements of the door. Since the doorways were big, they were arched; and, since the doors themselves, in order to be swung easily and closed tightly, were best made square-headed, under the arch would be a horizontal lintel over the door opening itself. The semicircle between lintel and arch was filled with a thin stone slab—the tympanum, always the center of the composition and the place where Christ reigned over the Last Judgment or sat enthroned in glory.

Since the stone walls of this early period were thick, the doorway was frequently stepped out in a series of ever-widening arches, with the door opening itself far back on the inner face of the wall; and these successive steps not only made a large and impressive composition out of a door of very modest size, but offered extraordinary opportunities for sculptural decoration. Below the lintel, statues of prophets or saints might decorate the steps, or panels symbolizing the Virtues and the Vices fill the jambs. By the twelfth century, the climax period of Romanesque art, these carved doorways had become one of the most perfect, as they were one of the most magnificent, combinations of structural architecture with sculpture that the world has ever known. In them the two arts are so inextricably combined that it is impossible to imagine one without the other.

Within, the same exuberant imagination and the same decorative skill produced the marvelous capitals which crowned the columns or piers between nave and aisles, and which form such impressive evidence of the decorative genius of the time. Reminiscences of the Roman Corinthian order still sometimes control the general shape of the capital or even occasional details. At other times the use of lacelike surface carving and interlaces reveals the influence of the Byzantine East. But the thing which controls both types of capital is neither Roman nor Byzantine; it is something new, a creative synthesis, filled with a complexity and a dramatic intensity that sometimes produces elements of horror and frequently the unbridled imagination of the grotesque.

In fact, to read aright the mental state of the Romanesque centuries, we must study its buildings as well as its literature. In them both we can read a story of idealism, of frustration, of naïveté, of ignorance, and of vision which together produced the extraordinary vitality of the time. They are evidences of some kind of mass neurosis, raised almost into frenzy. The conflict between luxury and asceticism, between bestiality and idealism, between unbridled imagination and disciplined thought, was far from solved. Indeed in the cloister it was perhaps raised to a higher pitch. For the monk, the world of magic was never far away. The ancient gods persisted as living devils, and the legends show that Satan himself was conceived of as a very real, present entity. Fear and hope fight in these sometimes tortured sculptures, as they fought in the minds of their makers; cruelty and sadism show in the terrible beasts devouring men or other animals, just as mercy is shown in the lovely carvings of many of the Biblical stories. And the fear of the end of the world and of an eternal Hell, pictured in very physical terms, is always hauntingly in the background to produce such terrible things as the figure of Vice devoured by serpents in the porch of Moissac.

The Romanesque world was essentially a man's world, in the castle as in the cloister; and, as the temptations of the flesh were ever present, so womankind herself became somehow, in the minds of these monastic carvers, to be associated only with sin and destruction. Only in rare cases, like those of certain queens or duchesses in their own right, did women achieve a position of honor or importance, and even the impossibly romantic idealism of women which gradually was growing up in the bosom of chivalry—especially in Provençal—was at heart an expression of masculine superiority on the one hand and an excuse for masculine dominance in the guise of worship on the other. It is significant that late in the twelfth century Eleanor of Aquitaine, who had been Queen of France and was Queen of England, one of the great women of history, sought to mitigate the brutality of the society of her time, to bring into it something of gentleness and a sense of individual worth, by instituting in the north the Courts of Love that had been developed in the more luxurious culture of the south; and it is significant that Eleanor had spent some of her most formative years in a visit to the royal court at Constantinople, where she had seen a life more polished, more gracious, and more sumptuous than any that the Western world knew.

Yet Eleanor was a symptom of a great civilizing movement in the twelfth century, a movement which had its roots in the growing breadth of view and the growing luxury of life that resulted necessarily from a new and rapid increase in commerce. This new commercial development was a challenge both to the feudal system and to the monasteries, for the merchant or the manufacturer could never fit successfully into the feudal framework. So much is this true that there have been many discussions as to exactly how the merchant class first grew up. They were neither feudal lords nor vassals. Under any strict interpretation of the feudal system they owed homage to no one, and it was inevitable that as the commercial class increased the feudal system lost prestige.

But at the beginning trade was also an opportunity for the feudal lords and the monasteries, which they were not slow to take advantage of. If the lords and the monasteries could control an important trade route, or assert their rule over a large market, their opportunities for tribute were enormous; and, instead of realizing that the whole trade system constituted a challenge to their very existence, the lords and the monasteries hastened to give trade a new importance by protecting it and cultivating it. Thus feudal castles and villages which were on important trade routes enjoyed a great advantage over others. There, markets began to grow up, merchants to settle, and skilled artificers to congregate, soon almost crowding out the old agricultural inhabitants. The market places increased in size and importance. Monasteries frequently held control over them, and, as a symbol of their control, would build in each a cross—the market cross. Houses grew closer and closer together within the walls of the town; streets were straightened, widened; often, too, outside the city wall at some favored point a separate community solely of merchants would grow up, to be eventually surrounded by its own wall, and at last incorporated into the city itself. In that way, under the magic touch of the increased exchange of goods and money, villages grew into towns and towns into cities, and the whole basis of life was changed. And, just as trade revolutionized the ordinary living of people by giving life a new freedom and the individual new luxuries, it also made over the architecture of the towns by the creation of new building types—the town, guild, and market halls, and the market crosses—and by forcing a closer and more urban type of building on the earlier villages, as well as by creating new types of city dwelling for the new wealthy trading class.

It is in these town houses of the bourgeoisie that the revolutionary character of this later Romanesque work can be most clearly seen. There are fragments of these buildings. often concealed by later work, all over Europe.

Metz, the Italian cities, and the towns of southern and eastern France are especially full of them. In them all the same character can be found—a new expression of urbanity, of gracious living. A number of houses in the wealthy trading town that grew up around the great monastery at Cluny, in Burgundy, are typical. They are not large, for land within the confines of the town walls was costly. Like the modern city house, their largest dimension was their depth, and from wall to wall they were not over twenty-five feet across. The greater part of the ground floor was occupied by a shop, opening onto the street by a large archway. At the side of the shop a door led to the

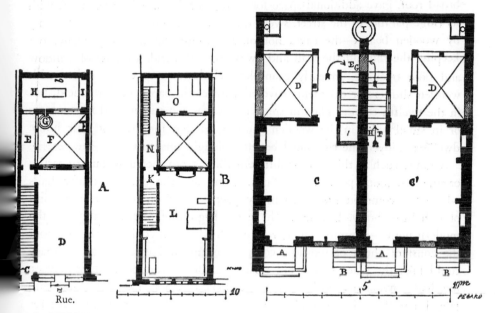

Rue.

56. TYPICAL ROMANESQUE HOUSES, CLUNY; PLANS. 12TH CENTURY. (Viollet-le-Duc.)

Left: HOUSE WITH SHOP	*Right:* A DOUBLE HOUSE
A. GROUND FLOOR	A. PORCH
C. ENTRANCE	B. CELLAR STAIRS
D. SHOP	C, c'. LIVING ROOM
E. PASSAGE	D. COURT
F. COURT	E, F, G, H. STAIRS
G. WELL	I. WELL
H. KITCHEN	
B. SECOND FLOOR	
K. STAIRS	
L. LIVING ROOM	
N. PASSAGE WITH ATTIC STAIRS	
O. BEDROOM	

stair to the upper and private parts of the house, and a passage went back to the court or yard behind, and by a gallery along its side to the kitchen at the rear. On the second floor, the front of the house had one large room, well lighted by a continuous row of arched windows. From it a smaller room, lighted from the court, opened out. Both had fireplaces. The front room served as living room, dining room, and bedroom for the master of the house; the rear room as a bedroom for the children. Another open gallery over the one below led back to the rear building, which contained above the kitchen a room for servants. Occasionally a third floor, or attic, under the broad roof, gave additional space for storage or for sleeping; the roof, with its ridge parallel to the street, swept down to wide projecting eaves held up by wooden beams—the eaves not only shading the windows below, but keeping the rain off the wall and away from the wide expanse of window and door opening. In early examples, windows were closed either with wooden shutters or casements covered with cloth, paper, or parchment, but in the twelfth century glass in small panes was sometimes used in transoms or in small holes in the wooden shutters, so that for the first time house dwellers enjoyed the combined benefits of light and warmth.

A house such as this is a far different thing from the rude country castles or the one-room peasant dwellings. Gone are the ancient, drafty halls where the common life of so many people went on together in a kind of rich hurly-burly. Instead we have the beginning of the concept of the modern home—a family center, where individualities could develop without the constant check of too-close companionship, and where quiet intimacy could take the place of the old roistering life in common. These houses, too, had conveniences unknown in the noble's manor. The little court contained a well or cistern head most conveniently related to the kitchen; for the first time adequate thought and care was expended on the problem of sanitation, and the individual privy became customary.

Later, this same care was more and more evidenced even in castle design, and the elaborate arrangements for castle sanitation in the great Gothic castles remain to tell us of the growing ideals of cleanliness and decency of the time. Thus, many a passage, shaft, and vaulted chamber, now carefully pointed out to tourists as a prison, dungeon, or a secret way, was originally nothing more or less than part of the old castle sanitary system.

This twelfth-century easing of manners not only gave rise to increasing demands for comfort, but also undoubtedly furnished an opportunity, such as had been unknown outside the cloisters since the Fall of the Roman Empire, for the development of personality and of original thinking. The movement seems to have begun in the bourgeoisie—the wealthy merchants, the skilled traders,—and it was a movement of the greatest importance, for to it, I believe, we may attribute the tremendous advancement in secular skills in building and the arts which brought in the next, the Gothic, period, as well as the creation of new municipal and governmental systems which replaced feudalism with the foundations of the modern nations, and which were symbolized by the great cathedral building of the period that lay ahead.

Chapter 13

DEVELOPMENT OF ROMANESQUE
ARCHITECTURE

THE greatest problem for the Romanesque architect was the church. The original inspiration behind most early Romanesque churches was naturally the early Christian basilica, with its low side aisles and its high nave with clerestory windows above the side-aisle roofs, and at the east end its large apse with the altar in front of it. Such basilicas as we have seen had been built in the Merovingian period in France, and the Carolingian builders had struggled to adapt the basilican form to their cruder construction and their differing decorative ideals.

Three things prevented a mere copying of the early basilica. The first was already present in the Carolingian period—the fact that the medieval masons liked to build thick walls of small stones and to arch over all openings, and the fact that their sculptural skill was not equal to, or perhaps their taste did not approve, the delicate classical carving of the earlier time.

The second great cause for change lay in the development of new rituals and new religious ideas, which followed naturally from the character of monasticism itself as well as from the importance given to the veneration of relics in the medieval church. At the basis of the monastic system lay the fact that many of the clergy lived together and served the same church. This led naturally to having more altars than one in this church, so that each of the monks might have sufficient opportunity for celebrating the mass. If more altars are necessary, the old single apse of the single basilica is manifestly inadequate, and we find that at an early date the rudimentary transepts of the basilica become real projections on each side of the church, and are furnished with little apses projecting from them. Similar small apses were added on each side of the main apse at the ends of the side aisles, and each of these minor apses, of which there might be as many as six, would contain an altar dedicated to a different saint, and therefore, in function at least, a separate chapel. Every altar was required to contain, prior to its dedication, some authenticated relic of a saint, and as the cult of the veneration of relics increased these new chapel altars might become magnets to draw to the church crowds of devout worshipers.

This reverence for relics had another important effect, for it led inevitably to a great increase in pilgrimages. The pilgrimage system had of course been in existence from at least the fourth century, but the early pilgrimages had had as their goal Rome and the Holy Land only. Now, in the early Middle Ages, all this was changed; and many churches, because of their possession of relics which were unusually famous or of great reputed power, might become pilgrimage centers themselves, or at least important stages on longer pilgrimages. Since pilgrims brought gifts to the shrines they visited, the church stimulated these pilgrimages by every means in its power, and churches began to be designed with especial regard to them.

One need was for a way of getting around the church from chapel to chapel without interrupting the ordinary services, which played such a large part in the monastic life and which must continue whether the church were thronged with pilgrims or not. A natural solution was to carry the side aisle completely around the apse to form an ambulatory, and then to open out from this a series of radiating chapels which would project from the apse wall. Thus, since the regular services were held in the choir, the pilgrims could be led around the ambulatory to all of the chapels without interrupting the chants and the music rising from the choir as they passed it. In this way, the entire east end of the old basilica was changed, and what was originally merely a semicircular apse became a long projecting arm with a high central choir, with a low side aisle leading continuously around it, and with a series of small chapels, usually of apse form, projecting from its outside wall. From this evolved that rich symphony of forms which is called the *chevet* (cradle), which was to have such a glorious development in the later Gothic era. This lavish east end can be well seen in such churches of central France as Notre Dame du Port at Clermont-Ferrand or St. Paul at Issoire, and in the great abbey churches of Burgundy like that at Cluny.

The third factor, which led to the change from the old basilica to the great medieval church, lay in the danger from fire. The early Christian basilica was wooden-roofed throughout, and if through the accidents of war or from lightning one of the great wooden roofs got well aflame the church and its contents were doomed; for, though the walls might stand, the roof would undoubtedly burn through and its great flaming mass of wood, crashing to the floor beneath, would consume everything within the walls. Such catastrophes had become almost a commonplace in early medieval times, and with the increase in the cult of relics, and the tremendous profusion of decoration which resulted from the wealth brought to the churches by the pilgrims, it became increasingly necessary to build at least the important churches in such a way that this danger could be obviated. Since vaulting was the only method of fireproof building known to the time, vaulted churches were the natural result.

But the building of vaulted churches brought great constructional difficulties, which were solved satisfactorily only in Gothic times. The whole history of Romanesque church architecture from the tenth to the twelfth century is the history of the experiments made in search of this perfect solution. The first difficulty was the mere weight of a stone vault. This meant at once that all the supporting piers had to be larger, and led to the gradual abandonment in many cases of the single column, in favor of a large pier built up of small stones. The second difficulty lay in the fact that a vault, like any arched construction as we have already seen (p. 14 and p. 15), exerts on its supports not only weight but a sidewise thrust, so that unless the supports are braced from falling outward the whole will collapse. A third problem lay in the high nave, which was an essential part of the basilica scheme. How could a vault be raised on walls extending high above the rest of the building, without danger of these walls being thrust apart? The fourth question to be taken into account was the fact that any arched construction has to be supported in place by a wooden framework, called a centering, until it is entirely complete; until the last stone is in place, the whole will collapse of its own weight unless such a support is present.

For 300 years the builders struggled with these difficulties. At times they approached success, at times they failed; and the history of medieval architecture is full of stories of catastrophic collapse due to bad design or bad construction. Many of the local differences between the various schools of Romanesque architecture depend upon differing types of approach to this central problem.

It is well to remember that not only had the old Roman skill in the building of vaults of brick and concrete long since disappeared, but also that only one of the great Roman basilicae, the Basilica of Maxentius,—and none of the early Christian—was vaulted; and the tradition of the basilica was very strong indeed.

The first thing which was done was to vault the side aisles, which, being comparatively near the ground, could be easily supported and the walls easily buttressed against outward thrust. Sometimes the mere weight of heavy walls was sufficient to withstand the thrust. In order to get arched windows as large as possible in the side-aisle walls, and also a continually arched passage running the length of the aisle, simple square intersecting groined vaults were used; this meant that the distance between the piers of the arcade separating nave and aisles was the same as the width of the aisles. When the apse ambulatory was reached, however, problems began to appear even in this simple portion of the building. Naturally, since the ambulatory ran around the semicircle of the apse, the segments or bays of which it was made up, instead of being square, became in plan wedge-shaped like the stones of an arch. The vaulting of these offered tremendous difficulties both structurally and aesthetically, because, instead of the simple diagonal groins of the regular intersecting vault, all sorts of queer-shaped intersections resulted.

But it was the vaulting of the central nave which was the supremely troublesome undertaking. The easiest way to vault it was of course by the use of a simple barrel or tunnel vault, supported on the side clerestory walls and running through unbroken. Yet how could the side walls be kept in place against the mighty thrust of this great stone tunnel? In many examples, the Romanesque builders confessed themselves defeated by this problem, and did one of two things—either they preserved the clerestory with its windows and used a wooden roof over the nave and choir, as in many of the Norman churches both in France and England; or else they abandoned the high clerestory entirely, as is the case in much of central and southern France. Even without clerestory windows, however, the Romanesque builders liked a higher central nave, and to produce this they would frequently make a sort of second story over the side aisles, roofed with a half vault—its low side at the outside walls, its high crown inward— and this half vault would serve to take the thrust of the nave vault out to the heavy outside walls. This upper gallery could then be opened out to the nave with a series of arches, and thus form what is called a triforium gallery. Churches constructed in this way were stable, but they were dark and gloomy—as one may see today in Notre Dame du Port or in St. Sernin at Toulouse—and they were extremely wasteful of material. Moreover, the barrel vaulting, running unbroken through from end to end, with nothing to emphasize its shape, appeared merely a formless heavy covering.

This led the architects to attempt to emphasize the shape of the vault by running a rib or additional arch, following the line of the vault but slightly smaller, over every support in the main arcade below. These ribs not only improved the appearance and gave grace and delicacy to the whole, but they also simplified the construction enormously. Once the ribs had been built, the vault was naturally divided into a series of individual units, and these units could be built separately, one by one; and the same centering, just large enough for one section, could be used again and again. The great forest of timbers required for the entire vault could therefore be much reduced.

57. NOTRE DAME DU PORT, CLERMONT-FERRAND; SECTION. 11TH CENTURY. (Viollet-le-Duc.)

We have already seen how the use of small stones and heavy walls led to the stepped arch. Precisely the same kind of thing went on in the interior construction, and led to stepping the arches between nave and side aisles, and breaking up the pier plan from a simple square into cross shapes, or even more elaborate plans as the number of steps in the arch above increased. With the addition of ribs for the nave vault, still more richness was suggested, for the ribs were carried on pilasterlike projections running down on the inside of the clerestory walls and thus furnishing another member to the pier below. Similar ribs could be added to the side-aisle vaults, so that eventually pier plans were of considerable intricacy, and the vertical lines of light and shade running up the piers and continuing around the steps of the arches and the ribs of the vaults began to create that vertical sense of upward growth and lightness which was such a marked beauty in later medieval churches.

However, the darkness of these early vaulted churches was a great disadvantage, particularly as these same Romanesque centuries saw the development of stained glass for window use, thus combining light and the glory of their decorative effect in one element. The clerestory window became more and more a necessity. Occasionally the attempt was made, successfully, merely to use low clerestory walls of extreme thickness, as in the cathedral at Autun, but this ordinarily was a manifestly illogical solution. Toward the end of the eleventh century, the architects of St. Philibert at Tournus hit upon another ingenious arrangement. After the ribs over the central nave were built, walls were carried up over them, running across the church, and from these walls little vaults, also running across the church, were turned, one to each bay. Since the thrust of each of these small vaults was balanced by the thrust of the one next it, the only thrust which had to be considered was that of the main ribs. These were, however, down low enough so that the problem was not difficult. The little vaults ended at the clerestory wall in arches and allowed ample windows, so that the whole church was light. Structurally this solution was almost perfect, but aesthetically it left much to be desired, for it broke up the nave too violently into separate units and destroyed the unity of the whole.

A more natural solution was of course the use of intersecting vaults over the nave, similar to those over the side aisles. Yet this, too, had its disadvantages, for the nave was usually twice as wide as the side aisles, and consequently each bay of the nave—since the piers on either side were only as far apart as the width of the aisle—was a long narrow rectangle. Manifestly, if round vaults of different widths start from the same spring (the level on which arches are built) they will rise to different heights and cannot be made to intersect in the middle. If the spring of the cross-vaults is raised sufficiently to make its crown at the same level as the crown of the main vault, the intersections between the two surfaces will be ugly and unnatural. And, since in an intersecting vault all of the thrusts are concentrated at the piers, the thrusts there become very great and require special buttressing.

The Romanesque architects struggled with these two problems with varying success. In Lombardy they tried making one bay of the nave equal two bays of the aisles, thus getting the square nave bay which would give simple intersections. This brought much more weight on alternate piers, for the intermediate piers carried none of the nave vault; and consequently the piers which carried the nave vault had to be made larger than the others or else, if the piers were alike, they were conspicuously overlarge and awkward. Nevertheless, this solution, found first perhaps in the church of San Ambrogio in Milan, marked a great step forward in the scientific solution of the nave vault problem. From Lombardy this form traveled to Normandy, perhaps through the influence of Abbot William of Volpiano, a Lombard, and from Normandy into England, where Durham Cathedral became another early example of a quasi-scientific solution of the vault question. The same Lombard influence followed a well-known trade route across the Alpine passes and down the Rhine, and controlled much of the German building there until well into the thirteenth century.

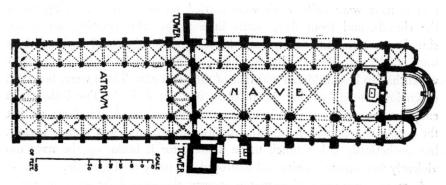

58. SAN AMBROGIO, MILAN; PLAN. (Simpson. Vol. II.)

The geometrical intersections of these vaults formed always a real difficulty to the stonecutter and the mason. With the rough building machinery at their command and the rather crude masonry techniques, it was hard to produce true intersection curves that were definite. Yet, aesthetically, these intersection lines played a tremendous part in the effect of the whole, because frequently the lighting on the two sections of intersecting vaults would be completely different, and if the line separating light and dark areas was wavy or unsure the result was painfully obvious.

To the Lombards, again, is probably due the credit for finding a simple answer to this problem—that is, building a separate diagonal arch or rib to the line of the groin, so as not only to emphasize its aesthetic function but also to serve in concealing the inequalities of the rough masonry vault surface. San Ambrogio in Milan probably is the first church to have these diagonal ribs in its nave vault, although they occurred at almost the same time in minor vaults in other parts of Europe. The vault of Durham Cathedral is especially interesting, because, although its lower part shows that it was originally intended to have the Lombard type of vault, in which two bays of the side aisle equal one of the nave, and its piers are alternately large and small, nevertheless its architects, having seized upon the idea of the diagonal rib, realized that to a large extent it solved the problem of difficult intersections in a rectangular bay; and therefore, although they built heavy ribs across the vault at alternate piers, the space between these two ribs was occupied by two complete bays of intersecting vaulting with rich diagonal ribs. Once the ribs were built, the vault forms could be waved or modified from the geometrical, cylindrical type to conical or other warped and distorted shapes without complication, and the eye saw only the intersection.

Another problem which this use of ribs—both groin ribs at vault intersections, and cross-ribs—helps to solve was the problem of the queer shapes in the vaulting of the ambulatory around the choir. Once the builders had grasped the conception that ribs could be carried up to form the desired pattern, and the vault surfaces waved or distorted to meet them, the question was almost settled. There still remained, however, both in this connection and in connection with the nave vaults, the problem that, with semicircular vaults, differences in width mean differences in height, and the fact that, even in a perfect intersecting vault, the intersection forms not a semicircle but an ellipse, which both structurally and aesthetically is less satisfactory than the higher, fuller curve. The only final answer to these questions, still unsettled, came with the adoption of the pointed arch; but, once the idea of the pointed arch and the ribbed vault combined had occurred, Gothic architecture was born, and the whole spirit and appearance of churches suffered a revolutionary modification. In a sense, then, the final solution of the problems which Romanesque architects faced was the signal for the death of Romanesque architecture as a style, and relentlessly forced the study of new aesthetic shapes and forms.

All of these changes in the interiors of churches made similar modifications necessary on the exterior. The east end, for instance, instead of being a simple half cylinder covered with a half-conical roof, became an intricate combination of radiating chapels and roofs of different heights—the chapels, the ambulatory, and the choir. Similarly, the need for withstanding the thrusts of the vaults, and the desire to avoid a wasteful use of stone, led to the development of exterior buttresses—that is, thicker portions of the wall, placed where they could give it extra stability. Naturally, with the intersecting vault concentrating the thrust at the lines of the piers, the buttresses began to divide up the exterior of the building into separate bays, just as the ribs and supporting pilasters divided the interior. The old horizontal quality began slowly to yield to the vertical accent that was to become one of the dominating characteristics of Gothic architecture.

The Romanesque architects used the buttress only tentatively at first, and experimented with all sorts of treatments for it, sometimes making it like an engaged column, sometimes as a projecting strip like a pilaster; and only gradually did they come to realize that its depth and not its width was the important element, and that the simplest way of treating it at the top was in a series of inclined surfaces to throw off the rain. Yet in the early attempts there is a certain charming naïveté and often great richness—a surface richness which characterized a large amount of Romanesque church work. At the eaves there would be little arcaded cornices, sometimes held up by grotesque brackets, with heads or animals carved upon them. Projecting horizontal moldings or string courses would divide the building and accent windowsill levels or the spring line of the arches. In some cases elaborate polygonal patterns of different-colored stones and marbles would fill the wall surfaces, particularly around the window heads and just under the cornice.

Among the exterior features in Romanesque architecture which grew to great importance during these three centuries was the bell tower. Starting in Italy, probably in the ninth century, as the simplest kind of square or circular tower, with little arched windows and repeated thin horizontal cornices to give it height, it gradually achieved, especially in France, a grace of outline and a growing lightness of structure which were the first steps toward the creation of the Gothic spire. The Italian towers had had very low-pitched roofs; in French work the pyramid-tops were given continuously steeper and steeper slopes, were more and more built of solid stone, and the openings in the sides became larger and larger. At the end of the eleventh century, for instance, the tower of Le Puy en Velay climbs, diminishing stage over diminishing stage, to an interesting top of intersecting gables and a small spire; and in Normandy it is the church towers, such as those of the famous Abbaye aux Hommes (St. Étienne), which give a new mark of distinction and beauty to these great churches, and point the way toward the magnificent monuments which were to follow.

The cruciform plan with many chapels, the general idea of a low side aisle and a higher nave and choir, the use of clustered piers and of round arches, a rich west front with an elaborately decorated portal and sometimes flanking towers, and ornament which is composed of elements derived from the classic world, from the northern grotesque, and from Constantinople—these qualities are well-nigh universal during the Romanesque period throughout Europe; but the exact character varies enormously from locality to locality, and climate and tradition joined to produce a series of important local schools.

In Tuscany, and generally through western central Italy, it was a combination of prosperity arising from the great Mediterranean trade of Pisa, together with a population which seems to have been less touched or less daunted by barbarian invasions than that of the rest of Italy, which controlled the design. The first brought wealth, which made possible a lavish use of the richest marbles and the most intricate carving, and a general gaiety of feeling that displayed itself in the black-and-white banding of building after building, and in the development of church fronts in which the actual wall is concealed by row after row of marvelous free-standing arcades. The second brought a skill in restudying classic forms—as it were, recreating them—that is remarkable, so that the Corinthian capitals and the carved acanthus bands of Pisa, although so obviously Roman in origin, are free and creative. In the Baptistry at Florence (*circa* 1050) the touch of Roman form is everywhere, and even the great simple inside space is not without its Roman grandeur; yet the impression of the whole is definitely that of something new. This Tuscan Romanesque is a style light, almost frivolous, but gracious, delicate, full of decorative genius; it can be seen best in the Baptistry at Florence, in the cathedral and leaning tower of Pisa, and in some of the churches at Lucca. It is characteristic of the dominance of decoration that the church fronts of this style are frequently mere screens, extending far above the roofs of the building behind as pure ornamental façades without structural meaning.

In Provence, also, the Roman ideals were pre-eminent, and in the palaces and castles a gay life went on, given to poetry and song; and, though a more serious and more structural sense appears in its churches than in those of Pisa, there is in both the same devotion to the Roman Corinthian capital and acanthus leaf, which reached its climax in the superb twelfth-century fronts of St. Gilles and St. Trophime at Arles, where the new Romanesque skill in figure sculpture and in the grotesque, the Romanesque desire to elaborate the main church entrance, and the classic forms were wed into a new synthesis of sublime power.

In Sicily and the south of Italy the Romanesque work reflects their confused history. The Byzantines, the Saracens, the Normans all left their imprint on that area, and occasionally sudden influences from northern Italy appear to complicate the picture. The pointed arch brought in by the Saracens is common; Saracenic, too, may be the intricate polychromed woodwork of some of the great church ceilings. But the greatest glory of the Sicilian Romanesque lies in its magnificent use of Byzantine mosaic. In the Capella Palatina at Palermo, 1132-43, and the cathedral at Monreale, 1171-76, the purely basilica-plan churches have Corinthian capitals of almost antique type and walls all sheathed above with glorious gold-ground mosaic, climaxing in the apse dome in gigantic figures which brood over the interiors with almost hypnotic powers; and the lower walls are sheathed in marbles in a way more Mohammedan than Byzantine.

In Aquitaine, far off in France near the Atlantic shore, there is another extraordinary development of Byzantine influence, and almost all the churches have the dome-on-pendentives of Byzantine building; yet, save for St. Front in Perigueux, the plan of which resembles so closely that of St. Mark's in Venice and, like it, is probably based on the Holy Apostles church in Constantinople, the churches are long and narrow, and seem to be trying to adapt the basilica plan to the dome construction. The experiment led to all sorts of interesting results, in churches as far apart as those of Poitiers and the cathedral of Le Puy en Velay; but perhaps its simplest versions, like Souillac and Cahors, where two or three simple domes crown the nave, are the most satisfactory. In these churches, too, the pointed arch is frequently found, and one can but surmise the traveling of monks from east to west, or the emigration of Greek masons to this distant land, to account for this unique and interesting local school and its use of the Mohammedan pointed arch.

Historically it is not these reflections of distant origins, nor the devotion to the Roman traditional forms, charming as they are, which are the most important Romanesque developments. There is something in all of these styles a little too superficial, a little too facile—something perhaps even expressive of decadence rather than growth. For the really significant developments one must turn elsewhere—to those lands where the impeding hand of tradition was less strong, where mankind had to face these new church building problems with a completely new approach, controlled by the materials at hand and by a lack of skill in building in the old ways. One must turn, therefore, to lands where barbarian destruction had been most complete, and the barbarian conquest most thoroughly successful—to Lombardy, to Spain, to northern and eastern France, to Normandy, and to England. It was these peoples who approached the problem of building a fireproof vaulted church with the most creative ingenuity, and who decorated it with the freest and most inventive forms.

The Lombard style is one characterized by great brilliance in vaulting, by comparative sobriety in exterior effect—with a large dependence on simple architectural forms, and by decorative sculpture which at the beginning is naïve and childlike. Its great contribution was the development of the ribbed vault, as we have seen, and along with that the discovery that buttresses as projecting strips could be made an essential part of the exterior decorative effect. Typical of this structural feeling, also, is the use of little arcades projecting slightly from the wall to form cornices and horizontal bands, instead of the carved and molded classic cornice. At the very end of the Romanesque period, long practice in decorative sculpture, combined perhaps with a great deal of fresh talent from other parts of Italy, produced a school of decorative sculpture as sure and as skillful as any in Europe, and in the late twelfth and early thirteenth centuries church fronts such as those of Parma and Modena and Verona were superbly decorated with sculpture, freely placed, in which all the possibilities of Biblical and legendary storytelling are realized. Significant not only of this skill, but also of the new wide internationalism brought by the pilgrimages, is the famous relief in Modena, showing scenes from the Arthurian legend.

The valley of the Rhine constituted the most natural trade route from northern Italy to the west and north, and it was natural therefore that Lombard influence should be the controlling element in the Romanesque of Germany. German Romanesque reached a first climax under the reigns of the Emperors Otto II and III (973-1002), and this earlier work is characterized by a skillful use of the simplest decorative forms, rich use of color, and a simplicity and power not unlike that of some of the Carolingian work. Later, in the twelfth century, a new flood of building swept across the Rhenish countries, and it is here that certain of the Lombard systems of vaulting and of church decoration reached their highest development. These later German Romanesque churches often have two apses and two sets of transepts, one at each end. Over both crossings there is usually a low tower or lantern, so that sometimes it is difficult to tell which end is to be considered the more important. Round, square, and polygonal towers are common; frequently a pair is placed at each end, so that the outline of the whole, with the high towers and the crossing lanterns, becomes extremely interesting.

Inside, these churches preserve many of the characteristics of Lombard churches—such as the common use of two bays of the side aisle to one of the nave,—but in general they are much higher and narrower in proportion, and the effect of this great height so strongly and simply treated is most impressive. On the exterior, the Lombard system of pilaster strips and arcaded cornices is carried to a high degree of development and gives an extremely interesting exterior pattern. At times, little open arcades in the thickness of the wall, perhaps borrowed from the Romanesque of Tuscany, give added richness. Roofs are generally high-pitched. Capitals and other architectural ornament are of the simplest; particularly common is the use of the simple geometric cushion capital. The figure carving is, however, often of great imaginative power, intricate in design, and beautifully executed, showing the influence of the magnificent Romanesque manuscript illumination in Romanesque Germany. This extremely vital school, represented in the great cathedrals and abbey churches of Mainz, Worms, Laach, and Speyer, lasted well into the thirteenth century.

In Spain, as we have seen, the Visigothic kingdom had already developed a distinctive and competent architecture, characterized by good building and rich decoration, in which the horseshoe arch was an important part. With the Moorish Conquest the kingdom came to an end, but the influence of its architecture went on, and it is probably from the Visigothic buildings that the Moors borrowed the horseshoe-arch form which they used so magnificently. Moreover, in those parts of Spain which had remained in the hands of the Christian powers, or were shortly reconquered by them, the old Visigothic skill had a profound influence in the Romanesque work which developed. This Spanish Romanesque of the eleventh and twelfth centuries is characterized especially by the boldness of its structure and the extraordinary vividness and dramatic power of its decorative sculpture. The climax of the style is best seen in the early parts of Santiago de Compostela and of the old cathedral at Salamanca, but numbers of other churches in Catalonia and the Spanish Pyrenees remain to prove its widespread power. In architectural form the style somewhat resembles that of southwestern France, especially of Toulouse; and, because of the fact that Santiago de Compostela was one of the greatest pilgrimage churches of Europe, the influence of Spanish decorative sculpture was spread wide all over the Western world.

FINAL GOTHIC ACHIEVEMENT: AMIENS CATHEDRAL, WEST FRONT, RISING ABOVE THE TOWN ROOFS.

FINAL GOTHIC ACHIEVEMENT: AMIENS CATHEDRAL, EAST END; VERTICAL ACCENT, POWER, LIGHTNESS.

PARIS, NOTRE DAME, INTERIOR; EARLY FRENCH GOTHIC; SIX-PART VAULT AND EARLY BAR TRACERY

LAON CATHEDRAL, INTERIOR; EARLY GOTHIC WITH UNUSUAL FLAT EAST END AND DOUBLE TRIFORIUM.

Plate 33

BRUGES, TOWN BELFRY; GOTHIC SECULAR
MAGNIFICENCE.

MODEL OF 17th-CENTURY NUREMBERG. (Metropolitan Museum of Art.)

FREIBURG-IM-BREISGAU, THE EXCHANGE;
LATE GOTHIC SECULAR STRUCTURE.

BRUGES, LATE GOTHIC TOWN HALL.

LUBECK, ST. MARY'S AND THE CITY SQUA
CHARACTERISTIC NORTH GERMAN BR
ARCHITECTURE.

Plate 34

CHARTRES CATHEDRAL, INTERIOR:
DEVELOPED EARLY FRENCH GOTHIC.

AMIENS CATHEDRAL, INTERIOR;
"RAYONNANT" GOTHIC.

PARIS, STE. CHAPELLE, INTERIOR;
"RAYONNANT" GOTHIC.

AMIENS, CHURCH OF ST. GERMAIN;
"FLAMBOYANT" GOTHIC.

BOURGES, HÔTEL JACQUES COEUR;
THE COURTYARD.

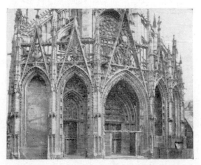

ROUEN, ST. MACLOU; "FLAMBOY-
ANT" PORCH.

Plate 35

SALISBURY CATHEDRAL; "EARLY ENG-
LISH" EXTERIOR.

SALISBURY CATHEDRAL; "EARLY ENG-
LISH" INTERIOR.

EXETER CATHEDRAL, CHOIR; "DECO-
RATED" MULTIPLE VAULT-RIBS.

WELLS CATHEDRAL, CHOIR; "DECO-
RATED" AND "PERPENDICULAR."

WINDSOR CASTLE, ST. GEORGE'S
CHAPEL; "PERPENDICULAR" GOTHIC.

WESTMINSTER ABBEY, HENRY VII
CHAPEL, EXTERIOR; "PERPENDICULAR."

Plate 36

COLOGNE CATHEDRAL; EXTERIOR AS COMPLETED IN THE 19th CENTURY,

CATHEDRAL; EXTERIOR BEFORE RESTION.

NE CATHEDRAL; INTERIOR.

NUREMBERG, ST. LAWRENCE CHURCH; INTERIOR.

Plate 37

FLORENCE, SANTA CROCE; INTERIOR.

SIENA, PALAZZO SARACINI; CHARAC
ISTIC ITALIAN NOBLEMAN'S DWELL

VENICE, THE CA D'ORO.

PALMA DE MALLORCA CATHEDRAL.

TOLEDO, SAN JUAN DE LOS REYE

Plate 38

CHES, CHÂTEAU; EARLY GOTHIC.

PIERREFONDS CHÂTEAU; LATE GOTHIC.

T ST. MICHEL, HALL OF THE KNIGHTS.

ROUEN, PALAIS DE JUSTICE.

LLE, HALF-TIMBER HOUSE OF FRANCIS I.

PARIS, CLUNY MUSEUM; DOOR.

Plate 39

OXFORD, ALL SOULS COLLEGE QUADRANGLE.

BOLOGNA, CASA ISOLANI.

Plate 40

In Burgundy a school of monastic church architecture arose, under the special impetus of the Cluniac monks, which had a tremendous effect on later architecture. Like the Lombard school, the Burgundian school was primarily interested in the construction of fireproof churches, but it was also interested in the whole problem of church planning and in such churches as the famous mother church at Cluny first developed the logical yet elaborate east end which was the foundation of the later Gothic chevet. Decoratively, too, the style is important, because although there is in many details a constant desire to imitate or adapt and modify traditional Roman forms—fluted pilasters, Corinthian capitals, and so on—nevertheless in the carvings of the great western portals, which in Burgundian churches were often under large porches, a completely new feeling enters in, based on the emotionalism and the dynamic quality of the north; and nowhere perhaps does this emotionalism achieve such superb results as in the doorways of Vézelay, Autun, and Aulnay.

Normandy was perhaps the least "civilized" of all the French provinces. The old Celtic population had there longest resisted the Frankish domination, and it was there in the valley of the Seine and along the banks of the English Channel that the half-savage Viking conquerors had settled. Yet this very quality of wildness and of lack of earlier traditions led the Normans, under the tutelage of Lombard monks, to attack the problem of church building with a surprising and ingenious vitality. The Norman churches are heavily built, of beautifully cut stone, and the richness of their arched interiors has a quality of power that comes largely from their structural form alone. There, in Caen, in the Abbaye aux Hommes and the Abbaye aux Dames, which William the Conqueror built to expiate his sins, a system of interior design that was to lead directly to the Gothic interior was first and most skillfully developed. Large pier arches below separated nave and aisles. Above them, in the space under the aisle roof, half vaults were turned to resist the thrust of the nave vault, and in front beautiful arcades formed a satisfactory triforium. Above, clerestory walls with large windows supported at first a wooden roof; but this temporary expedient was removed later, and the skill of the builders of the earlier work was proved by the successful vaulting of the nave in such a way as to preserve the large windows. In the Abbaye aux Dames, the concentrated thrusts of an intersecting nave vault at the piers were foreseen by making the half vault back of the triforium not continuous, but at the piers only. These half arches coming down from the piers of the nave to the outside wall, although concealed by the roof of the side aisle, are nevertheless the first flying buttresses.

In England the conquering Normans set about, almost at once, an enormous program of great church building. These abbeys were usually tremendously long and their side aisles unusually high, with arches held up, not on the clustered piers common in Normandy, but frequently on great round columns of colossal diameter. In most cases nave roofs are of wood. Only in Durham, as we have seen, was a complete stone vault achieved, and it is significant of the Norman building skill that this is one of the most advanced and highly developed vaults of its time in Europe. Decoratively, the Norman style is as untraditional as its building methods. Roman influence is very slight. Figure carving is uncommon and rather crude. Instead, we find geometric patterns of zigzags and similar forms worked out to the highest degree, and occasionally, especially in England, a kind of repetition of grotesque bird and beast forms unlike anything else, because of its basic geometric character.

Through central France ran a band in which almost all the influences of Rome and of Constantinople, as well as the structural ingenuity of Normandy, were somehow confused and mixed together. In the central uplands of Auvergne, the barrel vault of early Romanesque and variations of the dome are both found, as well as the elaborate east ends of the Burgundian type. Geometric polychrome masonry gives great richness to the exterior, and the carving has hints of the geometry of the north, the emotionalism of the Burgundian portals, and occasional beautiful developments of Roman forms. St. Sernin in Toulouse, somewhat to the west of this strip, became one of the climax buildings of the Romanesque because of its combination of these elements; but it was at the northern end of the band, in the Île de France, that the most important developments were to come, when the pointed arch and the ribbed vault were first combined together and the foundations laid for the Gothic architecture which lay ahead.

It is a characteristic of Romanesque architecture that nowhere does it seem to have entirely completed itself. Almost all Romanesque structures have something of a tentative quality, as though they were not quite sure of themselves—as though their builders were struggling with problems which they had not quite solved. In many ways the culmination of all of these elements of the Romanesque was reached in the great abbey of St.

Denis, begun by the abbot Suger in 1140. Since it was the royal abbey of France, Suger decided to outdo all previous churches, and collected together at St. Denis all of the best builders, sculptors, architects, and stained-glass workers he could find. Under his creative inspiration, their collaboration resulted in a building in which at last most of the problems that had plagued the Romanesque builders were solved. But this building is no longer Romanesque; in all its major essentials it is Gothic, and what was intended to be the summation of all the building culture of the Romanesque world became instead the first monument of the Gothic.

Chapter 14

GOTHIC ARCHITECTURE

THE growth of Gothic architecture is a clear example of how inextricably the structural and decorative elements in buildings are tied together. Almost all of those forms which we call Gothic—tracery, pointed arches, developed buttresses, tall slim columns or colonnettes, and decorated pinnacles—flowed somehow either from the structural necessities of the new type of church building initiated at St. Denis, or from simple attempts to decorate beautifully the structural forms there first utilized. To understand these forms, therefore, it is necessary first to understand something of this structural nature.

As we have seen, the use of the ribbed vault not only simplified the problems of vault building, but also gave it a brilliance and sureness of effect which were before unknown. Yet the full development of the Gothic vault was still hampered by the unfortunate fact that arches of different widths rise to different heights, as well as by the persistence of the old Roman desire to simplify the vault forms. None of the early experiments had been completely satisfactory. The old Lombard system, so frequently followed by the Normans, of combining two bays of the aisle to one of the nave, broke up the unity of the effect in a way that seemed unnecessary and complicated. In the aim to unify the church interior, the Norman builders once, in the Abbaye aux Dames at Caen, made the experiment of building another arch across the church at the intermediate piers of the old type of square nave bay, and on this they built a mere screen or web wall extending up till it met the surface of the intersecting vault. To be sure, this gave in perspective a cross-arch over the nave at every pier, but it also produced awkward and ugly shapes in the clerestory wall, each bay at the wall becoming only a half arch. A second and more advanced experiment was to use the arches and the main diagonal groins, but, instead of carrying a single vault across two bays of the side-aisle arcade created by the basic nave square, to put two little cross-vaults next each other, supported on the diagonal groins and the intermediate cross-rib. The crown of these small vaults, instead of running directly across the church, ran at an angle from the outside wall to the center of the main bay, thus creating what is known as the six-part vault, first crudely used in the Abbaye aux Hommes at Caen. The best example is the vault of Notre Dame in Paris. Yet this, too, gave nave bays which were of two kinds, according to the directions of the

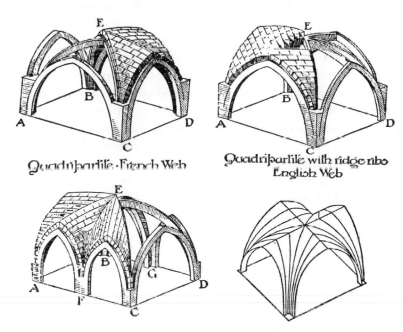

Quadripartile - French Web

Quadripartile with ridge ribs English Web

59. DIAGRAM SHOWING TYPICAL GOTHIC RIBBED VAULT CONSTRUCTION. (Bond: *Introduction to English Church Architecture.*)

Upper left: TYPICAL FRENCH 4-PART VAULT
Upper right: TYPICAL ENGLISH 4-PART VAULT WITH RIDGE RIBS
Lower left: TYPICAL FRENCH 6-PART VAULT
Lower right: ENGLISH 4-PART VAULT WITH RIDGE RIBS AND TIERCERONS

crowns of the cross-vaults, and still did not solve completely the bothersome question of unifying the design.

We have noted that the pointed arch, probably borrowed from Moslem prototypes, was used in some Romanesque work. Builders had invented it in Syria and Mesopotamia, possibly as a further development of Sassanian ovoid arches; they had discovered that it was both easier to build and exerted less thrust than the round arch of equal span, since its sides more nearly approached the vertical. As used in Romanesque work, the structural advantages of the pointed arch seem not to have been realized, and its adoption as a basic structural element crept in gradually during the twelfth century, especially in the Île de France, in the effort to solve the troublesome problem of the intersections of the ambulatory vault around the apse. The use of the pointed arch in this location enabled the builders, by varying the steepness of the arch, to bring all the intersecting vaults to the same height, irrespective of their width. This discovery was coupled with a second—namely, that the sides of a pointed arch are independent of each other and that, provided there is an equilibrium in the general balance of forces, the two sides can be set at angles to each other in plan; so that the center of the intersection of unequal or wedge-shaped vaults could be placed anywhere the architect desired, rather than at some point determined only by the vault curves. In that way the intersection could be placed in the visual center of each wedge-shaped bay, where it counted in the best possible manner, and the surfaces of the vaults between the ribs, built merely to connect them, could take any shape made necessary.

Just what importance in this development is to be given to native structural sense, and what to the simple artistic desire to produce a whole which would be visually beautiful, is a much debated question. The whole theory that the ribbed vault was a consciously scientific, rational solution to an engineering problem is now almost universally discredited. The builders did not know enough engineering to make any such approach possible, and furthermore there are so many tentative and illogical experimental solutions in existence that any such idea seems impossible. Moreover, the old theory that the filling of a vault is actually supported on the ribs and strengthened by them is untrue. The ribs simplify the vault-building problem by allowing a vault to be built in sections, and the pointed arch gave freedom of planning. Beyond that, it was probably the desire to accent the lines of the building, to make them count so that any observer could realize the pattern, that seems to have controlled the development of vault and rib design. What the Gothic builders did discover, also, was that, once the rib framework had been built, the filling between could be waved or distorted from true geometrical surfaces as much as was necessary, and that if these surfaces themselves were curved so that the stones which made them up could be of wedge shape they would still act as vaults no matter how distorted the surface.

The bearing of all this on the great church was enormous. It enabled plan areas of almost any shape to be satisfactorily vaulted, and it made it possible to build beautiful and unified vaults on the rectangular bays of the church nave. Furthermore, the pointed arch gave a dynamic vertical expression to the whole structure which was the exact reverse of the heavy horizontality of most Romanesque design, and the artistic possibilities of this change were almost at once realized. But the pointed arch was adopted only hesitantly at first, and many of the earlier Gothic cathedrals of France combine round and pointed arches in different parts of the building—the pointed arch being generally reserved for the major arches of the vaults, and the pier arches between nave and aisles, whereas the minor arches of windows and triforium might still be rounded. It was not until the last decades of the twelfth century that the pointed arch became universal in French churches, and not until well into the thirteenth that it was thoroughly accepted in England and Germany. In Italy it never completely superseded the semicircular form so deeply ingrained from Roman times on.

Another characteristic of a church roofed with ribbed pointed vaults was that the walls began to lose much of their structural significance, and the whole tended to become a framework of stone. The groined vaults concentrated the weight at the piers, and, since all the piers were connected by arches with each other, the system of piers, buttresses, and vaults became essentially self-supporting, so that the wall existed only as a filler between these other elements. The revolutionary character of this change also was realized but slowly, and outside of France and Germany hardly ever in a complete form. The Romanesque tradition of heavy walls was the direct opposite of this newer conception of the building as a stone frame, and walls of unnecessary thickness continued in use in many cases throughout the Gothic period.

The flying buttress was another element which made possible the Gothic church. The original of this we have already seen in the little half arches behind the triforium of the Abbaye aux Dames at Caen. If the buttresses on the outside of the side-aisle wall were heavy enough and carried above the aisle roofs high enough, such a half arch could be built connecting these buttresses with the nave piers at almost any desired height, and thus the tremendous thrusting-out force of the nave vault could be transferred across the side-aisle space to a mass of masonry—the developed exterior buttress—made large enough to receive and counterbalance it. In this way the height dimension was immediately freed from the hampering limitations of Romanesque building, and the heights of the naves of great churches, particularly in France, rose gradually all through the thirteenth century to reach a climax in Beauvais, where the ridge is 154 feet from the pavement. Even in the earlier Gothic churches this height dimension is consistently forced. At St.

Denis the ridge was around 90 feet, in Paris 110, in Chartres 114, in Rheims 125, and in Amiens 140.

Still another element added strength to this search for aspiring height—the growing skill of the workers in stained glass. From at least as early as the tenth century onward, French churches had been largely glazed with brilliantly colored stained glass; yet the early limitations of the craft had

60. DIAGRAMMATIC VIEW OF AMIENS CA-THEDRAL, SHOWING THE ESSENTIALS OF GOTHIC CONSTRUC-TION: RIBBED VAULTS, ISOLATED SUPPORTS, BUT-TRESSES AND FLY-ING BUTTRESSES. (Viollet-le-Duc.)

prevented any windows of large size. Fundamentally, a window composed of hundreds of pieces of colored glass, held together by flexible lead strips, is nonrigid and fragile. What enabled the craftsmen to contrive the large stained glass windows of the later Middle Ages was the fact that iron frameworks, called armatures, could be built into the stone, and the stained glass fastened to them by wiring where necessary. In the best Gothic work the design of these armatures had an important bearing on the stained-glass pattern, and its outline furnished the basic design for the stained-glass decoration. It is thus that the so-called medallion window was developed.

Later, the solid iron armature was sometimes replaced by saddle bars running straight across the window, and the change from the elaborate armature to saddle bar coincided with the change from rather set and small-scale designs to large, free compositions occupying the entire window area.

As the skill of the stained-glass designers increased, so did the desire of the church builders to increase the light in the churches, and windows both in clerestory and side aisle tended to become larger and larger. But even with the use of iron armatures it was difficult to get sufficient strength in openings over six to eight feet wide. Since the average nave bay was almost twenty feet, and since there was a desire to fill the entire bay width with the window, it became necessary to subdivide this large area into smaller widths—and thus tracery was originated. At first it was the custom merely to put two or three separate pointed-arched windows under the enclosed arch of the nave bay, with perhaps a circular opening to fill the space above them. The stone separations between these openings tended naturally to become thinner and more delicate, and the whole system was called plate tracery, because the effect was that of piercing holes of various sizes in a solid plate of stone. Sometime in the first half of the thirteenth century, an entirely different system, called bar tracery, was invented, in which the effect, instead of being a wall pierced with various windows and openings, is that of one great arch subdivided by a patterning of stone bars, big enough for the purposes of strength but just as thin as the architect dared to make them. At first these bars took simple geometrical forms; usually the lower part of the window would be subdivided into two or three "lights" with pointed-arched heads, and the space above would be filled with a great circular "rose." This combination of pointed arches and circles is the foundation of all geometric tracery. Later, by the use of cusps or inward-pointing projecting forms on arches and roses, great lightness and delicacy of effect was given; later still, the introduction of the reversed curve allowed an almost unlimited development of free-flowing forms (English "Curvilinear" and French "Flamboyant").

The outside of the church was as much modified by these changes as the inside. More and more, as the possibilities of the style were realized, the exterior became vertical in feeling instead of horizontal, for at each bay the great buttress, projecting boldly at right angles to the wall, tended to break up the horizontal lines. Between the buttresses, traceried windows began to fill the space, until the wall became merely a screen below the windowsill; and, above, the side-aisle roofs, the soaring buttresses, and the repeated half-arched flying buttresses gave a vivid, dynamic network of lines which revolutionized exterior design. Since lightness of structure came with growing knowledge, the architect's tendency was to exaggerate and emphasize this quality by pinnacles and crockets—little projecting leafed ornaments on the edges of gables or spires—just as he tended to emphasize the vertical feeling by the steep slopes of roof, of spire, and of pinnacle.

The west fronts, too, except sometimes in England and Italy, achieved a new character, because the great buttresses which withstood the longitudinal thrusts of the pier arcades necessarily gave these a vertical accent which repeated the verticality of the sides. Twin western towers, such as had been used in some of the Norman churches, were often supported on these buttresses, which served then a double purpose, not only to withstand the thrusts of the vaults within, but also to help support and to lead the eye up to the towers above. Between these buttresses the richest of gabled porches could be built; so that, although the old general sculpture arrangement of the Romanesque period was preserved (*i.e.,* a sculptured tympanum above the square-headed door opening, and rich sculpture or ornament around the molded arch and on the jambs at either side), the whole effect was completely different.

It is clear that the kind of ornament fitted for the heavy power of Romanesque buildings accorded but ill with the new light grace of Gothic. Besides, the entire popular feeling about life seems to have changed, and there is in all of the Gothic decoration the expression of a new-found gaiety, security, and integration. Men came to love nature, rather than to fear it; and natural forms, naturalistically carved, became the rule. The nightmare of the old grotesques, expression of such deep-held fears, yielded to a new kind of grotesque in which a sort of cosmic humor or of human satire takes the place of the old terror; and even the Biblical stories themselves undergo a subtle change in feeling, and there is less insistence on Hell, sin and damnation, and Satan, and more on the grace of salvation and the beauty of holiness.

Another significant element controls Gothic decoration—the fact that tracery, gable, buttress, and spire forms, originally developed in the design of large churches, were little by little taken over as decorative elements for secular buildings and even for furniture.

The rapidity of the change from Romanesque to Gothic in most parts of Europe was surprising. Several things account for this: One was the fact that, as the town importance increased, the cathedral (as opposed to the monastery church) began to have a greater and greater importance, and the bishop both politically and religiously became a man of tremendous power. The monastery remained the dominant element in Christianity while the feudal system controlled secular life; but, with the development of the town and the gradual change in the feudal system, the monastery, like the feudal castle, began to lose some of its pre-eminent importance. As a result, the traditional hold of conservative monastic opinion on building yielded too. Abbot Suger of St. Denis was an exception in this respect, and it is characteristic that he collected together an enormous number of lay craftsmen, for with the gradual wane of monasticism the lay craftsman was to have a much greater place in all building matters. Along with this change from lay brother or monastic craftsman to lay craftsman working for a wage, went another, the increase in the importance of the lay architect. Thus, just at the time when a tremendous number of new buildings came to be required for cathedral purposes, to enshrine the new dignity of the bishop, the work fell into the hands of lay designers unfettered by old monastic traditions.

We are coming to realize more and more that the medieval architect was a thoroughly professional man of great importance and held a position of considerable honor, receiving large wages. The few Gothic architectural drawings that have come down to us, such as the notebook of the thirteenth-century Villard de Honnecourt and the later drawings made for the west front of Cologne Cathedral, show that these great buildings are not the almost magical results of a folk movement, as used to be believed, but rather the results of careful study in advance, with the determination of all major elements by drawings before construction was started—in other words, that they were the result of exactly as conscious a design process as were the buildings of the Renaissance or of the present time.

The medieval worshiper in his cathedral saw an interior quite different in effect from the buildings as we know them today. In almost every case the choir and the clergy were shut off from the nave by solid screens; for the old separation of clergy and people went much further then than it does today, and the tradition of the monastic church, with its closed service for the monks, which the laity could hear and perhaps catch glimpses of through the open door in the screen, still held sway. In that way the sense of mystery was enhanced, and also the apparent size of the church was increased by its subdivision. Over the choir screen rose a cross, which gave it its name of rood screen, and there might be two flanking altars outside the screen at which services were occasionally held.

Moreover, in many churches there was much more color than can be seen today, except in such restorations as that of the Ste. Chapelle in Paris. The

61. CHARACTERISTIC FRENCH GOTHIC CHOIR, WITH ITS FURNITURE, FROM ST. DENIS ABBEY, RESTORED. (Viollet-le-Duc.)

rich clustered piers were colored, the vault frequently was decorated with stars or with foliage, and hangings of Venetian velvets or damasks or even lustrous textiles from the Orient gave warmth and color to the whole. The total impression, then, would be at once more personal, more emotional, more lavish, and more mysterious than the impression these great interiors make today, and the stained-glass windows would form but one note in a symphony of color.

Gothic architecture was much more than the solution of building prob-lems; it was also the expression of a new Europe that had been gradually coming into being—a new Europe which was the result of the gradual decay of the feudal system under the impact of trade, prosperity, and the growth of national feeling. From the time when the Saracens had been swept from the control of the Mediterranean Sea, about the middle of the eleventh century, the commerce of Europe underwent continuous growth. Markets increased, trade routes became settled, the benefits of trade per-meated more and more deeply into the countryside, merchants grew wealthy, cities expanded and flourished.

Now the merchant was necessarily outside the framework of the feudal system, for the feudal system had been essentially a matter of systematizing the development of the land through agriculture and of military strength through vassal service. The existence of trade and the development of local industries which naturally accompanied it was a threat to the entire system; for, if people entirely outside of either agricultural or military life became wealthy, and if the power of the municipalities which were rising increased, the lordship of the feudal seigneur inevitably lessened. However much the feudal lords may have realized this growing power of wealthy merchants and powerful municipalities, the benefits which trade brought to the nobles, through furnishing them with the luxuries and the arms they desired, made any actual hostility between them rare indeed.

Another element undoubtedly added to this break-up of the old tradi-tional feudal life—the Crusades. While pilgrimages cost money, which the pilgrims had to obtain somewhere, crusades cost enormously more; and one of the accepted methods by which the seigneurs raised the necessary amounts was by selling their feudal rights to towns, or by a system of mortgaging their lands which amounted in essence to sale. The change from land mortgaging to land selling was a gradual one, which went on naturally and spontaneously and was significant of the entire change from a land economy to a money economy.

In addition, the Crusades had a great educational value. Pilgrimages had entailed travel and had brought to the West a considerable knowledge of the East; but they were individual—their effect was bound to be a matter of limited scope based largely on hearsay. The Crusades, however, were mass movements, and for the first time since the Fall of Rome travel became a common and accepted part of living. The Crusades, too, took various routes to the East—some went over land via the Danube route and the Balkans, some went by sea from France or Italy;—but distances were great and travel was slow, and the actual business of the Crusades, the reconquest of the Holy Land, was delayed and hindered and finally defeated by the national and feudal rivalries of the most important of the crusading lords, as well as by the cupidity of the Mediterranean shipowners of Venice and Constantinople.

The result was that the Crusades spent large amounts of time in places like Sicily, southern France, various portions of Italy, Cyprus, and Constantinople—where one Crusade, the Fourth, took it upon itself to halt long enough to capture the city and set up a western dynasty, which ruled for seventy years. Thus, noble and soldier alike were brought in touch not only with the lavish architecture of Constantinople and the ideals of greater personal luxury which there held sway, at least among the rich, but also with the Saracenic work of Sicily, and from time to time with the highly developed Mohammedan architecture of Egypt and of Syria. Necessarily, too, in the course of these long journeys and wars, there was a tremendous interchange of knowledge among the Crusaders themselves, and the Crusades acted as a sort of gigantic melting pot despite the rivalries which cursed and destroyed them. The returned Crusader had a knowledge not only of the far lands which he had seen, but also of his neighbors in Europe, which was a new thing and naturally added to the feeling of individual responsibility, as it developed individual curiosity.

The world of the thirteenth century was thus a different world. In some agricultural areas the feudal castle, still of crude Romanesque type, with its little agricultural village around, persisted; but elsewhere the new life was creating new houses and new towns. Obviously, the earliest and the greatest advances were made in places where trade and industry were most highly developed; and, especially in northern Italy and in Flanders, the idea of the Gothic municipality, and of a life based on commerce and industry rather than on agriculture and war, was already well advanced a century before the Gothic style in architecture made its appearance; for it was in Flanders and in north Italy that the textile trade, then the foundation of so much other commerce, received its highest development.

To replace the feudal hierarchy, a new system based on the guild arose. The guild, essentially, was merely a corporation of the wealthiest or most powerful men in a town, formed for its administration; its perpetuation was assured in various ways, by election or appointment. Each industry, similarly, came to form its own guild, to regulate the rules and standards of work, the payment of employees, and the prices of goods and services. Sometimes, as in Italy, the governing body was made up of a representative of each of the major trade guilds. At other times the town guild remained a separate governing body, which itself regulated and correlated the functions of the trades guilds. The growth of the guild system was bound profoundly to change the whole outlook of the average man. In earlier days, the only outlet from the rigidity of the feudal system had been furnished by the monasteries, and in some cases even entrance into these was strictly limited. Now, however, through the apprenticeship system, any young man or boy who could manage to escape from the strict feudal round was assured of training, employment, and advancement through the stages of apprentice, journeyman, and master, as far as his talents would permit. Since it was frequently to the advantage of the landowner that the farmers who were his serfs or vassals should keep their holdings unbroken, it was also to his advantage to see that all the farmers' children except one were allowed or encouraged to leave the place and start self-supporting lives of their own.

In the towns, the physical results of these tremendous changes—this increased knowledge of the world, the increased freedom of human contact, and the vastly increased trade and commerce which accompanied them— were rapid and revolutionary. The market place, from a mere empty area, became a square or piazza, frequently surrounded with arcades for the more efficient display of goods. On it would be built the town hall, often with shops and a covered market on the ground floor and a great hall for corporation meetings above; almost always there would be an upper balcony from which the mayor or the councilors could address the citizens. Frequently the town hall would have its own city tower or town belfry, from which the town bell—a sort of symbol of new-found municipal freedom— would ring to tell the hours or to call the citizens together. Guild halls for trades guilds rose; in some places, especially in Flanders, they came to rival or to surpass in size and magnificence the town hall itself. The straggling towns of the early period began to achieve form. Streets were regularized. Arcades, or covered passages under projecting upper floors of houses, became common, to give protection from the sun and the rain to the pedestrian or the peddler. The "rows" of Chester and the *lauben* of Innsbruck and Berne are examples of these covered sidewalks, and occasionally in France, as in Vitry, portions of the old covered galleries still remain. In market places and other open spaces, town wells and pumps, or fountains, were placed, to supply water to the surrounding dwellings; and frequently, especially in Italy and Germany, these fountains became structures of great beauty and richness, new expressions of municipal pride and a sense of municipal decency.

A striking feature of the new prosperity was a corresponding rise in population, which led slowly but surely toward city congestion on the one hand and to the foundation of brand-new towns and cities on the other. These *villes neuves* are especially common in southern and western France, and in them, even more than in the more picturesque older places, one may see what the ideals of the town planning of the Gothic era really were. The typical *ville neuve* is placed on or near some trade route, preferably in a location easily defended. It is walled, with its walls carefully designed in relation to the existing topography. Thus, except in plain country, the general outline is likely to be irregular. Within the walls, however, the greatest regularity which the site would permit was sought. Streets ran straight from gate to market, and from market to gate again. Market places were usually rectangular, and set, not astride the main street—for the Gothic city planner knew enough not to desire traffic through the middle of his market,—but rather at one side of it. Generally there are arcades all around the market place, and often the houses are of similar or identical design. Sometimes, in addition to a market place, a large covered market hall is also furnished. Equal lots are laid out along the straight streets, and frequently building requirements compelled the man who leased one of these lots to build a house of a given size, often stretching across the entire width of the lot. Such a town had decency and regularity and was well ventilated; if it may have been monotonous at the beginning, it was not long before alterations and rebuildings brought variety into its street picture, and always there was the high bulk and perhaps the rich spire of the church to give it unity and character.

Today, Gothic towns look gray and old. In the Middle Ages these were far otherwise, for the Middle Ages loved vivid colors, and the gray wood was painted with bright reds and blues. Brilliant signboards hung over inns and taverns, and the coats of arms on nobles' houses glowed with blue and gold and red. The costumes were gay, too, in the fourteenth century reaching such a pitch of gorgeous elaborateness that power after power attempted to restrain their insane extravagance with sumptuary laws that seem to have been honored more in the breach than in the observance. Processions and pageants sparkling with banners and lavish vestments were common, too, and from time to time a lord's marriage or a bishop's or king's visit served as an excuse to deck the chief streets with painted cloth and to make, as it were, the entire city a stage setting for a city-wide festivity.

But there was a reverse of this picture of brilliance and beauty. In general, sanitation was little understood and less cared for, and the more advanced towns carried on a continuous losing battle against filth and smell. Gutters were little more than open sewers, and it is no wonder that plagues and pests swept over all of Europe and brought with them a terrible mortality. Moreover, the relaxation of the feudal system, while it opened the doors to new wealth for the trader, the manufacturer, the banker, and the land speculator, made inevitable, too, the development of a new class of town poor who lived a formless and hopeless life in unspeakable congestion in the rabbit warrens of the older parts of the towns, like the *Cour des Miracles* at Paris. The cruel contrast between the condition of the wealthy and the poor which seems to accompany almost all highly developed civilizations was already apparent.

Strange emotional instability seems to have been universally present, taking form in all sorts of odd religious enthusiasms, fanaticisms, and heresies, sending thousands of children to hardship and death in the Children's Crusade, causing all the extraordinary and terrible cruelties of the persecution of heretics which were a blot on the thirteenth and fourteenth centuries, and driving both the victims and the persecutors of the weird superstitions surrounding witchcraft. Despite the general wealth and the new integrations, all sorts of revolutionary ideas were abroad; and Wat Tyler's Rebellion, so beautifully told by William Morris, was but one example of the growth of popular protests against things as they were, which were to blossom later in the Reformation and the development of the concept of democracy.

Chapter 15

DEVELOPMENT AND DEGENERATION
OF GOTHIC ARCHITECTURE

DURING the twelfth century the nations of Europe were gradually struggling to birth, and the development of the different languages which gave rise to our present tongues was almost complete. Feudalism and the monastic system had acted to produce an international culture, with Latin as its official tongue. When both of these began to yield, under the impact of trade and new ideas, differences that before had been merely local tended to crystallize into differences that became national. Thus, in considering Gothic architecture, which came to birth in the middle of the century, one must see it not only as the expression of a phase of Western culture, but also as the product of the differing life and differing ideals of France, England, the Spanish kingdoms, Germany, and Italy. Since the ideas behind Gothic architecture first appeared in their full form in France, it is with France that we shall begin.

All the great Gothic churches of France have certain things in common—a great love of height, of large windows, and an almost universal use of monumental west fronts with twin towers and great doors between and below them. Transepts are short, the choir is almost always apse-ended, and there is an elaborate group of chapels surrounding its ambulatory. The whole history of Gothic architecture in France is also characterized by a spirit of perfect structural clarity, an attempt always to use a minimum of material and to allow all of the structural members to be controlling elements in the actual visual impression. Accordingly, we shall find the exterior walls punctuated by boldly projecting buttresses, rising high above the side-aisle roofs and often crowned with pinnacles, and we shall see the flying buttresses—those great half arches over the aisle roofs by which the nave thrust is carried out to the outer buttresses—exposed and made, in fact, one of the chief factors in the exterior effect. The transepts hardly ever reach far beyond the side-aisle buttresses, so that the entire result is compact and unified. The clear expression of the structure makes the eas

end, with its radiating chapels, its high buttresses, and the curving or
polygonal apse of the choir, necessarily a complex composition; yet in the
best work all of its vertical lines seem to combine with the separate roofs
of each chapel and the slanting lines of the flying buttresses, so that the eye
is led inevitably upward to the ring of great clerestory windows of the choir
and the high roof above them.

The west front has a similar power, due to its direct expression of the
lines between nave and aisles, and to the fact that in almost every case a

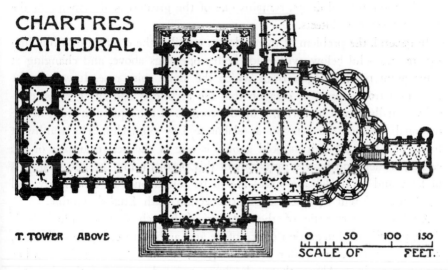

CHARTRES CATHEDRAL.

T. TOWER ABOVE

SCALE OF FEET.

62. CHARTRES CATHEDRAL; PLAN. (Simpson, Vol. II.)

great door opens into each of these three elements, the central nave door
naturally being larger than those on either side. Between the doors and at
the corners rise the great buttresses, which, sweeping up the tower, give
enormous lift to the design; but any danger of the lack of unity which these
three divisions might otherwise produce is obviated by tying the whole
together by strong horizontal moldings and arcades. At the end of the nave,
over the entrance door, is usually a great rose window, and the sharp gable
of the high roof above is often veiled by rich arcading and balustrades.

The French tower designs vary greatly. Few churches have their towers
complete. The famous square towers of Notre Dame, for instance, were
originally intended to have stone spires. Chartres completed its two western
towers by the end of the Gothic period in very different styles, but six other
towers originally planned—two at each transept and two flanking the choir
—were never carried above the clerestory level. Similarly, Amiens and

Rheims have uncompleted west fronts, and many people have felt that perhaps the completion of the towers planned might somehow have damaged the effect of the whole by overemphasizing the impression of verticality. Even at Laon, where the west front has its twin towers with their famous statues of the patient oxen, commemorating the animals which helped in the construction of the building, the spires and pinnacles that were to have crowned the whole were never finally built. Nevertheless, the French west front, with its clear divisions, its strong vertical and horizontal emphasis, and its monumental doors, remains one of the greatest achievements of the French Gothic architects.

In general, the problem of tower design entailed the erection of a building square and solid below, with wide belfry openings above, and changing at some point to an octagon from which the stone spire rose. It was in the transition from square to octagon that the architects had the greatest difficulty, usually solved by carrying up the corners of the square in front of the diagonal faces of the octagon as elaborate lacy pinnacles. The southwest tower at Chartres, with its bold gables, is one of the best examples of the earlier, cruder, and heavier solutions of this problem, but the best examples of later and more delicate spires are to be found only in Normandy and England, and will be discussed in connection with English Gothic.

Another characteristic of the exterior of French Gothic cathedrals is the extraordinary integration of sculpture and architecture. Figures of saints, vices and virtues, or similar sacred subjects are usually ranged on either side of the door. Above them, the huge pointed arches of the doorway splay are filled with row after row of adoring angels, and the tympanum contains either the Last Judgment, the Crucifixion, Christ or the Virgin Enthroned, or some such climax scene—or else, as in Rheims, is occupied by a large traceried rose. The whole composition is of course merely a more highly developed working out of the old Romanesque door scheme; yet the sculpture is individually so much more personalized, the general conception so much richer, and the sculptural and architectural elements so much more integrally wed together, that the French Gothic portals become new creations. Especially fine is the work at Notre Dame, at Strasbourg, and at Amiens; at Rheims the exuberance of the sculpture seems somehow almost to obscure the beautiful pure pattern of the conception, and magnificent as the figures are there is a little sense of display for display's sake.

The earliest Gothic churches—those of the period roughly from 1150 to 1200, notably Soissons, Sens, Noyon, and Laon—are all somewhat tentative in their approach to the Gothic ideal. In many of them round and pointed arches are mixed, as in Noyon, where all the windows are round-headed. Often, too, there is a sort of double triforium, due to the enlargement of the old Romanesque triforium into a full vaulted gallery the width of the side aisle. This manifestly had to have a roof over it, which made necessary a blank space in the wall between the top of the gallery arcade and the bottom of the clerestory window, and in this space another little arcade in the thickness of the walls was built.

In Notre Dame de Paris the architect, realizing the disadvantage of this double arcade, made another experiment—he opened the roof space over the gallery into the nave through large traceried circular openings, above which were the pointed-arch clerestory windows, and this constituted a definite gain in unity. Nevertheless, even this was not a perfect solution; and, when about 1230 a fire burned off this gallery roof, the design was changed and the roof flattened and covered with metal, so that the clerestory windowsill could now be brought down close to the top of the gallery arcade. Furthermore, by this time the use of bar tracery in windows had come in, and the opportunity was taken to enlarge the size of the windows and make them traceried windows. By 1240 Paris began to take on its present appearance, with long traceried clerestory windows, a large triforium gallery, and the great pier arcade below. Paris, like most of the early churches, used single round columns for its main arcade up to the height of the pier arch. From their capitals spring the vaulting shafts which run up the nave wall. These great round columns have a tremendous expression of dignified strength, but they are not logical expressions of the Gothic idea. It was natural, then, that as the feeling for this new pointed-arch architecture developed the vertical lines of the vaulted shaft should be carried down to the floor by adding colonnettes to the columns of the arcade, or else by using clustered piers.

The development of tracery has already been mentioned. The earlier cathedrals had little if any tracery. Those of the early thirteenth century, like Chartres, depended on plate tracery only, and it was not until the second quarter of the thirteenth century that bar tracery began to supersede the earlier, heavier form. Once the French architects had discovered the grace and the possible variety of this new form of design, they made it into a chief element in all of their churches, and it is the light and delicate, yet at the same time strictly geometrical, tracery of such cathedrals as Amiens, Rheims, and Beauvais which is one of their greatest beauties.

Especially impressive is the use of this tracery in the great rose windows that fill the ends of the transepts and the nave; and, owing to the radiating character of the design which these rose or wheel windows have, this highly developed style of French Gothic from the middle of the thirteenth century on is known as *Rayonnant*. The highest perfection of this style may perhaps be seen, not in one of the great cathedrals, but in the chapel which St. Louis (Louis IX) built in the palace at Paris to contain the Crown of Thorns— the little building we now call the Ste. Chapelle. Here, although the dimensions of the building are modest and its parts simple, the treatment of all is so carefully studied, all of the forms are brought into such a beautiful delicacy, and the fundamental structure of the whole is nevertheless so clear, that it has an effect altogether out of proportion to its size. In it, too, the sculptor, the stained-glass worker, and the architect have worked in such unified harmony that the building is unthinkable without its sculpture and its glass, as they are unthinkable in any other frame than that which here contains them. Of course the greater part of the glass, much of the carving, and all of the color decoration, as we see it today, is of the nineteenth century—a restoration by Viollet-le-Duc,—but its basic design and its controlling colors are right and can be accepted as showing us, if only imperfectly, the real glory of the Rayonnant Gothic ideal.

The great danger of Rayonnant architecture lay perhaps in the skill of its own architects and in the tremendous rivalry between towns and between architects each to outdo the other in lightness, delicacy, and height. Thus, at Beauvais, begun in 1247, only the choir of the enormous building contemplated was ever completed, and in the effort to obtain the maximum lightness of supports and the greatest possible height (154 feet) even that was only accomplished with great difficulty. When the vaults were built, they fell—the construction was too light. In 1272 they were rebuilt, and again twelve years later the supports cracked and the vault fell in. At last the builders were forced to double the number of supports and divide each bay into two, and finally the choir in this new scheme was completed about 1320. The rest of the church was not begun until 1500, when the transepts were started and a great spire 500 feet high was built over the crossing. This, too, was overambitious and crashed before the century was out. The nave was never built at all. The impression of this extraordinary choir is breathtaking in its height and the slimness of all of its narrow parts; yet it shows a kind of thinness in the moldings which pointed the way that fourteenth-century French architecture was to take—the way of wire-drawn complication of structure and detail that seems to have become a matter of display of skill rather than pure creation,—so that most of the fourteenth-century churches such as St. Ouen at Rouen seem by comparison with earlier work cold and uninspired, however brilliant.

In church architecture, in fact, the fourteenth century in France was a period of rest. Most of the greater cathedrals had already been built, as well as great numbers of parish churches. The English wars which devastated western France for a century had taken a terrific toll of man power and wealth; and, to cap the climax, the Black Death swept over Europe.

It was therefore not until the English had finally been thrown out of France and the country had begun to draw a free breath again, relieved alike of the ravages of enemies and of the plague, that a new epoch of building began, and when that came it was in a new style which we call the *Flamboyant*. Flamboyant work receives its name from the flamelike shapes common in its window tracery. The earlier tracery had all been based upon the arch, the circle, and the cusp, but by the introduction of reversed curves it was possible to interweave the tracery forms with graceful freedom, giving them all sorts of leaflike and flamelike shapes. This type of tracery was undoubtedly borrowed from the earlier English *Curvilinear;* the French, however, gave it a vitality and a fluid character of their own.

Along with Flamboyant tracery went a new feeling for ornament—a new effort, as it were, to separate definitely structural and decorative features. All capitals in nave piers or vaulting shafts were omitted, and the lines flowed unbroken from the base, up the piers, and around the vault ribs to the ridge. The piers themselves were changed, becoming either simple forms with rather soft curved moldings running up them, into which the arch and rib moldings died away without definite lines of demarcation, or else merely the duplication of the vault ribs and arch moldings themselves carried down unbroken to the floor. Along with this went a general dislike of horizontal lines, so that the triforium was frequently omitted; and, although the sense of dynamic height in such churches is most impressive, there seems to be something about them that is overintellectual and starved— a sort of artificial asceticism.

This restrained character in structural forms was compensated for by extraordinary lavishness in the decorative carving on doors, porches, choir screens, pinnacles, and the like. Pierced gables without roofs behind them became commonplace exterior decorations, and everywhere moldings of different elements were allowed to pierce and intersect each other in the most complicated ways. To this already complex network of decorative form was added a frosting, as it were, of carved ornament. Instead of the simple crockets of the early period, with their tight spherical forms, crockets were much broken up with deep indentations like seaweed forms. Leafage was naturalistic and often deeply undercut, so that the effect was lacelike. The change is especially obvious in the figure work, where a new feeling for dramatic emotionalism and individual expression is seen, affected perhaps by the realism of the early Renaissance in Italy, which tended to make figures stand out as individual objects applied to the building rather than integral parts of it. In technical skill the French stone carvers of the Flamboyant period have never been surpassed, and their endless care in realistic detail can be seen in the choir screens of Amiens or of Chartres, where the panels seem almost like "frames" from a dramatic moving picture. Thus, although the pointed arch and the ribbed vault of the early period were preserved, and the tall spires and rich west fronts still remained obviously Gothic, nevertheless the spirit of the whole was vastly different from the spirit of the Gothic of 300 years earlier. The new style had a flavor and an excitement of its own, but it was an excitement half of decadence. The Gothic style had lived through its course, and most of the elements which gave vitality to its later manifestations could only reach their highest expression in the Renaissance.

In secular work, of course, the great stone vaults of the cathedrals were unnecessary, except for such rare buildings as the large hospital halls. In fact, the basic plan types and structural ideas of the house, the castle, and even the town hall had been fully formed before the Gothic style held sway. What distinguishes the Gothic secular building from the Romanesque in France is not, then, a structural difference as in the case of a church, but rather a change in the detail by which the pointed arch, tracery, and the general type of ornament current in churches were naturally applied to secular buildings of the same period. Another great difference between the secular and the religious work lies in the fact that, although the fourteenth century saw little important church building, it was one of the great eras of secular building marked by the most extraordinary richness and luxury.

Gothic town houses of masonry, like the house of Count Raymond at Cordes or the House of the Musicians at Rheims, show how the banded windows of the upper floors and the simple arches below were treated in the new style. Windows became larger and the use of glass more common, especially from the fourteenth century on; and, in order to make windows that could easily be opened and closed, grouped windows with flat tops were usual, and more and more large openings came to be divided by mullions (upright divisions) and by transom bars (horizontal divisions) into smaller rectangular units which could be easily glazed. From 1400 on, wooden half-timber constructions began to replace masonry in town houses as both less expensive and more flexible, and the houses grew narrower and higher as land in the towns became more expensive. The exposed wooden members were often carved with little columns or buttress or pinnacle forms; and, when toward the end of the Gothic period glass became comparatively inexpensive, almost the whole front of the house between the supporting posts would be of glass, leaving only the panels between the

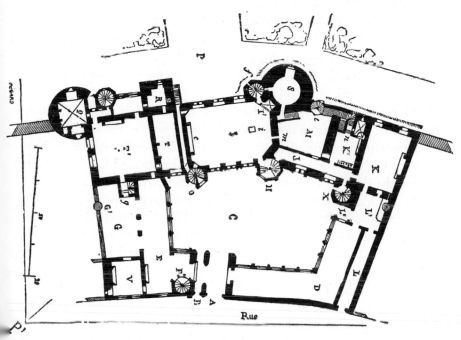

63. HOUSE OF JACQUES COEUR, BOURGES; PLAN. 15TH CENTURY. (Viollet-le-Duc.)

A. MAIN ENTRANCE	L. SERVICE ENTRANCE
B. PEDESTRIAN ENTRANCE	L'. SERVICE COURT
C. COURT	I. GREAT HALL
D. GALLERY	Q, S. BEDROOMS AND CABINETS
F, H, O, X. MAIN STAIRS	R, T. PRIVATE SUITE
K, K'. KITCHENS	T'. SECONDARY HALL

windowsill of one floor and the window head of the floor below to be filled with brick or stucco. The picturesque beauty resulting from these high narrow houses, in which the upper floors frequently project over the floors beneath, is well seen in such towns as Rouen and Lisieux.

The very large town house, the private palace, began to take form during the last half of the Gothic era. Usually built around a court, these large houses had elaborate plans with many different rooms for public and private use, and were frequently arranged with several spiral stairs so that any room could be reached from the ground with a minimum of corridor space. The sumptuousness of these houses can be seen in the Cluny Museum in Paris, once the town residence of the Bishop of Cluny, and in the even larger palace that the famous—or infamous—banker Jacques Coeur built for himself at Bourges. Magnificent halls, with richly carved doorways and enormous and beautiful mantelpieces, with lavish polychromed wooden ceilings, were characteristic of these buildings, and originally brilliant tapestries hung there. It is, in fact, typical of the extravagance of the fourteenth-century domestic work that it was in this century that tapestries began to replace the earlier and simpler printed or painted fabrics for wall hangings.

The history of the castle during the Gothic centuries tells vividly the story of the gradual change from the feuds and private wars of the feudal system to the more settled organization of royal France. The earlier castles, such as the famous Château Gaillard on the Seine built by Richard Coeur de Lion to buttress the English power in Normandy, were fortresses pure and simple, with the living accommodations entirely secondary. The characteristic castles of the middle of the thirteenth century, like the famous Coucy, show not only more advanced types of military construction, a more careful handling of gates and towers, and an enormously strong central keep or donjon, but also greater area and more careful study given to the living quarters, which take the form of a several-storied building on one side of the court, large enough to contain ample halls and chambers, furnished because of their protected position with large windows to give pleasant light within.

By the end of the fourteenth century, the residential portions of the castle have achieved richness and luxury as well as mere comfort, and in the great castle at Pierrefonds, built by Louis d'Orléans in the late fourteenth century, despite the careful study of the military necessities and the use of projecting masonry *machicoulis* at the tops of the towers to replace the older timber *hourds,* from which missiles could be dropped on besiegers below, the residential portion has become a true palace, with enormous, richly decorated halls for court ceremonials and a complex and convenient arrangement of the lavish rooms for private dwelling.

The château of Josselin reveals the change that the end of the Gothic period had brought. The river façade, which preserves the original twelfth-century plan, has the heavy walls, the great round towers, and the tiny openings of the fortress; but the land side, rebuilt early in the sixteenth century, has the great windows of late Gothic residential work and dormer windows of almost lacelike intricacy. Within, the story is the same, and the

origin of English churches shows most strongly. Many of the famous English Gothic churches were built by Cistercians, and the Cistercian order had come to the general use of a square rather than of an apse east end. It is the square east end of English churches which allows the great east windows that are so frequently their crowning glory. Moreover, since the monastic churches needed many altars, the east end of the choir is often but the beginning of a whole series of retro-choirs and chapels which sometimes seem to be almost little separate churches of delicate loveliness added behind the main fabric.

The love of the horizontal also influenced the interior design of the nave. There is none of the French effort to emphasize the separate bays. Instead, the horizontal line of the bottom of the triforium frequently carries through

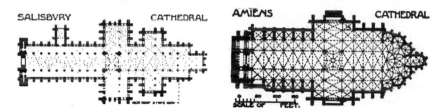

65. COMPARATIVE FRENCH AND ENGLISH GOTHIC CATHEDRAL PLANS: AMIENS AND SALISBURY. (Simpson. Vol. II.)

unbroken, and the vaulting shafts end at its level, supported on carved corbels. The triforium galleries are relatively higher than in the French examples, and the clerestory windows smaller.

The English love of decoration also had its effect in the interior design. The old idea of heavy walls, taken over from the Romanesque style, continued to exert a marked influence throughout the Gothic period. As a result, the windows often have two separate planes of tracery, which may differ slightly in design, the window proper being on the outside face of the wall and a screen of tracery being built on the inside face. Arcading of all sorts, sometimes of the greatest complexity, is used under side-aisle windows and elsewhere.

But the special contribution to Gothic architecture made by this English love of richness lay in its treatment of the vault, through the discovery that additional vault ribs, besides the groin and cross-ribs, could be added. These additional ribs not only made the individual pieces of vault filling smaller, but also by their treelike branching from the top of the vaulting shafts gave many of the English vaults an exquisite and lovely patterning. These reduplicated vault ribs also made possible great variety in the handling of the basic vault shapes. Moreover, the usual English method of building the vault filling produced a zigzag joint at the crown of the vault; to cover this, ridge ribs were added, at the crown of the main vault and often also at the crowns of the other vaults as well. The result of all of this was a soaring magnificence above, which goes far to compensate for the general English lack of height. Ribs running from the vault shaft to the ridge, between the groins, are called *tiercerons,* and the result in such an elaborate tierceron vault as that found, for instance, in Exeter seems almost to resemble the branching trees of a forest—to which the romantic writers often attribute the invention of the Gothic vault.

Equally revolutionary were the exterior changes. Usually the English architects disliked the broken rhythmical quality of flying buttresses, and therefore almost always concealed them under the side-aisle roofs. The long sweeping lines of roof, broken so interestingly by the boldly projecting transepts and the occasional side porches—or Galilee porches, which the English loved,—gave an exterior at once picturesque and impressive. This long low composition also led to the English fondness for the central tower and spire, which became the ideal motif to tie together the whole picture, as we can see it today in Salisbury. In such a church the west end becomes of almost minor importance. Again and again the west ends of English churches give the impression that their design was an afterthought. Doorways are usually small, and instead of the monumental masses of the French west fronts one has what is in essence a screen, decorated with row after row of Gothic arcading and pierced by tiny doors beneath. In themselves, these west fronts are perhaps the least successful part of English Gothic churches; yet, with the long lines and rambling plan of the whole, a more monumental treatment for the west front would be definitely out of place. The east end, with its succession of small chapels and retro-choirs building up to the great east window of the main choir, also had a character all its own.

In the course of the development of Gothic architecture in England, at least four quite different characteristic phases occur. The first is called *Early English* and may be dated roughly from 1180 to 1240. The second and third together are called *Decorated* and roughly occupy the period from 1240 to 1360 or 1370. This period is again divided into two—*Geometric,* 1240 to 1300, and *Curvilinear,* 1300 to 1360, so called because of the characteristic window tracery. The last period is the *Perpendicular* and runs from 1360 to the gradual replacement of Gothic by Renaissance forms, during the sixteenth century. Many English churches were built, altered, rebuilt, and added to over the entire period, so that with few exceptions work from almost all of the periods can be found within each.

Early English work has the quiet charm of an English spring day. It is naïve at times, with an almost childlike love of the indefinite repetition of decorative arcades with high sharp arches. It uses tracery seldom if at all, and instead, where large window areas are desired, it ranks together tall, narrow, separate window lights in groups. It loves, too, extravagant richness

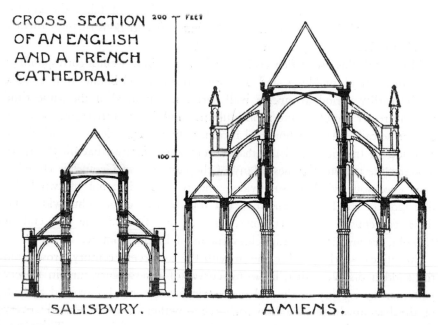

CROSS SECTION OF AN ENGLISH AND A FRENCH CATHEDRAL.

SALISBVRY.   AMIENS.

66. COMPARATIVE FRENCH AND ENGLISH GOTHIC CATHEDRALS; SECTIONS OF AMIENS AND SALISBURY DRAWN TO THE SAME SCALE. (Simpson. Vol II.)

in arch moldings and the change of color that can be produced by attaching black marble colonnettes to light stone piers. Its carving is generally simple, using thick, rounded-lobed leaves; but for pier and column capitals it prefers simple moldings, circular in plan, to foliated ornament. Its most characteristic monument is Salisbury Cathedral, built at almost identically the same time as Amiens, and the difference between the English and the French Gothic can nowhere more dramatically be seen than in the contrast between the bold height and daring construction of the one and the length and delightful simplicity of the other.

Once the English adopted tracery, in the middle of the thirteenth century, they carried its playful design to a much greater elaboration and used it more imaginatively than did the French. Geometric work employs tracery of curves based on the pointed arch and the circle. The patterns are at first similar to French patterns, but the English never had the French love for enormous top circles, and usually the main arch of the window and the arches of its separate lights spring from the same line. Again, cusps projecting inward from arch and circle are universally used and are sometimes brought out to the face of the arch, becoming larger elements than in French tracery. Sometimes, too, to give variety, the arch itself takes the cusped form; the result has that rather graceful but soft and nonstructural quality which the English designers seemed to like.

Along with this use of rich geometrical tracery there went a corresponding simplification of moldings and a change from the elaborate wall arcades of the earlier period to quieter wall surfaces, combined at the same time with a greater use of architectural sculpture and foliage ornament. Thus we get the so-called Angel Choir of Lincoln, with its large clerestory windows, its traceried triforium, and the magnificent angel figures that fill the space between the triforium arches. Many of the east ends of Geometric churches have enormous windows subdivided and re-subdivided, not of two lights like most of the French windows, but four, six, or eight lights wide; and these gorgeous traceried windows, such as one finds at the east end of Lincoln, are among the great achievements of English Gothic.

Curvilinear work, which came in with the fourteenth century, arose from the sudden discovery that, by using curves of reverse curvature in tracery patterns, the rigidity of the old geometric forms could be avoided and all of the bars made to flow into each other without breaks. This discovery threw the whole problem of window-tracery design wide open. There was no limit, except in the imagination of the designer, to the variation in types. The simplest kinds, in which there is an absolute regularity in the flowing shapes, are sometimes called net or reticulated windows, and are common in the smaller churches; but in the great east and west windows like those of York the most varied and even eccentric shapes are found. It was undoubtedly the influence of this English Curvilinear tracery which led to the French Flamboyant tracery half a century later.

The Curvilinear feeling exerted a tremendous influence over all design elements, and the reverse curve, known as the *ogee,* is applied to cusping and even to arch shapes. Along with it went an extravagance in decorative carving which is characteristic of the universal fourteenth-century luxury. Foliage carving was often realistic almost to the point of photography; at some places decorative suitability seems to have been forgotten in the search for rich, realistic leafage.

Later in the period, a change in the vaulting occurred through the addition, to the simple richness of tierceron vaults, of new little ribs called *liernes* ("ties") built between the tiercerons wherever the fancy of the architect demanded. With these small ribs, patterns of the most extraordinary intricacy could be produced—net vaults, star vaults, and so on, as one may see them in the choir of Wells Cathedral and the nave of Winchester.

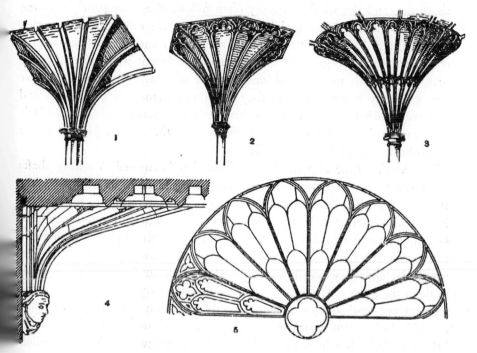

67. DIAGRAMS SHOWING THE DEVELOPMENT OF ENGLISH GOTHIC FAN VAULTS. 1, 2, 3. SPRINGING OF VAULTS. 4. ALL SOULS', OXFORD. 5. WESTMINSTER SOUTH TRANSEPT WINDOW. (Bond: *Gothic Architecture in England*.)

But the gain in superficial richness, magnified by the carving of rich bosses at every rib intersection, seems often dearly bought at the cost of a loss of clarity and structural expression.

The Perpendicular style crept tentatively, here and there, into buildings of the third quarter of the fourteenth century. In a way it was both a reaction against the overlush decoration of the Curvilinear period and also a development of it. It was a reaction because, for the soft lines of the earlier style, it substituted, for the first time in English Gothic, something of the strong structural membering and the powerful verticality of French work. It was a development, because it took the complexity of the lierne vault and, carrying it still further, produced the fan vault. Foliage carving tends to be minimized during the Perpendicular period, capitals are molded, there is little applied carving, and the leafage becomes flat and conventional. Everywhere moldings and architectural motifs tend to replace carved ornament, and there is an insistence on the vertical line which gives the style its name. Wall surfaces are paneled with long, narrow, high panels, arch-headed, tier above tier, and the window tracery often follows the same panel character, with mullions and horizontal bars intersecting each other at right angles, the horizontal bars supported by little arches over each light. Such tracery of course lacked the grace of Curvilinear work, but it was easier to build, structurally much more sound, and allowed windows of almost indefinite size, especially when braced as they sometimes were by vertical piers and buttresses carried up unbroken to the top. The panels of which the whole was composed served admirably as frames for the stained glass, a single figure being placed in each panel.

For the first time also the height dimension is stressed. Vaulting shafts often run clear from the floor, and everything is done to emphasize the vertical rather than the horizontal dimension. It is interesting to see how the Bishop of Winchester, in the early years of the fifteenth century, altered over his Norman church by carving from its great stone piers and arches a new architecture of delicate vertical lines and intricate panels. The Perpendicular churches have been criticized as cold, but it is wrong to apply to them the same criteria one applies to the earlier styles. What their architects set out to do they did magnificently and with a growing assurance. As skillful constructors and masons they were unrivaled, and it is characteristic of their facility in the use of stone that they revolutionized the whole vault conception. With the development of rich lierne vaults, the ribs had come to occupy such a great area of the vault that their original structural basis had little more functional part to play, the filling between the ribs being reduced to a matter of two or three stones, and the centering required for the ribs being so heavy as almost to equal the centering for a uniform nonribbed vault. The Perpendicular architects realized this and in the fan vault took the final step, making the ribs mere decorations carved on the surface of a homogeneous stone vault.

The type of vault used and the love of increasing the vertical lines to the greatest possible length led to another peculiarity of Perpendicular architecture—the use of low four-centered arches, which tended toward a flatter and flatter curvature as the style grew. The earliest stage of Perpendicular can be seen in parts of Gloucester Cathedral; a more highly advanced example is Winchester; but the three climax buildings of the style—St. George's Chapel in Windsor, the Henry VII Chapel of Westminster Abbey, and the King's College Chapel in Cambridge—are all of the sixteenth century, when Renaissance forms were beginning to be tentatively used.

Medieval England was predominantly a country of agricultural villages and prosperous market towns. The parish churches which were built in these centers by hundreds are among the most characteristic and beautiful manifestations of English Gothic architecture. Usually short, sometimes only three or four bays long, with wide side aisles, often reaching almost as high as the nave, they have a low and picturesque massing which seems to grow naturally from the ground. Frequently they were added to from generation to generation, a chapel here, an extra aisle there. The chief exterior feature in these churches is usually a single tower, often placed over the entrance, and on this tower the principal expenditure was lavished. Plain below, with a rich belfry opening above, and crowned more often than not with a spire of slim and graceful proportions, these church towers, rising from among the heavy foliage of embowering trees, form a constant note of interest in the English landscape. The spires themselves are usually beautiful in proportion, and the handling of the connection between the octagonal spire and the square tower is brilliant in its use of little cut-off pyramidal sections called broaches, or by some other means more simple than those found on the Continent—but nearly always more charming because of their simplicity. Notable examples exist at Louth, and at Patrington.

Another characteristic feature of many of these country churches is their beautiful exposed timber roofs. The English were perhaps the most skillful boat builders of the Middle Ages, and wood was always a congenial material for them. In the bracing of the roof trusses went much of the skill and much of the grace found in their boats, and these roofs were frequently decorated with carved angels on each side of every truss, and by inserts of wooden tracery and cusping. The result is not only richness of texture but warmth of color from the wood itself, often further emphasized by the painting of some of the moldings, or of the panels between the structural members, with red and blue and gold. These trusses are of various types; the majority have some kind of arched brace connecting the lower parts with the ties across above, which gives them unusual distinction of line and acts as a pleasant connecting element between the wall and the roof. Sometimes the trusswork is hidden by a paneled ceiling of the most complex cabinetwork.

The largest trusses are of the type known as the hammer-beam truss, with intermediate uprights bracketed out from the side walls to help reduce the span, and all of the members carefully tied together by elaborate diagonal or arched braces. These hammer-beam trusses, though not scientifically efficient, because they exert an outward thrust on the walls just as a vault does, are nevertheless extremely rich and beautiful and offer all sorts of opportunities for carved drops, pierced fillings, and applied figures. Hammer-beam trusses can also be used on very wide spans. Perhaps the finest of all these roofs

68. ENGLISH OPEN-TIMBER ROOFS, FROM BRINTON (*left*) AND WYMONDHAM (*right*). (Bond: *Gothic Architecture*.)

covers Westminster Hall, almost the only part of the old royal palace at Westminster left to us. The magnificent apparent strength and the shadowed depths of these trussed ceilings are among the finest creations of English Gothic work.

The generally rural character of medieval England affected its secular architecture profoundly, and the straggling early medieval village has remained in many places almost unchanged in plan or general aspect to the present day. Individual or paired cottages of the simplest type flanked a road, and perhaps a few minor streets. In the middle an informal open space with a market cross, served as the village center. The market crosses were frequently elaborately decorated and sometimes combined with a hall where the accounts of the market could be kept and the taxes received; but, gen erally speaking, both the houses and the other secular buildings were of the simplest type. In larger market centers and in the walled towns, the spirit was necessarily different and the effect more nearly that of the contemporary French community. Half-timbered houses, their gable ends to the street, were common from the fifteenth century on; and sometimes, as we can see from examples in Salisbury and Chester, they were skillfully carved and all of the English love of surface ornament appeared in their treatment. As in the churches, there is less structural feeling in the half-timber design of England than in that of the Continent.

The feudal conservatism of English life shows in the English castle, where the basic old Norse plan of a great hall remained a controlling element through the Gothic period. Conservative too was the occasional preservation of a single high Norman tower-keep as the castle type; as late as the fifteenth century Tattershall Castle preserved the old type of plan almost unchanged, with one great room to each floor, stairs in a corner turret, and a certain number of smaller rooms in the thickness of the wall itself. The other type of Norse castle—the walled enclosure containing a great hall, subsidiary buildings, and a keep which was fortification alone—was developed into such Gothic examples as Stokesay Castle, where we still possess a great timber-roofed hall of the thirteenth century with its smaller adjoining buildings. Little by little, especially during the fourteenth century, this type was given more amenities. The hall was entered through a vestibule, separated from the hall proper by a screen of paneling. Above it was the open musicians' gallery. From the vestibule opened out the service rooms of the house—kitchens, pantries, breweries, and so on. At the hall end opposite the screens was the lord's dais, raised a step or two above the rest of the room, and in the later examples often lighted by a tremendous bay window of Perpendicular tracery. From the dais doors led into the private rooms of the house, often on two floors—two or three bedrooms and a chapel.

As the luxury of living and the idea of privacy both increased, the use of the great hall for dining became increasingly irksome. Gradually it came to be used only for ritual occasions, but it still remained a vast, wasteful area to plague later designers. Just as in France, however, during the fifteenth century, the old castle idea gave way to the idea of the country house. The private rooms were increased in number and made more livable by wooden sheathing, a freer use of textile hangings, and greatly enlarged window areas, usually in long rows of little casements. Although in the greatest ducal mansions the old feudal uncomfortable magnificence

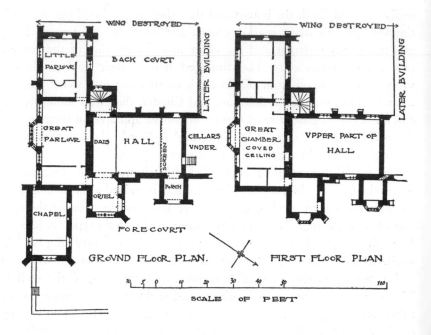

GROUND FLOOR PLAN. FIRST FLOOR PLAN

SCALE OF FEET

69. CHARACTERISTIC GOTHIC ENGLISH MANOR HOUSE; PLAN AND VIEW
LYTES CARY MANOR. 14TH AND 15TH CENTURIES. (Garner and Stratton:
Domestic Architecture of England during the Tudor Period.)

may have continued to rule—as late as the middle of the fourteenth century the great hall of Penshurst Place retained the old central hearth,—nevertheless, in the smaller houses the move toward comfort was irresistible, and in such a fifteenth-century manor as Cothay or Nappa Hall in Yorkshire a house type had been achieved which is livable even today. In livability and comfort these later Gothic English manors were probably the most advanced houses of their time in all Europe, and they set a standard which has had an extraordinary influence on all country-house design ever since.

Nowhere were feudal relationships so confused, or conditions so unsettled, during the Middle Ages, as in Germany under the aegis of the Holy Roman Empire. Nowhere, therefore, is Gothic work more varied and more expressive of local differences. The Gothic came into Germany slowly, for under the Empire the twelfth century had seen a Romanesque style so vital, so effective in both church and secular design, as to make a departure from it a matter of fashion rather than of need. The influences for the new style came from France, and it is naturally along the Rhine that the Gothic had its earliest developed movements. Thus, Strasbourg and Cologne—and, further east, Regensburg—all reveal the importance of French precedent. There is, accordingly, practically no real transitional work in Germany. The monuments are either all Romanesque or suddenly all Gothic, for at the time when they were built French Gothic, their precedent, had already reached almost its climax stage.

Yet Cologne and Strasbourg reveal, too, subtle differences from the pure French designs—a general trend toward broken silhouette, picturesque outline, and the development of geometrical window tracery to a point which becomes at times almost bizarre.

The moment we get away from the Rhine to the north and east, the changes become greater. Liking internal height, the Germans developed in the thirteenth century the so-called *hall church,* in which the nave and aisles rise almost to the same height, so that the church is lighted entirely from the side-aisle walls, and there is neither clerestory nor triforium, but only slim columns rising sheer from the floor to the spring of the branching vault ribs. Such a church could then be roofed with one huge gabled roof, stretching from wall to wall, and these colossal roofs, set so high in the air, form the most striking element in many a German view. This system allowed, too, a new type of exterior wall treatment, for the aisle walls now rose unbroken to heights elsewhere unknown, and the side-aisle windows could be made immensely tall. The cathedral in Munich is characteristic of the enormous bulk such a great church possesses and the tremendous impressiveness of its clifflike walls, pierced by their long windows. Even when side aisles did exist in the nave of the church, they were frequently omitted around the choir, so that at this point at least the tall unbroken windows which the Germans loved could rise a full sixty feet or more to the vaults. The effect of such an apse, with its high, slim windows, is magnificent; and in Erfurt, where two such churches flank a great flight of steps connecting two different levels in the town, the result is breathtakingly dramatic. With roofs of such bulk, necessarily tower designs were altered, and again and again a single tower in front of the nave replaces the twin towers of the French churches or the central tower of the English. Even when twin towers are used, they are often low and stubby, rising only slightly above the aisle walls and owing their effect today to the elaborate Baroque broken spires built later to crown them.

But the Germans nevertheless were among the most skillful tower designers in all Europe, as they were among the most skillful masons. It is to them that the open, pierced spire is due, as it is found in Freiburg or Cologne, and the delicate airiness of the best of these German spires is exquisitely fitting. Their ideals for these towers were, in fact, so ambitious that many of them remained unfinished. The whole west end of Cologne was only completed in the middle of the nineteenth century, from drawings which were fortunately preserved and which show the meticulous, careful detail of the Gothic architect. Similarly, the tower at Ulm waited until the nineteenth century for its completion. Three of the fifteenth-century architect's studies were preserved, and it was on the basis of one of these that the present tower, rising to a height of 528 feet, was carried out. Of the towers completed during the Middle Ages, those of Freiburg, of Regensburg, and of Vienna are probably the most graceful as well as the most typical.

It was in the fifteenth century that the independent genius of the German Gothic architects achieved its fullest results. Tracery became a network of dynamic lines, and all sorts of bizarre experiments—such as "branch tracery," and tracery formed, as it were, of two intersecting patterns—were made. Especially lavish were the late Gothic altarpieces, pulpits, choir screens, and similar church fitments, both of wood and stone, in which there is an extraordinary display of imagination, a lacy delicacy almost unreal, and great decorative effect. Town fountains and church screens in metal showed the same qualities.

The most interesting of the local variations was the creation of a special type of brick-built Gothic in the Baltic towns, where the architects, though accepting the ribbed vault and the pointed arch, and even the tracery of the more traditional Gothic, nevertheless realized so well the possibilities of their favorite building material, brick, that all of these forms are modified and the total effect is always essentially that of brick. A characteristic feature is a substitution of straight stepped gables for sloped gables, and the decoration of these with recessed panelings in the brickwork.

A delight in town life and prosperous commerce made the German medieval towns perhaps the richest and the most nobly built of any north of the Alps. Here the German genius for picturesque composition, whether conscious or not, is everywhere apparent. The towns are nearly always walled, and the resultant limited space led eventually to the most congested type of town building, with the houses rising three or four stories to the roof, and with perhaps another three stories in the roof itself. The great gables faced the street, and the façades below were banded with large windows framed in the half-timber that was the usual construction, or in beautiful tracery if the front were of stone. The variety in detail in these houses is exceptional, and their basic form gives them a controlling unity.

Especially interesting are the town squares or market places where were grouped the public buildings which the advanced city life demanded—a city hall, perhaps several guild halls, and sometimes a separate town belfry tower, as at Halle, where the tower, with all its lower portion a covered market hall, rises stage on stage high above the town. The town halls usually had an open loggia for a market, or shops, beneath, and great meeting halls above; almost always there was a balcony at this upper level overlooking the square, from which the burgomaster or the councilors could address the assembled citizens. Municipal pride poured more and more money into these municipal buildings, until we have such superb creations as the great L-shaped town hall that frames two sides of the market place in Brunswick, with the rich pierced tracery façade of its upper loggia, or the sheer simple height, beautiful windows, and graceful tower of that at Frankfurt. So lavish, so beautiful, so harmonious were many of these German towns that—as we see them today in part of Nuremberg or Frankfurt, or drawn with such loving and meticulous detail in the pictures of Albert Dürer—they have come to seem perhaps the most perfect incarnation of the secular life of the Middle Ages that we know.

Despite this advanced type of city building, the German castles remained generally at a much lower stage of development. Usually placed on high pinnacles commanding important river crossings or riverside roads, their growth and their plan were drastically limited by the site; and as generations passed, with each adding its suite of rooms or its new wing, the whole eventually became a confused and crowded mass of rather non-descript character, with narrow courts surrounded by high buildings, and with a skyline of exaggerated irregularity. Yet the interiors of these castles were sometimes of great beauty. Roof and ceiling beams were carved and molded. Intricate hardware decorated the doors. On the protected courts, projecting bays or wings of half-timber served as a pleasant contrast to the stone elsewhere. The halls seem to have been more frequently decorated with mural paintings than was common elsewhere, and in the Tyrol many precious fragments of this rich medieval secular mural painting have come down to us.

If we might sum up French Gothic as an architecture of clear and structural power, and English as the architecture of personalized rural charm, German Gothic would be the architecture of experimental and dynamic zest.

The Low Countries—the Netherlands—on the North Sea had been famous for their textiles since Roman times, and shared with northern Italy the honor of being countries where established, highly developed trade first challenged and conquered military feudalism. This quality gave to the medieval architecture of Belgium and Holland a special note. It is an architecture essentially urban and largely secular. In church design it is derivative, from both French and German sources.

Especially in Belgium, such structures as Ste. Gudule in Brussels or St. Bavon in Ghent, or the cathedral at Antwerp, seem merely modifications, not always successful, of pre-eminently French types. There is the same search for height and for logical exterior expression. There is the same general proportion of pier arch, triforium, and clerestory. There is often the same type of west front. Yet the whole seems frequently heavy-handed in detail, almost a little second-hand. The church of St. Bavon is especially interesting because it preserves a choir screen and rood loft, and although these are Baroque and not Gothic they enable one to gain a picture of the general mystery and richness which the Gothic churches had when the old Gothic screens were still standing.

In Holland, the rarity of stone forced a brick architecture, although the Dutch used stone whenever they could get it, and the choir and tower which are all that remain of the great church at Utrecht are perhaps the purest examples of "French" Gothic in the Netherlands—exquisite in their delicate verticality and their rich yet disciplined detail. The cathedral at Leyden has something of the same quality of height; but elsewhere the brick Gothic churches of Holland are relatively low and broad, often with timber ceilings, and interesting chiefly because they seem to foreshadow the open, "comfortable" breadth of later Protestant buildings.

The most interesting Gothic in both Belgium and Holland is undoubtedly domestic and civil, and—especially in Belgium—the great town halls and guild halls achieved a gorgeous monumentality seldom found elsewhere. Thus, the Cloth Hall at Ypres, destroyed during the Great War but now rebuilt, had a total length of almost 500 feet, with open vaulted loggias below and a tremendous wooden-roofed hall above; its perfectly symmetrical exterior expresses these elements with unflinching directness, and the hall is given centrality and unity by the colossal tower which rises in the center. Such a building could only be built by a very wealthy and very self-conscious community. Nor is Ypres a unique example. At Bruges the town hall and the guild halls, though smaller, are just as carefully designed and richer in detail. The late Gothic town halls of Louvain and of Brussels both demonstrated to what heights of imagination the lacelike intricate ornament of the late Gothic could be carried, and also the tremendous importance which such buildings must have held in the eyes of the citizens in order to justify the expenditure. It is noteworthy that in all of these town halls there is no attempt to copy ecclesiastical motifs. Windows are of the size and shape which the rooms demand. Walls are frankly walls, and arcades occur only where they form passages or covered walks. Roofs are usually simple gabled or hipped roofs. Yet over these elements there plays such a wealth of delicate carving, of applied sculpture, of rich metal crestings and the like, that they form perhaps the most extravagantly ornamented group of buildings in all Gothic Europe.

A great gulf separates the medieval life of the Mediterranean countries from that of the countries farther north. Everywhere the stamp of the Roman Empire and of Roman forms was still strong, and the climate itself was so different from that of northern countries as to make differences in building methods inevitable. Gothic architecture had primarily arisen in France as the result of efforts to erect buildings suitable to the French light and the French climate. Where both of these elements were vastly changed, as they were everywhere south of the Pyrenees and the Alps, and along the Mediterranean shore, such a Gothic as that of France or England or Germany would have been absurd, if not impossible. Where the north seeks large windows to welcome the sun, the south strives to soften the midday heat;

and, where the north uses high roofs to shed the winter rains and snows, the drier south remains loyal to the classic roof of lower slope. In the Mediterranean countries, too, many more buildings remained which dated from the Roman Empire, and the influence of such superb structures as the Pantheon at Rome should not be underestimated.

In Spain, the architectural problem was further complicated by the tenacious persistence of Mohammedan forms and the continued use of Mohammedan craftsmen, even after Moorish rule had been overthrown and the greater part of Spain had come again under Christian domination. The exquisite beauty of the best Moorish work—its love of surface ornament and of dramatic contrast, its method of carrying door decoration up the entire height of a wall, the skill of its carpenters, and its brilliant wall tiling —all left an ineradicable mark on Spanish taste.

Gothic forms undoubtedly came into Spain from the north, probably through the influence of the Cistercian order; and the monastery of Poblet, dating from the beginning of the thirteenth century, is a powerful example of Cistercian building, with its great simple pointed arches. Other Gothic architects in Spain, of a later and more highly advanced period, were often men from France or from Germany. In the latest period, at the end of the fourteenth and the beginning of the fifteenth century, Flemish designers and workmen were favored. But, despite this use of foreign architects and craftsmen, the actual work which the Spaniards built becomes at once characteristically their own. The most French, and in a sense the most Gothic, of Spanish medieval churches are those of Burgos, Leon, and Toledo, all built in the thirteenth century, where the forms, especially inside, are based on those of the French Gothic cathedrals. Nevertheless, climate forced smaller windows, and this immediately led to changes in proportion within. On the exterior, the almost universal use of flat roofs and large, simple wall surfaces gave an effect essentially different from that of the north. The fifteenth-century spires of Burgos are pierced spires of the German type and were designed by a German, John of Cologne; but even these have a kind of massive richness which has the true Spanish character.

As the style developed, the differences from northern work grew still greater, and the influences of Moorish precedent increased. Especially noticeable is the trend away from the clear northern Gothic differentiation of nave, transept, choir, and side aisles, and toward an effect which is essentially that of a great many-pillared hall in plan not unlike some of the Moorish mosques. In fact, the cathedral at Seville almost duplicates the plan of the mosque which it replaced, and, despite its enormous size—it is the largest Gothic church in Europe—and its lavish pointed-arch treatment, its interior effect is that of the mystery resulting from widespread views in all directions rather than the accented climax of the northern choir. Exterior design in these later churches is also very different from the design of the north. Great areas of plain wall are left without opening or decoration, and the windows which pierce them are small, buttresses are reduced to mere

70. CATHEDRAL, GERONA, SPAIN; INTERIOR. (Street: *The Gothic Architecture of Spain.*)

strips, and all of the decoration is concentrated around the doors, where ornament and sculpture and tracery are massed with an exuberance that is the result of Flemish influence.

Only in one section of the Iberian peninsula was a Gothic style developed which recognized the essentially structural origin of Gothic work—in Catalonia. Here the fourteenth century saw erected a series of great churches superbly original in design, beautifully adapted to their climate and materials, and yet preserving the clear structural membering of the best French

Gothic. The windows are small, the pier arches unusually high, and to give them scale in almost every case there are two bays of side chapels for each bay of the church proper. The result has something of the airy openness of the German hall church, but the heights are handled with greater subtlety, and the retaining of small clerestories adds enormously to the dramatic power of these churches. Characteristic examples are the cathedral and Sta. Maria del Mar at Barcelona.

The cathedral at Gerona started with a choir and ambulatory of normal type; but when it came time to build the nave the Chapter wished something different, something breathtakingly original. The architect decided to vault the nave in one great vault the entire width of the choir and its side aisles together, and this tremendous Gothic vault, seventy-three feet in span, is the widest vault of medieval times. The grand simplicity of this bold interior, given scale by the triple arch which leads into the choir, reveals the originality and skill of the Catalonian architects.

The cathedral at Palma de Mallorca, begun toward the middle of the thirteenth century, is the climax building of Catalonian Gothic, and one of the most beautiful of medieval churches. The piers which support the nave arcade are simple octagons and rise unbroken to a very great height. The scale is large, and the whole soaring interior is one of the few examples of medieval building which successfully combine something of the simple grandeur of Roman architecture with the structural feeling and innate lightness of the Gothic.

In the smaller churches and in secular building, the Moorish influence is much stronger than in the great cathedrals; here a style called *Mudejar* was evolved, in which the Christian builders made intelligent use of the Moorish craftsmen. Panels of decorated brickwork, elaborate wooden ceilings, and a wealth of surface ornament distinguish this work. It is interesting to see that in some domestic work, even of Christian date, the old Moorish forms are used almost unchanged, as in the Alcázar of Seville.

Spain is also noted for the high development of its military architecture, its elaborate castles and city walls. The castle of Coca, with its extraordinary symphony of polygonal brick projections running up its towers, is a typical example. Many beautiful town houses of the later Middle Ages also exist, which show varying degrees of Gothic influence, but which indicate even more clearly than the churches the growth of the Spanish feeling for plain wall and for inward-turning courtyard plans, and the persistence of Moorish ideals of house design and decoration. Especially remarkable are certain late

Gothic court arcades and the intricate carpentry ceilings or *artesonados* which cover the principal rooms.

It was the Cistercians who seem to have brought the first Gothic into Italy, as they did into Spain; and the monasteries of Fossanova, 1208, and San Galgano, 1218, preserve the characteristic Cistercian power and make use of the pointed arch and ribbed vaults in almost the northern manner.

Nevertheless, the whole theory of Gothic structure was essentially contrary to the Italian building tradition. The Romans had loved buildings of enormous dimensions, with all their parts widely spaced and open; they had built most often in brick or concrete, and veneered their structures with marble, mosaic, and painted plaster. The tradition of building of this type, as well as of the Roman system of proportions, was still strong, and no Italian medieval architect ever seems to have realized the true nature of the ribbed vault and buttress system that is the essence of Gothic, or even of the tracery and the naturalistic ornament which were its chief decorations. The most "Gothic" of Italian cathedrals is Milan (late fourteenth century). The Chapter wished it to rival the great cathedrals of the north and, after laying foundations on a typical Italian plan, called in various German and French architects (Heinrich von Gmunden the most important) to advise them. In its height and tracery Milan is Germanic, yet characteristically the advice of these foreigners was generally discarded. Heinrich suggested a high nave design "ad quadratum"; the French criticized the piers and buttresses. A lower scheme "ad triangulum" was proposed, but the actual church is lower than either. Italian taste dictated the lavish spires, pinnacles, and crestings, and even the interior with its small clerestory, its omission of a triforium, and its strange capitals is completely Italianate.

Elsewhere, Italian Gothic is a thing in itself, not to be judged by the criteria of the French or the English. It is merely another play of superficial ornament over the old traditional Italian structure.

Yet this is not to deny the extraordinary beauty of many Italian Gothic works; it is merely to place them in their proper perspective. Rome has but one church, Sta. Maria Sopra Minerva, which even faintly approaches Gothic; and, while Amiens and Rheims were rising across the Alps, Roman architects were building the exquisite Romanesque cloisters of St. John Lateran and St. Paul's Outside the Walls, with their almost classic cornices and their brilliant inlaid mosaics.

Italian Gothic work can be divided roughly into three types: the Central type, represented by Orvieto and Siena, which carries over the old hori-

zontally banded black-and-white marble sheathing of the Tuscan Romanesque, and combines with it an overlay of Gothic pinnacles, crockets, and
tracery; the Lombard type of brick Gothic, which controls also the great
Gothic churches in Florence; and the Venetian Gothic, which consists
largely of the adoption of tracery and the pointed arch and their application to the continuing Byzantine tradition. These three types are not strictly
separated geographically; each reacts on the other, and many localities may
have work of two of them.

In a sense, the brick type is that in which the pointed arch of the north
and the ribbed vault achieved their simplest expression, as one sees them for
instance in Sta. Croce or the cathedral at Florence. Here, simple piers
carry simple pointed arches; there is a small clerestory; everything is consistently in the one vein—yet no one entering these churches would for a
moment confuse them with the Gothic churches north of the Alps. It is the
old Roman desire for great dimensions which has controlled. The bay widths
are much greater than in northern work; all of the parts are simpler; there
is much more plain surface. As a result, to one accustomed to the work of the
north these buildings seem to lack scale, they never seem to appear their
true size. In the Florence cathedral, for instance, the bays are over sixty feet
from center to center; and, although the size of the church is colossal, the
fact that it has so few parts—however enormous each part may be—makes
it seem smaller than it really is.

On the other hand, the great size of the parts and the simplicity of the
wall surfaces in these Italian churches offered an opportunity for mural
decoration which no northern church could equal. It is no accident that the
greatest mural decorators arose to fill this need, or that Giotto, perhaps the
first great figure in the long tradition of Italian painting, found his most
congenial opportunities in the church of St. Francis at Assisi or the Arena
Chapel in Padua. This mural decoration, with its rich, solid color, its
glories of blue and red, of green and tan, picked out here and there with
golden halos, made perhaps for a total gorgeousness of interior effect unique
in history; and it is only where that decorative painting has been completed,
as in Assisi, in the Padua chapel, in the Spanish Chapel in Florence by
Andrea da Firenze, and in parts of Sta. Croce at Florence by Giotto and the
Gaddi, that the true aspect which was in the mind of the Italian Gothic
church builders can be realized.

In the Central Italian type of church, such as that of Siena or Orvieto,
the sizes of the units are smaller and the scale is therefore better; moreover,
the horizontal banding of colored marble gives at once the sense of size

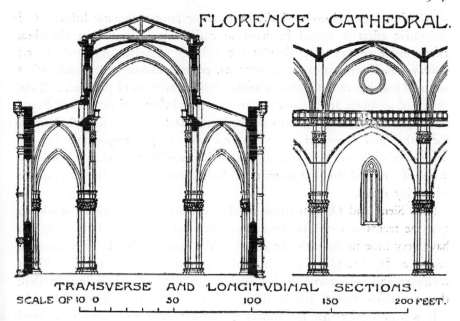

FLORENCE CATHEDRAL.

TRANSVERSE AND LONGITVDINAL SECTIONS.

SCALE OF 10 0   50   100   150   200 FEET.

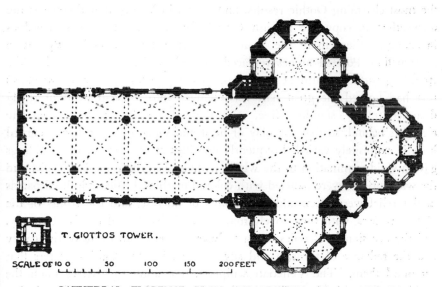

T. GIOTTOS TOWER.

SCALE OF 10 0   50   100   150   200 FEET

71. CATHEDRAL, FLORENCE; PLAN AND SECTION. (Simpson. Vol. II.)

which the plainer churches lack. In fact, for pure chromatic brilliance of decorative effect it would be hard to equal these magnificent churches, either inside or out. Yet, despite the richness of spire and crocket and tracery which ornaments their exteriors, pointed arches and round arches are used together in them almost without differentiation of purpose, and the details of sculpture and decoration are far more influenced by ancient Rome than by what we know usually as Gothic. In fact, the Pisani, both Niccola the father and Giovanni the son, who were largely responsible for the decoration of Siena, were among the sculptors who most clearly gave evidence of a careful study of Roman work and foreshadowed the Renaissance which lay ahead.

Both Siena and Orvieto show another characteristic of Italian work, in that the fronts of each are mere decorative screens, the outlines of which have very little to do with the shape of the church behind. They are conceived as façades, places for the elaborate ornamentation which brilliant sculpture and mosaic could give, and not as parts of a building. In that, they reveal the typical Italian disregard of the structural basis of Gothic.

It was in Venice that the Italian genius for surface decoration achieved the most charming Gothic results, and it was in Venice that there was the least effort to copy the foreign Gothic forms and the greatest freedom in changing them to fit the Venetian needs and the Venetian Byzantine construction. Pointed arches replaced the old semicircular arches, but the sparkling surface treatment remained. In the palaces, the row of windows that had lighted the great hall was changed into a broad band of richly designed tracery, standing free, with the window frames set as separate elements behind, so that the play of light and shade over the lovely curved lines is exquisitely varied. Frequently crestings at the tops of the buildings gave a vivid termination to the whole without disturbing its flat façade, and the wall surfaces were paneled with colored marbles. Little sculptured panels in flat relief were often added at points of interest; and the fronts of the Gothic palaces, with their lovely marbles, their horizontal bands of tracery, and the occasional balconies, seem to have in them something of the gaiety and the radiance of the sun and sky reflected in the laughing waters that surround them. The Venetian sculptors, too, flung themselves upon the problem of Gothic decorative detail with a gay abandon little found elsewhere, avoiding the bad copies of northern crockets or the flat imitations of Roman work so often met with in Italy. The capitals of the great open loggias of the Doges' Palace are among the most beautiful medieval architectural sculpture anywhere in Europe; and, even where the northern forms are more definitely adopted, as in the Porta della Carta, both the figures and the foliage are so imaginative and so free that the result is perhaps less Gothic than Venetian, yet altogether delightful.

The great wealth and the high level of development of the Italian cities gave rise to a tremendous amount of public and domestic building, which is in many ways the most distinguished contribution of Gothic architecture in Italy. Each town had its municipal palace, usually built around a court, with enormous upper halls for council meetings, courts, and the like. Each town had also its *palazzo del podestà*, the combined police station, prison, and palace of the military governor, a building usually more somber than the municipal hall but often equally grand. A great tower rose above the city hall, and often above the podesta as well; in addition, many noble families built treasure and fortification towers in the Italian cities, giving their sky-lines an extraordinary quality of dramatic contrast between these upright lines and the long horizontals everywhere else supreme.

But it was in the private palaces of the wealthy that the true character of this secular Italian Gothic most clearly appears, and it is in these that we see, too, most clearly the persistence of essentially classic ideals. Usually these palaces are four-square and simple, built around an arcaded court. The story heights are enormous and the stories are clearly differentiated from each other on the outside. Moreover, the principles of symmetry and regularity control the design again and again, and the palace fronts consist of rows of equal windows, equally spaced, separated by ample wall surfaces. It is an architecture of monumental repose, a repose essentially classic, and these palaces require but slight change in detail to become the more famous palaces of the Italian Renaissance.

BOOK V

The Renaissance

Chapter 16

THE DAWN OF THE RENAISSANCE

ALL through the Middle Ages the memory of classic culture still lived on, a sort of unreal will-o'-the-wisp that reached occasionally a more actual existence in the studies of the schoolmen and the poems which wandering scholars and ne'er-do-wells continued to write. Aristotle and Plato, Seneca and Cicero, were known, if not in the original, at least in early summaries and digests. Virgil was read; had he not prophesied the coming of Christ? And in the Goliardic verse which the wandering scholars sang as they traveled over the face of medieval Europe, a scandal to their more religious brethren, the nymphs and satyrs, with Diana and Aphrodite, still lived.

There are evidences of this afterlife of the classics even in some of the medieval buildings. Many of the capitals of Romanesque Languedoc still to be seen in the museum at Toulouse, as well as in the country churches, are carved with the creatures of classic myth, and centaurs and mermaids glance out of the intertwined foliage. Later, much French Gothic sculpture of the late thirteenth and early fourteenth centuries shows signs of a careful study of the classical drapery seen probably on Roman sarcophagus figures. So long as Latin remained the language of the church and of the learned, and the great international medium of intellectual exchange, the memory of Greece and Rome and the art which they had produced, even the forms and myths and legends of paganism, could not altogether die.

In literature at least, this consciousness of the grace and the beauty of classic form continued to increase all through the Gothic period. In the *Divine Comedy,* who guided Dante through the horrors of Hell but Virgil, still apparently to Dante the summit of all that was gracious and dignified and beautiful? Chaucer was obviously a deep scholar of classic poetry; and, a pure Gothic figure, true northerner as he was, nevertheless he filled his verse with references to pagan myth and devoted one of his most famous long poems to the tale of Troilus and Cressida in ancient Troy.

Especially in Italy was this growing interest in classic elements a marked and decisive cultural feature. Italy was still full of the ruins of Roman buildings, many in a much more fully preserved state than that in which they now exist, for the great building period of the Renaissance and the Baroque did more to destroy Roman buildings than twelve centuries of time and all the barbarian ravages. In many parts of the peninsula, as we have already seen, the Gothic hardly existed at all save as an imported style, and in Tuscany especially the Romanesque style had preserved again and again elements of detail as well as general structural methods which were essentially classic. The great Pisano family of sculptors, in the decorative carving with which they enriched so many churches in northern central Italy, show even more strongly than do the French sculptors the definite influence of classic sculpture; and the carvings on the façade of Orvieto Cathedral, in their treatment of drapery, in their handling of relief, in their brilliant and delicate carvings of the nude form, are much more classic than medieval.

That this study of classic forms, this acceptance of classic beauty as an inspiration, should eventually appear in buildings and become the governing force in architecture was inevitable. The cities of northern Italy were at the height of their prosperity; the textile industry was bringing them unprecedented wealth, and the position of some of them as the great commercial centers between the East and the West made thriving commerce almost a commonplace in their economy. Moreover, as "free cities," where the conservatism of feudal life was less highly developed, where wealth was more broadly held, and where there was a growing class of newly rich commercial families and of skilled craftsmen, conditions were ripe for a change. It is characteristic of the period and of Italy that the Medici family was the most powerful banking house in Europe and at the same time a ruling family in Florence, and it was no accident that Cosimo added to his abilities as financier and municipal dictator a keen, sensitive, and enthusiastic patronage of the fine arts. In this he was assiduously followed and imitated by every Italian nobleman or wealthy citizen who could afford it; and the Sforzas, the Viscontis, and even the hated Borgias must share with the artists of Italy some of the credit for making fifteenth- and sixteenth-century Italy such a land of architects and painters and sculptors as had never been known before nor was to be known again.

The actual incentive toward the architectural development of the Renaissance came from the desire to complete at last the greatest of the Gothic cathedrals of Italy, Santa Maria del Fiore in Florence. This great church, built in the fourteenth century and designed by Arnolfo di Cambio, had

remained incomplete for half a century. The architect had surpassed in
conception the ability of his time; he had created a great central crossing,
the roofing of which presented apparently insuperable difficulties, demanding as it did a vault 138 feet in span. The pride of Florence at the beginning
of the fifteenth century could not leave this challenge to its power unanswered, and it was decided to hold a competition for the completion of
the church. Among the contestants were the sculptor Donatello and the

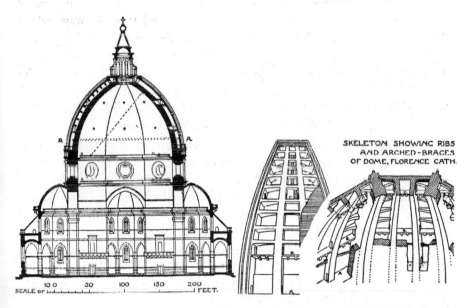

SKELETON SHOWING RIBS
AND ARCHED-BRACES
OF DOME, FLORENCE CATH.

72. CATHEDRAL, FLORENCE; THE DOME, DIAGRAM OF CONSTRUCTION. Brunelleschi, architect. (Simpson. Vol. III.)

architect Brunelleschi, and together they made a trip to Rome, hoping to
find there the solution to the problem. Together they studied the Roman
antiquities, such as they could find, and especially the great dome of the
Pantheon. This study trip was perhaps the final stimulus which the growing
admiration for classic things needed to break down the last traditions of
the Gothic in Florence; it introduced a new day in building, through the
work of Brunelleschi, and also because of the immense prestige of Donatello
it made all the younger sculptors and decorative carvers follow his footsteps, at least in style, to Rome.

Brunelleschi's design entailed the building of a huge octagonal vault, a
sort of eight-sided dome, with deep solid stone ribs at the corners, intermediate structural ribs to give strength, and two thin shells between—one

e out. The great stone ribs carried a stone lantern to cap
vith a note of sufficient decorative richness; and in this lantern
han orders—base, shaft, and capital; architrave, frieze, and
the first time appear. The dome of Santa Maria del Fiore is
f the Renaissance in Italy, because it was in no way a copy of
any given Roman building. It was a strictly original, daring, constructively
brilliant solution. Its scale was undoubtedly influenced by the great scale
of the Roman monuments, and the details of its moldings were inspired by
ancient work. It used the ancient orders, but it used them in ways which
the Romans had never dreamed of, and its whole constructional basis was
as Romanesque or Gothic as it was classic. Its scheme was obviously influenced by the dome of the Baptistry at Florence, then already four centuries
old. The Early Renaissance never copied ancient Rome; it merely turned,
in Italy, from the Gothic inspiration imported from the north to the ancient
Roman inspiration which had never been entirely forgotten.

Of course Brunelleschi's local fame as an architect was established by
his winning of the competition, and this became but one of a great series
of buildings erected in the first half of the fifteenth century in Florence
in which this same formula—a new attack on building problems in the
light of fresh inspiration from ancient Roman remains, with a free and
modified use of the classic orders—was used. The enormous beginnings
of the Pitti Palace, which Brunelleschi designed for the Medici, with its
powerful walls and arches of rough hewn stone, show his power in a
building of great scale. His beautiful chapel for the Pazzi family in the
church of Santa Croce shows the exquisite delicacy of his sense of detail;
yet even here, in this little domed building, which might so easily have
been copied from some Roman tomb or temple, the originality of the
Renaissance is clear. The columns, though manifestly of Corinthian type,
are like few if any actual ancient columns; there are subtle differences of
detail throughout. The bold design of the portico with its central arch is
new and fresh, and inside he daringly made use of a dome set on Byzantine
pendentives.

This building is evidence, too, of another quality which the Early Renaissance of Florence possessed to the fullest degree—a dainty luxuriance
of carved detail. Door frames, running horizontal moldings, pediments,
and friezes are everywhere decorated with either beautiful resurrections
of the old classic molding decorations—eggs and darts, the water leaf, the
acanthus leaf, the acanthus scroll—or with the most charming and delicate
figure sculpture—winged cherubs' heads, flying angels, and the like. At times

this carved decoration is of such extraordinary richness that the effect is almost unarchitectural—the work seems almost goldsmith's work, as of a jewel box;—and this quality creates much of the dreamlike, exuberant, springlike beauty of tombs, of altarpieces and pulpits in any number of north Italian churches, and of carved doors and courtyards in the great Italian houses of the time.

For part of this character the Italian system of apprenticeship for the crafts—the so-called *bottega* training—is responsible. Under this system, a young man who showed signs of promise in drawing or modeling was apprenticed to a goldsmith. His apprenticeship there took the form not only of working with metals, but also of a great deal of drawing—even to the copying of famous paintings—and considerable modeling and carving; in other words, it was an all-round fine-arts training of the greatest value, especially because it necessarily brought to the student's mind the qualities of all kinds of materials and techniques. A man so trained, if his talents pointed one way, might become at the end of his apprenticeship a painter; another, with precisely the same training, might develop into a sculptor; and still another into an architect. That is why, during the Renaissance, one finds so many stories of architects who were great painters, like Peruzzi, or painters who were occasionally architects, like Raphael. Even when the artist had received training only along his single art, the whole system had produced such a strong sense of the sistership and close relationship of all the arts that each specialist in one art could at a pinch deal with almost any of the others. The training led also to a kind of common-sense attitude toward the artist; he was admired and worshiped as a genius if his talents warranted it, because the Renaissance was a time when the highest awards in life were given for fine-arts skill. But the artist was never set apart on a pinnacle; he remained part and parcel of the life, and even the industrial life, of his city and his time. The goldsmith, or the craftsman in any other field, of superlative degree was honored as much as the painter or the sculptor, and in Benvenuto Cellini's *Memoirs* it is difficult to tell of which he is the more proud, his goldsmith work or his sculpture.

The great fault of the bottega training was almost inextricably bound up with its virtues. "Jack of all trades and master of none" is an accusation easy to make against some of its products. Its generalized basis was not adapted to make the painter think primarily of what is painterlike, nor the architect know what is buildable, what is essentially architectural; and the jeweled delicacy of some of the earlier architectural detail in the Italian Renaissance, however delightful, has a quality of not altogether admirable naïveté. Much of the ornament is overloaded, and seems to destroy the materials of which it is made rather than to express them.

Thus, as skills in the Renaissance fine arts increased, there was bound to be a greater and greater specialization leading to greater technical skill. The Medici themselves realized this fault of the old training and established their famous Academy of the Fine Arts, where brilliant young painters and sculptors could work along their own special fields unhampered; and, though with this new attitude something of the earlier, childlike, exuberant beauty naturally disappeared, it alone made possible the High Renaissance mastery of the century that was to follow.

The architecture developed in this way was necessarily an architecture of individuals. From the very beginning of the fifteenth century on, the individual designer, through the patronage he received, became much more of a power in his own right than earlier architects of the Gothic era had been. The age of self-expression had begun. The Renaissance itself, with its insistence on individual thinking, on personal independence, in matters religious and philosophical—a movement which eventually produced the Reformation,—built up the confidence of the individual creator, supported him in his departures from earlier accepted canons, led in other words to a period of the most rapid progress and change in design. From now on, the names of architects become growingly important, for each architect almost of necessity developed his own personal style, his own characteristic approach to the great building problems.

Accordingly, Brunelleschi was followed by a large group of individual architects—first in Florence; then, as the fifteenth century progressed, throughout northern Italy; and eventually even in the south. Rome itself at the beginning of this period was hardly more than a sprawling, down-at-heels, rather formless country town. There were undistinguished buildings scattered among the ancient ruins, punctuated here and there by the large forms of the early medieval basilicas. The period when the Popes were at Avignon had left it desolate and dying; but when the Popes returned from France it became their policy to rebuild Rome in its old grandeur. If there is little Early Renaissance architecture of distinction in Rome, it is only because this movement had just begun; but, as a series of Popes brilliant in their political skill gradually succeeded in bringing back to the Eternal City something of the wealth and all the prestige it had enjoyed before, this condition rapidly passed away, as new palaces and churches in the new Renaissance style rose along its once deserted streets. For this development the Popes and the Cardinal builders had to depend almost entirely upon architects trained in the north, and again and again the builders of the great Roman Renaissance movements were men from Florence, from Milan, or from the little hill towns like Perugia. Thus, the Renaissance came to birth first in Florence, had its exuberant trial generally in the other great free cities of northern and north-central Italy, but for its maturity needed the challenge of the rebuilding of Rome.

The Early Renaissance in Italy was essentially a decorative style. Except for the dome of the Florence cathedral there are few great structural triumphs among its works; and, except for the combination of the Byzantine pendentive, the drum, and the dome, there are few structural methods which are characteristic of it. The late Gothic builders of north Italy, as we have already noted, were skillful and adaptable, and the types of palace construction which they had developed allowed almost indefinite decorative change without affecting the basic building methods. Much of the old Roman feeling, with its large-scale structure in cheap materials faced with those more rich or decorative, still controlled, although in the hill towns where stone was common a great skill in masonry wall treatment had arisen, as can be seen, for instance, in the Palazzo Vecchio in Florence. Almost all Early Renaissance palaces in Italy are mere modifications of earlier types; classic cornices supersede the old Gothic battlements, moldings of classic profile are used instead of medieval moldings, round arches take the place of pointed arches, and the Corinthian capital or, more frequently, a simplified modification of it, which is usually called Corinthianesque, takes the place of the Gothic capital. In plan, too, slight changes occurred. No architect could study the Roman remains without being struck by the essential monumentality which results from the consistently excellent planning and the forthright directness of having opening directly behind opening, centers of rooms behind centers of courts, and the courts themselves centered on the front. Consequently, the occasionally incoherent plans of the old Gothic palaces yield to a greater and greater systematization, a more and more careful study of plan relationships. In almost every case, a simple vaulted vestibule leads directly into the center of a rectangular court with an arcaded, vaulted colonnade around it. At one end of the front colonnade of the court, broad stairs lead up the main floor, the *piano nobile,* which is always placed one story above the ground. Usually the arcades of the court support walls with windows in them, so that there is no outer gallery on the upper floors.

Just as there was this growing search for axial, symmetrical, carefully organized plans, just so the elevations tended similarly to be regularized. Windows were placed above each other and equally spaced horizontally, so that their regular rhythms controlled the entire façade. Windows usually consisted of two small round-headed openings under a single great enclosing arch—a distant classicized version of the Gothic tradition of tracery.

The Renaissance architect studied the details of this comparatively simple general scheme with ever-increasing care. It is extraordinary what variety

STROZZI PALACE, FLORENCE.

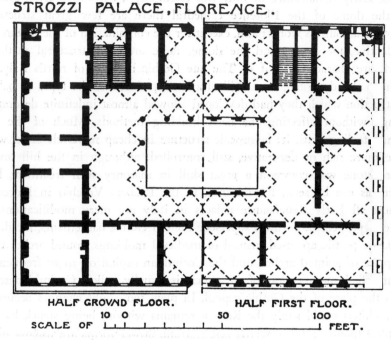

HALF GROUND FLOOR. HALF FIRST FLOOR.
10 0   50   100
SCALE OF └┴┴┴┴┴┴┴┴┘_____┘ FEET.

73. STROZZI PALACE, FLORENCE; PLAN. Benedetto da Maiano, architect. (Simpson. Vol. III.)

of detail can be achieved within it. Almost all the palaces consisted of three stories of enormous height; but by the careful handling of the roughness of the wall surface, the heavier and rougher stones being used below and a smoother masonry above, an attempt was made to lighten that brute heaviness which had characterized some of the Gothic palaces. All sorts of rustication were used—that is, systems of masonry in which the central part of each stone is raised above a narrow band at its borders; sometimes the raised portion is rough, sometimes smooth, and sometimes the little faces connecting the raised and the low portions will be straight and sometimes beveled or curved. Michelozzo's Riccardi Palace in Florence, built in 1444, is typical, with its surrounding bench at the bottom serving as a magnificently strong foundation, its beautifully profiled base course, its tremendous rough stones of the ground floor, the smoother rustication of the second floor, and the still smoother masonry on the top floor, all capped by a marvelously profiled, tremendously scaled classic cornice. The Strozzi Palace by Benedetto da Maiano, somewhat similar in general scheme, is nevertheless totally different in effect because of its different texture treatments and the shorter and higher proportions of the whole. And both of these are different from the earlier part of the Pitti, with its clifflike grandeur, its huge, almost brutal moldings. In the Rucellai Palace, Leon Battista Alberti—of whom more later—introduced a revolutionary element in emphasizing the rhythm of his palace front by placing delicate pilasters between the windows, which broke up and humanized the whole continuity of the rusticated stone surfaces. In Pienza, Rossellino followed him in this treatment; but as yet such a bold classic feature for exterior work was rare, and the Early Renaissance palaces that rose in town after town through central and northern Italy still generally followed the lead of the Pitti or the Riccardi.

But, if the exterior of these palaces was thus simple, almost heavy, the minor works of these Early Renaissance architects went to the other extreme. Interior doors, wall tombs, altarpieces, and reredoses were carved with an extraordinary luxuriance, and their forms were as imaginative as they were delicate. One characteristic shape which is used again and again is that called the Florentine pediment. It consists of a semicircular form placed above the entablature, and as wide as the enclosing columns or pilasters. Usually a simple band of moldings runs around it, and the semicircular field below is often decorated with a shell, although sometimes molded panels and even figures are found. Little rosettes and leaf and flower forms are usually used to fill the corner between the ends of the semicircle and the cornice below; and also as a finial at the top. The pilasters, which are common, are often carved with an elaborate scrolled pattern of the greatest delicacy, distantly based on Roman work, but always full of personal touches and exquisite in its relief. In these, very frequently, a slim candelabrumlike shaft runs up the center, and on either side of this are scrolls of acanthus and garlands. Even the Corinthianesque capitals are infinitely varied. Almost always the reversed S-scrolls rise from the center to the upper outer corners, as in some small ancient Roman examples, but with greater delicacy; and beneath these are acanthus leaves or anthemions or even shells, as the fancy of the designer might suggest.

The works of Desiderio da Settignano, Donatello, and Mino da Fiesole—

perhaps generally better known as sculptors than as architects—reveal the variety of decorative invention of which these Early Renaissance architects were capable. The works of the Della Robbia family in glazed and often polychromed terra-cotta show the same delicacy, the same fanciful invention. the same use of sensitively modified Greek and Roman forms. Brunelleschi used terra-cotta roundels designed by Lucca della Robbia in the lovely arcade which he built as a loggia for the Foundling Hospital in Florence, the Ospedale dei Innocenti. The wide, finely molded arches; the slim columns, with capitals almost crude in their simplicity; the roundels between the arches, on the rich blue background of which are the famous images of babies in their swaddling clothes; and the beautifully proportioned wall above and the wide and ample cornice—all form a composition which, in its personal quality, in its regularity, in its gracious yet dignified unpretentiousness, and in its creative modifications of ancient forms, is most characteristic of the entire spirit of the Early Renaissance.

But it was not only the city palaces which evidenced the spirit of the new time, for nothing shows more clearly the change from the earlier feudal conditions to this later era of commercial prosperity and comparative individual security than the change which the Renaissance brought from the old and fortified castle in the country to the new residential villa. Almost all of the larger castles of the Middle Ages had had elaborate gardens, small and necessarily outside of the inner fortifications, but nevertheless an important part of the whole composition, and much of the pleasantest part of the secular life of the Middle Ages was passed in these carefully cultivated pleasure spots. Manuscript illuminations show us the type—a walled space with rigidly geometrical beds of flowers and carefully placed trees, oftentimes with grass walks and raised benches of grass; in the center there was usually a fountain or a well, or even a pool where the castle folk sometimes bathed. Outside the palace walls a wooded park might stretch, filled with game for hunting, but between the two portions—the strictly planned garden and the wild forest—there was never any connection, and the garden itself seldom became part of the house design; it was a separate unit placed where the terrain suggested.

The whole spirit of the Renaissance was against any such separation of units, and in the fifteenth century there began to grow up around Florence and other cities a series of lavish mansions, half castle in origin perhaps, but—as time went on—with designs more and more open, with larger windows, with open loggias, colonnaded or arcaded, with broad cornices and sloping roofs instead of the earlier battlements. From their portals, and an integral part of the conception as a whole, stretched the new kind of Renaissance garden, which borrowed from the earlier medieval tradition the rigid geometrical beds, the central fountain, and the importance of water, but, in Italy at least, added to this original residuum a new monumentality of plan, a new variety, which brought into the whole as framing elements the high green walls of almost wild woodland. To the Italian Renaissance architect, building and foliage and water, hall and loggia and path, even the view of distant landscape, were all part of one well-considered composition. This ultimate ideal was reached only in villas of the later period, but even in the fifteenth century the beginnings of this movement from castle and garden to the villa—the Italian villa—were evident on the hillsides around Florence.

Early Renaissance church design follows two general types. The first is based on the early Christian basilica and, like it, uses long rows of columns to separate nave and aisles, and a flat wooden nave ceiling. The great new thing in these churches, as we can see them in Brunelleschi's San Lorenzo and Santo Spirito, is the treatment of the nave arcade. Brunelleschi wished his columns to carry arches, but he also felt that the simple column capital was ill-suited for the direct support of the arch moldings; therefore, he placed over each column a little piece of entablature—architrave, frieze, and cornice—and on this started the arches which held up the clerestory wall. It was a solution far from perfect, overcomplicated perhaps in outline; yet it illustrates, as does so much else in this world of the Early Renaissance, the architect's efforts not to copy Roman architecture but rather to create out of classic forms, and with the inspiration furnished originally by classic buildings, new and original answers to the building problems of the time. The side-aisle treatment of these churches is also different from that of the early Christian basilicas, owing to the fact that the side aisles in the Renaissance churches are vaulted, sometimes with little domes, sometimes with a simple groined vault. This use of the vault was prophetic. Vaulting was one of the chief sources of the effect of Roman buildings, and it was not strange that, more and more, the Renaissance architects began to study its possibilities for them.

The other type of church was more important, for from it grew all the great Renaissance churches of the later time. It accepted the vault as the essential controlling form in church planning, and frequently abandoned even the possibility of side aisles in order to emphasize the importance of the nave vault. The nave, transepts, and choir would be barrel-vaulted, with a half dome over the apse. At the crossing, a dome on pendentives would inevitably be raised. Often low chapels opened from the nave through arches, and the nave walls would be delicately patterned with pilasters carrying a slight entablature, from which the vault would rise. Sometimes paneled arched ribs carried across the vaulting over each pair of pilasters. The Badia di Fiesole is an early and primitive example of this type.

Yet all through the fifteenth century the church remained a comparatively unimportant problem, and little was done toward developing these beginnings so encouragingly made. Except in the work of Alberti, the architect's genius seems to have been directed almost entirely to palace planning, and to the addition of those lavish and delicate wall tombs and altarpieces bestowed on older churches which give them today so much of the atmosphere they possess. The day of the domed and vaulted Renaissance church lay still ahead.

Because the Italian cities were largely free, independent entities, often with violent rivalries between them, and because Renaissance architecture was so definitely an architecture of individuals, necessarily local styles developed characteristic of the people and city which gave them birth. The most important, just as it was the earliest, was the style of Florence. There seem to be periods in history when a single locality will have a sudden and exuberant blossoming for which it is difficult to plot the exact causes, a blossoming and an exuberance which often expresses itself in art. During the fifteenth century Florence was the scene of such a blooming. Wealth was there, leisure was there, and art appreciation—not limited to the wealthy, but apparently extending down through all classes of the populace—was there. There was a feeling of enormous creativeness, a kind of civic outburst of joy and pleasure, in which the appearance of things played a great part; the whole city seems to have been art-mad. The great families began collecting; and, significantly enough, they collected not only Roman antiques, classic sculpture, classic manuscripts, but they collected with an equal avidity and an equal rivalry the works of living artists. They outrivaled each other in commissioning altarpieces, in building tombs for themselves and their relatives, in constructing palaces and villas.

This outburst was much more than a matter of a few individuals. I produced a series of great annual pageants or fiestas, celebrated by the whole town with parades and games, and in these the most celebrated artists of the time were commissioned to design costumes and paint banners; the plaudits of the weaver and the farmer in from the environs, the shouts of delight from even the city poor, greeted each new creation as it moved through the gray, stone-walled streets, bringing into their midst an almost iridescent glory of color and gold, of free-flapping crimson banners, of prancing chargers, of knights in gilded armor, of chariots—or, as we today would call them, floats—bearing the effigies and insignia of Jupiter or Aphrodite or Mars; and the artists who conceived or who painted these great popular shows received enormous honor and considerable wealth.

It was all perhaps a little overlush, this art-madness of fifteenth-century Florence, and its character is mirrored in the exquisite, overluxuriant carvings of the tombs and altarpieces and picture frames and doors; yet it was, despite its richness, always superbly composed. The Medici ideal was the Greek measure, the Greek proportion; and, though there is little in the architectural work which bears any real mark of a knowledge of things Greek, there is a general sense of proportion, a general delicacy, which disciplines the luxury, that is not without its Greek analogies. It was the graduates of this great school of Florence who went out from city to city and spread abroad the artistic gospel of the Early Renaissance; the early Florentine Renaissance is the parent style of all.

To see the real worth of the Florentine sense of proportion, one has but to travel north to Milan and study on the Lombardy plain the Early Renaissance works that arose there; for there, again and again, what one gets is all the luxuriance, all the lavishness, the overdecoration, of the Early Renaissance, with little controlling discipline behind it. For one thing, the land was further from the inspiration of Roman remains, and the Gothic in Milan, as their cathedral bears witness, was one of the liveliest and most vital of the Italian Gothic styles; so that we find in such early buildings as the courtyard of the great municipal hospital in Milan a structure essentially Gothic, still retaining the old pointed arches but with every molding of the most elaborate Renaissance detail, executed in terra-cotta. The same prodigality can be seen in Santa Maria dei Miracoli in Brescia, or in the prison loggia there; and, even as far east as Bologna, the ease of making terra-cotta ornament led to the same kind of rather flat, involuted decoration of acanthus scrolls that is so frequently found in Milan. The whole emphasis was toward surface decoration; and, though as in the case of Santa Maria delle Grazie a lovely kind of semi-Byzantine effect is produced, and though Bramante, who became one of the greatest of the later Italian architects, had his original rise and his essential training in the Milan neighborhood, nevertheless the general sense of the Early Renaissance of Lombardy is of a rather thoughtless urge to overrich decoration.

This love of elaboration persisted for a century, and the façade of the church of the Certosa at Pavia is perhaps its greatest and most fascinating work. There one finds hardly a single molding over the great front which is not carved; one finds the moldings themselves duplicated and reduplicated, and the whole front is conceived not as a sober construction in stone but as a riotously rich casing of sheet marble, paneled and decorated with pilasters, architraves, pediments, acanthus scrolls, the whole a gorgeous decorative picture which leads eventually to a kind of aesthetic indigestion. Especially interesting is the fact that in this building, as in much other Lombardy work, a kind of enlarged, lavishly decorated candelabrum shaft is used again and again for all sorts of purposes, appearing at one moment as the column separating twin windows, at another as the ornament on a vertical pilaster panel, and at a third as a finial or pinnacle. This use of the candelabrum shaft was to have its later important repercussions in the Renaissance in France.

A somewhat similar inchoate ornateness distinguishes the Early Renaissance of Naples. There, tradition was strong; the older buildings still stood, so that little new building was done and the Early Renaissance appears chiefly as a mere decorative overlay, of which the richest example is the Triumphal Arch of Aragon that serves as the entrance to the famous old Castle of Naples. Here the sides are treated in a series of panels, each containing a historical group; the whole is overlaid with figure carving, and all of this sculpture is of distinguished quality both in composition and in execution. Nevertheless, the architecture seems to exist only as a picture frame for sculpture; of a real architectonic conception as to what a great triumphal entrance might be, there is little evidence.

Next to Florence, it is Venice which produced the most important, as it is one of the most gracious and inviting, of Early Renaissance styles. Though its old political power and some of its wealth had waned, Venice still stood primarily as the great connecting link between the East and the West, a city famous then and for centuries after as perhaps the most luxurious city in Europe. Its peculiar situation, its canals and encircling lagoon, had given to its buildings from the beginning a character different from that to be found anywhere else; and this tradition, set so strongly in the Byzantine and the Gothic periods, was still a living and vital thing.

The Early Renaissance came to Venice merely as another opportunity for a new kind of decorative detail, to be applied to the marble sheathing of the palaces. In general, it came late. The best of the work—that of the Lombardo family, especially Pietro, the architect of the Vendramini Palace and the charming little church of Santa Maria dei Miracoli—dates only from the last quarter of the fifteenth century. Perhaps it was because of this late flowering that the style was so exquisite; its designers were enabled to get without effort all the lessons which fifty years had taught the earlier architects of Florence. But, whatever the cause may have been, the Venetian architects of the Early Renaissance showed an amazing skill in the creative modification of classical forms and in the adaptation of these to their almost Byzantine type of building.

The Venetian work has a remarkable gaiety, if not frivolity, of feeling. The School of St. Mark, for instance, has a front membered, correctly enough, with entablatures and engaged columns; the skyline is fanciful, with half-round Florentine pediments and finials; and the lower panels have low reliefs in which lions look out of arcaded halls carefully carved in perspective. The use of colored marble panels was continued almost unchanged from the earlier styles, so that there is no definite break in the general appearance of the palaces that rose along the shores of the canals, with their brightly painted mooring posts in front; only the classic columns on either side of the windows, the classic arcade replacing the old band of traceried windows, show the coming of the new style.

Yet some of its works are much more advanced, without at the same time breaking the lovely Venetian continuity. Of these, the church of Santa Maria dei Miracoli is perhaps the purest. It is a simple rectangle, crowned with a semicircular roof of wood, paneled in wood inside and merely covered with lead on the outside. The chancel, slightly less wide than the church, is raised high above the nave floor; square in plan, it is crowned by a dome and drum on pendentives. At the end opposite the chancel a musicians' gallery is placed, carried simply on two columns. This simple conception is treated everywhere with the most impeccable refinement. The walls, both outside and in, are paneled simply in marble, and the inside marble is lovely in the subtle color of its veining. A wainscot of delicate cornice and widely spaced pilasters gives a slight emphasis on the interior. This simplicity of form and subtle richness of color acts as an admirable foil to the lavish carving of the sanctuary. Here, the architectural forms— the pilasters under the arches of the dome, the entablature, and so on—are of the same simplicity, but the wainscot which they enframe and the railings at the break in level are amazingly carved with intricate designs; dolphins and shells, cushion forms on the convex moldings, mermaids and tritons, all tell of the maritime site of Venice, and every panel bears its arabesque, each slightly differing from any other but all together united by the same basic composition. In the chancel is an altar surrounded by a parapet, and here the carving reaches its climax of prodigal and gracious complexity. Perhaps nowhere else in Italy have the Early Renaissance forms been used in such a disciplined manner to produce, by the contrast of restraint with lavishness, by the uniform delicacy of feeling, the greatest possible emotional effect of which they are capable.

Pietro Lombardo's same sense of architectonic form controlled his other greatest building, the Vendramini Palace, and here for the first time a complete break from the flat surfaces of the Byzantine type occurs. The whole palace is decorated with three stories of engaged orders, beautifully spaced about arched windows. Especially noticeable, and characteristic both of Pietro's originality and his sense of basic form, is the way in which the windows at either end are treated in a subtly different fashion from the windows in the center, thus expressing the central halls and creating an accented composition of two end bays and a connecting link of three central bays, so that the whole palace, though small in width, has a true monumental effectiveness.

Thus Venice, through the Early Renaissance period, continued to preserve its early charm, and little was done to injure the exquisite harmony of its marble-faced palaces that line so beautifully the busy waters of its canals.

Through the fifteenth century, almost until its end, Rome remained the straggling town of medieval days. Out of its hilly landscape rose the great hulks of the ancient Roman buildings, often built into and forming part of medieval castles, and here and there rose the castellated towers that the great Roman families had built as city strongholds. Between were wide stretches of farmland or dusty and grassy wastes, save near the river, where the old medieval houses shouldered each other in a crowded, nondescript mass. This was the town which the Popes were determined to make the first city of Europe. The task was a long one, and during the Early Renaissance period only a small beginning was made on the tremendous undertaking.

Early Renaissance building in Rome is but scanty—a certain amount of work on the Popes' Vatican Palace; a church or two, like Santa Maria del Popolo, simple, with its delicate pilasters, its plain vault forms, yet characteristic of Early Renaissance lavishness in some of its walled tombs; here and there a small palace; and, most important, the beginning of the great Palazzo de Venezia—the palace of the Venetian ambassador, where a new courtyard was built, added to the old Gothic fortress, and a new wing begun. Yet, small in amount and generally elementary in type as this Roman work is, already its character is beginning to be differentiated from that of the rest of Italy. The impact of the Roman remains upon the north-Italian artists who were brought in to do the work was too strong to be neglected. Of necessity, the work in Rome had to be more monumental, less frivolously lavish, more architecturally firm than the work to the north.

In the Santa Maria del Popolo tombs, engaged columns replace the pilasters of Florence, and there is a new power in the conception; and in the courtyard of the Palazzo de Venezia, for the first time in the Renaissance, there appears the full Roman arcade of engaged columns framing the ranged arches and giving strong lines of light and shade to the composition, quite different in character from the lacelike patterning of the Florentine Renaissance. The details of this courtyard are simple and crude enough, but the whole thing has the true Roman monumental tang. Any development further along that line was bound to produce, not merely a further efflorescence of the overlush ornament of the north, but something entirely new, something which had in it, along with the grace of the new, the power and the monumentality of the ancient. In other words, it was bound to produce what we call today the High Renaissance.

By the end of the fifteenth century, throughout Italy, the decorative Early Renaissance style had reached its apogee, and had begun to decay. All the possible changes seem to have been rung on the purely decorative use of Roman forms, seen through the imaginative eyes of the Early Renaissance artists. Only monotony could result from the continuation of the movement. New breath of life was necessary, new ideas; and, since the Early Renaissance had arisen through a turning back for inspiration to ancient Rome, so at this time only a further, a more intensive and careful, study of the actual architecture which the ancients had produced, a new and growing knowledge of the real monumental aims behind it, of its true basis in composition and not in detail, could serve to give the Renaissance the turn it needed toward the great fundamental questions of architectural composition. This study was made by any number of architects and artists, whose sketches of ancient Roman remains can still be seen in the Uffizi and elsewhere. From their study arose the new growth, the High Renaissance.

Chapter 17

THE HIGH RENAISSANCE

LEON BATTISTA ALBERTI conceived of architecture as something quite different from the usual lavishly decorated, but sometimes superficial, Early Renaissance design of his time. His ideal was prophetic of the High Renaissance architecture that was current in Italy during, roughly, the first half of the sixteenth century. In many ways he was one of the type figures of the Renaissance, a gentleman, a scholar, as well as an architect; of noble birth, with the best education the period afforded, he was a writer, a Latin scholar, a student of manuscripts. It was characteristic of him that one of his famous essays, on the dog, written in Latin, was accepted by many of his contemporaries as a piece of original ancient Roman authorship. This fundamental breadth of mind, this endless curiosity, and this intimate acquaintance with classic authors gave him quite a different approach to the art of building from the bottega training which was the usual education of his fellow artists. It made him naturally a student of the ancient Roman author Vitruvius and inevitably flowered in his own work, *De Re Aedificatoria* (Concerning Things Pertaining to Building), in which he set down his own theories of what architecture should be. This book, printed in 1485, after its author's death, became the first work on architecture ever to be printed from type, and anticipated the first printed edition of Vitruvius by a year. In form Alberti's treatise is similar to that of his famed Roman predecessor, yet it is more logical, more carefully thought out, better expressed; its general basis is the fact that *beautiful architecture is that from which nothing can be taken away and to which nothing can be added without harming it,* together with the idea that the chief elements in architecture must always be careful planning, good construction, and consistency between a design and its purpose. Now buildings conceived in this manner must necessarily be fundamentally designed; surface ornament, according to Alberti's ideas, takes a definitely minor position.

In the best of his own work Alberti applied these principles with revolutionary effect. Thus, in the church which he altered at Rimini as a mausoleum for the Malatesta family, the ornament of the exterior is limited to a few moldings; the effect results from the beautiful proportions of powerfully conceived, deeply shadowed, arched recesses along the walls, and on the uncompleted front from the application of the purest and simplest classic columns. In the great church of San Andrea at Mantua, Alberti produced a building which for the first time showed the grandeur of interior aspect made possible by the unpretentious and direct use of great vaults, a dome on pendentives at the crossing, and vaulted side chapels—the walls between the chapels constituting the buttresses necessary to withstand the thrust

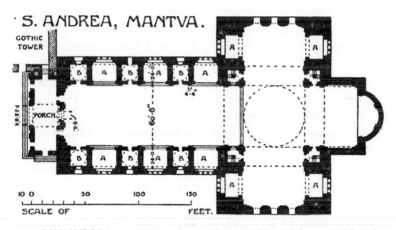

74. SAN ANDREA, MANTUA; PLAN. Alberti, architect. (Simpson. Vol. III.)

of the nave vault. This interior, like the exterior of the Rimini church, rightly deserves the term "monumental," and as such these two buildings foreshadow the ideals of the generation ahead.

It was, however, only the necessity for enormous amounts of construction in the rapidly growing city of Rome under the munificent auspices of the Pope himself, and of the Papal court, which brought the High Renaissance into final flowering. Although in that respect essentially a Roman product, it was produced almost entirely by artists and architects who came from the north, brought down either at the direct invitation of a Pope or a Cardinal or else in the search for the magnificent opportunities which the growing city offered. Arrived in Rome, the study of ancient Roman monuments seems to have impressed upon them all a new sense of greatness in form, and the ideals of the Papal court itself were on the side of simple grandeur coupled with exquisite restraint of detail rather than of the florid luxuriance of the earlier Florentine and Lombard work.

The greatest of the early architects thus to come to Rome to carry out their work, in which the principles of Alberti could be freely embodied, was Donato Bramante. Bramante had already achieved fame in the north because of his exquisite church work in Milan and Como—work in which, underneath the current panoply of rich surface ornament, there may be seen something of a new power of composition depending on large masses and simple lines, as in the exterior of the church of Santa Maria delle Grazie in Milan, with its simple brick walls and the careful and rhythmical placing of its decoration. With Bramante's arrival in Rome, about 1500, the last vestiges of the earlier northern overornamentation seem to have slipped away from his work forever. The cloister of Santa Maria della Pace in Rome, with its beautiful Roman arcade on the lower floor, capped with an open loggia on the second, with two openings over each arch, reveals the mastery which was his. It is in no sense a copy of ancient work, its pilasters have the slightest possible projection, its moldings are reduced in scale below ancient usage, and every profile is exquisitely modulated; yet, despite the beauty and the perfection of detail, the chief source of the effectiveness of this cloister lies in the originality of its conception and the perfection of its proportions. In restraint, in emphasis on proportion, it set the note of all of the best High Renaissance architecture in Rome.

Bramante's principal importance comes from the fact of his employment by Pope Alexander VI to build the Papal palace at the Vatican, and by Pope Julius II to develop a plan for rebuilding St. Peter's. The Vatican work consisted largely in two immense wings with a building connecting them at the further end, enclosing a long narrow terraced garden. The whole plan—the simple regularity of the Roman arcades of the wings, the great terrace wall and stair connecting the two levels of the garden, and the tremendous recessed niche of the connecting building—reveals a genius for conceiving things in a large way, for establishing a composition as grand as it was ambitious. Later building has cut the old long garden into three courts, but even today Bramante's Roman arcades—which Raphael so beautifully decorated with a delicate phantasy on Roman themes—and the enormous niche at the end with the ancient Roman pine-cone fountain in its center have a commanding beauty of their own.

This skill at large-scale composition received an even grander opportunity in St. Peter's. The old Early Christian basilica had fallen into an almost ruinous condition. In its place Pope Julius decided to construct the greatest church in the world, as if to symbolize the newly found and rapidly growing wealth and worldly prestige of the Roman Papacy. Bramante was but the first of a series of Roman architects to work on this huge creation, but to him is due the controlling scale and the choice of the width of the nave and the size of the great domed crossing, and during his lifetime several of the great piers were constructed and one of the arches begun. The important element in this great interior—a tremendous Corinthian order ninety feet high—was part of this original conception, though other portions of the church were considerably changed from the original design. The Bramante designs which have been preserved show an endless ingenuity in the use of buttress forms lightened with niches, and in the formation with them of all sorts of chapels separated by screens of columns. In these minor portions the great scale of the central crossing was lost, and the original design, clever though it was, would have been monotonously confused; later architects did well to change it gradually, omitting more and more of the nonessential details, until Michelangelo's final design of almost brutal simplicity.

Raphael, Baldassare Peruzzi, and Antonio da Sangallo the younger all worked on St. Peter's, gradually simplifying Bramante's conception, but keeping its big central elements and experimenting with all sorts of different arrangements for the nave and front. Particularly interesting was Sangallo's scheme of a short-armed Greek cross for the church itself, and a domed vestibule as an entrance treated almost as a separate unit. But it remained for Michelangelo, who was architect from 1547 till 1564, to give it its final beauty. He saw the church as a simple Greek cross, with all its parts as large, grand, and monumental as possible. Coffered barrel vaults covered nave, transept, and choir, and the great masses of the piers were given interest by niches and shrines between their coupled pilasters. The climax was the great dome at the crossing, 140 feet in span. Michelangelo realized that such a width demanded great height; and, whereas Bramante had planned a low dome of the Pantheon type, Michelangelo had the daring to rest the whole on a high drum. The dome itself was in two shells, the interior almost hemispherical, with the exterior raised to a pointed oval form so as not to appear too squat when seen from near at hand. The dome was to be crowned by a great stone lantern, and an opening in the inner dome allowed the eye to carry right up into the interior of the lantern.

Michelangelo prepared a careful wooden model of this design, but never lived to see its conclusion. The dome was completed by Giacomo della Porta and Domenico Fontana in 1590. They raised the dome still more, probably

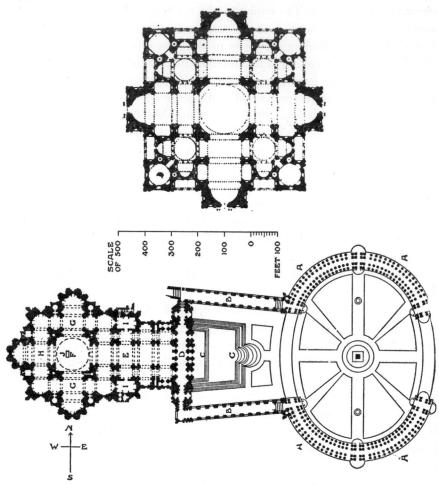

75. ST. PETER'S, ROME. *Above:* PROPOSED PLAN. Bramante, architect. (Anderson: *The Architecture of the Renaissance in Italy.*) *Below:* PLAN AS FINALLY CONSTRUCTED. (Simpson. Vol. III.)

improving the Michelangelo design. But the west end of the church still remained incomplete. Michelangelo had planned a simple narrow narthex in front of the nave, and a front with a great free-standing columnar portico, the whole being short enough so that the dome would count to its proper height even from fairly close to the façade. Unfortunately, successive Popes and successive architects failed to realize the vital importance of the preservation of this proportion, and in their ever-increasing search for grandeur, lavishness, and mere size decided to add several bays to the nave, so that the old Greek cross design became a Latin cross, and to build as a front a vast screen-type façade with colossal engaged columns, crowned by an enormous out-of-scale sculpture, with two all-too-small campaniles at the corners. Yet even this somewhat inept existing front cannot hide the majestic power of the whole conception, and, once the door is entered, the amazing monumentality of the whole becomes ever more apparent. It is an interior the beauty of which grows upon one gradually, as its sense of size continually increases. All of its forms are so immense that at first one has but a slight realization of its great dimensions; it is only as one walks around it and sees people small, like ants, within the same enclosure, especially when one sees the crowds at a service there, that some real idea of the building's area begins to develop.

The later building periods of St. Peter's hardly fall within the High Renaissance. They more properly belong to the Baroque era, and it was in this Baroque period that the church was gradually filled with sculptured monuments and tombs of all sorts, which, although they may somewhat fog the original big dignity of its earlier conception, nevertheless somehow by their very presence add to its total impressiveness. St. Peter's was the climax building of the High Renaissance and set a general pattern of church design which held true over almost all of western Europe for two centuries.

In the growing emphasis on the dome which is recognizable as the design of the church progressed in the hands of its successive architects, St. Peter's was merely following an almost universal Italian Renaissance path. From the days when Alberti built San Andrea at Mantua, the dome came to have a greater and greater importance in Italian church design. Nave, aisles, transept, and choir were all diminished or sacrificed in favor of the central rotunda. The scheme varied, from the Greek cross with filled-in corners— such as one gets in Santa Maria della Consolazione at Todi, where four apses crowned with half domes at the ends of the four arms give interest to the whole, or in the Madonna di San Biagio near Montepulciano, where the arms of the cross are square-ended and covered with pediment roofs—to designs more frankly circular or polygonal in character where the cross idea has entirely disappeared, as in Antonio da Sangallo's Santa Maria di Loreto in Rome; but in all cases it was the dome on pendentives, raised high on a window-pierced drum and carrying a decorative lantern, which was the chief feature of the exterior. Nevertheless, the old basilican idea of nave, aisles, and chapels had ritual advantages which could not be overlooked, and from the middle of the sixteenth century on the architects seem to have somewhat modified their church ideal, striving now for a design which would combine the grandeur and the openness of the dome with at least something of the feeling of a nave and aisles. The history of St. Peter's itself is significant, for the seventeenth century found Michelangelo's Greek-cross plan with the consequent enormous dominance of the dome not to its liking, and three bays of nave, side aisles, and chapels were added, to make the church as we know it today and thereby to wreck the magnificent simplicity of its original conception.

Yet the architecture of the High Renaissance was perhaps almost more an architecture of palaces and villas than of churches. The Papal court that set the fashions was vastly wealthy, vastly luxurious in its tastes, vastly given to the ideals of lavish living. The Cardinals outdid themselves, vying with each other in building palaces and gardens and in entertaining on a scale of ostentatious extravagance perhaps unknown since the days of ancient Rome. They poured money into jewelry and furniture, paintings and sculpture. With such exalted examples, it is not strange to find that all the secular nobility followed suit, and part of the extraordinary productivity of the Italian Renaissance is due, at least in some measure, to this widespread and munificent patronage.

In the main, the city palaces followed the general lines of the Early Renaissance palaces of Florence in the north, being built around large and dignified courtyards surrounded by arcades. Like the earlier palaces of Florence, they are generally simple on the exterior, gaining their effect more from beauty of proportion and exquisite restraint of detail than from any elaborate carving or ornament. Instead of the arched windows of earlier Florence, High Renaissance windows usually have square heads and are surrounded by architraves and sometimes capped by friezes and cornices. In the richest examples there are pediments over the windows as well; the Farnese Palace, perhaps the greatest of all High Renaissance palaces, surrounds each window with a projecting architectural frame of engaged columns carrying alternate round and pointed pediments.

Occasionally pilasters are used to decorate the front, as in the Cancelleria, the earliest of the High Renaissance palaces of Rome, begun in 1494 and perhaps owing its design in part to Bramante. Raphael, too, like his pupil Giulio Romano, liked pilasters or engaged columns as exterior wall decorations; but in general the other architects—Peruzzi, the Sangalli, and their like—preferred simple brick walls, with beautifully profiled stone-band courses to divide the façade into stories, simple stone architrave window frames, and a stone cornice, often of great size and richness.

The courtyards were usually relatively larger than those in Florentine palaces, and their arcades more severe, more monumental. The plans, also, were more carefully studied, so that vistas through the entrance doors should be carefully preserved and made important, and axes through important points should be clear and well defined. Stairs were large, monumental, and usually placed at the end of one of the main court arcades. The ground floor, as in most of the Florentine palaces, was reserved for stables, storage,

76. MASSIMI PALACE, ROME, THE GREAT HALL. Peruzzi, architect. (Letarouilly: *Édifices de Rome moderne.*)

and service. The chief floor, the *piano nobile,* was above, at the head of the grand stairs, and often included one or more halls of great architectural magnificence. But it is characteristic of the whole spirit of the High Renaissance that, outside of occasional rich coffered ceilings and still more occasional delicate pilasters, the decoration of these rooms was almost entirely through frescoes, and the architectural ornament was reduced to the least possible amount, in the most restrained possible manner.

Despite the similarity of the general type, it is amazing what variety, what individuality, was achieved by the designers of the Roman palaces. Not all are large like the Cancelleria or the Farnese; some attain grandeur with comparatively modest dimensions, and always the personality of the designer is revealed so strongly that the student finds little difficulty in picking out the work of each. Peruzzi, for instance, one of the most characteristic figures of the High Renaissance, designed always with a feeling for delicate restraint or perfection of detail that was almost Greek, and preferred always human scale to monumental scale. His two neighboring palaces for the Massimo brothers are characteristic in their little courtyards and the beautiful curved loggia through which one of the palaces is entered,

PALAZZI PIETRO & ANGELO MASSIMI, ROME.

A. ENTRANCE
   VESTIBVLE
   P. MASSIMI.
B. ENTRANCE
   VESTIBVLE
   A. MASSIMI.
C.C. COVRTS.

GROVND FLOOR.

77. THE MASSIMI PALACES, ROME; PLAN. Peruzzi, architect. (Simpson. Vol. III.)

as well as its lovely flat, coffer-ceiled great hall with delicate Ionic pilasters; within the courtyards, tiny as they are, the moldings are so rhythmically spaced, the supports and openings handled with such perfect proportion, that there is never a sense of being cramped, never a sense that the architect was trying to do more than the space allowed—instead, there is achieved an atmosphere of gracious and ample size. The Villa Farnesina, which Peruzzi designed for the Chigi family in some kind of association with Raphael, who painted there his famous ceiling with the story of Cupid and Psyche, has a similar quality of unassuming beauty, a modesty which almost belies its real size. The work of Antonio da Sangallo the younger, in its basic correctness, its somewhat heavy restraint, is similarly individual, as is the more imaginative, more willfully varied work of Raphael and his eccentric follower Giulio Romano. It is this variety in design, this sure expression of

FLORENCE, PAZZI CHAPEL; VIEW IN COL-
ONNADE. Brunelleschi, architect.

FLORENCE, MARSUPPINI TOMB; CHARACTER-
ISTIC 15th-CENTURY FLORENTINE DETAIL.
By Desiderio da Settignano.

FLORENCE, STROZZI PALACE; EXTERIOR. Bene-
to da Maiano, architect.

FLORENCE, STROZZI PALACE, COURT; CHAR-
ACTERISTIC FLORENTINE ARCADE.

Plate 41

PAVIA, THE CERTOSA; CHURCH FAÇADE.

VENICE, STA. MARIA DEI MIRACOLI; DETAIL. Pietro Lombardo, architect.

VENICE, VENDRAMINI PALACE. Pietro Lombardo, architect.

Plate 42

RIMINI, MALATESTA CHURCH. Alberti, architect.

ROME, THE VATICAN; LOGGIE. Bramante, architect; decorated by Raphael and his pupils.

ROME, STA. MARIA DELLA PACE; COURT-YARD. Bramante, architect.

MONTEPULCIANO, MADONNA DI SAN BIAGIO; INTERIOR. Antonio da San Gallo the Elder, architect.

Plate 43

ROME, MASSIMI PALACE; EXTERIOR. Peruzzi, architect.

ROME, MASSIMI PALACE; COU
YARD.

ROME, ST. PETER'S; INTERIOR. Bramante, Michelangelo, and others, architects; the baldachino by Berni

Plate 44

ERONA, PALAZZO POMPEI; EXTERIOR. Sammichele, architect.

VICENZA, VILLA CAPRA; EXTERIOR. Palladio, architect.

ENZA, THE BASILICA; EXTERIOR SHOWING THE "PALLADIAN MOTIF." Palladio, architect.

Plate 45

BLOIS CHÂTEAU, LOUIS XII WING; LATE GOTHIC FORMS WITH SOME EARLY RENAISSANCE DETAIL.

AZAY-LE-RIDEAU, A CHARACTERISTIC FRANCIS I COUNTRY HOUSE.

BLOIS CHÂTEAU, FRANCIS I WING, STAIRWAY; GOTHIC FORMS IN RENAISSANCE DRESS.

BLOIS CHÂTEAU, FRANCIS I WING; CHARACTERISTIC MANTELPIECE WITH OVERMANT AND DECORATED BEAMED CEILING.

Plate 46

PARIS, LOUVRE, PETITE GALERIE.
Chambiges, architect.

PARIS, ST. ÉTIENNE DU MONT; JUBÉ OR ROOD SCREEN.

FONTAINEBLEAU, GALLERY OF FRANCIS I. By Il Rosso and
Primaticcio.

PARIS, LOUVRE, FIRST WING; COURT FAÇADE. Lescot, architect.

Plate 47

BREMEN TOWN HALL, CHARACTERISTIC DELICATE
GERMAN RENAISSANCE ELABORATION.

A PLATE FROM WENDEL DIETTER
LIN, 1598; GERMAN PHANTASY AT
ITS HIGHEST PEAK.

HEIDELBERG, HAUS ZUM RITTER; TYPICAL
SCROLLED GABLE, WITH STRAPWORK.

HEIDELBERG CASTLE, DETAIL OF THE O
HEINRICHSBAU; GAÎNES, STRAPWORK, VE

Plate 48

DELFT TOWN HALL. Hendrik de Keyser, architect.

ANTWERP TOWN HALL. Cornelis Floris, architect.

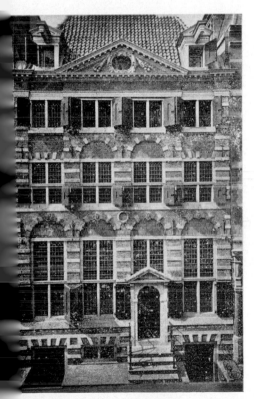

STERDAM, TYPICAL RENAISSANCE HOUSE; CK AND STONE, LARGE WINDOWS, IRON CHORS.

ALKMAAR, WEIGH HOUSE, WITH TYPICAL DUTCH TOWER AND GABLE.

Plate 49

THAME PARK, THE ABBOT'S PARLOR. (Garner and Stratton.)

CREWE HALL, CHESHIRE; THE CARVED PARLOR. (Nash: *Mansions of England in the Olden Time.*)

LONDON, THE BANQUETING HALL, WHITEHALL; PAL-

Plate 50

VILLE AYUNTAMIENTO. Diego de Riano, archi-
t.

TOLEDO, HOSPITAL OF SANTA CRUZ; COURT.
Henrique de Egas, architect.

.MANCA, THE LESSER SCHOOLS; DOOR.

VALENCIA, AUDIENCIA; GOLDEN HALL.

Plate 51

SEVILLE, HOUSE OF PILATE; REJA.

GRANADA CATHEDRAL; REJA.

THE ESCORIAL; COURT OF THE EVANGELISTS.

THE ESCORIAL; CHURCH FAÇADE.

THE ESCORIAL; GENERAL VIEW. Juan Bautista and Juan de Herrera, architects. (All photographs courtesy Carl Feiss.)

Plate 52

HAJURAHO, THE TEMPLE; AT LEFT, TOWER OVER THE SANCTUARY. (Metropolitan Museum of
rt.)

NTA, CHAITYA CAVE TEMPLE; BUD-
IST.

TRICHINIPOLY, TEMPLE; EASTERN GOPU-
RAM. (Metropolitan Museum of Art.)

Plate 53

PEKING, DRUM TOWER.

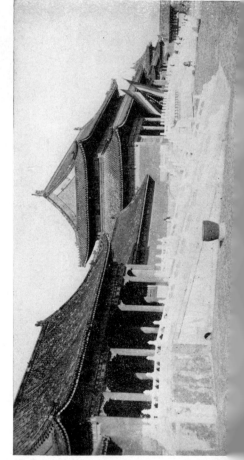

MT. ABU, JAIN TEMPLE; INTERIOR.

Plate 54

UJI, BYODO-IN; PHOENIX HALL. (Courtesy Dr. Ryusaku Tsunoda.)

KYOTO, BUDDHIST TEMPLE OF KYOMIDZU JI

PEKING, SUMMER PALACE; GENERAL VIEW.

KYOTO, KATSURA PALACE; SHOKIN-TEI INTERIOR. (Courtesy Dr. Ryusaku Tsunoda.)

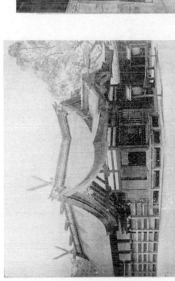

PEKING, 10,000-BUDDHA TEMPLE: INTERIOR.

OSAKA, SHINTO SHRINE. (Courtesy Dr. Ryusaku Tsunoda.)

Plate 55

ROME, CHURCH OF THE GESU; INTERIOR.
Vignola and G. della Porta, architects.

ROME, CHURCH OF SAN IGNAZIO; BAROQU
ALTARPIECE. Pozzo, architect.

ROME, SANTI MARCELLI CHURCH; FAÇADE.
(De Rossi: *Insignum Romae Templorum Prospectus.*)

GENOA, THE UNIVERSITY; ENTRANCE V
TIBULE AND STAIR TO COURT. B. Bianco,
chitect.

Plate 56

the personality of the architect, which makes the character of the Roman streets.

The High Renaissance found Rome an overgrown, formless country town. The Sack of Rome by Emperor Charles V in 1527 came as a terrific blow, as though almost to make for naught all the beginnings that had thus far been accomplished in creating a city out of this waste. Yet the fact was a blessing in disguise; the wealth and power which followed it were far greater than those which had preceded, and palace after palace rose rapidly along the streets, each grander than the one before, each more carefully designed, each gifted with greater and more imposing spaces.

In these great halls only a most brilliant, a most highly colored social life could exist, and one need only go to the pages of the *Memoirs* of Benvenuto Cellini, or even the more staid paragraphs of Vasari's *Lives of the Painters, Sculptors, and Architects,* to realize the gorgeousness which made these enormous, richly decorated interiors possible and a fit frame for the life that went on in them. Grace of line and lavishness of color characterized the costumes of the rich, and a similar mingling of graceful personality and radiant exuberance distinguished the social intercourse. There was not yet the heavy, ponderous formality that was to come later. The ideal of the time was to combine the delight of personal conversation, of poetry and phantasy, of philosophy and speculation, with the glorious excitement which could come only from the display of unlimited wealth in almost unlimited spaces, and to season the whole with an ample spicing of intrigue and sensuality.

For such a life as this, these great palaces were the only suitable frame. Into their capacious courts rode lord after lord, their torch-bearing outriders ahead, to dismount gaily at the foot of the wide stair. In the great halls tables piled with food and superb silver and gold and jeweled bowls and dishes, made by distinguished artists of the time, lay open to the multitude of guests, and pages dressed in black and white, or purple and gold, or red and green, stepped busily back and forth with pitchers and decanters of wines from Tuscany or the Sabine Hills or Naples. In the shadowed loggias, where the evening breeze swept in, or in the upper arcades of the great court, were abundant spaces for those who sought companionship more close, hidden from the public throng. Even today something of this tradition still remains in Rome, and the Swiss Guards of the Vatican wear still the noble red-blue-and-white costumes which Michelangelo designed for them nearly four centuries ago.

But if it was the public, gregarious side of Roman life which showed itself in the great palaces of the sixteenth century, it was a quite a different side of life which found expression in the Italian villas. Already in the fifteenth century the main elements of Italian villa design had been set—the comparatively minor scale of its *casino* or residence; the absolute unity of the architecture, natural landscape, and garden as parts of one composition; and the use of water in pools and fountains. The High Renaissance found new and stimulating arrangements of these elements, developed forms so perfect in the blending of their various portions that they have remained models ever since. Pirro Ligorio showed in two examples—one small and one large—what genius could do in making man the ally of nature. The one was the small Villa Pia in the Vatican gardens; a little oval terrace, a small casino, three arched entrances, a fountain and a few stairs—that is all, yet with what gaiety the whole is conceived, with what graciousness one is led from level to level, and even the florid stucco decoration of the walls comes to seem an integral part of the whole design!

The large example, the Villa d'Este at Tivoli, had the advantage of an everlasting and almost overcopious water supply from the Anio River, which flows past the town to fall in a magnificently romantic glen down to the level of the plain beneath. Ligorio took this water, broke it into many channels, carried it down from terrace to terrace through fountains, some spurting high, some barely trickling, some spouting out horizontally. An endless phantasy characterizes these fountain-lined terraces, which climb down almost clifflike hills. Between the paths and the terraces the foliage is left to grow almost wild, giving even greater emphasis to the artificial vivacity of the terrace figures. At the bottom of the hill the garden extends out on a wide terrace almost flat, through the middle of which, at right angles to the axis, runs a series of wide basins to reflect the trees around. At one end these basins are fed by the most extraordinary water piece of the whole composition, the famous "water organ," where tremendous volumes of water fall in cascades from level to level, emphasized by vertical jets. But how simple is the basic scheme of the whole! From the palace, which opens directly off the town street at the top of the villa, a clear axis runs through the whole composition unbroken, so that from the loggia at the center of the rear of the palace one looks out over the garden below, miles across the Campagna to the blue hills beyond, with the view framed by tall cypresses on either side.

The Italian villa designer evidently cared little for flowers except as flowers might incidentally decorate shrubs. The flower garden as such was unknown. His palette was simple: the creamy gray of Italian stone in buildings, terrace walls, balustrades, benches, fountain bases; the varied greens of foliage, always punctuated and climaxed by the rich dark tones and the sharp vertical forms of the cypress trees which he planted so skillfully to emphasize his design; and the ever-changing color and shimmer of water. Of these he made his garden, his villa; house and grounds and view always one unit indissoluble.

Throughout the sixteenth century the individual cities of Italy still retained their old independence. Although Roman fashions naturally affected them, and although Rome called to herself many of the best of their architects and artists, nevertheless local styles, local habits, and local traditions were too strong to allow the architecture of Italy to become one homogeneous thing. The visitor to Florence finds a city the character of which is unified. The stone façades of its palaces, though yielding in detail to Roman restraint and Roman accuracy of antique reproduction in molding and capital, remain essentially Florentine; and even Raphael's Pandolfini Palace, although in its pedimented windows Roman in type, nevertheless, by virtue of its material and a certain simple strength, seems to belong primarily to Florence. And later designs such as the Ugoccioni Palace by Buontalenti, with its coupled columns and its broad flat projecting cornice, built as late as the beginning of the seventeenth century, preserve on their ground floors the heavy rustication of the earlier period and take their places perfectly on the narrow, stony Florentine streets.

What is true of Florence is true generally of the other cities of Italy: Milan, with its Lombard love of rich, concentrated decoration and its almost universal use of brick and terra-cotta; Bologna, with its more restrained taste, also building brick and terra-cotta palaces with Roman details artfully modified for the different material; Naples, with its crude effulgence. It was only in the later period when the Baroque movement overwhelmed earlier Renaissance ideals that any national uniformity began to develop.

Especially interesting and individual is the High Renaissance work of Venice, of Verona, and of Vicenza, each under the influence of a single great creative mind: at Venice Sansovino, at Verona Sammichele, at Vicenza Palladio. In all three places the High Renaissance work is later than most of that at Rome, for all this portion of Italy found the lavish ornament and rich material of the Early Renaissance much to its liking and held to it nearly fifty years after it had given way in Rome to the restrained architectonic work of the High Renaissance. And even when the High Renaissance finally triumphed the old ideals modified it, enriched it, made it more luxuriant than elsewhere in Italy.

Just as the painting of Titian has a glorious radiance of color, a noble opulence of form, which is different from the character of contemporary painting elsewhere in Italy, so the architects of Venice strove for a similar imaginative magnificence, embroidered with delicate detail and expressed in the rich marbles which Venice so loved. Sansovino's library at Venice and his little loggia at the base of the Campanile are both expressive of this lavish yet delicate taste. Sansovino was sculptor almost as much as he was architect, and in both cases depended largely on sculptural detail for the totality of his effect. The library is especially significant because in it the "correct" antique order details in their boldest and most architectonic forms, engaged and free-standing columns and beautiful arches arranged somewhat after the manner of the Colosseum, are combined in a free composition with the richest possible ornament to form a whole which is not only successful and powerful in itself, but also completely different from any contemporary Roman work.

In Verona, Sammichele established a different character, partly perhaps influenced by the somewhat eccentric quality of the ancient Roman detail to be found in the ruins there, especially the famous Porta Borsari, an ancient Roman gateway. In his palaces he combines strength almost brutal in the lower portions—heavy rustications, bold square cap-molds, tremendous consoles under the windows, and so on—with upper portions of engaged columns and arched and square windows which approach, though never quite pass, the bounds of eccentricity; and these upper portions he decorates with unwonted delicacy, as though by the contrast to enhance both the power below and the delicate richness above. In the city gates which he built for the new fortifications of Verona, it is the atmosphere of power which rightly controls, and by relentless rustication of every portion, including even the engaged columns which stand between the arches, he achieves a character which was at the same time magnificent and military. All of this work dates from between 1525 and 1540.

It is noteworthy that in all of this work the orders—that is, columns and pilasters—played a more important part than in Rome or Florence. Roman remains were being more and more excavated and studied; the power of Roman scale, the impact of Roman grandeur, were more and more becoming obvious to the Renaissance designers. To many, the beauty of this ancient work seemed inextricably combined with the use of columns, and it is not strange to find that as the sixteenth century wore on the column came more and more into use, even in Rome itself.

At the same time there developed a growing search for originality in design. The restraint of the best High Renaissance work had come to seem dull, the careful beauty of its design niggling. This search for novelty gave rise to developments that historians call *Manneristic* and the whole movement *Mannerism,* perhaps because so susceptible of personal vagaries. The movement took two forms. One was a search for originality at all costs, even if it involved willful eccentricities; Michelangelo in some of his architectural work like the Porta Pia is its climax figure. The other was a trend toward an even greater classicism, a freer use of columns and colonnades, a more precise study of ancient buildings; Sansovino and later Palladio are its greatest exemplars. In many architects both trends are combined, as in the case of Vignola or Giulio Romano. Vignola published a definitive treatise on the orders, setting rules for their proportions; many such works were published all over Europe later, often based on Vignola's book, so that its influence was tremendous even outside Italy. But Vignola in his own work introduced all sorts of charming variations of freely created detail, and he always designed his orders with an immaculate sense of proportion to fit his buildings and not the reverse—as some of his followers did. The Villa of Papa Giulio just outside Rome which he designed, with its delightful semicircular colonnade and its rich and inventive ornament, its dramatic contrast of rusticated exterior and delicacy within, is characteristic of the best Mannerist combinations of classicism and imagination.

This classicizing tendency reached its climax in the work of Palladio. Confronted with the problem of designing a new front to the old regional palace at Vicenza, he solved it by surrounding the old great hall with an arcade in two stories, in which the bays were nearly square and the arches were carried on smaller columns that stood free between the larger engaged columns separating the bays. It was this bay design which gave rise to the term "Palladian arch" or "Palladian motif," and has been used ever since for an arched opening supported on columns and flanked by two narrow square-headed openings of the same height as the columns. This was only the first of a large number of buildings by Palladio in Vicenza and Venice. All of his work was characterized by the use of the orders and similar ancient Roman details expressed with considerable power, severity, and restraint. The work was mainly built of brick and stucco, and much of the detail was formed in the stucco. To that extent Palladian architecture was superficial; yet the composition is so strong, the proportions so harmonious and the detail always so apt that, despite any criticisms of its superficiality, the Palladian work has been considered worthy of study and emulation by large numbers of architects ever since his day.

But the work of Palladio was essentially a protest against a fashion which was irresistibly growing. In the book which he wrote he inveighs against what he terms the licentiousness of contemporary detail—its use of shields, of broken pediments, of unreasoned and eccentric curves. In Italy his protest was of no avail. The forces of individual creativeness unleashed by Michelangelo and stimulated by the changing conditions ushered in with the seventeenth century were too strong to be defeated. The future belonged to the Baroque.

Chapter 18

THE RENAISSANCE IN FRANCE

ALL through the Middle Ages, France had been struggling toward nation hood and power, and, just as the English were gradually forced back and out of the western portion of the country, so at the same time, under the leadership of a series of brilliant rulers, feudal power was little by little yielding to a national and royal centralized government. Exuberant with their newly gained supremacy, the French kings of the end of that period were not content with the territory of France itself. Through various marriages they claimed a dynastic right to the crown of Naples and to certain powers over other portions of Italy in addition. As a result, there followed a series of elaborate military expeditions into Italy under Charles VIII, Louis XII, and finally Francis I. The military results of these expeditions were unimportant and at the end disastrous, when Francis I was captured in the battle of Pavia by the new emperor of the Holy Roman Empire, Charles V, and held captive in Madrid for a year.

But, if the military results were small, the cultural results were enormous, for all the wealthiest and most powerful nobles of France, the flower of the French upper class, were for the first time brought into intimate contact with the civilized and cultivated life of the cities of northern Italy. Here they found amenities which medieval France had never known—cities with streets paved throughout, clean, well planned, dignified. Here they were entertained in the noble palaces of the Italian generals or in the luxurious villas which dotted the Italian countryside. Brantôme tells of the deep effect made upon them by the beautiful manners of their Italian foes and friends alike, their admiration of the general cleanliness and beauty of this new and Renaissance country.

And, having seen, they could only long to imitate—to develop the same polish of manners, to build the same gracious and dignified homes, decorated with the same richness of lovely fresco, the same daintiness of carved ornament. What more natural than that Louis XII should have invited

Leonardo to come to work at the French court, or that his successor Francis I should welcome to Fontainebleau and Paris Primaticcio, Il Rosso, Serlio, and even for a brief and stormy period Benvenuto Cellini himself? And these were but the famous names among a much greater number of carvers and metalworkers, draftsmen and painters, who found in the French court at the beginning of the sixteenth century not only employment but honor and appreciation.

Thus, Italian Renaissance ideas began gradually to creep into French building. For nearly a half century these appeared in details only, as was natural, for the new decorative forms could be carved by Italian workmen or by the infinitely clever French carvers whom the Italians trained, with no fundamental change in building conception or building technique. That was to come only later; for the Flamboyant Late Gothic of France had been perhaps the most vital and the most creative of all the Late Gothic traditions, and, especially in residence work, was still a living thing throughout the country, preserved by the traditional conservatism of the guilds and stimulated and made even more creative by the high standards which the guild training demanded. To substitute acanthus leaves, classic scrolls, the egg-and-dart molding decoration, and Corinthianesque capitals for the intricate stylized leafage, the undercut vines, and the complicated seaweedlike crocket capitals of the Late Gothic was a change in outward form only, and the same skill which had produced the exquisite complexity of Late Gothic carving found equally congenial and perhaps even more stimulating opportunities in carving the new, delicate, classic ornament, giving it a refinement of low-relief, a beauty of light-and-shade patterning, a contrast between leaves raised high above the background and casting deep shadows with stems and scrolls almost dying into the background (where they were hardly more than indicated) which even the best of the Early Renaissance carving in Florence had not known. There might be produced occasional works of almost purely Italian type, like the beautiful tomb of the children of Charles V in the cathedral at Tours, carved in 1506 by the Italian Girolamo da Fiesole, or the few works executed by Luciano da Laurano of Florence in Marseilles and Le Mans some twenty years earlier. Yet these were exceptional; in general, the vitality of the French building tradition and the persistence of French building types imposed upon this new Renaissance work, even when designed and executed by the traveling Italians, its own specific and individual character.

A typical example can be seen in the wing which Louis XII built at the Château of Blois, with its high roofs, its mullioned windows, its rich Gothic

dormers and enormous chimneys, its lavish use here and there of decorative Flamboyant tracery, of pinnacles, buttresses, and spirelets, its low oval
arches. It is a rich work of the most luxurious Late Gothic, even to the somewhat Rabelaisian humor of its famous carved grotesques; nevertheless, as
one compares it with such other Late Gothic Châteaux as Josselin, one is conscious of subtle differences in spirit—the horizontal lines are much more
definitely stressed, and something of the classic feeling of membering has
controlled the rhythmical spacing of its windows, the continuity of its horizontal band courses, the strong accent on its arched entrance. To that extent
the general design has felt the new classic winds blowing over the face of
Europe. But, even more important, alternate piers of the court arcade are
decorated with purely classical acanthus-leaf, scroll, and candelabrum-shaft
pilasters—definite copies of a type invented by the ancient Romans and developed even further by the fifteenth-century Florentines. The extraordinary
thing is that this purely classic ornament is used with such brilliant decorative skill that somehow it seems quite at home even amid the wealth of
Gothic carving which surrounds it.

With the accession of Francis I in 1515 the atmosphere changed, for
Francis was not only a frank innovator, a vivid, energetic personality continually on the search for the new and the exciting, but he was also a
tremendous builder, almost obsessed with the creation of new châteaux; and
one of the surest ways to his favor on the part of his courtiers was the construction by them of new houses or palaces in which he could be received.
During his reign the advent of Italian artists and craftsmen into France,
which had been but a trickle before, became a little flood. The love and use
of classic details, which had been the exception, became the rule; and all
over France, but especially in the Loire valley, his most favored residence
spot, château after château arose, preserving, it is true, the towers and the
pavilions, the high roofs, and the construction of the old Late Gothic tradition, but one and all decorated entirely with ornament borrowed from the
new Renaissance alphabet.

At Blois, the king himself built a new wing, as if to outrival and excel the
huge addition which his predecessor had constructed. The difference between
the two is instructive. Both preserve the high steep roof, the great chimneys,
the tall rich dormers, the mullioned windows of the Gothic tradition; but,
whereas in the Louis XII wing the ornament is chiefly on the Gothic basis,
in the wing which Francis I built the ornament is all of classic inspiration.
A balustrade replaces the traceried parapet at the eaves. Classic modillions
and little arches with classic scallop shells are used instead of the Gothic

corbels of the earlier cornice. At the dormers, scrolls are found in lieu of flying buttresses, and pilastered piers carrying candelabrum shafts instead of Gothic buttresses and pinnacles. Corinthian pilasters frame each window, and horizontal band courses of sill and head begin little by little to take on the look of classic cornices and pedestal courses. As the chief feature of his court façade, Francis I had his architects build a great spiral stair in a polygonal tower, open to the outside air through wide arches. In some ways this stair is the masterpiece of the early transitional Renaissance of France. Structurally, it has all the ingenuity of the Late Gothic; decoratively, all the delicate lavishness of north-Italian ornament. It is almost unbelievably rich in detail; even the stair balusters are carved with little Corinthian capitals. Its statues, on corbels and under canopies, are purely Gothic in idea, but the canopies are built with classic arches, classic colonnettes and niches, and classical fittings; and the statues have a kind of ineffable grace which is the result of the attempt to merge classical drapery and classical beauty with the exuberant realism of the Late Gothic. The whole is splendid with the sala-mander and the crowned F which were the special, favorite badges of the king, with lozenge panels, and with friezes and pilasters of the most delicate acanthus ornament. Slightly incoherent as it is, the whole breathes; it is vital with the life of a style in the process of birth.

A similar vitality characterizes the other châteaux which were rising so swiftly up and down the lovely Loire countryside. Less rich they might be, for few nobles could hope to command the resources which the king pos-sessed; but all without exception strove to follow the king's fashion in being homes which were Renaissance, at least in their ornament. In all, the win-dows are framed by Corinthian pilasters; there is the same approximation to the classic entablature in horizontal moldings, the same substitution of pilasters for buttresses, of classic candelabrum shafts—perhaps based on the lavish use of the candelabrum-shaft motif in the work of Lombardy, espe-cially in the front of the Certosa di Pavia—instead of Gothic pinnacles; and around the doors particularly was decoration composed of pilasters, entabla-tures, pediments, and round arches. The best examples are Chambord, built by the king, in which a naïve attempt is made for classic symmetry of plan as well as classic detail, Azay-le-Rideau, and the earlier portions of Chenonceaux.

It was a prodigal period, careless, carefree, wealthy; the peasantry were prosperous, the bourgeoisie gaining in wealth and importance; as yet there were no signs of that concentration of wealth and power, that gradual im-poverishment of the countryside which was later to wreck the land; and even the wealthy peasants and the bourgeoisie took delight in aping as far as they could the Renaissance manners of the nobles. Accordingly, within a very short time manors and large farms, from the Mediterranean to Normandy, and city halls and town houses in the growing towns, where commerce was booming, began to show the Corinthianesque pilasters, the strangely lovely combinations of Gothic form dressed in the new classic garb, the delicate acanthus leaves and scrolls, that distinguished the work of the court.

In the interiors the story is the same. The simple rectangular halls, the large chimney pieces, the beamed ceilings of Late Gothic type continued in use, but they were decked with an array of delicate Renaissance ornament, and many delightful mantelpieces like those in the château of Blois remain to show the rich beauty which this transitional work produced. Little by little, too, tapestries were passing out of fashion, being replaced by hangings of woven damask or by tooled and gilded leather, or by simple painted plaster. Furniture still remained elementary. Long tables on heavy legs, stools and chests, dressers, and one state chair comprised all the furniture of even important rooms in royal residences; but, like the mantelpieces, their still conservative general forms were richly ornamented with the exquisite fine Renaissance carving.

Conservatism remained even more strongly entrenched in the churches. There at least the Gothic reigned for another half century, almost unchanged save for the occasional occurrence of a classic tomb or choir screen and the rare carving of vertical panels with Renaissance pilaster decorations. Only gradually did the new style break through this conservatism, and even then in ways more hesitant than in the case of the châteaux. The church of St. Eustache in Paris is the largest, the most magnificent, and perhaps the most daring of these transitional churches. With a plan based definitely on that of Notre Dame, with all its structure and its proportions Gothic, with traceried windows and a ribbed vault, it has nevertheless every bit of carved ornament classic in inspiration, every molding profile based on classic forms. Its piers are decorated with ranges of pilasters one over another, broken into complex plan to give the effect and to serve the purpose of the older Gothic-membered piers; its exterior buttresses are decorated with pilasters and entablatures, and its entrance doors are little gems of Francis I design. The effect is superb, interesting, and in the main beautiful. Yet there is about it still something which seems almost eccentric; the effort to apply the classic details to forms manifestly so ill-suited to them is too great—the whole seems a *tour de force* almost more than a work of art.

In the Paris church of St. Étienne-du-Mont greater liberties have been taken with the Gothic structure, and the classic elements seem less forced, less perhaps out of place. Here too the effect is of something attempted without complete success; yet the experimentalism is along the line of creative structural thought and not merely an attempt to apply alien forms to Gothic structure. Its simple round piers are struggling toward classic grandeur, and its rich *jubé,* or rood-screen, is a masterpiece of Early Renaissance design. Elsewhere, the few new churches built were pure examples of Flamboyant Gothic. The most successful Early Renaissance ecclesiastical work is minor; it lies in the occasional screens of chapels or walled tombs, or little added details like the exquisite doors and organ gallery of the church of St. Maclou in Rouen.

Yet Francis I could not remain forever satisfied with this straining and tentative approach to the Renaissance, however charming its details might be. He set himself the definite task of establishing in France a center of Renaissance influence, as though in his own way to rival the Medici of Florence; and he chose his hunting lodge at Fontainebleau as the place where his Italian artists should gather and work, the place from which a purer, a more Italian, Renaissance might flow. The resulting work, in architecture as in painting, which now is grouped together under the name, the School of Fontainebleau, has a character quite different from the stumbling steps toward the classic one finds in the Touraine châteaux. At Fontainebleau the two most important Italians were Il Rosso and Primaticcio. For a while Serlio, the great Italian architect and author of architectural books, worked there, till he retired in his old age to Lyons, and it was during his residence in France that many of his most important books were produced. Among these was one devoted to domestic architecture, never published and existing still in two manuscripts, one in the National Library in Munich and one in Columbia University. This is a most significant work, for in it one can see how the Italian architects attempted to apply their Italian training, their sound classical skill, to the new French problems. They were too wise to try to impose upon France the mere copying of Italian designs. They knew full well the extraordinary importance in architectural design of such matters as climate, materials, and the ways of life of the client. They designed, therefore, not Italian palazzi, but châteaux which were still French—French in their large windows, their great chimneys, their whole basic plan conception. Yet on this they imposed a pattern in which they sought to gain the symmetry, the dignity, the perfection of proportion, the regularity of Italian Renaissance work. Serlio's book on domestic architecture starts with tiny houses—farmhouses and small town residences. For each plan he works out two exteriors, one based on the low-pitched tile roofs and the small windows of his own Italian south, and the other on the high roofs, the big chimneys, the large windows of the north of France. The same character runs all through the work of the painters of the School of Fontainebleau, and even the French artists who studied there were imbued with it. A sort of luxuriance, a delight purely pagan in free classic sensuality, runs through it all, but in addition there is always that touch of sure precision which is essentially French, and the subjects—so frequently portraits—are French men and women, unmistakably.

The enlargements made at this period in Fontainebleau itself are interesting. In some ways less successful than the Loire châteaux—more awkward, occasionally overheavy,—they are, nevertheless, more creative even in their failure, and the search for simple composition, for symmetry and regularity, is obvious. The best of the Francis I work here is on the interior—especially the lovely long gallery called the Gallery of Francis I, with its rich paneled wainscot and its lavish stucco figures above, forming frames for brilliant paintings, and a paneled ceiling crowning the whole, of exquisite delicacy of design, no longer the beamed ceiling of the Gothic and yet entirely different in character and design from the heavy coffers of Italy. Other characteristic work of the period includes the erratic but interesting design for the Paris Hôtel de Ville (the city hall), by Il Boccador; and the Château de Madrid in Paris, heavily symmetrical, but complicated and forced in its efforts to gain this symmetry. The best example is probably the Château of Ancy-le-Franc, designed by Serlio himself, where the whole scheme of the French courtyard château has finally been resolved into a simple, direct, four-square whole, symmetrical, dignified, and gracious, where for almost the first time the high roofs, the projecting pavilions, the dormers, and the chimneys of the French home have been combined, perfectly and without strain, with the simple dignity of the classic tradition.

The final triumph of the classic came only in the last years of Francis I, in the design for the enlargement and rebuilding of the old château of the Louvre, just outside the city walls. There the architect, Pierre Lescot, achieved a blend so perfect that it appears no longer as a blend but as a new thing, a new creation; it is no longer transitional, it is full-grown and mature, an exquisite piece of Renaissance that is purely Renaissance and yet purely French. It set a type which exercised enormous influence for many years to come. Each floor is carefully distinguished from the other floors by strong horizontal cornices, and each floor has it own order of pilasters. The windows are large, filling almost the whole height of the wall, and close together so that the pilasters and engaged columns which occur between them have a pleasant, close rhythm. The third floor, which is above the main cornice, is treated as a minor story in a sort of attic which carries its own little pilasters, treated with a special new kind of capital characteristically French. Above this is a rich metal gutter, and then a high slate roof crowned with a decorative cresting of lead. The wing which Pierre Lescot constructed was broken into a central and two end pavilions, with connecting links between, but the breaks are so subtle that no sense of disunity results, and the whole

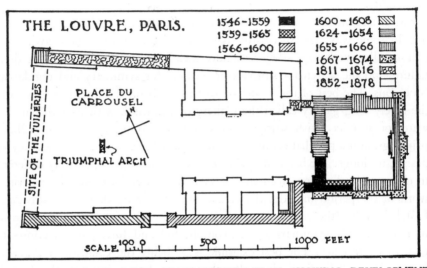

THE LOUVRE, PARIS.

1546-1559	1600-1608
1559-1565	1624-1654
1566-1600	1655-1666
	1667-1674
	1811-1816
	1852-1878

PLACE DU CARROUSEL

SITE OF THE TUILERIES

TRIUMPHAL ARCH

SCALE 100 0   500   1000 FEET

78. LOUVRE PALACE, PARIS; DIAGRAMMATIC PLAN SHOWING DEVELOPMENT (Redrawn from Simpson. Vol. III.)

merely seems an extraordinarily interesting façade, full of vivid accents and almost perfect in proportion and detail. In this work he had the co-operation of one of the great architectural sculptors of the world, Jean Goujon. Both Lescot and Goujon had learned well all that the Italians of the School of Fontainebleau could give, and all that their knowledge of classic form could offer, but both remained primarily and essentially French; and this first wing of the Louvre is the first monument of a Renaissance which is at last truly at home and truly French.

The reign of Henry II, Francis I's successor, marks the high-water mark of this French Renaissance. Under him the first part of the Louvre was finished, another great palace, the Tuileries, for the queen, was begun near by, and an enormous amount of country-house building went on all over

France. The best of it is by French architects, of whom Philibert de l'Orme and Jean Bullant are the best known. The period is distinguished by the perfect assimilation of the classic orders and complete mastery in their correct use. The last vestiges of Gothic ornament disappear, except in occasional churches, and yet the French château tradition of high roofs and large windows controls all. Philibert de l'Orme's Château d'Anet, built for the king's mistress, Diane de Poitiers, is typical in its free and daring composition, in its bold use of arcades and porticoes, which are given new rhythms because of the large windows that surround or enframe them, and in its playful use of *quoins* (projecting rusticated corner blocks), moldings, and panels. There is something of the phantasy of the Baroque about it, but none of the Baroque heavy-handedness.

The work of the Henry II period is all full of invention, almost of caprice, and yet of delicacy also. Only in its occasionally ponderous devotion to the orders themselves, which it uses with an ever-increasing frequency, can it be severely criticized. This fault is especially common in the work of Jean Bullant, de l'Orme's famous contemporary, as in the façades he added to the Château of Écouen. But, generally speaking, restraint and good taste prevailed. De l'Orme's tomb of Francis I and his magnificent plan for the Tuileries palace, only a fraction of which was built, are eloquent evidence of the high quality of Henry II design.

With the death of Henry, France entered a period of civil and religious war, of virtual anarchy, of economic and cultural depletion. He ended an epoch; the forces which had reached their acme in the brilliant reign of Francis I and of Henry himself had spent themselves, and new impulses and new forces were at work. The Reformation and the Counter-Reformation were much more than religious manifestations; they were symptoms of a profound new feeling about life, a new feeling that was bound to produce eventually a new and different architecture. The period of the civil wars under Francis II, Charles IX, and Henry III, of the insensate struggles of the Guises and their opponents—that period of sadistic intrigue which was so well expressed by the Massacre of St. Bartholomew,— was little fitted to produce architecture. For forty years there was an almost complete stagnation of building in France, and the building which followed was to be a building of a different kind and controlled by different ideals from those which had gone before.

Chapter 19

THE RENAISSANCE IN
NORTHERN EUROPE

ALL through the fifteenth century the independent German cities had been growing rapidly in population and wealth through commerce and industry. The essentially urban civilization of Germany had produced cities and towns ample in size, closely built, with houses picturesque yet logical, and churches clothed in a vital Flamboyant style that was one of the richest expressions of Late Gothic architecture. There was a tremendous vitality in this work, and the high-gabled towns of late medieval Germany, with their winding streets and beautiful city squares, remain in large part today to show the reality of this life. To such towns and to such a life the intellectual movements which produced the Renaissance came as no violent revolution, for that independence of thought which gave rise eventually to Martin Luther and the Reformation was merely a logical development of the independence of culture and the independence of trade which had characterized the whole period in Germany.

Nevertheless, the new classic forms which had been developed in Italy crept inevitably into the Germanic territories. Wandering Italian artists and architects, searching for fame and fortune in the courts of the German principalities and dukedoms, helped the aristocracy in that search for the new and the smart which seemed so frequently to be a concomitant of Renaissance courts. Books, too, began to play a greater and greater part in the distribution of this classic lore, and, especially from the middle of the sixteenth century on, the much translated works of Serlio and Scamozzi, added to the basic knowledge in Vitruvius, gave a foundation for classic design quite apart from the work of the traveling Italian architects. The northern painters as well, who so frequently traveled in Italy to learn there the secrets of the new and popular Italian painting, exerted a tremendous influence, and architectural forms of classic type appear frequently in the engravings and paintings of Dürer, of Van Orley, of Blondeel, of Memling, and of other German and Flemish artists of the time, decades before those same forms became popular in actual building.

All this combined to give a peculiar character to the Early Renaissance of the north, which may rightly be called "picturesque." It was largely independent of Italian and French influence, except that found in the occasional works of the traveling Italians, and it was chiefly designed by Germans and Flemings for a vivid and prosperous city civilization, which had already worked out adequate and beautiful fundamental forms. There was accordingly even less attempt to imitate Italian buildings than there had been in France. Instead, the architects and builders of the time, generally speaking, realized full well the beauty and the adequacy of the high-roofed, many-windowed houses of the Late Gothic, of the town halls with their balconies and great halls and ground-floor markets, of the fountains and the beautifully composed public squares which distinguished the cities of their fathers. What interested them was an examination of how best the classic details, the perfection and beauty of which they well realized, could be applied to their own traditional buildings. They wished to be "up to date," their princes and dukes wanted to be as modern as those of France or Italy; yet no revolutionary change in building types was desired or even contemplated.

In a sense the problem was simple. The half-timber construction of the Late Gothic German houses had already established a tradition of design based largely on vertical and horizontal lines, the posts and the beams of the timbering. It was a simple matter to put classic pilasters on the vertical posts, and classic entablatures on the horizontal bands; it was simple, too, to substitute for the intricate leafage of the Late Gothic foliage which had sometimes decorated the horizontal members a leafage of a distantly classic sort. A similar process had distinguished considerable work in Early Renaissance France, but in Germany the approach was more fundamental, the classic forms more thoroughly changed, modified, and adapted to their new and strange positions on group-windowed, peak-roofed houses. The German architect and builder was never content merely to accept the orders as he found them in the books. He reserved always the right to alter them to fit the new positions, and the exuberance of the civic life of the sixteenth century is reflected in the vivid imagination with which he played over the classic tunes.

Another element which aided in this creative modification of the classic forms was the fact that much of the German knowledge of actual Renaissance work came from textiles and metalwork rather than from buildings.

Now, Italian textile design and Italian metalwork had been perhaps the freest in design of all types of Renaissance craftsmanship. They had been, through the medium of Venice, deeply affected by many oriental ideas and by that complicated interlace of pattern which only later and in a tentative way came to be a part of Italian architecture, but which in the sixteenth century almost controlled the elaborate inlaid armor, the exquisite enameled jewelry and goldsmithing, and the brocades and velvets of northern Italy. All these the Germans knew well through their important commercial connections; and this free, complicated type of Renaissance design, so thoroughly imbued with the idea of interlacing patterns, of contrast and conflicting lines, seemed but one step removed from the intricacy and the involvement that had typified Late Gothic German tracery. Thus, all of these elements combined to give the Renaissance in the Germanic territories an entirely different character, a basically different color, a particular flavor of its own; and, at least throughout the sixteenth century, despite the occasional Italian work by Italian artists, German Renaissance architecture as a whole remained essentially and entirely of the north, so that there seems less difference at first sight between an Early Renaissance and a Late Gothic German house than between either and a similar building in France or Italy. It is this character which preserved the unity and the consistency of the appearance of the German towns, in spite of the change in style, and it is this which has led to much of the winning charm that marked such towns as Hildesheim, Nuremberg, Rothenburg, and the old part of Frankfurt.

Yet the tendency toward an increased use of classic form was too strong to be resisted. The more classic type of work came in especially from the east, because it was in Austria and in the Bohemian cities that the Italian architects played the greatest role. Scamozzi himself made one design for the cathedral at Salzburg, and the Italian influence remained dominant in some of the Austrian cities ever after, giving to Salzburg and to Vienna their own special tone of monumental and classic dignity, as opposed to the high-roofed picturesqueness the rule elsewhere. In Prague, the architect Paolo della Stella designed for the royal palace a large garden building, called the Belvedere, where he combined most successfully the large scale and serene arcades of Renaissance Italy with the high hipped roof of more northern climates.

The compositional quality of this work was too strong to go unnoticed. The largeness of its scale, the repose of its general arrangements, so different from the dynamic, piquant quality of the more native work, had necessarily an enormous appeal. This appeal was especially strong in the courts of the counts and dukes and princes. There was perhaps in it a quality which seemed congenial to the growing centrality of power for which they were gradually struggling. If the modified classic of high-roofed houses and town houses was in a sense expressive of the secular bourgeois prosperity of the independent cities, so the new search for greater classicism became characteristic of the gradually changing political climate, the gradually growing power of the nobility, the gradual formation of military dictatorships which eventually, complicated by religious differences, were to lead inevitably to the Thirty Years' War.

But even here the classic of Italy was much modified by existing traditions, and the independence of the northern designers is well expressed by the publication in Germany and Flanders of other books on architecture besides those of the Italians—of books by native architects, who issued with perfect confidence and aplomb plate after plate of the most extraordinarily fantastic phantasies on the classic orders. Typical works are the books by Wendel Dietterlin, issued at the end of the sixteenth century, in which, classified under the headings of the five orders—Tuscan, Doric, Ionic, Corinthian, and Composite—and perhaps starting out from forms based on the classic proportions, designs of greater and greater complexity, of a wilder and wilder fantastic quality, bear witness to the amazing inventiveness of the time. In Flanders at the same time Vredeman de Vries (1528-1607) was producing work somewhat similar, although controlled by more architectonic ideals; and the Dutch were soon to follow suit with the books of Danckerts and de Keyser.

Dietterlin was essentially a painter and engraver. His plates are *tours de force* of engraving rather than serious architectural designs; yet the interlacing arches, the occasional presence of Gothic forms in new and pseudo-classical guise, the extraordinary lavishness of rustication and broken entablatures, the weird combinations of doors and niches, of columns and pilasters, with figure sculpture, the strange caricaturing of the classical capitals and even the columns and pilasters themselves, which abound in these plates, exerted a remarkable influence on German architecture, and the books were published and republished to fill the need their popularity brought.

A little later, Daniel Maier republished many of the Dietterlin plates reengraved by himself; but the change in taste which had occurred in the two decades between the two publications, the greater and growing architectural feeling behind the work of the seventeenth century, is shown by the fact that, in addition to the plates of grotesque ornament, Maier illustrates actual elevations of proposed buildings, and his forms have gained thereby something of the discipline which the feeling for actual structure and actual material inevitably give. Thus, as happened again and again in the history of the Renaissance, forms first loved and used purely as ornament eventually worked out into simplifications dependent upon actual structure, and in that way gave rise to new and creative architectural syntheses.

The high-roofed houses of Hildesheim, Nuremberg, and Frankfurt offer beautiful examples of the earlier bourgeois type of German Renaissance. In

79. CHARACTERISTIC GERMAN RENAISSANCE DETAILS. *Left:* GAÎNES. *Right:* STRAPWORK. (A. D. F. Hamlin: *A History of Ornament.*)

many the material of the front is stone, although the ranked windows, the large glass areas, the steep roofs, and the general rectangular pattern are due to the half-timber origin of the type. There is considerable elegance in the details to be found, and it is noteworthy that, instead of depending entirely upon pilasters or columns for the decoration of vertical supporting elements, there is often a use of *gaînes*—that is, combinations of the upper part of a human figure bearing a column capital and the lower part of the figure apparently surrounded by a rectangular sheaf tapering downward. Characteristic also, and perhaps borrowed from certain ideas to be found in Italian inlaid metal and Italian leather work, is the growing use of a kind of flat ornament called "strapwork," formed of queer-shaped projecting scrolls and panels, with the flat surface varied by projecting "jewels" and bosses at important places where shapes intersect.

The gable too became endlessly varied. A sharp-pointed gable, following absolutely the shape of the roof behind, was not a typical nor even a logical stone form, because stone is cut only with difficulty in forms that have sharp feather edges; therefore it soon became a custom to run the façade above the roof behind, as a screen and parapet, either stepping the edges to form that stepped gable which later became common in Holland, or else treating the slope with a series of pediments and half-pediments. In both cases, finial-like forms made of little obelisks, statues, or pedestals, or balls and urns, are frequently used to emphasize the steps, or breaks in line; and, since the gabled fronts of these houses were almost always toward the street and the houses close together, the street views became wonderfully rich, interesting, and nervously dynamic. When the house was large, the steepness of the roof forced a ridge so high that frequently there were three stories in the height of the roof construction itself, and the little dormers which lighted these form a typical feature in any view of an old Germanic town.

The period produced also a large number of beautiful civic structures. The commercial prosperity of these busy towns is reflected again and again in the construction during the sixteenth century of larger and more magnificent guild halls and town halls, of richer and more elaborate town fountains. In almost all of these, classic forms decorate the essentially Gothic structure. Even as early as 1508, the exquisite bronze monument in Nuremberg, the St. Sebald shrine, by Peter Vischer, though basically Gothic, has occasional details that reveal the new tides in the sea of taste that were flowing over Europe; and in later work the classical elements become more and more distinct, although the intricacy of the composition, the love of picturesque skyline, and the accent on the vertical still remain as evidence of the traditional Gothic. The town halls form an especially interesting series. At Cologne the old Gothic structure was allowed to remain, but there was added to it a new wing with a loggia in which the Roman arcade, with fairly classic orders, unusually restrained for Germany, is combined attractively if erratically with the pointed arch; and new interiors with lavish wooden paneling, in which the modified orders of the time are freely used, were added inside.

At Rothenburg, in 1572, a new town hall was built, unusual in the quiet restraint of its wall surfaces and the more tempered quality of its classical doorways; but the most beautiful example is probably that at Bremen, built in 1612, where the old Gothic hall, a single great rectangle of superb scale, had new window frames and dormers and a new surrounding arcade added to it in a most exquisitely delicate, a most imaginatively complex style based on a modified German Dietterlin kind of detail. Only three years later, the town hall at Augsburg, by Elias Holl, shows a spirit entirely different. Here, for the first time in German civic building, appears something of the real monumentality, something of the definite emphasis on the horizontal, the regular rhythm and serenity of classic form. Yet this was and remained an exceptional building, the product of an individual designer rather than the normal expression of the period.

The other type of work, the aristocratic type, in which a more definite classicization of form is present, characterizes especially the great ducal residences such as those of Heidelberg and Wismar. It was the German nobles who had employed the Italians to produce such works as the Belvedere in Prague, or the extraordinary Early Renaissance doorway of the Piastenschloss at Brieg, and had outdone even the town halls in the luxury of the intricate classic interiors they had added to older buildings. It was natural that the castles should remain of a different character from the ordinary town houses and the city halls, varying from such Italianate courtyard-surrounded buildings as some of those in the Tyrol or the so-called Mint at Munich to works in which, although the high roof of traditional Germany and the rich dormers are found, there is nevertheless a regularity of membering, an attempt at correctness in placing one order over another, a certain heaviness and monumentality, which belonged definitely to the classic tradition. Such a castle as Hämelschenburg is typical. Its windows are regularly spaced and separated by simple pilasters, its high roof comes down at the sides to a long horizontal cornice, and the high dormers which decorate and light it, although with scrolled and elaborated sides, seem none the less solid and impressive.

This early German Renaissance castle style reached its climax in the castle at Heidelberg, where two large wings—one the Otto Heinrichsbau, 1556, the other the Friedrichsbau, 1601—show the combined richness and monumentality of the type. In both there is a correct use of the orders, with windows regularly spaced in the classic custom, but in both the detail is complicated far beyond the Italian or the French manner, with elaborate small-scale rustication and with a substitution of niches with statues for pilasters on the alternate piers. In both there is considerable strapwork and a use of the *gaîne,* so that the whole has an appearance totally unlike any building in any other part of Europe. This we may accept as almost the high-water mark of the German Renaissance.

Forces were at work which were to change the whole make-up and basis of Germanic life and alter its architecture as well. The military rivalry and territorial greed of the nobles found excellent stimulus in the religious struggles and differences to which the Reformation had given rise. International intrigue—on the part of the Holy Roman Empire, the French, and the growing powers of the north—was rampant; the whole medieval equilibrium which had led to the prosperity of the free cities and little independent principalities was facing new strains and stresses too great for it to bear. People losing their sense of security plunged into the most preposterous extravagances of eccentricity in costume and design, of which the prints of the period are sufficient evidence; and all this confusion, cultural and religious, was seized upon as mere additional fuel on the fires of dynastic intrigue. The result was the horror of the Thirty Years' War. In its meaningless slaughter there died not only unnecessary thousands of individuals, but the whole life which had produced the Renaissance in Germany. What was to follow was new and different—the architecture of the Baroque.

In Flanders and the Netherlands, the coming of the Renaissance in the early sixteenth century found a vivid late Gothic tradition deeply installed—a tradition as vital as the Flamboyant of France or Germany, but differing markedly from the French and German types because of the extraordinary local economic developments. The towns which are part of what is now Belgium had been from the early Middle Ages the centers of a prodigiously busy local textile industry, which had been the means of producing a town life more free, more in a sense "modern," than that of almost any other part of Europe, with the possible exception of north Italy. Holland had been less industrial, but it had preserved many of the same liberal and advanced social characteristics, and its limited area and growing population had early forced the Dutch to a remarkably socialized attitude toward land, and to such communal efforts at increased land area as the building of the dikes and pumping the water out of low-lying lands, called *polders,* which could be thus freed for agriculture or cattle raising. Thus these two countries, and to a less extent Denmark, had already by the sixteenth century created a kind of life so different from that of the rest of Europe that even the Late Gothic forms wore a new and strange dress. There was less emphasis on church building, more on the construction of houses and civic buildings, and in these the growing cheapness and availability of glass was rapidly leading up to the use of larger windows than were customary elsewhere. Wealth showed itself in exuberance of carved detail and in the development of a craftsmanship in woodwork, in brick, and terra-cotta, and tile which was largely independent of similar work in other parts of Europe, because devoted chiefly to secular rather than religious ends.

Into this world of busy and prosperous burghers and farmers the Renaissance brought at first changes only superficial. The tall Dutch houses, with their steep gable ends toward the streets, with stone outlining windows and forming copings for gables, could be treated with Renaissance detail almost as readily as with Gothic; and, in fact, the general type persisted in Flanders and Holland much longer than it did elsewhere in Europe, because the newer fashions of the Renaissance and Baroque could flow so easily over the surface of this constant pattern without forcing any radical changes in composition. Windows were greater in number and larger in size than elsewhere, so that they fitted more easily into ordinary classic proportions than did the Gothic windows of Germany or France, and the simple surfaces of brick or of stone which ran between the windows could be considered as belonging equally well to any style at all. Thus both the Netherlands and Holland were spared the artificiality of attempting to reproduce Italian models on the one hand, and, on the other, avoided the worst extremes of German Renaissance phantasy. Superficially there were many resemblances to early German Renaissance forms, as can be seen, for instance, in the books of the German Dietterlin and the Flemish de Vries; yet the more one studies them the more one realizes that, despite the use by both of *gaînes,* of strapwork, and of richly decorated Baroque gables, there was none the less a profound difference, for the Flemish work seems somehow more rooted in the soil, more natural, less forced and self-conscious than the German.

This difference reveals itself even more strongly in the actual constructed work. There is a placid firmness about the Renaissance houses that line the older canals of Amsterdam or Leyden; for, even in the extremely rich Renaissance houses on the Grande Place at Brussels, it was founded on the strength of the economic life of the Low Countries, their common sense, their basic realism, their love for quiet progress without strain—qualities which lasted all through the tragic and disastrous period of the wars of liberation from Spain and the Holy Roman Empire, and indeed were the cause of their final success. Against such firmly based common sense, such true socialized co-operation, such self-possession, all the power and grandeur of Spain was unavailing.

For a people with this foundation the only architecture possible was one in which local materials were dominant, and an architecture which could count always on excellent, careful craftsmanship. Accordingly, the similarity in certain details to the Renaissance details of Germany is fundamentally a deceptive similarity; the moment one finds himself in front of such a building as the Town Hall of Delft, or the early seventeenth-century houses along the canals of Amsterdam, one realizes the striking difference in spirit. The Delft town hall has much of the imaginative naïveté in the use of the classic orders that is to be found in Heidelberg Castle; yet its whole scale is smaller, it looks more solid and earthy, it is essentially human and its basic composition more straightforward. Similarly, though one occasionally finds the obelisks and scrolls of the German gables on the Dutch houses, or along the Belgian streets, the buildings which they decorate, with their large, clear, simple glass areas, their high ceilings and the simple walls that frequently show between, have an unmistakable local character.

Once the Renaissance had taken root in the Low Countries, these differ-ences became even more emphatic. Belgium and the Netherlands seemed to have a greater ability to digest classic form and re-express it in an unpretentious, direct manner, which at the same time combined perfectly with the native traditions. It is interesting to see that, in the Netherlands at least, this ability to take many different artistic impulses, to domesticate them and make them seem at home and part of the landscape, has continued even to the present time, so that the best of the contemporary work, with its large window areas, its beautiful brickwork, and its gay painted trim, takes its place without uneasiness or shock among the seventeenth- and eighteenth-century buildings.

Both Belgium and the Netherlands, moreover, had the good fortune to develop during the sixteenth century a number of architects of taste and skill, whose work went far to assist in this development of a new kind of Renaissance. In Belgium the greatest was probably Cornelis Floris (1514-75)—also known as Cornelis de Vriendt,—whose master work, the Antwerp City Hall (1561-65), is a splendid creation in which classic Doric and Ionic orders of fairly correct proportions are used brilliantly to enframe long ranges of large windows, and the central portion is raised to form a sort of tower. The whole is original, effective, characteristic. The guild houses that front on the *place* before the city hall are similarly varied and vivid, fantastic but somehow restrained as well; and the same is true of the guild houses of Brussels. The Town Hall of Leyden—now, alas, destroyed,—completed by Lieven de Key (1560-1627) toward the end of the sixteenth century, like the slightly earlier City Hall of The Hague, is more naïve but equally interesting, and equally creative in its discovery of new applications for, and new effects from, the classic orders.

The greatest of the Dutch architects was Hendrik de Keyser (1565-1621). In his work all that had been tentative before became definite, full-formed, mature. At last, in complete command of this new modified Dutch classic, he could force it to do his will in any way he pleased. With him architecture became much more than a mere matter of the detail treatment of the front of a building in the traditional shape; it became a matter of the total mass composition. In the series of churches he built at Amsterdam, on which his reputation chiefly rests, he revealed how brilliantly he could handle the contrast of the large mass of the church with its high tower, how magnificently he could handle the balance of plain wall against large window and crowning roof, with what sureness of touch he could place pilasters and buttresses so as best to develop a sense of the whole. The interiors of these churches are as remarkable as their exteriors. Varied in plan, the great simple scale of their high naves, the sure power of the interior pilasters and columns, the sense of control of interior view shown in his treatment of side aisles and transepts—all of this reveals an architect of the first magnitude.

Especially interesting are the de Keyser towers. Holland, like many flat countries, had always been distinguished for its tower building, and for de Keyser the task was clear—to produce towers and spires as impressive and as beautiful as the earlier Gothic examples had been, and yet to make them essential parts of his Renaissance churches. The greater number of de Keyser towers rise as simple square structures to a considerable height. Above this point a series of square and octagonal stages are found, of gradually increasing lightness and delicacy, and the whole is usually crowned by a pyramidal spire or a Baroque finial. Each stage is treated with its own pilasters or columns, and the diminutions in width accented and decorated by urns and obelisks at the corners. These upper portions are frequently framed in wood and covered with metal. They are important not only in themselves as essential parts of the Dutch landscape, but also because they probably were the inspiration for many of the tower types which Wren, a little later, developed so strikingly in England.

The wealth of craftsmanship in Flanders and Holland is nowhere better seen than in the richness and individuality of the secular interiors. Tiles, usually with a white background, painted with patterns in blue, but sometimes also in luster or full color, were used freely as wainscots; wood screens and wainscots of the greatest richness decorated the lower parts of walls or separated the interior spaces of the long narrow houses; and there was a mingling of warmth, of human personal quality, with great lavishness of carving and of color that was unique in Europe, so that the Dutch house of the end of the sixteenth and the beginning of the seventeenth centuries, as we can see it today so beautifully in the clear light of the paintings of Vermeer, had an amenity, a livability, that was a perfect frame for the opulent yet unostentatious life which went on within it. To produce all of this tile, this carved wood, required great numbers of craftsmen trained not only in technique but in design as well, and their influence went far beyond the bounds of their own countries. The Flemish woodcarvers and stone-masons played a great part in the Early Renaissance of England; and Dutch architects, carpenters, sculptors, and potters worked in the British Isles, and far to the north in Denmark and Sweden as well, where much of the Early Renaissance work can be traced to their hands and their brains.

As the course of the Renaissance developed and the classic forms became more and more common, it was only natural that some of this earlier, characteristically Netherlandish charm should disappear, to be replaced by a stricter following of classic canons, a greater attempt to follow the European fashions of the day; but the culmination of this classicizing influence in both Belgium and the Netherlands was to come only later, after the middle of the seventeenth century, and to be part and parcel of the Baroque interna-tionalism which lay ahead.

When Henry VIII came to the throne of England in 1509, the country over which he ruled was still a Gothic country, still largely feudal, still in all the main patterns of its existence medieval. And, despite his own desire for change, his restless search for the new, his devotion to what seemed to him the more advanced Renaissance cultures of France and of Italy, England remained in many ways essentially feudal and essentially medieval for another century. Like Francis I, Henry VIII patronized Italian artists and sought in the tomb which he built for his father in Westminster Abbey to create a new pattern. Torregiano, the sculptor, a schoolmate with Michel-angelo at the Medici Academy, produced in that tomb a work of exquisite beauty, but a work essentially Italian. Giovanni da Maiano made delicate terra-cotta roundels of the heads of great generals surrounded by wreaths, which decorate the octagonal towers of the entrances to Cardinal Wolsey's Hampton Court; but the towers which they adorn are in all other respects Gothic, and the whole of Wolsey's great building was merely a more elabo-rate example of the English Late Gothic residential castle, with grouped and traceried windows, tapestried rooms, and a great hall complete with dais and oriel—an oriel unusually large and unusually rich, to be sure, but still all Gothic in its tracery and its fan vault. Only in occasional details here and there, such as the pendants to the open-timber roof, is there a trace of classic feeling.

The pattern of the Early Renaissance in England, so set, was to continue throughout Henry VIII's reign and well into that of Elizabeth. In all basic respects, the houses and the churches remained Gothic; only in incidental details did early-sixteenth-century England use the new and classic forms. Nevertheless, literary England, learned England, was passionately devoted to

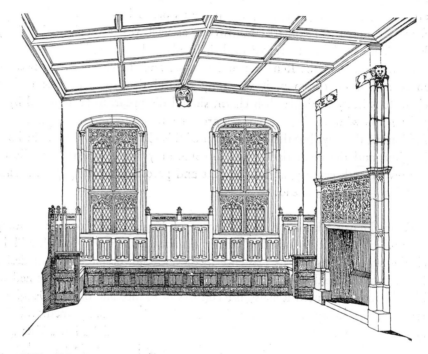

80. THE ABBOT'S HOUSE, MUCHELNEY, SUSSEX; INTERIOR OF THE ABBOT'S PARLOR, SHOWING LINENFOLD PANELING AND BEAMED CEILING. (Garner and Stratton.)

Renaissance ideals. The nobles who built themselves great houses wanted to be classic, but they wanted, too, to be correct, and they feared to change the excellent patterns of domestic architecture which their fathers had developed. The whole period was architecturally one of confused and yet at the same time strangely logical paradox. The large Tudor English house was, so far as comfort was concerned, perhaps the most livable of all of Europe, granted the feudal living system that was current. Its grouped windows, its flexible plan, its many chimneys and large fireplaces were pleasant to live with; its complete freedom in arrangement of rooms, large and small, was an advantage not to be easily renounced. How, then, could all of this purely Gothic scheme of things be combined with the new classicism that was becoming fashionable?

The first answer was, of course, by classicizing details—by adding pilasters or columns on either side of a Tudor-arched mantelpiece or door; by making horizontal moldings with classic profiles; by placing occasional pilasters between the panels of the wainscot. At times the classic additions might be of considerable size, as for instance in the exquisite chancel screen which was built across King's College Chapel at Cambridge at the beginning of the second quarter of the century. The screen is purely classic, probably designed and perhaps even executed by Italian workmen. Its classic detail is impeccable, graceful, combining delicacy with dignity. Yet the chapel itself, which had not been completed more than twenty years, was purely Gothic, and perhaps the noblest example in all England of the developed fan-vaulted Perpendicular church. In all cases, the additions were minor and superficial. The wall treatment of Layer Marney Towers, a characteristic great house of the period, is typical. Pure Tudor in basic design, with grouped Perpendicular traceried windows and battlements, the wall surface is decorated—in the spandrels between the windows and in a band which acts as a cornice—with terra-cotta panels of obviously classic design.

At the same time, the interior detail of houses was in a similar state of transition, but in this work it was less the Italian than the Flemish influence which was paramount. Many Flemish workers came to England, fleeing from Spanish persecution, and the works of Vredeman de Vries seem to have been much followed by them and their patrons. To them was due the quantity of *gaines,* of strapwork, of little pinnacles and scrolls and niches which decorate many a mid-sixteenth-century fireplace, and sit but oddly on the quiet oak surfaces of the wainscots; and to them was due the whole confused pattern of Jacobean interior design, which at times achieved masterpieces of exquisite carved and inlaid woodwork in which these Flemish and Germanic Renaissance forms were completely integrated, and at times descended to carnivals of the crudest elaboration, ill-conceived in design and crudely handled in execution.

By the middle of the century the pattern began to clarify; the Renaissance began to affect basic conception as well as details. Men who had traveled—and it was the custom even then for the sons of the nobility to travel for a year or two in France and Italy as part of their education—could not help realizing that the Renaissance of France and of Italy was a far different thing from the tentative experiments thus far made in England, that the classic feeling was based on matters much more fundamental than the mere use of the classic orders or the following in detail of Flemish or German Renaissance models. To any sensitive person who had seen in Rome the works of the Sangalli, Bramante, and Peruzzi, or the structures that de l'Orme and Bullant were building in France, the basic inconsistency of the English attempts to combine classic detail—often poorly conceived—with Gothic structure and planning must have seemed puerile and unsatisfactory. Regularity, the traveling Englishman must have realized, symmetry, and composition played as important a part in the effect of the Renaissance as did the character of the details. On his return to England, when he too came to build, it was these elements that he now sought to gain. Longleat Hall, built between 1567 and 1578, was typical of the new feeling, for in it not only did the orders decorate the exterior walls in a regular rhythm of evenly spaced window and pier, but also there was complete symmetry in the exterior composition, so that although the details are still crude and naïve the result at last was pure Renaissance.

Yet to produce designs requires more than imported or even native trained carpenters and masons; it requires architects, designers. John Shute was apparently such a one, and the fact that he was sent to Italy to study in 1550, by the Duke of Northumberland, bears witness to the realization of this fact by at least some of the great lords. In 1563 Shute produced his *Chief Groundes of Architecture,* the earliest book published in England in which the orders were accurately shown at large enough scale so that the English workman was at last liberated from the Flemish and German influence. Of Shute's work we know little, but much of that of his contemporary John Thorpe, whose sketches—many of which still remain—show the working of a mind thoroughly architectural, thinking as much in plan as in elevation, and struggling manfully, and at times brilliantly, with the problem of how to impose symmetry on the basic English house plan. Two architects named Smithson are also known to have designed many houses of the time in which the same effort is obvious.

The great difficulty lay in the hall. The traditional English great hall had had its entrance at one end, through the screens, with a service wing opening at the entrance end and the residence rooms opening from the dais at the other end. This, of course, brought the main entrance near one end of the whole composition. How could such a plan be reconciled with classic symmetry? John Thorpe's Kirby Hall shows one characteristic solution. The main building is approached through a courtyard with a central monumental entrance and a vaulted Renaissance arcade. Long galleries, somewhat in the French manner, border the courtyard on each side. The main living portion of the building is at the back of the courtyard, with the hall portion directly on the main axis. Thus the lack of symmetry between the service wings on one side and the residential portion on the other was concealed by the courtyard. The whole of the building is a most delightful and characteristic piece of English seventeenth-century work, preserving in its grouped mullioned windows, its brick walls, and its many chimneys much of the charm of the earlier Late Gothic houses, but with horizontal classic cornices, pilasters widely spaced to decorate the long wings of the court, and an elaborate scrolled cresting and gable ends of strapwork in the German manner, which show the Renaissance feeling.

In smaller houses, similar attempts to gain symmetry were made by placing the hall at one side, with its entrance on the center. But all of these seem somehow forced. The great hall was too large an element to be summarily placed at one side, and a full solution of the problem came finally only because of a change in living conditions that made the old feudal great hall itself an anachronism.

For, feudal as England in many ways remained, the old wholesale living of the feudal castle was slowly passing. In the great halls of earlier castles, the lord and his family ate at least one meal daily with as many as fifty or sixty vassals and dependents. The new economy which was gradually growing up all over Europe, owing to the development of trade and the increasing specialization in crafts, could not, even in the houses of the wealthy, indefinitely stand such a strain. The great estates were becoming less and less patriarchal, self-supporting communities, and more and more of the materials of life and even of food itself were being purchased, as the land of the estates was more and more let out on a system of money rents rather than feudal tenures.

The new ideals called also for the greater importance of private family living. Personality development demanded that, and personality development was one of the great aims of the best type of Renaissance life. Privacy, intimacy, gentleness of manners—all of these were coming to be factors in ordinary life, and none of them could fit well into the chilly great spaces of the old feudal hall. Little by little it was deserted, used only for great parties two or three times a year—the coming of age of a son of the family, a Christmas rout, entertainment of the sovereign, or some such occasion— when at least a pretense of reviving the "good old customs" was made. At other times the hall was forsaken, a great wasteful area, which nevertheless controlled the whole plan of the house, making service difficult and cramping design.

Accordingly, the hall, from being the chief living place of the family, gradually came to be, at first, merely a symbol—to be preserved in the largest houses as a sign of aristocratic standing—or else a mere formal entrance hall. In Wollaton Hall, for instance, by the Smithsons, there is still a great hall, an enormous room directly in the center of the compact block, rising

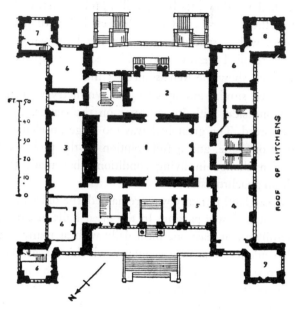

81. WOLLATON HALL, NEAR NOTTINGHAM; PLAN. The Smithsons, architects. (Gotch: *Early Renaissance Architecture in England*.) 1. GREAT HALL. 2. ENTRANCE HALL. 3. GALLERY.

above the roofs of the surrounding rooms and lighted by clerestory windows. Still it is obviously here a great hall, a formalized, symbolic area, no longer the place where the family lived or ate. In Aston Hall, near Birmingham, the final step is taken; the hall is on the center of the front, with the door in its center and stairs on either side—it has become merely the monumental vestibule to the house. As such, its importance waned, and little by little the old tradition disappeared.

Another type of room began to take the place of the old feudal hall as the center of social entertainment—the long gallery. This occurs in many seventeenth-century houses—a long narrow room, sometimes extending the entire length or width of the house, lighted by many windows, comparatively intimate in treatment, with wainscoted walls and an enriched plaster ceiling. For a century or so these long galleries formed an essential part of any large nobleman's house. Yet, as the family ideal became stronger, the intimate personal life of each individual a more important part in the whole national culture, even this gallery, pleasant and lovely as it frequently was gradually disappeared, and houses of what seem to us more livable, more modern types began to be common.

These great houses were usually placed in the center of a beautifully decorated, carefully gardened area of the greatest formality, based largely on the French gardens of the time, with formalized terraces, geometric beds of flowers, and great tree-lined avenues stretching in straight lines across the country. It was all on a scale of enormous grandeur. The garden was a place often more for show than for enjoyment, and there was frequently a definite clash between the formality and the geometric quality of the garden and the many gables, the rich chimneys, and the grouped mullioned windows that still characterized the greater number of houses.

This somewhat confused, but often charming, modified Renaissance of the English rapidly became domesticated over the entire country. It was in no sense limited to great houses; more and more the small manors, the parsonages, the inns, and even the tenant cottages on the estates took on the same general quality. Usually, the smaller the building and the further it was from the great centers, the more was the old Gothic feeling preserved, the Renaissance influence being limited to molding profiles here and there, and occasionally a pilaster-bordered or round-arched entrance door. Much of the most beautiful of the seventeenth-century work is to be found in these smaller buildings. Manifestly the living conditions in the country villages, as in many of the towns, were undergoing a revolutionary change for the better. The new amenities which specialization and growing efficiency were bringing, the freedom which the change to money rents brought in its train, all united to improve the lot of large sections of the population, and this change was reflected in the increased size and decency of cottages and small town houses; so that many an English agricultural center, such as the stone-built villages of the Cotswolds, has even today a feeling of coherent and gracious loveliness which is unique in Europe. Moreover, except in London and perhaps one or two other centers, there was not in England that crowding into walled towns which produced the terrifying congestion of such continental Renaissance cities as Frankfurt or Paris. The country remained dominantly agricultural; the towns were essentially market towns; there was still space for ample planning.

The interior work in the houses, both large and small, is always impeccable in craftsmanship, and reveals the integrity and artistic conscience of the English workman. Especially remarkable is the woodwork of wainscot and screen, in which Renaissance details—acanthus scrolls, occasional strapwork, little round arched panels, medallions, and vertical pilasters—are combined in the most delightful and natural way with the linen-fold and the simple panel patterns of the Late Gothic. The plasterwork is also remarkable, and the extraordinary number of beautiful examples of richly decorated plaster ceilings reveals how broadly spread this skill was in the England of that time.

82. STONE-BUILT COTSWOLD COTTAGES IN WILLERSLEY, GLOUCESTERSHIRE; drawing by Sidney R. Jones. (Holme: *Old English Country Cottages*.)

Even comparatively modest houses will often have a decorated frieze of plaster around the top of the room, and in houses of any pretension room after room has ceilings enhanced by interlacing moldings, combinations of squares, diamonds, and polygons, freely drawn and modeled vine patterns, little heraldic figures, and touches of naturalistic foliage, which are full of an exciting variety and verve.

Nevertheless, despite all of this excellent transitional Renaissance crafts-manship, there were places where the Gothic still lived on all through the sixteenth and well into the seventeenth century. Occasional houses in the remoter parts show no signs whatsoever of the new style, and the new work built in Oxford during this period seems almost self-consciously Gothic, especially the extraordinarily elaborate fan-vaulted interiors of the stair hall of Christ Church at Oxford, 1640.

A change from all of this world of tentative though charming transitional classic detail was inevitable. English interests were increasingly bound up with those of the continental powers. English scholarship was in constant and close touch with continental Renaissance writings, and young Englishmen were more and more commonly traveling widely through France and Italy. The change to a new and more classic type of Renaissance came almost suddenly, shortly before the middle of the seventeenth century, and largely through the work and the influence of one individual, Inigo Jones (1573-1652). A naturally imaginative draftsman, he came first into public notice in connection with the court masques. These lavish entertainments depended largely for their effect upon the most gorgeous scenery and costumes which the time could produce, for, unlike the drama of the period, the masques demanded visual beauty and visual illusion, in addition to the magic of their poetry and their music. His designs for these masques, many of which are still preserved, show not only an exquisite sense of composition, but also a sophisticated knowledge of the theatrical designs of contemporary Italy. It is not strange, then, that in 1612, when the death of his patron, Prince Henry, left him without work, he set out for Italy, where he remained for three years. On his return, James I appointed him Surveyor-General—that is, architect-in-chief of the entire royal undertakings. Jones had developed in Italy a passion for the work and the writings of Palladio; and the Palladian teachings, of strong classic propriety combined with dignified reticence, strong composition, and a complete renunciation of the broken curves and tortured detail of the Baroque which was beginning, seemed to him especially necessary in England, where the combination of Gothic, Italian, Flemish, and German influences was producing work which, however attractive, was often incoherent and sometimes forced and eccentric.

Jones, too, had the good fortune to be presented almost at once with a superb opportunity—the complete design of a great palace at Whitehall on the site of the old palace which had suffered from fire. For this, Jones developed an enormous scheme of seven courts—six small, and one in the center, large. In plan it was based, obviously, on some of the schemes which de l'Orme had made for the Tuileries in Paris. In it there is not a trace of the old English house or palace conception. With this one design Inigo Jones broke forever from the earlier feudal great-hall type of building. Only one small section of the palace was ever built, the famous Banqueting Hall at Whitehall, begun in 1619 and finished three years later; and, just as the plan of the entire scheme was revolutionary, so were, even more, the exterior and the interior of the banqueting hall. Its two chief stories have simple windows of classic proportion, surrounded by classic architraves and crowned by classic cornices, ranged in regular rhythms, with correctly proportioned engaged columns and pilasters between them. The lower floor is Ionic, the upper floor Corinthian, and the whole is topped by a classic balustrade. In the purity of its classic composition it may well be compared with much of the work of Jones's master, Palladio; in subtlety of treatment it is in some ways even more advanced. Wishing to give an emphasis to the center without disturbing the regularity of the whole, he made the orders decorating the four central piers engaged columns, while those at the ends are pilasters; this refinement is characteristic of his imaginative quality.

Jones designed a number of other works of importance, in which the same qualities of reticence and monumentality are to be found. The Queen's House at Greenwich is even more delicate and restrained than the Banqueting Hall. In 1631 he designed the first of London's beautiful squares, that of Covent Garden, the quiet arcades of which are climaxed by the powerful Tuscan portico of St. Paul's Church; and during the period from 1630 to the outbreak of the Revolution in 1642 he also designed a number of country houses, in which all of the elements of the later English Renaissance and Baroque houses are to be found in a remarkably developed form. In general, these houses are simple symmetrical blocks, without courts or great projection to the wings, with rooms large, to be sure, but still definitely rooms for family living and entertaining, and not great feudal halls. The great hall has finally disappeared completely. In its place there is usually a central entrance leading to a monumental vestibule, richly decorated classic stairs, and ranges of symmetrically disposed rooms. The rooms are almost all wainscoted in large simple panels, with bold projecting moldings. Classic cornices run around at the ceiling, and the ceilings themselves use the natural craft skill of the English plasterers in ways that are classic and monumental, founded originally on the inspiration of the lavish Renaissance ceilings of Italy. The outside walls are usually of simple brick, often with stone *quoins* (stones at the corner, usually alternately long and short, set one above the other, to strengthen the corner both practically and aesthetically), and there is often a decoration around the door of rather quiet Baroque character. The roofs, of slate, are generally hipped; and the chimneys, instead of having the multiple flues of Elizabethan and Jacobean work, are great masses of simple brick, crowned with a cornice.

Thus, the English great house, as designed by Jones, became for the first

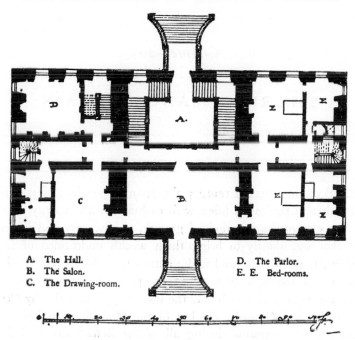

A. The Hall.
B. The Salon.
C. The Drawing-room.

D. The Parlor.
E. E. Bed-rooms.

83. COLESHILL, BERKSHIRE; PLAN, CHARACTERISTIC OF THE INIGO JONES
TRADITION. (Gotch: *Old English Houses.*)

time the dignified gentleman's residence, fundamentally unostentatious,
planned for use as a residence and not as a great feudal center. Later followers of Jones still further refined and simplified the type, cutting its scale
to even more intimate and human proportions, until a type of English
manor was developed which was the prototype of the great houses of
late-seventeenth-century and early-eighteenth-century Virginia and Massachusetts.

The Revolution put an end to Jones's work, as it did to almost all building
in the country, and Jones died before the Restoration in 1660. Yet in his
work he succeeded in setting the course English architecture was to follow
for another century, and it was largely because of him that the later architecture of the Baroque period followed rather the serious lines that Palladio
had set than the vagaries of the developed Baroque of Bernini or Borromini.

Chapter 20

THE RENAISSANCE IN SPAIN

AT the end of the fifteenth century the Spanish people, at last masters of the entire Iberian peninsula, filled with enthusiasm and energy, were starting on that extraordinary period of growth, of discovery and imperial expansion, that was shortly to bring them wealth undreamed of from the mines of Peru and Mexico, and make almost the whole New World south of what is now the State of Georgia the property either of Spain or of Portugal. The same year which saw the discovery of America by Columbus saw also the fall of Granada, the last of the Moorish strongholds, so that the entire Iberian peninsula during all of the Renaissance period was at last Christian again. Yet, though the Moorish power had fallen, Moorish influence still remained active, for the Moors themselves were not finally expelled from Spain for over a century; and the superb craftsmanship of Moorish carpenters, cabinetmakers, and potters, together with the fact that already in the Gothic period works of combined Moorish and Christian influence called *Mudejar* had been common, gave to the entire output of Spanish Renaissance architecture a unique character.

Nor must the influence of the land itself be forgotten. Spain was, and is still, a land of the most vivid and dramatic contrasts—windswept and barren upland plateaus, rocky and forbidding mountains, valleys of great fertility; cold and blustery in the northern uplands, warm and balmy and almost tropical along the southern Mediterranean shore. It was a country, too, with a rich and confused cultural background; Roman, Visigoth, Moor, and later the Christian chivalry of the conquering kingdoms had all left their mark; and the fifteenth-century inhabitants, many with mixed blood from all of these sources, had been welded together by the Moorish wars into a strange and complex brotherhood, fanatical in its devotion to military prowess, to the idea of an aristocracy almost divinely appointed, and to the church. All of this gave the Spaniard a certain driving intensity of feeling, a certain dynamism, a special kind of dramatic power, that was in a sense the human analogy of the drama of his natural surroundings. None of the quiet regularity and delicacy of the north Italian Renaissance could ever satisfy him; he must have something with more definite life, more violent contrasts.

Nevertheless, the Renaissance, which finally arrived in Spain about the end of the fifteenth century, came directly from Italy; for Spanish bonds with the Roman church were strong, and the Spanish ruling house claimed—and for many years preserved—political hegemony over parts of Italy itself. Thus Spaniards knew Italy, and Italy—sometimes to its distress, as when Charles V sacked Rome in 1527—knew Spaniards. A goldsmith, Pedro Diez, who worked in Italy for some years and returned to Spain about 1460, is supposed to have been the first to bring into the peninsula something of the Italian feeling and a few minor fragments of Italian detail.

The Early Renaissance in Spain is usually termed the *Plateresque*. Some people base this on the fact that Diez had been a goldsmith, a *platero*, but it is more likely that the name came from the circumstance that so much of the architectural detail of the Early Renaissance has the intricacy, the delicacy, the surface quality of goldsmith work rather than the architectonic character of architecture. The connection of Diez with the style is indeed slight, for there is little Renaissance work in Spain that can be dated prior to 1500; and the real impetus seems rather to have come from the tomb of Ferdinand and Isabella in the royal chapel at Granada, carved by Bartolomé Ordóñez but probably designed by the Italian Dominico Fancelli, for whom Ordóñez had worked earlier in Genoa. This tomb was built in the early years of the sixteenth century, and after it more and more work of Renaissance character began to be erected in all portions of Spain. Various Italians were working there, and, as we can see from the cases of both Diez and Ordóñez, many Spaniards had been working in Italy as well; so that, once the long reign of the Gothic tradition had been broken, the natural extravagance of the time and the people led to enormous amounts of building in the new style, especially in Salamanca, Toledo, Granada, and Seville.

The qualities of Plateresque architecture are the inevitable results of its makers and their background. Borrowing superficial details from the Early Renaissance of Italy—the use of the orders, the classic moldings, acanthus scrolls, candelabrum shafts, for instance,—it transformed them all in the search for the dramatic contrast it loved. Moorish ways of composing exerted a tremendous influence. Tiles of Moorish manufacture, and often still preserving Moorish patterns, were used widely for floors and wainscots; and that Moorish skill in carpentry which had produced such exquisitely lovely and intricate paneling of many-pointed stars and intersecting lines found ready use in the new Renaissance buildings, transforming the coffered ceilings of Italy into the many planes and complex carving of those wooden ceilings which are called *artesonados* (from *artesón,* a kneading trough). The Moors had loved to carry the decoration around a door, up the wall clear to its top; so the Early Renaissance architects of Spain did likewise, and made of the door merely an incident in a centerpiece of rich decoration that covered the whole height of the wall. The Moors had loved the contrast of plain wall without cornice or molding, with lavishly decorated notes at doors and windows; so also the Spanish architects of the first half of the sixteenth century often left the greatest area of the wall simple and undecorated, concentrating their ornament around the openings.

The elaborate Late Gothic of Spain, which owed so much to Flemish and German influence, left its mark as well, and varied forms of Gothic crestings and cuspings, pinnacles, and tracery forms continue in use or are shifted and changed into a new guise. Ribbed vaults continue to be built, and certain architects like Enrique de Egas worked equally and apparently with equal facility in both styles—the rich Late Gothic or the new Plateresque. When Granada Cathedral was begun in 1520, Enrique de Egas started it as a Gothic church; his successor Diego de Siloë, who followed in 1525, changed over into Renaissance and decorated the clustered piers of the Gothic structure with classic bases, beautiful Corinthian capitals, delicate variations of the classic entablature. In Seville the Gothic was even longer-lived, and good Gothic work was built there as late as 1580, although secular work by this time was entirely Renaissance.

The greatest amount of Early Renaissance church work was in the nature of screens, chapels, and altars and altarpieces or *retablos.* In all of this work the Spanish exuberance, the love of surface decoration, the passion for dynamic line had almost unlimited opportunity. Even more than in Italy, sculpture and architecture became one thing, for the Spanish taste for the dramatic led to an unusual amount of figure sculpture and even figure ornament. Wherever possible, the Spanish designer substituted human figures for the Italian foliage ornament. If figures were too difficult or the scale was too small, animals or birds were used—everything must be alive. There was, of course, foliated ornament, in capitals and bands and friezes, but most of it was listless and uninteresting. That which excited the maker and the designer, and through the contagion of its power remains still thrilling, is in Spanish work always animal or human.

If we except such purely Italian compositions as the altarpiece which Francisco Niculoso of Pisa did in a chapel in the Alcázar at Seville, in colored tile (*azulejos*), the individuality of the Spanish work becomes apparent at once. The altarpieces frequently climb, story after story, high up the rising chapel walls almost to the vault; each story has its columns and its entablature, and each surrounds a relief or a series of reliefs. The play of light and shadow over the deep carving is extraordinarily complex and vivid, especially if the carving was gilded and polychromed, as it usually was. Nevertheless, the main decorative forms are clear and sure, carrying through and articulating the whole complexity into one. In the chapel screens one comes upon another striking Spanish element, for the chapel screens were then almost all of iron and reveal the amazing skill of the Spanish decorative ironworkers. These screens, called *rejas,* as the whole art is called *rejeria,* in the Early Renaissance work are generally of wrought iron, though occasional cast elements appear in later work. They usually consist of vertical uprights, closely spaced, molded like extremely elongated balusters and broken here and there by widely projecting moldings that give in the repeated bars interesting broken horizontal lines, carrying across and tying together the whole rich composition. At the top these uprights support an entablature of metal moldings, often with a pierced frieze, and the richest possible cresting of wrought iron—scrolls, figures, leaves and flowers, decorative finials—crowns the whole. One of the earliest of *rejas* is also one of the greatest—the tremendous screen which closes off the royal chapel at Granada—and these chapel screens again and again give the interior of the great Spanish churches a mystery, a richness, and an individuality that are unique.

The same general type of metalwork is used commonly on house exteriors also, as window guards or as balcony railings; but it is interesting to note that the extraordinary decorative skill of the Spanish designers always keeps the *rejeria* simple when the architectural surroundings of carved stone are complicated, and only uses the richer forms when the window that is screened or the balcony that is railed are on walls of perfectly plain, simple, undecorated stone.

The building types which grew up in this new and prodigal country were largely mere modifications of earlier and traditional forms. As in the Moorish house, the central court or *patio* became an essential portion of all but the smallest dwellings, and in the arcades that surround these patios the Spanish designers tried some of their most original and charming experiments in blending Gothic ideas with Moorish intricacy and Renaissance details. Thus, sometimes a lower story of classic columns will carry an upper arcade with Gothic arches, and in many cases the classic column capital will have a long bracket beam over it to reduce the span of the wooden balcony floor above. The court of the Infantada at Guadalajara, long since taken from its original position and now in Paris, is characteristic.

Exteriors, too, show the same zest, the same confusion of influences, in their detail. Enrique de Egas decorated the long stone front of his Hospital of Santa Cruz in Toledo with a rich door and window combination in which classic orders, Gothic moldings, Gothic figures under canopies, and classic entablatures form a focus almost bewilderingly rich yet decoratively sound; and again and again in the smaller houses and palaces of the period the doorways have a similar lavish decoration, which runs up to the top of the wall. Typical examples, more restrained perhaps than some, which show perfectly the ideals of the designer, are two doors to the University buildings at Salamanca—the great main door, with its tier above tier of heraldic shields and intricate surface scroll ornament, its profuse pierced cresting, and its double arched doors; and the little doorway to the Irish College, more modest in scale but equally brilliant as a decorative composition.

In the Saragossa region, carved wood plays a great part in Spanish exteriors, producing magnificent bracketed cornices of extreme richness, like that of the *Lonja,* or Exchange, and the Argillo palace, or in the form of elaborately carved balcony brackets. Elsewhere wood is chiefly used for interiors. The marvelous *artesonados,* in which the geometric interlaces of Mohammedan art are combined with classic coffers, have already been mentioned; but elaborate wall paneling is also found, and the Golden Hall of the *Audiencia* or Court House at Valencia, with its lovely open arcade and its rich wood wainscot, shows with what skill.

Nevertheless, soberer, more classic, more architectonic design was bound to develop. Charles V's Italian adventures and ambitions had their cultural side as well. Thus the sculptor and architect Alonso Berruguete spent fifteen years in Italy studying with both Bramante and Michelangelo, returning in 1520 to Spain, where his work exerted a tremendous influence. Pedro de Ibarra followed him in the generally more classical coloring of his design; and the courtyard of the Irish College at Salamanca, although still lavish in detail, has a serenity, a consistency in its combination of classic columns below and Renaissance candelabrum-shaft colonnettes above, which shows the line that fashion was taking. In the University by Rodrigo Gil de Hontañon and the Archbishop's Palace by Covarrubias at Alcalá de Henares, the designers went one step further. The last of the Gothic feeling has departed and obvious Moorish borrowings are no longer apparent. The courtyards are quiet, the Corinthian columns with varied but consistent capitals carry bracket beams, but the whole is schooled and disciplined. Proportion is at last beginning to take its place with lavishness of decoration as an essential means of architectural design.

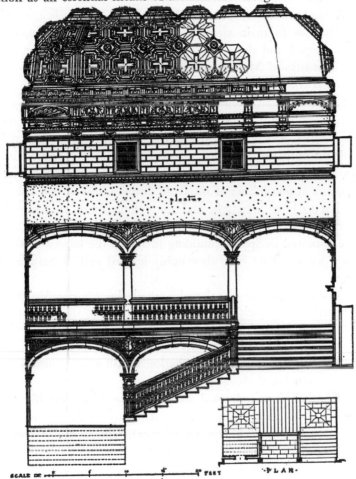

84. ARCHBISHOP'S PALACE, ALCALÁ DE HENARES; SECTION THROUGH STAIR
Covarrubias, architect. (Byne and Stapley: *Spanish Architecture of the Sixteenth Century*.)

The ideals of Charles V himself were entirely along these more classic lines. Diego de Siloë had shown in his Granada Cathedral work of 1525 something of the beauty that lay in classic detail, even when used in a non-classic way; and Diego de Riano, in the *Ayuntamiento* or Town Hall of Seville, had succeeded about the same time in giving his work not only the decorative lavishness which was characteristic of Spain, but also a sober and well-proportioned architectonic basis for this ornament. In 1527 Charles V started a new Alhambra, tearing down a large section of the old Moorish palace to get space for it. His original plan was to destroy the whole, but fortunately this was never carried out, so that the best portions of the Moorish Alhambra still remain to us. The palace which he began and never completed had as its main element a square block of buildings, entered through developed and decorated entrance pavilions—no longer the mere decorated doorways of Moorish tradition in a classic guise—and enclosing a large circular court surrounded by a two-story colonnade. In the planning of the whole there is an attention to axial symmetry, an attempt at monumental grandeur, and a logical yet beautiful relation of interior rooms of interesting shapes, which all form a new note in the Spanish Renaissance. The pavilions, with their coupled pilasters and columns and their arched entrances, are naïve in detail but monumental in conception; some notion of the compositional possibilities of the large simple forms of true classic work seems at last to have been felt, and the colonnade of the court itself is both pure and correct in detail and finely proportioned. Here for the first time there appeared in Spain a building in which the lessons of the Italian Renaissance seem to have been thoroughly learned and its beauties entirely appreciated.

In Toledo, the Alcázar was largely rebuilt by Charles V. Completely destroyed during the tragic civil war, it still remains in pictures to show a simpler, a more natural, but an equally sure application of classic form; and its courtyards, surrounded by two tiers of arcades on slender Corinthian columns, had the classicism of the Charles V Alhambra court without its derivative or even banal characteristics.

Yet, if Charles V was devoted to the Italian idealisms, his successor, Philip II, was even more passionately attached to them; and with a grim fanaticism almost if not entirely pathological, which reveals one side of the intense Spanish character, he set out to show that all the previous Spanish Renaissance work was worthless because it was not Roman. Perhaps himself a most typical example of the extremes to which the Spanish are addicted, he nevertheless set himself the task of weeding out every last element of a purely Spanish nature from the architecture of his time. The result was a style personal to him rather than to Spain, with his disciplined power and something of his fanatical asceticism, Italianesque if not Italian, the only truly classical High Renaissance which Spain ever developed. It produced, significantly, but one great monument, the Escorial, a unified composition containing, besides a royal palace, a college and a monastery grouped around a central church. But, in addition to being a unique monument, the Escorial was also one of the greatest examples of formalized and unified planning which the world up to that time had known; it was as though, almost because of its solitary eminence, into it had been poured with a characteristically Spanish intensity all the building skill, all the

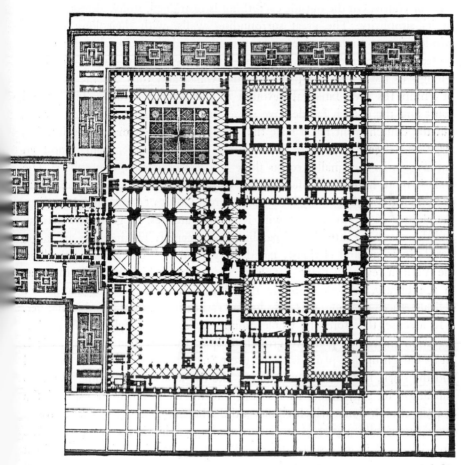

85. THE ESCORIAL, NEAR MADRID; PLAN. Juan Bautista and Juan de Herrera, architects. (Byne and Stapley.)

imaginative genius, which the time possessed. It became one of the noble achievements of man's building ability anywhere.

Conceived and carried on first by Juan Bautista, and later finished by Juan de Herrera, it took thirty years to complete, from 1550 to 1580. The remarkable thing is that during this long period of construction the artistic ideals it expressed remained so consistent and so definite. The Escorial forms a rectangle 675 feet wide and 525 feet deep. One enters, through an entrance pavilion, into a tremendous central court, at the end of which rises the powerful façade of the church. To the right lies the monastery, to the left the college and the royal palace, all grouped around their own separate interior courts. On the outside everything is restrained, stony, almost craglike in its simplicity. The great surrounding walls, with their long rows of windows, are emphasized by corner towers and the colossal order of the central entrance motif; but the dome and towers of the church are large enough to rise above the plain external walls, and thus become a symbol of Philip II's own fanatical devotion to the Roman Church. The central court and the church façade have something of the same restrained power, but the church front has a scale that is gigantic, which makes the interior, large and dignified as it is in its purely Roman scheme, seem almost an anticlimax. In the smaller courts there is a less oppressive atmosphere. The scale is more human; one feels at last within them that here is a possibility of human living. Especially lovely is the great Court of the Four Evangelists, the cloister of the monastery, with its simple arcades, its geometric garden, and the charming little domed pavilion in the center. The interiors are large, simple in form, and obviously based in type on the contemporary work in the Vatican, even to many details of decoration, which in some cases, as in the library, is extraordinarily rich, but rich in the Italian manner of delicate stucco and gorgeous polychromy rather than in the Spanish manner.

In a sense, therefore, the whole monument seems in style almost an importation instead of a native growth, despite the fact that—placed as it is on its barren upland plain, with the great Spanish clouds sweeping overhead and the stark, rocky landscape around, like the landscapes in some El Greco paintings—its gray walls, its restrained form, its towering roofs, and the Roman church dome which climaxes the whole somehow seem perfectly at home, essentially a part of their surroundings. This is the paradox of the Escorial, as it is in a sense the paradox of the Philip II ideals, and in a sense the paradox of much of Spanish Renaissance culture: on the one hand a passionate devotion to an Italianate church, a wistful longing for the serenity of Italian culture; and on the other a native background savage, sometimes almost pagan, and founded deep in the contrasting ideals of Roman, of Visigoth, and of Moor. The greatness of the Escorial, like the greatness of many architectural masterpieces, lies on planes far above national differences. The Escorial is interesting as an expression of the Spanish paradox, but it is great only because of the superbly imaginative quality of its plan, the basic simplicity of scheme which underlies its complexity, the perfect adjustment of its parts to the purpose and the appearance of the whole, and the brilliant way in which all of its manifold details are disciplined to lead inevitably to its climax, the church. The relative sizes of its courts, the manner in which its parts are distinguished from each other, the magnificent handling of scale, the variety and yet the unity, all of these make the Escorial one of the greatest architectural creations of its time.

The architectural development in Portugal somewhat paralleled that in Spain. Portugal too had its own Plateresque, its own tentative applications of Italianesque forms to native structures; but the underlying basis in Portugal was different, for the end of the Gothic period had seen in Portugal an extraordinarily imaginative kind of Flamboyant Gothic developed, known as the *Manuelino* style, in which the buttresses, the tracery, the pointed arches, and the grouped moldings of the Gothic are surrounded and sometimes almost smothered under great rounded masses of the richest ornament, in which ropes and figures and foliage are combined in a theatrically effective, almost unreal, manner. The Manuelino style, which had reached its Gothic climax in the monastery at Belem, appeared in a Plateresque guise with many Renaissance details in the great monastery at Thomar. The architect, João de Castilho, who had designed the Late Gothic work of Belem and the even richer similar work at Batalha, was also the architect at Thomar, built between 1520 and 1530, where, characteristically enough, parts like the church gates seem almost pure Gothic, while other parts like some of the courts and the details around some of the windows are just as definitely pure Renaissance. Elsewhere, in smaller work, there is much more resemblance to contemporary work in the neighboring kingdom of Spain, though everywhere something of that quality of luxurious and almost unlicensed imagination which gave rise to the amazing exuberance of the Manuelino style is to be found. Of sixteenth-century High Renaissance architecture there is scarcely a trace in Portugal. The classicizing tendency did not come in until later, in the Baroque period, under the direct influence of imported Italian architects.

Thus, in the Iberian peninsula, the Renaissance style during the sixteenth century developed to produce the exquisite, rich, but perhaps superficial style of the Plateresque, to bloom briefly in the ascetic grandeur of the High Renaissance of Philip II; but the blossoming, great as it was, seems almost like that of a foreign graft on a native plant. The High Renaissance was never at home in Spain, for the qualities of restraint, of disciplined form, of architectonic logic, which are its great characteristics, were not Spanish virtues, and all the Spanish genius, which had flowered in buildings of many different types, in many different styles, from the Alhambra on the one hand to the Cathedral of Seville on the other, could find little opportunity for self-expression in the quiet forms of the High Renaissance. Once the heavy hand of Philip II had been removed, there came the reaction, partly back to a kind of developed Plateresque, and later into the extraordinary richness of the Spanish Baroque.

The Architecture of Further Asia

Interlude C

THE ARCHITECTURE OF FURTHER ASIA

FROM the earliest times, India had its own highly developed civilizations. The excavations at Mohenjo-Daro and Harappa have shown that at least as early as the third millennium B.C. there was in the Indus valley a city-building culture closely related in many ways to the contemporary culture of the Tigro-Euphrates valley; there are evidences that both were local variations of a general central Asian primitive civilization which spread over vast areas the archaeology of which is still but vaguely known. We are aware, too, that various peoples from the north came down through the Himalayan passes into the warm and fertile lowlands of the Indian peninsula;—the Dravidians, whom the Aryan invaders found inhabiting the country, were apparently themselves immigrants of an earlier time who had mixed with the still earlier peoples, much as the first waves of newcomers from the north into the Mediterranean mixed with the local tribes there.

The later Aryan invasion is better known, though its details are still legendary; for, although the power of the former Sanskrit-speaking rulers was limited to the northern half of the country, the Aryan settlers themselves scattered widely over the peninsula, establishing small semifeudal states. By the force of their imagination and character, by the purity and sincerity of their religious and philosophical beliefs, they exerted a cultural sway far broader than their political power, and gave a dominant element to that culture which became the characteristic expression of historic India. Accordingly, behind all the varied religious and philosophical faiths of India and of those parts of Asia which came under Indian influence, there is always the same underlying background—the Vedic hymns and the early Sanskrit religious writings.

This fact is of profound significance even in the architecture, for it is impossible to gain any true understanding of the development of Indian buildings without realizing something of the ascendancy of mystical idealism in Indian art and the importance of religious symbolism in the building forms. To the Indian, the whole world of natural phenomena is hardly more than a fortuitous event, ruled by its own mundane laws, to be sure, but interesting and significant to the religious man (and every man was supposed to be religious) merely as it expressed or gave a foretaste of that underlying unitary reality which, undisturbed by chance, was not only the essence of the divine but somehow also the essence of the human soul and of all of nature. To the Indian philosopher, perhaps more strongly than to one of any other race, was given a vivid appreciation of the eternal differences between the subject who sees and the things seen; but, paradoxically enough, the Indian also realized that the things seen existed, as it were, only for the seer, and were in a sense manifestations of him, just as all of nature was a manifestation of the single divine reality—the absolute peace, absolute truth, absolute bliss. The artist, therefore, or the architect must infuse both himself and deity into his creations, and they have meaning to the observer only as he too is able to merge himself in them, so that they become a part of him as he becomes a part of them. This intermingling, this complete identification, is to the Indian the only valid aesthetic experience.

It is thus clear that it is fruitless to seek in Indian architecture for those qualities of structural logic inherent in the close relationship of scientific construction and appearance which have formed so much of the content of Western architectures; for the Hindu architect counts no cost too great, no extravagance too excessive, if thereby more of this almost hypnotic identification can be achieved. Thus we get the endless repetitions of molding on molding, of form on form, and sculptural decoration so enormous in quantity as to defy all but the most patient analysis. It is only by long contemplation that little by little the meanings become clear, the complexities resolve themselves into a unity, and the endlessly differing manifestations of the *Karma,* or physical considerations and results of the building, reveal themselves as merely crowded revelations of the single and unitary truth.

The earlier Aryan architecture must have been almost entirely of wood, for it is wooden constructional forms which generate, time after time, the controlling features of Indian detail. The curved lines of window tops and roofs go back to a primitive system of building, with curved wooden rafters and a roof of reeds; it is natural, therefore, that almost all the great cave-temple interiors built for both Buddhist and Brahmanist worship, and dating perhaps from the period 200 B.C. to 600 A.D., have great high curved roofs the vaulted appearance of which is purely accidental, for they are carved with carefully executed reproductions of the earlier wooden framing and covering.

Into this world of wooden building came two different influences from the north: one from Persia, that of the colonnaded halls of Persepolis or Susa, with their column capitals of coupled horses or bulls; the other from Greece, through the conquests of Alexander the Great and the Greek kingdoms which were set up in northwest India after his death. Although recent research has tended to discount the importance of the contributions of classic architecture to Indian detail, and to restrict this influence to a small area around Gandhara, nevertheless it is hard to deny that certain ways of carving leaf ornaments, certain tricks of scale decoration on bases and moldings, owe their origin to these two exterior forces, for the Greco-Buddhist art of Gandhara was one of the greatest early bonds between the West and the East.

Indian architecture began to take definite form only after the emperor Asoka had made Buddhism the official religion of India in the third century B.C., and most of the great Indian monuments of the next 600 years are Buddhist buildings. These take three chief types: first, the meeting hall or *chaitya* hall; second, the *vihara* or monastery; and, third, the *tope* or *stupa*, a development of the primitive tumulus.

The characteristic chaitya is a hall with a round-arched top, imitating in stone its wooden original, often with side aisles, and ending in an apse in which there is a small stupa as a symbol of the Buddha. The greatest of these halls are in the rock-cut temple groups of Ajanta and Elephanta. Lighted entirely from the front, they have a great horseshoe-arch-shaped window over the entrance; nowhere is the wooden origin of the form more clearly expressed than in its enclosing projecting hood. The decoration is simple and the forms of the whole are dignified, but there is considerable rich sculptural carving, often of an extremely naturalistic type. These cave temples probably represent the ordinary meeting halls of the early Buddhist village, which because of their fragile temporary materials have all disappeared. Occasional ruins of actual constructed examples do, however, exist.

The viharas were of two types. In one a stepped pyramid was constructed, which gave a series of terraces on each of which were the cells of the monks, in long lines around the mass. Later, after this form itself had acquired a certain sanctity, little shrines containing statues of Buddha began to replace the earlier monks' cells, and the edifice became a pure temple. The great Javanese temple of Borobudur, dating probably from the seventh century, is such a structure. The other type of monastery had its cells opening on colonnades around a court, and is well represented in rock-cut examples in the cave groups.

The stupa or tope was reserved for the most sacred relics of the Buddha. It consisted of a great hemispherical construction, usually of brick, built around an inaccessible central chamber in which the relic was placed. The whole was in a circular enclosure surrounded by a railing, and entered through four gates, at the north, south, east, and west. The tope at Sanchi, from the third century A.D., is the best preserved, and the exquisite workmanship on its railing and its gates, carved with vivid Buddhist reliefs, reveals both the amazing skill of the Indian sculptors and stonecutters and the particular combination of imaginative realism and exaggeration which were the result of the artists' philosophical approach. The tope railings and gates show, too, as the rock-cut temples do, the purely wooden structural basis of the whole design. They are mere stone representations of wooden details. Later, the hemispherical part of the tope form was raised higher and higher on a vertical drum, until an almost towerlike form resulted; this high stupa became a common element in Buddhist architecture all over eastern Asia.

But there were other forces at work in this early period. Buddhism never completely superseded Brahmanism, and Brahman religious ideas were developing their own special architectural expressions. Each religion deeply influenced the other, in architecture as in doctrine; and, although some of the earlier Brahman temple caves are only to be differentiated from the Buddhist caves by the fact that a statue of the deity replaces the Buddhist stupa in the apse, it is also true that in the famous temple of Bodhgaya, one of the most sacred sites in all the Buddhist world, the high, pyramidal structure, lined with horizontal moldings and rich with ornament, is of definitely Brahman origin.

The early Brahman temples apparently included a shrine and a hall or porch. The shrine was often roofed with a corbeled vault of stone, and in the effort to give this the greatest possible stability the slope of the vault sides was very slight and its height therefore very great. Naturally its exterior rose high into the air, and over this basic idea the Hindu love of symbolization played with striking results. In the development of this form, the obvious symbol of creation, the *lingam,* had an important place, and combined with it was the other great Indian nature symbol, the mystic lotus; a great many Indian temple forms, complicated as they may seem, can be analyzed into these two elements—the one leading to the use of great vertical shapes; the other to the elaborate oval finials with which they are frequently crowned.

Often the hall or porch was reduplicated on four sides, giving a kind of star-shaped plan, and over these porches two smaller towers—or, rather, masses of masonry—were built. The temple was usually placed in an enclosure entered by gates, and over each gate an additional high structure, the *gopuram*, was erected, so that the silhouette became immensely varied and powerful, the goourams and the smaller towers over the porch leading

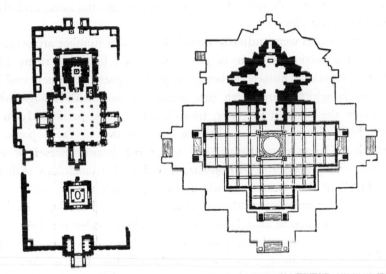

86. CHARACTERISTIC INDIAN TEMPLE PLANS. *Left:* GREAT TEMPLE AT PURUDKUL. *Right:* GREAT TEMPLE AT BAILLUR. (Fergusson: *A History of Indian and Eastern Architecture.*)

up inevitably to the great *vimana,* the tower over the shrine itself. In later periods, flat-roofed, pillared halls were added, connecting the gates with the shrine, and often smaller shrines to other deities were built within the same enclosure, as well as a great tank for ritual bathing; so that the final result, as seen in the seventeenth-century temple at Madura, was almost a religious city in itself.

Over these elements the Indian decorative genius played with the most fantastic and yet disciplined imagination. Especially characteristic is the horizontal banding of these great vertical masses, with line on line of projecting molding, and band on band of rich sculpture in which all the activity of life as well as all the legends of the gods are portrayed—for, according to the Indian, all of life is divine. The details of the design were controlled by strict canons, and carefully preserved from age to age. Each molding had its own name; each was arranged in accordance with a definite rule. The vertical surfaces were broken, too, by projections; bays and, as it were, "dormer windows" gave variety to the plan and carried vertical bands of light and shadow up the great forms, to contrast with and accent the horizontal moldings. Thus an enormous diversity was produced, and no two temples are exactly alike; but behind them all, even when they show the widest extremes of local variation, is a basic harmony resulting from the same general attitude toward life and religion, and the same underlying architectural principles.

The columns also were endlessly varied. The greater number are octagonal for at least a portion of their height; and capital forms of many kinds are found, especially numerous being those like great decorated cushions and those in which there is an urn brimming over with foliage which pours down the sides. In the later, more lavish periods, particularly in the pillared halls, the columns are broken up into two or three parts, the column itself being often fronted by sculptured beasts (horses or even elephants) or by good and evil spirits, carved with tremendous skill and verve. In all of these minor details the wooden original of the style remained as the controlling tradition. Brackets are used freely, carved out of stone in forms almost as delicate as those which wooden brackets would take. Roofs are often made by piling long narrow slabs on each other in interesting ways, as though they were wooden beams. Out of these there were often produced almost domelike forms, especially in the work built by the sect of the Jains, who were co-rebels with the Buddhists from the idolatry of Brahmanism. In the great Jain center of Mount Abu the interior work is especially rich, and the lacelike delicacy of the brackets and the "domes" is of unbelievably intricate beauty.

Little secular architecture remains from times prior to the Mohammedan conquest; yet the continuation of the Hindu building types and decorative skills exerted an even more powerful influence on the Moslem palaces than it did on the mosques. Curved roofs, projecting bays, rich sculpture, complex banded columns—all of these, preserved from pre-Moslem days, added not a little to the picturesque and romantic glory of the Moslem palaces and castles, and gave to all the Indian cities, no matter what their age or foundation, some underlying harmony that makes them what they are. Above all else, whether Christian or Mohammedan, Jain or Brahman, they were and remain essentially Indian.

The Indian influence, especially the Buddhist influence, spread far and wide outside of the peninsula, over the Eastern world; and, although Buddhism itself died out of India almost completely before 800 A.D., it was only to gain still more vigorous life in the countries to the north, Nepal and Tibet, to the south in Ceylon, and all over the Far East. With Buddhism went Indian culture and Indian building ways and forms, and Ceylon, Burma, Siam, Sumatra, and Java still preserve many ruins of Buddhist structures of early date. Borobudur is by far the greatest of these, and the exquisite perfection of the reliefs which band its several stages is eloquent evidence even today of the power of the central tradition which inspired them.

Yet in this diffusion the Indian motifs slowly changed as they came in contact with local needs and local ways. In general, the decoration becomes more suave and delicate, almost feminine in type, while there is a tendency toward exaggeration in building shapes. Stupas become higher and are frequently crowned with tall slim spires, which give them an entirely different expression from the solemn curves of Sanchi. Buddhist temples often consist of great groups of small stupas around a central one, and the slim gilded tops make an almost bewildering complexity of richness against the sky. The native wooden construction also had its effect, and high roofs with broad projecting eaves are often found. Later, and in the eastern regions, Chinese influence is also strong, and the curved roofs and dragons, the elaborate eaves, the wooden columns of Siamese work often recall more clearly the Chinese inspiration to the north than the original Indian impetus behind their design.

The area, too, gave birth to a type of building quite unique, in the great structures of the Khmer empire in Cambodia, built between the eleventh and fourteenth centuries. Here Buddhist ideals direct from India and the classic influences of the Greco-Buddhist art of Gandhara were given a new direction and achieved completely new expressions, due to the extraordinary building genius of these peoples who had come down into the country from the west and the north. Angkor Wat, the great temple of the capital city, Angkor Thom, is one of the most superb architectural creations of the East. Laid out on a plan of magnificent formality, its tiered, colonnaded terraces, detailed with an almost classic simplicity, act as perfect foils for the rich triple towers which rise above them, and the sculptural decoration throughout has a vivacity and a grace unlike either the lush profusion of the Indian or the almost effeminate delicacy of the Javanese. And near by rises another great temple, carrying on its gate tower the colossal quadruple head of Brahma; its serene, enormous faces gazing out in four directions seem somehow to express permanence and magnanimity—almost tenderness —in a way that belies and yet results from their size. The composition is one of the great *tours de force* of the combination of sculpture and architecture. However, after three centuries, the Khmer power and the Khmer civilization vanished, and the jungles grew up and swallowed the great Khmer cities,

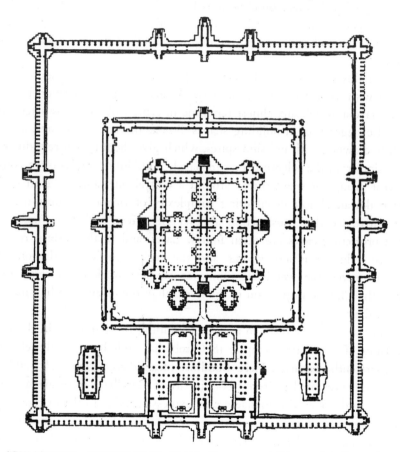

87. THE TEMPLE, ANGKOR WAT; PLAN. (Fergusson: *A History of Indian and Eastern Architecture.*)

so that it is only recently that they have been cleared, to disclose the ex- quisite beauty which must have surrounded the life of a people unusually sensitive to aesthetic form and yet filled with some truly Eastern serenity of soul.

Like the United States, China covers a vast area of many climates and great differences of surface. From north to south it embraces regions with temperatures as severe as that of Montana and more tropical than that of Florida. From east to west it includes the coastal plain, river deltas, fertile river valleys, huge plateaus, and high rocky mountains. For long centuries in its development, much of its territory was heavily forested, so that wood came to play a tremendous part in the evolution of Chinese building. Between the wooded hillsides were thickly populated fertile valleys with terraced gardens, so that every possible square inch of land was brought under cultivation. In these valleys and the great river plains the population increased rapidly, supported by perhaps the most intensive agriculture the ancient world knew.

In this rich country there grew up highly developed arts and crafts, drawing from different sections of the enormous country all the materials which they needed—copper, tin, building stones and marbles, iron, precious stones. In the great alluvial plains there were clays of all kinds suitable for brick-making and pottery. The population, supported by this wealth of natural resources and the great agricultural yield of the productive fields, was enabled to develop over long centuries an artistic culture unique in the world for its continuity, and characterized by a continual search for greater and greater perfection based on the slight variation of earlier achievements.

Here, as well, there grew up a governmental system, based on many early experiments and reaching its first full flowering under the Han dynasty about the beginning of the Christian era, which was admirably designed to combine the virtues of local responsibility and centralized efficiency. From the lowest peasant to the emperor himself there was a continually ascending series of officials, with definite powers and obligations. Theoretically, the only requirement for entrance into official position was merit, and merit was conceived largely as a matter of learning. The new officials required each year were all selected on the basis of public examinations which anyone could enter—examinations largely literary in character and based on the classic Chinese writings. Thus, an early type of civil-service system was created which produced a constant flow of new blood into the system; and, although the examinations tended to make the official class a group perhaps too wedded to mere academic excellence, the long continuation of the system, despite changes in dynasty and foreign conquerors, proves the strength of its foundation. It necessarily gave a kind of democracy, at least a kind of sympathy between the rulers and the ruled, which no purely hereditary system can ever achieve. It guaranteed a respect for the learned man, a respect which was paralleled by the almost universal admiration of the artist. It meant a culture basically conservative, but still a culture willing to progress.

The conservatism of Chinese life had still another basis: the system of ancestor worship, which enters so largely into Chinese life even today. A people keenly aware of duties owed to their grandparents are a people who are also deep students of all that their forefathers have written, and eager to take advantage of the lessons to be gained from them. Ancestor worship and respect for the ancient classics, combined with a free and democratic civil service, formed here an admirable basis for cultural development—slow, to be sure, but irresistible.

For this highly organized life many different types of architecture were needed, and to build them the Chinese possessed ample material of all kinds. They were excellent builders in brick, in stone, in marble; but fundamentally it was wood which set the structural forms, and even the most monumental buildings were frequently wooden constructions, set of course on masonry basements and perhaps surrounded by masonry walls, but held up and supported by wooden columns, beams, and girders. This has made the tracing of the exact historical growth of Chinese forms extremely difficult, for wood rots and the old structures need constant repair and rebuilding. Of the great monuments one sees in Peking today, many are eighteenth-century and by far the greater number of the rest go back no further than the Ming dynasty of the fifteenth and sixteenth centuries. But general plans remain constant; even now one can almost use Marco Polo's description of thirteenth-century Peking and the Imperial Palace as a guide around the present city.

Yet there have been many important changes. Incised slate reliefs, preserved from Han dynasty tombs, show many illustrations of Chinese palaces and houses. Tomb offerings from even earlier periods frequently include house models, and the striking thing about both the Han dynasty pictures and the early clay models is the fact that the curved roof does not appear in them. The buildings have simple one-sloped roofs, distinctly "classic" in general appearance, with almost the same roof slope that distinguished the Greek temples. The earliest existing temple structure of Chinese type stands in far-off Japan—the prayer hall of the Horyuji temple,—and this, which dates from the seventh century, already shows the complete curved roof we have come to associate so definitely with the Far East.

No one has yet solved the great problem of how and why the straight roofs of early China gave way so generally to the curved roofs of the later time, although the curved roofs were more difficult to build. It is possible that, in the search for broadly projecting eaves to give shaded porches, the lower parts of roofs were set at a different slope from the upper portions, and that little by little a curve replaced the break in the roof thus developed. Since this sweeping line seemed lovely to the builders, they took the same curve and applied it to the roof corners, so that gradually it became the custom to sweep up all roofs not only at the outer edges but also at the corners, to give that characteristic graceful curve which is almost universal. It may be that invaders or new settlers from the nomad steppes to the west brought with them the curved forms of tents, and sought to combine these curves with the carpentry building of early China. Whatever the reason, the fact is sure.

Early Chinese culture was centered in the northern and western regions of the country; the southern and eastern areas were only conquered and civilized or settled at dates much more recent than the original birth of the culture. And the north has always preserved earlier types of building and architectural design than central or south China. The majestic, suavely curved roofs of Peking and the north—the "classic" architecture of China— and many of the details used there have both a more monumental and at the same time a more primitive appearance than the florid, almost rococo archi- tecture of parts of south China and the Yangtze valley. The more delicate roof curve—the first and the most successful development—has remained in use in north China almost to the present day, whereas the builders of Canton and Amoy, and even of the Yangtze river towns, outdid themselves in the most eccentric and almost decadent variations on the theme. Thus, the outer corners of the roof were curved up in extravagant rising sweeps, defying any real sense of structure whatsoever, and the upward curve of the eaves was continued by long, hornlike projections in tile or metal. Roof ridges, too, were treated with a lavishness entirely lacking in the north; often the central part of the roof ridge would be stepped up high above the roof, and the space between filled with pierced ornament in stucco, either of geometric type or of naturalistic figure relief work. At the same time, roofs full of reverse curves came into use, so that the silhouettes of these later buildings of the Yangtze and south China are bizarre to the last degree.

In the neighborhood of Canton another local style evolved, in the effort to use stone structural members where the northern styles had used wood. Extraordinarily skillful masons, these south China builders were able to create light and delicate structures with all the posts and beams carved from granite; yet, despite this skill in carving, the forms remain essentially wooden forms, and there seems to Western eyes to be an underlying conflict between the material and its expression.

This southern work was but one phase of a certain tendency toward rich and almost rococo decorative treatment. Nowhere in China did carved wooden screens achieve such a lacy delicacy of complicated openwork. Nowhere else were naturalistic foliage and animal forms used with such a free hand, and in all the details of furniture and interior furnishing there is an enormous contrast between the simple severity of the typical north China large house and the extravagant ornamentation of the merchant's residence in Canton. Nevertheless, in both there was always the same insistence on strict formal regularity of planning and a search for rigid axial symmetry. Since it was at Canton that the Western nations had their great commercial centers, and since it was the Cantonese or at least people from south China who settled most in Western lands, it was this fantastic quality of south China architecture which first aroused European interest; and it was this local work which gave rise to the *Chinoiseries* of eighteenth-century Europe and which still is the picture which most Westerners have of Chinese design.

Chinese construction makes use freely of masonry materials. From an early period the Chinese understood the principle of the arch and the vault, and used it freely in bridge design, in tombs, in city and palace gateways. They liked especially to build tremendous basements to monumental buildings, and then pierce them with great vaulted tunnels of entrance, and sometimes with vaulted halls within. Such solid structures, often with walls sloping subtly inward, perforated by large arches, are among the most characteristic features of Chinese town walls, of palace gates like that of the Forbidden City in Peking, and of the drum and bell towers frequently built in Chinese towns, from which alarms could be given and the watches of the night sounded.

Vaulted masonry halls were even occasionally used for temples; especially impressive are the great halls of Wu Tai Shan, one of the sacred mountains of China. Occasionally these temple vaults have spans as great as fifty or sixty feet. Many smaller constructions also were vaulted, especially the first floors of towers and occasional pagodas.

But the Chinese thought chiefly in terms of wood. Even the exteriors of the great vaulted temple halls have on their façades, carefully cut in stone, the columns, beams, brackets, and eaves of the current wooden forms; and tile roofs, gabled and swept down in curves like the wooden roofs of houses or temples, cover them. To the Chinese, evidently, the honored part of a building should be essentially a wooden construction or should look like a wooden construction, even if it was of stone or of brick and faïence tile.

Chinese wooden construction was based fundamentally on the post, the beam, and the projecting bracket. Trussed forms were never used; to roof a wide hall, the wooden posts were made to carry great girders straight across it. These girders in turn would each carry two smaller posts of lesser span, and these would bear another girder which would carry other smaller posts still closer together, until little by little the triangular shape of the roof was built up. Purlins or horizontal beams would rest on the

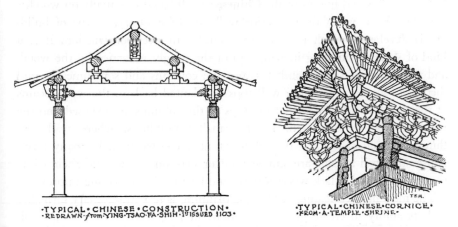

·TYPICAL·CHINESE·CONSTRUCTION·
·REDRAWN·from·YING·TSAO·FA·SHIH·1ª ISSUED 1103·

·TYPICAL·CHINESE·CORNICE·
·FROM·A·TEMPLE·SHRINE·

88. CHARACTERISTIC CHINESE ARCHITECTURAL FORMS. *Left:* TYPICAL CHINESE ROOF CONSTRUCTION. *Right:* CHARACTERISTIC BRACKETED CORNICE, FROM A SHRINE IN THE TEMPLE HUA YEN SSU AT TA T'UNG, PROBABLY 11TH CENTURY. (Drawn by the author from the *Ying Tsao Fa Shih* and from the *Bulletin* of the Society for Research in Chinese Architecture, 1934.)

posts, and on these the roof rafters would be laid. Perhaps it was this trick of construction which helped in the development of the curved roof, for there was no engineering gain in such a construction to be achieved through having the rafters straight. The wide eaves typical of all Chinese work were formed by the use of an elaborate system of wooden brackets projecting from the posts and the beams connecting them. The lowest bracket would be a simple projecting piece of wood, curved up at the outer end and carrying a kind of cap. This again would carry other brackets similar to it and running in both directions, so that, by piling tier and tier of these brackets on each other in the general form of a sort of inverted pyramid, great projections could be produced. The last brackets would carry horizontal beams, on which the roof rafters were placed. This system of brackets occurs in all sorts of forms. In the earliest work the bracket systems were simple, relatively large in scale, and the groups of adjacent brackets relatively far apart. As time went on, the brackets became smaller and their number increased, until forms of almost bewildering complexity were composed. Much of the richness of effect of the exteriors of Chinese buildings comes from these brackets; and, when they are gaily painted in ultramarine, emerald green, and white, as they usually are in northern Chinese work, the result is a unique kind of jeweled magnificence, and the small bright forms break up the deep shadow of the roof delightfully.

The temples and houses of the Chinese are all based essentially on wooden structure. Even when their exterior walls are of masonry, a type of building is developed which is in its way similar to steel construction. It is a kind of skeleton building in which all of the weight is carried by the wood, and the walls are simply built between the columns and sometimes around them; but almost always the wall tops are slanted back to the wood beams of the roof, in such a way that the tops of the columns are exposed and the real construction expressed. In the smaller buildings, where walls are thinner, the effect is often that of half-timber construction. In many farmhouses the wall screens are simple mud or clay on wattle, and their white shapes lined by the dark wooden posts and beams give a striking impression.

The most marked feature of Chinese planning is its extraordinary formality and its ability to create great conceptions in large terms. In a temple, all the main halls and gates are centered on one chief axis, with roofs running across the axis rather than, as in most Western buildings, parallel to it. Minor buildings at right angles to these connect the halls to form a series of courts, and the progression from one court to the next through halls of growing richness or sanctity is an impressive experience, especially since the doors between the courts are usually not on the axis but on either side, so that one is continually forced to turn away from the great axis, to pass through a decorative side door, and then to come back to the main axis with fresh delight. The same system applies to the large houses of the north, and gives them a kind of gracious dignity combined with a sense of privacy which is out of all proportion to their size.

The same system of planning controls the Chinese ideals of city design. In Peking one great north-south axis carries through the entire city a full seven miles long; on it are the chief gates, the courts and halls of the Forbidden City, the artificial hill crowned with five pagodas made when the palace lakes were built, and the city drum tower and bell tower. The impression on a visitor of this succession of horizontal roofs, one behind the other, some—on the larger buildings—raised high so that they show over the

lower, smaller roofs in front, is the result of a kind of artistic creation un-
paralleled in the architecture of any other people. It is this formality, coupled
with the graceful sweep of the gently curved roofs and the richness of the
decoration, which makes Peking one of the great architectural cities of the
world.

To this formality of plan is added an amazing brilliance of color decoration. The wooden columns are almost universally lacquered red, though
occasionally green- and even black-columned buildings are found. The beam

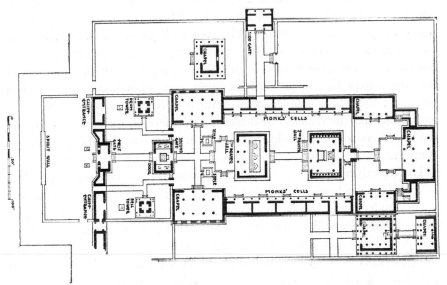

89. TEMPLE BO LIN SSU, WESTERN HILLS NEAR PEKING; PLAN. (Drawn by E. P.
McMullin, Jr.)

and bracket work of the eaves is usually blue and green, gold and white,
with here and there touches of red and yellow; and the roofs above, if
the building is a palace or a temple with imperial sponsorship, are usually
covered with glazed, shiny tile of golden yellow. The roof ridge is stopped
at each end by a great dragonfish form. The big hip moldings stop before
the corner of the roof is reached with a somewhat similar animal, and from
there to the corner the hip carries a row of little dogs or horses or other
small animals, that punctuate the skyline in a delightful manner.

It is typical of Chinese life that all of its temples, whether Buddhist,
Taoist, or Confucian, have essentially similar plans. In front is a "spirit
wall," a solid wall closing the axis, designed, the legend goes, to keep evil
spirits out of the temple, because evil spirits can only travel in a straight

line. Sometimes a monumental gateway or *pailoo* covers the entrance way. Beyond is the gate proper, usually a hall, and through this the first court is entered. This court contains, on either side, a little tower—one for the great temple bell and the other for the temple drum. The sides of the court are closed by minor chapels and residences for priests or monks. Directly ahead rises the first prayer hall, on its marble-railed masonry terrace. One enters the hall through a series of wide grilled wooden doors, and finds facing him a long altar covered with altar furniture—candles, incense burners, offering vases, and so on—leading up to the climax, which in the Confucius temples is a simple tablet containing the Confucius name, in the other temples a group of three statues. The roof high above one is paneled with small square panels of wood, often polychromed and gilded. If the temple has more than one court, each is in a sense a repetition with variations of the first, except that there is usually only one drum tower and one bell tower for the whole temple. If the temple belongs to a monastery, court after court may be required to house the dormitories, the eating halls, and the schoolrooms of the monks, but in all the same basic formality of design controls.

The underlying quality of the Chinese house is its inward-turning nature. Like the Roman house, the larger Chinese houses, both north and south, are always built around one or more courts; and the view down upon a Chinese city from a hill is strikingly like looking down upon a model of Pompeii. The result is that streets of Chinese towns or villages are often mere passages between long unbroken walls, with here and there a lovely polychromed entrance door. The visitor walking through the city may be delighted with the life of the Chinese shops or with the gorgeous signs in blue and green, and red and gold, which hang over the street; but of the real pleasantness, the real wealth even, of the town he will get no impression. For that he must climb a pagoda or a near-by hill, from which a glimpse of richly decorated courtyard and the green of lush gardens makes the town seem quite another thing from what it appeared in its own streets.

The influence of Chinese architecture spread widely, far south to meet and mingle with the Indian work of Indonesia, north and east into Korea and Japan. Japanese architecture is essentially the result of the assimilation of Chinese influence by a culture which had already produced its own characteristic architectural forms, and the history of its development is often a history of the changing values given to either the one element or the other at different times. In general, the native Japanese influences continued to dominate the domestic architecture field and the building of Shinto shrines. The Buddhist temples, on the contrary, were more likely to develop still further the Chinese precedents.

Landscape and climate undoubtedly affected this blend enormously. Japan is a land of steep slopes, of mountains, of rapidly changing terrain, of picturesque views, to which the natives have always been extraordinarily sensitive. The sea is almost always present or near by, and lakes and rivers and waterfalls have always had a tremendous charm for the Japanese. Almost necessarily, therefore, the strict formalities of Chinese design were hardly suitable to the Japanese countryside. A sense of the picturesque, of the free balance of dissimilar things, of the dramatic relationship of building to tree, to slope, to water, became a basic feature in almost all Japanese design. Although here and there there are temples with the symmetrical general plans the Chinese loved, and although almost everywhere there seems to be an attempt to get at least one of the main halls on a controlling axis of approach, usually the balance across this axis will be unsymmetrical; and again and again trees, groups of stone lanterns, and little shrines will be used to make beautiful picturesque compositions in which the distant landscape often plays an important if not a controlling part. That is why Japanese architecture generally photographs better than the architecture of the Chinese, although in many ways the Chinese compositions may be sounder and perhaps in the long run, after many visits, at least as satisfactory.

Like the Chinese, the Japanese were fundamentally builders in wood, but they used wood with an entirely different feeling, seeking everywhere to bring out its natural characteristics of grain and color, loving plain, undecorated, velvety-smooth surfaces and a simple rectangular framework of delicate members. Thatched roofs were originally universal, and still give color and character to many Japanese villages, as they do to the Shinto temples. Everywhere it seems that lightness and delicacy are sought, whereas in China it is solidity and dignity.

The Japanese house is thus the most typical production of Japanese design. Its sliding paper screen partitions, its sliding wooden outer shutters, its immaculate mattings, and its clear simple wood panels are eloquent of a people acutely sensitive to the values inherent in the material, wood, and loving a life fastidiously and elegantly unpretentious. Characteristic, too, is the free way in which these houses are planned, with space added to space as the site and the size demand, each space arranged for its use and its view of garden or surrounding country. Equally typical is the careful, sensible planning of the house conveniences. Of rooms in the Western sense there is hardly a trace in the characteristic Japanese house, for the system of sliding partitions allows the whole to be thrown open into one airy unit at will.

With the development of the tea ceremony in Japan, under the influence of the Zen sect, ascetic Buddhism had an important role in the evolution of Japanese house ideals; and the usual tea ceremony space, with its raised platform for flowers, its little cabinets and shelves, and its one naturalistic, untrimmed, unsquared tree-trunk post to bring into the interior the sense of outdoors, forms a lovely climax for the house.

In all of this traditionally Japanese work there is no sign of the curved roof of China; that is reserved for temples, for palaces, and occasionally for the details of castles. The curved roof came in with Buddhist influence in the seventh century, and at first, as was natural, the early Buddhist temples were as perfect reproductions of Chinese models as the Chinese monks who had brought Buddhism with them could contrive. Later, however, as the style developed in Japan, changes became inevitable. In accordance with the Japanese devotion to picturesque and informal composition, planes are broken up and varied. Instead of the elaborate Chinese *pailoo* with its complicated brackets and cornices, one has the simple Japanese *tori,* with its two simple posts and crossbeams. Roofs also change, generally becoming slightly flatter, with eaves more developed; and, because the Japanese love wood surfaces, much of the elaborate polychromy of Chinese architecture gives way to plain uncolored wood, here and there heightened with a touch of gold or of color. The marble balustrades of Chinese terraces yield to wooden railings with brass-topped posts, and occasionally thatched roofs replace those of tile.

Later still, there began to creep into Japanese architecture a new drive toward lavish and almost eccentric complexity. Greater and greater amounts of carving were scattered profusely over the buildings. Roofs took more and more complicated shapes; often dormerlike gables projected rather arbitrarily over the entrance in a long roof, and sometimes these were reduplicated one over the other. Ridgeless roofs of soft curves came into use, until a climax was reached in the period of the Tokugawa Shoguns in the seventeenth century, when there occurred a marvelous explosion of luxurious richness well illustrated in the much photographed gateways and halls of Nikko, and shown too in the reduplicated roofs and dormers of the white towers of the feudal castles. It is this latest and most lavish development of the Buddhist temple style which has frequently won the foreigner's unthinking interest; its elaborate naturalistic ornament, its white paint and gold, and its fantastic roof shapes have all given it a perhaps unmerited acclaim.

For the real contributions of Japanese architecture, for a truer understanding of the aesthetic ideals of Japanese building, it is better to turn back to the earlier temple work of Nara or Kyoto, and still more to the beauty of the traditional Japanese house and the exquisite if artificial subtleties of the Japanese garden; for it is in these that one may best see the amazing sensitiveness of the Japanese artists and craftsmen in their use of natural materials and the astonishing felicity with which they adjust their buildings to natural surroundings. To sit, shoeless and cross-legged, on a Japanese mat in these serene and lovely house interiors, looking out through half-opened sliding screens into the water and green of the house garden; to stand in a temple court and see the exquisite harmony between spreading roof and the spreading branches of the ancient pines beside one; to look out over the inland sea with its steep, pine-clad, rocky islands, past the great *tori* standing with its feet in the water—these are experiences which only the Japanese could create; these are their great contributions to architecture.

BOOK VI

The Baroque and the Eighteenth Century

Chapter 21

THE BAROQUE SPIRIT

ALL through the seventeenth century the Renaissance world was falling into ruins, as a new life came to bloom in its place. Discovery after discovery of new and strange lands in America and in the East, undreamed-of wealth flowing into the coffers of Europe, adventurous traders and conquerors opening up new territories to European penetration—all these created economic stresses and strains, national rivalries, which grew into national wars. Even more powerful in the disintegration of the old and the creation of the new was the final result of an essentially Renaissance movement, the trend toward free inquiry, with its natural result, the theory of the supremacy of the individual mind and the individual conscience. Inevitably these led to differences in philosophies and religions, to savage questioning of old and accepted creeds, to the destruction of old loyalties, and to a consequent, almost universal, feeling of instability.

The Reformation was but one result of this movement which disturbed a cultural equilibrium that had been built up for centuries. Faced with new questions difficult to answer, deprived of old securities, men's minds became fanatical, human energy turned naturally to violence. All over Europe the middle of the seventeenth century was a period of war, of what seems sometimes almost senseless destruction and mass murder. At the basis of most of these wars—the Thirty Years' War, the Revolution in England, the Huguenot wars of France—was the great religious ferment of the Reformation and the Counter-Reformation, the Protestant and the Catholic; but in every case these wars, entered into perhaps in a spirit of misguided but sincere religious fervor, soon degenerated into struggles for dominion on the part of greedy and power-drunk leaders. Religious and social differences became mere pretexts for cruel struggles for military control.

The powers thus built up by long years of military conquest were, perforce, powers of a different kind from those which had grown up in the slow and gradual transformation of the feudal system during the Renaissance. Founded on military might, they were essentially military dictator-ships; created frequently by personal greed or personal brilliance, they were of necessity personal and individual. The divine right of kings, in its modern sense, was a natural product of that period, for the king was the leader and the creator of the army, and the army had created the country over which he ruled, and was its only guarantee of survival. Such a monarchy as that of France under Louis XIV would have been unthinkable a century before. Behind it lay a new kind of army, designed for the first time with some logical relationship to the use of gunpowder, dispensing for the first time with all the older panoply of chivalry; and the French monarchy was the model which almost every power in Europe, large and small, with the possible exception of England and the Low Countries, was striving to follow.

Into the hands of these military rulers came, naturally, the greatest share of the new-found wealth which new trade and the discovery of new worlds were bringing. A Versailles would have been impossible without this new centralization. In such a large country as France it was perhaps understand-able enough; what is extraordinary is the enormous number of little palaces like Versailles—smaller perhaps, but as luxurious, fundamentally as ex-travagant, and in relation to the impressiveness of their buildings and the size of the countries over which they presided just as gargantuan.

The new Baroque world was thus a profoundly different one from the Renaissance world that had preceded it, and architecture could not but reveal the difference. The new world was a world of paradoxes, of centralized national or ducal power, and of international chaos; of extraordinary and vaunting wealth on the part of kings and dukes, and a certain number of fortunate merchants; and of increasing poverty, squalor, and misery for millions of peasants, whose taxes supported the armies and the leaders who overtaxed and oppressed them. It was a period of tremendous public im-provements combined with incredible public impoverishment; for the army is a jealous god, and military power is an insatiable maw into which to pour the riches and the energy of a people.

Nevertheless, the Baroque period had its redeeming sides. If Louis XIV said, *"L'État, c'est moi"* ("I am the State!"), it naturally followed also that the reverse was true—that, if the state was the king, the king became also in a new sense the representative of the entire nation—and no man in his senses could fail to realize the prodigious responsibility of such a position. Rulers were forced by their new status to think in terms of their people's welfare in a different and more profound way than had frequently been the case earlier. It is no accident that the Baroque era was the first great period since the Fall of Rome when city planning and even national planning on a grand scale became an essential part of the architectural picture, when kings not only built palaces but laid out great streets and squares, built bridges and roads and harbor works.

Emotionally, too, there were compensations. The intellectual questioning and the emotional anguish which in many cases accompanied the struggles surrounding the Reformation gave a new kind of value to living, a new kind of intensity to little things in life. The world was full of violent contrasts; the very paradoxes of its condition emphasized, even if they did not create, a universal sense of the dramatic, the tragic; personal salvation became of huge importance, somewhat resembling the importance it had held in the Romanesque period; and the striving architecture of Baroque churches —the broken lines and twisted contours, the dramatic contrasts of dark and light—became in a way an externalization of this sense of the drama of salvation.

The stage also played its part, for the stage is dramatic necessarily, and the whole theatrical atmosphere of the new time is expressed and aided by the great increase in the importance of the stage, the development of opera, and, following Shakespeare, the new dignity and popularity of dramatic tragedy. The seventeenth-century world may have been a world full of "battle and murder and sudden death," of poverty and exploitation and misery, but it was also a world of vivid excitement and dynamic living. And it was a world, too, of constantly broadening horizons, physically and mentally. A world sense for the first time began to appear; the amazing variety of this earth—its countries, its oceans, and its peoples—was becoming known. Telescopes were gradually piercing the enigmas of the skies, giving a new vision of the greatness of the cosmos. The foundations of modern science were being laid. Never perhaps since Greek days had there been a period when human curiosity along so many lines was alike so aroused, so stimulated, and so satisfied. Life became an intellectual as well as an emotional adventure.

Renaissance architecture, especially in Italy, had reached, about the middle of the sixteenth century, a point of such perfection, such refinement, such delicate study of detail, and such a generally high standard of conventional taste that, without new and revolutionary ideas, the only advance could be along the dangerous road of further refinement, and progress showed danger of becoming merely a repassing again and again of old landmarks. Sterilization and boredom could be the only results of such a process. The experiments of the Mannerist architects were the answer to this danger, and Michelangelo especially was searching always for new, vivid, inventive, revolutionary ways of doing things. Without doubt, according to the cannons of Renaissance taste, some of his experiments were outlandish. His strange and erratic wall-paneling motifs, his repetition of niche on niche, his broken pediments and heavy cornices, compared to the details of such of his contemporaries as Peruzzi, were crude if you will. In the vestibule of the Laurentian Library in Florence, he even went to the extent of setting engaged columns back into recesses sunk into the wall, so that the wall face and outside edge of the columns are approximately in line—a kind of almost arrogant flouting of all the conventional ideals of what columns were and should do;—and in the Porta Pia at Rome he piled motif on motif in a way that was vivid but almost uncouth. Michelangelo obviously realized the danger of the Renaissance of his time, the danger of standardized, uncreative good taste. He evidently realized that within the Renaissance itself lay the seeds of its own decay, through the pitfalls of floridity on the one hand and of listless good manners on the other. He had little patience with either, and rich as most of his work is it is never florid. In his greatest work, like the magnificence of his conception for St. Peter's and his designs for the completion of the palaces on the Capitoline Hill, all his creativeness appears and a few of his extravagances.

The Capitoline Hill work is especially significant of the new spirit, the spirit of the Baroque. It is essentially a sculptural composition—no longer a mere combination of flat façades, but a creation in three dimensions, with all of the space qualities of the open square, the loggias of the buildings, the great flights leading up on either side to higher peaks, and the long axial ramp approach essential parts of the design. The placing of statues; the handling of balustrades; the contrast in style between the front of the senatorial palace, which meets one at the end of the axis, and the two palaces at the side; the change of levels; the fact that the entrances of the side palaces are on the ground floor, whereas that of the senatorial palace is one story up, at the head of a monumental flight of steps and a fountain—all these are most cunningly contrived in relation to the changing perspectives of the individual coming up the ramp and into the square. It is a composition of great richness, continually changing as the spectator moves around; and it is this quality of design with regard to motion in space—in which space and movement become, as it were, two controlling factors in the design—that sets the piazza apart from any earlier composition of the

Renaissance. It is that which makes many people call Michelangelo the father of the Baroque; for, space and movement in increasing proportion, dynamics and drama, these are the great qualities of Baroque life.

In Baroque buildings the time element becomes a basic part of the design, as it had been to a less extent during the Roman Empire. The architect's

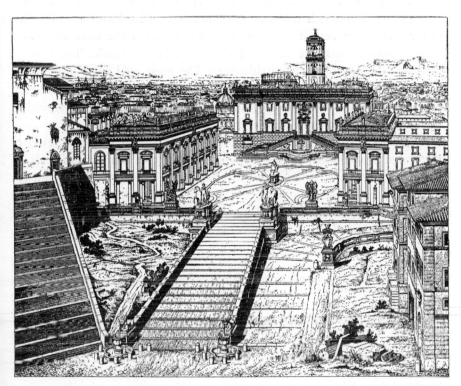

90. CAMPIDOGLIO, ROME; BIRD'S-EYE VIEW. Michelangelo, architect. (Letarouilly.)

interest was no longer in the single room or the one façade, or a single enclosed court; it was rather in the relations between façade and court and room, in the building up of artistic experiences in time as one approaches a building, enters it, goes through its great open spaces. At its best it thereby achieves a kind of symphonic quality, building always by means of carefully calculated curves, by strong contrasts of light and dark, of big and little, of simple and complicated, a glow, an emotion, which finally reaches some definite climax. That is why Baroque buildings more than any others suffer in photographs, for the photograph is static and the building is designed with all its parts so interrelated that the static unit often seems complicated, bizarre, or meaningless when taken away from its proper context in a continuing single artistic experience.

Accompanying this feeling for motion runs its inevitable concomitant drama. The Baroque church became an expression of the great drama of individual salvation through the church; the center of the mystery through which salvation was to be achieved, the altar, was surrounded with a lavish frame of gold and rich color, of swinging lines, of colorful marbles, just as the symbolic drama of the mass was surrounded at the same time with the gorgeous splendor of new and complex religious music. The two go together—the music and the architecture. The great gold-rayed glorias, full of winged cherubs and flying angels, the broken pediments on twisted columns, the tense and vivid emotional sculpture—all of these are typical of this new Baroque sense of individual drama.

And what is true of the church is true also of secular buildings, even of the design of whole cities. The drama of the court, of court ceremonials, of flashing costume and stilted, codified gesture; the drama of military guards in brilliant uniforms lining a straight avenue, while prancing horses drag a gilded coach up the wide esplanade to the castle—these are essentially Baroque conceptions, part and parcel of the whole Baroque feeling for life. Within the house or the palace, the same search for dramatic effects controls the design. The new emphasis on motion led inevitably to a new study of the relations between rooms in buildings. The anteroom, instead of being a mere vestibule, becomes a prologue; the stair a grand setting for a royal progress, with wide flights and broad landings all set in a hall of enormous size and richness. In the details of the working out of these units the Baroque architects expended the best of their brilliant invention. Rooms and vestibules that are dark or dim contrast with spaces where the light is a blaze from large windows, the cold gray of cut stone or the sharp white of unpainted plaster contrasts with the warm richness of carved wood or the radiance of gold in the rooms which follow. So square rooms alternate with round, vaulted rooms lead into higher chambers with flat ceilings richly painted; everywhere this search for dramatic interest seems the first aim in the designer's mind.

In order to obtain this contrast, this dynamic sense of motion, this emotional drama, the simple forms of the classic orders and the unchanged classic forms were manifestly insufficient. It seems almost a general law that styles of quiet restraint and unified simplicity develop later into styles of complexity, experimentation, and contrast. So it was in the ancient Roman world, where a sort of Baroque conception both of space and of detail controls much of the work after the time of Trajan. So it was in the Gothic period, when the fifteenth and sixteenth centuries saw arise the intricacy of the Flamboyant styles. So also it was in Italy in the latter half of the sixteenth century, when, little by little, the restraint of the architecture of the Sangalli and of Peruzzi gave way to the new experimentalism of Michelangelo and his followers. This first breaking away from the strict categories of classic form was shown in Mannerist architecture, as has already been mentioned. It gave rise to many important buildings and many fresh details, different alike from the Renaissance which preceded and the Baroque which followed. Historically, however, Mannerism is most significant as the first step on the way to the developed Baroque, the first effort to inject into the simple straight lines and round arches of the High Renaissance a new feeling of flexibility and emotional power.

Baroque detail thus became a matter of the increasingly free modification of forms originally classic, to make them sensitive to every possible nuance of emotional expression. Pediments were broken and their sides curved and scrolled, separated by cartouches, or urns; columns were twisted, moldings duplicated and reduplicated to give sharp emphasis, and broken suddenly out and in where a complexity of shadow was desired. Then decorative sculpture of all kinds came more and more into use; figures filled the spandrels of arches or the fields of pediments. Leaves and scrolls, increasingly free from the original acanthus inspiration, were sometimes poured around the architectural forms. Curved lines more and more took the place of straight lines—lines curved both vertically and horizontally. Inside, the old simple painted planes began to yield to an ever-increasing richness. Paneling, pilasters, engaged columns, projecting cornices, complicated ceilings became common; and the facility with which such forms could be modeled in stucco and plaster gave stuccowork a new importance in interior design.

Later still, entirely new architectural forms, bearing little relation to the ancient classic details but still distantly under their influence, began to take the place of the old orders. The *gaine* form replaced pilasters and columns, and even when the orders were used they were often made to taper downward. More and more, especially in interior work, an atmosphere almost as of some extraordinary extemporaneous creation was sought, instead of the careful restraint of the Renaissance; forms were softened, and the interest was not on the form itself but on the light and shade which it produced, so that some of the richest Baroque work—like that of late seventeenth-century

Spain—looks almost more like a drawing in charcoal or soft pencil than an actual material object.

With this emphasis, any feeling for the expression of structural materials became entirely secondary to the effect which was desired. The Baroque designer, therefore, had no hesitation whatsoever in using plaster or stone interchangeably at will; in carving stone, if that happened to be his material, he proceeded so lavishly and with so little regard for strength that the stone became soft in appearance, or, on the other hand, he modeled his stucco into severely architectural forms which imitated and symbolized structure without becoming structural. The whole atmosphere was a little bit that of the stage; the typical large Baroque building was a stage setting for a drama.

Against the unbridled imagination, the loss of the restraint of the old taste, there were, naturally enough, many protests. The most famous rebels were Vignola and Palladio, who in the second half of the sixteenth century sought in vain to change the course of inevitable development and to preserve in their work the dignified greatness which they deemed to be the essence of the classic. In this effort, Vignola published a work on the orders, attempting to codify and regularize; and Palladio produced his four books on architecture, modeled on the work of Vitruvius and taking every opportunity to deprecate and condemn the broken pediments, the restless lines, the overloaded ornament used by many of his contemporaries. But with their death in 1580, for both died the same year, the last protest against the coming of the Baroque seems to have passed, and the seventeenth century became the Baroque century *par excellence*. The new freedom of details, with the aim of greater variety and greater drama, was universal.

The first of the great Baroque churches was the church of the Gesù, in Rome, built between 1568 and 1584, from designs of Vignola and Giacomo della Porta. To Vignola is due its great scale, the general dignity of its façade, the tremendous simplicity with which its nave leads to the great dome. Nevertheless it is a Baroque church, and as completed by his follower della Porta all of the dynamic possibilities of the scheme are emphasized. Later churches took this formula of a nave flanked by arched or domed chapels, leading into a crossing crowned by the largest possible dome on a drum, and behind that a choir and domed apse, and on this rang all the possible changes of which the Baroque imagination was capable. The lines of the nave might be waved, the barrel vault interrupted with interesting penetrations to receive clerestory windows, and every available free space filled with sculpture in violent action. Sometimes the dome was exaggerated to a point where the nave almost disappeared, and always the climax of the main altar and the lesser climaxes of side-aisle altars became increasingly rich in color and shape.

Eventually it was the decorative effect which alone controlled; the entire structure and composition became entirely secondary, until such an absurdity resulted as the vault of the Roman church of San Ignazio, over which was painted an elaborate composition in the most carefully calculated vertical

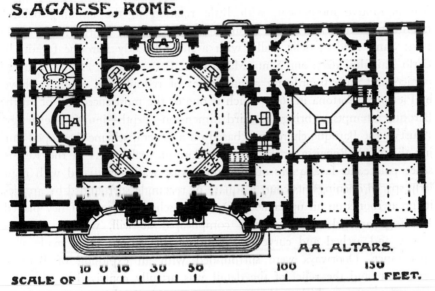

S. AGNESE, ROME.

AA. ALTARS.

SCALE OF 10 0 10 30 50 100 150 FEET.

91. SANT' AGNESE, ROME; PLAN. Borromini and the Rainaldis, architects. (Simpson. Vol. III.)

perspective, so designed as to eliminate the visual effect of the vault shapes entirely, and in their place attempt to give the effect of open sky above elaborate colonnades, filled with clouds and flying figures. In this same search for producing an unreal effect, the plaster would sometimes be swept out over important structural moldings, and painted as though the mural painting itself—of clouds and figures—were an actuality which hid the building. The result is often disturbing to the last degree, one of those artistic curiosities in which the aim to astound had overcome the ability to create.

Especially interesting are the façades of these Baroque churches. The basic shape of nave and side aisle is difficult to treat with classic forms. The Early Christians had been content with simple brick walls frankly expressing the building behind, and adding to them an entrance portico or a rich porch. The Renaissance architects had usually used two orders—one below no higher than the side aisles, and one above across the front of the nave. To fill the awkward space in between the two, they had made all kinds of experiments—half-pediments in front of the side-aisle roofs, or great ungainly scrolls. It remained for the Baroque architects, with their skill in free plastic composition, to take this simple formula and make it an opportunity for almost unlimited variety. Decoratively these Baroque façades are a great advance over the earlier ones, with more coherence, more unity, and naturally more dramatic effect. Often they are mere screens, almost like a free decorative monument, with little relation to the building behind. Excellent examples are: Santa Susanna, designed by Carlo Maderno in 1603; Sant' Andrea della Valle, with a magnificently Baroque façade, by Carlo Rainaldi, 1665; and Santa Maria della Pace, with an exquisite curved portico and an extraordinary arrangement of reduplicated columns above, by Pietro da Cortona in 1657, which is one of the most successful of all the Baroque attempts to bring the third dimension—depth—into façade design.

Just as the Baroque church was based on a general scheme developed during the High Renaissance, so was the Baroque palace. As in the Renaissance palace, its façade was often a mere vast wall punctuated with regularly spaced openings, its court a square or rectangle surrounded by arcades, its great rooms on an upper floor. Over this scheme Baroque fancy played. Moldings around windows were complicated at will, windows became larger, and arched and curved-top windows of various types made their appearance. Doorways were surrounded with an explosion of Baroque ornament, and the relief of the detail was artfully contrived to give that dramatic contrast which was so necessary an aesthetic element. In the court, arcades supported directly on columns were frequently found, and columns were often coupled to give variety of rhythm. Balustrades of all kinds came into greater and greater use. But the most profound changes were in the interior, for here the Baroque desire for progressively related spaces led to an entirely new kind of study of interior rooms. There is more directness as well as more complexity; and, since the ideal was the close artistic relationship of all the rooms, naturally a more studied, a tighter, a more completely composed interior plan resulted.

Of particular interest is the treatment of stairs, which were so frequently a dominant element—stairs curved and straight, stairs in one flight or several flights, but always stairs given an importance both in placing and design which was previously unknown. Often, it would seem, hillside sites were preferred because of the opportunity they offered for gorgeous interior stairs. The Barberini Palace, for instance, in Rome, in which three of the greatest Baroque architects—Maderno, Borromini, and Bernini—all had a hand, has a superb sequence from the recessed entrance, through a series of arcaded vestibules, up a complicated monumental staircase, to the upper level of the garden behind. This love of stairs and of hillside sites is especially shown in the palaces of Genoa, where palace after palace, as in the famous University, owes the greatest part of its effect to the magnificent

PALAZZO BARBERINI, ROME
PLAN OF CENTRAL PORTION

TERRACE
PORTE COCHERE
VESTIBVLE
GRAND STAIRCASE
GRAND SALON
ENTRANCE VESTIBVLE
½ FIRST FLOOR. ½ GROVND FLOOR
10 0 10 20 30 40 50 100
SCALE OF FEET

92. BARBERINI PALACE, ROME; PLAN. Bernini and Borromini, architects. (Simpson. Vol. III.)

stairs between the lower-level entrance at the street, the interior court on a higher level, and perhaps a garden behind on a higher level still.

To this desire for important sequential architectural effect, everything else in palace design was secondary. There was as yet little study of real functional relationships, little attempt to solve the problems of ease of service. Privacy did not exist; it seems hardly to have been desired, and almost always rooms were entered through other rooms. The average living spaces were designed in suites—always an anteroom, then a bedchamber more monumental than comfortable, then perhaps a retiring room or cabinet, used alike as studio, as informal bedroom, and generally as a retreat from the crowd. Kitchens were relegated to the ground floor, with the stables, and a multitude of servants was depended upon to make these vast piles function.

Given the governmental ideals of the Baroque age, and its architectural aspirations, it was only natural that city planning began to have a new value. The city itself was an opportunity for grandiose dramatic design which no individual building could ever offer. Moreover, the ruling lord, king, or count, as himself the embodiment of the state, had a new responsibility toward his own citizens, and again and again the better and more creative rulers expended as much time and thought and money on the beautifying and systematizing of their cities—on road building, on the creation of plazas and markets and great avenues, on bridges and dams and canals—as they did on their own palaces. Military requirements and the growing substitution of wheeled vehicles for horseback, at least for the wealthy, all forced a new consideration of what a city demanded and what a city should be.

The Renaissance cities had in many cases merely been enlarged medieval towns; where the original medieval town had had an adequate plan, the Renaissance city was adequate, as for instance in the case of Florence; on the other hand, where the growth had been too sudden or the medieval center ill-designed and congested, as in the case of both Paris and London, the Renaissance cities were even more ill-designed and congested because of their rapid growth. Rome itself remained a rather formless conglomeration of old and new, ancient ruin and modern palace, with a few large streets which had more or less happened by accident. In every case, one of the great tasks which faced seventeenth-century Europe was the necessity of bringing order out of this urban chaos. The mere growth of commerce and trade, the mere increase in population, made necessary a kind of town which was a new thing. Thus the artistic ambition of the architects, the new position of the despots, and the needs of the towns themselves combined to force Baroque designers to a conclusion that the city itself could be made a work of art, arrived at by means of conscious planning, to the combined end of greater convenience and greater beauty.

This was of course a conception that had been a commonplace in Hellenistic and Roman times; yet it seems to have broken upon the seventeenth-century world like a new and revolutionary discovery. All over Europe towns were opened up, squares built, avenues cut through. The Piazza del

Popolo, designed probably by Carlo Rainaldi, dates from about the middle of the century; the Piazza of St. Peter's was regularized and surrounded by its magnificent colonnade by Bernini in the 1660's; and the great steps of the Piazza di Spagna were built about forty years later to form a necessary connection between two separated parts of Rome—a connection as magnificent as it was necessary. So, in Paris, Henry IV built the Pont Neuf, the Place Dauphine, and the great Place Royale, now the Place des Vosges; and after him, in the latter half of the century, Louis XIV built the Place Vendôme, the Place des Victoires, started the great circuit of boulevards to replace the earlier fortifications, and established the beginnings of the Champs Elysées. Thus the city-planning movement spread out from Italy north and west, and each local ruler tried to outdo his neighbor not only in the magnificence of his palace but also in the beauty and regularity of his capital.

At times this effort at town creation, or town regularization, was not altogether a blessing. It could be too drastic, too artificial, with too little regard for the practical needs of the present. The time had come obviously when the imposition of definite form on the rapidly growing urban centers of Europe was necessary; but in the process frequently unconscious and useful form, which had grown naturally, was destroyed and the whole balance between town and country, between formality and informality, was upset. The great avenues and squares of the Baroque town not only produced open areas and necessary military and traffic thoroughfares, but sometimes they were not without their share in producing slums hidden behind them as well. Sometimes the improvements themselves increased the population. The movement from the country to the cities, which had been a trickle, began to be a flood. In the capitals were centered the great opportunities for gain, for acquiring culture, for pleasure. They formed a magnet too strong to resist. For these people who were thus thronging to the cities, the Baroque architects seem to have had little regard—even less than the architects of the Renaissance who had preceded, as the book of Serlio on houses shows, with its designs for carefully planned small dwellings as well as for palaces.

Even artistically, this imposition of form could go too far. In the hands of great designers it could produce much of beauty, which still makes Paris a center of pilgrimage. The new squares and avenues of Rome seem to have been an unmixed blessing; and the same kind of skill, though in a different expression, created the exquisite related open spaces of Nancy and Copenhagen. Nevertheless, the radiating avenues and the tremendous open spaces in front of the palace at Versailles are fundamentally inhuman, bleak, out of scale; effective on paper as a plan, but in reality a dreary waste. The climax was perhaps reached in Karlsruhe, where a town was placed at a castle gate and so arranged that all of its chief streets were radiated to a common center at the palace. Across this fan ran two or three longitudinal streets necessary for traffic, and the result was impractical, strange-shaped blocks, as well as a basic, devouring, and finally depressing monotony.

In Italy a characteristic feature of the new town planning was the growing importance of fountains and of water. There was something especially congenial to the Baroque love of motion and of power in the disciplined use of water, trickling from basin to basin, spouting up in vertical jets, forming complicated arcs as it rushed out of pipes artificially concealed in sculpture, or pouring in a tremendous cataract from the mouth of an aqueduct. Bernini, great as sculptor and as architect, created fountain after fountain in which architecture and sculpture and flowing water were combined into a single entity. The Acqua Felice, by Domenico Fontana, *circa* 1585, was perhaps the first of the great fountains, where the water pours out of a great architectural frontispiece into an enormous basin; the Paolo Quinto ("Acqua Paolo"), by Maderno and Fontana, in 1612, was somewhat similar in general scheme; and the largest of the group was the Fountain of Trevi, built in 1732, probably after a Bernini design. Yet it was the smaller, more intimate fountains which were probably the best, and if Bernini had done nothing else except the Fountain of the Triton, or the two magnificent undecorated jets of water falling into superbly simple basins in the Piazza of St. Peter's, his reputation would be sure.

Such an architecture as that which Baroque taste demanded was necessarily an architecture highly individual. Its products, infinitely varied, are the results of definite, varied personalities. In Italy, the list is extraordinary in its length, its variety. In Rome the greatest were Maderno, da Cortona, Borromini, and Bernini. Maderno stands generally for a tighter, more classic type of Baroque; da Cortona for the most dramatic contrasts of simple classic details, with eccentric and bizarre general composition; Borromini, whose greatest work was the façade of Sant' Agnese on the Piazza Navona, was perhaps the most eccentrically imaginative of all the Roman designers, and even in his own day was frequently criticized as violating good taste in his pursuit of the new.

Of them all, Bernini is undoubtedly the greatest figure. His anguished, tense, emotional sculpture is superb in the way its flowing of dynamic line is used to express and to heighten its emotional purpose. Architecturally, his mind was large; bigness, simplicity, disciplined power were his methods of gaining effect, whether in the great bronze baldachino of St. Peter's, with its daring open-scrolled top, or in the severe regularity of the Doric colonnades which he swung around the oval piazza in front of the church. It is no wonder that during his lifetime Bernini commanded the respect and lived the life of a prince, and that when Louis XIV called him to France to furnish a design for the completion of the Louvre palace—a design which was never built—his trip to Paris was told of almost in the terms of a royal progress.

Chapter 22

BAROQUE INTERNATIONALISM

OUTSIDE of Rome, Europe was ripe for the Baroque influence. Even in Italy the northern cities had never become so attached to the High Renaissance as had Rome, and the signs of a growing desire for experimentalism were more and more apparent in the second half of the sixteenth century. Galeazzo Alessi, though in many ways belonging to the Renaissance rather than to the Baroque world, had shown in his Genoese palaces and in the Palazzo Marino in Milan a sense of exuberant and creative detail, which indicated that same wish for plastic richness so frequently to be found in the work of Michelangelo. Even Giulio Romano (1499-1546), the follower and favorite student of Raphael, in the brutally effective decorations of the Palazzo del Té had shown signs of the change which was to come, although the exterior of the building is comparatively simple; and in 1568 Ammanati had added wings and a courtyard to Brunelleschi's Pitti Palace in which he not only rusticated the whole elevation throughout, but also enframed his windows and doors in double frames—architrave, frieze, and pediment of the normal type within, and rusticated arches without. All of these were not yet in the full current of the Baroque, yet they showed that the taste of the north of Italy was even then striving for new and experimental forms.

It is not strange, then, to find that the cities of the north welcomed Baroque freedom in the following century—in Genoa the rising wealth brought by her growing commerce led to the building of palace after palace in which the dynamic space planning and the emphasis on the stairs already mentioned reached their highest points, as for instance in the University, by Bartolomeo Bianco, in the 1620's—not strange that, to the east, Venice, Genoa's great rival city, despite military and political setbacks, was developing a vital and characteristic Baroque style of its own. Especially remarkable were the great Pesaro Palace and the domical church of Santa Maria della Salute, both designed by Baldassare Longhena. In these, the simple order treatment developed earlier in Venice by Lombardo and Sansovino was preserved, but handled with a boldness of projection, a richness of architectural sculpture, a kind of arrogant heaviness of detail that is eloquent of the new style. In Santa Maria della Salute, Longhena went even further, and no Baroque church is probably more indicative of the Baroque ideals than this. Its two domes, one over the nave and one over the chancel; the chapels which project around its octagonal plan, each treated as an independent unit; the bold height of the dome drum; and the great buttresses which render its support possible, treated like enormous scrolls, each carrying a figure—all of these combine to give it a variety of silhouette, an interesting dramatic unity, a power and a richness which are perfect expressions of the Baroque spirit. Inside also, the Baroque love for changing views, for the interesting and interlocking relationship of differing spaces, is obvious. The way in which space opens from space, and views of the high dome can be gained through the side-aisle arches; the manner in which the chancel, the nave, and the sacristy are related—these are original, unlike anything in any other church, and owe their peculiar climax effectiveness to Baroque design and to Baroque taste.

The culmination of the Baroque in Italy came in the far south and the far north—in Turin, where the growing importance of the House of Savoy was rapidly creating a capital which rivaled and exceeded in its luxurious life and its wealth the earlier cities of Lombardy or Tuscany, and in the far south, in Sicily, where the seventeenth century brought a new outpouring of construction in which the Baroque ideas had full sway, expressed with a particularly fantastic and lively imagination. The architects of Turin and of Sicily both went further even than Borromini in their extraordinary phantasies on classic themes. This movement reached its height in the buildings of Filippo Juvara, whose work extended into the eighteenth century. The Madama Palace and the church of San Filippo are as far removed from the Baroque of Rome as the Baroque of Rome is from the High Renaissance work which had preceded it, for in these Turin buildings one gets not only a use of all the standard Baroque elements—the succession of varying spaces, the elaboration of stairs, the rich contrast of differing interior details—but also a new element, an emphasis on curved rooms, on broken exterior surfaces, and especially on larger and larger windows. In Guarini's Palazzo Carignano the great oval room, projecting as the main feature of the façade, gives at once a vitality to perspective lines, a lightness and playfulness of exterior aspect, quite different from such a façade as that of the restrained, classically decorated Barberini Palace.

In this work in Turin the Baroque style had reached a level of flexibility which was unsurpassed. The architects who worked with it were now masters of every trick of light and shade, of plastic variation, of interior space composition, and their danger lay in this very mastery; the last elements of structural expression sometimes disappeared entirely in the search for the new and strange. Form, which must be the basis of any great architecture, showed signs of disintegration; the architects, immersed in the creation of interesting and fanciful details, of successions of varying spaces, achieved variety and a fantastic quality at the expense of unity and fundamental harmony. Only minds of the greatest imagination could command the enormous architectural resources which the wealth of the day and the taste of the time had put into the architects' hands; and again and again work of the late seventeenth century or the beginning of the eighteenth shows a kind of restless megalomania, a kind of forced drama, that approaches stridency in the obviousness of its effects, a kind of disregard for structure and material which has almost become an insult to structure and material. It is this work which has brought to the Baroque expression a popular condemnation frequently undeserved. It is not merely that it is "not in good taste," for good taste changes from decade to decade, almost from year to year, and there is no style that man has ever created which is continually and always good or bad; it is something deeper than this which troubles us in front of some of the Late Baroque work, especially of northern Italy and of Germany—it is the fact that the architect, in gaining this amazingly skillful intricacy, has lost the one absolutely necessary architectural quality, harmonious interrelated unity. The details have swallowed the whole.

From Italy the Baroque influence swept rapidly over Europe. The end of the Thirty Years' War saw the Roman church and the Roman influence dominant over vast sections of central Europe. The "Holy Roman Empire," centered in Vienna, became in one sense the greatest living expression of that centralized power which was at the heart of Baroque life. To the west of Switzerland, Louis XIII was rapidly building a similar centralized France, and under Louis XIV the ideal of the state as both patron and dictator of the arts was finally built into the firm system of the French Academy. The power of the Jesuit order was wide and deep, and the Jesuit architects—men of amazing competence though perhaps little originality—filled Europe with imitations, big and little, more or less good, of their Mother Church, the Gesù, in Rome. Italian architects again were in demand throughout Germany and north as far as the Russian Empire; and, even where local tradition was strong, the local architects, whenever they could, traveled to Rome, studied there, and on their return re-expressed the ideals of the Roman Baroque in their own architectural language.

Thus, in Austria, Fischer von Erlach, Lukas von Hildebrandt, and Jakob Prandauer, learning all that Bernini and Borromini had to offer, developed their own personal interpretations of the Baroque, which in flexibility, in decorative richness, and especially in dynamic drama of effect excelled some of the work of their teachers. Von Erlach, who worked in Prague and in Salzburg, as well as in Vienna, was the most restrained of the three, superior always in the astonishing skill with which he alternated the most delicate architectural members with boldly projecting, vivid, almost tortured sculpture, or else, if the architectural members were emphasized, kept the sculptural detail simple and refined, so that never is there a conflict between the two. In the Karlskirche he produced one of the most brilliant church exteriors of the Baroque, using a simple pedimented portico, widespreading *porte cochère* wings, two high free-standing columns (reduced copies of the Column of Trajan), and yet somehow subordinating all of this to the great oval dome that crowns the whole. It is theatrical, of course, but it is good theater, and the skill with which its various parts are related, the way in which the dome from any point of view forms the climax, is matched in Baroque church design only by Longhena's Santa Maria della Salute. Within, the same dramatic skill controls, and the plan has that quality of contrast of simple large forms with rich detail which is of the essence of von Erlach's spirit.

The loveliest of his secular buildings is the royal library of the Hofburg palace, where the wings are treated with the greatest simplicity, and the suave projecting curve of the central motif—outlined and emphasized by delicate rustication and crowned with its richly decorated curved slate roof —gives just the right touch of climax. Inside, the great hall of the library, divided into five parts by interesting columnar screens, is perhaps the most magnificent library room in the world. Its walls are still lined with its original books, exquisitely bound in royal bindings; its cases of intricately carved oak, its curved gallery, supported on rich wooden posts, the oval arches of the screens, the combination of gray marble, bronze, the soft tones of the old oak, the glint of the book bindings, and the soft rose and blue of the painted ceiling—all flooded by light from large well-spaced windows— make a picture one can never forget. There is something especially significant in this room, for it reveals the Baroque ruler not only as a man of wealth, which of course he was, but also as a real patron of literature and all the arts, and perhaps sincerely attempting to be something of a scholar as well as a ruler.

The genius of Lukas von Hildebrandt is different. Here one gets the full unashamed phantasy of Baroque imagination. Curved and scrolled

93. THE MONASTERY, MELK; VIEW FROM THE DANUBE. Prandauer, architect (Briggs: *Baroque Architecture.*)

pediments, interiors with sprawled, struggling figures holding up the great stair runs and landings, forms eccentric and vivid—these are the elements which he loved. In the upper Belvedere palace a most interesting combination of low towers, projecting pavilions, and curved roofs shows the characteristic Baroque plastic imagination, the desire to create a building that is as interesting as a piece of sculpture in its silhouette and light and shade.

Prandauer was essentially a designer of monasteries. Melk, Dürnstein, and St. Florian were all his creations. He is perhaps the most original, one might almost say the most northern, of the three men, combining something of von Erlach's sense of contrast with something of Hildebrandt's fantastic imagination, and adding to the mixture a love for bulbous forms, for high pinnacles, and for sharp accents that seems both distantly Gothic and distantly Slavic. He appears to have had also an uncanny ability in adjusting buildings to their sites. Since his work was chiefly monastic, it is also chiefly in the hilly, river-scored Austrian countryside; and the way the twin towers of the Melk chapel, with the forecourt in front of them, climb up from the cliffs of the Danube shore, and are buttressed by long lines of perfectly simple, many-windowed monastic buildings, is one of the greatest examples of a complete merging of site and building into one artistic whole.

Further west the story is similar. In Munich, the Italian architect Agostino Barelli started the greater Theatiner-Kirche; another Italian, Zuccali, completed the dome and designed the façade. It all has a superb bigness of scale truly Italian, and at the same time just those touches of eccentric imagination which indicate something of the taste of Bavaria. Later, a whole school of extraordinarily skillful native architects developed in Bavaria and Württemberg, until there is hardly a town in the neighborhood, however small, which does not possess some trace of their work, some church with dome and bulbous spire, with intricate curved-line plan, with amazing Baroque decoration around its altar and its entrance. The most remarkable of these men were the Dientzenhofers, who built church after church in which the German love of vertical lines and of fantastic ornament more and more freed itself from Italian precedent. Typical are the abbey church at Banz and the west façade of St. Michaels-Kirche at Bamberg, by Johann Lionhard Dientzenhofer; the cathedral at Fulda and the schloss of Pommersfelden, by his brother Johann; and the church of St. Johann am Felsen, Prague, by Kilian Ignaz, their nephew.

In Würzburg, the Residenz, begun in 1720, designed by Germain Boffrand and Johann Balthasar Neumann, forms, next to Versailles, the greatest single palace of the Baroque period. Late though it is, the Rococo style shows only in its interior decorations. The whole plan, with its superb staircase, painted by Tiepolo, leading up to an enormous oval throne room, is of the essence of Baroque planning, and shows the dramatic skill of the Baroque architects as well as the fact that these Baroque palaces were built for pageants, in a sense for the drama, of the court of an absolute ruler rather than as houses in which to live pleasantly or even comfortably. If comfort and convenience had to conflict with this impersonal court pageantry, it was always the comfort and the convenience which yielded.

In Prussia the influences at play were entirely different. There the Jesuit example had little effect. Instead, political attraction was all toward France and the West, so that the influence of the Louis XIV buildings was supreme, and many French, Flemish, and Dutch names appear among those who worked in Berlin and Potsdam.

The end of the Wars of Religion in France and the coming to the throne of Henry IV initiated a new epoch. The Baroque political idealism which was almost inevitably building up the conception of highly centralized governments, under the personal sway of an absolute monarchy, ruled the political development of France, eventually creating from the chaos of the Wars of Religion the extraordinary governmental structure of Louis XIV. Yet, because of the very perfection of this structure, Roman influence was bound to be less than in Germany, for the essence of the royal power under the Louis was its firm foundation in French nationalism, conceived as a cultural as well as a political factor. Henry IV, idolized by his people, himself idolized France and, lighthearted and erratic as he undoubtedly sometimes was, held as perhaps his major ideal the development of a French life for French people. Some of his improvements in Paris have already been listed. He set a fashion that his successors could hardly do more than follow.

What is perhaps most interesting architecturally in the work done under Henry's reign and that of Louis XIII is the astonishing and perhaps voluntarily sought Frenchness of it all. Local materials and local conditions everywhere controlled, and the French architects of the period were fortunately men of unusual ability, equal to the task which was thus set before them. To be sure, Salamon de Brosse, when he built the Luxembourg Palace for Marie de' Medici, gave her the rusticated stonework which Ammanati had used in her earlier favorite home, the Pitti Palace, but with what a different touch does it appear here! The building is designed as the typical French château, with boldly projecting corner pavilions and high slate roofs with large chimneys. The windows are much larger, so that the whole rhythm of wall and window is more like that set by Pierre Lescot under Francis I, years before, than like that of any Italian palace; and this great rusticated building was set at the head of an enclosed courtyard of French rather than Italian type, the Henry IV expression of the old idea of the castle courtyard or bailey. The court has to the outside simple rusticated walls, and in the center a beautiful gateway carrying a dome—a gateway which combines monumental grandeur with a kind of delicacy that is somehow characteristically French.

In the Temple of Charenton, which de Brosse designed as the first great monumental Protestant church in France, his originality is easily seen, for the building was a simple rectangular hall surrounded by galleries on all four sides, lighted by large windows, crowned with a high roof, and having in its midst a central raised pulpit. In this building the quality of logical analysis of a problem, which so frequently has distinguished the academic architecture of France ever since, showed itself unmistakably, for de Brosse realized at once that for congregational worship—in which preaching was perhaps the chief element—a far different type of church was necessary than for the Roman rites.

De Brosse was but the first of a long series of brilliant Baroque architects who served the kings of France so well. Jacques Lemercier, the great architect of Cardinal Richelieu and Louis XIII, had a similar independence, emphasizing even more strongly than de Brosse the high roofs that seemed to him native to France. He designed a huge enlargement of the old Louvre, more than doubling its size, and had both the genius and the modesty to make the greater part of it a mere reproduction of the Pierre Lescot portion already built. To connect the old and the new he designed a new high entrance pavilion, with a great arch through which the Louvre court was entered, raised it high enough above the wings to count as the central motif and bring them into proper subordination, and crowned the whole with a high curve-sided slate roof—a sort of square "dome" which he used again and again in other works as well. For Richelieu he built not only the great Château Richelieu, now destroyed, which was in its size, the richness of its gardens, and the extent of its dependencies the first step on a path that was to lead eventually to Versailles, but also the little neighboring town of Richelieu, built complete from his designs, with its brick walls, its lovely brick-and-stone gates, and its simple, regularly spaced houses. In this there appears a kind of wall treatment that is especially characteristic of the native quality of much work built under Henry IV and Louis XIII. The walls are chiefly of brick, undecorated, but emphasized by stone frames around the windows, stone quoins at the corners, and stone cornices and bases. A building so built, because of the richness of the color patterning, has little need for other architectural ornament; there is an almost total absence of columns or pilasters or all the ornament usually associated with Renaissance and Baroque work. The emphasis is on proportion, necessarily, and the discipline of working in this simple style undoubtedly did much to clarify and to refine the French architects' skill. Another exquisite example of work of this type is the great service court at the château at Fontainebleau, where the brick is stuccoed and the stone window frames and quoins left in slight relief.

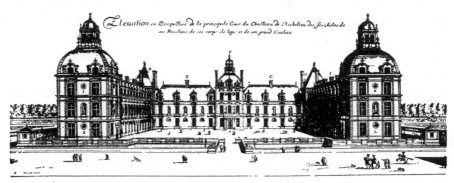

94. CHÂTEAU OF RICHELIEU; VIEW IN THE COURT. Lemercier, architect. (Marot: *Le magnifique chasteau de Richelieu.*)

But there was another tendency at work in the architecture of the time, a more direct reflection of the Baroque revolution elsewhere—a tendency toward experimentalism in detail. Although wall compositions were commonly simple, again and again doors, dormer windows, even chimneys were treated with the greatest variety of scrolls, broken pediments, masks, and those shields on curved panels surrounded by elaborate scrolled frames which are called cartouches. It was all vivid and personal, but frequently erratic and, in the sense of scale especially, tentative and unsure. It was as though the French architects were making all the possible experiments they could, with the complete freedom which their French tradition and the new Baroque forms alike allowed. Often moldings and cartouches were over-large; there is a sense of the heavy-handed in much of this work. Yet through its very uncouth variety the French architects were learning priceless lessons in what good detail and harmonious scale are and are not. At times effects of great interest were gained. Pierre Lemuet was the architect who distinguished himself particularly in the variety and the ingenuity of his experiments, seeking new ways of using even the most common classic details, as for instance in the château of Pontz, where he covered the wall surfaces between the windows with slightly projecting pilasters, jammed as closely as they could be put, so that their old semistructural expression disappears entirely and they become mere decorations of the wall.

Indoors, the same sort of experimentalism prevailed. Wood wainscot began to play a greater and greater part in interior design, and painted walls and tapestries were less and less used. The fireplaces lacked the monumental heaviness of the earlier period, but still frequently retained an elaborate paneled overmantel, often decorated with cartouches and sculpture. Toward the end of the period, delicate monochrome painted patterns appeared over the panels of the woodwork, and a great sense of lightness and delicacy crept into the moldings, as though little by little the experimentalism of the period that had passed was gradually resulting in a growing simplicity, a growing sense of human delicacy, of proper scale, of refinement.

The end of the period, which covered roughly the first half of the seventeenth century, saw a succession of great architects, who, making use of the results of the experiments which had preceded them, succeeded in imposing a new discipline on the variety of forms. There was, all through France, a new turning back to classical ideals, but classic ideals which had become thoroughly assimilated and were themselves a part of the French tradition, so that the work which was produced not only had a new dignity of formal planning and careful composition, but was equally well a purely French expression. The Baroque elements were used with discretion, and the flurry of Baroque freedom which had characterized the early part of the period left as a permanent result a freedom in the handling of detail which is one of the marks of succeeding French architecture.

The three greatest architects of the time were Jacques Lemercier, already mentioned, Louis Levau, and François Mansart. Besides his work at the Louvre and the château of Richelieu, Lemercier is best known for the domed chapel that he built for the Sorbonne (the University of Paris). Here appeared for the first time in France a fully developed domical church in the Baroque manner, with a high drum, a dominant dome, and a façade with a well-designed pediment, side scrolls, and two tiers of classic orders. Although in size comparatively small, the chapel has the true French sense of perfect scale. It is essentially monumental, and, especially on the interior, there are many elements which differentiate it drastically from the contemporary churches of Rome, particularly a restraint in the use of the orders and a simplicity in the treatment of structural elements which are characteristically French. For the French architects even at the height of the Baroque never lost their sensitiveness to the material and to structure; they never sacrificed, as the Italians so constantly did, the feeling of structure to the search for drama. Lemercier also had a part in the designing of another great domical church in Paris, the convent chapel of the Val-de-Grâce, although the chief credit for its final design and completion must go to François Mansart. The Val-de-Grâce is a church much larger than the Sorbonne chapel, and its dome is plainly based on Michelangelo's design for the dome of St. Peter's in Rome. Its façade, too, is Roman in spirit. Nevertheless, in the whole church there is a character essentially Parisian, and the originality with which the nuns' chapel is treated as an enlarged transept and the altar is placed in the center, directly under the dome, so as to be on the axis both of the nuns' chapel and the public nave, shows the inventiveness of the French designers. The conventual buildings that surround the chapel are equally French and equally monumental, and the contrast of the low, restrained, arcaded wings with the high chapel façade is an exquisite example of that mastery of basic mass composition which was more and more a French quality.

Louis Levau was perhaps the most erratic and in some ways the most original of the three men. He did a vast amount of work at the Louvre, completing its court with a simple treatment which is almost banal but has the virtue of restraint. In the Collège des Quatre Nations, now the Institut de France, Levau had a better opportunity to show his merits; on a most irregular piece of ground he erected not only a college building surrounding a simple, well-designed court, but also a college chapel entered from an impressive semicircular forecourt. The whole exterior composition, with its strong corner elements, its arcaded curved connecting wings, and the high dome and simple strong front of the chapel in the middle, forms still today one of the most powerful and attractive elements in that magnificent architectural panorama which the banks of the Seine unfold. Levau was, in fact, a marvelous architectural composer, at times heavy-handed in detail, but full of imagination and with an unusual sense of varied and monumental design. The ingenious planning of his city houses, like the Hôtel Lambert; his free yet powerful use of the classic orders; his sense of classic structure used in new ways, so beautifully shown in the great church of St. Sulpice, where on a plan almost Gothic he produced one of the largest, most Baroque, and at the same time most restrained of the classic churches in Paris—these are all characteristics of the man. His masterpiece was probably the château of Vaux-le-Vicomte, built for Nicolas Fouquet, whose not-too-well-gotten gains were expended there in the most lavish manner. The essential element which sets Vaux-le-Vicomte apart from most of the châteaux of its time is the tremendous oval salon, two stories high, in the center of its garden front, and the effective way in which a severely classic wall is combined with the traditional high roofs of earlier palaces.

The most polished designer of the group was undoubtedly François Mansart, whose work bridges the gradual change from the style of Louis XIII, still somewhat tentative, to the fully developed academic classicism of the Louis XIV period. François Mansart (Mansard) worked in both veins. The château of Balleroy is perhaps the last word in the brick and stone quoin construction that had been popular under Henry IV, but the château of Maisons and the wing of Gaston d'Orléans at Blois are equally remarkable examples of the classical approach, in which the walls are treated with correct orders and the whole effort is toward simple and monumental dignity.

Louis XIV (*Le Roi Soleil*) was unquestionably one of the great monarchs of history, as he was one of the most characteristic expressions of Baroque culture. Large-minded, his ambitions were not limited to political and military ends; it was his desire to make France as unified and as powerful a cultural force as it was a military regime. Under the influence of his adviser Colbert, little by little the whole machinery of the French Academy of Arts arose. At first this academy was a discussion group of the best-known architects and artists of the time, to which all important architectural questions, both aesthetic and structural, could be submitted for discussion and eventual decision. Through an elaborate series of royal licenses, the whole architectural profession was brought into the closest relation to the academy and the court itself. Later, classes for teaching promising young men were added to this framework, until the academy found itself running what amounted to a real professional school, or rather a series of professional schools, of architecture, painting, and sculpture. Furniture design and decoration also were taken under the royal sway, and this combination of aesthetic and intellectual stimulus, added to the almost unlimited funds for expenditure on buildings and furniture over which the court had command—for Louis XIV was an inveterate builder,—rapidly produced an amazing unity in the architectural and decorative work in France; and the style of Louis XIV became an official style, the result of the royal authority and the expression of the royal taste.

This is well evidenced by the story of the completion of the old Louvre. The simple façades which Levau had given the outside of the palace did not at all appeal to the luxurious taste of the French court. All of Louis's artistic taste was founded on classic principles, and all of his influence and that of his advisers and naturally of the royal Academy was more and more directed toward a monumental classicism which should combine dignity and grace, restraint and power. The Louvre became the subject of great controversy; it had to be the best palace in the world, so Bernini, the most famous architect in the world, was invited to come to Paris and prepare a design. Bernini's design, of which drawings still exist, was a tremendously powerful conception, with a colossal scale almost equal to that of St. Peter's itself; but it was utterly un-French, and it either destroyed or hid behind its gargantuan forms all the earlier work that had previously been done. Fundamentally it could never please the French court, for Louis was as insistent on developing an architecture truly French as he was on seeing that it was also truly classic; so Bernini was paid well and sent home. Finally a design by an amateur, a famous anatomist and doctor, Claude Perrault, was adopted, in which for the first time the new ideals achieved an almost perfect architectural expression; and the east colonnade of the Louvre, at that time the main front, with its simple basement, its ample yet human scale, its magnificent range of coupled Corinthian columns, and the brilliantly original and thoroughly French treatment of the central motif and the corner pavilions, is even today considered by many one of the most beautiful façades in the world.

The final expression of such a centralized taste must inevitably come from a great centralized architectural office, and such an office rapidly grew up, under the control of Jules Hardouin Mansart, a nephew of François. The amount of work which flowed through that office was prodigious. In it were employed the most brilliant designers and draftsmen of the period— men like Lassurance, Antoine Lepautre, and Robert de Cotte. There has been much controversy as to the exact amount of credit due to Mansart and his assistants in the varied productions of the office. Mansart was evidently more the administrator than the designer or the draftsman; however, the complete harmony and unity of character of all of these royal buildings must be due in some small measure to the taste of the head of the firm.

Mansart's most original design was the domical chapel he added to the great military hospital another architect, Libéral Bruant, had built a few years before on the outskirts of Paris. This domed chapel, known as the Dôme des Invalides, or simply the Dôme, and famous now because within it lies the tomb of Napoleon, is one of the great domed churches of Europe, different in conception from any other, more daring structurally, with the complexities of its composition more perfectly solved. Mansart simplified his building by making it absolutely square in plan—a nave, transepts, and choir of identical length, with four chapels in the corners covered by low domes. This gave to the central area where the great dome rises a simplicity of form, a unity of feeling, which is one of its marked qualities, and allowed a certain suavity of treatment not only characteristically French but also the direct result of the simplifications of the basic plan. The dome itself is triple—an inner dome on a high drum, with a great opening in its center; above this an intermediate dome of masonry, carrying a painting on its under side, where it could be seen with typically Baroque dramatic effect through the opening in the lower dome; and above this again an outer

95. DÔME OF THE INVALIDES, PARIS; SECTION. J. H. Mansart, architect. (Ward: *The Architecture of the Renaissance in France.*)

dome and lantern of timber covered with lead and richly gilded. The intermediate dome is most cleverly arranged with windows to light its mural. The combination of daring and simplicity in the plan and structure is paralleled on the exterior. Two stories of orders form the entrance porch and decorate the simple square of the external wall. Above this rises the dome drum, boldly; and the silhouette of the outer dome and its lantern is audacious in its height and the projection of its details. The whole, both outside and in, shows the extraordinary command over classic form which these Louis XIV architects had developed, and reveals as well a certain conscious restraint and delicacy in detail, combined with largeness of general conception, which is typical of the work of the Mansart office.

The great work, not merely of the office but perhaps of the whole period in western Europe, was the palace at Versailles, where, around the kernel of a hunting lodge designed by de Brosse, there grew up little by little the world's greatest palace, a half mile long, set in a garden that is one of the Renaissance wonders of the world. Nowhere else has a single formal pattern of such variety and yet such unity been so arrogantly imposed on, and yet so harmoniously blended with, a whole countryside, and nowhere else perhaps has so much money, so much labor, so much intelligence been applied to the problem of creating a framework for a great royal court. As a residence the palace is absurd; as a setting for royal pageantry, few suites can be imagined more perfectly fitted than the great sequence of halls across the garden front, with the *Galerie des Glaces* as its climax element. There is here a combined richness and simplicity, a bigness of scale, a variety of form which are remarkable.

The outside of Versailles, like the east front of the Louvre, reveals the new form that architecture had taken. Gone are the high roofs, the dormer windows, the large chimneys, the brick and stone of the earlier period; instead, the whole is flat-roofed, with a crowning balustrade, and the walls below treated with an exquisite yet powerful simplicity; a rusticated basement supports a single tier of pilasters and engaged columns, artfully arranged in slightly projecting pavilions to give variety to the whole and centrality to the axis, yet in themselves all delicately detailed and human in scale, in spite of the enormous extent of the entire building. It is manifestly a structure not to be seen from any single point of view, but so designed as to produce interesting forms from almost any position. It retains a strong French character notwithstanding the quiet classicism of its detail, a character to be seen in the ample window sizes, the rhythmical change of wall and window, and a certain neat perfection of execution.

In a sense the palace is meaningless without its garden, and the genius of the architect needed the genius of André Le Nôtre, the landscape designer, to complete the whole. The French Baroque garden was essentially different from the Italian garden, though it retains the Italian formality, the Baroque geometry, and something of the Italian feeling that building and garden are but parts of one composition. The French gardens sought for greater breadth, wider views, and more extended continuous axes, and used water in wide quiet canals and large spreading pools as well as in elaborate fountains. Grass, too, for the first time in garden work came into its own. To give scale and human quality to such vast and open expanses of water and path and lawn, the French garden architect developed the idea of the bosquet—the thick woods out of which could be cut, almost carved, outdoor rooms embellished with their own fountains, their own pavilions and colonnades, and entered mysteriously through curving or narrow paths. And the woods could be clipped at their sides to form vertical walls to frame the great axis, thus bringing the necessary sense of power and of growing things into the whole picture. At Versailles, some of the bosquets are of colossal size, and an exquisite series of engravings exists showing the superb pageantry of the great parties which Louis XIV liked to hold in them.

Almost the same kind of plan composition was applied to civic design. Great avenues were cut through towns and projected out into the country beyond, just as the axes of the gardens were carried across the hills and valleys. Squares were opened up among the city buildings, as the bosquets and *carrefours* were opened up in the gardens; and the drive toward unity and monumentality of effect which is seen so plainly in the royal buildings of the Louvre and Versailles can be noted equally well in the outside façades of the Place Vendôme and the Place des Victoires, in Paris, or the Place Royale in Bordeaux.

In such a civilization the residences of the ordinary people are relegated to an entirely secondary position. The court was the center of all things, and only those nobles or merchants who had achieved court dignity and the wealth which usually attended it built important houses. These must be big and formal, for formality was of the essence of life at the time; yet it was wise not to have them too big. It is said that Louis XIV's envy of Vaux le Vicomte was not a little responsible for Fouquet's downfall and death! The characteristic Paris house of the great men of the court developed a typical form which was given many varied interpretations, especially by Lassurance and Lepautre. Several of them still remain on the Île St. Louis and along the streets of the Faubourg St. Germain. From the street one entered a wide court through a monumental entrance in a simple enclosure wall. On either side of the court rose service wings, one usually containing the stables, the other the kitchens. At the end of the court was the house proper, generally two stories high, though sometimes an attic existed above the main story. The house was only two rooms deep, so that it was long and narrow, and the windows of its chief entertainment rooms, all arranged *en suite,* looked out over a terrace and garden behind. In many cases the entrances were at the corners of the court rather than in the center, with perhaps twin monumental staircases leading up to the main floor. Of privacy there was little or none, and bedchambers were often as formal and public as the entertainment rooms themselves. What privacy there was came merely from the multiplicity of units of the same general type.

The interior treatment of all of these large houses, like that of Versailles, was unified, classic, dignified, impersonal. Rooms were now paneled clear from floor to ceiling, usually with large vertical panels. A rich cornice and sometimes a sweeping cove above it connected walls and ceiling; pilasters often flanked the fireplace and sometimes were used elsewhere in the room. Almost universal features were painted or sculptured panels above the doors and large mirrors over all the fireplaces. The wood was almost always painted ivory white, with many of the panel moldings and much of the ceiling decoration picked out in gold. Occasionally rich marbles were used as wainscoting, especially in the more public rooms and halls; and, little by little, more and more naturalistic ornament crept into the whole—bunches of flowers, hanging garlands, and the like. At the same time, the acanthus leaf tended to disappear in favor of palm leaves and the newer naturalistic ornament. It was all extremely profuse, rather overwhelming, courtly in all the senses of that word, dignified and never frivolous. It was a fit frame-work for the bewigged men with their flaring coats and rich satins, brocades, and embroideries, and for the voluminous skirts and tall headdresses of the women, who carried on within it the monotonous, the exciting, the dreary, the dramatic, the essentially unreal life of the court.

Nowhere was Baroque exuberance more at home than in Spain. The High Renaissance, which had been so assiduously cultivated by the architects of Charles V and Philip II, had never become a really general Spanish style. It lacked opportunities for the expression of that vividness of invention, that dramatic contrast, that naïve combination of influences from so many sources—Gothic and Moorish—which was so dear to the Spanish heart. To the Spanish architect or sculptor the categories of High Renaissance classic could never seem more than irksome restrictions. As a result the spirit of the Baroque brought with it a feeling almost as of one coming home again after a visit to strange and not too well liked foreign parts. Now again the Spanish fancy could flow freely over an architectural problem, could concentrate luxuriant ornament to form a smashing climax in a quiet wall; now again stone and wood and plaster could be carved or modeled into forms which had no limits except those of their creator's desire.

And it was a time of opulence in Spanish life. The Spanish colonial empire was at its height, pouring into the country—into the coffers of the church and of the great noble families—a steady stream of wealth which seemed to have no end. The effect was inevitably great growth in the cities, with an enormous amount of new building everywhere. New chapels were added to the churches; new altarpieces rose along the walls, tier on tier of rich carving.

Of course, this Spanish Baroque ornament was quite different in character from the Plateresque ornament of a century earlier. Nevertheless, in basic decorative ideals there was much in common between them. Just as the Plateresque style had used the orders less than they had been used in the Early Renaissance in Italy, so in the Baroque period the Spanish architects took much greater freedom with the orders than did the Baroque architects elsewhere. Just as the Plateresque artists had never been afraid of large areas of surface ornament, provided there was always the contrast of plain wall, so now in the same way the Baroque designers, using an even richer, much more varied, much more dynamic type of detail, liked to contrast it with simple stone surfaces on either side. The result is that, again and again, a distant view or a superficial study shows little to distinguish buildings of the earliest and of the latest of the Spanish Renaissance styles; it is only on closer acquaintance that the tremendous differences in the ornament used become apparent.

The style is usually called *Churrigueresque,* from Jose Churriguera, one of the most important Spanish architects of the time. Fundamentally the style is much wider than its name would indicate, and, indeed, differentiated by many characteristics not to be found in the more restrained works of Churriguera himself, who tended more to design in an all-over, rather Italianized style. Of works of the larger type, church façades are the most important. The Spanish architects, like the Italians, often treated church fronts as a mere decorative screen, with little necessary relation to the roof and wall lines behind, and the Spanish love for lavish decoration found in these screen façades admirable opportunities. Often, as in the cathedral of Jaen, the whole front is treated as though it were a great niche, so that vivid changing light and shade plays over the whole surface, and the rich ornament that decorates it appears now in bright sun, now in half light, now in shadow, as the curve changes. The skyline is broken up and sometimes bizarre, and often the church façade is composed with a bell tower at its side or near by.

The most elaborate of these church fronts is that which was added to the famous pilgrimage church of Santiago de Compostela, by Fernando Casas y Novoa, *circa* 1730. It is pure surface decoration of the most skillful type, a sort of fretwork of light and shade, in which every part is beautifully related to all the rest in scale and in its sense of balanced motion; and the whole is so designed that it is equally satisfactory both from a distance, when only its major lines can be appreciated, and from near by, when the extraordinary jeweled intricacy of it comes into view. And it has an extremely emotional and romantic quality, not too common. The stairs, the severe plain basement walls of the flanking buildings, the open loggias at the sides, the original treatment of the vertical lines on the towers, the balance between the horizontal and the vertical, the strong focus of interest on the center—all of these unite to form an unforgettable picture.

A characteristic feature of almost all Spanish towns is the design of the Baroque church towers which so frequently give them lively interest. In a sense, these towers are merely higher developments of a type of Renaissance composition developed first in the Giralda at Seville. The lower part of the Giralda is the plain square Moorish minaret of the original mosque. On this the Renaissance architects had placed a series of square setback elements, each smaller and more open than the one beneath it. The contrast achieved between the simplicity below and the broken outline and airiness of the upper portions is most effective. In the Baroque period, this same general scheme —plain, almost heavy simplicity below and more open stages above—was used again and again with all sorts of interesting varieties. Especially fre. quent was the use of octagonal instead of square upper portions, and the whole was usually crowned with a dome. In small examples there was but one upper stage, often rather low, while in larger towers there might be two or three; but always the characteristic Baroque contrast between the plain lower portion and the decorated upper part was stressed.

Yet perhaps the most typical of the Spanish Baroque buildings are the town houses of the smaller towns, and the little monasteries and country houses of the villages. The growing wealth and vitality of Spain did not limit itself to the larger cities, the great cathedrals, and the huge palaces of ducal families, but seems to have spread itself over almost the entire country. In town after town the streets are lined by houses of the seventeenth or early eighteenth century, with plain walls, large but widely spaced windows covered with exquisite grille work, or balconies of the most delicate wrought iron projecting over the sidewalk, and with an entrance door enriched by the reduplicated moldings, the broken lines, and the lavish exuberance of the Spanish Baroque. In town after town, too, one may come almost unexpectedly on a gateway in a long, plain, unbroken white wall—a gateway, frosted with the most profuse Baroque ornament, which leads into a monastery church. In the smaller houses of the country, the same love of balconies is seen, but here again and again it is wood which is the controlling material, rather than iron; and, especially in northern Spain, these village houses, with their wood-beamed balconies projecting so frankly from the wall and crowned with railings of slim turned wood pilasters, are charming examples of a kind of Baroque that owes its loveliness to simple economy.

The climax of Churrigueresque richness came in the church interiors— in the tombs and altarpieces and the sacristies. Here the classic orders almost disappeared under the floods of foliage, figures, and reduplicated moldings which surrounded them. Reduplication of line became almost a fetish of the designers. Niches and doors were surrounded, not with one, but with three or four or even five separate frames, each different from the other, each full of sudden breaks of light and dark, in and out. Often the columns were twisted, with ornament carried spirally around the twist, filling its hollows; and there was a tremendous use of hanging swags, as though of drapery, carved in the stone or the wood. Even lines originally structural, such as architrave and cornice lines, would be bent up or down in sudden breaks and curves, so that the eye becomes almost bewildered; and, if the basic decorative compositions had not been so sure and strong, the result would have been mere chaos. In the sacristy of the Certosa at Granada, by Frey Manuel Vasquez, the boundary was almost passed, for here not only the cabinets, the cases, and the details were so treated, but the basic architectural features of the room itself; and the "columns" (if one may call them so) at the corners from which the vault rose were a confusing mass of twisted and contorted moldings and leafage, which climbed unbroken from the base to the spring of the vault. At a distance, with half-closed eyes, one can pick out of this maze something of the fundamental light and shade which define the cornice, the frieze, the architrave, the capital, and the base of the order; but, from near at hand, even this system-giving appearance is lost—one is only conscious of elaboration.

Beyond such work as this, human imagination could go no further; the end of the period saw a general veering away from such cloying enrichment, and turned almost abruptly to more restrained and more French types of design. This last type of French-inspired Baroque can be seen especially in Valencia, in the house of the Marqués de Dos Aquas, where the ornament of the exterior is full of tricks which the French used for interior work only, and where the great door is surrounded by a mass of sculpture in which architectural forms are completely forgotten and replaced by an accumulation of seminaturalistic ornament.

The parliamentary system in England was too deeply ingrained in the English character to permit a great development of the Baroque type of centralized and autocratic government. Charles I tried it and was beheaded; Cromwell tried it, and popular support swung over to the Royalists and brought back Charles II. Charles II was too interested in his own pleasures, too mentally curious about all the manifold artistic and cultural advances of the time to be much worried about government at all. His successor, James II, tried it, and the result was the Revolution of 1688 and the bringing of William and Mary from Holland, with the parliamentary system stronger than ever.

It is not surprising, therefore, to find that many of the ideas of Baroque architecture found but a grudging welcome in the British Isles, and only appeared there later at the very end of the seventeenth and the beginning of the eighteenth century, when English wealth, largely centered in the hands of a few great families, enabled the dukes and wealthy lords to build themselves houses in which they and their architecture could play with the ideas of Baroque grandeur. In general the Baroque, then, came to England only as a matter of superficial and fashionable details, and the quiet Palladianism introduced by Inigo Jones continued to be developed for nearly a century.

The history of the design of St. Paul's Cathedral is itself significant. After the Great Fire of 1666, in which such a large proportion of the city of London was destroyed, the old Gothic cathedral was a dangerous ruin, and its reconstruction became an absolute necessity. Sir Christopher Wren, the architect-in-chief of the court, prepared a design which was thoroughly Baroque in its conception. He envisaged a great domical area of enormous scale, so as to allow large unbroken congregations to attend the service. He surrounded this with a ring of eight chapels, four larger and four smaller, so arranged that the relation of each to the center was emphasized, and the variety of views to be gained as one walked around was extraordinary. The diversity of shapes, the interesting diagonal and transverse arches, the alternation of dome and groined vau , all of this formed an artistic unit full of the true Baroque symphonic quality, and the domination of the central dome over this rich side aisle had the true Baroque drama. But the king and the clergy and their advisers could not see the magnificence of this conception. They wanted a traditional English cathedral, fashionable, to be sure, in *its* use of the current classic idiom, but still in plan the typical English church with long nave and side aisles, transepts, crossing, and a deep chancel. The king also wished a high central tower, and the design which Wren eventually prepared and which the king signed—the so-called "warrant design"— gave the king exactly what he asked for. The crossing was the most interesting part of this design, for Wren realized that English congregational worship needed a large unbroken central space. For this reason, instead of a central dome at the crossing of nave and transepts, such as the Italian Renaissance churches had used, he developed a great central octagonal space as wide as the combined nave and aisles, and over this he raised his great dome. In accordance with the king's wishes, the warrant design crowns this interior dome with a most amazing collection of forms—dome and spire— which pile up into a real central tower quite absurd in effect, and one feels sure that Wren presented this scheme with his tongue in his cheek. Once the design was accepted, this central-tower idea was promptly forgotten and the great present dome system designed. Elsewhere the church as built follows the warrant design exactly, and Wren's brilliant originality can nowhere be better seen than in the way he took this essentially Gothic plan and on it created one of the loveliest Renaissance church interiors in Europe.

Sir Christopher Wren was as much mathematician and scientist as architect. His early interests had been in mathematics and mechanics, and his early reputation was based on mathematical and scientific achievements. He seems to have taken up architecture almost by accident. He was requested to make a design for his Oxford college chapel, and produced a very simple, straightforward solution, with lovely interior paneled walls, a rich plaster ceiling, and an exterior in which engaged Corinthian columns carried a rather Baroque pediment and central belfry. From this he went on to the design of the Sheldonian Theater at Oxford, and because of his mathematical and mechanical skill was enabled to roof it simply and with comparatively little expense by means of excellently designed wooden trusses. This made his reputation, for it was a structural triumph in the England of that time.

It was the Fire of 1666 which brought him his great opportunity, for not only did it result in the rebuilding of St. Paul's, but it also allowed him to present a plan for the rebuilding of the city, which was intelligent despite its formality, and it also forced him to design in short order an immense number of new churches to replace those destroyed in the fire. The plan for the city, like several other excellent plans submitted at the same time, came to nothing. Speed, English traditionalism, and the difficulty of rearranging land titles combined to enforce a rebuilding largely on the old plan; but St. Paul's and the city churches were actually constructed, and they remade English taste, as the work of Inigo Jones had remade it fifty years earlier.

The greatest of the monuments is, of course, St. Paul's; and the most interesting, significant, and characteristic part of St. Paul's is its central area

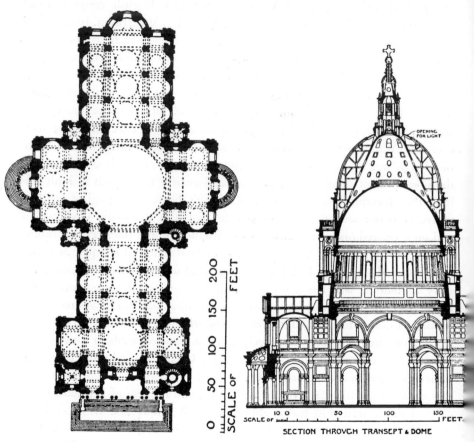

96. ST. PAUL'S, LONDON; PLAN AND SECTION. Wren, architect. (Simpson. Vol. III.)

and great dome, for it shows so well the efforts of a man with splendid analytical powers, unusual structural engineering knowledge, and a rather unsure artistic sense unequal to solving the problems his structural ability could create. From the structural point of view the design is daring and extraordinarily successful. Supports are kept slim, with their long direction always at right angles to the thrust which such a great dome was bound to exert, and they were so disposed as to interrupt as little as possible the great vistas through the church. Light perfectly equal geometrical pendentives rise above the arches which crown the octagon sides; and, to soften the angle between the side aisles of nave and transepts and the forty-five-degree corners of the octagon, niches were built, into which the aisle arches opened. Yet the very simplicity and logical nature of this solution brought artistic difficulties which Wren could solve only in an awkward fashion. The whole system of the niche tops, the last arches of the side aisles, and their relation to the angular arch above is ungainly, complicated, and unsatisfactory; and, because it was manifestly impossible to carry the great weight of the dome above on the thin points established between the pendentives, the canted corners of the diagonal sides were filled in with vertical piers. Obviously, the regular pendentives delighted his geometry-loving soul, but it is equally clear that they were no real solution for the excellent plan he had established.

Above the great circular cornice from which the dome drum rises, the impression is different, because here everything is simple, straightforward, and logical. The dome system consists of an interior dome of hemispherical shape, supported on a drum the walls of which slant inward toward the top so as to reduce the span of the dome itself and still, because of the increased perspective, emphasize the height. Above and outside this inner dome rises a great brick cone, supported on the main nave arches and the walls of the drum. This cone, braced and tied with stone bands here and there, is crowned at the top by a smaller dome far above the opening of the inner dome, and carries in its turn the stone lantern which caps the entire composition. The outside is formed by a vertical drum, built almost independently of the inner one and by its weight helping to withstand the dome thrust. This outer drum carries the exterior dome of timber covered with lead, which is braced out from the brick cone for additional strength. The lower part of the drum is surrounded by a free-standing colonnade of great scale, with certain solid portions tied into the drum itself by cross-walls, so as to furnish still greater buttressing for the thrust. The whole formed an amazingly successful solution of one of the most difficult structural problems in architecture—how to support in a stone-vaulted church a great central dome and lantern, above the nave and aisles of a typical church plan, without using excessively heavy and constricting crossing piers.

The same kind of geometrical imagination, the same love of varied geometrical shapes, is to be seen in the extremely diverse interiors of his city churches. These were built rapidly and cheaply, with wooden roofs and plaster ceilings. The structural problems involved were therefore simple, and allowed the architect the greatest freedom in developing ingenious interior shapes. The dome form is the basis for most of the plans. Oval domes and round domes were combined with polygonal or square plans in the most interesting way, and usually the central part of the ceiling was raised high on slim columns to allow clerestory lighting. In other examples a simple nave and aisle scheme is used, with the addition of a gallery on three sides; and these simple rectangular churches, usually barrel-vaulted, with the vaults and arches carried on simple columns, and intermediate

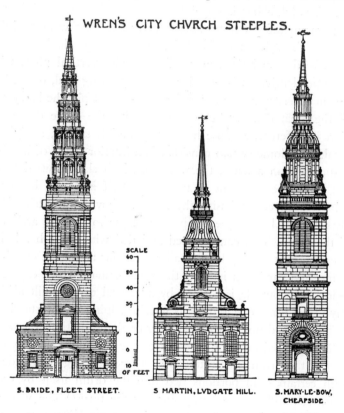

† WREN'S CITY CHVRCH STEEPLES.

SCALE
60
50
40
30
20
10
0
10
OF FEET

S. BRIDE, FLEET STREET.   S MARTIN, LVDGATE HILL.   S. MARY-LE-BOW, CHEAPSIDE

97. CHARACTERISTIC WREN TOWERS. (Simpson. Vol. III.)

galleries running around over the side aisles, formed the essential pioneer examples of a type which was to be so much more highly developed during the eighteenth century in England, as in James Gibbs's famous London church of St. Martin's-in-the-Fields. Both the Gibbs and the Wren churches exerted an enormous influence on the Colonial architecture of America.

The Baroque influence shows itself also in the Wren towers and spires for the city churches. The towerlets on the front of St. Paul's are quite

TURIN, PALAZZO MADAMA; STAIRCASE.

TURIN, PALAZZO CARIGNANO; EXTERIOR.

EINSIEDELN MONASTERY, CHAPEL INTERIOR; TYPICAL GERMAN BAROQUE.

RIER, ST. PAULINUS, EXTERIOR; CHARAC-RISTIC GERMAN VERTICALITY.

VIENNA, KARLSKIRCHE, EXTERIOR; AUS-TRIAN BAROQUE BRAVURA. Fischer von Erlach, architect.

Plate 57

VERSAILLES, THE PALACE SEEN OVER THE ORANGERIE.
J. H. Mansart, architect.

PARIS, DÔME OF THE INVALIDES;
EXTERIOR. J. H. Mansart, architect.

VERSAILLES, GALERIE DES GLACES. J. H. Mansart, a⊀

PARIS, LOUVRE; EAST FRONT. Perrault, architect.

Plate 58

ILLE, ARCHBISHOP'S PALACE; ENTRANCE.   BURGOS CATHEDRAL; ALTAR OF ST. TECLA.

MA DE MALLORCA CATHEDRAL; CHAP-   GRANADA, CARTUJA; SACRISTY INTERIOR.
HOUSE DOOR.

Plate 59

LONDON, ST. PAUL'S; INTERIOR UNDER TH
DOME. (Metropolitan Museum of Art.)

LONDON, ST. PAUL'S; EXTERIOR. Sir Christopher
Wren, architect.

GREENWICH HOSPITAL; VIEW OF THE COL-
ONNADE. Wren, architect. (Belcher and Macartney.)

OXFORD, TRINITY COLLEGE CHAPEL;
TERIOR. (Belcher and Macartney.)

Plate 60

h-CENTURY BEDROOM FROM A VENETIAN
LACE. (Metropolitan Museum of Art.)

PARIS, HÔTEL SOUBISE; SALON OVALE. Boffrand, architect.

SAILLES, THE CHAPEL; INTERIOR. De Cotte,
tect.

NANCY, GRANDE PLACE. Héré de Corny, architect.

Plate 61

DRESDEN, THE ZWINGER; A PAVILION. Pöppelmann, architect.

DRESDEN, FRAUENKIRCHE. Bähr, architect.

MUNICH, NYMPHENBURG; AMALIENBURG INTERIOR.

MUNICH, NYMPHENBURG; AMALIENBUR EXTERIOR. Cuvilliés, architect.

Plate 62

KEDLESTON; FRONT ELEVATION. James Paine, architect. (Paine: *Plans...of ...Gentlemen's Houses.*)

LONDON, KEW GARDENS; THE RUIN. (Le Rouge: *Jardins Anglo-Chinois.*)

LONDON: RED LION SQUARE. (Kip: *Britannia Illustrata.*)

SALISBURY, HOUSE IN THE CLOSE. (Belcher and Macartney.)

Plate 63

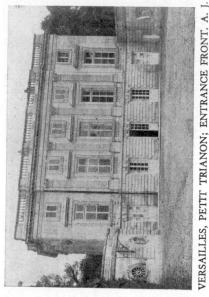

VERSAILLES, PETIT TRIANON; ENTRANCE FRONT. A. J. Gabriel, architect.

PARIS, PANTHÉON, EXTERIOR; CLASSIC PORTICO, UNBROKEN WALLS. Soufflot, architect.

PARIS, PANTHÉON, INTERIOR; LIGHT SOLID MASONRY CONSTRUCTION AT ITS HIGHEST DEVELOPMENT. Soufflot, architect.

Plate 64

Roman in feeling, not unlike those Borromini had used in the front of Sant' Agnese; but in the city churches the problem was different, and the traditional desire for a high spire-crowned tower for parish churches was still strong. For these churches, accordingly, Wren designed a series of extremely varied towers. They usually start as simple rectangular masses, often topped with a stage decorated with orders. This carries in turn an element that is either octagonal or circular. above which is the spire proper. The octagonal or circular element may itself be in several decreasing stages. In Amsterdam, as we have seen, Hendrik de Keyser had already built a number of classic spires in which a somewhat similar scheme had been used, and it is more than probable that many of the Wren steeples owe their original inspiration to these Dutch examples.

Wren worked in the Gothic as well as in the classic spirit, and of his Gothic work it is difficult to say whether it is the first stumbling example of the Gothic Revival or the last awkward expression of a rapidly dying tradition. St. Dunstan's-in-the-East in London is all Gothic, with a remarkable spire carried on four flying buttresses, a characteristic Wren geometric and structural "stunt." In Oxford, Wren completed the Perpendicular-style gateway of Christ Church, with a lantern and a finial in which, although classic general form is apparent, the detail is adequately accurate Perpendicular Gothic; and he also made a design for the west front of Westminster Abbey. Wren's Gothic is immature, rather wire-drawn and thin, with an overemphasis on the horizontal lines, but it is sincere.

Besides his church work, Sir Christopher Wren designed an enormous number of other buildings, varying from the delightful simplicity of the Blackheath Alms Houses (Morden College), with their quiet brick walls, their great sweeping entrance pediment, and an attractive colonnaded court, to the magnificence of the buildings he planned to add to the king's palace at Greenwich. This palace, which later became a hospital and home for ill and retired sailors and still stands as Greenwich Hospital, has a surprisingly mature grandeur of general effect; and, though other architects followed him in its construction, and it was never completed until long after Wren's death, its essential merit—the beautiful perspective relationship of the wider court below nearer the water and the narrower court on a slightly raised terrace behind, with an open avenue through the middle leading up to Inigo Jones's Queen's House on the hill—is due to Wren, and to Wren also are due the little domes which accent the corners of the inner buildings, as well as the larger and simpler scale of those closer to the river.

In many ways one of his most charming and successful works is the huge addition to Cardinal Wolsey's palace, Hampton Court, which Wren built for William and Mary. Here the Dutch influence is even more obvious than in the tall spires of the city churches; and the unassuming red brick walls, the large, closely spaced windows, the discreetly applied carving, and the delicate stone entrance motifs all combine to make a palace which seems also to be really a residence. Nowhere can the difference in the basic ideals of the Baroque of France and of England be seen more readily than in the contrast between Versailles and Hampton Court.

The most Baroque and the most brilliant of Wren's immediate successors was Sir John Vanbrugh, famous as courtier, wit, and dramatist as well as architect. Vanbrugh's hand was heavier than Wren's, and his imagination both bolder and more sure. He was always seeking for Baroque drama, even in comparatively small houses—for the contrast of strongly accented central wings, for skylines broken with massed chimneys, trophies of arms, and projecting clerestories. He was much criticized during his lifetime for the extravagance of his creations, and some wit of the time wrote of him,

Lie heavy on him, earth, for he
Laid grievous heavy weighs on thee.

Yet his great houses, like Blenheim, Seaton Delaval, and Castle Howard, have an originality of conception, a power in the relation of low wings to the main building, a fundamental grandeur of scale, both inside and out, which is unique in England.

But such great ducal mansions were really exceptional. In ordinary town houses and the smaller country estates a far different tradition prevailed, and quite different buildings were the result. Inigo Jones set the style before the Revolution, in his simple massing of rectangular elements, with the most reticent possible walls, a cornice, a slightly Baroque entrance door, a hipped roof, and large chimneys. This type continued in vogue almost up to the nineteenth century, and all through England example after example exists to show how the later-seventeenth- and eighteenth-century architects took this elemental form, refined it, and made it even more simple. Proportion tended to become more delicate, stonework and moldings less heavy; and much of the charm of English eighteenth-century towns and villages, as of some of the older squares of London, comes from this gentlemanly, restrained dignity. It is this simple brick architecture which is really the heart of the English Baroque style. These buildings remain essentially homes; they look and are comfortable, and their wood-paneled walls, their plaster ceilings, their ample classic fireplaces make them as pleasant inside as they are lovely without. Like the Wren churches, these buildings exerted an enormous influence on the American colonies, for it was not dukes who settled America, but plain people; and the best, the most elegant, models on which they could form their work were these quiet, unassuming, yet refined and dignified houses.

It is work like this which forms the real architectural expression of the Baroque in England. For the typical Englishman of the end of the seventeenth century is not James II, with his delusions of grandeur and absolute rule; not even his predecessor, Charles II, with his mistresses and his playful court. The typical figure is a man like Pepys, hard-working, ingenious, devoted to his job, but essentially home-loving, essentially humane; or, on a different plane, his contemporary John Evelyn, scientist, traveler, essayist, but like Pepys a distruster of the overgreat or the overgrand.

Chapter 23

THE EIGHTEENTH CENTURY

BETWEEN the spirit of the Baroque and the spirit of the eighteenth century there was an enormous gulf. One might choose the *Levée du Roi* in Versailles as perhaps the most expressive, if not the most important, of Baroque scenes. In that square monumental room, crowded behind the white-and-gold balustrade which cuts it in half, stand the favored few of the vast court, to watch in silence as the king gets up from his gorgeous satin-hung bed, aided by the correct court officers, with a ritual which controlled almost every motion. But the typical eighteenth-century scene, by contrast, would perhaps be Casanova in the villa which he had rented from the English ambassador, near Venice, waiting alone in a small room almost incredibly rich in delicate paneling, in mirrors, in decorated tiles, for the coming of his inamorata of the moment. For the Rococo period of the eighteenth century was as private as the Baroque was public; it made of personal privacy, of secrecy, of intrigue, of personal experience almost the highest aims in life, dressing them gaily and luxuriously, but in ways designed to emphasize their quality. Rococo architecture became, in a very real sense, an architecture of intrigue, as Baroque had been an architecture of pageantry.

For some time before the death of Louis XIV, a revolution against the ponderous ceremonials of court life had been brewing. Men and women, even of the court, were sated with drama, exhausted with spectacles, depressed and listless because of the total want of privacy. People began again to demand private lives. Even at the height of the period the demand had arisen, and in place after place the kings and dukes who had built those great palaces to enshrine regal ceremonial had been forced to erect for themselves smaller residences, often within the palace gardens, in which for a day or a week they could get away from the terrible impersonal drag of constant publicity. So the Grand Trianon and later, in the eighteenth century, the Petit Trianon were built at Versailles; and, at Marly, Louis XIV tried another scheme to gain privacy, constructing a simple square building for himself in the center, with twelve smaller private houses on the borders of the formal garden, so that even the selected few whom he invited to visit him could have their own privacy at least for a moment. So in Munich the little Amalienburg was built to give a relief from the miniature Versailles of the Nymphenburg.

By the end of Louis XIV's reign this longing for personal lives and personal privacy had become universal. A complete revolution in social life occurred. People were suddenly interested in individuals and individual relationships, in intimate conversation. Wit began to take the place of eloquence. This personal interest was somehow combined with a new attitude toward the world, a new curiosity in things, particularly in small and dainty things, in fine discriminations. The seventeenth century had been a great era of scientific discovery, but it was the eighteenth century which systematized and analyzed these discoveries and made them usable; for, if the seventeenth was one of the great ages of discovery, the eighteenth was rightly called the century of reason.

Naturally all of this affected architecture deeply. No era devoted to reason and not drunk with the love of insensate pageantry could ever conceive of a Versailles as anything but a piece of monumental waste and extravagance. Of true comfort it had none, save what had been laboriously introduced by later followers of its original builder. It was notoriously without any sanitary conveniences whatsoever, and eyewitness descriptions of the stench and filth which sometimes resulted are almost unbelievable.* Rooms were arranged in magnificent suites, to be sure, but there was no functional differentiation between them, and the amount of unnecessary labor involved in such a simple thing as serving a small meal was colossal. Memoirs of the time show the actual living in such a place as hardly more than a rather inconvenient camping out in the midst of luxury.

The eighteenth century would have none of all of this, for the idea of functionalism in planning—that is, of arranging spaces in a building in such

---

* It is characteristic of the period that, although Sir John Harington had invented a workable water closet as long before as 1596, describing and illustrating it in a quaint pamphlet published in that year, entitled *The Metamorphosis of Ajax*, it was not until nearly the middle of the eighteenth century that conveniences of this type began to be common, at least in the more luxurious houses. The habit of installing them started apparently in England, for all over the continent they were known in the eighteenth century as *chaises à l'Anglais*. Published house plans, from the 1740's on, show them almost universally in large houses both in France and Germany; and the revolution in ways of living, the extraordinary increase in cleanliness, decency, and good health which these appliances, crude as they were, brought into society can be easily imagined.

a way that each is designed for a specific use—reappeared. Roman planning, as both the writings of Vitruvius and the buildings themselves tell us, was to a large extent functional. The medieval planning of monasteries and houses was also dictated to a large degree by the actual necessities of living. But seventeenth-century palace plans seem to have been prompted by nothing except megalomania and a superb imagination in creating a setting for official functions. Now, with the eighteenth century, there was a sudden turning back, a sudden desire to make buildings work, to produce convenience and beauty in small spaces with economy. The eighteenth-century house became livable, and it is a significant fact that many eighteenth-century dwellings can be lived in conveniently today with but slight alterations and modernizations, whereas the seventeenth-century house can become at best a museum.

This quality affected all of architecture. Churches as well as houses were designed for definite purposes. The sermon became more and more important, and the individual's reaction was stressed. Thus the tendency was to make churches smaller, to bring the people into more intimate touch with the preacher or the rite, to give even to the church services a quality not unlike that of a salon. This movement can be well seen in the beautiful chapel which was added by Robert de Cotte to the château at Versailles. It forms a church of considerable size, yet on the interior every effort has been made to keep its scale small and human, its detail delicate and personal. Moldings are refined and their relief diminished, and the lovely marble columns of its upper floor carry, not the powerful arches of an earlier period, but a simple straight horizontal entablature. It was not that the eighteenth century forgot the old ideals of big composition and monumental grandeur; it was merely that it strove to realize these ideals only in places to which they were peculiarly adapted—that is, in the largest churches and in city beautification. The period produced no Versailles, but it did produce the Place de la Concorde, in Paris, one of the most beautiful of all city squares, characteristic in the restraint and discretion with which its architectural framework—a mere balustrade—is treated; and in Nancy it gave birth to the imposing series of open squares which Héré de Corny designed—the Place Royale, stretching in front of the noble Hôtel de Ville and leading through a great triumphal arch into the long, narrow, simple Place de la Carrière, and that in turn debouching into the Place du Gouvernement, with the town governor's palace closing the vista at one side and with lovely hemicycles of arcading at either end.

The revolution against ceremonial was accompanied inevitably by a revolution against the limitations of the strict architectural standards which had been so carefully built up by the Academy. The rebellion had started much earlier. Claude Perrault, the architect of the east front of the Louvre, had himself been perhaps the original rebel; his skeptical scientific mind, examining the theories of architecture, could not accept the academic dogmatism, and in a book which he wrote on the Orders of Architecture he not only pointed out with apparent delight the extreme differences between the proportions set up by various so-called authorities, but he went much further and in his foreword claimed that beauty in all such matters was entirely dependent on custom and usage, and that the only absolute beauties were those resulting from perfection of construction, grandeur of size, and beauty of material.

During the eighteenth century this controversy about the nature of beauty suddenly achieved renewed vitality. François Blondel had been the great supporter of academic authority under Louis XIV, and in his *Cours d'Architecture* had sought to place the problem of architectural proportion on a basis as definitely arithmetical and invariable as that of harmony in music. His work had been, throughout the reign, accepted as an authority almost equal to Vitruvius, but in the eighteenth century new voices acclaiming freedom arose. Germain Boffrand upheld the Perrault ideals of freedom in design, and brought into architectural discussion the whole concept of taste as something personal and fluctuating, yet somehow through usage achieving a real validity. He gave evidence of the new freedom from Baroque dogma by even including words of appreciation for the Gothic cathedrals. Briseux countered with a treatise not only upholding the Blondel dicta but going even further, to an almost absurd extent, in paralleling architectural proportion with musical harmony, illustrating his work with many designs in which the arithmetical relationships were meticulously worked out and graphically displayed.

These two men were, of course, as much architectural theorists and critics as practicing architects, but the attitude of the practicing architect is magnificently shown in another *Cours d'Architecture* written by another Blondel of the eighteenth century, Jacques François Blondel (probably not related to the elder Blondel), who for many years conducted an actual professional architectural school in Paris, and who achieved a somewhat different fame in a different walk of life, as the lover and eventually the husband of one of Casanova's most attractive sweethearts. Jacques François Blondel's *Cours d'Architecture* shows vividly the new emphasis of eighteenth-century architecture. It is essentially practical; it devotes many pages to building materials and their qualities and proper use, to foundations, to structural economy and strength; in its sections dealing with planning it insists above all else on convenience, on the correct relationships of the various parts of a building, so that whatever activities are pursued there may be carried out with the least effort and the least waste motion; it emphasizes orientation, view, wind, drainage, and all those qualities that add to the pleasantness of ordinary everyday living; in its consideration of decoration it stresses the quality of character—that is, the exact consistency between the purpose of a room and its decoration, between the wealth of a client and the lavishness to be displayed, in other words between the whole function of a building and its design. The Reason which had begun to occupy such an important place in the philosophy of the time has become the guiding light of architecture.

Over this bedrock of rationalism played the phantasy of the Rococo imagination, as though to express the unconscious feeling of a world which was losing its old standards with amazing rapidity. The revolt against dogma in architecture produced an extraordinary wave of ebullient, at times uncontrolled, imagination. The delight in the small and the dainty made this imagination take small and dainty forms, and exoticism in detail, orientalism, even here and there touches of Gothicism, crept inevitably in. The world was enlarging, discovery giving place to commerce; travel was becoming more and more common, and a new pleasure in the strange and the foreign was born. *Chinoiseries*—decorations that are fantastic modifications of the scenes on Chinese pottery, or fairy-tale interpretations of the stories of China published in the "travels"—became popular in interior decoration, in wall panels, furniture, and ornaments. *Singeries*—decorations based on the antics of somewhat humanized monkeys—enjoyed an almost unexplainable vogue. Straight lines broke into curves. Delicate naturalistic ornament supplanted the old Roman acanthus leaves. The corners of panels were all broken with C-scrolls, and the tops and bottoms filled with lavish decorations, and panel molds were doubled or trebled. Asymmetry began to creep in, too, especially in the work of such decorators as Meissonier; and only the superb French sense of decorative composition still holding true saved the period from a complete deliquescence into meaningless and formless confusion. Yet the decorative sense did hold true, forcing the new luxuriance and imagination into firm and lovely patterns. Such an interior as the oval room in the Hôtel Soubise by Boffrand, with its simple panels below breaking into an exuberance of carved decoration above that led to plaster ornaments running up to a center flower in the middle of the domed ceiling, and surrounding on the way exquisite paintings of the myth of Cupid and Psyche by Natoire, was a *tour de force* of decorative skill in which architecture, sculpture, and painting were perfectly blended to produce a general effect delicate, even frivolous, but perfect in its harmony nevertheless. And this is not an isolated example.

Louis XV decoration must not be judged by the stupid modern imitations, filled with women in tailored clothes and men in the characterless costume of today. It must be seen in its best original examples, in place; it must be imagined in relation to the people for whom it was built, with the beautiful women Nattier painted, in their daintily flowing brocaded gowns, ensconced on its elegantly fragile chairs and sofas, exchanging cynical but witty gossip; or it must be seen in its more intimate sides, as Casanova tells about it inimitably in his memoirs, or as one can see it—at second-hand, perhaps—in the lovely green-and-gold, much bemirrored bedchamber from Venice in the Metropolitan Museum. Looked at in that way, Louis XV design becomes, not the silly mass of curlicues which it must sometimes appear to modern eyes, but rather as a charmingly playful frame for a witty, skeptical, luxurious, and sensual life, a frame revealing brilliant decorative ability and yet never meant to be taken too seriously.

Luxury was almost its first, most necessary, quality, for growing trade and international commerce was making luxury possible for people who had never known it before. The wealthy commercial bourgeoisie in the eighteenth century demanded amenities which only the court and the nobles had enjoyed a century earlier. The results can be seen all over Europe— in the rows of red brick houses with exquisite Rococo doors that line the canals of Delft; in the beautiful stone-fronted, restrained hotels that are so numerous in Bordeaux; in house after house in Paris, Vienna, London. And in all of Europe, since it was in France that the greatest skill was to be found in supplying the needs this luxury produced, it was French taste which was supreme and French fashions which controlled.

And with all this indulgence in pleasure there was necessarily developing also a new poverty, a new poverty of workers in the industries—sweated at miserable wages,—a new poverty, in the countryside, of peasants whose farms could hardly pay the growing taxes forced upon them. The mad extravagance of Baroque monarchs had already gone far to break the equilibrium of centuries; it has been said that it was Versailles which produced the French Revolution. Despite the new industries, eighteenth-century statesmanship did little to help the basic evils, and beneath the luxury of city and country châteaux was an increasing force of bitterness, disillusion, and poverty which might soon be galvanized into revolt.

But the eighteenth century was the age of reason. No eccentricities, no prodigality of detail, could completely fog that concept of reason; and, as though almost in revenge for the frivolous luxury of interior detail, at least as a sort of countermovement, the love of reason made the architects aim for the greatest possible exterior restraint, coupled with the greatest possible convenience of plan.

The movement toward restraint in exterior design had begun in the reign of Louis XIV, and Versailles, in spite of the magnitude of its dimensions and the splendor of its interior suites, had had an exterior quietly classical. The Louis XV architect seems to have wished to mute the exteriors of his buildings even more, to avoid as far as possible any unnecessary architectural elements. Frequently walls are without pilasters or columns and have the simplest moldings around the closely spaced windows; only a delicate cornice and richly scrolled wrought-iron railings in front of the lower parts of the story-high windows give a touch of elegance here and there. The tops of windows and doors are often segmental arches instead of the rectangular- or semicircular-headed windows common earlier. Often the only hint of the lavishness and the untrammeled detail within is contained in the interior door and its immediate frame, where touches of Rococo detail are used. When the orders are used, it is usually only to emphasize a central element in a long wing or to give a necessary touch of decorative weight over an entrance. These Louis XV house exteriors are almost aggressively well-mannered; reasoned restraint has brought them at times almost to the threshold of dullness. Yet as one goes through the French provincial towns or strolls along such an old street in Paris as the Rue de l'Université, or leafs through the gorgeous books in which the period delighted to publish its architectural achievements, one's chief impression is that of a kind of humane urbanity, a kind of gentleness, a sure reasonableness, that ends up by seeming almost noble.

Naturally these new houses were much smaller than their predecessors of the reign before. Instead of stabling for 100 horses, stabling for eight or ten was sufficient; instead of great suites of a dozen entertainment rooms, two or three now sufficed for the more intimate functions. In many ways the general system of planning remained, at least in the larger houses, similar to the earlier work. One usually entered a forecourt through a large gate, and found on either side low buildings containing stables and the kitchen services; before one rose the higher block devoted to the actual residence—reduced in size, to be sure, and more intimate and human in its scale, but still essentially the same *corps de logis* which had been traditional. In the growing congestion of the eighteenth-century city, this extended plan was not always possible, and the French architects especially exerted an amazing ingenuity in adapting these basic requirements to the small sites which they were now forced to use.

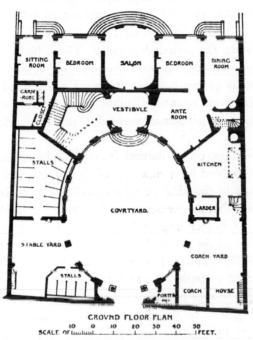

98. HÔTEL D'AMELOT, PARIS; PLAN. Boffrand, architect. (Simpson. Vol. III.)

A characteristic example is the Hôtel d'Amelot, designed by Germain Boffrand. The forecourt is oval and the whole building compact and unified, the dining salon is easily accessible from the kitchen, and a monumental but delicate flight of stairs leads directly up from the entrance vestibule to the chief rooms along the garden front. All of the lines of travel within the house were simplified and made direct, so that there was the least possible waste space in area and the fewest lost steps in service; and the whole had not only a new convenience, a new efficiency, but also a new kind of privacy and intimacy. In the smaller houses of the bourgeoisie, who could not expect to support the elaborate panoply of coaches and horses and the extravagant service arrangements of houses like these, the forecourt came to be eliminated entirely, and the whole house developed into a simple rectangular block directly on the street; yet even in these smaller houses the new ideals of convenience, of intimacy, and of privacy controlled the arrangement of the rooms and the decorative aspect of the whole.

For the social life of the eighteenth century, the imposing sweeps of gardens of the Louis XIV type were manifestly ill-suited. Bosquets as large as those at Versailles, where in one bosquet a great court fête for the entire population of the château could be held without crowding, had little of the privacy which the personalized social intercourse and the love of personal intrigue dominating the period demanded. There had to be a change—a general reduction of sizes, a general renunciation of the Le Nôtre idea of imposing enormous geometrical patterns on a whole landscape. The great Le Nôtre gardens were essentially public parks and, as such, superb; but the eighteenth-century gentleman wanted a private garden, not a public park.

Moreover, new concepts of natural beauty combined rather oddly with the exoticism stimulated by a new knowledge of the Orient to produce a complete overturn in the ideal of what gardens should be. It was in the eighteenth century that the romantic garden came into being, almost simultaneously, both in France and in England. The most important French garden publication of the second half of the eighteenth century was a periodical magnificently illustrated with engravings both of designs and of actually constructed examples, entitled *Jardins Anglo-Chinois,* which sufficiently reveals this strange mixture of oriental flavor and English romantic taste. Gardens began to be thought of, first, as imitations of uncultivated nature—imitations, that is, of lovely natural landscape—and, in the second place, as opportunities for developing the most romantic and exotic incidents by building Chinese pagodas or teahouses, Turkish bath buildings, or artificial ruins—*hermitages.* The straight line suddenly disappeared in garden design, to be replaced by serpentine, spiral, or circular paths, and the old Le Nôtre bosquets by circuitous passages cut in wild foliage, leading to concealed glades where rose a little shepherd's cote or a temple of love— places where enamored couples could find themselves shut off from the prying eyes of all the world, or where two amateur philosophers, surrounded by the thick greenery and listening to the songs of birds, could discuss the relation of man and nature, the happiness of the noble savage, or the abstruse mathematical theories of Descartes.

Thus society, at perhaps one of its most unreal and artificial periods, attempted somehow to compensate for its own loss of touch with life by the artificial naturalism of its gardens, the sophisticated primitivism and promiscuity of its conventional life. Of course it took no great imagination to realize the underlying superficiality of this kind of design; it was obviously a play kind of landscape architecture, devoted to little things. It became a fruitful source of satire. The growing romanticism of the age is nowhere better shown than in the enormous literary reflections of the new kind of garden design; and the debate which arose between the supporters of artificiality and of naturalism became strangely enough one of the great inspirations toward a new examination into the basic problems of aesthetics, and so added to the older aesthetic categories new titles, especially the "picturesque" and the "sublime."

Accordingly, the individualism, the emotionalism, and in a sense the confusion of the modern world were little by little expressing themselves in building, and to this confusion the latter part of the eighteenth century added another element—archaeology. The discovery and the early excavation of Pompeii and Herculaneum showed the eighteenth century a kind of ancient life quite different from the monumental magnificence of the greater Roman buildings which had formed the taste and been the authority of seventeenth-century theorists. Here was an ancient classic life of small houses, colorfully decorated, indeed, but fundamentally informal; here was a Rome of shopkeepers, craftsmen, wealthy dilettanti, and businessmen, instead of the Rome of the half-legendary figures of history. Such a discovery could not help having tremendous popular repercussions. The ordinary educated man who had looked up to Cincinnatus at the plow, Augustus, and even Vitruvius the architect, as gods, saw in these new Romans of Pompeii and Herculaneum not gods but fellow men. A kind of romantic friendship toward the ancient world took the place of the old Baroque worship, and Pompeiian elements began to appear in furniture and interior design.

But there was an even deeper aspect to this new discovery of the ancient world. Winkelmann in the middle of the century had begun to differentiate between Greek and Roman work, and laid the foundations at least of scientific archaeology. The world began to realize that artistic styles changed as the years passed; had their birth, their climax, and their decline, as the life of the people who produced them developed or disintegrated. Thus a new sense of time gradually permeated European thought. History became not only military and political narrative, but inevitably began to absorb some idea of continual flux and change, some dim appreciation of the fact that all the manifestations of human life—military, political, and artistic—were alike functions of a continually changing equation, to be understood only in their relation to the other elements of that equation, in any specific case, at one and only one particular time.

The architectural implications of this revolutionary time concept became apparent only gradually, but intimations of the change were immediately visible. Up to the middle of the century architects had designed directly within the current tradition, almost unconscious of any possibility of choice or change. The basic classicism of the Renaissance had paraded down through the Baroque period and into the eighteenth century unchallenged, completely dominant, its conclusions, its absolute authority, disputed only by occasional rebels like Perrault. Now suddenly, with the new concept of time and history and architectural style as a continual flux, with a new knowledge of beautiful buildings of different periods all over the world, this authority of classic precedent, as interpreted by the academies, disappeared. In a world of change, how could any absolute standards of taste survive?

The architect, then, was faced with a new task, that of a personal critique of authority, of a personal choice on the basis of his own knowledge and individuality, of his entire approach to design. He was freed from the rules of the past, but as yet little had arisen to take the place of those rules in guiding him. He had to fall back upon his own personal taste and the personal taste of his clients. Connoisseurship and scholarship became inevitable requirements for "good" design, and the thinking architects realized that in the final creation the taste of their employers was as important as their own. Every educated man realized this also and became, if not an amateur archaeologist, at least an amateur connoisseur; and the education of these amateurs in matters architectural was responsible for the extraordinary flood of marvelous architectural books which the eighteenth century produced, alike in France, England, and Germany. Jacques François Blondel, in Paris, went even further, and established, as a sort of supplement to his professional school of architecture, courses of lectures for the layman.

In that way an attempt was made to substitute intellectual knowledge for the acceptance of seventeenth-century architectural dogma, and sometimes even to substitute a similar intellectualism for the processes of creative design. For a time this effort had its desired result. Popular taste was educated, connoisseurship did prevent the worst results of intellectual confusion, and the new freedom of thought produced original and useful experiments; but the disintegrating forces which were building up behind the whole body of eighteenth-century culture were too great to be permanently defied. No mere personal taste, however exquisite, could defeat the industrial revolution on the one hand, and the crowding new knowledge of all kinds of architecture—Gothic, Romanesque, Byzantine, Egyptian, even Chinese—which the new archaeology and the new curiosity were making known, on the other. The eventual end could only be chaos, or else a re-examination of the entire bases of architectural form.

Chapter 24

THE ROCOCO IN GERMANY AND ENGLAND

THE eighteenth-century ties between Germany and France were close. Frederick the Great, in Prussia, worshiped French culture, wrote and spoke largely in French, and carried on a voluminous correspondence with French thinkers from Voltaire down; in Bavaria, the whole orientation of the court, politically and culturally, was toward France rather than toward Austria; and it was the fashion for the princelets and dukelets of the German regions along the Rhine to imitate French manners and to patronize French artists. It was natural, therefore, for French Rococo ideals to play a large, even a dominant, part in the eighteenth-century architecture of great areas in Germany.

Nevertheless, the tradition of the Germanic Baroque was too vital to disappear, and the best German work of the time often combined many of the basic compositional qualities of the earlier Baroque with a superficial overlay of Rococo decoration, and also at times with something of the more human scale, the more intimate quality, for which French architecture was famous. And fundamental regional cultural tastes also played their part in changing the earlier French forms. From the time of the Late Gothic on, the German designers had loved broken, picturesque outlines, emphasized verticals, and a kind of fantastic exuberance. Just as they had refused in Austria to accept the Roman Baroque forms unchanged, and out of them had created the daring and effective massing of such buildings as the monastery of Melk or the Karlskirche in Vienna, so now throughout Germany they refused to accept the delicate details of the French Rococo without giving to them their own personal and regional character.

It was in Saxony that the change from French ideals was greatest, for in the court at Dresden the Baroque ideals were most deeply fixed, and Dresden is today a city in which the eighteenth-century work has its most individual expression. From the Baroque inheritance came a continuing love of dynamic power, of great scale, of superb plan conception; from France came a new luxuriance and fertility, a new delicacy of detail. The Zwinger Palace, built by Daniel Pöppelmann in 1711-22, is typical. It was an addition to the residential palace of the king, made purely for entertainment purposes, and consisted of a series of lavish pavilions and halls for court festivities, connected by one-story arcades, and entered through a gateway which is an almost riotous combination of columns, broken pediments, scrolls, and sculpture, so designed that its first apparent confusion becomes as one looks at it further a magnificently disciplined composition, leading the eye in- evitably to the rich bulbous roof which crowns it. The same quality of monu- mental basic organization, expressed in and yet almost hidden by elaborate detail, is seen in the rest of the structure; the crowded caryatids and *gaines*, the bold carved foliage, the cupids, the cartouches, the curved roofs with their broken silhouettes, all unite to make a single and coherent production of which almost every square inch is carved with swirling line and bulbous form.

Strangely enough, the court church, built three decades later, is much less touched by the new floridity. Designed by an Italian architect, Chiaveri, it nevertheless retains the purely Baroque character of the Viennese work which it so closely resembles. The Protestant Frauenkirche, designed by Georg Bähr and completely demolished by bombing in the last days of the Second World War, was one of the most extraordinary and successful origi- nal compositions of the period. It was a large, unified, stone, vaulted build- ing, with a tremendous dome the lantern of which rises to over 300 feet. The central dome was surrounded by several tiers of galleries in lofty side aisles, and the exterior wall was broken by several radiating projections to take care of the stairs, the approaches, and the chancel. The large scale, the great simple windows, the upsweeping curved roof, and the enormous dome were of course typically Baroque, but the whole spirit of the interior both in plan and aspect reveals the new Rococo feeling. Since it was designed for Protes- tant worship, its architect has evidently taken the theater rather than the ritualistic church as his fundamental inspiration, and the seats for the 5000 people who could be accommodated were arranged on the floor and in the circling galleries so that the greatest possible number of worshipers could see and hear the preacher; even the shallow chancel, with its remark- able Rococo fittings and organ case, was planned with the same basic con- ception in mind. The great piers which supported the dome were without classic capitals; the ornament throughout was purely Rococo in type, and combined with the boxlike arrangement of some of the gallery seating to produce an effect strangely personal and intimate, despite the vast size of the edifice.

The same general character of vivid and sometimes erratic Baroque, decorated with Rococo details in Rococo profusion, controls the greater amount of eighteenth-century work in all the northeastern German lands, and is evident even further east—deep into Poland. In some of the Polish great houses, however, as in the eighteenth-century work of Moscow and St. Petersburg, more direct French influence is apparent, for French artists and craftsmen were as eagerly patronized by the Russian and the Polish dukes as they were by the nobles of the Rhenish towns. Catherine the Great, especially, was a patron of foreign artists and architects, and was in constant communication both with Italy and Paris in order to insure a constant supply in Russia of thoroughly trained Italian architects and French craftsmen.

Like Saxony, Bavaria also had its characteristic eighteenth-century expression, for in Bavaria—although French craftsmen were all the fashion, and much of the most important work was designed by either François Cuvilliés, a pupil of Robert de Cotte, or his son—Vienna was geographically very near and the earlier Baroque churches of Bavaria continued to exert a strong effect on ecclesiastical design; and, just as, earlier, Serlio on coming into France had designed French buildings and attempted to create, by means of his Italian knowledge and taste, buildings which should be French rather than Italian, so these Cuvilliés, notwithstanding their French parentage and training in French taste, designed public buildings which remained essentially Bavarian. They were responsible, however, for the general change in the character of exterior design, as well as for the introduction of the C-scrolls and the delicacy of French Rococo into Bavarian interiors. Their exteriors were quieter, more classic, more restrained than those of half a century earlier; they liked flat roofs with balustrades—with a refined classic quality in detail quite different from the older Baroque heaviness. François Cuvilliés the elder was, in addition, a maker of plans of the most amazing ingenuity, and invariably seized upon the opportunities offered by the fantastic taste of his clients to produce, especially in country-house design, a new kind of freely planned structure. Triangular, circular, and polygonal buildings were common in his work, and he delighted in oval, circular, or circular-ended rooms. That he could also on occasion be monumental and restrained—as in his Archbishop's Palace, and in his work in the Residenz, especially the Residenz theater, in Munich—is only an additional evidence of his underlying skill.

Perhaps his most expressive work is a little pavilion called the Amalien-

burg, which he built in the gardens of the Nymphenburg for the Elector of
Bavaria in the 1730's. It is a one-story building, with interesting and sometimes oddly shaped rooms grouped on either side of a circular domed reception room in the middle of the front. Each room has its walls covered with
exquisite Rococo stucco reliefs, the exuberance of which is rendered not only
tolerable but pleasant by their singular delicacy and the lovely color treatment. Each room has a different scheme, but in general the reliefs are silver
and the ground sometimes of soft yellow, sometimes of green-blue, sometimes of bluish gray. Even the kitchen is lavishly decorated, with lovely blue

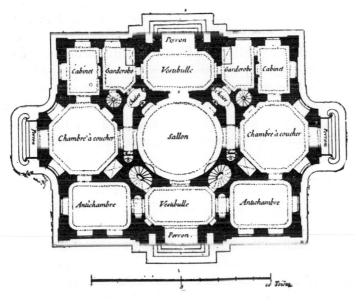

99. CHARACTERISTIC BAVARIAN ROCOCO GARDEN PAVILION; PLAN. Cuvilliés,
architect. (Cuvilliés: *École d'architecture bavaroise.*)

Dutch tiles, and the combination of luxury, rare refinement, mild color, and
interesting form makes of the whole both a decorative jewel and a small
house of no little personal charm.

In ecclesiastical architecture the Baroque elements had a longer life; but
the little church of St. Johannes-Nepomuk and the adjoining house, in
Munich, designed by the Asam brothers, shows how consummately Rococo
decoration could be added to Baroque conception. In the church the lighting
is so designed as to be concealed and yet to throw brilliant dramatic climax
on the altar. The walls wave in plan and are decorated almost bewilderingly
with carved wood, modeled stucco, and rich marble. The result is typical

of the Bavarian eighteenth-century love of almost frivolous detail, used skillfully to produce theatrical effect.

In Prussia, the life of the court of Frederick the Great was a far different thing from the often flighty luxury of Bavaria and the Rhine country. Prussia was beginning to march toward the domination of the Germanic lands. Frederick, though his amusement lay in French philosophy and Rococo culture, was essentially devoted to ideals of centralized power. He was a great builder, adding largely to the castle at Berlin and building a whole group in Potsdam for his summer court; and his buildings reveal the trend of his aims. They were planned by a whole group of foreign designers as well as by German architects. The Berlin palace had been begun by Andreas Schlüter at the end of the seventeenth century, and the exterior of the building had been largely completed under the predecessor of Frederick the Great, from designs by the Swedish architect Eosander and the German Boehme. It was severely classic, large in scale, and with few Baroque tricks. It revealed early something of the basic austerity and power of the Prussian court. Undoubtedly it must have influenced Frederick the Great tremendously and given a character to all Prussian eighteenth-century work, which places it at the opposite pole from the intricacies of Munich.

Thus in the new palace at Potsdam, which Frederick the Great built in the 1760's, there is the same strong classic exterior, rich in material but with no concessions made to Rococo taste—except perhaps the free-standing colonnade at the terrace end. Even this, however, maintains a sober classicism of style which its decorative detail cannot conceal. Behind stretch the great stable and barrack buildings for the royal retinue, as though to rival, not the delicate, humanized French work of the time, but the tremendous royal structures of Versailles. These side buildings, with their picturesque outline and their applied classic detail, may perhaps indicate a little of the informality and experimentalism that was current in other eighteenth-century work, yet the whole group possesses the impersonal monumentality of the Baroque more than it does the picturesque humanity of the Rococo.

It is only in interiors and the minor, more or less recreational, buildings that Frederick's admiration of French culture is allowed free rein. The little palace of Sanssouci, the king's personal residence, designed by Knobelsdorff —according to legend, after the king's own sketches,—is competely a Rococo structure. One story high, it is human in scale despite its length. Its classic details are intimate rather than impressive, and its interior is a gay medley of Rococo phantasy. The same riotous Rococo appears in many of the interiors built by Frederick the Great both in Potsdam and in the Berlin palace, and all of it is of a kind that reveals how far the Germanic Rococo style could depart from the French precedent. It spreads the ornament over entire wall surfaces, instead of restricting it to the tops and bottoms of panels as the French had done; it becomes a kind of web of scrolls and foliage, the lines of which wander rather aimlessly over all the apparent surfaces of a room, so that the eye becomes finally sated and longs for repose. The hand of the modeler in this Prussian Rococo is heavier too. Projections are greater; and, whereas in the Amalienburg in Munich delicacy and taste have made exuberance lovely, in many of the Prussian rooms the lack of it has made exuberance only ostentatious and sometimes dangerously close to plain vulgarity. There is something of the *nouveau riche* in its expression, for in Prussia Rococo seems more than anywhere else in Europe to have been the mere plaything, almost the vicious appetite, of people whose minds were basically hostile to it and given to more austere ideals. Perhaps the added violence of this Prussian Rococo was a necessary antidote for the impersonal regularity of the almost sadistic military drills in which Frederick so delighted.

Just as England had never had a true Baroque, so England never developed a native Rococo. The quiet development of English individuality and English home life went on, forcing an architecture which could express these rather than the grandiose fashions of the seventeenth century or the frivolities of the eighteenth. Samuel Pepys in his garden of a summer night, playing on his flute, while his wife and her maid sang madrigals softly in the dark, and the neighbors opened their windows around and listened with delight, is just as true an English seventeenth-century character as King Charles II himself; and in the eighteenth century, though the field of knowledge had widened and growing business brought an opportunity for comfortable living to great numbers, the same ideas of home and the household, of close individual contacts, as the central things in life continued undiminished. Perhaps the great characteristic expression of the English eighteenth century is Boswell's *Johnson*, a book by one eccentric, even cranky, individual about another still more erratic, though infinitely more witty. Dr. Johnson was a man of his time; his delight was in people, his most pithy sayings were about people. His literary criticism gave something of a new slant on the problem of personalities in literature. Character was his great passion; and, if he was egregiously and almost continuously wrong in all matters of politics and economics, Dr. Johnson was almost always inevitably right in matters dealing with individual character.

This continuity of feeling about life gave a continuity to architectural development far stronger than any changes of superficial fashion. English eighteenth-century architecture pursued, therefore, a quiet and almost unwavering course, developing and refining, restudying and recreating the ideals which had been first incarnated in English buildings by Inigo Jones and by Wren. Little by little the superficial Baroque ornaments which both those masters had occasionally used slipped away. What remained was their essential common sense, their essential desire to create buildings dignified, classic, unostentatious, and adapted to English life. English customs and English manners were more and more against the extravagant, more and more striving for a kind of sophisticated moderation in all things; and, as always, the concept of good manners played an enormous part in English art.

Yet Rococo fashions were bound to have their English effect, for in matters of fashion at least London was already under the sway of Paris, and English costume was based on the French. The Englishman with typical simplicity solved this puzzle of how to be at once Rococo and yet not Rococo. His buildings remained classic; in their furniture he allowed the new fashion to have its way, provided of course that it could be changed and modified to give the solid usability which the Englishman demanded. The work of Chippendale was the perfect answer, for Chippendale combined with an extraordinary imagination a magnificent sense of the structure of furniture and a manifest delight in its materials, which saved him always from any mere French frivolities. The Chippendale furniture, especially such things as bookcases, brackets, side tables, candelabra, and minor furnishings, makes lavish use of all the tricks of C-scroll, broken line, shell patterns, and naturalistic carving which the French Louis XV designers had developed; but it makes use of them in new and simpler ways, so that Chippendale furniture is always definitely English, without affectation, and his strongly built mahogany chairs with their carved Rococo backs of intersecting ribbons and delicate moldings are unique in Rococo furniture because of their preservation of powerful structural lines. Chippendale's feeling for the Rococo was, then, merely that of one who finds a new article to play with, and the other fashions which came along during his busy life he played with in the same way, transforming them to reveal his own skill and to express the English taste. Thus Chippendale's Rococo work went along with and was followed by work which he called Chinese, and even some which he termed Gothic, in response to the shifting demands of English fashion; still, whether Rococo or Gothic or Chinese, the greater part of it is instantly recognizable as good Chippendale.

The English combination of good manners and a delight in character explains the rapid development in eighteenth-century England of a tremendous number of excellent architects, all of them producing work polished, harmonious, and charming, yet none of them actually great. They were men of taste, assuredly, but not one of them had the amazing vitality, the gorgeous imagination, that Vanbrugh had had earlier. Few English eighteenth-century buildings are truly great; by far the majority are lovely and livable.

It was for the most part a prosperous period for England, this eighteenth century; the Peace of Utrecht in 1713 had opened numerous opportunities for foreign trade, the beginning of industrial manufacture in the north was creating new wealth, and agriculture was still flourishing and vital. Generally speaking, the wealth was distributed more widely than in earlier periods, and the new commercialism was producing not only occasional families of great wealth, but also large numbers who possessed a modest and assured comfortable competence. And so the architects were busy and well paid; they were admired and looked up to, and both their wealth and their influence was important. James Gibbs told his friend Vertue that he had made £1500 from his *Book of Architecture* and expected to sell the plates for £500 more. If we multiply these figures by five or six, we can get some approximate knowledge of the actual cash income which would be today's equivalent of the income Gibbs received from but one literary venture.

And the influence of these eighteenth-century architects was increased by the number of books they produced and the wide distribution which these works enjoyed. The eighteenth century in England was a century of artistic connoisseurship, as in France, and every nobleman as well as every shopkeeper who aped the ways of the nobility either set himself up as an authority on architecture or strove to learn all that he could about it. Book after book came off the London presses and was apparently eagerly snapped up by this alert, curious, and insatiable public; it was an ignorant fellow indeed who could not at need discourse learnedly on the orders, or at a pinch plan and direct—often not badly—the erection of his own house. These books were of three basic types: the theoretical treatise, the compilation of designs, and the builder's or architect's handbook.

The best examples of the first type of these books are Sir William Chambers's *Treatise on Civil Architecture* and Roger Morris's *Lectures on Architecture*. The two are characteristic of two sides of English eighteenth-century architectural thinking. Sir William Chambers had been brought up originally in the business world, and had traveled widely in Europe and

Asia. His treatise is therefore eminently practical. In his foreword he even hints at the economic implications of the profession. Roger Morris is as theoretical as Chambers is practical, and in his lectures, intended for laymen, he sets out systematically and with a kind of thoughtful dogmatism a whole doctrine of good proportion and consistent detail, giving formulas for window sizes for a given room, for the relative height, width, and length of apartments and buildings, and telling what is the proper order to use for different types of site, quaintly relating the quality of the order to the character of the landscape.

The most famous of the second type of book is the great *Vitruvius Britannicus,* started by Colin Campbell and extending eventually over a period of nearly a century, in eight great volumes, in which one can see in magnificent plates drawings of all the greatest English buildings, especially the large country houses. Individual architects like Gibbs and James Paine, and later the Adam brothers, also published superb presentations of their own work, so that the educated Englishman who could afford these expensive books was never at a loss to find the current ways of designing or the current standards of taste. The best of the last class of books is Isaac Ware's *A Complete Body of Architecture.* Simple, systematic common sense distinguishes it and makes it almost a model of its kind, discussing structure, building materials, and design with equal emphasis.

Besides these, there was a flood of smaller publications, coming out every year in greater number, by such men as the irrepressible Batty Langley, William Pain, and William Halfpenny. These minor works usually contained great numbers of examples of details—cornices, mantels, doors, windows, and so forth, as well as considerable valuable structural information;—because of their small size and low cost they were extremely popular with builders, and the general high quality of the details they show is reflected in the quiet streets of any number of English provincial towns. They were imported into the American colonies in large numbers also, and had an almost equal effect there.

Few churches were built during the eighteenth century in England, until the very end of the century. Those which were constructed generally followed the type James Gibbs established in St. Martin's-in-the-Fields, with its columns, its plaster vault, its side galleries, its elliptical arched chancel, and its high spire. It became the precedent for numbers of churches built on this side of the Atlantic also, where the Gibbs *Book of Architecture,* which illustrated St. Martin's, was evidently widely known. Most of the churches were as definitely preaching churches as the contemporary Protestant churches of Germany. In many the pulpit stood on the main axis of the church, and even where the service was Episcopalian the altar was reduced to a mere communion table. This old arrangement has been preserved in few churches, for everywhere, both in England and America, the ritualistic furor which followed the Oxford movement of the nineteenth century forced changes in the original plan, pushed the pulpit to one side, and gave the altar the importance which it had lost.

Many charming smaller eighteenth-century public buildings bear witness to the general high level of taste. Customs houses, town halls, and markets all evidence general restraint, dignity, and good manners. Brick is the usual building material. Sometimes stone trim and a decorated stone door-way, with pediment and cartouche, give emphasis and richness; and almost always these little public buildings have cupolas above the roof, distant symbolic reminiscences of the days when the lord's great hall, with its cupola through which the smoke escaped from a central hearth, was the center for all local administration. These tranquil red brick buildings, often with high slate roofs, fit most attractively into the little villages in which they are placed, harmonizing perfectly either with the grouped windows and Gothic tracery of Tudor times or with the restful red brick houses—so like them in general character—that the eighteenth-century businessmen were erecting along the main streets.

It was in house design that the period achieved its most brilliant results, and strangely enough along two absolutely different and conflicting paths. The great English noble families, through their enormous holdings of productive land, were piling up colossal fortunes. Each noble seems to have felt that building was the most worth-while as well as the most showy way of spending his money. The wealthy dukes built not one but several great houses for themselves, and the Earl of Burlington, a student of architecture and a passionate connoisseur, patronized a whole group of architects, sometimes satirically spoken of as his "stable"—Kent, Leoni, and Campbell the best-known among them;—and their work fills a large part of the early volumes of the *Vitruvius Britannicus*. Indeed, the Earl of Burlington, through his prodigious architectural patronage, did not a little to set the fashion in these great houses.

In most cases a central building, which was the residence proper, was flanked by two side wings, often only one story high. One of these contained the stables, the other the kitchens and food services. Sometimes in separate buildings, these were connected to the main house by colonnades or arcades, and thus a forecourt was created. All sorts of arrangements of these basic elements were found, the two favorite types being: one in which quadrant-curved colonnades connected the elements, and one in which the elements were in a straight line. The houses could be as huge as the wealth of the client permitted, but they must be quietly Palladian classic, without Baroque frippery; and colossal they were, many of them, with tremendous Roman colonnaded halls eighty feet long by sixty feet wide, immense two-storied salons, great impressive areas of corridor, monumental stairs, and rooms as big as barns. All of this magnificence was clothed in the most discreet classic dress; serene walls, simple colonnaded porches, several wings—even more restrained—connected to the main building by arcades, these are the main characteristics of the type. Working at such a large scale and with such simple shapes, these English eighteenth-century architects were forced to a careful study of proportion and skill which makes of many of these houses some of the most advanced, carefully composed, and successful pieces of large-scale and varied classic design; but as houses they were obviously absurd—uncomfortable, impossible to heat, inhuman within—and even the rich plaster ornament used to decorate the walls could not make these great houses human.

Characteristic examples can be seen in the long façade of Wanstead House, with corner pavilions and a central portico, designed by Colin Campbell; in Holkham Hall, by William Kent, famous for its tremendous basilican entrance hall, its great state galleries, and its four minor wings; and in Kedleston Hall, begun by Paine and finished by Robert Adam in a later style, with two sets of quadrant arcades leading to four minor buildings.

The satirists of the time attacked the faults of these ducal mansions unmercifully. Pope, in the Fourth Epistle of his *Moral Essays,* addressed to Richard Boyle, the Earl of Burlington, writes,

> *You show us, Rome was glorious, not profuse,*
> *And pompous buildings once were things of use.*
> *Yet shall (my Lord) your just, your noble rules,*
> *Fill half the land with imitating fools;*
> *Who random drawings from your sheets shall take,*
> *And of one beauty many blunders make;*
> *Load some vain church with old theatric state,*
> *Turn arks of triumph to a garden-gate;*
> *Reverse your ornaments, and hang them all*
> *On some patch'd dog-hole ek'd with ends of wall;*

> *Then clap four slices of pilaster on't,*
> *That, lac'd with bits of rustic, makes a front:*
> *Shall call the winds through long arcades to roar,*
> *Proud to catch cold at a Venetian door;*
> *Conscious they act a true Palladian part,*
> *And if they starve, they starve by rules of art.*

And later,

> *But hark! the chiming clock to dinner call;*
> *A hundred footsteps scrape the marble hall:*
> *The rich buffet well-colour'd serpents grace,*
> *And gaping Tritons spew to wash your face.*
> *Is this a dinner? this a genial room?*
> *No, 'tis a temple, and a hecatomb;*
> *A solemn sacrifice, perform'd in state;*
> *You drink by measure, and to minutes eat.*

The other type of house is the more characteristic, as it is the more common—the smaller, restrained, reticent building of town or country. Red brick, with slate or tile roof, with a simple cornice of stone or wood, with small-paned windows, often the only decoration upon it is a little architrave frame and a bracketed hood at the door; but the proportions are so unpretentious and regular, the relationships between all the parts so just, that the eye is satisfied, and the spirit of the whole—with its large chimneys, its ample warm red walls, its large many-paned windows—is essentially and definitely that of home. It is architecture at its simplest, and for that very reason these houses go on pleasing from year to year, no matter what the current fashion, while the great ducal mansions, with all their panoply of classic detail, are already white elephants and seem strangely out of date. The same artlessness which controlled the outside usually governed the rooms within as well; but the smaller houses were more resistant to changes in fashion, and in them the use of the large wooden panels which Inigo Jones had loved in the middle of the seventeenth century often continued well down into the eighteenth, when in the larger buildings wooden paneling had almost entirely passed out of use. Modest plaster cornices, classic architraves around doors, sometimes in the more lavish houses crowned with cornice and pediment, and fireplaces of the greatest variety, but all distantly Baroque, gave the necessary notes of interest. Fireplace design, indeed, during the eighteenth century became almost a special branch of the art, and the books and the houses are both filled with beautiful examples. Almost all have an architrave or molding around the opening, a frieze and a projecting cornice to serve as a mantel, and the greater number have an overmantel, usually with its own panel mold, cornice, and broken or scrolled pediment. Sometimes sculptured figures or columns hold up the cornice at either side of the opening, sometimes scrolls flat against the face

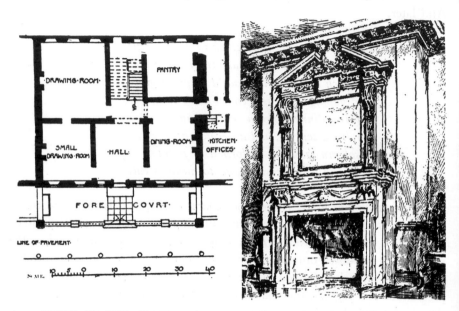

100. HOUSE IN THE CLOSE, SALISBURY; PLAN AND LIVING-ROOM MANTEL. (Belcher and Macartney: *Later Renaissance Architecture in England.*)

of the wall give a sense of support; but always the touch is sure and firm, the decorative composition excellent. In the second half of the century moldings tended to become more and more delicate, and naturalistic ornament crept in; thus far the Rococo fashion was accepted, but the basic designs remained always simple, strong, and classic.

Eighteenth-century house stairs were also typical examples of the English taste. Delicate turned balusters, usually three to each stair tread, rested directly on the treads and carried a molded handrail, which curved up at landings and breaks in the stair, and at the bottom often swept out in a gracious horizontal scroll supported on an elaborate carved newel. The balusters were often of three different designs, according to their height, so that the changing rhythm gave variety and lightness without interrupting the continuity. It was these stairs, as it was these newels, published so care-fully in the builders' handbooks, which became the models for any amount of American Colonial house detail.

In garden design, as we have seen, the eighteenth century in England really initiated the change to informal gardens that extended over all of Europe. In this shift of taste, the satirists too played their part, and Pope's famous picturesque garden at Twickenham had a large role in the transfor-mation. Pope himself was a passionate supporter of the new and informal landscape architecture, and in the same epistle to Burlington which has been mentioned before takes great delight in pointing out the absurdities, the inconveniences, and the stiffness of the old formal arrangements. The whole great house he calls "a labour'd quarry above ground," and of its setting he writes,

His gardens next your admiration call;
On ev'ry side you look, behold the wall!
No pleasing intricacies intervene,
No artful wildness to perplex the scene;
Grove nods at grove, each alley has a brother,
And half the platform just reflects the other.
The suff'ring eye inverted Nature sees,
Trees cut to statues, statues thick as trees:
With here a fountain, never to be play'd;
And there a summer-house, that knows no shade.

Kent, in the gardens of Stowe, applied informal design to a vast area and established for decades to come the English ideal of the noble's park—grassy glades, embowering trees planted in artful clumps, distant prospects of hill and valley, and always a lake or stream wandering in willful curves through the whole. Grottoes and hermitages, little bathhouses and tea-houses, or oriental pavilions gave variety and interest to the scene; and the underlying confusion between the artificiality of the whole conception and the naturalness it was supposed to imitate seems hardly to have been real-ized. Kew Gardens followed, and the Chinese pagoda at Kew still stands as a monument to that romantic time. Sir William Chambers had seen Chinese gardens and written a little book that is an excellent description of them; on this slight basis the Chinese passion flourished, and made his modest and accurate description the excuse for the most extraordinary and unreal de-signs. The entire garden-design picture became a conglomeration of the exotic and the picturesque, the picturesque and the natural, as though the designers and the lords who paid them well were all drunk with this new idea of a garden or a park as a piece of nature, and with the sudden discovery that nature itself was beautiful, that the ruined or the imperfect might be "picturesque," and that the awful or even the unpleasant might be the "sublime." The famous landscape architect who perpetrated perhaps the greatest number of the most confused designs was a man whom his contemporaries called, because of his supposed ability to do almost anything, "Capability Brown." Of course the satirists again found endless opportunities here as well, glad to be able to take a deserved crack at their chief exemplar and rival, Pope. Lady Mary Wortley Montagu, for instance, wrote of the grotto in Pope's own garden,

Adorn'd within with shells of small expense
(Emblems of tinsel rhyme and trifling sense)
Perpetual fogs enclose the sacred cave,
The neighboring sinks their fragrant odors gave.

It still remained for Humphrey Repton, in the nineteenth century, to give real form and cogent artistic meaning to the English informal landscape garden.

But, if informality more and more controlled garden design, it had little effect upon city planning; and one of the great contributions which eighteenth-century English architecture made to the town concept was that of the residential square. London and many other towns were growing enormously; acre after acre of country land had to be built upon, and since most of this land was in immense single-ownership areas it could be laid out on a definite, unified, planned basis. The result is to be seen in the beautiful squares of Mayfair and of their later descendants in Bloomsbury. The essential thing was to build a city of homes. Numberless quiet and reticent houses, ample in size, comfortably planned, with large back gardens—their façades all alike, or else, more commonly, portions of a single dominating composition running from street to street unbroken,—were arranged to front an open square of large size, planted thickly with trees and gardens. To these squares each householder had a key (they were not public); and, though this type of co-operatively owned open space may by now have outlived its usefulness, it was probably their protected and private character which preserved so many of them unharmed till our own day. In many ways these eighteenth-century residential districts of English towns represent a very high standard of town planning. Everywhere there is greenery, open square succeeds open square, broad streets connect them, and the placid harmony of the uniform façades around adds to the gentle graciousness of the whole picture. Outside of London, where there was more available land, designs could be freer; and here, as in Bath, the same kind of unified thinking has produced not only squares but also "crescents" and "circuses," in which the sweeping curve made by the fronts of the unvaried adjoining houses gives lovely change of light and shade, so that Bath today has come to be considered one of the most charming small cities anywhere.

In the smaller countries of northern and western Europe, the French Rococo fashions, radiating outward, produced small changes similar to those made in England. Nowhere did Rococo intricacy of wall panel, door molding, and carved decoration achieve the sway it enjoyed in either France or Germany. Always in Holland and the Scandinavian countries it appears as a sort of light dusting over of the surface with a frosting of delicate whimsicality, but the essentials of the buildings remain as they had been set in the seventeenth century. If anything, walls are even simpler, moldings more refined, and only a careful study of detail reveals the new Rococo trend; for the Rococo demanded for its full expression a type of luxury and a type of life—even a whole moral outlook—quite foreign to these grave and contented peoples. For them the practical, the comfortable, the home-like remained the desired ideal, and farmhouses throughout Denmark, like the eighteenth-century houses of Amsterdam or Delft, show the serene beauty to which this ideal gave rise. In the more monumental work, like the famous series of eighteenth-century squares in Copenhagen, it is only the delicate classic side of the Rococo which finds expression. There, as in England, all the Baroque eccentricities are forgotten; quiet lines, simple surfaces, the orders used unaffectedly and directly, these are the elements which create the characteristic elegance which this work possesses.

Chapter 25

THE EARLY CLASSIC REVIVAL

WITH the decline of the eighteenth century the Rococo flame began to flicker and wane. Exuberance so unrestrained could lead only to satiety, and ᵗhat atmosphere of excited, neurotic personal intrigue—the inevitable reaction from Baroque pomposity—could only produce a greater and greater disintegration. And other elements in the eighteenth-century mind were coming more and more to the front, exerting wider and wider sway over man's activities—the knowledge of archaeology, the love of reason, and the sense of democracy.

The new knowledge of the architecture of the classic world could not but have important results. Greek architecture, unknown for centuries, was suddenly discovered; archaeologists and architects from both France and England were measuring and publishing exquisite engravings of the great Greek monuments; book after book brought before architect and layman alike the delicate loveliness of Pompeiian wall decoration and the simple and homelike rectangularity of Pompeiian house designs; and in the last quarter of the century the magnificent etchings of Piranesi were coming off the press to sell like hot cakes through England and France, with their gorgeous blacks and whites, their virile if romantic presentation of Italian antiquities. There was a sort of intoxication in all of this sudden new knowledge, and little by little direct imitation of antique form began to creep into decorative motifs as it had never done before. In the beginning, architecture itself was affected only in detail; the Renaissance tradition was still too strong, the academic training founded deep in Louis XIV traditions too sound, to allow direct copying of ancient work.

Moreover, there were other elements in the culture of the period which accompanied this new knowledge of the classics and gave their own twist to the architectural development. Reason, for example, had gradually become the great criterion of the philosophers; the reasonable man became the ideal man. But no sincere reasoning analysis of Rococo architecture could fail to see its vast shortcomings or fail to realize that, although it was far from perfect, any direct imitation of ancient work would be equally or more unreasonable. Reason had, it is true, clarified and rationalized the plans of houses and produced, almost for the first time in centuries, workable, efficient homes; but it had stopped there—in churches and the large palaces and public buildings the old Louis XIV conceptions of grandeur still largely controlled. The first violent attack on the whole Baroque tradition, from the point of view of reason, was made not by architects but by one of those all-round scholars, critics, and connoisseurs of whom the eighteenth century was full, Père Marc Antoine Laugier. Once a famous Jesuit scholar and diplomat, he later left the Jesuit order, trammeled by its limitations, and became a sort of free-lance art adviser to municipalities and princes. As a result of his study of architectural problems, he published two works— *Essai sur l'Architecture*, in 1753, and *Observations sur l'Architecture*, in 1755. The two together actually constitute one work, which forms one of the most piercing, forthright criticisms of a contemporary style of architecture ever made. These books are distinguished not only by their clear-sightedness, but even more by their positive, constructive tone. Instead of merely stating his disapproval of the conditions he found, he goes ahead to set up certain standards of design which he felt to be reasonable and acceptable, and on their foundation to erect a series of imaginative structures which he describes carefully and at length. One of his chapters, significantly enough, is entitled, *On the Disadvantages of the Classic Orders*. He was enough a man of his time not to condemn the use of the classic orders because they were classic, and he accepted the general beauty of the standards which had been established. What he did do, however, was to show how utterly absurd it was to use the orders merely as decoration, how contrary to the real spirit of reason to make of them a dogmatic religion or to demand that they be used on every building. Columns to Laugier were essentially posts, to be used as supports and for nothing else; and in the ideal church which he describes he attempts to use the same common sense as the guiding principle in the design. The columns which separate nave and aisles should be used as the actual supports of the clerestory, and should carry a horizontal beam or architrave. There should be no cornice on this interior order, because cornices are essentially meant for the eaves of buildings, and not only are a logical anomaly in the interior but also diminish the apparent width of the building and thus destroy its open airiness of effect. The same kind of thinking lies behind his consideration of all the other elements in the church, and the church which he pictures is both absolutely unlike any contemporary eighteenth-century church on the continent, and unlike any other church building of any period; he had been daring enough to realize that architectural forms of a new kind could flow simply and naturally from the application of reason and logic to the problem in hand, and that in these forms there would be no loss of beauty but rather an enhanced effectiveness.

He even goes so far as to develop the implications of this logic on the whole problem of city planning. Streets and squares and gates are not to him primarily royal monuments; they are essential functional parts of the machinery of the city, and their placing in design should be determined by the whole question of communication, good ventilation, and general convenience. Just as these elements should be functionally considered, so should the position of important buildings within the city. Residential quarters should be placed in healthy, well-ventilated positions, where prevailing winds will blow away vitiated air; hospitals should be placed downstream from a town, so that any polluted drainage will flow away from rather than into the city. Now, to a modern, these concepts are almost axiomatic, but to eighteenth-century architects they must have come as a thunderbolt; and notes in the second edition of his works reveal the savage attacks which he had brought upon himself. Just how great the effect of Laugier upon his contemporaries was, it is difficult to say, but his effect on later designers was real and direct; Sir John Soane, the great revolutionary architect of England at the beginning of the nineteenth century, kept a large supply of Laugier's books with him and gave a copy to every one of his favored assistants.

And even in the actual architectural work there are evidences of the effect of similar thinking. Where the great temple of La Madeleine now stands, a church was planned, dedicated to the same saint, during the concluding years of the reign of Louis XV, and its construction begun though it never got beyond the foundations. Drawings of it which are preserved show a radical approach to church design. As in the case of the Laugier ideal church, rows of columns separate nave and aisles, and carry a horizontal entablature instead of the traditional arcade. The crossing of nave and transepts is handled in a most original way, so that the central dome, instead of being a great climax, becomes merely a sort of externalized baldachino or ciborium over the altar, which was centrally placed, surrounded on all sides by a wide open area. The detail was all restrained and classic; in it there is scarcely a trace of the delicate exuberance of de Cotte's Versailles chapel. Here classic serenity and reasonable dignity have controlled.

The design is far from perfect, and the whole handling of the central area inconclusive and experimental; perhaps the fact that it was never completed is not an irretrievable loss, but the design is extremely significant as revealing the trend of taste.

A little bit later another church was built in Paris, in which structural ingenuity, classic restraint of feeling, and an attempt to create new forms through a reasonable use of original structural conceptions were given extraordinarily complete and successful expression. That was the church of Ste. Geneviève, now the Panthéon, designed by Soufflot and built on the highest point of the Left Bank hill. This was an epoch-making building. As in the Laugier church and the design for the Madeleine, columns are used to separate nave and aisles, but the whole method of vaulting the arms of the cross of which the church consists and the great dome at the center is amazingly creative. Soufflot used shallow domes on pendentives, carried on arches and piers the dimensions of which were cut down to the smallest possible sizes. The great stone dome at the intersection of the cross is triple-shelled; it is a further development of the scheme originated by Wren in St. Paul's. A high drum supports the inner hemispherical dome, with a large opening in the center. Above this rises a tall ovoid dome, shaped generally like the small half of an egg, but with its four sides so cut away in great arches as to give the effect of a small shallow dome supported on four sloping legs. It is this structure which supports the stone lantern that shows on the outside. The outer dome is also of cut stone of almost unbelievable thinness—the shell is not more than five or six inches thick at the crown—and it is further lightened by arched recesses on the underside. All of this elaborate combination of elements, each one of which is necessary to the effect and to the structure, is bound together by the most ingeniously arranged masonry. Thrust is minimized, and what thrust there is counter-balanced by the weight of a free-standing colonnade which runs around the outside of the drum like that at St. Paul's. The whole structure is so relatively light in weight that the architect cut down the four piers which support it to a small size which seems almost incredible; in fact, in this case he went too far, and when these small piers showed signs of overstress and failure they had to be reinforced by increasing their size, and a new shell was built around them almost doubling their area. Even today, however, with this enlarged area, the effect of the mass is amazingly delicate and light; the entire building is a *tour de force* of brilliant engineering combined with unconventional form imagination, so that the views from any part of the church through the colonnades and up into the vaults are entirely different from those in any other church. Around this rich yet logical and delicate structure runs an unbroken exterior wall of tremendous dignity and power, ending in a simple cornice and parapet and decorated with great classic garlands. At the front is a classic porch of impressive Corinthian columns supporting a straightforward pediment. Here the influence of ancient architecture is apparent. The whole design, in its classical exterior with its almost artificial refinement of detail, and in its light, delicate, originally conceived interior in which the logic of construction plays such a large

101. CHARACTERISTIC LOUIS XVI ARCHITECTURAL FORMS; MAISON THELUSSON, PARIS. Ledoux, architect. (Krafft and Thiollet: *Choix des plus jolies maisons.*)

part, is a characteristic example of early Classic Revival architecture at its best.

The effect of the new classic inspiration on secular architecture was more uncertain. Even before the death of Louis XV, the architect Ange Jacques Gabriel had designed in the Petit Trianon at Versailles a charming little palace in which rectangular openings and a simple composition of pilasters, a classic entablature, and a flat roof gave a cubical geometric kind of expression that is essentially new. Horizontality and rectangularity became more and more the rule in the architecture of Gabriel and his followers. With this there was also evident a growing love of refinement in detail, of diminished projections, of flattened moldings. The colonnade with a pediment in the classic manner was frequent; and the contrast between the beautiful buildings which Gabriel designed at the head of the Place de la Concorde and the east front of the Louvre, on which they are undoubtedly distantly based, shows perfectly the changes in taste which had occurred between the two periods. The more modest scale of the Place de la Concorde buildings, the use of single instead of coupled columns, the avoidance of Baroque innovations, all make the difference plain. Gabriel also designed a new wing at Versailles to contain the palace theater, which is equally expressive of his ideals. It carries simply around it all the horizontal moldings and cornices of the original Louis XIV Mansart-designed façade; yet somehow, in its treatment of the windows and piers, in the use of the engaged columns and the subtly wider spacings, in the simpler surfaces, there is produced in this theater wing a sense of classic serenity, of delicacy, which is a new thing, indicative of a style we call Louis XVI. Inside, too, the theater itself shows the same characteristics. It is large, gracious, simple, despite the lavish use of marble and gilt. The proscenium arch is flanked by columns and topped by a simple entablature, and Gabriel has done everything to bring the lively curves of box frontals and rear wall into a quiet harmony.

By the time that Louis XVI ascended the throne, the reaction against the Rococo had become complete; and successive architects more and more strove for what they deemed the classic spirit, and sought everywhere for continuity of line, simplicity of surface, and archaeological accuracy of detail. The great theater in Bordeaux, still in use, which was designed by Victor Louis, is an excellent example of Louis XVI architecture. It is superbly planned, with ample entrances, foyer spaces, and so on, all contrived so that the shape of the building as a whole becomes an absolute rectangle, with continuous arcades around the outside and a beautiful front of Corinthian columns. The skyline is unbroken; the whole is regular, impressive, dignified, and yet, because of the exquisite restraint of its detail, never heavy. Within, the same spirit rules, in the monumental staircase and the auditorium room itself. Victor Louis also designed large portions of the present Palais Royal in Paris; and there too, though the motifs are more personal, more original in a way, the spirit of restraint and of classicism is the same.

The Hôtel de Salm, now the Palace of the Legion of Honor, designed by Rousseau, shows another typical effort of the new classicism—the desire to produce a one-story building. So many of the houses at Pompeii had been one story high, and even where two stories existed the upper story had been clearly only a service mezzanine, that the French architects conceived of classic design as essentially design in single one-floor masses. Of course these one-story houses had to be much more spread out and took larger areas than the old-fashioned multistoried dwellings. Service in them was equally difficult. Fundamentally they were impractical; yet the influence of the movement was tremendously wide, and it is probable that it was because of his admiration for the Hôtel de Salm that, in America, Jefferson tried to make his own house, Monticello, as much a one-story dwelling as he could, and where two stories were necessary carefully concealed the upper story behind the roof balustrade.

The most telling changes which the Louis XVI style brought with it were those inherent in interior finish and furnishing. These had begun to appear before Louis XV's death, and the new style can be seen in an almost fully matured state in Gabriel's Petit Trianon. From that time on it ruled all French interior design until the Revolution. It marks an even more profound break from the style that had gone before than the break between the Baroque and the Rococo. Gone were all the C-scrolls, the elaborate intricate ornament of panel tops and bottoms. Gone were most of the reduplicated moldings that had given Louis XV paneling such a sense of overlavish richness. Instead, all wall panels suddenly became rectangular; the cornice, which had largely disappeared from Louis XV work because of a desire to soften the corner between walls and ceiling, suddenly came back into use again, as though the simple rectangular geometrical forms were again welcome.

Everywhere, classic details superseded Rococo ornament, but the interior classic of Louis XVI was a very different thing from the monumental classic of the exteriors. In it, refinement was sought at the sacrifice of strength; moldings frequently looked pulled out and thin, as though smallness of size were somehow itself a virtue; rich, delicate little reedings and flutings were used to ornament faces and bands, as though the designer were afraid of plain surfaces; and the cornices usually used over doors were simplified in profile beyond the classic wont. Occasional naturalistic carvings still remained from the older period—bunches of roses, or lilies, wreaths and garlands—and, particularly in mirror frames which stood over the mantels, garlands of leaves and flowers often hung down over the mirror face under the arch which crowned it. The fireplace itself went through the same metamorphosis. Instead of the waving, vital lines of the Louis XV fireplaces, there was verticality and horizontality supreme. Little posts replaced the old side scrolls, and a straight-faced mantel shelf, perhaps molded like a little cornice, took the place of the earlier curved outline. The posts which held it up were sometimes treated like little columns, sometimes like bundles of reeds, sometimes like mere delicately molded furniture legs which tapered gradually downward. And, just as the straight line replaced everywhere the Rococo curve in this paneling and interior architecture, so in furniture the Rococo swing and verve, the bowed legs, the scrolled aprons, the convex-curved chair tops gave way to the straight line, to the vertical leg, the square or rectangular chair back, the horizontal molded apron. The old color schemes—white, gold, and pastel shades—remained, and the new furniture of the Louis XVI period preserved with those some quality of the old Louis XV richness. These Louis XVI interiors had manifest charm, but somehow it was an old, a sick, a decadent kind of charm. Refinement is a

102. CHARACTERISTIC LOUIS XVI DETAIL; THE ELEVATION OF A ROOM. (De Neufforge: *Recueil élémentaire d'architecture.*)

quality which, undisciplined by other, more vital drives, leads inevitably to weakness; and refinement in many of these Louis XVI interiors became maddeningly effete.

The culture that produced this work was sick. Democratic ideals had wakened the populace to a sense of its own tyrannical suppression, but in the minds of the rulers and the wealthy had aroused only romantic play-acting and a sense of guilt. The good ladies of Paris might acclaim Rousseau in their salons, but they could only shudder and feel a baffled fear at the growing riotous clamor that was rolling up from below. Marie Antoinette might play milkmaid with her maids of honor in the Trianon gardens, and delight in the absurd dolls'-house country village which the romanticism of the time had built there; perhaps she felt sorry, even, for the plight of real country folk; but taxes remained high, discontent grew, the leaven of democracy and reason was working in the mass of the nation. Fundamentally these three ideals of early pre-Revolutionary Classic Revival—archaeological knowledge, love of reason, and democracy—had led only to a kind of faded decadence, of charming refinement, that had in it the seeds of death. Outside of a few exceptional buildings like the Panthéon, it was a style that could have no issue.

The new classic enthusiasm came to England suddenly, in the work of one man, Robert Adam. Adam had spent several years in Rome, about the middle of the eighteenth century, and had also visited Diocletian's great palace at Spalatro, in Dalmatia, which he sketched, measured, and later published handsomely. In Rome he seems to have been especially struck by the exquisite plaster relief ceilings of some rooms of Nero's Golden House, which had been, as it were, for the second time discovered (for they had been discovered earlier in the sixteenth century and then reburied). Both of these influences—the delicate refinement of the work of the time of Nero in Rome, and the modified Byzantinesque classic of Diocletian's palace—affected him deeply and gave to his work its peculiar character of combined decadence and delicacy. He loved to modify the Roman orders; and, though his touch was different, more sophisticated, more graceful, nevertheless the modifications which he used were inspired by the modifications that Diocletian's builders had made in the Roman orders 1400 years before.

But Robert Adam, later assisted by his brother James, produced work which proves him much more than a clever alterer of old garments. He was brought up in an architectural atmosphere, for his father had been a well-known architect of Edinburgh before him; and, in addition to his great decorative genius, he was a planner of extraordinary skill and originality. Into the staid tradition of the English house he brought the oval rooms so popular with Louis XVI of France, and the circles and octagons and niches of Rome, and of them arranged houses with a convenience as yet rare in the England of his day. Especially in his city houses this ability is remarkably expressed, for on the narrow lots of the typical London streets he was able to produce houses—like that of the Earl of Derby, for instance—in which not only was there a new sense of privacy, a new ease of service, through a carefully considered arrangement of service stairs and the relations of kitchens, dining rooms, and so on, but one in which the rooms were of unusual and lovely shapes, with the most interesting vistas from one room into another, so that the aspect of the house inside seems to indicate a much greater free space than is actually present. These city houses have been the inspiration of many large city houses ever since; in their stair placing and general arrangement they anticipate and furnish precedent for a great number of the so-called English basement houses of almost our own day. The Adams' ability to think in a larger scale is shown both by the Adelphi Terrace development in London (only recently destroyed) and the two great public buildings which they designed in Edinburgh—the Register Office and the University.

Adelphi Terrace reclaimed a large area of the Thames bank, building up a great vaulted substructure, which was directly approachable from the water and admirably fitted for warehouse use, and on its roof laying out

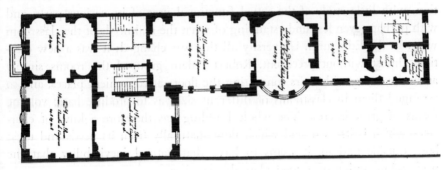

103. THE EARL OF DERBY'S HOUSE, LONDON; PLAN. Robert Adam, architect.
(The Works in Architecture of Robert and James Adam.)

blocks of almost identical houses along new streets. The architects, heavy investors in their own scheme, lost heavily in its unfortunate and undeserved bankruptcy, but the buildings which they erected remained as a blessing for that part of London for over a century. It is perhaps no mere accident, but rather a well-earned tribute to the pleasantness and the graciousness of the atmosphere of the Adelphi buildings, that they were for many years a chosen residence area for many of England's most brilliant writers and thinkers. The Adelphi houses were for the most part almost bleakly simple on the exterior, though the street fronts were ornamented here and there by projecting pavilions decorated with characteristic Adam pilasters. The interiors, on the other hand, were rich with that special kind of delicate classic ornament on which the Adam fame so largely, and in some ways so unfortunately, rests; and the world, in its delight at these exquisite, perhaps overdecorated, marble mantelpieces, these rich ceilings with their little

garlands, their circular moldings, their tiny painted panels, tends to forget
that the man who had exulted in Diocletian's brutal palace could compose
strongly, simply, and with dignity. This quality is naturally best seen in the
Edinburgh buildings, for there the architects were working at large scale
on designs for public use. The Register Office is restrained but powerful,
and well-proportioned; and the façade especially, with its central pavilion
crowned by a dome, is among the best works of the time.

It is the plan which pre-eminently distinguishes the University buildings.
Here, almost for the first time in Europe, the planning of a large educational
building was conceived as a functional study in the proper relation of well-
lighted, conveniently arranged, and efficient classrooms. The old colleges at
Oxford and Cambridge had been allowed to grow. They have the charm of
natural growth; but college after college had been built in the same tradition, with little study of the actual functional uses of its various parts, and
with perhaps even less understanding of what the real needs of the classroom
were. In the Edinburgh University all this was changed; it was a new creation almost without precedent. Robert Adam grouped the rooms simply
around a court, with stairs connecting the floors at convenient places, and so
arranged them in classrooms of different sizes as to produce basic volume
forms of great interest. The whole building has therefore a kind of character which is its own, and which flows naturally from its needs and uses;
both outside and in, it seems to have that natural inevitability that the
perfect integration of a good plan always gives.

Something of the same quality of simple and monumental largeness can
be seen in much of Adam's country-house work, especially in the halls and
front which he added to James Paine's Kedleston house. The original house
was a typical piece of English eighteenth-century country-house work—large,
dignified, classic, and inconvenient. To it Robert Adam added a south front,
with a composition daringly based on the Roman triumphal arch, detailed,
however, not with Roman grandeur but with a quiet and restrained delicacy
almost like that of Louis XVI interior work. Through this front one enters
a great domed hall, rising the full height of the building, its circular walls
lightened by large niches, but with moldings and other applied decoration
reduced almost to a minimum. This superb vestibule leads to the great hall
behind. It stretches through the middle of the house to Paine's older north
portico. The hall has a nave and aisles like a basilica; the roof is supported
by two rows of stately Corinthian columns of almost Roman scale; the walls
are broken by doors and Adam's favorite decorative motif, the niche; and the
whole forms an interior which, no matter how unsuited to a residence, has

in its own forms a dignity and a beauty of proportion that are truly architectural.

Yet in other country work Adam's detail becomes oversmall, too dainty—although it may have charm, like the orangerie at Bowood, with its simple arched windows and delicately detailed pavilions. Nevertheless the detail tends to seem almost effeminate, as though designed for interior rather than exterior use.

In fact, Adam was as a designer a double character, never entirely integrated. Often he seems to be striving for two opposite and conflicting effects. He loved classic dignity, he delighted in using classic columns as decorative screens or in projecting them boldly into a hall as simple sculptural masses, as in the vestibule of Syon House; but he also could seldom restrain himself, if money was plentiful, from piercing the wall surfaces with a superabundance of niches and panels, and tracing over ceilings and walls alike the delicate moldings, the dainty garlands, the oval fan patterns which he was so fond of. The result was sometimes finicking. The interiors were sometimes a little overrich, like the work of an unusually talented cakemaker displaying his skill at frosting a wedding cake.

And these motifs which Adam used in this decoration—these intersecting circular curves, the fan and half-fan motifs, the garlands, the alternations of square and circle—had the additional misfortune of being easy to copy in a superficial manner. Much that passes for Adam work in late eighteenth-century houses, and practically all that is called Adam work which has been done in the past century, should not be credited to Robert and James Adam; it is frequently only a caricature of their work, badly applied and crudely executed. Even at their most decorative, the Adams retained that sense of decorative balance, that contrast of plain surface and ornament, which is the basis of good taste; and after looking at pseudo-Adam one comes almost with surprise upon the true Adam interiors, to find so much clear untroubled wall surface, to see the ceilings so basically strong in design, to realize that almost never does the Adam decoration degenerate into fussiness. The hall at Boodle's Club in London is characteristic.

The Adams were not satisfied with merely building the shells of houses; they insisted on doing the furniture also, and in this furniture the combination of influences from ancient Rome and Louis XVI that distinguished the early Classic Revival of England can easily be seen. The work never becomes as frail as some Louis XVI work; its forms are more virile. But essentially there are many similarities. In the Adam work there is more direct imitation of ancient Roman detail, and usually a greater simplicity of line; but the tapered legs, the use of cast metal to decorate wooden pieces, the frequent supports, made like a bundle of reeds, all show strong French influence.

The Adam work became such a violent rage in the last quarter of the eighteenth century that it is not strange to discover imitators, good and bad, springing up all over the land. Even James Paine, who had worked earlier more or less in the Kent or Gibbs manner, worked later almost entirely in the Adam vein, retaining, however, something of the old sense of Baroque form in his planning and never quite achieving the gay and personal charm, a little cold, which had characterized the best Adam work. Books, too, began to popularize the style in growing quantities, especially the works of William Pain, of which Pain's *British Palladio* was perhaps the best known. Pain was an assiduous draftsman. Handbooks for builders, in which fashionable detail was shown, were coming out in great numbers every year. To these Pain added his own spice of modified Adam classicism. His books are full of fantastically delicate cornices, with new flat-molding profiles. Many he called "fancy" cornices and decorated with scrolls, beads, almost microscopic little leaves, or anything that seemed to come into his imagination. All of it has a character distinctly based on Adam prototypes, but it is by no means Adam design; it all has a kind of capricious, chimerical quality of its own, and its effect on interior design especially was enormous both in England and the American colonies, where the works of Pain were favorite hand-books.

But Adam and his followers were not the only influences behind the later eighteenth century of England. Other, more French fashions were at work. Chippendale yielded in favor of Hepplewhite and then to Sheraton; both the latter not only made large amounts of furniture themselves but issued richly illustrated publications of their own work; and, just as Chippendale chairs and bookcases had flooded England from all the furniture factories on the island in the 1750's and '60's, so the 1770's and '80's were distinguished by a similar flood of furniture and decoration in the Hepplewhite and Sheraton styles. Both had the advantage over Adam of designing pieces which could be made for reasonable sums, for almost all the Adam furniture was enormously rich in carving and specially designed for special houses. The Hepplewhite chairs, with their feather- and urn-ornamented back slats and their oval backs, or the greater simplicity of Sheraton's delicate mahogany, on the other hand, could be readily duplicated and through their basic simplicity would fit well into almost any interior. It was for this reason that the Adam furniture exerted little subsequent influence, whereas the designs of Hepplewhite and Sheraton, like those of Chippendale before them, injected important and long-lived elements into the whole stream of furniture design both in England and America.

England never capitulated to this early Classic Revival movement as completely as did France. The old eighteenth-century tradition of Palladio, on the one hand, and of simple red brick buildings almost undecorated, on the other, was too comfortable, too basically sound, to be easily destroyed. Adam all his life remained the darling of the wealthy Tory nobility. Even Pain's *British Palladio* at first affected only the more radical builders and architects. Other architects continued along all through the century in the older tradition, further studying and refining it, making it continuously more flexible, and learning from the new work of Adam, if anything, only the advantages of occasional restraint and delicacy. Sir William Chambers was perhaps the greatest of these later architects. His Somerset House, the tremendous archives office of Great Britain, is brilliantly conceived both in plan and exterior mass, and the huge rusticated riverside terrace on which it stands easily bears comparison with the Adam Adelphi Terrace not far away. Yet the classicism of Chambers is in general along the older lines. Only here and there a new note creeps in, which reveals the growing sophistication, the growing style self-consciousness of the time. Such are the wide arches springing low down near the ground, unconventionally combined with the orders on the river front. Such too, and prophetic perhaps of the nineteenth-century eclecticism, is the great arcaded entrance from the Strand, which is based neither on the classic work of the ancient Romans, nor on the earlier Palladian work of England, but on Sangallo's vaulted entrance to the Farnese Palace.

In the smaller work, the new feeling showed itself chiefly in a move toward greater and greater restraint in detail and a gradual diminution in the size of all moldings. Cornices became thin, following the William Pain types. Windows were frequently set in arched recesses, and tended to become larger and fewer in number, so that the wall surfaces were less interrupted. This trend toward simplicity, toward unbroken wall and serene mass, accented by the minimum of delicate ornament, was still a trend only, all through the century, and only achieved its final expressions at a later time, when the entire fabric of European life had been shaken and torn by the stresses of the French Revolution, and when the new world of the nineteenth century came into being.

Elsewhere in Europe the new discoveries of archaeology received less rapid architectural application. In Germany there was a swing from French to English inspiration, and the last years of the century saw a sudden flurry of building in which obvious imitations of Adam work were common. Most of these German buildings were at once simpler and more heavy-handed than their English prototypes; but occasionally they had the beauty which quiet walls and well-distributed windows can give, and especially in the minor work, the smaller country houses and the little residences of city and town, work of great beauty was achieved, particularly in northern Germany. Indeed, the placid, tree-lined streets, with their rows of similar houses, all so homelike, so perfectly unassuming, so regular in their alternation of pier and window, with here and there a touch of classic detail, remain to show some of the pleasantest residential quarters of the entire eighteenth century.

But the great effect of the new discovery of the ancient world was to come later and, when it did come, to sweep over Germany with an irresistible flood born of a vast romantic enthusiasm. The new, more accurate Classic Revival was essentially a nineteenth-century phenomenon, but in Germany its first great monument occurred before the eighteenth ended; and, just as Winkelmann of Germany was perhaps the first scholar to attempt a new kind of archaeology, more scientific and more precise than the antiquarianism which had preceded it, so the first monument of the new archaeological revival was German too—the Brandenburg Gate in Berlin, done in a variation of the Greek Doric order by K. G. Langhans in 1788-91. Its archaeological correctness was not yet complete; nevertheless, what makes it significant was the fact that Langhans was trying not merely to be classic but to be Greek as well, and thus in this building he forecast the style trends of the century that was to come.

Chapter 26

COLONIAL ARCHITECTURE
IN AMERICA

THE Western world was a long time in being settled by the Europeans. Little by little, in the sixteenth century, Spanish power and Spanish culture percolated into Central and South America, where the lure of gold tempted adventurers into Mexico and Peru, and large pagan populations seemed to offer unlimited opportunity to the missionary zeal of Jesuits and Franciscans. By the beginning of the seventeenth century the Spanish power in Mexico and Central America was secure, and gradually its influence radiated outward to outlying and near-by countries through the fervor of the missions and the continuing greed and curiosity of the fortune-hunters. Outposts became settlements, settlements changed into towns, towns became cities, in which the native populace, laboring for their new European masters, were gradually giving birth to a new culture basically Hispanic but modified in detail through the continuing vivid native traditions.

What gives especial character and marked vitality to the Hispano-American culture is the fact that the Spanish settlers had no wish to eliminate native populations; they found their hands too willing, and—seeking either souls or wealth, and ofttimes both—were forced to make unwitting partners of the very native peoples they were striving to exploit. Thus, in the Spanish lands, the Indian populations continued to thrive, though half-enslaved, and more and more brought to their Spanish masters not only the labor of their hands, but something at least of their old artistic skills and their basic agrarian nature feeling. Eventually the two peoples were bound to mix increasingly; and in all of Spanish America, though Indians and Spaniards still existed pure-blooded side by side, great sections of the population owed their inheritance to both.

The English settlements of North America had different ends and necessarily different methods of achieving them. Land hunger or the search for religious freedom brought the northerners to what is now the United States and started the great plantations of Virginia; to these settlers the forest-dwelling Indians of the East, with their primitive agriculture, could be of little assistance; sooner or later they were sure to be seen as nuisances to be eradicated. And, where the Spaniard at first exploited the Indians and later mixed with them, in North America the English depended for their labor on their own hands, on indentured servants, and later on negro slaves. The sparse population of Indians was pushed gradually westward, as lands were either bought or seized. Although there are a few noble exceptions to this general course—although Penn attempted in Pennsylvania to treat fairly with the Indians, to consider them as people and brothers, and although occasional missionaries of exalted character attempted to convert the northern Indians to Christianity and somehow to make them productive members of the new communities—for the most part the history is one of complete and callous disregard of Indian rights or Indian personality, so that the new English colonies of the northern states became English and English only. For different reasons perhaps, the Dutch on the Hudson and the Swedes on the Delaware followed the English lead, and when they mixed it was with the English, not with the Indians.

Colonialism in architecture is, first of all, the result of homesickness; second, of national pride. The colonist, surrounded with the sights and sounds and smells of a strange country, dreams of the reassuring, accustomed environment of his youth, and when he builds sets out to build, in nine cases out of ten, a building as much like those which he remembers as his skill and his means allow. It is only a sophisticated colonizer of a later and more analytic age who realizes the inexorable needs of a new climate or of new materials, and creates new forms to fit them. The seventeenth- and eighteenth-century colonizer learned these lessons of local necessity but slowly, and to understand the buildings which he built one must understand the buildings in which he grew up. Usually these were buildings that the generation previous to him had erected; so that it is an almost universal rule that styles in colonial architecture are, in the early periods at least, a generation behind those of the mother country, and that it is only at a later time when expanding commerce and rapidly expanding settlement bring over a constant flood of contemporary goods from the mother country and a growing flood of young, well-trained artisans that this cultural lag shortens and finally disappears.

In the Spanish colonies architectural development was extraordinarily rapid, not only because the Indians of Mexico and Peru were accomplished builders themselves, easy to train, apt in handling and cutting stone, but also because the whole colonial structure was more highly centralized; and many designs for at least the most important Spanish edifices in Mexico, the West Indies, and South America were prepared by architects in Spain itself, and the buildings supervised either by highly skilled monks or craftsmen sent over especially for that purpose. This close architectural tie beween the Spanish colonies and the mother country persisted long after the period when most of the designs were made in the colonies, and it was the general custom to send back to Spain, for record, complete drawings of all the important structures designed in the new country; so that in the Archives of the Indies at Seville there can be found thousands of careful drawings— plans, elevations, and views of the churches and the monasteries and public buildings of San Domingo, Mexico, Cuba, and the South America settlements. All of this argues a very high level of architectural skill, and in the colonies themselves the superb Spanish Colonial buildings of the seventeenth and eighteenth centuries are eloquent witnesses of it.

Yet even in these Spanish colonies the colonial cultural lag is noticeable; for the first exuberant building was so skillful, so beautifully executed, so full of verve, that it formed a new center of tradition in which the native colonial architects were brought up. It formed standards which held sway in America long after the similar standards had failed and died in Spain, undermined by the changing tides of European taste. Thus, gorgeous Baroque work in churches and monasteries continued to be built all through the eighteenth century, and the façade of the church of the mission of San Jose de Aguayo in San Antonio, Texas, although completed later than 1731, is as rich, as perfect, and as sophisticated a piece of Spanish Baroque design as one would find in the Spain of half a century earlier. Similarly, the mission at Carmel, California, not constructed until 1797, is a beautifully executed work in the Spanish style of a century before, and has a baptistry with a ribbed vault essentially Gothic in its construction.

It is in the great centers of the Spanish colonial world that the work is to be found in its highest perfection—in Cuzco, in Havana, in the rich cities of Mexico, Peru, and Ecuador. In Brazil the dramatic work of the sculptor-architect Aleijadinho, especially at Ouro Prieto, is outstanding. Everywhere rise late Baroque church façades, with tier on tier of dynamic ornament; within, lavish altarpieces of carved wood covered with gold fill the chapels and the church apses with a glory of rich subdued light, alive with twisted columns, scrolls, and figures. Sometimes, particularly in Mexico, the richness seems even greater, the intricacy more elaborate, than in Spain itself, for Aztec carvers inevitably instilled the feeling of their own native pre-Columbian buildings, something of their magnificent power, almost brutal, and of that kind of geometric carving which had decorated their own temples. The cathedral of Mexico rose on the exact site of their chief temple; in this there is a symbol of the entire output of the developed Spanish Colonial architecture. Behind its Baroque enrichment lay the memory of the Aztec and the Mayan, and the handiwork of Indian carvers.

At its start, when most directly under the influence of the architects of old Spain, Mexican architecture parallels in its history the architecture of sixteenth- and seventeenth-century Spain. One finds the ribbed vaults of the Spanish Late Gothic, something of the delicate all-over patterning of the Plateresque; later the extravagance of the Baroque dominates all, and, since the great era of Mexican wealth fell in the latter part of the seventeenth and the beginning of the eighteenth centuries, it is this most elaborate kind of Churrigueresque which predominates, for many of the earlier, quieter works were rebuilt or altered beyond recognition in the new period of immoderation. The traveler in Mexico, then, whether in Mexico City, Queretaro, Tasco, or Oaxaca, in a way learns more about Spanish Baroque, sees more of its amazing creative imagination, than the visitor to Spain itself, although a greater and closer acquaintance brings out an ever-deepening importance in the variations due to the Indian workmen, to the growth of the native Colonial architectural tradition.

This same sense of the assimilation of Indian skills creates marked local differences between the Spanish colonies. In Cuba, where the native Indians were savage, unskilled, and rapidly eliminated with utter ruthlessness, the work is closest to that of Spain; and the harborside streets of Havana, with their grilled balconies, their plain wall surfaces, their occasional rich Baroque doors, can be almost exactly paralleled in town after town in Spain. In Brazil and the Argentine, where great feudal ranches and missions were the rule, the work is definitely cruder, the carving naïve, the whole effect wilder and more picturesque. In Peru, there is a special quality of sharp dramatic contrast, a special use of great walls of unbroken stone, from which project carved wooden balconies and bay windows almost jewel-like in their bossy richness, which owe their character only to the special skills, the special artistic sense of the Incas.

In Mexico, too, despite the high general quality, the effervescent, lavish, extravagant culture of the great cities, the extraordinary number of magnificent churches, colleges, monasteries, and palaces, there is a subtle differentiation brought by the native workmen; and, as one goes out into the countryside from the great cities, as one follows the gradual radiation of this culture northward over the Mexican deserts into the rolling hills of Texas, the deserts of Arizona, the rich fertile valleys and grassy mountains of California, there is a constant increase in simplicity, a constant lessening of the power of the central tradition, a constantly growing naïveté, simplicity, directness. The outlying missions which brought Spanish power and Spanish culture alike into the waste spaces, and supported themselves by agriculture or cattle raising, depended for their design almost entirely on the mission priests and for their building upon the local Indians. If the priest were especially learned or possessed of especially good architectural books, the work would reflect this in the skill of its design or the correctness of its detail, as was undoubtedly the case in the mission of San Xavier del Bac in Tucson, Arizona, or San Carlos Borromeo in Carmel, California; but usually the padre, relatively unlettered, would build at least for permanence. Structures like the crudely powerful churches of New Mexico resulted, full of native Indian pueblo influence, with great thick walls, tiny windows, flat timber ceilings, crude belfries, balconies over the doors, and here and there touches of remembered Baroque detail.

Indeed, much of the charm of many California missions comes from just this combination of sincere effort, naïve ignorance, and unskillful execution; for, untroubled by prejudice, the general pattern of the mission—its walled compound, its long narrow chapel with heavily buttressed walls and arcaded belfry, and the cloister with low, wide, simple arches—developed a kind of simple directness altogether lovely. The rich sophistication of the San Antonio missions remained exceptional; they enjoyed obviously a much closer touch with the sophisticated Mexican centers, and their exquisite execution reveals the hand of trained sculptors as well as accomplished designers. Yet even they are simpler than the wealthy Mexican churches. The Purisma Concepción, for instance, has a purity in its simple vaulted interior which seems almost like country work of the early Italian Renaissance than like the Baroque of Spain. San Xavier del Bac is as rich in design as the Texas work, but here the greater distance from the Mexican center shows in the naïveté of the execution, which indicates clearly the decorative sense of the desert Indians of Arizona and New Mexico, just as much of the Mexican work reveals the differing skills of the Aztec.

All the missions as we see them today, cool and white and simple, are far different from what they were at their height, for all apparently without exception were covered with vivid wall painting, the faded remains of which can sometimes be seen; great scrolls crudely drawn in brown and red, black and white, spread over the interior walls, and even sometimes over exteriors as well, with crude stone jointing indicated in awkward rectangular panels.

Here the Indian workmen dominated; again and again the originally Baroque or classic forms are strangely modified with easily recognizable Indian patterns taken from basketwork or pottery, for the Spanish missionaries sought in every way not to alienate their Indian converts by imposing upon them a complete set of strange forms and strange customs, but rather to assimilate them and encourage them to make whatever use they could of their own native festivals, their own native decorative skills.

The secular work in the Spanish colonies was necessarily more affected by local conditions and materials. For one thing, the builder of a ranch house or a town dwelling could not command the almost unlimited wealth which the great religious orders possessed; he was forced to build economically. His wealth, such as it was, he used to provide furnishings or to decorate little special portions; but the structure he usually kept absolutely simple. The Spanish governor's house at San Antonio, like that at Santa Fe, is an example. Both have exteriors absolutely simple, flat roofs, and a kind of "rough-and-ready" atmosphere. Only occasional bits of wrought iron or carved wood show the Spanish influence. In Santa Fe the result was a building which is in large measure indistinguishable at a distance from the adobe pueblos which the Indians had built there for centuries; only the doors and windows identify it as a Europeanized structure. In such simple buildings the Spanish owner would surround himself with furniture, rugs, hangings, and metalwork which was essentially Spanish, so that once within the simple walls he could feel himself still a Spanish grandee, despite the deserts and the ocean between.

Even in the Mexican houses where there was wealth, this same tendency toward plain construction holds true. The building is better, more accurate. Colored tiles are often lavishly used to wainscot interior walls, or occasionally even to face the entire exterior. Sometimes there will be Baroque ornament around the door or a Baroque wellhead in the court, and often wrought-iron grilles at the windows recall the *rejas* of Spain. Nevertheless, almost nowhere except in an occasional viceroy's or bishop's palace is there that enrichment of the courtyard posts, that panoply of cornice and molding on the exterior, that architectural as distinguished from decorative richness, which was usual in houses of equal pretension in Spain. In Peru, to be sure, there was an amazing display of decorative woodcarving, which established a tradition of lavishness in interior design that has held true continuously ever since. Even this, however, was a purely local manifestation, a new creation of the colonial conditions, and even more unlike the house design of Spain than the simple dwellings of Mexico.

The further one gets from the great cultural centers in the Spanish colonies, the more evident is the search for simple solutions of building problems. The secular Spanish colonist in eighteenth-century California, without the force of ecclesiastical tradition behind him, built as best he could for the conditions at hand. Greater rainfall made the flat roofs of the desert country often impossible, so the sloped roof became universal. If tile could not be obtained to cover it, wood shingles would do equally well. He liked as far as possible to keep his courtyard or patio, but often he abandoned even that in favor of the economy and the directness of a simple single rectangular plan, to be roofed with a single gable roof. If he wanted a porch, he built a simple structure of timber posts, bracing it as necessary, as in the old Spanish governor's house at Monterey. Or, if more space were desired, he ran up his building two stories, and put a projecting covered timber porch on the second floor, where both airiness and privacy could be combined.

The result was, of course, an entirely new kind of building, which is "Spanish" only in that it was built by Spaniards, and "Colonial" only because constructed in a colony. By the middle of the eighteenth century, at least in California, the Spanish settlers and rulers seem to have almost entirely rid themselves of the control of any parent Spanish architectural tradition. The especial quality of what they built comes from the simple directness with which their buildings solve the local problems at hand; and, strangely enough, many of them, just because the problems were similar, resemble more closely the simpler buildings of the English colonies to the east than they do the work of Spain or Mexico.

This is an inevitable development in all colonial architecture where the colony is of long standing. At first the colonist built what he remembered in the "old country"; later, he established his own colonial cultural tradition based on that of the mother country as a controlling factor, but modified it to fit local needs; later still, after several generations, when the memory of the parent culture has become but a distant, vague thing—hardly more than an aroma—he comes to realize that even the modified tradition of colonialism entails compromises or sacrifices in comfort or economy, and, the whole past apparently forgotten, he designs new buildings of new kinds for his new and different life.

The same process went on in the colonies of the eastern coast, producing the same phases. In the French, English, and Dutch colonies, however, the first stage was of shorter duration, for the severity of the climate and the plentifulness of wood alike forced early modifications in the copying of the mother-country buildings. The second phase, on the other hand, that of a modified architecture still in close touch with the work of the old country, lasted much longer than in the Spanish colonies; and, in fact, the third phase, the complete liberation from the traditions of Europe, occurred generally only after the Revolutionary War had closed and the architecture was no longer colonial but American.

To each colony the colonists brought their own culture, their own memories. The French, settling a semicircle up the St. Lawrence Valley, down the Mississippi, and along the Gulf Coast, built in this varied terrain buildings not too unlike their homeland dwellings, but changing details and construction to fit the region. In Quebec they built stone hipped or gable-roofed houses, sometimes with the round towers of French manors, or smaller story-and-a-half houses based on French village precedents. The most polished Canadian building was in the churches, where, even long after the English conquest, French Canadian architects, like the Baillargé family, developed a simple, high-gabled, towered type with interiors of pure pre-Revolutionary French Baroque and Rococo. But in Montreal and the Maritime Provinces, meanwhile, the English were building their own severe versions of Georgian themes. In New Orleans, French colonial work reached its highest peak of elegant sophistication, and many buildings were designed by French architects and engineers sent out specifically for the work. This was frequently formal and correct, like the Archbishopric, and several exquisite drawings still exist. In the connecting link, through Michigan, Illinois, and down the Mississippi, the buildings are simpler and cruder; a few existing examples in Ste Geneviève, near St. Louis, and in Illinois remain to show the types. Much of this work was in a sort of half-timber, stuccoed.

The Dutch, settling along the Hudson, came as traders, and New Amsterdam was essentially a trading post; later landed proprietors—patroons—came, and Dutch manors bordering the Hudson brought in a new element of wealth and culture. In New Amsterdam the Dutch invested ample means in their buildings and built more solidly than their British neighbors. They established a brick kiln at the start and made beautiful brick out of which almost all the houses of the young town were constructed. These were purely Dutch in type, with ends to the street and stepped gables, with grouped leaded windows and doors arranged so that the bottom part could be closed for security while the top was open for light and air. Of this Dutch building in New Amsterdam, as in Albany, not a single example exists save in old pictures. Fort Crailo, at Greenbush, and a single example in Schenectady survive to show something of the type.

But the sturdy Dutch temperament preserved Dutch habits in many places long after New Amsterdam had become New York, and after floods of new colonizers from England and from New England were filling New York, the Hudson River towns, and even the manors. The simple low stone houses of Kingston and Old Hurley are essentially Dutch in character, whatever their date may be. The same habits affected even the building of wood houses in the seventeenth and eighteenth centuries, giving in those parts of the colony which remained dominantly Dutch new types of dwelling different both from those of New England to the north and Pennsylvania to the south. The love of the low wall remained, and the idea of the Dutch stoop or front porch made the builders again and again sweep out the lower portions of the roof in a wide curve to give wide eaves to shelter the front door. Later, these eaves became so wide that posts were added to support the projection; the stoop had become the porch. And still later, toward the end of the eighteenth century, when the increased width in the house plan tended to make the single-slope roofs too high, the *gambrel* roof was developed as a method both of saving material where roofs were wide in span, and also of making a greater proportion of the inside of the roof space usable. Fundamentally the gambrel consists in giving the lower portions of the roof a very steep slope, which carries up to the attic ceiling; above this the slope of the roof is made comparatively flat, so that waste space in this upper portion is reduced. In the so-called Dutch gambrels the lower slopes approximate 45 degrees, the upper slopes between 20 and 30; in the gambrels of New England the lower slope is steeper, usually about 60 degrees.

Thus, gradually the purely Dutch elements in the work of the New Netherlands yielded to the influx of English fashions, and ended up by becoming merely one of many local variations of the general body of English Colonial architecture in America; and much of what is called today Dutch Colonial is Dutch only in the fact that it was built in areas where the Dutch originally held sway.

The Swedish settlers along the Delaware River had an even smaller part in forming American Colonial architecture, and left even fewer results. Perhaps something of the quaint, rather crude heaviness of the Old Swedes' Church in Philadelphia can be credited to them; certainly its low, massive brick walls, with the windows widely spaced, its boldly projecting cornice and comparatively steep roof, its cross-shaped plan, and its miniature tower, crowned with a spire that is hardly more than a low pinnacle, make up a whole which would be more at home in Upsala or Stockholm than in London or Bristol.

Germans, too, came in great numbers to the Delaware and settled the rich valleys of Pennsylvania west of Philadelphia. In these German towns, like Bethlehem or Ephrata, one is conscious of differences between them and other colonial centers; yet the difference is hard to express in strict architectural terms. There is perhaps less ornament, a greater severity, in these German settlements, for many of them were founded by members of religious cults in which asceticism was strong. Only in Ephrata does one get a sudden breath-taking reminiscence of the fascinating Renaissance towns of Germany, for there three great buildings were erected as a kind of Reformed monastery for the followers of Pastor Johann Conrad Beissel—a Brothers' house, a Sisters' house, and a guesthouse and administration building. Only one of these stands today, but in its high walls, in its small windows, in its whole sense of proportion, and especially in the towering steep-sloping roof which crowns it there lives the same spirit which built the tall houses along the streets of Rothenburg or Frankfurt. It is perhaps significant, too, of the German feeling for materials that one of the few pieces of true half-timber construction, dating from the colonial era, which still stands today is a building at Oley, Pennsylvania, constructed originally in the 1740's as a Moravian schoolhouse. Nevertheless, in Pennsylvania, the strict German forms tended more and more to be modified by and finally to be merged also with the general trend of American design.

The great underlying strain of Colonial architecture in eastern America is therefore predominantly English. It is this which formed alike the architecture of Virginia and the Carolinas, of Maryland and Pennsylvania, and of all New England; and it is this which, behind all of the local differences, forced by different types of economic make-up, by different conditions, by different materials, makes all of it so basically harmonious.

When the Pilgrims came upon the Massachusetts coast, they found a country of salt marshes and of rolling hills and valleys almost entirely covered with forest. It had good harbors, plenty of fish, plenty of game, and plenty of timber, but very little else. It had also a bleak and violent climate, of cold winters and hot summers. Out of this apparently uncongenial environment they started gallantly to create a new England. Their first buildings were of the simplest—logs pointed and driven into the ground to form enclosures, roofed with rough thatch, or even huts half-excavated in the ground to reduce the amount of necessary wall. But as their sphere of influence gradually widened, as more and more acres of forest fell before them and fields and pastures came to take their place, as they were followed by hundreds more in ship after ship, in a surprisingly short time the essentials of the New England Colonial village began to take form. Framed houses succeeded the crude huts and stockades, and it was only natural that these timber structures should be built like the half-timber houses of distant England, with the same posts and horizontal girts or girders, the same summer beam carrying across the main room to divide its long span in half, the same diagonal braces, even the same overhanging second floor which had originally been developed because it was in some ways simpler to frame and, where lots were small and the house wall directly on the street as in many of the English towns, gave more space above. The fundamental conservatism of early colonial taste can nowhere be better seen than in this preservation of the second-floor overhang in New England, where land was then almost unlimited. These early houses had, too, like the older English buildings, casement windows, in many cases with the sash covered with oiled paper, in the better houses glazed with small panes set in lead in diamond or other small patterns. For filling the spaces between the timbers the early builders undoubtedly used wattle-and-daub; later, after brick kilns had been established, brick filling—or *nogging,* as it is sometimes called —was used. And some at least of these houses of the middle seventeenth century in Salem or Boston must have once seemed almost like those of the village streets of England, with the same many gables, the same steep roof slope, and the same casement sash. Even thatched roofs were common, and were only gradually replaced with shingles or occasionally tile or slate.

But this half-timber construction, however suited to the English climate, was ill-fitted for the severe winters and the icy northwest gales of an American winter. The wood shrank, the filling cracked, the winds felt out and penetrated every crevice; and, no matter how great the fire which roared in the enormous fireplace, drafts and the dampness of driving rain must have made these houses uncomfortable indeed. Thus, to answer the first great pressing problem of climate, the colonists were forced to their first great modification—the covering over of these half-timber houses with boards, those overlapping boards we call *clapboards*—and at once the entire aspect of the towns changed; and, though the picturesqueness and variety of the half-timber was lost, a new charm, a new beauty, was developed in the quiet silver-gray of the weathered boards, or through painting their simple continuous surfaces dark red or brown, or even, in later periods when taste was gayer, white.

It may have been the same problem of warmth in winter and coolness in summer which forced an eventual change in the roofs. The old many-gabled houses were designed to give pleasant well-lighted rooms on the attic floor; but, if these rooms were uninhabitable for a large part of the year because of blazing sun beating down on the unprotected roofs in summer or the wild winter gales blowing through their unheated spaces, they became essentially useless. There may have been difficulty in flashing and making water-tight the joints in the roof surfaces which these complicated many-gabled plans produced. In any case, again and again the old houses were changed, the front gables stripped off, leaving only the plain, gabled roof running from one end of the house to the other unbroken, and the roof space made a simple attic for storage. Again the new condi-

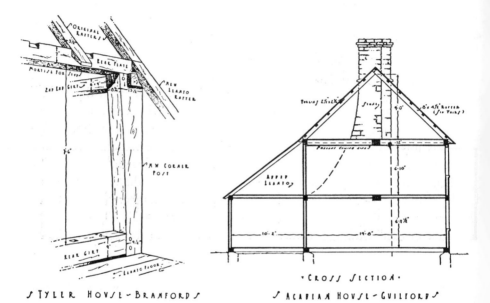

ﾉTYLﾐR HOVﾉﾐ-BRAﾊﾊFORDﾉ   ﾉﾑCﾑﾊﾉﾑﾑ HOVﾉﾐ-GVﾉﾊﾉﾑRﾊﾉ

104. DIAGRAMMATIC SECTION SHOWING CHARACTERISTIC COLONIAL HOUSE FRAMING. *Left:* TYLER HOUSE, BRANFORD, CONN. *Right:* ACADIAN HOUSE, GUILFORD, CONN. (Kelly: *Early Domestic Architecture of Connecticut.*)

tions enforced a change in the old traditional work and produced a house which had a new kind of simple beauty, due to the uninterrupted sweep of its roofs and the simple straightforward outline, obstructed only by the great central chimney, which carried flues from all the house fireplaces.

Perhaps the ideal example of such a house is the Capen house at Topsfield, Massachusetts. It preserves the second-floor overhang from the older tradition, and it has overhangs at the top of the second floor at the base of the gables as well. The roof sweeps through in single unbroken planes; only its steep slope recalls the English work. The central chimney of brick is divided into several receding and projecting planes, as though to recall the individual flues that had been used on the houses of Tudor England. The walls are clapboarded, and casement windows of comparatively small size give to the whole a great sense of warmth and comfort and dignified enclosure. Striking also is the fact that this house, with its central door and two windows on each side, approximates the composition of the standard five-bay house which was soon to become well-nigh universal.

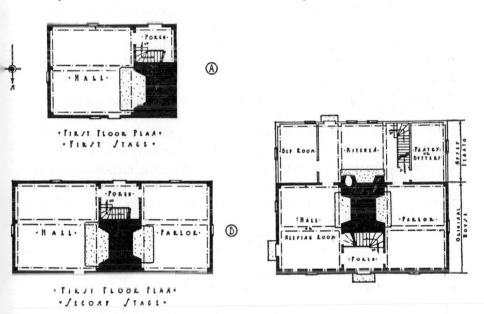

105. GROWTH AND DEVELOPMENT OF EARLY COLONIAL HOUSE PLAN TYPES
Left: LEE HOUSE, EAST LYME, CONN. *Right:* A TYPICAL CENTRAL-CHIMNEY HOUSE, SHOWING ADDED LEAN-TO. (Kelly.)

This plan itself was the result frequently of gradual development. Many houses were added to as the colonist gained greater security or wealth, and as his family increased. Some began as one-room cottages, with a tremendous end chimney, and in front of it, just behind the door, a little winding stair leading up to an upper room or loft. Later the house would be doubled in size lengthwise, and the old end chimney became a central chimney. Sometimes a porch with a porch chamber would be added in front of the door, as in many English manor houses. Later still, if more space were needed, a lean-to would be extended across the house at the back, and the roof slope would be continued down over it to a low eaves line at the back; thus the "salt-box" type was developed. If still further room were needed, the main portion of the house would be built two rooms deep instead of one room deep, and this would give in the already elongated house four rooms to a floor. But in many cases the original structures were of this larger, developed type, and there were occasional houses in Saybrook, Connecticut, or Salem, Massachusetts, of marked architectural pretensions. With the four-rooms-to-a-floor plan, however, the plan offered difficulties, for the great central chimney prevented any through hall to give communication to the rear rooms. The central chimney was therefore split and placed either in the center of the partitions between the front and back rooms, with a fireplace in all four, or else on the end walls of the house. A continuous hall through the building was possible in that way; and the stair, for convenience, was usually placed at the rear of the hall. But this came only later, in the eighteenth century, when the second phase of the Colonial was thoroughly developed.

All of this New England work was based on the simplest town and country houses of seventeenth-century England; for in the main the New England settlers were a modest folk, coming from families of little means, and the architecture they developed was therefore the architecture of the small people of England—the little shopkeepers, the smaller farmers, the poorer professional men. Even when in the new country, after a century, some of them acquired great wealth and built large and lavish mansions, this original derivation from the smaller houses was still plain; for the great houses of the wealthy hardly ever attempted the complexities of the large English house plan, but merely enriched, enlarged, and made more monumental the essentially simple type with which they had begun.

By the last quarter of the seventeenth century New England communities had gained a remarkable degree of security, of comfort, of the essentials of well-being. Skilled craftsmen had begun to come over, finding new opportunities for work; and the older crudities rapidly gave way to greater perfection of execution, greater amenity of plan. The essentials of such a community were simple. A series of houses kept close together to give social intercourse as well as greater security against Indian attack, a meetinghouse which served both for church and for village meetings and courts, and a common for pasturing the village flocks and herds—the whole system of land allotment was based on these requirements. And there were even dim reminiscences, in the land system, of the old feudal type of land development, through the fact that frequently the villages had an "in-lot" on which their houses were built, and an "out-lot" of larger size outside the village for larger-scale agriculture. The common rapidly became the center of the growing town. Around it would be placed other churches if such were needed, and public buildings when civic development made them necessary.

Sometimes it straddled the main road, which was taken around it on either side; sometimes it opened off the road on one side only. In a few cases in the Connecticut valley, as in Old Hadley, the road itself was widened to the proportions of a great monumental avenue, with a cartway on each side and a common strip of grass and trees—the common pasture—between, running the entire length of the village. Whatever the details of the layout, the aim to produce a community seems always to have been paramount; and much of the charm of these New England villages, both in appearance and in essential livability, comes from this fact, for it brought the houses close together, it produced a real center of culture and civilization in the middle of the New England wilds. Little by little the larger villages, of course, developed commercially too, and the port towns and the fishing towns necessarily had a character quite different from that of the agricultural villages; but the common remained an important feature of all, and the sense of community life affected all. The typical New Englander of the seventeenth century was usually not a lonely farmer living apart on his vast acres, but basically a citizen living in surroundings which he made to resemble the little market towns and harbor villages of England as closely as his materials would let him.

It is difficult for us to reconstruct today the extremely English character of these towns. Old engravings and occasional early photographs preserve for us the aspect of such many-gabled, stuccoed buildings as the famous old Feather Store of Boston, and here and there a building like the House of the Seven Gables in Salem retains the picturesqueness of the older time; in the Essex Institute in Salem one of these old houses—the Ward house—has been restored to what the indications showed was its original form, and here and there casement windows have been replaced where the eighteenth century had installed double-hung windows in earlier buildings; yet, by and large, later alterations and much later building have given a new character to these old towns—a character that is essentially that of the eighteenth century.

It was perhaps the Peace of Utrecht, in 1713, that gave the greatest impetus to this change in New England ideals; for the Peace of Utrecht threw open the seas to commerce again, with a freedom that had not been known for almost a century. The little high pooped boats that had shuttled back and forth spasmodically between England and New England became suddenly a large fleet; the boats were larger and better designed, made quicker trips, carried greater cargoes; and the New Englanders themselves became expert in building vessels which rivaled the ships of old England in speed and seaworthiness. The new country offered endless opportunities; thousands of new settlers came, and among them were many craftsmen skilled in all the arts. Books were imported in great numbers, and new shops dealing in all kinds of goods opened almost daily in Salem and Boston. The harbor towns grew; Portsmouth and Portland and Nantucket were added to Salem and Boston; and fortunes were made in commerce. This new trade brought with it much more than increase in population and growing money wealth; it brought a sudden new close touch with English culture, and the colonists discovered that, since they or their fathers had left the old country, the old country had undergone an architectural revolution—the last of the old Gothic, Tudor, Jacobean ideas had perished and in their place Classic architecture ruled supreme.

The first of the great Classic houses, naturally in Boston—the Hutchinson house—had been built some years earlier, in the 1680's. Its three-story façade, crowned with a cornice and a balustrade, was decorated with Ionic pilasters, carved richly and with no little skill. Its door had a balcony over it, and above this on the second floor an arched window with a curved pediment. All the panoply of the English Palladian Baroque thus suddenly broke upon the gaze of the good Boston citizens, and all of them naturally who could afford it set out before long to imitate or to surpass it. After the Peace of Utrecht, the new influx of trained craftsmen and of English architectural books made it possible for them to do so. The first half of the eighteenth century shows many of these large Classic houses. Such is the McPhedris house in Portsmouth, built before 1728; such was the Hancock house in Boston; and Salem and Newburyport were by the middle of the eighteenth century entirely made over in the new Classic vein. This movement reached its height during the third quarter of the eighteenth century. It was reinforced, if not indeed initiated, by the growing flood of architects' handbooks that were being published in England, and by the rapid imitation in America of the English notion that part of every gentleman's education was some knowledge of architecture. Thus the cornices, the doorways, the mantelpieces, and the orders shown in the works of Batty Langley and Halfpenny, of Swan and Isaac Ware, became the generally accepted standards for similar work in New England, and the twisted balusters and rich newels which ornament the stair rails of New England as well as of Virginia are copies of those in the houses of England.

One great difference between English and American conditions still made a chasm between them—the question of materials. For 100 years America had been developing skilled carpenters of its own. To use wood in buildings had a double utility; not only did it furnish excellent buildings well suited to the climate and the conditions, but it was a further inducement to additional forest clearing, and since every tree removed meant just that much more land given to field or pasture the colonists were loath to abandon their timber building. Nevertheless almost all of the building in England had been masonry building, and the details shown in the handbooks were masonry details. The New England builder was therefore in a quandary. Only seldom, in the largest houses, was he building even in brick, and cut-stone was an almost unknown luxury. Yet here were these magnificent plates of beautiful classic detail, and classic was what his clients demanded. Thus he was almost forced to copy these classic elements in wood, and in many houses there is an almost naïve simplicity in the way the masonry details are directly taken over into the new material with no changes whatsoever. The use of quoins cut out of boards for the corners of frame houses became almost universal; and in some cases, as in the Lee mansion in Marblehead, the whole front of the house is treated in boards as though it were cut-stone ashlar slightly rusticated. The pilasters, the heavy cornices, the pediments of English eighteenth-century masonry work all appear in wood in New England. Little by little, of course, modifications crept in. These carpenters were too highly skilled in the use of their material not to detail almost unconsciously in tune with its qualities. Cornices became smaller and more delicate; the orders grew slimmer in proportion; and the wooden mantelpieces had more refined moldings, began to look more and more like wood and less like stone. This development reached its highest point just before the Revolutionary War, when a beautifully subtle relationship existed between the material and the detail; and although the forms are still basically the old English forms, and even the proportions preserve much of the robust British quality, there is nevertheless somehow a controlling sense of consistency, of harmony, as the old attempts at pure imitation yielded to more rational detailing.

In exterior composition there is great similarity between the eighteenth-century houses. Almost all are symmetrical, with a central door and two windows on either side. Usually, though not always, the roof eaves cornice is placed close above the second-floor windows, and the roof slopes are broken by rhythmically spaced dormers, which have little pediments over them and little pilasters at each side. The roof is sometimes a single-gable roof, sometimes a gambrel, and occasionally balustrades are placed at the break of the slope in the gambrel to make a "captain's walk" of the upper, flatter slopes. Sometimes a central cupola is used. The chimneys are either two at each end, with windows on either side of the fireplace in each room, or else larger chimneys in the centers of the two side rooms. Within this general frame there are endless varieties. The simpler village houses are entirely undecorated, depending almost wholly for their effect on subtle proportions. Often even the cornice is hardly more than a projecting board with a mold above and below. In the richest examples, not only is the door enframed by pilasters or engaged columns and crowned by a pediment, but even the window frames may have pediments over them; and the cornice boasts the entire classic array of modillions (little brackets), dentils, and carved moldings. Sometimes pilasters are applied running the whole height of the wall, at the corners or to enframe a central pavilion, which may project and be crowned itself by a pedimented roof, as in the Craigie-Longfellow house at Cambridge or the Lady Pepperrell house in Kittery. Toward the end of the period the three-story house became more common, and roofs were flattened, but otherwise the general elements of the composition remained constant; and the beauty of street after street, in Portsmouth, in Deerfield, in Hadley, in Nantucket, in Edgartown, comes from the quiet repetition of this general pattern, subtly varied by modifications of detail and changes in proportion.

In the Middle Atlantic colonies the conditions were different. In New York and New Jersey the Dutch influence colored not only the seventeenth-century architecture but also much eighteenth-century work, and the existence of the semifeudal patroonships gave an entirely different character to the villages. Tenants tended to live on their own farms; the villages which grew up were little market centers or port towns along the Hudson, in many cases repeating central European village types straggling along a single road. Even today they reveal this difference; seldom do they have that organized, planned look which one becomes used to in New England. In New York City the work of the last half of the eighteenth century was more closely modeled on English prototypes than was usual in New England, for New York seems to have retained a continuously closer touch culturally with England than did Boston or Salem, and its wealthy businessman landowners delighted in building along Wall Street and lower Broadway houses—such as the Kennedy house on the corner of Broadway and Battery Place—which would have graced any English town. The orders were more used; the detail had generally a more definitely Wren or Gibbs cast. In the country houses these magnates built along the banks of the East River and the Harlem, though the interiors were of the expected paneled lavishness, the exteriors were usually of wood and seem almost undesigned, as though they were the comparatively unimportant caprices of men whose real interest was centered in the city.

Pennsylvania had its largest settlement only toward the end of the seventeenth century and in the middle of the eighteenth, so that there are few remnants along the Delaware of that kind of almost Gothic construction which one finds both to the north in New England and to the south. The Pennsylvania work is either rather heavily correct and English, as in Philadelphia and its neighborhood, or else distinguished by that staid, reticent quality which characterized the structures built by the German settlers of Lancaster, Bethlehem, and York and the great barns of the Lancaster Valley.

Philadelphia claimed to be the cultural center of the continent, prided itself on keeping up to date in its following of English fashions, and succeeded in attaining in its red brick architecture a purely correct English character which distinguished it for many years even after the Revolution. British travelers of the early nineteenth century, like Mrs. Trollope and Thomas Hamilton, always felt themselves most at home in Philadelphia first, and in Boston second. It is typical of Philadelphia that nowhere else did a carpenters' company achieve such power and wealth as to enable it to build for itself America's only guildhall—Carpenters' Hall, where once the Continental Congress met. There a handsome architectural library was collected; there the most recent publications of the English architectural writers could always be consulted. It is no wonder, then, that nowhere else in America can be found such correct classic detail, such a complete recapture of the atmosphere and the forms of the provincial towns of England. The simple red brick houses which line the Philadelphia streets, with their beautiful brickwork, their restrained doorways, their white marble steps, have the same serene, almost self-conscious respectability which is to be found in street after street of eighteenth-century London. And in the larger houses the story is the same. Cliveden House and Mount Pleasant both show a kind of architectural grandeur, in their stone details, their urns, their four-square masonry dignity, which may be seen nowhere else.

Even when the prosperous and busy members of the Carpenters' Company were forced, as they usually were, to substitute wood for the stone which would have been used in England, they hesitated to make any concessions to the new material, and preferred to stick as closely as they could to the details published in the English books. In Independence Hall itself, for instance, built as the provincial capitol, the severity of the Doric order used throughout, the scale of the detail, is all essentially more fitted for stone than for the carved wood of which it is made. It is characteristic, too, that in Christ Church Dr. Kearsley, its amateur architect, produced perhaps the most Wrenlike of any church in the colonies. Its sophisticated molded brick detail, its arched windows, its little Baroque key-blocks, and especially the rich and powerful chancel end—with its brick pilasters, its pediment, its carved cartouches and urns, and its great Palladian window—all have a monumentality which is the direct descendant of the more expensive Wren city churches in London.

In the German districts the spirit is inherently different; for, although there is in the exterior little evidence of direct German inspiration, there is always a controlling sense of quiet, almost ascetic, restraint in detail. Many of these German settlements were the direct result of religious movements; a kind of mystical austerity characterized them, and this feeling was bound to express itself, if only unconsciously, in the wide, serene surfaces, the plain trim, the simple roofs which these people so loved.

Farther south there was a different expression. The first settlers in Virginia were adventurers under aristocratic sponsorship, and the aristocratic stamp persisted for long. Jamestown was a close-built village of row houses, but later, when defense against Indians was less important, the country was developed in great estates; towns were minimized except for port towns like Norfolk, Yorktown, or Alexandria and the small but lavishly planned and built provincial capital, Williamsburg, now so brilliantly restored. Situated there is the only building in America—the College—for which Sir Christopher Wren is known to have made plans. But the typical buildings of Virginia were the great houses, set on vast estates, each with own landing on tidewater. These were essentially feudal manors. The workers, first indentured servants working out their time, and later Negro slaves, were miserably housed. Almost all of these servant and slave quarters have now disappeared, but the great houses remain—big, luxurious, high-ceilinged, rich with paneled walls and carved mantels and stairs.

Westover is a good example. It is approached through a rich iron gate, perhaps forged in London. The great red-brick hip-roofed central building, seven bays long, has unwonted scale and dignity; two flanking buildings furnish service areas and extra quarters. The doorway, with scrolled, split pediment and central pineapple, recalls the Baroque doors Inigo Jones liked to use. Mount Airy, later in date by over three decades, built of cut stone, has an even more academically formal plan; quadrant garden walls conceal service colonnades that connect the central block with side service buildings. The source of its design was probably a plate in Morris's *Select Architecture*. Other houses vary greatly. Many earlier seventeenth-century examples in

Virginia and Maryland have cross-shaped plans. Some, like Bacon's Castle or Bond Castle on Chesapeake Bay, have the separated chimney stacks of Tudor and Jacobean England and the traditional porch and porch chamber. In Bacon's Castle the curved, stone-coped gables are pure Jacobean. In other early houses the tradition of the old feudal hall persisted and, as late as the time of Tuckahoe and Stratford, gave rise to large central halls with projecting end wings—a plan already obsolete in England.

Southward, the low coasts of the Carolinas and Georgia were settled along the bays and rivers with great estates even more isolated and larger than those in Virginia. Because of their wild surroundings and the sparseness of the white population, the houses were generally simpler than those to the north, but they were planned with the same ideals. Exceptional was the palace built for Governor Middleton, of which one wing—a large house in itself—still stands. It combined eighteenth-century formality with the curved gables of Jacobean England. At Edenton and on Edisto Island were other large and impressive mansions. Exceptional, too, was the founding of Savannah by General Oglethorpe; here a carefully planned town with ample open squares and wide avenues gave promise of settled urban living.

But, for the most part, it was not until the middle of the century, when Charleston, South Carolina, had grown to be an important shipping port, a cultural center where the great estate owners could collect in the "season," that the architecture of the Deep South achieved characteristic expression. The warm damp climate of Charleston made imperative a different kind of architecture from that further north; and, although there are all over the South the same kind of mantelpieces founded on the books of Swan or Kent, the same Chippendale plaster ceilings, the plans and the exteriors are totally different. In Charleston the houses are raised high above the damp ground, they are compactly planned as befitted their city environment, and always—usually at the side—there are galleries or piazzas, often in two stories, to allow ample space for outdoor living. The individual luxury of detail to be found in such a Charleston house as the Miles Brewton house exceeded the lavishness of detail of even the richest Virginia mansions, and in this work of the latter part of the eighteenth century in Charleston there is an urban sophistication which discloses the existence of a true metropolitan feeling.

Something of the same spirit, the same knowing sumptuousness, is to be found in the great houses of Annapolis. Maryland had been founded by wealthy Catholics, disgusted with the intolerance of the time both in England and in the other American colonies; from the first it was the only colony with complete religious tolerance, and the great families who were influential in its founding saw to it that their own houses were a true expression of their wealth and culture. Fundamentally, many of the country mansions along the Chesapeake shores of Maryland are similar in type to those of near-by Virginia. It is in the towns, and especially in Annapolis, that the differences most surely show, for these houses are as unlike those of Charleston or Richmond as they are unlike the homes which the merchant princes of Salem and Boston and New York built for themselves. They have a high-ceilinged dignity all their own; and, though in general their plans are compact and their exteriors severely restrained in composition, the rich Rococo nature of their detail sets them apart.

Gradually the sources of this colonial building are being discovered in English architectural books, in English houses; even the names of some of the designers are known. Thus Richard Taliafero did some building in early Virginia; his name is associated with the Carters, and he may have designed some of the Carter mansions. Later, in the mid-eighteenth century, John Arris is known to have designed many houses; Mount Airy is probably his, as are the enlargements that Washington made to Mount Vernon.

William Buckland was another important figure at the end of the colonial period. He was primarily a cabinetmaker and woodcarver, and responsible for much of the lavish ornament in Annapolis houses. But he was an architect as well, and Peale's famous portrait shows him holding the plans of the unusual Harwood house there.

Colonial builders used many English architectural books—naturally the builders' handbooks of Halfpenny, Batty Langley, Pain, and others, but more important works also. Among the most popular were Ware's *Complete Body of Architecture,* Adam's *Vitruvius Scotius,* Gibbs's *Book of Architecture,* Morris's *Select Architecture,* and Swan's *Treasury of Staircases,* the last reprinted in Philadelphia in 1775 as the first architectural book published in America.

But colonial America needed more buildings than mere houses to dwell in. As its commerce grew and its government became inevitably more complicated, all kinds of civic structures became necessary. The old simple meetinghouse had sufficed for a town hall in early theocratic days; but, when the theocracy of the seventeenth century yielded to the plutocratic republicanism of the eighteenth, these simple expedients no longer sufficed. Customs houses, town halls, provincial capitol buildings, all made their appearance. The old New York City Hall, once standing at the corner of Nassau and Wall Streets where the Sub-Treasury now rises, is typical. An

H-shaped building, its lower floor was almost all open arcaded loggia for general meetings and market purposes. In the wings on either side were public offices and stairs which led up to the main council hall and court-rooms on the floor above. In the attic in the roof were the cells of the jail. Simply detailed in brick, its size gave it dignity, and its official character was made sure by the cupola which crowned it, as it crowned all the little town halls and customs houses of England. The little courthouses of the Virginia counties are also interesting examples of simple public buildings designed for specific uses. Hardly more than a single room, with a porch in front and a cupola on the roof to give the necessary public quality, they neverthe-less possess the beauty of grace and simplicity.

Commerce also demanded its buildings. Inns rose along the post roads, designed like great overlarge dwellings; and warehouses began to line the water fronts of harbor towns, usually simple structures of brick, with many windows and gabled roofs. Markets, too, were built, and in Philadelphia the little market house of the old Pine Street Market, with its open arcade through the middle, its meeting room above, and its cupola, shows a type that was once much more common. In Boston, Faneuil Hall was constructed as early as 1741, from designs by the painter Smibert. The original struc-ture was but a fraction of the present building, with a front only three windows wide instead of seven, and one entire story lower. It was enlarged and reconstructed by Bulfinch half a century later. Nevertheless, the pilasters which decorated its walls, its carefully correct Doric entablature, its simple pedimented roof, all gave even to the original small building a spirit of pleasant but unostentatious formality.

Four of the original provincial capitols remain: the old State House in Boston, the old State House in Newport, the Capitol in Annapolis, and Independence Hall in Philadelphia.

The old Boston State House is remarkable because of its strong Baroque character, given by the stepped end walls and the carved lion and unicorn which flanked the royal arms. Beneath them a large window, pediment-crowned, leads out to a balcony from which the governor could address the people; and above the roof rises the ubiquitous cupola—here taller, slimmer, more graceful, as well as simpler in its plan than many others. The building is small but obviously a public official structure, an excellent example in its quality and expression of what the unassuming public building may be.

The Newport State House, designed by Richard Munday, is hardly more than an elaborated house design, with a balcony over the door for official speeches, strange snub-nosed gable pediments with queer circular windows, and Baroque detail in door and window frames.

The Annapolis Capitol was begun as an enormous Governor's Mansion, later taken over by the Province. Its immense timber dome, rising high in air, is a later, post-Revolutionary addition. It is heavy-handed, composed with a naïveté expressive of its comparatively untutored designers, yet its size and its unusual silhouette give it great power. The exquisite earlier details of the rooms beneath show how skillful the builders were in those crafts to which they were more accustomed.

The state house in Philadelphia—Independence Hall—is undoubtedly the best designed, the most beautiful, of all of these colonial public buildings. Its plan was made by the lawyer Andrew Hamilton, whose independence of mind was evidenced in its design just as much as in his better-known defense of the New York printer, Zenger, a case that formed the basis of the American democratic belief in the freedom of the press; and it is perhaps more than an accident that the man who was thus responsible, at least in part, for such an important element in American democracy should also have been the man who designed the hall in which the Declaration of Independence was signed. The design of the building, too, is independent; instead of the cupola, which was the almost universal badge of English public buildings, Hamilton had the daring to use a complete tower, projecting from one side of the building, and by placing the great stair within this tower he freed the entire rectangular area of the building proper for a monumental central corridor and important courtrooms and council chambers. The outside he treated with the greatest simplicity, although the little panels below the second-floor windows give the whole a rare sense of European sophistication. And he arranged for the interior a paneled wall-covering of the most severe classicism; the exterior and the interior became two parts of one composition, related in style and spirit as they seldom had been in any other colonial building. Hamilton also planned side buildings, connected to the center by a colonnade. Although the present side buildings are of later date and designed by different architects after the War of the Revolution had been won, the essential conception was Hamilton's, and Philadelphia had thereby a state house dignified, beautiful, almost magnificent. Soon after it was built, the upper part of the tower was destroyed, and for years the building stood with a stumpy tower roof. Later the original Wrenlike top was reconstructed, fortunately in almost exact accord with the old lines.

Williamsburg, of course, had the most sophisticated, the most elegant capitol of them all. Now rebuilt in as close a reproduction of the original as the existing foundations, contemporary engravings, and descriptions could make possible, the existing structure is not, however, old. The original had been destroyed to the foundations over a century before. The designs for the capitol, the governor's palace, and William and Mary College in Williamsburg were probably by Sir Christopher Wren. In the last case there is strong documentary evidence, and these three buildings remain the only ones in the American colonies to which Wren's name can be even distantly applied. Yet even here modifications from the Wren design were made, and the commissioners' reports tell of these changes—probably reductions in size and richness in detail, to bring them within the scope of the labor and money available. In any case, the reconstructed buildings show a quality in the proportion of window and wall, an originality and daring in the use of carved forms, a dexterity in the handling of arched and square-headed openings which is all unique in America, and because of its English design perhaps hardly to be included in the true thread of American colonial tradition.

And the men of colonial America needed not only to be governed and to govern themselves; they needed also to worship, especially since the religious motive was so strong behind so much of the colonial effort. In New England the earliest churches were all of the strict meetinghouse type—buildings square or nearly square, with galleries around three sides and a pulpit in the middle of the fourth. Usually, at least in the earlier buildings, the pulpit was contrived to be against one of the longer sides, so as to bring the preacher into the closest possible touch with all the members of his congregation; and these buildings, simple as they were, were admirably suited to their purpose—more so perhaps than the long narrow churches of more thoroughly Georgian type which succeeded them. The meetinghouse walls were simple; rows of plain windows showed the two levels within, and the plainest of doors on one, two, or three sides gave entrance. A little cornice crowned the walls, and above this rose a hipped roof to a central cupola or belfry. The "Old Ship" meetinghouse at Hingham, Massachusetts, shows the type perfectly, although its belfry, simple as it is, is richer than that of many of the earlier buildings. The same meetinghouse type was found all through the northern colonies—in New England, even in urban Boston, in New York, in Albany.

In Philadelphia the Swedish and German and Quaker settlers all furnished their quota of influences in changing this meetinghouse type. Especially interesting are many of the simple Quaker meetings—perfectly plain, rectangular buildings with gabled roofs, which somehow show in the quiet loveliness of their proportions, as they do in the asceticism of their detail, that delightful quality of gracious living which so frequently distinguished the early Friends themselves.

In Virginia the early churches were under entirely different auspices; the official, the quasi-aristocratic type of the settlements is evidenced by the fact that all of the earliest churches are Church of England—Episcopalian. Among them a pre-eminent example is St. Luke's at Smithfield, Virginia, built in 1632 and thus one of the earliest datable standing buildings in the English colonies. St. Luke's is remarkable as perhaps the only true Gothic church in America. It is late debased Jacobean Gothic, to be sure; it has a round-arched door with a naïve pediment above it, but it also has true offset buttresses at the sides, a high-pitched roof, and traceried windows. Its brick tracery is unsophisticated like its door, and the windows, starting as though with pointed arches, end in the center with a strange and awkward curve; but its parentage is obvious—the little village churches of England. It is late English Gothic seen through a haze of Jacobean Renaissance and built by untrained masons in a far-off land. St. Peter's of New Kent County still retains some of this earlier feeling, although built nearly seventy years later. Here the builders were trying as hard to be Classic as in the earlier example they were attempting to be Gothic. Yet the old medieval church plan tradition—the great central tower, the projecting buttresses, and the high spire—still shows in the crude workmanship of this naïve building and in the heavy pinnacles which crown the tower buttresses.

Later, of course, in the full high noon of the eighteenth century, all of this early artlessness was left behind, and the Georgian type of church, first established by James Gibbs in St. Martin's-in-the-Fields in London, swept over the country north and south alike. The Gibbs book must have had a tremendous circulation, and rumor has it that some of the architects of these later Colonial churches—like Thomas McBean, the designer of S⊦ Paul's Chapel in New York—were draftsmen or pupils of Gibbs himself. St. Paul's is of course an unusually perfect and lavish example of the type, just as Dr. Kearsley's Christ Church in Philadelphia is an unusually perfect example of the Wren influence; nevertheless the general scheme—a rectangular building divided into nave and aisles by columns carrying arches or plaster vaults, with galleries over the side aisles, and with a tall steeple and tower over the main entrance—is well-nigh universal. It appears in many strange guises, indeed. In the Old South Meetinghouse in Boston, a high entrance tower and steeple is joined to a building of almost purely meetinghouse type; the delicate arcade around the base of the spire gives promise of the exquisite wooden New England steeples that were to be built later, like that of the Congregational Church at Farmington, Connecticut, or the somewhat similar spire in Kennebunk Port. A completely sophisticated example appears in the First Baptist Church in Providence, designed by Joseph Brown; Trinity, in Newport, by Richard Munday, is transitional. The complete Gibbs church type is climaxed by King's Chapel, Boston, and St. Paul's, New York, both of stone. King's Chapel was designed by Peter Harrison, also the architect of the Newport market and the Touro Synagogue and Redwood Library there, as well as of the unusual Christ Church in Cambridge. The colonnade of King's Chapel was added after the Revolution.

Further south, in Charleston, the churches have greater heaviness. St. Michael's is a characteristic Gibbs design, widened and flattened, so that the proportions of its windows and its interior have a strangely depressed, awkward, low line; and its tower, rich as it is, seems overheavy, although the Doric portico is correct and monumental. This search for monumental magnificence went further still in St. Philip's, built a little later. Oddly situated, in such a way that it projects into a street intersection, its designer gave it three complete porticoes, one in front and one at right angles at each side facing down the interrupted roadways. The conception was grand, and the detailing more elegant than in the earlier building. The church was burned in 1835, but was rebuilt the next year, following much the same exterior scheme though with changes in detail and interior.

Thus, the eighteenth century brought a similarity of church inspiration all over the American colonies, an inspiration which revealed itself in similarities in design; and the foundations were laid for that enduring tradition in church design which was to last for half a century more and raise the white spires which show themselves above the village trees in so many parts of eastern America.

This fact, this gradual unification of tradition, as eighteenth-century sophistication crept in, characterized the whole field of architecture. Communication between the colonies was becoming continuously easier, continuously more frequent. Commercial bonds, similarities in political ideals were gradually overcoming the earlier differences in colonial impulse, were gradually welding together, all through the eighteenth century, the various colonies into one nation. This cultural unity is nowhere better shown than in interior work and furniture, for there the fashions of the day had far more sweep than in the design of the more permanent buildings themselves. Local furniture makers there were, of course, like the Savery establishment in Philadelphia; and the expert antiquarian can frequently judge correctly the original source of much Colonial work. But the general styles remained constant. The Elizabethan court cupboards and the carved flat oak chests of the seventeenth century gave way to the walnut of Queen Anne, as the crude painted plaster and grooved, molded wainscot boarding and the feather-edged planking partitions gave way to the dignity of large wooden panels with chair rails and carved cornices. At first the paneling covered only the chimney end of the room; later, examples almost as rich as any in England are found, like the so-called mahogany room in the Lee mansion at Marblehead. Later still, the paneling itself came to seem over-heavy, and little by little disappeared except for a low wainscot; and the wall above was painted or, in the more expensive houses, papered with paper from China or England. So, too, the colonists' Queen Anne furniture gave way to the mahogany of Chippendale—the ladder-backs, the carved, bowed legs, the rich Rococo detail—to match the Rococo ornament on occasional ceilings; and, just as in England the Rococo yielded after the middle of the century to more quiet and restrained work, so in the American colonies very shortly afterward the Rococo Chippendale yielded to the more classic American copies of Hepplewhite and Sheraton.

Yet the basic architectural taste of the colonies remained generally conservative, preserving its new-found simplicity, its classic dignity. The new English fashion of Early Classic Revival, due to the influence of the Adam brothers and Pain, came but slowly into America. Though occasional individual buildings give a suggestion of this trend, like the two-story portico of Whitehall in Maryland or the slim colonnade of the Jumel house in New York—the only free-standing two-story colonnades built in America prior to the Revolution—in general the Adam influence became a ruling factor only after 1785, and the Classic Revival in America therefore is no longer a colonial matter but part of the architectural history of the United States.

BOOK VII

Nineteenth Century Architecture

Chapter 27

THE SPIRIT OF THE NINETEENTH
CENTURY

ONE cannot play with ideas indefinitely without being changed, and all of Europe for the last half of the eighteenth century had been playing with revolutionary ideas. Without knowing it, quite, all of Western culture was altering, for reason and individualism as set forth by Voltaire and Rousseau were sapping the foundations of all previous traditions. Voltaire's intense skepticism, rationalism, and tolerance were common coin among the intellectuals; and Rousseau's doctrine of individual rights, his theories of a society based on the free contract of individuals, and his willful, romantic primitivism had alike become the plaything of fashionable salons. Yet Voltaire and Rousseau became the two matches to set fire to the great mass of revolutionary fuel that a century of oppression had been storing up, and the last quarter of the eighteenth century saw the constant piecemeal disintegration of the entire Renaissance and Baroque system.

The American Revolution was but one symbol, Thomas Paine's voice but one of many. Everywhere men were questioning existing governments, existing social systems, and finding them wanting. When at last the French Revolution swept over France, carrying away the old Bourbon monarchy in a flood of disastrous destruction, the old system received its deathblow. All over the Western world, what was to come after was to be different; and, even in countries which seemed as yet untouched, the leaven of reason and individualism was deeply at work.

A new physical world was arising, too. The great scientific discoveries of the seventeenth century and the ingenious mechanisms of the eighteenth were beginning at last to have their effect on ordinary living, the bases of production were changing, a new world—the industrial world—was coming to birth. Newcomen's steam pumping engine had been puffing away in the English mines for more than a half century. James Watt, taking the basic ideas of steam power, refined them, made the steam work more efficiently, introduced the rotary flywheel, created in fact the fundamental elements of the steam engine of today in patents which he obtained between 1769 and 1784. Later, the refinements of Cartwright, Radcliffe, and Tolman had by the end of the first decade of the nineteenth century produced steam-power units which were freed from their early, limited uses and could now be applied to almost any purpose for which power was necessary. Power looms clattered in Yorkshire at least as early as the 1790's, and more and more the textile industry was becoming a matter not of cottage manufacture or even of small groups of hand looms in local mills, but rather a true factory industry where the power of each individual to make things was increased many times. Unemployment was rife; if one person could do the work that ten had done before, what were the ten to do? No wonder the introduction of the factory system into the textile industry brought riots, the wrecking of factories, the destruction of machines!

These are only samples of a movement which was as wide as Western civilization, a movement which was making the manufacture of things of all kinds easier and cheaper, producing floods of new goods at low prices, and doubling, tripling, multiplying manifold the manufacture of iron and steel. Steam power was making over the world more rapidly than the changes could be digested.

And, just as there was a change in the industrial basis of the manufacture of almost everything men needed, so the new movement brought with it new ideas of trade and commerce and business. Adam Smith published in 1776, the year of America's Declaration of Independence, his *Inquiry into the Nature and Causes of the Wealth of Nations*. It was an epoch-making book; for, loosely constructed though it was, it nevertheless for the first time patterned out the necessary business background of an industrial civilization. The ideas of profit and loss, of cost, of wages and rents, of the nature of capital were there set down simply and directly; and from his observations Smith developed the theory that in business at least that government was best which governed least, and thus gave a sort of quasi-respectable rationalization of that profit-seeking greed which was the curse of the employing class. Adam Smith had started out as a moral philosopher; his book became a sort of eagerly quoted Bible for a rampant commercialism, and the concept of free competition as a necessary element to preserve standards and prevent monopoly prices became a ruling tenet of all orthodox business people.

Thus the new nineteenth-century world was furnished at once with the enormous industrial potentialities of the factory system and an economic theory which induced, and in fact almost justified, the unlimited exploitation of workers, to the end of an unlimited distribution of goods. Since the workers could not buy back the goods they made with the wages paid them, new markets had to be sought, and a new kind of imperialism arose as an unavoidable result; so that even international affairs and international thinking were completely altered, the old ideas overset, and what came later to be called "dollar diplomacy" was born. Nor did the changes stop with manufacture and selling. The application of the steam engine to railroads and to steamships made over the geography of the world, brought suddenly a new nearness between places, made travel easier and quicker. The beginning of the nineteenth century saw the world a leisurely place of stagecoaches and canalboats; the middle of the century found it netted with railroads and saw steamships shuttling across the oceans. The first public railroad, the Stockton and Darlington, was opened in England in 1825; four years later the London and Manchester Railroad gave tremendous publicity to the new form of travel and became the first of an enormous series of railroad systems that grew up with almost unbelievable rapidity all over Europe and even in America. With the railroad, manufactured goods could be distributed in a way that older methods had never equaled. Immediately, local traditions of craftsmanship and design were influenced; the local existence of some special material no longer conveyed special advantages. Generalization of forms and manufactures, of fashions and tastes, became inevitable over large areas where previously local ways had held sway.

The architectural effects of such deep-seated changes in living were, of course, profound. They influenced both the content and the manner of building. They made necessary entirely new types of structures—factories, railroad stations, great industrial warehouses, new kinds of houses for factory workers;—and they gave rise to utterly new kinds of towns, the industrial towns which sprang up like mushrooms, all over England especially and to a less extent along the Rhine and in parts of the New World. The steam engine made large factories more economical than small ones. The presence or the easy availability of fuel forced steam engines to group together. The result was naturally the concentration of manufacturing units, great series of huge mills, and around them all the buildings found necessary for the people who worked there. And people flocked to these new centers. What else could they do? Their old local industries or cottage crafts ruined, they moved perforce where work was to be had; and congestion became the usual, one might almost say the necessary, accompaniment of every single new industrial town. Out of congestion was born land speculation; out of land speculation, and the attempt to wring the last penny of profit from every square foot of ground, were born the nineteenth-century slums of the world. For example, Middlesbrough, in Yorkshire, had in 1801 a population of twenty-five people; but there was iron ore in the hills near by and a river to make a harbor, and today the city has over 130,000 people. The greater part of this growth occurred between 1830 and 1870, and, with exploitation in the saddle, forty years' building for 70,000 or 80,000 new people could only produce the cheapest, the ugliest, the most crowded, the most depressing of towns.

Other elements added to this confusion. Somehow the new distribution of goods, the new ways of living, and perhaps the growing development of scientific medicine increased birth rates and populations with frightening rapidity. Thomas Malthus had observed the beginnings of the phenomenon and in 1798 had published his *Essay on Population*, based on the alarming and pessimistic theory that population was bound to increase faster than the means of supporting it, and that every increase in available food or amenity brought an increase in population which more than outweighed it. The fecundity of the slums became proverbial. Workers increased faster than jobs, wages went down, and at times there seemed no possible answer to the growing problems that confronted the new industrial world. Only the existence of vast, still undeveloped spaces in Asia, in Africa, in Australia, in the Americas, which could receive surplus people, saved the system.

But there was another side to this development. Adam Smith had seen that at least a modicum of education was necessary to produce efficient workers, and had somewhat tentatively set out the ideal of universal education. Had this ideal not been in the closest harmony with the Rousseau concepts of individual growth that had so deeply affected all Western thinking, it is probable that Smith's suggestion would have been neglected; but the power of the Rousseau theories was still alive. Universal education, then, became first an ideal, then a slogan, finally a fact. The world became in a few decades a literate world, and more and more people sought release from the thronging practical problems that industrialism and trade were bringing upon them in their eager and enthusiastic search for the stored wisdom of the written word.

In architecture the results had already begun to be apparent in the early Classic Revivals of France and England; but the popularization of the knowledge of history, of the architectural work not of one but of many previous civilizations, was sure to produce startling results. One showed one's culture by a knowledge of the past, and the ideal of "culture" was an ideal to which everyone could aspire in an era of universal education.

EIGHTEENTH-CENTURY ARCHITECTURAL PHANTASY; SPACE, LIGHT, THREE-DIMENSIONAL FORM, SCALE. (G. B. Piranesi: *Prigioni*.)

Plate 65

PIRANESI PLATE, THE FRONTISPIECE TO *LE ANTICHITA ROMANE*, 1756.

LONDON, LORD DERBY'S HOUSE; A TYPICAL ADAM DETAIL. (*The Works in Architecture of Robert and James Adam*.)

LONDON, LORD DERBY'S HOUSE; DRAWING ROOM INTERIOR. (*Ibid.*)

Plate 66

CHOLULA, CAPILLA REAL; PURE RENAISSANCE IN MEXICO. (Courtesy Carl Feiss.)

HAVANA CATHEDRAL; EXTERIOR AND ARCADED PLAZA.

TEPOTZOTLAN, A REREDOS; THE JEWELED LAVISHNESS OF MEXICAN BAROQUE. (Courtesy Carl Feiss.)

SAN ANTONIO, TEXAS, MISSION OF SAN JOSE AGUAYO, DOOR; COLONIAL BAROQUE EXQUISITELY EXECUTED. (Photograph by author.)

Plate 67

SMITHFIELD, VA., ST. LUKE'S CHURCH; "COLONIAL GOTHIC." (Frances Johnston.)

EPHRATA, PA., SISTERS' HOUSE AND THE SAAL. (P. B. Wallace.)

SALEM, MASS., WARD HOUSE. (Essex Institute.)

Plate 68

WESTOVER, A GREAT VIRGINIA HOUSE. (Frances Johnston.)

PORTSMOUTH, N. H., THOMAS BAILEY ALDRICH HOUSE.

ANNAPOLIS, MD., CHASE HOUSE. (Hayman Studio, Annapolis.)

NEW YORK, N. Y., THE APTHORP HOUSE (DESTROYED).

Plate 69

HINGHAM, MASS., OLD SHIP MEETINGHOUSE; SIMPLE SERENITY OF PURITAN NEW ENGLAND.

NEW YORK, N. Y., ST. PAUL'S CHAPEL; INTERIOR. McBean, architect; chancel by L'Enfant. (Wurts Brothers.)

BOSTON, MASS., OLD STATE HOUSE; BAROQUE PROVINCIAL DIGNITY. (Halliday Historic Photograph Co.)

PHILADELPHIA, PA., INDEPENDENCE HALL. Andrew Hamilton, architect. (P. B. Wallace.)

Plate 70

PARIS, CHAMBRE DES DÉPUTÉS, ENTRANCE
COLONNADE; EMPIRE CLASSICISM IN ARCHI-
TECTURE. Poyet, architect.

CLASSIC REVIVAL ORIGINALITY: HOUSE FOR
A RIVER SUPERINTENDENT. (*L'architecture de
C. N. Ledoux.*)

PARIS, TRIUMPHAL ARCH OF THE ÉTOILE.
Chalgrin, architect.

PARIS, THE MADELEINE; INTERIOR. Vignon and
Huvé, architects.

Plate 71

MUNICH, GLYPTOTHEK. Von Klenze, architect.

REGENSBURG, VALHALLA; INTERIOR. Von Klenze, architect.

BERLIN, COURT THEATER; CLASSIC DIGNITY AND CLASSIC REVIVAL ORIGINALITY IN WINDOW TREATMENT. Schinkel, architect.

Plate 72

LONDON, BRITISH MUSEUM; COLONNADE. Sir Robert Smirke, architect.

LIVERPOOL, ST. GEORGE'S HALL. Elmes and Cockerell, architects.

CLASSIC REVIVAL ORIGINALITY IN ENGLAND; ROW OF FOUR HOUSES FROM GANDY: *The Rural Architect.*

DERBY, EARLY RAILROAD STATION; CLASSIC REVIVAL DESIGN APPLIED TO AN IMPORTANT NEW PROBLEM. (Ackermann aquatint, Parsons Collection.)

Plate 73

WASHINGTON, THE CAPITOL; STATUARY HALL. Latrobe, architect.

WASHINGTON, OLD PATENT OFFICE; EXTERIOR. Mills, architect.

CHARLOTTESVILLE, UNIVERSITY OF VIRGINIA; ROTUNDA. Thomas Jefferson, architect.

PHILADELPHIA, MARINE EXCHANGE. EXTERIOR. Strickland, archi-

Plate 74

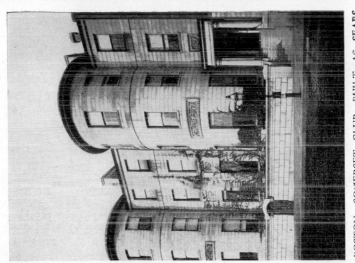

BOSTON, SOMERSET CLUB, BUILT AS SEARS HOUSE. Alexander Parris, architect.

NEW YORK, TREDWELL (OLD MERCHANTS') HOUSE: PARLOR. (Courtesy Historic Landmark Society.)

NEW ORLEANS, "THREE OAKS" PLANTATION; GREEK REVIVAL IN THE SOUTH. (Ricciuti: *New Orleans and Its Environs.*)

NANTUCKET, MAIN STREET; GREEK REVIVAL HARMONY AND GRACIOUSNESS. (Photograph by the author.)

Plate 75

FONTHILL ABBEY, INTERIOR; RO-MANTIC EXAGGERATION AND PICTURESQUENESS. James Wyatt, architect.

FONTHILL ABBEY, EXTERIOR: THE CASTEL-LATED MANSION IN ITS MOST EXTRAVAGANT FORM.

CONTRASTED ALTARPIECES; A PLATE FROM A. W. PUGIN: *CONTRASTS*. AT THE LEFT, 18th-CENTURY CLASSIC; AT THE RIGHT, THE PERFECTION OF GOTHIC RICH-NESS. PUGIN'S PROPAGANDA FOR THE GOTHIC REVIVAL WAS BRILLIANT AND SUCCESSFUL.

Plate 76

VIENNA, VOTIVKIRCHE. Von Ferstel, architect.

NEW YORK, TRINITY CHURCH: RICHARD UPJOHN'S RENDERING. (Courtesy Professor Everard Upjohn.)

NEW YORK, OLD NATIONAL ACADEMY OF DESIGN. Wight, arch't.

MANCHESTER, ASSIZE COURTS. Waterhouse, architect.

Plate 77

BRIGHTON, THE PAVILION; EXOTICISM IN ENGLAND. Nash, architect.

PARIS, THE OPÉRA, EXTERIOR; EXPRESSION ON THE OUTSIDE
OF INTERIOR ARRANGEMENTS. Garnier, architect.

PARIS, THE OPÉRA, GRAND STAIR; SECOND EMPIRE LAV-

Plate 78

DRESDEN, THE OPERA HOUSE; ECLECTIC CLASSIC IN GERMANY. Semper, architect.

PARIS, SACRÉ COEUR; ECLECTIC ROMANESQUE. Abadie and Magne, architects.

LEIPZIG, CITY HALL; ECLECTIC GERMAN RENAISSANCE. Licht, architect.

Plate 79

CHICAGO WORLD'S FAIR, 1893; ADMINISTRATION BUILDING. Hunt, architect.

NEWPORT, "THE BREAKERS." Hunt, architect. (Courtesy Prof. H.-R. Hitchcock Jr.)

NEW YORK, VANDERBILT HOUSE. George B. Post, architect.

Plate 80

Governmentally, too, there were changes. The democratic myth in various phases became more and more widely accepted; and, though pure democracy was frequently still frowned on, various forms of representative government through parliaments were almost universally accepted as the proper means of government. And the electoral basis on which these parliaments were founded was constantly widening. Everywhere this movement was resisted by the entrenched power of a hereditary nobility, and later of a plutocracy of wealth. Yet the enthusiasm behind the movement was too strong to withstand, and little by little the older forces yielded grudgingly. To dream-making and imaginative minds there seemed no end to this gradual development of popular sovereignty, as there seemed no possible limit to the advantages to be gained by increased power and the broadening and deepening of education. What if slums were being built and spawning millions of unkempt, unwanted, pitiful, undernourished children?—greater knowledge, greater education, better distribution would solve these problems.

So that everywhere, even among the oppressed themselves, there was hope —hope expressing itself in strange and thwarted attempts at self-improvement, hope setting aflame all sorts of queer Utopian cults that started out here and now to build the promised land on the basis of socialism, communism, religious enthusiasm, or what you will. If Malthus was stating what he felt to be the fact, that human physical improvement was bound to defeat itself through increasing population, at the same time men like Shelley were holding flaming aloft like a torch the concept of eternal progress to constantly greater happiness and accomplishment; for Shelley is as truly a son of the early nineteenth century as Watt or George Stephenson (who perfected the locomotive), and the idea of this magnificent forward march of humanity dazzled the eyes of people of all classes. The French Revolution had established the watchword, "Liberty, Equality, Brotherhood." To these ideals popular education was giving wings, and men like Shelley or Robert Owen (with his socialist Utopias) a new vision, a new mythology. With democracy, brotherhood, education, science, mutual understanding and love, humanity it seemed could march ahead straight into heaven. It was the tragedy of the nineteenth century that the evils of industrialism, of the slum, so early put out this blazing flame, and that Darwin's new theory of evolution, which might have fired the old Shelleyan hope with new brilliance, became merely an excuse for a popular business psychology of "the devil take the hindmost."

In architecture the tragedy is easily seen. Confusion of ideals produced confusion in building types and building integrity. The profit system, as de-

veloped in the early rampant industrial and commercial world, made cheapness in itself an ideal to strive for, as though cheapness were ever anything
but an unfortunate necessity! It made men feel that cheapness and economy
were the same thing, although the world's history existed to prove their
infinite separation. The new education gave architects and laymen alike a
new smattering of archaeological knowledge, which they could ill digest,
and the new problems of new building types and new city concepts came
pressing so fast that the architectural mind of Europe faltered and finally
fell before them. Moreover, a new client class was growing up, a class of
suddenly wealthy, successful businessmen, who more and more came to
control not only the construction of their own houses, but the building
of the courthouses and city halls and churches which the new towns made
necessary. These clients lacked entirely that kind of sense of architectural
merit which somehow the old Baroque courts had consciously developed
and the eighteenth-century nobility had largely maintained. Lacking standards and tradition, their only standard could be merely the superficial one
of fashion, and even this criterion was often vitiated by their arrogant
sense of their own power and their own uncertain and limited knowledge.
The client has the last word in any actual building. What he says goes,
necessarily, for it is the man who pays the piper who calls the tune; and no
architectural training, however severe, however effective, could produce
anything, save exceptionally, which was not in the final analysis that which
a client desired. Hence the ill-ventilated, ill-lighted mills, the showy but
inconvenient public buildings, the pathetically cheap and crowded schools,
the rows of back-to-back houses sitting dank and grim in the factory smoke;
the public houses, gay with bright lights and bright tile, but innocent of
any real beauty; the country houses, aping the castles of the medieval
nobility or the villas of Florence or Rome; the cardboard churches in
classic or Gothic or any other style, built like cheap dolls' houses to have
an "effect."

The architectural picture, like the emotional and cultural picture, is not
all one-sided. In the beginning at least, architects met the problems thrust
upon them with extraordinary flexibility and imagination, and not all clients
were blind to decency or common sense. It is extraordinary, for instance,
to notice how many books were published in the first half of the nineteenth
century dealing with the comfortable and pleasant housing of laboring
people at small cost. Many of the earlier mills, both abroad and in the
United States, are dignified in form, simple and efficient in plan, adequately
lighted, and possessed of a definite architectural beauty of their own. The

earlier railroad stations such as those built in the 1830's for the London and Manchester Railroad, and later for the Birmingham Railway, were excellently designed, sensible, beautiful, facing and solving the special problems of planning and appearance simply, directly, and without trickery. Science and engineering alike were suddenly making available metals and glass for building purposes, and again and again nineteenth-century architects seized eagerly the opportunities these new materials offered and produced with them buildings which were as fresh, as simple, as logical, as expressive as anyone could wish. Just as there was a Shelley in poetry to point the new path, so in architecture men rose up like Sir John Soane in England, K. Friedrich Schinkel in Germany, and Latrobe, Mills, or Strickland in America —who designed sincerely and well, making creative use of the extraordinary new opportunities which their age offered. At the beginning of the industrial revolution, it was its sudden new opportunities which seem to have chiefly struck the architectural mind. It was only later, when the new industrial plutocrats had come to dominate the scene, that unmixed confusion set in.

All nineteenth-century work, good or bad, was bound to have one element in common—its complete separation from the traditions of Renaissance and Baroque Europe. Life and people had both changed. The great gradual development of traditions, from the Middle Ages, through the Renaissance, into the Baroque, had lived its life and died in the welter of revolution, industrialism, and education. Nineteenth-century architecture was sure to be a new and a different phase.

Chapter 28

CLASSIC REVIVAL IDEALS

WHEN the old aristocratic architectural tradition passed away in the revolutions of the end of the eighteenth century, there was but one valid architectural influence still alive and still sufficiently unconnected with the older and hated forms to warrant a fuller, victorious development. That was the classic tradition—not the classic of the Renaissance or the Baroque or the Rococo, but the classic architecture of the ancient world, which archaeology was bringing to a new life. Of this new knowledge of the classical world the popular mind was deeply sensitive, the critics deeply appreciative, and the architects enthusiastically admiring. The result was inevitably a Classic Revival spreading over the entire Western world with a surprising unanimity and speed.

The name by which this movement goes, however, is essentially a misnomer. The ideals of the real thinkers of the time, as of the most skilled designers, were not ideals of mere imitation. What the student saw in the ancient buildings of Greece and Rome was not merely a set of forms to copy, but rather a whole new language in which the ancient peoples had expressed an infinitude of differing conceptions as they built temples, market places, theaters, amphitheaters, baths, palaces. Realizing, accordingly, the flexibility of the ancient Greek and Roman architecture, the creative architects of the early nineteenth century were at once conscious that this same kind of language could be used to express the new problems and the new conceptions of their own day. They must have realized, too, the fact that the old academic classicism of the end of the Rococo period, in which most of them had been trained, was fundamentally a sterile style, dependent for its exiguous life upon the existence of the great aristocratic courts in which it had been developed, and through its own dainty refinement somehow basically unsuited to the new ardent hopes of the emerging industrial world.

This enthusiasm for the ancient classic world was not limited to the architects, the archaeologists, or even the educated amateurs, it was almost as wide as culture itself. Greece and Rome became more than ancient civilizations long dead; they became living symbols of a successful democracy and a successful republicanism. They came in a sense to have a life of their own in this new time. As symbols they developed an essentially imaginary quality, which might have little to do with the actual historic or archaeological facts. Greece and Rome together formed a sort of golden age to which perplexed philosophers and puzzled politicians could turn for inspiration, and this golden age came to stand for the entire liberalizing tendency of the beginning of the nineteenth century, the whole notion of a new culture unfettered by a limited aristocracy. The old standards, the old criteria of judgment, were dead. Clericalism was fighting for its life; the new skepticism which followed the "reason" of the eighteenth century was attacking even the basic concepts of Christianity itself. The people needed new ideals, a new mythology, and these they found in this vision of the golden age of the classic world. When the French Revolution was at its height, the worship of Reason was enthroned in the place of Christianity, and, it is said, Reason herself in the form of a naked woman was worshiped publicly on the Champs de Mars. Thus the Paris mob set its approval on a kind of new paganism founded intrinsically, at least in its forms, on the ideals which the time had discovered in classic art.

It is not strange, then, that architects the world over felt the magic of this nostalgic dream of a golden age, and that everywhere in buildings they sought to use the newly found language of the architectural forms of Greece and Rome. Nor is it strange that the earlier ideals of the classic forms as a liberation from earlier style trammels should tend later to become lost in a flood of archaeological fervor. No sensitive designer could fail to be moved by the exquisite loveliness of the best Greek detail and to see in it qualities of imagination, discipline, refinement, and perfection of a high order. No traveled amateur could stand unaffected before the Pantheon, the Maison Carrée at Nîmes, or the ruins of the Parthenon, the Theseum, and the Erechtheum in far-off Athens. Here *was* the Greek, the Roman, ideal, apparently at its best and noblest; how better could the new language be used than in such ways as the Greeks and Romans had themselves worked out through centuries of effort? The amateurs, accordingly, became obsessed with the ideal not only of using the new forms, the new language, but of building as the ancients had built, of creating new modern temples like those of Athens or Rome, of imitating classic architecture at its highest peak. This second-hand, imitative phrase of Classic Revival architecture was essentially a lay movement. Again and again the architects themselves protested against it, for the great architects saw clearly the underlying stupidity of trying to imitate old buildings in new structures built for entirely different uses; but, after all, it was the client who paid for the buildings, and it was his taste which must in the long run govern. So that all over the Western world, in case after case, direct imitation of classic structures—classic temple porticoes especially—came to supersede the earlier, clearer, nobler conception of the classic movement as a liberating force.

Books, too, added to the force of the Classic Revival in architecture. Everywhere, the results of archaeological effort were being published in greater and greater amounts, in books with engravings that showed, exquisitely drawn, the beauties of the ancient works; and it became the fashion for the amateurs as well as the architects and the scholars to own these sumptuous publications. In that way, educated men of the end of the first quarter of the nineteenth century knew almost as a matter of course the appearance of the houses of Pompeii and their decoration, the Greek ruins of Athens and Asia Minor, the great Roman monuments of Syria as well as of Rome itself. Even if the more technical volumes escaped them, they would own, if they could possibly afford it, the folios of the collected etchings of Piranesi, where the delineation of ancient ruins had become itself no longer a mere documentation but rather almost a new fine art. It was important, also, that in many of these books it was not considered enough to present the ancient ruins as they stood; they must also be shown, if possible, as they had existed before ruin had overtaken them—that is, the books must give "restorations" as well as the actual existing conditions. Now the pictorial restoration of ancient buildings is an extraordinarily technical task, requiring the deepest knowledge of structure, living ways, decorative ideals. It is also an imaginative enterprise, for in few cases could mere logical deduction give the complete original expression. Therefore, in many cases, these restorations were as much a commentary on the taste of their time as they were a statement of inevitable fact; and in the case of the amateur, leafing over these books, it must have been very largely the restorations rather than the presentations of the ruined work which interested and excited him. Seeing there these exquisitely engraved presentations of sober classic temples, it was natural when he came to build that he should demand that his architect reproduce them. Thus the taste of the time unavoidably affected the restorations and they in turn necessarily reinforced and deeply modified the actual architectural work.

The Classic Revival in its earlier and more creative phases is excellently expressed in the architectural work of France under the Empire of Napoleon I. Napoleon himself was a Roman enthusiast, either because of his own taste or because he recognized in the Roman predilections of the French people an excellent tool of which to make use. In the inevitable development of the Roman Empire from the chaotic confusion of the last years of the Republic he found a model for his own seizure of power. From the glory of the Roman Empire he borrowed glory for himself, and somehow over it all there still remained in the eyes of the people the glow of the old Roman inspiration. Empire costume was supposedly as classic as possible; Madame Récamier reclining on a classic couch in flowing draperies embodied the ideal.

In buildings it was the same. Napoleon wished Paris made over anew with that great monumental dignity, that sense of lavish, magnificent greatness, that obvious largeness of scale which characterized Roman architecture. Only in the great forms of the Roman Empire could the glories of the new Empire be adequately expressed. Accordingly, one of the most important of the monuments of the Empire style is the enormous colonnaded porch and the great blank wall with which Napoleon's architect, Poyet, surrounded the old Chambre des Députés. This was to be the new capitol of the French Empire, a symbol of the power and the magnificence of the new government. Brilliantly, by clever planning, the whole was arranged to center on the Place de la Concorde across the river, and an imposing bridge built to connect the two banks on the main axis. The old palace, the product of various dates and various architects, was thus given a front of a monumental power that was a new thing in European architecture. Its colossal unbroken stone walls, the enormous columns of its portico, all together make up a new kind of architecture, neither a straight copy of Roman ideals, nor a development of local French traditions, but rather something essentially fresh, showing a new sensitiveness to the power of simplicity and great scale. Such a note at one end of the axis demanded a huge counterpoise at the other end, and this was furnished by the new Madeleine, where Napoleon planned a tremendous temple to the armies of France. This vast work, designed by Vignon, was only completed by Huvé after Napoleon's fall and its purpose was changed; it became the great fashionable church of Paris. Yet in understanding it one must bear in mind that it was intended not as a Christian church but as a tremendous national memorial. It took the form of a temple larger in scale and in some ways more magnificent than any but one or two in the ancient Roman Empire.

With its unbroken stone walls pierced only by doors, the problem of lighting became naturally acute. The nineteenth-century world demanded an amount and a quality of lighting which the Roman temples had not had, and the greater the size the more difficult the problem. The architect borrowed the idea of top lighting from the Roman Pantheon, and made the interior into a great nave of three successive domes with large central skylights, ending in a domed apse. It is a superb interior, rich in material, interesting in basic form, fresh and creative, honest in structure; but it is not Roman. In it the architect's designing function has controlled; he has created new forms to fit his problem. But the outside of the building was Roman—it was a Roman temple. And in this dilemma between modern purpose and ancient effect, which is so perfectly expressed in the Madeleine, lay the root of the future failure of the style. The Madeleine is two buildings, not one: outside a magnificent Roman temple, within an equally magnificent nineteenth-century interior. Between the two there is not only no organic connection but even a marked conflict in aim and artistic purpose.

The Bourse, which Brongniart designed, is altogether more satisfactory and in its way a more perfect expression of the real ideals which underlay the work of the Empire architects. Simplicity of form, monumentality of scale, and Roman detail are used for a building well planned and simply organized to serve its purpose. Its wide nave, skylighted through an iron-and-glass ceiling light, serves as the Exchange room. Around it vaulted chambers on two floors hold the brokers' offices, and a vast colonnade surrounding the whole becomes the place where brokers and their clients meet. It is a copy of no Roman work, although Roman in scale and dignity; it is essentially a new and effective creation.

This same sense of the double aim of Empire architecture can be seen in the two great triumphal arches built to celebrate Napoleonic conquests. The smaller of the two—the arch of the Carrousel—is a strictly Roman work almost archaeological in its duplication of the forms of well-known Roman triumphal arches. Only its differing sculpture, which sets forth Napoleonic campaigns and uses soldiers in Napoleonic uniform instead of classic figures for its decoration, makes it a building of the new period. It is truly a piece of "Classic Revival" work. The other, greater, arch—the Arc de Triomphe de l'Étoile, by Chalgrin—reveals equally well the other creative drive. A gigantic structure, many times larger than any Roman work, it produced problems of design, in scale and arrangement, quite different from any which the Romans had solved, and Chalgrin had the temerity to abandon entirely all Roman precedent in its design. The molding profiles and perhaps something of the basic arrangement are Roman; but the plain wall surfaces decorated with colossal sculpture brilliantly applied, the regular rhythms of the attic, these are elements as new as they are successful. The great merit of the Arc de l'Étoile resides in the fact that it is equally effective when seen from the end of the Champs Élysées a mile away and when studied from near at hand.

106. TYPICAL EMPIRE INTERIOR; A PARIS BEDROOM BY PERCIER AND FONTAINE.
(Percier and Fontaine: *Recueil de décorations interieures.*)

Napoleon's favorite personal designers were Charles Percier and Pierre F. L. Fontaine, to whom he entrusted practically all of his decorative and interior projects. In their work a different and more personal side of the Empire style is incarnated. Their task was to develop interiors for luxurious, comfortable living, embodying the new conveniences which the nineteenth century was making available, and to do it in a way essentially in harmony with the Roman enthusiasm of Napoleon and the graceful classic costumes of the women of the court. It is to their endless credit that they put aside the easy temptation of merely copying Pompeiian interiors and produced work as freshly creative, as ingeniously inventive, as any of the French interior styles which had preceded it. They worked for large simplicity of effect, decorated with intricate classic details. They loved sweeps of hanging drapery, in rich colors, bordered with classic patterns, and powdered with Napoleonic emblems. They liked simple, delicate metal supports based on Pompeiian candelabra, and furniture in which a new comfort and solidity appears, with simple surfaces of rich wood ornamented by cast-bronze appliqués. Roman and classic emblems are everywhere used—laurel leaves, the Roman eagle, the acanthus rinceau. Occasionally, too, forms of Egyptian parentage recall Napoleon's campaigns in Egypt, and the sphinx joins the Roman eagle on this elaborate and solid furniture. Generally there is little use of the orders. Percier's and Fontaine's skill in exterior design had few chances in which to express itself, but their innate taste is well shown in certain of the works which they published—especially a book on the country houses of the Roman Campagna, where they took the greatest delight in setting out that beautiful relation of completely simple, undecorated wall with well-spaced openings and low-pitched tile roofs.

This last enthusiasm, this trend toward simplicity, toward the avoidance of extraneous ornament and a delight in plain walls, illustrates another characteristic of much minor work of the Empire style. Charming houses, largely of unornamented stucco wall, with here and there a delicate loggia or a classic cornice, became the rule. And nowhere else can the liberating effects of the early Classic Revival be better shown than in these lovely simple dwellings which rose in such numbers not only in France but in Germany and England as well.

The architects of the period seem to have found in the new Roman fashion a congenial and exciting inspiration. Most of them had been trained in pre-Revolutionary times, and almost without exception dropped the tired Louis XVI style with apparent relief. The career of Claude Nicolas Ledoux is characteristic. He had been the favorite architect of Madame du Barry and through her wide influence had designed the great national salt plant, Salines de Chaux, where already his independence of mind and his desire to make architecture expressive, simple, and big showed itself in unconventional shapes and vivid imaginative detail, as though of stalactites and congealed fountains. In Paris he did groups of houses based on simple cubes and other geometrical forms with an almost perverse lack of ornament, as though to seek the more strongly for expressive form because of his avoidance of decoration. As he grew older his own style matured and he built for Paris a series of gates or *barrières* which were amazing in their imaginative, creative, unconventional buildings, in which classic details appear in queerly changed guise. Columns carry walls without any intervening moldings. Great walls pierced with simple rectangular openings rise to cornices almost barbaric in their powerful simplicity. And his imaginative power was expressed only partly by his executed works. He published a vast volume of his designs, both actual and imaginary, which is one of the epoch-making architectural books. Its text is confused and metaphysical, based on the close association of architectural form with the customs and ideals of the people. He sought to make his architecture talk, to tell its story by obvious definite symbolisms of shape. He tried to ring all the possible changes on pure geometrical forms, even showing a spherical house designed for barracks for *gardes champêtres*. The work is so unusual in its personal quality, in its complete freedom from either archaeology or traditionalism, that certain modern scholars have claimed him as the first modern architect, the direct precursor of such revolutionaries as Le Corbusier today. What is significant is the fact that apparently in this period of the Classic Revival his work was appreciated and admired, and that Louis XVI himself commissioned him to design the great Paris *barrières*.

In Germany the Roman influence had little effect. It had been Winkelmann, a German, who had first, in the eighteenth century, attempted a complete differentiation between Greek and Roman classic art, and had given his preference to the Greek; and it was the Greek phase of classic design which remained always dominant in the minds of early-nineteenth-century Germany. Langhans had built the Brandenburg Gate in Berlin in a modified Greek Doric in the eighteenth century, as we have seen. The path which he there indicated was followed by all of the greatest of the German early-nineteenth-century designers. It is possible, too, that hatred of Napoleon had much to do with the German coldness toward the Roman Revival. In a very true sense, Napoleon had made Roman classic his own; all of Germany, therefore, turned to other ideals. In Berlin, in the north, the two great figures are Gilly and Schinkel. Both fell completely under the sway of classic detail, but both remained architects enough never to try direct imitation. Gilly's vast scheme for a monument to Frederick the Great combined a Greek classic temple with tremendous substructures of more than Roman power, and he had no hesitancy whatsoever in using the Greek

Doric order with the vaults and arches which in the ancient world were only Roman.

Schinkel went further. To him, more perhaps than to anyone in France save Ledoux, the classic forms were merely a new language in which to express current thoughts. The Court Theater in Berlin, the Potsdam houses, and the old Berlin Museum all are definitely modern works built for modern use by nineteenth-century people, and never merely the attempts to recreate forgotten glories in a new period. Even at his most archaeological, as in the Berlin Hauptwache (or police station) where the German World War memorial is now enshrined, there is no direct copying, and eagles boldly take the place of the triglyphs on the great Doric entablature. Schinkel of course was even more daring than this in his experimentation. He worked equally in other styles—Gothic and Renaissance—and was not averse to inventing brand-new forms where he felt the need. He was one of a group of early-nineteenth-century architects in whom the revolutionary promise of scientific discovery and technical advance was already evident; one of a group of whom we shall hear more later, who stood essentially for a modern architecture for a modern world.

In Bavaria the conditions were entirely different from those in Prussia. King Ludwig I, who came to the throne in 1825, was passionately devoted to Greece, the Greek ideals, and Greek independence; and one of his sons, Otto, became the first king of liberated Greece. Ludwig was also a great builder and during his reign completely transformed his capital city, Munich. It is easy to understand, therefore, how one of his favorite architects, Leo von Klenze, was perhaps the most archaeological of all the great designers of the Classic Revival period in Europe, and how in the Valhalla, a great national shrine built at Regensburg, he should attempt a line-for-line imitation of great Greek Doric temples, or that in the National Monument in Munich the same search for archaeological correctness is completely dominant. But even von Klenze was more than the mere archaeologist. In the two museums, the Glyptothek and the Pinakothek, for sculpture and painting respectively, the very names of which are characteristic of the Bavarian Greek enthusiasm, von Klenze designed museums which for their time are excellent—well lighted, conveniently arranged—and the Greek details used in them are used simply and without strain. Classic details govern, too, such structures as the triumphal arch at the end of the Ludwigstrasse and the Odéon (concert hall) with its superb portico.

It was in the closest copies of ancient work that the greatest difficulties arose. The archaeological quality of the Valhalla and the National Monu-

107. PROPOSED DESIGN FOR A CHURCH AT THE ROSENTHALER GATE, BERLIN; INTERIOR SHOWING CHARACTERISTIC FREEDOM IN HANDLING CLASSIC MOTIFS. Schinkel, architect. (Schinkel: *Sammlung architektonischer Entwürfe*.)

ment brought with it problems basically insoluble. For one thing, there was the matter of site and climate. The Valhalla, standing so impressively on the height of a great series of terraces on the Danube bank, looks somehow strangely out of place by the German stream, embowered in the soft foliage of German trees. Its site was romantic, full of characteristically northern natural beauty. The forms which the Greeks had developed in other and sunnier climes, designed to look well with the different greens of Mediterranean foliage, with all the details calculated for the blazing and continuous sun, look oddly pale, gray, and indecisive under the soft grays of northern skies. Moreover, of the color which originally decorated the Greek Doric temples, and made their beautiful surfaces sing with blue and red and gold, there is no trace, for the importance of color decoration in Greek architecture was then but little known and little understood. The Greek Doric temple had needed for its complete effectiveness a gorgeous panoply of harmonious sculpture. Sculpture filled the metopes and the pediments of the Greek temples, giving point and emphasis to many of their architectural lines. In nineteenth-century Bavaria mere expense prevented the use of a sufficient amount of sculpture, and the new temples look necessarily bare. Even where sculpture was planned and used, it soon became evident that even the best sculptures of nineteenth-century Bavaria were utterly unqualified to attack the problems offered by the decoration of these new Greek buildings. The Bavarian Monument is itself the perfect expression of this fact; and the great soft forms of the colossal female who impersonates Bavaria, with the lion sitting beside her like an amiable Newfoundland dog, can arouse only the sense of levity. No, manifestly the Bavarian sculptors could never equal Phidias!

Between the eighteenth-century English classic of Adam and Chambers and the Classic Revival work of the nineteenth century there was a gulf almost as great as that in France between the Louis XVI and the Empire. The Adam movement had been too definitely an architecture of great houses and depended too much on fine-scaled and expensive detail to allow of more than superficial popularization; by 1800 it was quite dead. The movement which took its place owes its birth to a new search for daring simplicity and large, imaginative compositions. Sir John Soane was its first and in some ways its greatest exponent. Soane's influence was supreme in England for a period of almost thirty years, from 1790 to 1820. A man of large ideas and sound academic background, a careful student of the ancient work of Greece and Rome, he was nevertheless at heart a revolutionary, one of those rare architects whose restless mind was always striving for new and more perfect architectural solutions, for a more rigid logic, a more realistic attitude toward style. He did not fight the new materials that were coming in; he welcomed them and used them. He tried to find for iron an appropriate expression in the large interiors which he designed for the Bank of England, and the availability of glass enabled his naturally dramatic imagination to develop all sorts of the most brilliant systems of clerestory and indirect lighting. He loved plain wall surfaces, liked to strip from his buildings every atom of superfluous detail, so that their own geometric shapes would count strongly and simply. Generally, where he used detail, he turned back to the ancients for inspiration, but this inspiration he employed in the most creative and imaginative ways. He had, for instance, no objection whatsoever to combining the Greek Doric order with bold vaults of Byzantine or Roman fashion. From the Romans he learned the lesson of great scale and wide unencumbered interiors, and several of the great public rooms of the Bank show most ingenious compositions of vaulted surfaces, clerestory lighting, and detail almost twentieth-century in its simplicity. He liked to use columns carrying simple walls or lintels without entablatures, and where he wished emphasis often used simple projecting bands instead of moldings, as in the superb arched gate to Tyringham.

108. THE BANK OF ENGLAND, LONDON; A CHARACTERISTIC INTERIOR. Soane, architect. (Soane: *Designs for Public and Private Buildings.*)

Soane had a large practice and a large office. The students whom he trained played a great part in the architecture of early-nineteenth-century England, and it is characteristic of his logical and revolutionary attitude that he is reported to have given the works of Laugier to his students, as has already been noted. Soane conceived of himself as a prophet and a missionary for simple, straightforward, and logical architecture and the right use of ancient inspiration. He was a great collector, and on his death left his house, which he had largely transformed into a museum, to the nation. The house itself, in its strange, high, arcaded porch, the original type of ornament which he had gradually evolved, and the ingenuity of its arrangements to give light to its contents and to exhibit them properly despite the smallness of the area, bears witness to his realistic mind.

This simple rationalism had its prototype in the work of George Dance, Jr., such as Newgate Prison; Dance had been Soane's employer and teacher. Henry Holland was another architect with somewhat similar ideals, but Soane was the greatest of the group. Among Soane's draftsmen his favorite was Joseph Gandy, whose superb renderings of the Bank are among the most valued exhibits in the Soane Museum. Gandy carried the Soane doctrines even further than his teacher. He published two books of designs for rural buildings—farmhouses, gate lodges, cottages—in which many elements of much of today's architecture prophetically appear. There are no orders; instead, simple posts and beams. The wall surfaces are unbroken, and wherever possible the windows are combined into long horizontal panels; the roof eaves project markedly, without moldings; and the horizontal dimension is always stressed and simple geometric volumes are emphasized. These features show how closely Soane's revolutionary Classic Revival could approach many of the controlling forms of the architecture to come a century and more later.

This movement toward simplicity became almost nation-wide, and distinguishes thousands of the smaller houses built in English towns during the period from 1800 to 1820. Few if any of these buildings achieved the revolutionary synthesis which Gandy had foreshadowed, but all reveal unmistakably various steps on the same path. The use of stucco became common in the designs of this period—usually termed the Regency period, and its style the Regency style, however much they may overlap and extend beyond the actual date of the Regency. Stucco, by hiding inequalities in masonry and by substituting plain surface for interesting texture, necessarily emphasized geometrical composition, and geometrical composition in turn led the architects again and again to use few and large openings instead of the many and small windows prevalent earlier. Along with this growing quietness and simplicity of wall surface went a similar quietness of detail. Cornices became simple roof eaves, or at most a delicate projection supported on simple, widely spaced brackets. Windows were often grouped three together under a single segmental arch, or occasionally—a rare sign of Adam persistence—were set in a semicircular-headed recess. Porches of all kinds came into use, often projecting boldly to form real outdoor rooms, and thus expressing an entirely new conception of the relation of man and the outdoor world. In these porches iron is often used for supports, for railings, and even for the roofs themselves. Its strength was recognized in the delicacy of all the parts; and many of these Regency porches, with latticed supports, sometimes decorated with cast-iron ornaments, with light and open railings, and with curving, upsweeping metal roofs, are miracles of grace and refinement. Even where brick and stone were exposed, they were treated in such a way as to emphasize this uniformity; and the brick wall was considered as a mere field of uniform color, stressed by judicious accents of white marble bands, key-blocks, imposts, and so forth. Often, in the search for quiet rectangular composition, the roofs would be hidden behind parapets, with simple undecorated stone copings, to form a subtle line at the top. This Regency work is a perfect expression of that atmosphere of logic, of hope, of modesty which characterized early-nineteenth-century English life, when the possibilities of liberation inherent in industrialism had become already apparent, but before its abuses had made men hopeless or cynical. It was full of the promise of a new architecture founded on the new conditions that confronted the world, an architecture vivid and delightful, which can be seen in many of the squares which were being built as London grew toward the west, the north, and the south; but the promise was never entirely realized—it was soon to be buried under other and alien influences.

One of the factors which killed this promise was the enormous popular ardor for things Greek, a passion diligently stimulated by the poets from Byron on, and assiduously cultivated by the aestheticians and critics. Byron had perhaps a greater influence on his contemporaries than any other poet in English history. His flamboyant notoriety inevitably created almost a cult. Byron made Greece fashionable; and when to Byron was added the effect of the successive volumes of the *Antiquities of Athens* and the *Antiquities of Ionia,* which were coming out at that time under the distinguished auspices of the Society of Dilettanti, an architectural furor was produced impossible to withstand, and the fickle English public swung rapidly over into an unthinking demand for Greek forms. The Greek-drunk public could appreciate Soane's use of the Greek orders much more easily than they could appreciate the daring innovations in his buildings, and more and more they clamored for the pure Greek forms. An archaeological conception of architecture was as typical of the amateurs of the 1820's and 1830's as it is of our Colonial enthusiasts today, and architecture became for a few years largely a matter of adjusting copied Greek detail to nineteenth-century English buildings.

Sir Robert Smirke's work on the British Museum is characteristic. To its fundamentally workable and functional plan he added a tremendous monumental frontispiece of Greek Ionic columns. It is magnificent in scale and unusually perfect in execution. It forms a superb street decoration, which gives character to the entire section of London in which it stands. Nevertheless its connection to the building behind is of the flimsiest kind, and it darkens galleries already none too light. From the point of view of integrated architecture it is an absurdity, for it entails a sacrifice of workability to the parade of archaeological display.

Once this superficial idea of architecture as a mere clothing had taken hold, the entire intimate relation of structure, use, and beauty which is at the foundation of good design disappeared, and it seemed no inconsistency to design a fish market for Billingsgate formed like a great classic temple, or to think that the mere addition of a pedimented portico to any building conferred upon it thereby timeless beauty. However, this disintegration of architectural taste never became universal, and few British Museum colonnades were built. The natural common sense of good architects, fashionable or otherwise, saved most buildings; and an instinctive feeling for the larger elements of composition, even of city planning, made other structures, if superficial, at least extraordinarily effective. The first is frequently the case in Scotland, where Greek inclinations almost exceeded those in modish London; and, despite the unfinished Parthenon intended as a memorial in Edinburgh, the greater amount of Scottish work in the Greek Revival is direct, simple, strong. The high school in Edinburgh by Hamilton is an example. To be sure, it uses all the machinery of the Greek Revival, but the whole building is planned as a unit and arranged so that no sacrifices are occasioned by the archaeological ornament. Typical also are various squares and terraces in Edinburgh and Glasgow, in which the Greek ornament is used discreetly on houses that retain all the simplicity, the clarity, and the basic intelligence of the earlier Regency work. The second quality— skill in composition—is especially to be noted in the London work of John Nash. Here, in the great houses surrounding Regent's Park, in the quiet continuous façades of the Regent Street quadrant—alas, no longer standing, —and in many of his Classic Revival churches, there is such a loveliness of relationship, such a skillful adaptation of classic forms to the needs of the problem, such unfettered imagination, that one hesitates to inquire more deeply.

The archaeological Greek Revival in England was comparatively short-lived. Stimulated primarily by literary enthusiasms, it was bound to fall when this literary fervor changed; and the change was not long in coming, as the new medievalism, giving rise to a new nationalism, which sought for the native rather than the alien inspiration, swept increasingly over the country.

The tale is largely the same all over the remaining parts of Europe. Alike in Italy, Russia, and Scandinavia, a flare of Empire style work followed the victories of Napoleon, and George Cameron built for the Russian court those exquisite combinations of Greek, Roman, and Adam forms which were among the most charming buildings and interiors in Russia; and, just as the Pantheonlike church of San Francesco di Paola had risen in Naples, so the Cathedral of St. Isaac with its four Corinthian porticoes and its great dome was built in St. Petersburg (now Leningrad). As in England, much of the best of the work lies in the smaller structures—country houses, the natural forms of which are given a little fillip of interest by a Greek portico; little market and town-hall buildings, and the like. Especially delightful are some of the country houses of Denmark and northern Germany, where accents of restrained classic detail are used with naïve frankness on long, low, rambling structures, often of wood. Of the more important buildings, the Thorvaldsen Museum and the Vor Frue church in Denmark, both by Hansen, and the work of Engel in Finland reveal creative ability in producing fresh and inventive designs with detail based on classic inspiration. Much of the St. Petersburg work by Russian architects of the time deserves similar note, for the Russian architects seem to have had uncommon skill in using Greek details in nonarchaeological and sometimes strikingly dramatic ways, often emphasizing the effects by brilliant color, as in the great Admiralty Building, designed by Adrian Sacharoff. All the countries, too, suffered from occasional sterile and purely literary classic enthusiasms, which gave rise to ill-adapted archaeological attempts to copy ancient forms, like the tomb of Canova in Italy, with its Greek Doric Parthenon portico so stupidly attached to its Roman dome.

It is the custom today to deprecate all the work of the Greek Revival period as a senseless and reactionary turning to the past. The briefest glance at the work of Schinkel or Soane or Ledoux should reveal how silly any such wholesale condemnation is. Again and again, too, in the smaller work of the time—the little houses, the smaller business buildings, all that array of anonymous structures which go to make up the total effect of any town— there is a restraint, a wise fitness of form to use, and a quiet harmony that fills one with a sense of easy serenity. The classic detail is used without strain, without sacrifice; evidently the classic inspiration had come, not as a new set of rules to hobble design, but rather as a fresh new stimulus to put an end to the last expressions of Rococo feeling and bring people back to the bigger questions of building itself.

And there were always the great men, the men who used classic inspiration as they would have used any current fashion, merely as a springboard from which to leap into new creation—men like Schinkel, with his daring experiments in all the styles, his basic sense of functional planning, of restraint, of fitness, his anticipation of so many forces which were to mature later—men like Ledoux, who created out of the ancient forms a new language of almost pure geometry, in which he felt the voice of the new age speaking—men like Soane, whose space conceptions are as daringly untrammeled as his detail is free, or like Gandy, his pupil, with his plain walls and strip windows—men like H. L. Elmes, who in St. George's Hall in Liverpool ventured to combine a brilliant plan with classic detail freely used in fitting places, so that the whole was perhaps the finest of the monumental works of the English Classic Revival school.

There was still another factor which made the period of enormous importance to later architecture—the development of firmly based architectural schools, in which professional training of a new breadth and soundness was available. Especially this was true of France, where the École Nationale des Beaux Arts, resurrected by Napoleon from the ghost of the old Royal Academy, became the model. In these schools the young architects learned, among other things, to plan, and the concept of planning taught there was based on the old Roman conceptions, that that planning was best in which practical necessity, convenience of relationship, construction, and an interesting succession of beautiful interior spaces were most closely integrated so that each helped the other. The new world of the nineteenth century demanded great numbers of new kinds of buildings, and behind their design there had to be new ideas of plan. The problems of the circulation of large numbers of people, of the convenient placing of mechanical equipment, of ease and rapidity of service, all imposed themselves on the new architects with growing importance, and all demanded a kind of planning which was at once more complicated and more restricting than the old, but at the same time offered new opportunities for characteristic beauty and superb interior effect. That the early nineteenth century so frequently found beautiful and simple solutions for these problems reveals the fact that the Classic Revival was no mere thoughtless reduplication of a style long dead. At its beginning, and wherever the deadening hand of the literary fads of the amateur or the restrictive claims of unmitigated and greedy profit-seeking did not control, the architecture of the time was remarkably flexible and logical. Some of the early mills are excellent constructions, well-lighted, simple, straightforward; and almost without exception the earlier large railroad stations, like those of the London and Birmingham Railway and the railway between Paris and Havre or like Philip Hardwick's Euston, were buildings of dignity and unpretentious good taste, which worked well and which were not afraid to use the light delicacy of cast-iron columns and wrought-iron trusses.

It is the fate of early-nineteenth-century architecture that its great excellencies have been largely forgotten. To see the style at its best, to realize the simple logic of its work, one must turn less to the great structures, where the taste of the royal client or wealthy amateur controlled, less to the British Museums and the Bavarian Valhallas, and more to the minor work—the small houses, the less ostentatious churches, the residential quarters of the cities built between 1800 and 1840. There, in the serene harmony, the unstrained occasional delicate ornament, the regularity, the simplicity, one finds a spirit that is fresh and lovely and free.

Chapter 29

THE CLASSIC REVIVAL IN THE
UNITED STATES

THE winning of the Revolutionary War freed the United States from Great Britain in more ways than those any mere political change, however drastic, would indicate. The new country was founded in a real enthusiasm that envisaged a true national culture almost as soon as it achieved national status. The bonds which had held it so closely to England were loosed, in architecture as well as in government. To what, then, should the young country turn for architectural guidance? The tradition of country building in the old Colonial styles was still vivid. The builder-architects of towns and cities were just becoming aware of the Adam details, and were destined in the more conservative regions to work them over for another twenty years. But this persistence of English form could never for long satisfy the young country; it must have an architecture of its own. The inspiration of Rome and of Greece belonged to the Americans of the time as much as it did to the Europeans, for were they not all children of the same basic heritage? And the ideals of Roman republican austerity, of Greek democratic enlightenment, were ideals most congenial to the American spirit of the period. The New World should have a new architecture as grand as that of Rome, as delicate and lovely as the architecture of Greece.

Fortunately, neither discerning cultural leaders nor skillful architects were lacking to make this effort fruitful, and the building of the new capital city of Washington, with its ambitious public structures, furnished a magnificent challenge to the ability of the nation's architects. Jefferson and Washington were alike agreed that the new city should have buildings not of the older Baroque Colonial types, but buildings of a new kind, in which the ancient ideals of Greece and Rome received new, creative expressions to fit the new needs. Jefferson's hatred of the general standards of Colonial architecture is well known. To him it all appeared either crude and barn-like, or decorated with unnecessary and frivolous fripperies. He had been a student of architecture for years before the Revolution, and after its successful close continued his studies and increased his capabilities until he became an excellent architect himself. His long residence in Paris gave him an unusual chance to realize the organic, architectonic character of the best eighteenth-century French building. It had filled him with a desire to see in America that freedom of shape, that close organization of details into one unit, which lay at the base of the best French architecture. Moreover, Jefferson had been to Nîmes and with his own eyes seen there the Maison Carrée, the best preserved of all the Roman temples. It had excited in him a deep and sensitive admiration. He saw at once, in its beauty of proportion, its perfection of detail, and its fundamental simplicity, a quality that was a new thing in the Rococo world, and from that time on he was a confirmed classicist. Nor was he satisfied with mere admiration, and in the building of the State Capitol at Richmond, Virginia, his first opportunity in public architecture, he found a chance to express his taste by creating in that building one of the epoch-making structures of the Classic Revival movement. The whole design was directed toward the aim of building in Richmond a classic temple of great size, dignity, and beauty, which should at the same time contain the necessary meeting halls and offices.

Jefferson's importance as an adviser in connection with the early work at Washington was great. Washington, too, found in these new classic forms ideals extremely sympathetic to his polished austerity, so that the two men were in perfect agreement. It is not strange, therefore, to find that, when the competition for the United States Capitol was held, it was won, not by the exquisite, accomplished McIntire design, which was in the continuing vein of English Palladianism, but by a design of totally different character, in which the Roman- dome and classic porticoes played the chief parts. Essentially, then, the first great national building enterprise of the young country was a monument to classical inspiration.

Nevertheless the older tradition lived on, especially in New England, and the Adam ideas were given new and charming embodiment by the American house builders; in many localities the great change in architectural forms came only later, and the work of the first two decades of freedom is in perfect harmony with that done earlier. A tremendous amount of this delicate "Late Colonial" work was built in those years. Yet even in this the new nationalism is frequently apparent, for the builder-architects did not follow along with the current styles of England, but rather took the Adam influence which they had received earlier and went on refining the forms, adapting the details to wood and the plans to the American climate, until the result was a completely new thing. True, they retained some of the Adam

tricks—the windows in arched panels, the slim proportions, the subtle ornament—but, out of these, men like McIntire created a new alphabet of
shapes; and the best of the McIntire houses in Salem, like the earlier houses
of Bulfinch, could never be mistaken for English homes.

This movement was given enormous impetus by the early American
architectural books of Asher Benjamin in Massachusetts and of George
Biddle in Philadelphia. It is noteworthy that in all of these works the authors

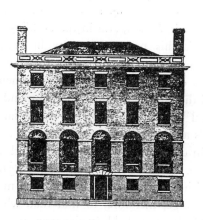
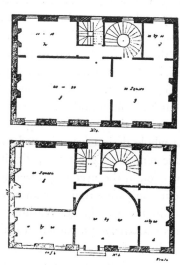

109. A CHARACTERISTIC ASHER BENJAMIN DESIGN; ELEVATION AND PLANS
FOR A TOWN HOUSE. (Benjamin: *The American Builder's Companion; or, A New
System of Architecture.*)

insist upon the fact that there are American books designed for American
conditions, and that they have no hesitancy whatsoever in changing the
English standards as they see fit. It was these books, with their exquisite,
delicate details, which made possible those chaste wooden houses with slim-
columned porticoes and rich cornices in which for the first time the stone
details of the original English inspiration have finally evolved into some
of the most perfect expressions of wood which architecture has known. And
it is this fitness of detail to material, so beautifully shown in these widely
distributed books, that made the style last on in country villages long after
it had passed in the great urban centers, and which enabled the settler of
the Western Reserve in Ohio to build there the gracious white houses which
distinguish so many of its towns.

But the general movement of taste was more and more toward classic ideals. There was something a little too thin about this refined Late Colonial to satisfy a young and pushing nation. In its richest examples it becomes almost decadent and effete, and the whole elaborate carving of oval rosettes, of fans, of reeded moldings became a mannerism which at times grew monotonous and unpleasant. The architects of the country and the men of means and power who were most fitted to employ them demanded something more virile, more simple, and this combination they found in the ancient classic forms. Thus American taste swung gradually more and more toward ancient Roman ideals of grandeur in the first place, and later—after the War of 1812, and especially after the enthusiasm aroused by the Greek Wars of Independence in the 1820's—to the beautiful serenity of Greece. The prophetic judgment of Washington and Jefferson was vindicated.

Well-trained architects from both England and France came to the country in its early days seeking employment and honor amid its growing success. They brought with them the polished urbanity of England, the technical skill and the classic tradition of France. A Frenchman, Pierre Charles L'Enfant, was the architect of the first national building of the United States, Federal Hall in New York, as well as the city planner of Washington. A Frenchman, Joseph François Mangin, was co-designer with McComb of the New York City Hall, and to him is due its exquisitely delicate Louis XVI character. Another Frenchman, J. J. Ramée, designed the earlier buildings of Union College at Schenectady and laid out there the first large-scale general plan for any American educational group. A British colonial, William Thornton, won the competition for the United States Capitol. An Irish architect, James Hoban, designed the White House. And Benjamin H. Latrobe, of a Huguenot family resident in England and with a mother born in Pennsylvania, after an excellent general and architectural education in England and on the Continent, came to the United States in 1796 and eventually became an important architect, the teacher of many others, and the real founder of the American architectural profession.

Thus, early America became a sort of cultural melting pot. The most significant thing about this process was the fact that, despite differences of background and differences of training, the most successful of these architects never attempted in their American designs to reproduce the buildings of their homelands, but rather sought to create a new architecture instilled with the classic spirit and adapted to American conditions. Many of these foreign architects finally returned to their original homes disillusioned; they had not been able to adjust themselves, they had remained foreigners at heart. The successful ones, like the Englishman John Haviland, like Latrobe, became thoroughly American, devoted citizens of the new country, fervent in the creation of an American architecture.

Jefferson's main enthusiasms had been Palladian and Roman; yet the Roman influence in American architecture was comparatively short-lived. After all, the great buildings of Rome were imperial structures, requiring wealth and materials the young nation could never command, and the Pompeiian houses as they were known in those days were anything but suited to the American climate. What the Roman taste did give to American architecture was a controlling sense of scale. In details its prestige soon yielded to the newer passion for the Greek. Greek details had appeared as controlling elements in Latrobe's Bank of Pennsylvania, Philadelphia, as early as 1801-02 and in much of his work on the United States Capitol (where he had succeeded Thornton in 1803) before 1817—the Senate, the House, the Supreme Court—and other architects also studied the beautiful plates of the *Antiquities of Athens* with growing excitement. Gradually Greek forms became a universal fashion and by 1830 reigned supreme in the United States.

There were three great centers from which this Greek impulse radiated. The first was in the area bounded by Washington and Philadelphia, and is especially connected with the work of Latrobe and his two most famous pupils, Robert Mills and William Strickland. The second was in Boston, where in the work of Benjamin, of Alexander Parris, and especially of that strange genius, Solomon Willard, the late Colonial was gradually giving way, day by day, almost unconsciously, to the Greek expression. The third was in New York, centered around the personalities of Ithiel Town, originally a Boston-trained man, Alexander Jackson Davis, and Martin Thompson. Town had invented an ingenious bridge truss, which he had patented, and from his royalties had accumulated a considerable fortune, which he spent in European travel and the purchase of architectural books and prints; by 1830 he had what must have been one of the largest private art libraries of the time, running to over 15,000 volumes, and this store of architectural knowledge and inspiration was kept so as to be readily available to all interested people. Little wonder that from the architectural rooms of Town, Davis, and Thompson influences of immense value were sent forth far over the country and generated a new sophistication, a new high standard, in both planning and exterior design.

The first group, the Philadelphia-Washington group, was enormously productive. John Haviland, English trained, did much distinguished Greek

Revival work, later using also Egyptian and Gothic forms; he became inter-
nationally famous as a designer of prisons. William Strickland was the
architect of important public buildings in Philadelphia—the Exchange, the
Mint, the Naval Hospital—and of the Mint in New Orleans; he climaxed
his successful career by becoming architect of the Tennessee Capitol at Nash-
ville. Robert Mills was famous as a church designer, creating the circular or
octagonal auditorium church in America. He was also the architect of the
Washington Monuments in Baltimore and Washington, and subsequently
as architect for the national government he established much of the later
character of Federal buildings by his monumental designs for the Treasury
Building, the Patent Office, and the Post Office in Washington, as well as
by his customs houses, such as that at New Bedford, and his marine hospitals. From Strickland's office came not only Gideon Shryock, who was to
be the great Greek Revival architect of Kentucky, but also Thomas U.
Walter, designer of Girard College in Philadelphia, who was to become the
last major architect of the United States Capitol, adding the present Senate
and House wings in the 1850's and the great cast-iron dome which was
completed during the Civil War.

The Boston group was distinguished by the strong individualities of its
members and by the direct New England simplicity of their architectural
approach. In many ways the most important member of the group was
Charles Bulfinch; yet he was hardly typical. A man of fine Boston
family, he had traveled in Europe, and it had been in England that his
architectural taste was first developed, so that the English background exerted a continuing influence on him. His houses designed prior to the War
of 1812 represent perhaps the highest development of the modified-Adam,
Late Colonial style, but they are quieter, simpler, more powerful than the
work, say, of McIntire. Later, he too of course came strongly under the
sway of the classic, and between his design for the Massachusetts State
House (which is purely English in its inspiration, though new and American in its expression) and the serene walls and pedimented portico of the
Massachusetts General Hospital there is a great gulf. He was for many years
architect of the United States Capitol, and to him is due the credit for the
first completion of the edifice in 1830 and the design of its western front,
which looks out so proudly over the Mall. Yet he never became a thorough
Grecian; and where he is most Greek, as perhaps in the Maine State House
at Augusta, he is least happy. His best work undoubtedly lies in the perfect
adjustments he made between quiet brick walls and refined detail discreetly
used, as in the meetinghouse he designed for Lancaster, Massachusetts, in

which the old New England Colonial church tradition reached perhaps its most perfect, as it was its most restrained, expression.

In the 1820's Benjamin's books began to show Greek detail along with his slim wooden adaptations, and his later works spread the Greek gospel as extensively as his earlier works had popularized his modified Adam and Pain details. Parris became an accomplished planner, whose work is always characterized by solidity, dignity, and a kind of almost aristocratic restraint. Willard, starting as a carpenter, became figurehead carver for ships, then sculptor, then architect, then scientist, then quarry master, and ended as a scientific agriculturalist in Quincy. His architectural work is as uncompromisingly solid as the native gray granite he loved to use; yet he was capable of modeling the delicate, almost Rococo ornament that Godefroi used on the domed Unitarian Church in Baltimore. Willard traveled widely; worked in Washington for Bulfinch, in Baltimore for Godefroi; and, though his own architectural work is all but forgotten except for the Bunker Hill Monument, his influence on his contemporaries was tremendous. From the Boston group, too, came Isaiah Rogers, one of the most flexible and imaginative architects of the entire period. His first important work, the Tremont House in Boston, set in 1827 a new standard for hotel design; it was in many ways more advanced than similar work of the time in Europe, well planned and beautifully detailed. It was famous, as well, for its elaborate mechanical equipment and its lavish plumbing facilities. Rogers also lived for some time in New York and was the architect of the old Astor House and the imposing building erected for the Merchants' Exchange after the Great Fire of 1835, which had a lovely Exchange room with a brick dome eighty feet in span and a monumental colonnade which still stands as the front of the National City Bank. He was, for years after, the great hotel architect of the country, and to him more than any single person is due the credit for the first establishment of American hotel standards of luxury, privacy, and mechanical equipment. His long life was crowned with appointment as Government Architect during the Civil War, and to his taste is due something at least of the underlying quiet classicism which kept much mid-century government work from the complete banality of the then current styles.

In New York, although McComb continued for years a practice in which the older conventional ideals of English origin were still accepted, the younger men were all thoroughly imbued with Greek Revival ideals. The firm of Town and Davis had a huge practice, public and private. They were the architects of several state capitols, of much educational work, of any number of houses; and all of it is distinguished by flexible and ingenious planning and by daring innovations in exterior detail. Thompson is famous for his design of the Assay Office, originally built as the Bank of the United States, the front of which now decorates the south side of the American wing of the Metropolitan Museum. He was the architect, as well, of many churches, and undoubtedly much of the charm of old New York in certain streets of Greenwich Village and the lower East Side, or of Chelsea, is due to his quiet taste. Another New York architect, Minard Lafever, famous for

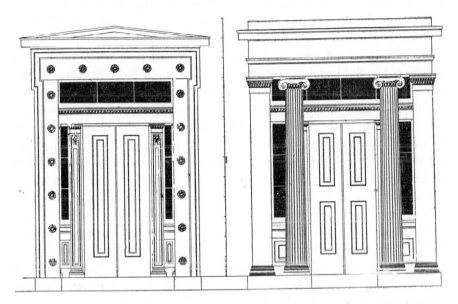

110. TYPICAL GREEK REVIVAL DETAIL BY MINARD LAFEVER, SHOWING CHARACTERISTIC CREATIVE SIMPLIFICATIONS AND MODIFICATIONS OF GREEK PRECEDENT. (Lafever: *The Modern Builders' Guide.*)

his Gothic churches in Brooklyn, is perhaps more important as a classic designer. He, like Thompson, probably designed many New York houses, and the standard achieved in them is high. Detail is graceful, reserved, beautifully placed, and the houses are well planned, as may be seen in the Old Merchant's House (Tredwell House), now a museum. He was also the architect of the unusual Whalers' Church and the Huntting house in Sag Harbor, both with creative "Greek" detail. But his national importance is due to the three books which he produced, showing perhaps the most exquisitely drawn and engraved illustrations of the freely modified Greek Revival detail of the period. Lafever's Greek is more fluid, more delicate, than that shown in the Benjamin or Haviland books. Again and again it is anything but archaeological, although perhaps more than any of the three he had absorbed and could re-express the essential combination of refinement, restraint, accent, and delicacy which is at the foundation of the Greek charm. The Lafever books were widely distributed; and time after time, in Louisiana, in Ohio, in Michigan, in Kentucky or Tennessee, one comes suddenly upon doorframes or mantels, cornices or porches, or even entire house designs, taken almost bodily from his beautiful plates. New York was a training ground, too, and the pupils and associates of Davis and Lafever—like Dakin, the Irish Gallier, and R. C. Long—were busy in many places.

There is a fourth center for Greek radiation, slightly less important and more local in its influence, in Savannah and Charleston, where an English architect, Jay, did exquisite work of a character both more Regency in feeling and perhaps more original in detail than the work in other parts of the country. Without doubt, his work exerted enormous influence in the more easterly group of the Southern states, though often the plantation houses of Georgia and Alabama of the 1830's and 1840's seem almost independent creations, as though designed by their owners and erected by local builders or builder-architects, with details picked up here, there, and everywhere, from Benjamin, from Lafever, or direct from the *Antiquities of Athens*.

The growth of the young country was admirably fitted to hasten dissemination of this Greek Revival building. The population was increasing by leaps and bounds. Immigration was continually growing. Surplus population in the easterly states was pouring over the Alleghenies. Ohio, Tennessee, and Kentucky were no longer frontier communities, but places where in growing towns a society of culture and urbanity was rapidly developing; and the rich Michigan lands and forests supported town after town, like Dexter or Ann Arbor, in which Greek buildings quickly replaced the shacks and cabins of the first settlers. By the middle of the century the whole country east of the Mississippi was a settled and civilized region, and the old frontiersmen were pushing westward over the plains and into the Rockies and beyond to the very shores of the Pacific. It is perhaps well to remember that the first carefully considered buildings erected by the United States citizens in Oregon and California were in the full tradition of the Greek Revival.

The whole period was also one of comparatively harmonious prosperity. The development of industrialism had begun, but it still seemed the complement to agriculture rather than its hostile rival. People still sought to dwell in communities rather than on individual farms of great size, and much of the older community spirit characteristic of the New England tradition was vitally alive in Ohio and Michigan and Indiana. Wealth from the opening of new territory, from the growing exploitation of natural resources that seemed almost endless, was flowing into the country; and, although great fortunes were in the making here and there, the old revolutionary tradition of equality governed a great deal of popular thought and prevented the worst forms of plutocratic snobbism, and to those who somehow could not adjust themselves to life within the communities—to those who failed—there was always the hope of the unopened West beckoning.

In the main, these people of the United States of the 1820's and 1830's were people with a deep, honest, and simple culture, with a natural-born respect for learning, innate good taste, and a growing appreciation of the arts. The pioneers carried good books with them on their travels, and the new towns demanded schools, academies, and colleges as soon as their permanence was assured. Local papers were founded, and almost all carried a page each week devoted to literature and the fine arts; this was as true of Ohio or Michigan or Missouri as it was of New England itself. It is significant that Mrs. Trollope comments that Americans were more insulted if you deprecated their achievements in painting than if you cried down their political system. Naïve the Americans may have been in this new artistic enthusiasm, but it was an enthusiasm that could only have been possible in a country sincerely attached to the ideal of beauty, sincerely clamoring for surroundings which should be formed and designed and organized. This was the reason for the harmony that controlled so much of the work of the time, whether in painting or in architecture. It was this sincere spirit which sought for beautiful houses, dignified public buildings, attractive and well-designed academies, and found in the modified Greek details of Benjamin or Lafever elements admirably suited for their decoration. It was a period, as well, of tremendous hopes. Utopia seemed just around the corner, and Utopian communities sprang up under the influence of religious or political theorists. Almost anything seemed possible, and the freedom and variety of architectural design represents and expresses the exuberant vitality of popular feeling.

This same spirit accounts also for the great local varieties existent within this general harmony. Artistic culture was not standardized or centralized; it was a living thing in each community, and every town of every size had its own architects and architect-builders of which it was proud. These may have been trained elsewhere, perhaps in the Eastern centers, as Shryock was trained in Strickland's office; but, once settled in the new localities, these men became inevitably the creators and the developers of local styles to fit the local tastes and needs.

Of these regional variants, those of New Orleans and the plantation houses nearby deserve special notice. New Orleans had been under both French and Spanish sway; there was a strong Latin feeling at its base. Its special climate and its position by a river subject to destructive floods combined to give its buildings a distinctive character even before the Louisiana Purchase; and the immigrants who flowed into the city by the hundreds, often from New York or New England, though they brought with them the traditional skills and the detail forms of the towns in which they were brought up, seldom tried to do more than modify the older types which had proved satisfactory. Thus, in houses with arcaded courtyards one will come upon details straight from the books of Lafever; and in the work of architects like Gallier and Dakin the blend of sophisticated "Northern" Greek Revival detail, with plan types and proportions characteristic of the place, achieved a loveliness which is unique. Similarly, in the plantation houses on the bayous and the river shore, the earlier type of a single rectangular building with cross-corridors and four rooms to a floor, surrounded on all sides by a portico, remained in use all through this busy time, and only the details revealed the swing from French provincial or Roman forms to those of Greek inspiration.

This period saw the almost complete disappearance of the old type of Colonial house design all through the United States. Its simple forms were too hampering to the demand for invention. Instead, there is the most complete freedom. Compact houses, rambling houses, houses on one floor or on several, houses with a pediment to the street or with the long eaves of a gable roof, can all be found. A frequent town type is T-shaped in plan, with the vertical bar of the T parallel to the street and forming an ell to the main portion, which is long and narrow and has a pediment on the front The entrance door is usually not in the center but on one side of this front, and often there is a porch fronting the ell. Another type, symmetrical, has a Greek portico two stories high across the front of the main portion of the house, with lower, one-story wings on either side. In other types simple rectangular plans produce continuous gabled roofs of almost Colonial type. The farmhouses are equally varied and usually equally gracious in detail, although they dispense with the magnificence of columns and depend for decorative effect upon simple Greek moldings at the door and on the mantels inside. The remarkable thing about the domestic architecture of this period is not its standardization but its variety. The complete temple type of house is comparatively rare; and even when it is to be found, as in the case of Nicholas Biddle's great mansion Andalusia, with its Parthenon portico, it was the desire of the client rather than the wish of the architect that had so carefully and so illogically dictated the copying of the ancient forms.

In general, church design remained more true to the earlier traditions, and Greek Revival churches generally preserved the plan types and basic arrangements of the Colonial buildings. Naturally the proportions changed; the buildings were usually wider and lower, the towers more squat and heavy. Frequently recessed colonnaded porches with Greek Doric columns shielded the doors. Sometimes the temple colonnade was carried completely across the front. There is something beautifully simple and almost "homey" about many of the smaller churches of this period. They are less finicky than many Colonial examples, quieter and more serene. Only in a few large city churches could the architect afford stone; and how brilliantly the Greek Revival architect rose to the rare opportunity which a complete stone church afforded can be seen in the Lafayette Street Church in New York by Isaiah Rogers, now alas no longer standing but preserved to us in photographs which show its grace, its richness, its beauty.

Like the churches, the courthouses and town halls also were largely mere variations on basic types developed earlier. In them the cupola remained as an almost universal badge of official usage and public character, the Greek fashion showing itself only in the porch or portico that often stretched across the front. Ohio is especially replete with these small courthouses and town halls, and their dignified, massive fronts and their white cupolas rising above the pedimented roof give charm and dignity to many a town green.

It was in state capitols and the buildings erected under federal auspices that the new style received perhaps its most outstanding results. Many of these have already been mentioned. Some preserved a reminiscence of the federal Capitol in Washington by using a domed central portion with two flanking wings, but this was by no means general. The New Haven Capitol, by Ithiel Town, was a simple colonnaded temple. The Tennessee Capitol, by Strickland, is a long, narrow, rectangular building with beautiful Ionic columns at its ends and in central porticoes on either side. The whole is crowned by a slim and graceful cupola. The greatest of the Greek Revival capitols is probably that of Ohio at Columbus, designed by Henry Walters. It was twenty years in the building, and during its construction other architects like West and Isaiah Rogers worked on it. Its strikingly simple rectangular form, with recessed entrance colonnades of the most severe Greek

Doric, and its brilliant and unusual plan combine to make it one of the most impressive governmental buildings in the United States.

It is in this public work that one distinctive feature in the building of the time can best be seen: its structural and engineering integrity. Latrobe, Mills, and Strickland all prided themselves on being as much engineers as architects, and they and their followers sought always to build their structures in the most permanent, the most fireproof, the strongest possible manner. Whenever the need arose they were not afraid of building daring masonry vaults. It was perhaps only in that period that the masonry vault really became at home in American architecture, and a visit to the Sub-Treasury building in New York, to the old Treasury in Washington, or to the superb and daring Girard College building in Philadelphia, designed by Thomas U. Walter, will show at once with what extraordinary ingenuity masonry vaults were used to cover over large spaces with a permanent, fireproof, and impressive covering. This same quality of good building runs through almost all of the engineering works of the period—bridges, canals, viaducts—which the growing country needed in ever-increasing numbers; for in those days design and structure were still considered as one thing.

Basic harmony in color and material, in detail and spirit, makes town after town of those days an oasis of real beauty. Indeed, many of those cities which have become pilgrimage places because of their gracious charm, and are usually considered typically "Colonial," owe their present beauty not to the Colonial period but to this very period of the so-called Greek Revival. Nantucket, parts of Portsmouth, New Hampshire, and much of New Bedford did not achieve their present wealth of characteristic harmony until the 1840's. It was a harmony largely instinctive, an architectural expression of one of those rare short intervals of unified development in popular life before the stresses of sectionalism or of industrial growth had become too violent.

This quality of concord, of beautiful adjustment of the means to the end, even pervades the industrial towns of the time. As we have seen, early industry frequently preserved a rather noble kind of paternalistic idealism. The employer frequently felt that he had the same kind of responsibility to his employees that the landed estate owner had to his tenants. He must see that they were well housed and had at least some of the advantages of social life, some education and amusement. That is the reason why, in Manchester, New Hampshire, in Lowell, in Nashua, in some of the early industrial towns of the Hudson Valley, there are streets of simple, quiet houses, beautifully proportioned, adequately planned, set in ample yards, yet built as industrial housing—as we should call it today. That is why there are so frequently, in the older parts of these industrial towns, so many evidences of careful planning and of beautiful building.

Of course the amateurs, the *cognoscenti,* could not entirely appreciate the really creative qualities of the Greek Revival—its freedom in planning, its magnificent integrity in construction. They were bound to think of architecture in more literary and sentimental ways. In them, enthusiasm for Greek detail developed a desire for imitation; they could not understand that to the architect the new fashion of Greek forms was merely a new and liberating alphabet to be used in forming new words and sentences. Philip Hone wrote in his diary on February 14, 1838, of the Bank of the United States in Philadelphia, later the United States Customs House, "How strange it is that in all the inventions of modern times architecture alone seems to admit of no improvement—every departure from the classical models of antiquity in this science is a departure from grace and Beauty." What struck him about this edifice was its templelike façade, its eight serene Doric columns carrying their proper entablature and pediment. He could never realize that the great virtue of Strickland's design lay in the planning of the interior to give efficient arrangements in beautifully shaped and well-built halls, which were Greek only in the sense that they had used Greek detail almost as freely as Soane had done in the Bank of England. With similar misguided enthusiasm, Nicholas Biddle had made Thomas U. Walter surround his own house with a great Parthenon colonnade and, as a consistent learned amateur, had suggested the temple form for the Girard College building. Walter's genius shows, not in the immaculately detailed exterior colonnade, but in basic plan and in the daring vaulted construction and the beautiful fireproof masonry stairs. The architects themselves were almost unanimously vocal on these points. Even A. J. Davis, though often superficial in his construction, was courageously original in plan and in the exterior treatment of his "Greek Revival" houses. And other architects were much more definite. Latrobe wrote, "My principles of good taste are rigid in Grecian architecture ... [but] our religion requires a church wholly different from the temples, our legislative assemblies and our courts of justice, buildings entirely different from their basilicas. ..." In an essay which was written as a foreword to a proposed publication of his own designs, Robert Mills stated, "Utility and economy will be found to have entered into most of the studies of the author, and little sacrifice to display; at the same time his endeavors were to produce as much harmony and beauty of arrangement as practicable. The principle assumed and acted upon was that beauty is founded upon order, and that convenience and utility were constituent parts." A little later he adds, "... The author has made it a rule never to consult books when he had to design a building. His considerations were—first, the object of the building; second, the means appropriated for its construction; third, the situation it was to occupy; these served as guides in forming the outline of his plan." No stronger statement could be made of the essential creative nature of the architecture of this time, or the basic reasons behind its best works.

With all these qualities of creativeness, of harmony, of simple logic, it would seem strange to find the style so rapidly disintegrating as the mid-century come on. The Greek Revival died because other influences stronger than any mere architectural fashion were more and more becoming the governing qualities of American life. The character of immigration was changing; exploitation of labor was beginning to take the place of the earlier paternalism; extraordinary westward expansion was bringing with it prob-lems of distribution and of use faster than they could be solved. The old feeling of the aristocracy of the learned, of the professional class, was giving way rapidly to a new feeling of the dominance of wealth. It had been the lawyer and the minister who had ruled; now it was to be the wealthy in-dustrialist. In such a society the old standards ceased to command; the new plutocracy sought architectural expressions more ostentatious, more blatant, than the careful harmonies and the muted details of the older type. And they wanted results in a hurry. If cheap methods and imitative construction could make more noise with less expense, then by all means the cheap and tawdry! The money saved could be used to produce all the greater show in fittings and furbelows. And of course there was the growing tragedy of sectionalism, the growing burden of slavery. These were things no thinking man could neglect, forces which were to lead eventually to the Civil War; and the Civil War itself was still more to enrich the Northern plutocrats, still more —indirectly—to assist in the ruthless exploitation of the West. Before these forces the old harmony collapsed, and with it collapsed that style which had been its architectural expression—the style so mistakenly entitled the "Greek Revival."

Chapter 30

ROMANTICISM

BEHIND romanticism in nineteenth-century architecture lay a long literary parentage, and this literary basis inevitably affected it profoundly. The eighteenth century, as we have seen, made a new discovery of the past, and sooner or later the Middle Ages were bound to share with the classic period in the attention of the learned. In England, eighteenth-century antiquarianism turned with growing excitement back to medievalism; and Sir Horace Walpole, who combined the functions of critic, amateur, and wealthy patron, gave this new medievalism respectability. He gave it, too, one of its most important and characteristic, though not most beautiful, architectural expressions in the rebuilding of his own house, Strawberry Hill, where, employing various designers, he produced a strange combination of picturesqueness, imitative Gothic detail, and lavishness of Gothic ornament sometimes as naïvely incorrect as the Gothic of Batty Langley or Chippendale already referred to. In free response to his own whims, and with an almost complete neglect of such architectural qualities as good planning and construction that was in any real way integrated with the forms, he was after "effects," as a writer goes after effects, and the means by which the effects were gained apparently meant nothing whatsoever to him.

Thus, from the very beginning the revival of medieval architecture was cursed with the complete separation of the appearance and the construction. It became a kind of plaything for the wealthy; and the lords and rich gentry who strove to follow the new fashion could not conceive of the "castellated" mansions which they built in any different terms. They were out to produce the "picturesque," to outdo even the eighteenth-century romantic gardeners in their search for that kind of emotional, even sentimental, reaction toward things antique and strange which is at the basis of the aesthetician's definition of the word. This character pervades almost all the early Gothic Revival work. It is true, of course, of the great English castellated mansions, like Wyatt's Fonthill Abbey, designed for William Beckford. It is true of Davis's

111. THE "ARMORY"; THE STAIRWAY AT STRAWBERRY HILL. Horace Walpole, designer. (Robins: *Catalogue of the Classic Contents of Strawberry Hill Collected by Horace Walpole.*)

Gothic mansions in America built a third of a century later, and even such fundamentally creative architects as Latrobe in America and Schinkel in Germany were influenced by the trend; and Latrobe's Sedgeley in Philadelphia, built in 1790 as the first Gothic Revival house in the country, and Schinkel's castles were essentially but superficial applications of Gothic detail. Schinkel, to be sure, had achieved in the freedom of his planning a quality of mass which had in its free, informal effectiveness something of the true medieval character, but the construction is as routine as in the other cases.

Only two possible advances could be made in the Gothic Revival so conceived—one a growing facility and knowledge in the use of detail, and the other an increasing freedom in plan which broken-up, picturesque outlines allowed—and both of these advances were rapidly made. Living rooms could be placed to the best advantage; if they projected from the main block of the house, so much the better—another opportunity for picturesqueness was achieved. A new freedom, then, entered design, particularly domestic design, and the whole concept of convenience which had been so insisted upon by some eighteenth-century architects was allowed to govern more and more. Wings, towers, oriels, and bay windows not only seemed medieval, picturesque, and inspiring to people filled with the new enthusiasms, but also allowed plans in which service relations and problems of aspect, connection, and arrangement could be handled with complete ease.

Increasing accuracy of detail was aided by a great flood of architectural books, in which plans, elevations, and details of medieval buildings were presented in exquisite plates which sometimes, by their own beauty, belied their inaccuracy. For the expenditure of a few pounds, the English architect of the 1830's had command of a surprising new collection of forms. In these books he found ready to his hand Gothic molding profiles, tracery details, the proportions of arches and of group windows, diagrams of vaulting systems, and outlines of battlements or the details of half-timber houses. Although a knowledge of the great underlying principles of medieval building was lacking, at least archaeological accuracy in detail became almost a commonplace. Wyatt's great design for Fonthill Abbey was perhaps, in spite of its early date, 1790, the climax building of the earlier castellated mansions. Built for one of the great romantic eccentrics of the time, a man of vast wealth and a prodigal spender, the building seems to have had no limits save its architect's imagination. It was a huge pile—half house, half stage set—culminating in a great Gothic tower over 200 feet high, and entered through an impressive entrance hall and a superb stair, which led into a tall octagonal Gothic vaulted hall beneath the tower. The hall must have been breath-taking in its vertical accents, in its tremendous heights and soaring lines. But, alas, the vaults were of lath and plaster; and even the great tower itself, the climax of the whole, though it was apparently of masonry and faced partly in stone, was held up on a great wooden framework. As a piece of pure picturesque architecture, a symphony in emotional design, the whole conception was magnificent; and the artful way in which the lower portions were balanced against the higher masses, and the various Gothic details applied to the fabric, was admirable. As a house it was probably as inconvenient as the great eighteenth-century ducal mansions, but it did have wainscoted halls, bay windows and oriels, vaulted corridors, and even a cloister where the owner might imagine himself enshrined within an ancient monastery. The detail was freer, in some ways more creative, than the more archaeological ornament which was to come later, for no mere archaeological correctness could ever have satisfactorily clothed such a structure, so basically unreal, so obviously built as an expression of an individual's passion for the medieval rather than as a house; and the whole was overvaunting, attempting more than its construction could withstand. There came a day of high wind and the great tower crashed to the ground, bringing down with it large parts of the building in common ruin. The fall of Fonthill Abbey must have been an event almost as emotionally exciting, as dramatically impressive, as picturesquely thrilling, as to satisfy even the most extravagant fancies of the most immoderate searcher for the romantic or the sublime. Its fall somehow symbolizes the entire inherent unreality, the literary quality, of the movement. It is all as right as a drama.

Of course, this new interest in medievalism was destined for other developments than the mere literary gestures of a Walpole or a Beckford. Two other factors entered the picture: one a new concept of nationalism, the other a new desire for a characteristically "Christian" art. The antiquarians felt, more and more, as they studied the remains of ancient buildings —of monasteries, and castles, and churches—that they were studying the work of their own ancestors. French Gothic, they saw, was a different thing from English Gothic, and both were entirely removed from the traceried arcades of Venice. Each country came to feel that its own kind of Gothic was somehow a national possession; and, as the national feeling which followed the Napoleonic wars became ever more strong, it was only natural that this feeling that the Gothic somehow belonged to the nation itself increased also. These Gothic buildings of the olden time, men felt, because they were the products of one's own predecessors and built in one's own country, were necessarily closer, necessarily more fitted to act as an inspiration than the work of Greece and Rome, produced by differing peoples in more distant parts of the world. To be national in architecture came almost to mean the same thing as being Gothic, and when Queen Victoria and Lord Palmerston made Charles Barry abandon the Renaissance design which he preferred and build the present Houses of Parliament in English Perpendicular they were only expressing the wide popular feeling.

The religious facets of the movement had an even greater importance. The whole English church was exercised more and more about the fundamental problems of ritualism and historical tradition. The most important ecclesiastical thinkers were reacting against the routine secularism of the eighteenth-century church, demanding not only greater seriousness and a more intense devotion to Christian ideals, but also expressing their conviction that the medieval church had been a vital force and medieval devotion a vivid experience that had been subsequently lost, and that therefore the easiest way to reform the church was by a return to medievalism. Of the religious controversies these ideas aroused it is not necessary to particularize. The history of the first Oxford Movement is well known and the importance of the Cambridge Ecclesiological Society, its great rival, fully realized. In France, Chateaubriand in the *Génie du Christianisme* was giving his own interpretation of similar forces. Also important is the fact that everywhere these religious controversies focused attention on medieval church architecture, and that there was the closest relationship between architecture and ritual. Therefore, the theory went, if it was necessary to return to the medieval conception of Christianity, it was equally essential to return to medievalism in church design.

There was a third, more subtle, factor behind the Gothic Revival in architecture. The word "romanticism" has accumulated so many different meanings in the course of a century of criticism that it is necessary to be more precise. Behind the new interest in medieval architecture went a search for emotional expression which was a new thing. Romanticism means many more things than mere antiquarianism, for from the point of view of a mere turn to the past the Classic Revivals might also be considered romantic; but, as we have seen, the architects of the Classic Revival were striving primarily for form which should be serene, well composed, consistent, harmonious, adequate. The true romanticist is not satisfied with this. He demands more; he demands that architecture shall be "expressive"—that is, that it shall aim definitely at expressing specific emotions such as religious awe, grandeur, gaiety, intimacy, sadness. He seeks to make architecture as expressive and as personal as a lyric poem, and oftentimes this demand for emotional expression he makes superior to any other claims. All architecture is expressive; but, whereas the classic architect allows the expression to arise naturally from forms developed in the common-sense solution of his problem, the true romantic seeks expression first, with a definite self-conscious urge. To the romantic architect of the mid-nineteenth century, Romanesque and Gothic had somehow come to seem more emotional than the other styles.

Eventually the structural basis of medieval architecture was sure to be realized. Students of the great cathedrals could not help realizing that buttress and pinnacle, vault rib and tracery, existed at least in part because of the structural demands of the building, and that their forms had arisen largely because of such structural necessities. In England the younger Pugin (Augustus Welby Pugin) understood this with growing intensity throughout his short and checkered career, and in his superb satirical books like

Contrasts and *On the State of Christian Architecture* took delight in poking as much fun at the earlier castellated Gothic of the mansions and the thin lath-and-plaster Gothic of the earlier Revival churches (such as the famous Commissioners' churches built so widely in the early nineteenth century in England) as he did at what seemed to him the stupidities of the Classic. He came more and more to realize that no revival of medieval architecture, in the older sense, was possible, because conditions and structural methods had so deeply changed, and that the only thing which was possible was a new architecture beginning where the Gothic had left off. Using Gothic ornament and the pointed arch—for these seemed to him essentially Christian elements, and he was looking for a Christian architecture above all— but trying always to design honestly and creatively in accordance with the necessities of the individual problem, it was the tragedy of Pugin that in his own work he was so seldom able to rise to this ideal. He complained savagely that his clients wanted cathedrals for the money which could only build a modest parish church, and that consequently he was forced time after time to compromises of which he did not approve.

In France, the greatest student of medieval buildings was Viollet-le-Duc, and he too became progressively more conscious of the enormous importance of structure in the development of Gothic architecture, even carrying the theory to extremes hardly tenable. Yet, in essence, his approach was sound; he was a profound scholar not only of medieval architecture but of medieval literature and life, and in the *Dictionnaire raisonné de l'architecture française du XIme au XVIme siècle* he set a new standard in imaginative speculative archaeology; he built an entire coherent theory of architecture on the basis of the most minute factual study of medieval buildings. His architectural work was comparatively unimportant; even the great restoration work which he did to preserve and to protect monuments falling into ruin, like the work at Carcassonne and the reconstruction of the château of Pierrefonds, is today looked upon with considerable skepticism as being often more the product of his own creation than the necessary carrying out of archaeological evidence. But his great literary work, his Dictionary and a long series of books on building types and architectural education, not only prove him one of the greatest architectural thinkers of the world, but also the man who recreated the idea of logic and structure as the basis of any living architecture. Viollet-le-Duc, like Pugin, realized that no complete revival of medieval styles was possible. He went much further, however; his sure logical sense made it obvious to him that any revival of the past was impossible, and that the great task of modern architecture was the creation of a new style fitted to its own needs.

The Gothic Revival in France was more a matter of intellectual approach than of architectural work, except for the restorations by Viollet-le-Duc and Lassus, but these were of extraordinary extent. The sudden new enthusiasm for medieval work made all France passionately aware of its amazing architectural wealth, and also acutely conscious of the disintegration which threatened ruin to so many of the medieval structures. The French government, accordingly, set about the work of putting these into condition, and, in the course of what started out to be simple repair work, eventually attempted more and more restoration, in the effort both to preserve the buildings and to make vivid to all who saw them their earlier appearance when they were in their prime. In some cases this work was brilliant in its discretion; in others, unfortunately, zeal got the better of the restorers, and large amounts of new buildings were added the forms of which were actually new designs. Even in detail the restoration was carried to such a degree that frequently almost the entire exposed portion, where weathering was serious, was replaced with new stonework. In Notre Dame, in Paris, for instance, the present detail of the front entrances dates largely from this period, and all but a few of the famous *chimères* which look down from the towers over Paris were carved in the 1850's. Similarly, the metal-covered timber *flèche* of Notre Dame is a new creation by Viollet-le-Duc, based on the scantiest of records, for the old one had long before disappeared; and the present interior appearance of Ste. Chapelle, with its glory of rich painting and its red, blue, and purple glass, is almost entirely the result of the nineteenth-century "restorations."

Of course the minute study of the actual work which these restorations made necessary gave the French architects an unprecedented command of medieval detail, but it also probably trained many of them to think too much in terms of this detail itself, and when new work in the ancient style was begun the danger always existed of making it an opportunity to display the architects' knowledge. Of the economy, the restraint, found in so much real Gothic work, there is in this nineteenth-century Gothic little trace; and in such new creations as the west front of St. Ouen at Rouen, with its two diagonally placed towers, built in the middle of the century, the impression is less of a coherent, simple, and dignified church front than of a museum of Gothic ornament applied in a too-crowded way, designed with a strange kind of wire-drawn, meticulous, intellectual frigidity. Even when earlier and more naïve French designers set out to work in the medieval style, the same preoccupation with detail is evident, as in the great iron spire which rises over the center of Rouen Cathedral. Precisely the same feeling, too, controls the few churches built in the style. The richest example and the most characteristic is the large church of Ste. Clotilde in Paris, designed by Gau and Ballu, a building impressive in its scale and unity, but somehow giving the effect even today, when eighty years have aged and softened it, of something new and arrogantly ostentatious.

Despite the small amount of new building in the Gothic style in France, the medieval enthusiasm had its architectural repercussions. Thus in small house design half-timber and high gables began to replace the quiet, dig-nified, geometric forms of the Empire and Classic Revival periods. The search for picturesqueness brought in all kinds of eccentricities of plan and detail, and the lesser architects learned just enough of Viollet-le-Duc's theory of freedom in design to cut themselves loose from both dignity and tradi-tion at the same time and develop a vogue for the bizarre whimsicalities, erratic projections, exaggerated eaves, and caricatures of wood framing in gables which make up the perky incoherence that still today curses so many of the French suburbs and resort towns. The study of medieval structure, the development by Viollet-le-Duc of the theory of a structural architecture, was to enter into the tradition of later nineteenth-century architecture and was pregnant with many important elements for the future, but the actual building result of the Gothic Revival in France disintegrated into mere eccentric show and vulgarity.

In Germany and Austria the medieval revival had as literary a basis as the movement in England. Goethe had been one of the pioneers in a sym-pathetic understanding of Gothic buildings; his apostrophe to Strasbourg Cathedral, in its lyric ecstasy, was epoch-making. The same furor of restora-tion and reconstruction which had played over France activated the Ger-mans too; and, though the Germans had no Viollet-le-Duc, they had what was perhaps almost as valuable, several important medieval architectural drawings still preserved in the cathedral and monastery archives. Especially noteworthy were the elaborately detailed drawings for the west end of the uncompleted Cologne Cathedral—drawings which should forever set at rest the popular misconception of the Gothic architect as a mere handy man, a sort of super-mason—and studies showing three possible completions for the unfinished façade tower of Ulm Cathedral. Working from these medi-eval drawings, nineteenth-century architects completed Cologne Cathedral and the great tower of Ulm, which reached a height of 528 feet. At the same time an aroused interest led to the restoration of various castles. The Wartburg was perhaps the greatest of these. It was reconditioned between 1840 and 1870, so as to show impressively the dignified lavishness of the great Romanesque palace.

Nationalism lay behind much of this ardor and a great deal of actual work was done. Significantly enough, one of the first important monuments of the German Gothic Revival was the elaborate iron spire and pinnacle which Schinkel designed as early as 1818 as a national monument to commemorate the War of Liberation. Nationalism in Germany led naturally to a broader stylistic study than did the Gothic inspiration in France, for the Germans in their nineteenth-century attempt to create an enthusiasm for the true *Deutschtum* were almost equally interested in the Romanesque, the Gothic, and the early German Renaissance; and, while Frederick William IV might rebuild the castle at Hohenzollern—an almost completely new design, though on ancient foundations—in the Gothic style, the authorities were just as much attracted to the Early Renaissance work of Frankfurt, Nuremberg, and Rothenburg.

Thus, almost the only examples of pure Gothic Revival new building are a few churches, of which the greatest is undoubtedly the Votive Church in Vienna, designed by Ferstel, a great cathedral-like structure, with twin western towers, which is in some ways the finest, as it is the most lavish, of all of the nineteenth-century archaeological Gothic Revival buildings, distinguished by excellence of proportion and beauty of detail. Somewhat exceptional in its free Late Gothic style is the great Vienna City Hall, designed by Friedrich von Schmidt in the third quarter of the century, a tremendous edifice of imaginative Gothic detail, but one which reveals in its free borrowing from many sources, as well as in the classic symmetry of its plan, the influence not of the pure Gothic Revival spirit but rather of the eclecticism which so frequently followed it.

Nowhere did the Gothic Revival have a greater and a more revolutionary effect than in England, which had given it its first expression, for nowhere else were the forces behind it so irresistibly strong. In Germany, nationalism had led the architects of the romantic age into the byways of Romanesque and of Renaissance. In France, the strong classic traditions of the École des Beaux Arts held firm against all the attacks of the romanticists and gave, at least to the official work, the requisite classic stamp. But, in England, religious fervor, so closely allied to the desires of the court and the government, made the drive toward Gothic design irrepressible, and there was no

academic and classic tradition powerful enough to withstand it. Furthermore, the movement was blessed with extremely brilliant and articulate
writers, who had the gift not only of interesting the specialist but of moving
the general population. The younger Pugin, at the center of a storm of
religious controversy, produced book after book of spirited writing illustrated by lively engravings in which he lampooned the classic and upheld
the ideals of Gothic architecture as the one possible inspiration for a modern English Christian who sought to build. Ruskin, that strange and un-
balanced genius whose criticism bestrode the whole last half of the nineteenth century, was equally eloquent and more persuasive. It is hard to
develop a coherent theory from his successive works. His own rationaliza-
tions of his admiration for medieval architecture swung widely from base
to base, as his religious and social ideals changed and matured. Gothic
architecture was best now because it was the most Christian, later because it
was the most creative and least imitative, then again because it was the most
honest—whatever that might mean. Essentially, his theory of art was a
moral theory, based on radical economic ideas, a passionate disgust at the
horrors of rampant industrialism, and a feeling that somehow Gothic architecture was godly and produced by happy workmen, while classic buildings,
with the possible exception of the Greek, were pagan, unlovely, and the
product of unhappy slave labor. But, incoherent as he sometimes was,
Ruskin's magnificent passion, so manifestly sincere, swayed the hearts of
his contemporaries as few critics have stirred their readers and hearers since.
His aims were so clearly noble, his integrity so exalted, his words so eloquent, that few could find it in their hearts to question the logic of his
superb periods.

Fortunately, Ruskin was no narrow archaeologist. Like Viollet-le-Duc, he
realized that some kind of honesty was at the core of all the best architecture
—that is, some kind of consistent agreement between the forms and appearance of a building and the forces (the life, and the construction) which
had given it birth. He knew that a modern building could not ever be at
the same time an honest nineteenth-century building and also a mere copy
of any model, however lovely. He felt more deeply than Pugin, for instance,
that the new world demanded a new style, and this style he set himself out
to envisage. It must be basically Gothic, he thought, in the sense that the
construction should be as honest as Gothic construction, its composition as
free as the composition of medieval buildings, and its ornament based on
natural forms. It should probably use the pointed arch, because of the
greater freedom in design which the pointed arch allows. But, being built

for modern uses in modern ways, its forms must arise naturally from the demands of the building. It must have more horizontal accents than the medieval Gothic of France or England, because modern buildings were so frequently of several stories, and honesty demanded that they be separately expressed. Modern buildings, too, were seldom vaulted, and thus the whole system of buttress and screen wall must necessarily disappear and a new kind of flat-walled Gothic arise. This was all sound enough, save for its insistence on the pointed arch and naturalistic ornament; and it had the great merit of making many people think of the essential bases of architec ture rather than of mere style preferences. But Ruskin was not content with that; and, as his own travels had brought him perhaps his greatest happi ness in Italy, it was to Italian Gothic he turned again and again to illustrate his points, especially to the polychrome surface ornament and the vivid decoration of Venetian Gothic palaces. His followers, and indeed all the architects of England who came under his influence during the third quar ter of the century, could not help being aroused by his enthusiasm, so that various forms of polychrome Italian Gothic became the basis for the free medieval style which was the final flowering of the Gothic Revival in England, the style we know as Victorian Gothic.

Charles Barry had produced in the Houses of Parliament an extraordi narily brilliant design, largely in the English Perpendicular manner. Im mensely costly, lavish in every detail of decoration and ornament, planned with an unusual system and convenience to shelter its manifold activities, it had tremendous vitality. Its details were largely designed by the younger Pugin—indeed, he claimed that much of the entire design was his—and this detail gave to the building a popular appeal which was enormous. Yet, strange as it may seem, this precedent was little followed, and the archaeologi cal Gothic Revival died out completely except in church work. In church work, of course, the Gothic style marched on, receiving continually freer and more fluent expression in the works of Bodley and Bentley, and set a tradition in church design that is still alive, of which the last and perhaps the greatest expression is Liverpool Cathedral, by George Gilbert Scott, still under construction.

Elsewhere the free Victorian Gothic was supreme. House after house rose, all over England, in the new manner, with black and white marble arches over the windows, polished granite columns at the door, color patterns in the slate roof, naturalistic foliage in the ornament, and the utmost freedom in general composition—in the arrangement of windows, the addition of bays, the breaking up of the silhouette. Some, in the hands of men less skilled, descended almost to the depths of whimsical eccentricity to be found in the smaller French houses of the time, but generally speaking Ruskinian ideals of restraint and honesty, of directness and simplicity, were strong enough to curb the worst violations of taste.

The greatest achievements of this Victorian Gothic were undoubtedly in public buildings. The Assize Courts building in Manchester, by Alfred Waterhouse, was characteristic. The Manchester City Hall, by the same architect, was equally successful. In both a frequent characteristic of the style appears, in the low and stumpy columns which carry wide arches so that the tops may not pierce through the story above. In both of these buildings, essential simplicity and directness of plan is made to generate interesting and picturesque forms, and the detail is vivid, direct, and generally well applied, without too much spottiness from a forced search for polychrome effects. Ruskin had hoped to develop a method by which the old craft spirit could be revived among the stonecutters. He felt that the architect should indicate general types of capital and carved detail only, and that the individual carver or sculptor should work out the details himself, designing his own work and thereby making of each carved piece an individual work of art. In the Oxford Museum, the only building for which Ruskin himself might claim to be even in part the architect, the system was given a trial and some very charming naturalistic capitals resulted. But it was impossible to apply the same method of ornament design to the great public buildings the nineteenth century demanded. The hurry of the time and the necessity for accurate estimates and fixed price contracts made any such scheme obviously impractical, so that the carved detail is often hard and unsympathetic, almost more definitely so because of the too forced attempt at freedom and variety. The Law Courts in London by George Edmund Street reveal both the advantages and the difficulties of this Victorian Gothic style. They are picturesque, vivid; they do add a definite note of interest to the stretch of the Strand on which they face; but as a great public building they leave much to be desired. The search for variety, for picturesqueness, has led to confusion in plan, inconvenience in relationship, and a puzzling number of centers of interest. It is all too broken up; and though the search for honesty of expression in its design was sincere, it somehow fails completely to express its nature as a great courthouse. It is indicative of the aesthetic sense of the period that, in the competition to select the architect, Street's design was preferred over Gilbert Scott's; for Scott's design was magnificently planned, straightforward and logical, but it was "too classic" in plan, not nearly picturesque enough to appeal to the Victorian taste. Scott's own great work, besides a huge amount of church restoration and a superb design for the church of St. Nicholas in Hamburg, was the Albert Memorial, a tremendous structure largely of metal, rich with mosaic and gold, and lavishly decorated with inept sculpture, which stands in Hyde Park, a monument to Victorian fashion, to the futile search for a romantic exuberance, to which the underlying industrialism of the time was inevitably hostile.

Nevertheless, Gothicism had become such an intrinsic part of English architectural thinking that even railroad stations and hotels were built in the Victorian Gothic manner; and perhaps the last stage in the development—the final *reductio ad absurdum* of the whole movement—can be seen in the St. Pancras Hotel and Railroad Station in London, where Scott attempted to dress all the vast indispensables of a great modern terminal in the picturesque garb of the Victorian Gothic. In spite of the fine ideals, the sound bases, of Ruskin's architectural criticism, only his enthusiasm for Italian polychrome Gothic had won popular acclaim, while the great foundations of his theory were forgotten; and the style created with such sanguine hopes fell swiftly before other encroaching forces.

As early as the 1790's, the English fashionable passion for medieval buildings was mirrored in America, in Sedgeley, near Philadelphia, which Latrobe designed, where superficial Gothic detail was used to decorate a building otherwise quite conventional in its layout. It caused considerable talk; and more and more of the wealthy people, particularly those who claimed to have the most advanced cultural ideas, began to build houses in which they hoped to incarnate something of the quality of the English castellated mansions. This movement only became common in the late 1820's, and reached a climax twenty years later. But there were no real castles for Americans to see, stone building was expensive, and the American carpenter-craftsmen were forced into the same modifications of Gothic detail which their grandfathers had made in Baroque forms a half century before. Picturesqueness became a rival to Greek purity in house design; and, though the majority of houses in one way or another still followed the classic vein, there arose among them all sorts of rather charming Gothic cottages, such as A. J. Davis's Rotch house in New Bedford. This application of carpenter-Gothic detail is least successful when most correct, and most charming and effective when most naïve. Occasionally simple rectangular houses of perfectly traditional classical plan would receive a battlemented cresting, hood molds around the window heads, and perhaps projecting oriel windows and a lacy porch of carved wood or cast iron in which Gothic details were delightfully symbolized. Such is the Hermitage in Savannah, Georgia, which General Sherman used as his headquarters. Such is the so-called Wedding Cake House in Kennebunk Port, in Maine, where an ambitious sea captain added to his lovely square traditional house a rich frontispiece of jigsaw woodwork, which has a lacelike allure of its own. Or the changes might be more in matters of general form than in detail. High gables took the place of earlier flat or low-pitched roofs, and their fronts bore intricately carved openwork verge boards or barge boards, running up the slope; separate terra-cotta chimney caps recalled the independent brick flues of Tudor England; and diligent poring over the Gothic examples in the books of the elder Pugin (Augustus Pugin) and of Britton enabled the builders to use group windows with at least a recognizable Gothic feeling. Alexander Jackson Davis of New York, who had already won wide fame as a Greek Revival architect, took to the new style with reckless abandon; and many of its most pleasing results, which have a quaint and likable reality behind their superficial Gothic gingerbread, are due to his design or the extensive influence exerted by the drawings he made for A. J. Downing's much-read books on rural architecture. Occasionally Davis's houses, like the Hudson River mansion of Lyndhurst, later the residence of Mrs. Finley J. Shepard, attained a dignity and a truly Gothic character far beyond the carpenter-Gothic vagaries. But the style never became really at home in American domestic architecture; it was too foreign to the American tradition and the bonds between the new country and feudal England had been too long relaxed to give it even the traditional reality it had held in England. The Gothic houses were tempting targets for the satirist. Thus the *New York Mirror*, in reviewing *The American Architect*, a periodical publication of house designs, by Ranlett, which came out between 1846 and 1848, said of the first number, in 1846:

These cottages have nothing to commend them but a picturesque profile.... They are the most costly and least convenient houses that can be built.... They are the imitations of the natural expressions of an age of semi-civilization and gross ignorance.... It was quite pardonable in Horace Walpole and Sir Walter Scott to build gingerbread houses in imitation of robber barons and Bluebeard chieftains; they were poets and had written Gothic romances; they would fill their houses with rusty old armour, lances, drinking horns and mouldy tapestry, and they were surrounded by the memorials of the times they were idly trying to revive. But there can be nothing more grotesque. more absurd, or more affected, than for a quiet gentleman, who has made his fortune in the peaceful occupation of selling calicos, and who knows no more of the middle ages than they do of him, to erect for his family residence a gimcrack of a Gothic castle ... as though he anticipated an attack upon his roost from some Front de Boeuf in the neighborhood.

The problem was quite different when churches were considered, for the same arguments that upheld the use of the Gothic in England as the only true Christian church architecture applied equally well in this country. Latrobe had prepared a Gothic design for the cathedral in Baltimore during the first decade of the nineteenth century; and Godefroi, a French architect, had built there at about the same time a charming little Gothic chapel. In New York, the first St. Patrick's Church, the great original cathedral of the New York diocese, was built between 1809 and 1812, from the designs of the French Mangin. It was a large church of gargantuan scale, which was originally planned to have the same twin front towers as Notre Dame in Paris, but these were never built, and the detail which still remains from this first building shows an awkward caricature of Gothic forms, remarkable only in its rather ungainly power. In 1813 Ithiel Town built Trinity Church in New Haven, a typical New England meetinghouse decorated with Gothic detail; but it was not until the later 1830's that archaeologically correct Gothic came to be used with freedom. Certain earlier Gothic work in the Boston neighborhood, by Solomon Willard and Gridley Bryant, has a kind of brutal power because of its simple granite treatment. But these early gray and lowering edifices, despite their pointed windows and their primitive tracery, are scarcely within the true Gothic tenor. That remained almost unknown in this country until suddenly, between 1835 and 1850, it was given abundant expression in the work of three architects—Richard Upjohn, James Renwick, and Minard Lafever. Upjohn, in Trinity Church, set a tradition for American church architecture which has hardly died yet; and Renwick, in Grace Church in New York, showed the exquisite richness that Gothic could give. Minard Lafever's work is more daring, more original, and less correct, but in the Church of the Holy Trinity in Brooklyn, only slightly later than Trinity and Grace, he achieved a combination of lavish detail, imaginative variations on Gothic themes, and a general effectiveness of proportion and composition which make it one of the most successful, as it is certainly the most American, of all these early Gothic Revival churches. Yet even in these, correct as they were in detail, beautiful in mass and line, there was always a certain sense of unreality.

The old tradition of integrity in structure, on which the best Greek Revival architects had so insistently based their work, was breaking down. Romanticism, with its emphasis on the effect and its comparative lack of interest in how the effect was produced, was sapping at the whole integral basis of architecture. These attractive Gothic churches were, all of them, content with lath-and-plaster vaults. In them the last connections between building methods and building form disappeared, and in their very success they did much to establish in America the disastrous separation between engineering

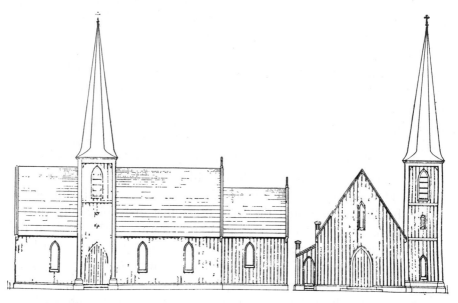

112. INEXPENSIVE WOODEN COUNTRY CHURCH. Richard Upjohn, architect. (*Upjohn's Rural Architecture.*)

and architecture which was to curse American building for two generations. The best of the American Gothic work remains in its simpler, its less ostentatious, monuments: the little churches in which wood was allowed frankly to be itself, as in the small frame chapels which Upjohn designed for country villages and distant mission stations; and the frank carpenter-Gothic of the picturesque high-gabled cottages which rose so bewitchingly embowered in heavy trees along many of our Eastern village streets.

The polychrome Victorian Gothic of England also became a brief American fashion. A number of architects, especially in New York and later in early Chicago, fell under the spell of Ruskin's persuasive writing, and sought as he did to create a modern, freely designed, inventive nineteenth-century

Gothic. But here also the strings that bound America and England seemed too tenuous to hold for long; and in spite of the occasional appealing successes of the style—such as the old National Academy of Design with its black-and-white marble front, designed by Peter B. Wight, and some of Renwick's city houses—the Victorian Gothic was doomed in America to swift disintegration into the cheapest and most illogical copying of its most obvious mannerisms, and a complete negation of its essential foundations. It became in a sense a caricature, to be rapidly swallowed up in the confusion of eclecticism which the last quarter of the century brought with it.

Chapter 31

ECLECTICISM

IN a sense, the Classic and Gothic Revivals themselves led inevitably to eclecticism in architecture, although the ideals of the great architects of both movements had been creative. They had all used inspiration drawn from classic or medieval sources as a stimulus to further invention, a means of overcoming traditions which no longer had validity in the nineteenth-century world. But the growing floods of books in which the details of the architecture of the past were so beautifully presented were insidious temptations to copying; and, as we have noted, many of the amateurs and the educated laymen of the period could see no finer aim in architecture than the imitation of past glories. And, once the idea of copying—reproducing even details unaltered—became accepted as the correct thing, why should one stop with the copying of Greek or Gothic? Napoleon's campaigns in Egypt had evoked the superb volumes of Mariette's *Description de l'Égypte,* and Egyptian detail began to be used, as in the famous old Tombs Prison of New York, designed by John Haviland, or the handsome gateways which Isaiah Rogers designed for the Jewish Cemetery at Newport and Henry Austin built for the cemetery at New Haven. And, if Egyptian, why not Romanesque or Renaissance? The Italian villa made its appearance early in the century in England, in all sorts of modified forms, and by the 1840's so-called Italian villa designs joined the Greek and Gothic forms as accepted models for country houses in Germany, England, and America. Many of these were as creative, as independent in design, as the best of the Greek Revival houses. Their usually flat or low-pitched roofs, their broadly projecting eaves supported on brackets, their ubiquitous square towers, their arcaded or colonnaded piazzas, and the general amplitude of room size and ceiling height which characterized them gave them a definitely homelike and livable quality. They were Italian in name only, but the name itself is significant of the growing passion for giving style names to buildings; and, when the style name becomes the important thing in a building design, creativeness and integrity are in danger.

There were many persuasive arguments in favor of the new movement. Eclecticism in architecture is essentially design by means of picking and choosing, from here or there, details of past styles which appeal, and recombining them as the essential elements of a new building. Under the stress of new problems and the growing hurry and bustle of an industrial age, the older Revival traditions had worn thin, just as the Rococo traditions had disappeared with the revolutions in France and America. People everywhere were perplexed. An increasing self-consciousness forced architects and critics to re-examine the whole problem of architectural design. As early as 1844, Gilman published an article in the *North American Review* which contains a reasoned support of the philosophy of eclecticism. In general, his argument was that both Greek and Gothic were the results of civilizations far different from that of the nineteenth century; that the entire series of necessities which the modern building must fulfill can be but ill satisfied within the categories of Greek or Gothic architectural forms. The Renaissance was much nearer our own time, he wrote, and Renaissance buildings might therefore furnish an even better source of inspiration, if only because they gave the window almost as important a place in design as do modern works. He even suggested that the earlier Colonial work of the United States might furnish a better basis than Greece or medieval Europe. He also argued that, since we were building for a day which was not the Greek day or the medieval day or the Renaissance day, there was no need whatsoever for archaeological consistency in the work we do. He expressed his theory in the Arlington Street Church in Boston, built a few years later, in which he modeled the exterior on the English work of Sir Christopher Wren and the interior on the seventeenth-century Italian Renaissance of Genoa.

Critics thus came to discuss all the styles of past architecture in the Western world, which archaeology and the new "science" of art history were bringing more and more into popular ken. Are we not, said they, heirs of all the ages? Are we not descended from the same peoples who created all of this Western pageant of architecture? If, then, our true heritage is the entire body of past buildings, is it not perfectly logical to use all of their own forms in our own work? Archaeology was continually clarifying the picture of the development of building. Art history was showing the phantasmagoric shift of styles from century to century. Art history was showing, too, that Mesopotamia borrowed from Egypt, and Greece from both, and that the whole process which had given rise to the great masterpieces of the world's architecture had always had in it something of a continual taking from the past to help the present and form the future. Should we not, the critics said, do likewise? Should we not select out of all of this past wealth what we need, and build an architecture out of it? Accordingly, the eclectic architects of the last half of the nineteenth century began to act like spend-thrift heirs. They failed to learn the real lesson which the past had to teach, that great architecture arose from great problems logically faced and creatively conceived, using the best and most inventive methods of construc-tion the time afforded. Instead, they saw only plates in books, or bits of detail in the actual buildings to be sketched carefully in notebooks, which could be brought out at the needful time to decorate nineteenth-century windows or doors.

And there was another tremendous impetus to this kind of superficial picture-puzzle design. Fundamentally it was extraordinarily expressive of the age which brought it forth. Industrialism had conquered civilization. The exploiting of new lands, the formation of modern empires, and the almost insane search for ever-broadening markets were sweeping vast wealth into new hands and filling the capitals of the world with a new class of restless, eager, half-educated millionaires. As the flood increased, the standards of living of the earlier aristocracy became more and more fixed and conven-tional as a protection of their own respectabilities. But the newly rich caught the infection and became themselves even more respectable than their men-tors. Their one aim seems to have been to hide their crudities under an enamel of propriety and what they chose to call "culture."

They set themselves diligently to acquiring these virtues, trying to buy them as they could buy almost anything else their hearts desired. They became collectors, for a great art collection was an almost infallible guar-antee of respectability. They became travelers, because travel was easily purchased and its results could be easily publicized in conversation. In a sense, travel was merely another way of making the whole world theirs, so that the well-to-do-people from the middle of the century on had, almost in spite of themselves, a wider knowledge of the strange places of the world than any equally large group of people who had preceded them. They were no longer dependent on books; they had seen the cities of the world with their own eyes. They had seen the piazza of St. Peter's with its magnificent sweep of colonnade and its superb fountains; they had admired, themselves, the suave curved front of Peruzzi's Massimi Palace; they had slipped along the Grand Canal at sunset, or when the moon was silvering the waters, and watched the splendid marble façades of the palaces slip by—the inlaid marble of the Byzantine, the traceried arcade of the Gothic, the verve and monumentality of the Renaissance;—they had wandered through the halls of Versailles and looked out over the great vista from the terrace to the lagoon, down the *tapis vert;* they had seen the purple light from stained glass dyeing the soaring columns of Notre Dame and Chartres; they had visited the Tudor of Hampton Court or strolled along the quiet brick length of its Wren façade; perhaps, if they had been lucky and had had the correct introductions, they had even been entertained in country houses three centuries old, with the warm oak paneling around them and the rich plaster ceiling above; or they had been received in the exquisite Louis Quinze cream-and-gold delicacy of the salon in an eighteenth-century house in the Faubourg St. Germain.

And these travelers photographed and bought photographs. The perfecting of the photographic process came, one might almost say, at the exact psychological moment when its repercussions on art would be greatest; for the photograph brought to architects and lay people alike a new kind of presentation of the buildings of the past, which seemed to have about it a sort of reality—a specious reality—which made the architecture of the whole world a familiar thing.

Of course, no person who had even the germs of aesthetic sensibility could fail to be impressed by the magnificence, the enduring living beauty, of these masterpieces of the creative building of the past, with which the whole world was thus becoming so suddenly familiar through travel and photography. No person could fail to make the most damaging comparisons between all of this beauty, this dignity, this lasting grandeur, and the squalid ugliness of most purely nineteenth-century cities or even the nineteenth-century parts of older towns. Industrialism was spawning its most evil results in them. Dirt and disorder, jerry-building, and congestion made architectural beauty an impossibility. "Where there's muck there's money," says an old Yorkshire proverb. One of the most obvious tragic results of untrained, disorganized, violently competitive industrialism was muck, carelessness with regard to appearance of any kind, slackness, and finally hopeless and stolid tolerance of unbelievable filth and hideousness.

To the industrialist of the nineteenth century, to the successful businessman fighting his way up in the relentless battle of commerce, any consideration of beauty *per se* appeared a meaningless waste of either good time or good money. Beauty came to be generally regarded as a sort of half-sinful luxury which the successful could afford, just as they could afford overrich food. Yet here in this same world, with slum and reeking factory, with open sewer and garish saloon, stood these buildings left from the past, endowed with a grace and a loveliness that somehow seemed still alive. The time came when the industrialists and the successful businessmen, or—what was perhaps even more important—their wives, began to taste a little of this forbidden fruit of beauty. Is it strange that they sought to regain it in their own structures by copying buildings or building details from the past?

And it was natural, also, that along with the *nouveau-riche* desire to gain beauty, respectability, and the respect due a successful man, all at the same time, by building a house larger, more ostentatious, and more covered with bits of remembered detail than any their neighbors had built, the habit spread from the rich to the jerry-builders. The desire to overcome the first terrible results of mass building for poor people, by providing some kind of exterior respectability, made the jerry-builders turn eagerly to the books and the photographs for details to copy. Cheap stamped-tin cornices decorated the fronts of tenements in New York; cheap terra-cotta insets in door and window frames made by the thousands began to appear on the façades of the slums in Germany and England.

Travel brought in another element, as well: the element of exoticism. The longing for distant places, the love of styles the direct opposite from what common sense would suggest, was a marked feature of nineteenth-century art. It was a reflection on the one hand of a kind of basic escapism; on the other, of a quite honest delight in the ever-widening horizons of the nineteenth-century world, the ever-growing acquaintance with places new and strange. A new era of exploitation was under way, something like that of the seventeenth century; and it was a part of the same world feeling that sent ill-prepared Polar expeditions to starve in the Arctic, or drove Stanley through the heart of Africa, which filled the Salons with Gérôme's paintings of Algerian harems and made Barnum build himself a Persian villa in Bridgeport. Exoticism had appeared early, as the plaything of eighteenth-century eccentrics; later, it had achieved respectability with Nash's extraordinary Oriental Pavilion at Brighton for King George IV. But, in general, the later nineteenth century was too wise, too superficially sophisticated, to accept any such playfully sincere oddities. It wished its exoticism flavored with learning; and, if it was to use new and strange and untried architectural styles as sources for its eclecticism, it must do it precisely, accurately, and from the best sources.

For all these reasons, the architect's attitude toward design inevitably changed. His library came to replace his imagination. If he needed a certain general type of door, it was convenient to be able to refer to a definite plate

in a definite book and introduce into the new building the details he found
in the source; for, the argument was, these old details had been proved good
by the approbation of generations and must therefore be good still. Taste
and authority necessarily became the criteria of beauty, and architecture too
frequently took on the aspect of a masked ball—nineteenth-century people
enjoying themselves in exquisitely chosen historical settings.

But there was another side to nineteenth-century architecture. Creativeness was forced upon the architects. No dilettantism, however discriminat-
ing, could ever completely hide three great forces—the tradition of creative
design, the development of scientific engineering, and the thronging demands
for new kinds of building. The individual architects might bow to current
fashions in detail, but more than ever before they had a bedrock of sound
traditional training. The development of architectural education was a very
important side of nineteenth-century educational idealism, and in general
professional education in architecture followed the lead set in France by the
national school of fine arts, the famous École des Beaux Arts. From the time
of Napoleon down, this school, the revived remains of the old Royal
Academy, had been constantly increasing in effectiveness; yet it had always
preserved the essential sanity of the old Louis XIV ideals. It taught its
pupils, above all else, to plan—to arrange the parts of a building with simple
directness, and to arrange them in such a way as to secure always the most
beautiful, most formally ordered succession of interior spaces. It emphasized
logic as the supreme quality, and interpreted logic not in the modern terms
of any absolute following out of functional and structural needs, but symbolically as referring to basic relationships in buildings founded on common
sense, directness, emphasis of the most important elements, and expression
of purpose.

The Opéra in Paris, by Charles Garnier, is an example of the results of
this thinking. He conceived the building essentially as of three parts—the
stage and stage services, the auditorium proper, and the vestibules and stairs
of approach. Each of these three units was then developed with the greatest
richness possible, but always in such a way as to accent its relationship to
the other two. The great stage house towers over the whole, and the court
behind it is flanked by wings containing the dressing rooms and other
necessary minor elements. The auditorium roof rises as a metal dome, buttressed against the front of the stage house and surrounded by the lower
mass of the lavish foyer, stair, and entrance elements. To obtain this effect
Garnier had to raise the metal roof over the auditorium to a height far above
the actual ceiling. The logic is one of expression only; it is a kind of architec-

tural rhetoric. Yet the essential elements become obvious to every observer; there is a magnificent clarity in the general appearance, both outside and in, despite the oversumptuous detail. This characteristic monument reveals the spirit that underlies all of the best nineteenth-century architecture of France; and, since France attained a greater precision in the expression of this logic than any other country, it was only natural that architects elsewhere should imitate the approach. For a half century Paris was the Mecca of architectural students, and the École des Beaux Arts the ideal on which new architectural schools all over the world were gradually formed.

This insistence on open and logical planning and on the clarity of basic expression was vitally necessary to the solution of new architectural problems. Many of the earlier romantic builders, in their search for appealing effect, had woefully neglected plan, had produced buildings that were complicated, inconvenient, often dark and labyrinthine. The new careful study of monumental planning destroyed at once the old tendency toward superficiality and made possible a whole series of great public buildings, like railroad stations and auditoria, admirably suited to the swift movements of crowds of people. Architecture became a matter of disciplined study of plan relationships; even the symmetry usually required in the school projects was a necessary discipline in teaching the young architect to think in large terms.

The development of scientific engineering during the nineteenth century had a profound effect upon all architecture. The discovery of the structural possibilities of iron and steel, and later of reinforced concrete, not only facilitated the building of enormous bridges—the mere existence of such a monument as the Brooklyn Bridge was an impressive lesson in the beauty of forms of great scale based on engineering design—but also set architecture suddenly free from the old hampering limitations of traditional masonry and wood construction. With steel, tremendous spans could be roofed simply with trusses or great girders. Concentrated weights of unprecedented size could be easily carried on small supports; unwonted lightness and delicacy of structural form and widths of unencumbered, sheltered open space became suddenly possible. Paxton's Crystal Palace of 1851, borrowing from conservatory construction the idea of combining light frames with large glass areas, introduced in its conjunction of metal and glass a new epoch in architecture; in Paris, the metal and glass of the great market, the Halles Centrales, by Baltard, was an early example of an attempt to find logical architectural forms for the new construction; and the large steel-arched train sheds of many nineteenth-century railroad stations were.

as expressive architectural form, magnificent, although the difficulties of ventilation have gradually rendered them obsolete and frequently gave reason for their destruction. Little by little the disadvantages of the old single train shed became increasingly apparent. The eddying coal smoke left within it a sulphurous smell that constantly grew from year to year. Then, new methods of steel design and reinforced concrete construction made possible the creation of simple platform covers, sloping up on either side to an opening over the center of each track, through which the engine smoke was easily discharged. Such a system was infinitely less costly than the old great sheds, and had the same advantage of giving perfectly protected shelter. The ventilation problem was readily solved, so that the old type of shed went out of use in spite of its formal beauty. Later still, the electrification of many railroads removed the smoke nuisance altogether, so that the designer today has almost complete freedom.

It was metal construction, of course, and another engineering development—the elevator,—joined to the ever-increasing land values of urban centers, particularly in America, which made the high building possible. Beyond heights of twelve stories or more, the wall thickness at the bottom of the building necessary to carry merely the crushing weight of the wall itself became excessive and the whole construction overexpensive and wasteful. Rolled-iron floor beams came into use gradually from the middle of the nineteenth century on, and the floors themselves were made of brick or hollow-tile arches, and later of reinforced concrete. Interior supports were of cast-iron or steel, but it was only the discovery that wall weights could be carried on the metal frame just as simply as the floors themselves which made the modern skyscraper a reality. In this type of construction, all of the weight of the building is carried on steel. The walls become mere screens between and around the steel members, to keep out the weather. They need be no thicker, therefore, than the walls of a two-story building, even when built of old traditional materials like brick, for they are supported at each floor by horizontal beams. A series of disastrous fires proved that the earlier hopes of unprotected steel or iron producing fireproof buildings were unfounded, and made it necessary to surround all of the steel, both in columns and beams, with a layer of masonry, as fireproofing; and this in turn made it impossible to design steel buildings with the extreme and almost fairylike lightness of form which the metal alone would have allowed. Yet the new type of construction which engineering had ushered in was so fundamentally different from anything that had gone before that it made eventual architectural design of an entirely new type inevitable.

The pressing new problems which the nineteenth-century industrial world gave to the architect were themselves a superb impetus toward creative design. And what problems they were! The railroad stations have already been mentioned. The new developments of national power and the increasing governmental complexity which resulted from commercial expansion made new demands on the designers of government buildings—post offices, customs houses, vast administrative centers. Congestion in cities, coupled with universal education, necessitated great school buildings, full of the most interesting architectural problems in the distribution of people, the arrangement of classrooms, the furnishing of adequate light and air. The apartment house itself offered a new field for creative design, and in Paris at least achieved from early in the century distinctive and stimulating solutions. Even the factories which were rising so swiftly all over the Western world, usually without benefit of architect, offered endless opportunities for creative architectural thought in the integration of their complex functions.

Above all, there was the city itself, this strange new growing organism of slum and palace, of amusement building, store, and factory, this crowding together of great masses of people dependent on mechanized transportation and municipal services. The old Baroque capital cities, fine as their vistas sometimes were, were ill suited to the new strains placed upon them. As a mere matter of self-preservation they *had* to change. Everywhere in Europe the authorities struggled with the problem, and fortunately in many cases saw that the question was primarily a matter of planning, and actually perhaps the world's most exciting architectural opportunity. The science and the art of city planning were born. Under Napoleon III Paris was made over and a whole new traffic system developed, by the piercing of great avenues and boulevards through its congested center. In Vienna the Ring-Strasse took the place of the old fortifications, and brought air and light and green into the middle of the vast agglomeration. That beauty and magnificence which for so many decades have made Paris and Vienna centers of tourist attraction are quite as much due to the vision of nineteenth-century city planners, to the daring of Napoleon III and Baron Haussmann, as they are to the munificence of Louis XIV and the Baroque emperors of Vienna.

City planning was still in its infancy, still superficial, seeing its problems as mainly those of communication, not yet realizing that communication itself is but a means. It still failed to understand the manifold bases of city deterioration and slum development; but it did perceive that the city was an organism and could be planned, it did appreciate and often magnificently expressed the conception that the city itself could be a work of art.

It is impossible to do much more than summarize the actual achievements of nineteenth-century eclecticism. The cities we live in are still largely of nineteenth century creation. The buildings we see every day are, many of them, due to the eclectic movement. And this movement had a sort of international character, which well expressed the growing internationalism in trade, commerce, and culture. It is one of the nineteenth century paradoxes that the same century which saw the advent of modern imperialism and nationalism, forces which still cast their sinister shadow over so much modern living, saw also the beginnings of an intellectual internationalism that found its expression not only in wide travel by millions of people, but also in the general parallelism of cultural movements in all parts of the civilized world.

Yet national taste differences in architecture continued to find an outlet. German eclecticism had its own special flavor, based largely on the persistence of certain ideals taken from the earlier Classic Revival of Schinkel, and on a later inspiration from the monuments of the German Baroque or even the earlier Germanic Renaissance. The nationalism of the empire of Wilhelm II and of the Hapsburgs in Vienna was especially influenced by the later of these phases. This Germanic eclecticism produced such striking monuments as the Leipzig City Hall, in lavish German Renaissance; the new parts of the Hofburg Palace in Vienna, inspired by the earlier work of Fischer von Erlach; the University and the Imperial Palace built in Strasbourg while it was a German city, rather vulgar and eccentric pieces of eclectic Baroque;—and it gave to Berlin much of its pre-war appearance, climaxed in the rather blouzy grandeur of the Cathedral and the old Parliament building. The other, sounder, tradition of a rather restrained classicism is especially noteworthy in the works of Gottfried Semper, such as the Theater and Opera House in Dresden; the Parliament building in Vienna, by the Dane Hansen, a superb piece of modified Greek Revival; and much of the nineteenth-century work in Munich, like the National Library, based on Italian Renaissance and the great classic basilicas. Schinkel had been one of the most original and creative forces in early-nineteenth-century continental architecture, and German design in the nineteenth century seemed always best when it followed most closely in his footsteps.

England, too, found a double inspiration for its eclecticism—in the rather Baroque classicism of Inigo Jones and of Wren on the one hand, and the charming informality of the Late Gothic and Early Renaissance of Tudor and Jacobean times on the other. The first gave rise to a tremendous amount of building in a rather uninspired official classic, such as the government buildings in Whitehall, London. Its more Baroque elements were worked over with greater and greater extravagance in a great deal of nineteenth-century commercial building, until in many of those which line the chief commercial streets of London or Manchester or Leeds the architects' aim would seem almost to have been that of covering every possible square inch of wall with column, entablature, garland, or broken pediment; and that controlling feeling of serene composition, which is the essential quality of all good classic work and even of the best Baroque, was lost entirely in the search for novel ways of using classic elements. Along with this new and uneasy classicism went a new sentimental Gothicism, which aped the forms and forgot the spirit of medieval architecture, and the combined impact of the two forces destroyed the last vestiges of Classic Revival harmony in most of the English cities. Typical was the fate of Regent Street in London, where the old, quiet, and uniform façades that Nash had designed for the new avenue yielded little by little to a carnival of heavy and misplaced Baroque, punctuated by the absurd imitation half-timber of the Liberty stores.

The other inspiration in England was much more creative in its effects. It was related to a new and important movement toward creative craftsmanship, of which William Morris was the most famous exponent. The architects under its influence, like Norman Shaw and Philip Webb, and the decorators, like Eastlake, sought in their work more than anything else to express their delight in lovely materials logically used and if possible handmade. The so-called "Queen Anne" style—the name of which is a mystery, for it had nothing in common with the actual work done under Queen Anne's reign, except perhaps a love of brickwork—gained whatever validity it had from this delight in materials and their use, coupled with a complete freedom in planning. It was a sort of wistful protest movement against the machine-made and the routine, and doomed by its hesitant attitude—half a nostalgic turning back to the past, half an attempt to anticipate the future. Yet in its best work it was the most creative element in the English architecture of the time. Even its eccentricities had behind them a definite creative aim; and in its best examples, like some of the long, rambling brick houses of Shaw, it showed a new kind of freedom. The climax of the movement came perhaps in the earlier houses of Sir Edwin Lutyens, in which the whimsicalities of the Queen Anne had completely disappeared, and, instead, there was merely the interest of varied forms resulting from free planning and expressed in beautiful materials exquisitely used. It is all recognizably English, distantly based on Tudor and Jacobean forms. It is one of the most appealing outgrowths of nineteenth-century eclecticism. The same quality distinguishes much of the church work of the period, where Gothic forms were used with a new kind of creative ingenuity and abandon, and archaeology became secondary to design. Little by little, as the needs of the modern church were realized, much of the ornament dropped away, until the church architects of the early twentieth century were able to produce church structures which in general form and sometimes in structure were still within the Gothic tradition, but in which every last trace of archaeological detail had vanished.

It was in France that the eclecticism of the nineteenth century attained its most triumphant heights, for it was in France that the old traditions and the new logic of the École des Beaux Arts combined to prevent the greatest excesses of the movement. The movement began brilliantly with the creation of the Nouveau Louvre by Napoleon III—a vast construction which cleared out the area between the Louvre and the Tuileries, made it one vast open space, and thus brought to a conclusion the scheme begun over three centuries earlier by Francis I. Visconti and Lefuel, the architects, rose to this magnificent opportunity and produced a design which, for all its over-lavish ornament, had the requisite dignity and great scale that the conditions demanded. Areas of simple wall with the most delicate and refined ornamentation gave contrast to the high-roofed corner pavilions and the monumental arched gateways which allowed the traffic of Paris to pass through the newly opened squares. The joining of the old and the new work was accomplished with the greatest skill; and, though the very exuberance of the Napoleonic court led to occasional extravagances in decorative sculpture and carved ornament, the general effect was imposing and fitted admirably into the new Paris of the great boulevards and avenues, leading from impressive square to impressive square, which Napoleon and Baron Haussmann had conceived.

The burning of the Tuileries during the Commune, and the final destruction of the ruins, threw open the new court to the Tuileries Gardens and the great vista up to the Arc de l'Étoile; and the tying of all this together with the rest of Paris, by new bridges, newly decorated quays, and the Avenue de l'Opéra, made a city center which was unique in its designed grandeur.

The new avenues themselves created endless opportunity for the exuberant classicism which France loved. Fountains, like the great fountain of St.

Michel by Davioud, decorated the places where streets met. New *mairies,* one for each *arrondissement,* or ward, in Paris, were built, usually with the refined classic detail and the high mansard roofs of slate made popular by the Nouveau Louvre. The old City Hall, burned and destroyed during the Commune, was rebuilt with new splendor and with a majestic plan of monumental corridors, great stairs, and a luxurious suite of official reception rooms which represented almost the best in the new kind of planning. It is characteristic of the period, and of the influence which the École des Beaux Arts had, that in these buildings mural painting and sculptural decoration were conceived of as having an importance almost as great as that of the architecture itself; and the delicate flat mural decorations of Puvis de Chavannes gave a new validity and a new direction to much nineteenth-century painting.

And, if Paris was made over, so were many of the French provincial cities—Lyons, Orléans, Tours, Marseilles;—and the pleasant tree-shaded boulevards, with their attractive sidewalk cafés, the little squares above which rise the dignified classic town halls which characterize so many of the cities of France, owe much of their present charm not only to the French way of living but also to the creative ability of these nineteenth-century eclectic architects. Typical monuments are the *Hôtel de Ville* of Tours and the railroad station there, by Laloux, and the great fountain of Longchamps in Marseilles, by Espérandieu.

But the eclecticism of nineteenth-century France did not limit itself to classic models. The domestic architecture outside of the great cities was frequently inordinately romantic, attempting to use medieval and Early Renaissance influence in the same creative way that the more classic and later Renaissance was used by the architects of the great official buildings. In general, this work failed of the success which the official buildings achieved; for that type of carefully studied, formalized planning which so befits great constructions, when used by many people, is frequently but a poor aid in laying out a house for an ordinary family. In many of these houses there seems to be an obvious and unpleasant conflict between the formalism of the plan and the eccentricity of the detail. The desire to be eclectically original led too often only to absurdities. In England, eclecticism had flowered most successfully in house design, but the new eclectic architecture in France was at its worst in domestic architecture.

The French were more successful with their churches. The Gothic Revival buildings, happy as some of them had been, had revealed all too clearly the huge expense which any Gothic work in modern times necessarily entails.

They had seemed to show, too, that Gothic was in a sense a completed style in which further advance was impossible. The French architects turned, therefore, to earlier styles—to the Byzantine and the Romanesque—for inspiration, finding there something of the ritualistic "Christian" character for which they were looking, as well as an opportunity for almost endless variation. Especially successful were a number of buildings designed in a modified version of the domed Romanesque of Aquitania, with borrowings from other Romanesque styles, especially that of Auvergne. This style seemed to lend itself to little churches as well as big ones, and was handled with the greatest skill by numerous architects. One of the best of the smaller examples is St. Pierre de Montrouge in Paris, by Vaudremer. The larger types are well shown in Tours in the basilica of St. Martin by Laloux, especially interesting in the free way in which the Romanesque ornament is used and the large simplicity of the interior, with its beautiful polychromed open-timber roof. In Paris, the church of Sacré Coeur, by Abadie and Magne, is another characteristic monument of the style, and its white domes gleaming on the heights of Montparnasse, which so frequently seem to float in the air above the mist and smoke of the lower town, are among the most distinctive features of the contemporary Paris skyline.

The influence of French work extended far and wide. In Bucharest, as in Rio de Janeiro and Buenos Aires, tree-lined avenues and rich classic sculptures imitated the boulevards and public buildings of Paris, as the young architects from Rumania or South America flocked to the Paris school and, after spending sometimes six or seven years in its ateliers, returned to their native countries to construct, as far as possible, an environment which would recall to them the nostalgic fascination of their Paris years and perhaps help to make in those far lands some such life of polish and tolerance and gracious art a possibility. "All good Americans when they die go to Paris," said a nineteenth-century aphorism. The very idea of that city had entered into the nineteenth-century mind as a kind of second and earthly Heaven, and in this vision the trees and buildings of the city played, albeit unconsciously, quite as large a part as the sidewalk cafés and the wines and the demoiselles.

The United States, too, fell under the sway of the enchanting, perhaps deceptive, spectacle of French eclecticism. Eclecticism itself had come into the country much earlier than the influence of the Paris school, for eclecticism was in a sense a normal expression of the young nation growing so rapidly in wealth, spreading out, settling cities in places where tradition had never been born. As we have seen, Davis had been eclectic, and Gilman had written a persuasive argument in favor of eclecticism before the middle of the century; but it took the Civil War and the emerging commercial and industrial expansion which succeeded it to put a final quietus on the old Classic Revival tradition, to tear up its last roots, as it were, so that the whole field lay fallow for new fashions. And the new fashions came in a multitude. Essentially they were European fashions. The Philadelphia Centennial Exposition of 1876 brought to hundreds of thousands of Americans a sudden consciousness of the vitality of European art. Disconnected as they were from earlier or rooted preferences in building, filled many of them with a real longing for beauty, they could do nothing but follow, willing slaves to the vision of beauty they found in the European exhibits, and still more, as travel became common, to the actual enchantment they found in European towns. There was building going on in America the like of which had not been seen. Villages were being founded, cities were growing and spreading out. Everywhere there was the sound of the hammer and the saw. New floods of immigrants landed weekly, new factories arose and their employees had to be housed. So the cities and towns grew, under frightful pressure for speed and for cheapness—formless, sprawling, incoherent, often shoddy as well. A false and superficial gimcrack ornament was applied to shacks in a frenzied effort to make them less shacklike. People brought up in communities like these could not but find in foreign architecture an amenity, a quietness, a sense of real beauty which they admired and sought to imitate. Then began the swarming of American architectural students to Paris, or if not to Paris to Italy and the "Grand Tour"—students who sketched and photographed assiduously and came back with their heads filled with an intoxicating confusion of Gothic spire and classic colonnade, of dome and pediment, of Tudor village or tree-lined boulevard, all gilded by the reminiscent excitement of carefree student life. It was this vision which they sought to incarnate in the buildings they designed.

The first of the important Americans to study in the Paris school was Richard Morris Hunt; and on his return, just prior to the Civil War, he began a series of buildings which were a new delight to his entranced clients. He joined a small circle of men, many of them foreign-born and trained in foreign schools, like Detlef Lienau, who were trying to preserve through the chaotic atmosphere of rush and greed some of the decencies of the architectural profession and to design buildings which had effective composition and appropriate though derivative detail. Hunt's houses, like the Vanderbilt house on Fifth Avenue, or Biltmore in North Carolina, or any number of Newport palaces, inevitably set the fashion for the great houses of wealthy industrialists. They were luxurious; they were costly and they showed it; they were magnificent and yet at the same time basically well composed; they gave their owners the sense of culture as well as furnishing a badge, as it were, of success. These vast structures are the true monuments of the so-called "Gilded Age," and their marble floors, their Baroque carving, their ranked columns, their bronze hand-railings and marble stairs, and their Louis XV salons were immensely important in setting the taste not only of the wealthy who could afford them, but of all of those who aped the ways of their betters and sought thus to step on the first rungs of the ladder of social success.

Other eclectic elements entered at this time also, especially the Romanesque influence brought in by Henry Hobson Richardson and first achieving tremendous popularity in his Trinity Church in Boston. Richardson of course was much more than an eclectic, as were all the greatest architects of the time both in America and abroad. He had a superb sense of rather monumental composition, an uncommon sensitiveness to materials, and a creative imagination in the way to use them. His stone detailing especially was unusually lovely, and it is not strange that his buildings were imitated far and wide. He was an independent planner as well, continually feeling for greater and greater originality. Perhaps his most inventive work was in his summer houses, in which for the first time there appeared that simple use of broad and spreading roofs, of shingled walls allowed to weather silver gray, of wide piazzas, of large low-ceiled rooms which came in the following decades to be the distinguishing marks of almost all the best American country work. But it was not these for which he was most admired. It is one of the characteristics of eclectic fashions that it is usually the nonessential details and not the essential thinking which give rise to them, so that "Richardsonian" came in the popular mind to mean, not sensitiveness to material, nor independence of design, but rather the indefinite repetition of low, wide arches, intricate Byzantinelike ornament, or dark and somber colors. Richardson himself climaxed his career with a great warehouse for Marshall Field in Chicago, an imposing business building that was one of the inspirations of Louis Sullivan and so of great importance in the development of a new architecture. But Richardson's followers dragged his influence down to the level of the most stupid and false imitative Romanesque forms, so that there is hardly a town in America from the Atlantic to the Pacific which does not possess some elephantine structure of dark brown stone, sullen and forbidding and badly planned, as a monument to eclectic medievalism.

But it was the classic vein in eclecticism which was bound in the long run to win out. Perhaps the strong early basis of classic Colonial and Classic Revival had something to do with it. Certainly whatever tradition the eastern part of the country had was classic in tone. Even the lovely Gothic Revival of the best of the work of Upjohn and Renwick and Lafever had been, seemingly, but a temporary rash on the body of American architecture; so that, superficially at least, the nation was prepared for classic form. "Italian villas" of the English type had become a commonplace in American suburbs in the 1850's and 1860's, and the only style of any vitality which had succeeded them was a kind of mansard fashion which owed its basis also to originally classic inspiration. Thus the classic work of Hunt and his fol-

113. TWO CHARACTERISTIC AMERICAN "ITALIAN VILLAS," GEORGETOWN, D. C. Vaux, architect. (Vaux: *Villas and Cottages.*)

lowers found a ready acceptance; and, when McKim in the 1880's designed the beautiful simple walls of the Boston Public Library and its delightful refined Florentine courtyard, the public welcomed it immediately. Here was a kind of architecture which somehow they could understand; and the building itself, perhaps the first important public monument of the new classic eclecticism, was of such a high level in design that it effectually silenced any criticism.

More and more, from the 1880's onward, Americans turned to classic forms in public building design, and the final high-water mark of popular approval was reached in the Chicago World's Fair of 1893. There, working on a superb general plan and toward an ideal already set in advance, numbers of architects from all over the country accepted the limitations of a uniform cornice line and a uniform material and color, to produce a group of buildings which were an extraordinary dream world somehow come true. Of course it was not real architecture in the strict sense of the term; the buildings were great sheds, the "architecture" merely a decorative frosting around their walls. But the decorative frosting was so harmonious from building to building, so effective because of its frank acceptance of unreality, that the consequences were sure to be tremendous. The Fair was seen by millions; from North and South, from East and West, they came flocking, to wonder and admire. Here for the first time most of these people saw a large group of buildings designed in unison and placed in accordance with a brilliant general plan intended to enhance the whole effect. Here they saw sculpture and painting combined with buildings, and a luxury of pleasing light-and-shade variation, which intoxicated them. The white buildings standing along the edges of the lagoon, with the colonnade at the end and the blue horizon of Lake Michigan beyond, formed a picture unforgettable, and it fixed the taste of a people for a generation. As usual, they returned to their homes ignorant that the real reason for their pleasure was to be found in the harmony of the general plan, and thinking rather, as people usually do, of the superficial elements of design—of columns and pediments, entablatures and arches. In these, they thought, lay the secret of the beauty they had seen; and so they decided, almost unconsciously, as a mass, to demand columns and pediments, arches and entablatures, in all future buildings, whether they were appropriate or not. The millionaire's palace and the Chicago World's Fair together made American classicism irresistible.

The classic eclecticism of the United States was different from that of England or Germany or France. Perhaps more than any other nation, the United States was in a position to realize the advantages of the French school training, its insistence on *logique,* system, and great scale, and yet to criticize the particular kind of Baroque with which the French had usually expressed that ideal. The American taste was for a classic quieter, more dignified; and there were few American sculptors who could be relied on to give that sense of surface richness which was so much a part of French design. Once the lesson of planning had been learned—and it was well learned—American architects tended more and more to turn for classic inspiration, not to the French styles, but to the severer Renaissance of Rome, or further back still to the great monuments of ancient Rome and the refined detail of ancient Greece. The architectural firm of McKim, Mead and White came especially to stand for this later, more restrained development; and the Renaissance of the Villard houses or the University Club, in New York, and the completely eclectic classic of the Columbia Library, which borrows and integrates details from so many sources, show the quality they were seeking and so frequently achieved. Other architects tended more to richer and rather flamboyant styles. Carrère and Hastings, in the New York Public Library, produced a design which was in planning and general mass an admirable example of French *logique* and French expressiveness, but detailed it in a manner in which French exuberance and a kind of harsh, cold, intellectual restraint are rather ill at ease together. Later architects seem to have turned more and more to the ancient sources, and as in some of the work of John Russell Pope, like the Scottish Rite Temple in Washington or the Richmond, Virginia, railroad station, composed almost all the possible variations on that theme. Perhaps the finest, the most sincere, the

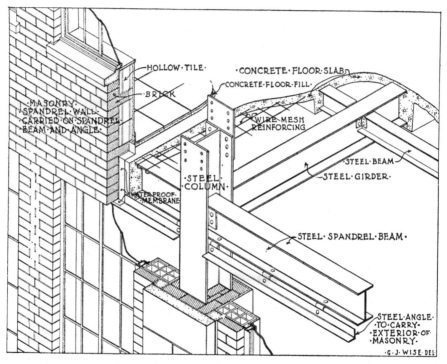

114. CUTAWAY DIAGRAM SHOWING THE CONSTRUCTIONAL ELEMENTS OF A TYPICAL STEEL SKELETON-FRAMED STRUCTURE. (Drawn by G. J. Wise.)

most lovingly detailed of all of these eclectic works based on the ancient styles is the Lincoln Memorial in Washington, by Henry Bacon.

The results of the movement in commercial buildings were less happy. The whole form and spirit of a great office building or a department store is so foreign to Renaissance or ancient conceptions that any application of classic detail could only be conceived as the merest surface frosting; and, being surface frosting, it was treated with less and less conviction. The powerful scale of great Roman arches in steel-supported walls twelve inches thick was an obvious anomaly, and to surround steel frame members with the forms of the Doric or the Ionic or the Corinthian order seemed hardly less absurd. The wonder is that out of this absurdity so many buildings which were at least passable in composition were produced. From a distance, many American city buildings look alike. The basic rhythms of their windows and their general forms are responsible for that, and it becomes wholly unimportant of what nature the frosting is. It was a foolish fashion, this surrounding of steel cages with all the pomp and majesty of classic colonnades, or the ringing of the top stories with a rich Baroque crown to form a sort of capital to the building; and it is therefore understandable why some of the first appearances of what we may call the "new" architecture arose in connection with office-building design.

But the problem of such vast buildings as railroad stations was different. Here the new sense of open planning could find congenial expression indeed, and there is magnificent impressiveness in the large open concourses and huge waiting rooms of many of our stations, however banal their ornament. This amplitude, this sense of direct planning, this desire to build practical necessities into a civic monument were all as much a part of the nineteenth-century movement as was the derivative detail; and we today can design new stations in new ways, using an architecture which arises naturally from our new materials and our new needs, with the necessary grandeur of scale, the desirable directness and simplicity, largely because of the work our eclectic predecessors have accomplished.

In house design something of the same double process is clear—enormous improvement in planning, and refined and derivative eclecticism in detail. The ordinary American middle-class house of the beginning of the twentieth century was better planned, better equipped, more comfortable than the similar house of almost any other country. Many of the elements, such as overformality, lack of attention to orientation, and inconvenience of relationship, which were common occurrences in European houses and gave rise to much of the protest leading to the modern architectural revolution, were absent in this country. That is why so much of our domestic work has remained conservative. The Colonial styles furnished the most fruitful source for emulation, and Colonial of all kinds was for twenty years the rage. Second to it came the influence of English domestic architecture; false half-timber sprouted on the walls, and plans were artificially complicated to create gables and rambling wings. Later still there was a Spanish flurry, especially strong in California and the Southwest; and so-called French Provincial types made their appearance. In general, the trend in the first portion of the twentieth century seemed to be toward a more and more superficial attitude about these borrowed styles, toward more and more rapid changes in popular fashion, until the problem of house design became so complex that laymen seized upon labels as almost the only guide in the whole problem, and came to demand houses which could be called "Colonial," or "English," or "French Provincial," or something else equally specific. The results of this were especially deplorable in speculative houses, where again and again the desire to produce a salable object led to insistence on meaningless and superficial elements, to the complete destruction of sensible planning and sound, economical building.

Thus, little by little, eclecticism was working out its own ruin, showing its own weaknesses, revealing only too clearly that borrowed clothes are a poor covering. The styles had run their course, and even in America the time for protest and rebellion in architecture was ripe.

BOOK VIII

The Architecture of Today

Chapter 32

THE REVOLT AGAINST ECLECTICISM

IF it had not been doomed by its own derivative nature, eclecticism would have died eventually because of changes in the world. The organization of industry, which had seemed so firmly based during the third quarter of the nineteenth century, was really changing profoundly throughout the period, sensitive to every new invention, every new discovery in the fields of physical science and psychology. The development of advertising and pressure selling produced almost as radical modifications in living as did the development of that kind of mass production which was necessary to supply the new needs. Population was growing amazingly; perhaps future generations will find that the most significant nineteenth-century phenomenon was not so much the development of industry as it was the extraordinary increase in the world's population. Nevertheless, by the beginning of the twentieth century the fallacies inherent in the Malthus theory had begun to be realized. The curve of population increase was declining almost as rapidly as it had climbed a century earlier. Both voluntary birth control and other little understood physiological and psychological factors were working toward a stationary population as the world filled up. In some countries the problem posed by the twentieth century was not to find living area for rapidly increasing masses, but rather to find ways in which the present population level could be maintained. Steam was yielding in many industries to electricity; the old centralization of industry required by the direct steam drive of manufacturing machines was no longer necessary. The force that led to the mushroom growth of manufacturing towns was thus no longer effective.

And the strains in human relationships which nineteenth-century industry had set up were slowly and tentatively working out new patterns of living. Protests against the unlimited exploitation of workers appeared early, and there was a tremendous excitement in early attempts to set up various types of socialist or communal developments grouped around industrial and agricultural centers. Robert Owen in England, and later in America at New Harmony, Indiana, and Fourier and his followers, in France, were patterning out types of Utopian community which they felt the new industry made possible; these were valuable not for their practical results, since without exception all the communities established in accordance with Owen and Fourier doctrines passed away, but because they were the first attempts to make the greatly increased productivity engendered by industrial manufacture and agricultural science available and useful to the entire community and not only to capitalist owners.

A View and Plan of the Agricultural and Manufacturing Villages of *Unity* and *Mutual Co-operation.*

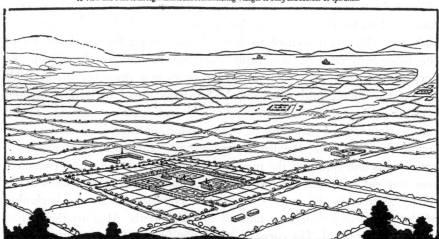

115. ROBERT OWEN'S SCHEME FOR A UTOPIAN COMMUNITY; A BIRD'S-EYE VIEW. (From a broadside of 1817, courtesy of the Seligman Library, Columbia University.)

Welfare paternalism also became an accepted type of industrial thinking; and the founding of many early American industrial communities, such as Lowell, gave evidence of the early appreciation that the welfare of workers and the well-being of industry went somehow hand in hand. But this early paternalism, hopeful as it was, failed under the stresses of too rapid development and the vastly augmented labor market produced by the increased population and the emigration of large numbers of people from country to city, and from old countries to new.

All of these movements meant planning—planning for communities, planning which should take into account architectural amenity as well as practical utility;—and every single example of these planned communities, like the ample and attractive industrial housing built in the 1830's and early 1840's in numerous American centers, was a gage thrown in the face of the nineteenth-century *laissez-faire* doctrines which in architecture had expressed themselves in eclecticism.

But none of these challenges succeeded. Their failure was the tragic result of an incapacity to forecast with sufficient reality the terrific undermining forces of nineteenth-century life—exploitation, real-estate speculation, the impersonal drive for corporate profits, and just plain greed. The planned community gave way to the slum, the socialist center to the chaotic city generated in the struggles of cross-purpose and conflicting opinions, religious, economic, social. It almost seemed as though every single answer made to a pressing question, however well it solved the problem it sought to attack, raised other, more urgent problems. Every solution of a city traffic problem increased congestion rather than lessened it, by giving greater means for people to throng to the city center. Steel and the elevator in creating the skyscraper established a building the economy of which was gained at the expense of overcrowded land, and the light and view of its upper stories were paid for by dark and canyonlike streets where the office lights burned all day long even through the summer. Similarly, every invention to make culture available to everyone seemed often to lead to the vulgarization of that culture itself. The aim to "give the people what they want" led on the part of many to a pandering to the lowest, most primitive, most socially undesirable traits of the population. Yellow journalism and crime magazines are but two examples. The mechanical diffusion of culture—by means of the printing press, cheap paper, the movies, and even the radio—and the importance of advertising as the main support of many of these activities not only colored the whole production, but also tended inevitably toward standardization and centralization of culture.

So commerce itself, spreading over the world, had only as a by-product the distribution of goods; its principal aim was the accumulation of profits; and, unavoidably, nationalistic rivalries grew up, as the "civilized" nations strove for the privilege of selling their goods to those more "primitive." Whatever the immediate cause of the World War of 1914, behind it lay a long history of commercial and financial rivalry; and in the long years of that terrible strife the old balance of the world was lost. That cataclysm, in a sense, was a blind alley which showed the utter falseness, the frightful instability, the sordid background of human greed which weakened much nineteenth-century culture.

Recent movements in architecture had this as their framework. All modern architecture, to a degree, is a protest against the nineteenth-century world entire, and an attempt to find creative expression for a new vision. In a similar way, all the old protest movements—the socialisms and communal communities which strove and failed—had about them some radical architectural vision. Owen's conception of a series of small industrial centers,

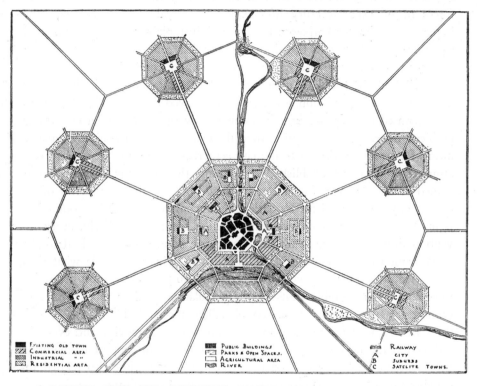

116. GARDEN CITY AND SATELLITE COMMUNITIES, AS CONCEIVED BY SIR RAYMOND UNWIN. (Drawing, courtesy of Sir Raymond Unwin.)

surrounded by carefully worked agricultural land, with industry and agriculture kept in perfect balance, is close to the more recent conception of the garden city; and the planning of some of the paternalistic industrial communities, such as the original Lowell, foreshadowed many of the aims and some of the forms of recent city planning, such as standardization of units with variation of effect, close relationship of work places and living places, and an appreciation of the necessity of parked open spaces.

Architecturally, too, there had been almost continuous protests against the sterility of the eclectic ideal. Every architectural rationalist, from the

BEVERLY FARMS, A SUMMER COTTAGE. H. H. Richardson, architect.

SAN FRANCISCO, PUBLIC LIBRARY. George W. Kilham, architect.

CHICAGO, MARSHALL FIELD BUILDING; BEGINNING OF A NEW STYLE. H. H. Richardson, architect. (Courtesy Prof. H.-R. Hitchcock Jr.)

WASHINGTON, LINCOLN MEMORIAL. Henry Bacon, architect.

Plate 81

MANCHESTER, N. H., EARLY FACTORY HOUSING; DIG-
NITY AND AMPLE SIZE. (John Coolidge.)

SOMERSWORTH, N. H., EARLY FACTORY HOUSING GROUP; PLEAS-
ANT SPACES AND FORMAL PLANNING. (John Coolidge.)

DOWNTOWN SECTION, NEW YORK, AIR VIEW; UTTER CONFUSION IN
THE TYPICAL 20th-CENTURY CITY. (McLaughlin Air Service.)

Plate 82

PARIS, NATIONAL LIBRARY, READING ROOM; CREATIVE USE OF IRON, TERRA-COTTA, AND GLASS IN 1850. H. Labrouste, architect.

VIENNA, PROJECT FOR FRANZ JOSEF MUSEUM, VESTIBULE; AN ADVANCED DESIGN AT THE BEGINNING OF THE 20th CENTURY, Otto Wagner, architect.

BUFFALO, GUARANTY BUILDING; THE BEST OF THE EARLY SKYSCRAPERS, AN EPOCH-MAKING WORK AT THE END OF THE 19th CENTURY. Louis Sullivan, architect.

VIENNA, SECESSION GALLERY; NEO-CLASSIC AND ART NOUVEAU IN AN EARLY WORK OF THE NEW STYLE IN AUSTRIA. J. M. Olbrich, architect.

Plate 83

BERLIN, TEMPELHOF HOUSING. Bruno Taut, architect. (Carl Feiss.)

"VILLA SAVOYE," NEAR PARIS. Le Corbusier, architect. (Museum of Modern Art.)

FRANKFURT, MUNICIPAL HOUSING. Ernst May, architect. (Carl Feiss.)

DESSAU, THE BAUHAUS. W. Gropius, architect. (Museum of Modern Art.)

Plate 84

NAPLES, POST OFFICE; INTERIOR. (Both photographs, Museum of Modern Art.)

LINCOLN, NEBRASKA STATE CAPITOL. B. G. Goodhue, architect. (Courtesy Mayers, Murray & Phillip.)

NAPLES, POST OFFICE. Vaccaro and Franzi, architects.

CHEMNITZ, SCHOCKEN STORE. Mendelsohn, architect. (Museum of Modern Art.)

Plate 85

BARCELONA EXPOSITION, 1929, GERMAN BUILDING. Mies van der Rohe, architect.

HILVERSUM TOWN HALL. Dudok, architect. (All photographs, Museum of Modern Art.)

ROTTERDAM, VAN NELLE TOBACCO FACTORY. Brinkman and Van der Vlugt, architects.

BRUNN, TUGENDHAT HOUSE. Mies

Plate 86

CHISWICK PARK STATION, LONDON UNDERGROUND. S. Heaps and Adams, Holden & Pearson, architects. (Museum of Modern Art.)

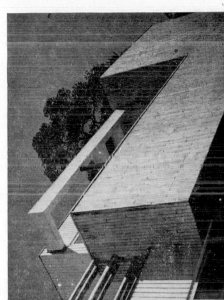

MALMO, RIBERSHUS HOUSING. Persson, Eriksson, Hellcen, and Welin, architects.

ARCHITECT'S OWN HOUSE NEAR HELSINKI; DETAIL. Alvar Aalto, architect. (Museum of Modern Art.)

LONDON, HIGH POINT I, AN APARTMENT HOUSE. Lubetkin and Tecton. architects. (Museum of Modern Art.)

Plate 87

PASADENA, MILLARD HOUSE; PRECAST CON-
CRETE BLOCK. Frank Lloyd Wright, architect.
(Museum of Modern Art.)

RACINE, JOHNSON WAX COMPANY BUILDING;
INTERIOR. F. L. Wright, architect. (Pictures, Inc.)

BEAR RUN, PA., KAUFMAN HOUSE, "FALLING
WATER"; VIEW FROM STREAM. F. L. Wright,
architect.

"FALLING WATER"; ONE END. (Both by John
McAndrew, courtesy Museum of Modern Art.)

Plate 88

eighteenth century Laugier down, had realized the necessity of new life pat terns giving birth to new architectural forms. Even when the social basis of architecture was overlooked, architects began to see that the new avail- ability of metal and glass as a structural material could only be considered a revolutionary architectural force, and that any new architecture must make full use of all the materials which science was preparing, must out of them develop forms based on these new materials and their structural qualities, and not merely try to dress them in the robes of the past. Architectural forms conditioned on iron and steel must necessarily be different from those founded on wood and stone; how, then, could the older styles be taken over for the new materials?

Thus a group of brilliant architects who worked in Paris in the 1840's— Labrouste, Hittorff, Duban, and Duc—strove to develop a fresh, new, and creative architecture which should learn from the past, not forms to imitate, but lessons in structural logic. Their work was called Néo-Grec, because it attempted to fulfill in spirit the honesty, creativeness, and restraint they claimed to find in Greek architecture. The products themselves vary—at times merely erratic, at times brilliant and revolutionary. When Labrouste built the iron, terra-cotta, and glass reading room of the Bibliothèque Na- tionale and the great storage stack behind it, skylighted and with stand- ardized metal supports and grated iron floors, he showed at once both the artistic possibilities of the new materials, logically conceived, and the enor- mous practical advantages of standardization and of the imaginative utili- zation of the new elements. Paxton, in the Crystal Palace in London, at about the same time, achieved the same revolutionary result.

It was Viollet-le-Duc, however, who gave the protest its most compelling form. Filled with a passion for logical analysis and the sense, which he had gained from his study of medieval buildings, that construction must be the basis of design, he set forth in his *Entretiens sur l'architecture* not only a closely reasoned analysis of the architecture of the past from the structural point of view, but also his conviction that iron and glass and baked clay had together inaugurated a new age in architecture, and he illustrated his work with a series of designs he prepared embodying the new materials as he felt they demanded. Viollet-le-Duc's criticism was largely ahead of his time. When he was appointed head of the architectural department of the École des Beaux Arts there was an immediate clamor of dissent, culminating in a students' strike, against such heretical leadership, and his appointment was withdrawn. The *Entretiens* were the course of lectures he had written for the school.

The whole movement of nineteenth-century protest in architecture, like the social protests of Owen and Fourier, was bound to fail. It was confused by the changing conditions of the life around it, puzzled by the contradictions of the nineteenth-century industrial world, largely blind to the social and economic forces which made popular taste what it was; it was too limited in its vision of architecture, too obsessed with pure structural methods. Nevertheless, the reasoning of Viollet-le-Duc lived on. His works were widely published, and the spirit of logical analysis, of daring revolutionary architectural thinking, with which they are filled was to have its reward, its final effectiveness, a half century later.

Another form of protest against eclecticism arose as the result of the Eastlake theories of decorative design and later the William Morris movement to uphold creative craftsmanship. The work of both Eastlake and Morris started out in an enthusiasm for the Gothic, but both men realized that any real truth to material, combined with the creative approach, must produce, in a modern world, work quite different from any that the Middle Ages had developed. In many of the products of Morris and Company, especially their textile and wallpaper designs, a complete freedom of design, generally on a naturalistic basis, was achieved. And such work was not unique. Louis Tiffany in America, in the 1880's, was feeling toward much the same aims in the glass and the metalwork that came from his shops, and many of the early Tiffany silverware patterns, especially, were graceful, free, unusually modern in feeling. They were evidences of a growing search for originality in architecture and the allied arts, a growing conviction that a modern world demanded its own expression—an expression which no past style, no matter how modified or adapted, could ever give.

This feeling reached its summit in the *Art Nouveau* movement which swept over the Western World toward the end of the century. If the reason for its origin is thus clear, the reason for the forms which it took is more obscure. A current penchant for Japanese art had much to do with it; indeed, one of its chief supporters was the Bing firm in Paris, who had achieved success first as dealers in oriental, and especially in Japanese, works of art. The Art Nouveau movement in architecture was frankly a rather negative kind of revolt. Art Nouveau architects knew very well what they did *not* want to be, and the kind of eclectic forms based on past styles which they did *not* want to use; unfortunately they were less clear about what they *did* want to design; and, interesting as some of the results of the movement were, this negative approach was an insuperable barrier to more than a superficial novelty. The craft basis was always present; significantly enough, the American magazine which chiefly upheld the Art Nouveau movement was called *The Craftsman*. There was much emphasis and occasional over-emphasis on daring and novel uses of all sorts of materials—glass, mosaic, the metals, and wood. There was an attempt to express the dynamic quality of nineteenth-century life in dynamic line; the famous whiplash line which became the hallmark of the style in many of its works was developed in an attempt to express the emotional tensions, the rapid unleashing of power, which seemed characteristic of the life of the time. Art Nouveau buildings were frequently overornamented, and in the ornament there was often a clear contradiction between the use of naturalistic forms, almost photographically presented, and queer contortions of swinging curved lines which expressed the dynamism of the period. Yet important results were produced.

The Paris Exposition of 1900 owed whatever quality it had, not to the overlavish semiclassic Baroque ornament with which it somewhat vulgarly abounded, but rather to the occasional vivid bits of Art Nouveau design which here and there crept in. Thus in the Grand Palais des Beaux Arts—which still stands, a monument to the taste of 1900—the exterior, with its rather inelegant and ornate Baroque stone architecture, is ostentatious and dull; but in the interior touch after touch, in the treatment of the metalwork, in the broad sweep of the arched trusses, in the balustrades of the stairs, shows a creative imagination struggling sincerely to find a new and a correct expression for iron and steel as used in the building of the modern world. And in furniture design and minor work much of the Art Nouveau design was more successful. Publicized widely in such magazines as *Moderne Bauformen,* started specifically to popularize the new and creative work, and the English *International Studio,* the style won considerable popularity, as evidenced in the erection of more or less successful Art Nouveau buildings all over the Western world during the first decade of the twentieth century, as well as in the broad distribution of a great deal of well-designed silverware, glassware, and pottery. The best American buildings of Art Nouveau type are the New Amsterdam Theater and the Hotel Belleclaire in New York. In themselves they are perhaps not particularly beautiful buildings, although the interior of the New Amsterdam had fresh qualities of design of great merit. Their importance lies in the fact that they showed a public trend, a public acceptance of buildings in which past precedent had little part. The people who bought Tiffany or Eastlake glass, or the later papers and textiles of William Morris, were coming to realize for the first time in a half century that beauty could be produced which was neither Gothic nor classic, nor Indian nor Chinese.

The Art Nouveau was the first great break in the popular dependence on eclecticism in art.

But more important protests, more fruitful for the future, were under way —protests based not on any mere search for novelty or any mere negative revolt against past forms, but on a true understanding of the tremendous changes in all of life which the nineteenth century had brought. It was as though all of the forces working for change, in economic relationships, in industrial production, in family living itself, were developing in the last twenty years of the nineteenth century at an ever-increasing speed. The "progress," if such it was, gathered speed with an almost frightening acceleration. Increasing power in the labor movement was forcing a shortening of the workday and increasing leisure. Women were flocking into the offices and factories of half the world. The entire foundation of the older patriarchal family was crumbling. Even the authority of religion was being criticized widely, and the church was rapidly losing much of its power, especially over the restless young people. Democracy was creaking under the strain, just at the moment when the new vision of the potential benefits of democracy was arising. Similar changes came apace even into the ideals of individual living. Old ideas of hygiene became suddenly personally important, and a new kind of athleticism developed all over the Western world. As city living increased, so also increased a nostalgic turning to nature and to the sun. People came to demand more and more fresh air, sunlight, greenery; and the more industrial life forced them to work and live indoors the more they clamored for the relief and the relaxation of outdoors. It was perhaps merely a natural reaction against the growing insistence of the regular mechanical rhythms of machinery that compelled mankind in its exhaustion to long for the spontaneous and unpredictable rhythms of nature. But, in any case, the more the machine came to dominate man, the more he turned to a kind of ideal primitivism for recreation.

It was the people who realized something of these new drives who became the real fathers of modern architecture. In Great Britain, Mackintosh went far beyond any mere Art Nouveau eccentricities in the sound structural basis of his revolutionary designs, such as the Glasgow School of Art. In Vienna, Otto Wagner gradually came to feel not only that a modern architecture must develop from the new world, and that its solid foundation must be sound engineering structure and a sound understanding of the quality of twentieth-century life, but also that sooner or later the true twentieth-century architect must become a city planner, must at least think in terms much wider than those of any individual structure. Otto Wagner's own buildings show a slow, gradual, and inevitable growth out of simplified Baroque and classic forms into shapes of continually increasing creative novelty, as he came with greater and greater certainty to express their structural principle. His Vienna Postal Savings Bank, in its handling of the exterior as a pure veneer over the metal frame, in its use of regular steel rhythms as the basis of its design, and especially in its simple, graceful, and delicate interiors, in which the slimness of the steel structure is so beau-

117. DESIGN FOR A PROPOSED UNIVERSITY LIBRARY IN VIENNA. Otto Wagner, architect. (Wagner: *Einige Skizzen, Projekte, und ausgeführte Bauwerke.*)

tifully expressed, anticipates in all of these qualities much of the architectural work of twenty years later in date.

In Holland, Berlage, working gradually out of the romantic nationalism of earlier nineteenth century Dutch architecture, came at last, in his design for the Bourse in Amsterdam, to a full expression of the theory that twentieth-century architecture must be based essentially on twentieth century construction, and that this construction, naturally and simply and openly expressed, will unfailingly create the new forms which fit it. In Germany, Peter Behrens, first painter, then designer, then later architect, used his post as Architect-in-Chief of the General Electric Company of Germany to bring similar ideas into industrial design, and proved the factory need no longer be the noisome, smoke-blackened confusion of building and smokestack and shop which the later-nineteenth-century factory had too frequently been, but could instead be clean, systematically planned, beautiful in its relationships, and creative and aesthetically effective in its individual units. His superb turbine assembly building in Berlin is characteristic.

In some ways the most important of these early pioneers was Louis Sullivan, in the United States, a dreamer, a revolutionary architect, a man passionately devoted to the ideals of democracy, full of trust in the endless potentialities of engineering and democracy, combined, to make a better life and a better architecture than the world had yet seen. He was a brilliant draftsman and ornamentalist as well, and sometimes it would almost seem as though his love of lavish decoration and his essentially sound feeling for structure were in conflict. More than anyone else, Louis Sullivan was the creator of the modern skyscraper, realizing in the early 1890's that any true office building of steel construction must be a totally different organism, founded on totally different sources, from any which had been known before. In the Guaranty Building of Buffalo he gave his ideal perhaps its clearest expression—lower floors with metal and glass shop windows, through which the columns which support the whole building are plainly seen; above, office floors of a simple plaid of windows in a richly decorated terra-cotta skin, with the vertical elements accented slightly more than the horizontal so that the height sense was emphasized; at the top a projecting cornice ending the composition with simple directness. None of the ornament with which the building was decorated is of purely historical inspiration; all of it is intensely personal, instinct with its designer's own sense of drama and delicacy.

Another of the important originators of contemporary conceptions of architecture was closely associated with Sullivan for several years. Frank Lloyd Wright, as Sullivan's chief draftsman, learned all that Sullivan had to teach, and became himself imbued with Sullivan"s passion for democracy as a means to finer living for everyone. When he left Sullivan, Wright branched out especially into the field of house design, and from the beginning, in the early nineties, produced homes daringly original not only in their decoration but even more in their basic plan. Wright, more than any architect of the time, realized the deep changes that were going on in family life, realized that houses must be closely related to the outdoors, that windows must be real connections between nature and man, and that the old kind of privacy which had divided up houses so often into little unappetizing separate boxes was no longer valid. Space, openness, horizontality, close connection between dwelling and site, dwelling and garden, interior and the open air—this was the vision which Wright had forty years ago, and this is the vision which has, more than any other, made over the best of twentieth-century houses.

The First World War put an end to an epoch. It left the world weary

and disillusioned, with faith in earlier ideals and earlier ways deeply undermined, and with a growing desire to find some better answer than any
which had gone before to the pressing questions of industry and human
living. With the old epoch, eclecticism in architecture died as a living force,
for present-day eclecticism is hardly more significant to vital design than
the twittering of very dead ghosts. Pursuant to the First World War the
impetus to a new architecture became an insistent clamor. On the foundations which had been laid by Mackintosh and Wagner, by Berlage and
Behrens, by Sullivan and Wright, the new architectural movement rapidly
attained stature. It had the tremendous advantage of a superb pamphleteer,
Charles Édouard Jeanneret, more commonly known by his pseudonym of
Le Corbusier. It had the advantage of the enormous advance in reinforced
concrete that had gone on in France and Germany even during the war,
and produced the effective and audaciously inventive work of the Perrets
in France and the earlier work of Walter Gropius and Mendelsohn in
Germany. It had the advantage of distinguished sponsorship, and above
all a crusading spirit which saw in nineteenth-century eclecticism only the
expression of a decadent civilization which had gone down already in well-
deserved ruin; it united in one intoxicating and beautiful ideal the vision
of a new world where the productivity of labor was used for the social
good, and where the new freedom and the new plenty were expressed in a
new architecture as gay and as logical and as free as the life which it
sheltered was to be.

"Architecture or revolution?" wrote Le Corbusier in his brilliant tract
translated as *Towards a New Architecture;* and, though other critics and
writers of the movement may have been less lyrically hopeful, in all there
was the common vision that modern life could be a good life and modern
architecture a new and magnificent expression of the human building instinct, provided that buildings were designed primarily for human use (the
house a machine for living, as Le Corbusier says), and that the machines
which are at the basis of modern productivity were not fought—as the old
handicraft people insisted—but were accepted. Machines, they asserted,
must be domesticated so that they no longer rule but only serve human
life; their spirit must be expressed in the new construction, as medieval life
had expressed the church in its own types of masonry building, or as the
Greek town plans had expressed the Greek concept of the city-state. Only
by such an insistence on frank acknowledgment and expression of the conditions of twentieth-century living could a new architecture be produced,
these people felt; and consequently, they argued, architects must resolutely

turn their backs on the entire past, must divest themselves of all their romantic conceptions of architecture as a series of pretty pictures, or as a way of evoking memories of times gone by. "All the past must be destroyed," wrote Lurçat; everything was to be gained by looking ahead. For discipline, the theory of functionalism was enough—the idea that forms must be designed for specific purposes first and foremost, and that the best answer to a practical necessity of purpose or structure would automatically create successful design.

It was an extreme doctrine, but the need was extreme. The faded reworkings of old themes in twentieth-century eclectic architecture had become a meaningless amusement of dilettante architects and clients, had substituted canons of arbitrary, learned-by-rote taste for any sense of creative design, had reduced architecture to the level of mere window dressing. When the functionalists insisted, as they did, on the avoidance of all ornament, because the world was not ready for ornament, they were really protesting against the use of silly, costume-party fripperies to conceal thoughtless and ill-planned buildings. When they sought to uphold functionalism as the one necessary discipline, they were fighting the current widely held notion of architecture as attractive pictures of past forms arranged in fixed proportions, which were good because they were old and time-tried.

Later, their teaching, with their practice, mellowed and broadened. They began to see how the aesthetic demands of architecture were on a different plane from the practical needs, not contradicting them but often complementing them. They began to realize that the strict geometrical formalisms into which their work had drifted were giving promise of too rapid crystallization into set forms as rigid as those of any of the earlier styles. They began to understand the danger of a new copybook eclecticism based on the rehash of their own revolutionary work. Lurçat expressed the danger well in an article on the development of French architecture, when he warned against the too-hasty fixation of the style and urged a continual flexibility in the approach to all problems of design. Wright, too, has realized the danger, and in his writings as in his work has gone on toward ever-growing and widening ideals of an architecture that shall be organic, in which structure and purpose and beauty are related as elastically but as inextricably as they are in a flower.

Thus the new work has developed and is continuing to develop, as the great architectures of the past have developed, with continually growing flexibility, harmony, and control. Thus, little by little, the new spirit of the twentieth century has come into architectural expression.

Chapter 33

THE ARCHITECTURE OF TODAY

⊁THE significant architecture of the twentieth century is much more than an architecture of protest. In fact, it was the basically negative approach of some early architects of the century which markedly retarded the popular acceptance of a new architecture for a new world. So much architectural criticism of the 1920's was devoted to attacking the superficiality of eclecticism that there was little space left for constructive concepts. Many persons said: It is easy to see what these people are *against,* but it is difficult for us to understand what they are *for;* until we are more sure, we will stick to what we have. But there were other elements in early "modern" which repelled the sensitive. All the early propagandists for modern architecture were united in attacking ornament; they felt that, for the time at least, every possible extraneous motif should be excluded from buildings and that architecture should be stripped to its bare essentials. Le Corbusier in his otherwise inspiring and extremely important book, *Vers une architecture* (Towards a New Architecture), one of the epoch-making architectural books of the twentieth century, had coined the unfortunate phrase that a house was a machine for living. But countless people did not wish to live in a machine (they had enough of machines in their workaday world), and many felt that the human spirit demanded more than the strict essentials, they did not wish to live in rooms resembling hospital wards.

Yet the whole of life after the First World War was different in essence from what it had been before. The rapidly mounting developments in industry and in science were inexorable forces; a growing population added to the building problems of the world; and the continuing impact of new materials and new building methods demanded architectural forms suitable to them. Change was to come, inevitably; social, economic, and industrial conditions saw to that. Thus, as the 1930's saw an increase in creativeness in modern architectural design, so also they witnessed a grudging but increasing acceptance of new architectural types by the people at large. During the 1940's this process went on with ever increasing speed—aided perhaps by the unsettled conditions surrounding the Second World War—so that by the middle of the century, to all intents and purposes, what are generally termed modern architectural forms were accepted in all significant work, and eclecticism remained only as a backward and often humorous force in the work of a gradually lessening number of speculative builders as well as in certain notoriously conservative fields like that of church design. Even here, however, the resistance to the new movement is now gradually weakening; synagogues and churches appear among the significant works employing the forms of today. In the United States, for example, Mendelsohn's synagogues for Cincinnati and St. Louis, Percival Goodman's synagogue at Milburn, New Jersey, the Tabernacle Church of Christ in Columbus, Indiana, by the Saarinens and Pierre & Wight, the Zion Lutheran Church at Portland, Oregon, by Pietro Belluschi, and the First Unitarian Church in Madison, Wisconsin, by Frank Lloyd Wright all rank extremely high in their imaginative forms and their expressiveness, and in the synagogues especially a new importance has been given to sculpture, painting, and decorative hangings.

From the beginning, of course, true architects realized that to protest against eclecticism was only part of their job, and they eagerly sought for sound foundations on which a new architecture could be based. Architecture must necessarily make beautiful and efficient objects of all those new buildings which twentieth-century problems have developed. Factories, for example, should be as appetizing and as good to look at as a house or a library. As the proportion of industrially employed persons increases, the problem of making their working environment not only pleasant but inspiring becomes a pressing one. For modern architecture in its truest forms is an architecture for the whole population and can draw no class lines. Any problem of the design of a necessary structure for modern life is by nature, therefore, an architectural problem.

This realization has brought engineers and architects more closely together. With the evolution of complicated manufacturing processes and the systematization of methods of manufacture, the correct diagramming of these processes and their relations is a matter of planning conception in which the architect's imagination is of great assistance to the technician. Moreover, the manufacturing system itself, if well planned, will develop a kind of form in the buildings that shelter it which has its own distinctive, expressive quality. To emphasize this is an aesthetic and architectural function, and only the collaboration of the employer, the employee, the engineer, and the architect can achieve the most successful results. Many of the great airplane factories built during and after the Second World War are in that respect magnificent works of architecture. And when to this basic problem there is added the inspiration of social purpose—as in the case of the great governmental power developments or the erection of bridges, dams, canals, and such works—then an architecture of surprising beauty and of real monumentality may result, as it has resulted, in the superb powerhouses and dams built by the Tennessee Valley Authority.

Another vital modern problem is that of housing the growing population. If, as many modern architects believe, the chief function of architecture is to improve and beautify the surroundings of human beings, what more noble or inspiring task can there be than the gracious housing of millions? Where can the architect find such an exhilarating opportunity to create beauty which shall enter into the very hearts of mankind? It is significant that it was in the housing field in Europe, in the years between the two world wars, that many concepts of modern architecture received their most important tests and achieved some of their most successful results. The Weissenhof housing exposition of 1927—a group of permanent houses and apartments designed by the best modern architects of Europe—not only was a remarkable monument to the progress of the new style but also did much to clarify its ideals, and the government and municipal housing of Frankfurt and Berlin, some of the groups around Paris, and many in England can be ranked among the most successful designs of modern architecture up through the early 1930's.

Equally important were revolutionary developments in building techniques and in new materials. The steel-frame skeleton structure had already been in use for thirty years and more, but only with the coming of modern architecture were its real implications in architectural design understood. All the proportions to which it gave rise were different from those current in the past. How could the tall narrow bays of classic or Gothic tradition fit naturally into the wide horizontal bays of the steel skeleton? An entirely new attack on this problem was necessary. Reinforced concrete, again, had for many decades been in use as a kind of misunderstood maid-of-all-work for the eclectic designer. The superb opportunities it offered for daring spans, for flat-slab ceilings, for shell domes and vaults again to bring the curved line into design and break the tyranny of the steel rectangle—all these needed the atmosphere of modern architectural thinking in order to come to fruition. Similarly, the development of rigid-frame construction and other forms of statically indeterminate structures brought a new need for imagination on the part of both the engineer and the architect, and made it feasible to produce large interiors with curved or slanting contours that were new elements in the architectural landscape. At the same time the development of new types of light metals and metal alloys gave new opportunities to the imaginative designer, and the new cheapness and perfection of glass manufacture made possible buildings entirely sheathed in this magic material. Insulation obviated the necessity for thick walls or roofs to keep out heat and cold. The whole movement pointed toward a refined delicacy within basically simple geometric patterns.

Modern architecture has often been associated with the concept of functionalism. Though Louis Sullivan, years before, had enunciated the provocative phrase, "Form follows function," and in the *Autobiography of an Idea* and *Kindergarten Chats* had given his interpretation of the concept a full expression, the architects of the 1920's—those who created what was frequently known as the International Style—gave the word functionalism a different and more limited meaning. Perhaps in following scientific thought in devotion to that which is measurable, they sometimes gave to function a purely physical meaning. Man became a mere physiological machine; work processes, even living processes, were measured, and spaces just adequate for them were developed. The architectural forms that followed any such analysis were bound to be minimal—economical. They might perhaps be "efficient," but there was often in them something harsh, stark, and cold. For designers and critics who supported this concept forgot—as Louis Sullivan never forgot—that imagination and emotion are also functions of a healthy human being, and that any architecture which starves these is as much a failure functionally as a factory in which a great deal of excess effort is necessary. At times this concept reached the point of a condemnation of any conscious aesthetic search in architectural design. Architectural beauty, the extremists felt, would be the inevitable result of the measurable physical functions economically related, and any conscious search for beauty of proportion, rhythm, or the harmonious relation of building and site was merely sentimental, backward-looking, and destructive of progress.

This extreme point of view, current especially in the 1920's, has fortunately almost entirely passed away; for architects in designing actual buildings came to realize that they were forced to make many choices for which functionalism had no answer. The size of doors, even the areas of rooms, and the relation of heights and widths were essential architectural problems for which often there were no measurable criteria. What is the purpose of space? How big is a room? Only wide limits to these vital factors could be set by any existing measurable criteria. In solving such problems, aesthetic discrimination crept in, willy-nilly, and by the middle 1930's all architects of any stature had begun to realize that architectural design must include a conscious search for the aesthetically satisfying.

The architects of the 1920's had another concept which was in its way a stultifying one: the theory that modern—that is, according to their interpretation, new—methods of construction and new materials must always be chosen for every problem that presented itself, whatever the local or regional conditions might be. Climate could be disregarded, for mechanical heating and cooling devices make a building independent of its region—provided there is enough money and space for them. In other words, instead of co-operating with nature, many architects of this decade felt that an almost arrogant disregard of nature was the only truly "modern" attitude. The elaborate studies of insolation made at the Bauhaus under Gropius were of course a counter movement of great importance, and where economic limitations were paramount—as in mass housing—co-operation with nature, in matters of heat and ventilation at least, was seen to be essential.

Later architects, from about 1930 on, have growingly disregarded these earlier attitudes. They have come to realize that any method of construction and any material, whether traditional or new, may be used creatively, and that conditions local to the site—such, for instance, as the availability of building stone or of brick or timber—may well indicate that the older and traditional materials and methods may be more efficient, more "modern," than a willful search for mere novelty. They have come to realize also that site conditions not only of climate but also of aesthetic quality—slopes, foliage, views—will be dominant elements in design, and that a building excellent for Florida may be absurd in Maine. Regionalism, in the sense of a frank acceptance of regional conditions of climate and site, therefore has become a universal element in the architecture of today.

But regionalism may go even further. It may bring in the concept of tradition, and here one enters one of the great current controversies in architectural thinking. Tradition has been defined as the living portion of the past. Can it, therefore, be disregarded? The problem reduces itself to an analysis of what is really still living and what pretends to live on merely as sentimentalism. Traditions of social relationships and of family and community mores are undoubtedly actual. Traditions in ornament, on the other hand, are generally sentimental only. But traditions of the use of materials and even certain basic concepts of composition may also be valid and operative elements. It is here that the architect's greatest imagination and discrimination are called for.

Besides social and functional reasons there was another extremely important influence behind the development of modern architecture. That was the development of painting. It is well known that changes in the ideals and methods of painting often precede those of architecture, and that was true in this case. Cubism, by virtue of its geometric basis, was bound to affect architectural design; but the other movements of that and a slightly later time, Expressionism and post-Impressionism, also had significant effects and parallels. It is noteworthy that Walter Gropius, with all his insistence on the close tie-up of architecture with industry—a connection that was at the basis of a great deal of the activity of the famous Bauhaus which he developed and directed—always kept a group of creative painters busy at the school, since he felt that their influence on the other projects of the organization was of primary importance. Eric Mendelsohn in the years immediately before the First World War was identified with the Expressionist movement in Germany, and German Expressionism colored all his earlier work. Le Corbusier was a distinguished painter before he was known as an architect, and with Amedée Ozenfant he founded a school called *Peinture Pure,* emphasizing the existence of each painting as a thing in, by, and for itself alone, achieved by pure color quality. And, finally, the Dutch group known as De Styl—whose most important figures were Van Doesburg and Mondrian, with their insistence on rhythmical organizations of pure line and area—had a tremendous effect on the architecture of J. J. P. Oud and Ludwig Mies van der Rohe. Frank Lloyd Wright from his early youth was not only an enthusiastic admirer of Japanese architecture but also a collector of Japanese prints, and without doubt some of the compositional values of his work were directly motivated by that influence. In other words, from almost the beginning the great architects of the whole movement realized that architecture as an expressive art must necessarily have analogies with the other expressive arts of its time. This of course was a purely aesthetic consideration, and to the best work of the time it gave the soul which some of the work so definitely lacked.

It may be well here to set out briefly the characteristics of various recognizably different manifestations included under the general head of modern architecture. The first prophecies of the work, naturally, came in the architecture noted in the previous chapter—the works of Otto Wagner, of Gropius, of Mackintosh, of Sullivan, of Van de Velde, and the early work of Wright—men sometimes associated with the Art Nouveau but whose work was soundly enough based to avoid most of the superficialities of the period. But the true movement, characterized by a complete break with the past, achieved its first successes in the buildings of those architects who are generally classed as belonging to the International School—Gropius, Le Corbusier, Lurçat, and Brinkman & Van der Vlugt especially, and in the United States Howe and Lescaze. The International Style has been so called because its practitioners felt that the important elements forming the essential quality of modern living—industry, a new knowledge of physiology, a new scientific approach—were fundamentally international in character, as true in Japan as in Germany or America. If architecture is to be a true reflection of contemporary life, these architects felt, then it too, like the forces that underlay it, must be international and take somewhat similar forms wherever built. The wide spread of the influence these men exerted reveals the basic truth of at least a part of the claim.

The work of the International School stresses four general concepts: pure geometrical composition; skeleton construction, with the wall merely as a screen; the use of large glass areas; and a general emphasis on interior volume rather than exterior mass. In some of its manifestations, as in the work of Bruno Taut, social relationships and the social basis of architecture are considered controlling elements in design; Le Corbusier, for example, in *Vers une architecture* has one section entitled "Architecture or Revolution?" It is also significant that the professional society which stems from the International School, the C.I.A.M. (*Congrès International des Architectes Modernes*), has performed its most valuable task in its continuing study of housing and city planning. It is this architecture of the International Style, with its occasional rigidity, its stripped bareness, its avoidance of interest in texture or expressive ornament, that came in many cases to be accepted as the "real" modern architecture. The true climax of the International Style was probably achieved in 1927 in Le Corbusier's competition design, unfortunately never executed, for the League of Nations buildings at Geneva. The brilliance of this scheme has since been realized, together with its prophetic quality with respect to many practical and aesthetic elements that were to come. Yet it is also significant that in that climax work there appeared many deviations from the strict functionalism and the strict geometry of more typical International School buildings. A superb and sympathetic use of the site, a search for a valid monumentality, and a delicate use of human scale gave it a character both of grandeur and of graciousness uncommon at its time.

A second group is more devoted to the development of interest in structural forms and methods and the use of these forms as controlling elements in design. Its greatest representative is Auguste Perret, who with his brother Gustave was among the pioneer innovators in the use of reinforced concrete.

Although he began by using all sorts of vaulted forms, his taste was fundamentally rectangular, and as his work has matured it has become so "classic" in feeling that some modern critics consider him a reactionary. Actually, Perret claims, the forms that reinforced concrete naturally takes are those of the simplest post-beam-and-slab construction. Since this is essentially the same kind of construction as the Greeks used, although the materials differ, it is not strange to find that a basically classic coloration pervades much of his work. Cornices and band courses protect the wall, he claims. Columns hold up things and should be emphasized as supporting members. Almost his whole architectural philosophy can be summed up in an apothegm of his: He who hides a beam or structural member hides the greatest source of decorative effect available to the architect; he who fakes a beam or structural member commits a crime. As a result, all his more recent buildings take the form of simple rectangular skeleton constructions with the spaces between the structural members filled in by panels of various materials and various types. He has had a wide influence on architecture in France and Switzerland but has gained few disciples elsewhere. In Switzerland, South America, and Italy concrete design has often taken the opposite turn. The Swiss engineer Maillart in bridges and industrial buildings developed extraordinary forms based on the fact that concrete structures are continuous—the supported and supporting members being identical—and, carrying such ideas further, in South America and Italy the most daring cantilevered rigid-frame structures for grandstands and similar buildings have been developed, as well as all kinds of parabolic-arched buildings. Pre-stressed and unit-type construction —the latter based on the erection and tying together of pre-cast elements into one rigid and interlocking whole—has also been fruitful in the creation of new and exciting forms. Another remarkable constructive influence has come, in the United States, from the revolutionary research of Buckminster Fuller, who has been working for years on the application of the latest scientific concepts to the whole problem of modern shelter. Recently he has devised a light hemispherical shelter of triangular units, metal framed and plastic covered, beneath which houses or other areas for human use can be arranged with complete freedom.

Wood also has led to fresh forms in the hands of many architects, especially in Scandinavia and the United States. Laminated arches and beams, glued up from relatively small pieces, have their own character; waterproof plywood and battened walls have generated new types of design. Even the simple post-and-beam combination has received new dignity. Alvar Aalto, in Finland, and Wright, Neutra, Rudolph, and Nemeny & Geller in the United States have pioneered in this kind of wood constructivism.

In a third category are the designers who, although they feel the necessity of new forms to express the new kinds of living and the new materials and techniques, are not won to the puritanical geometry of the International School or to the pure constructivism of Perret. To them, construction and materials are but means to the end of artistic creation and the development of a human environment for mankind. Expression, richness, variety—these all may be found in their work. They are likely to use traditional materials and techniques as well as those that are purely modern; the choice will be made on pragmatic rather than theoretical grounds. Eric Mendelsohn in Germany (and later in England, Palestine, and the United States) and W. M. Dudok in Holland are perhaps the most famous of this group, and Oud and Mies van der Rohe—though with some roots in the International Style— rapidly evolved into free creators in this vein. It is significant, for instance, that pure geometry, beautiful materials, and meticulous detailing have characterized the latest work of the latter, rather than any doctrinaire reasoning of efficiency or economy; whereas one of the most recent works of the former is the Shell Building in The Hague, in which unashamed ornament makes its unexpected appearance.

A fourth group is that in which Frank Lloyd Wright has been and continues (in 1953) to be the controlling figure. It sees a building as an organic whole, just as nature is organic; it must be living, it must be functional in the sense that its parts are there for a purpose, but above all it must be creatively one integrated whole, in which materials, plan, exterior and interior design, and even the treatment of the site exist only as they serve the total unity and as they express their relation to it. Practitioners of his philosophy have no prejudices in favor of new or old, straight or curved, or formal or informal, but they root their conception in that organic ideal and its execution by means of the most skillful and expressive use of structural systems and materials, whatever they may be. Typical American representatives of this group are Harwell Harris and Richard Neutra.

But there is a fifth group perhaps even more characteristic of the middle of the century, and the fact that this group includes probably the majority of architects practicing is sure evidence of the general acceptance of the ideals of contemporary architecture. These architects design almost automatically in the so-called modern vernacular. It is the natural way for them to create; though they may have little philosophy or ponder but little the reasons behind what they do, the fact that this is their natural vocabulary is extremely significant. For architects today will almost always design modern buildings unless specifically directed along other paths. Characteristic of this group in the United States are such architects as Edward D. Stone, Pietro Belluschi, Robert Law Weed, Burnham Hoyt, and Twitchell & Rudolph. Their common vocabulary is a simple one: glass to welcome in sun and views; structural materials obviously expressed (wood as wood, brick as brick, stone as stone); little dependence on applied decoration, but instead a trust in proportion and rhythm to give interest and vitality to the design.

The development of modern architecture in various parts of the world has proceeded along differing lines and emphasized different phases of the general concept.

In France the International School work of Le Corbusier and Lurçat and the reinforced concrete of Perret have dominated. In both cases, however, a national character has again and again been given by the strength of the tradition of classic planning and elegant detail which stems from the École des Beaux Arts. Le Corbusier was a painter and Lurçat a Beaux Arts graduate, and to neither was the limited geometry of the German group congenial. In the case of Perret the classic tradition completely triumphed, and in the best work in France between the two world wars the classic tradition exerted a salutary discipline. Elegance in the handling of both details and materials, at times to the point where mere fashionable *chic* is achieved, is typical of much of the work, especially in Paris, and even in the reconstruction work being carried on since the Second World War in France this same tendency toward elegance of detail often persists. In apartment house design this quality is especially marked, and Paris apartments by Roux Spitz or the more inventive and less conventional Jean Ginsberg have set high standards in elegance of plan and in exterior and interior detail. French churches, beginning with Perret's Notre Dame at Raincy, have sought for new kinds of richness and expression in the new materials, especially concrete. But in them the tradition of the height and the great glass areas of French Gothic, as well as a desire for rich adornment in sculpture and in color, has remained dominant; Paul Tournon's Ste. Geneviève, at Elisabethville, a sort of miniature Ste. Chapelle in concrete frames with a concrete shell vault and a richly sculptured façade, is typical. In the period since the Second World War, while the work of the Perrets seems to become more and more rectangular and classic—as in the reconstruction work at Le Havre—the work of Le Corbusier strives for the large-scale bravura best exemplified in the great apartment house erected for the muncipality in Marseilles.

Meanwhile many reconstruction plans by other architects show daring and interesting attempts to combine something of the constructivism of Perret with freer and more varied compositional forms. In almost all of this reconstruction work, the dominance of the tall elevator apartment house is noteworthy. A century ago, in Paris, Lyons, and certain other cities, the French had been the pioneers in developing apartment houses and apartment living; now this trend to urbanized apartments is apparently sweeping all of France. For many provincial towns it constitutes a major revolution in living ways. Typical are the plans for Lorient by Tourry, for St. Denis by Lurçat, and for Toulon by Mikélian.

In Germany three great influences have been at work. The first was the International Style, particularly as developed by the Bauhaus group. The second was Expressionism, to which reference has already been made. In addition to influencing the work of Mendelsohn, Expressionism gave rise to a series of remarkable church designs in light concrete construction by Dominikus Boehm, Martin Weber, and others. In these the utmost drama of form and light was sought. Boehm was especially fond of pointed vaults springing from near the floor and intersecting in strange geometric shapes like a sort of fantasy on the Gothic church, but in the funeral church for Hindenburg he produced a work extraordinarily prophetic in its somber, stark brick. The third influence was Nazi neo-classicism.

The Nazi interlude brought a tragic end to the greater part of the significant architecture in Germany, and most of the important German architects fled the country—Gropius to practice in England and the United States; Mendelsohn to continue his work in England, Palestine, and the United States; Ernst May, one of the great city planners and housing designers of the world, to go into retirement in Africa; and Bruno Taut to work in Japan and finally in Turkey, where he died while head of the national architectural school. Nazi architecture was in its way Expressionist also. It attempted to deify Hitler and the state and to resurrect the good old days of peasant art, eccentric individual craftsmanship, and in official buildings an overweening classic stripped naked and vain. In place of the broadly conceived and forward-looking city plans of Frankfurt, city planning ideals prevailed in which great Versailles-like avenues dominated one half of it and stupid little peasant villages the other. Since the war the appalling problems of reconstruction which faced Germany have prevented much large-scale construction. East Germany is of course entirely controlled by Russian ideals, but in West Germany definite signs of a renaissance are apparent in spite of the small amount of work done. In this the simplicity of the International Style is wed to a greater human variety and considerable elegance in detail. The Parliament buildings at Bonn by Hans Schwippert, in part an alteration of the old University, are typical in their simple and gracious geometry.

In Great Britain there has been an enormous variety, expressive of British tolerance and individuality. The ideals of the International School were accepted by many of the most forward-looking architects, like Lubetkin, Yorke, and others, but were given a flavor of individual vagary, at times verging on eccentricity. Constructivist ideals were often evident and in much English work of the early 1930's produced a sort of staccato feeling. But, in addition, traditionalism remained strong in public buildings and in church design, although greatly modified by modern ideals of simplicity and directness. Occasional public buildings resulted which combined something of classic official dignity with a great deal of freedom and freshness. In church work the simplified versions of neo-Gothic have continued to be dominant, varying all the way from those in which the pointed arch is found to those in which the Gothic flavor is only a faint aroma over simple forms of brick and timber. But it is in the fields of housing and works of social value that English architecture has remained outstanding. Large numbers of schools built both before and after the Second World War show a remarkable sense of child scale and of simple, charming details combined in plans which, while varied, are integrated and strong. Details frequently have an International Style character, yet the whole sense these buildings give is one of quiet charm and personality. Characteristic examples from the 1930's include many by Oswald Milne and by Curtis & Burchett; typical of more recent work since the war but carrying out the general ideals of the pre-war types is the Stevenage School for one of the New Towns, by Yorke, Rosenberg & Mardall. The housing movement has produced many stunning apartment houses, often almost French in their elegance—like the suave concrete of the Embassy Hotel at Brighton by Wells Coates. Other important examples are the Highpoint apartments in Highgate, London, by Lubetkin and his group known as Tecton, and others in London by Maxwell Fry, F. S. Yorke, and Norman & Dawbarn. But Britain's housing genius has gone into general plans rather than individual structures. The New Towns, Britain's answer both to the growing population and to the recognized evils of congested cities, were originally conceived prior to the Second World War and within five years after the war were under construction. Among them several different types of town planning have been developed, yet all aim to be true communities. Many make careful use of local traditions and even preserve some local buildings, and all of them stress the richness of family life rather than the mere efficiency of traffic distribution. They are aimed primarily at humanizing the machine in every way. Among them are Crawley, by Anthony Minoprio; East Kilbrige (in Scotland), by Donald Reay; Harlow, by Frederick Gibberd; Ongar, by C. Macgregor; Peterlee, by Lubetkin; and Stevenage, by C. Holliday. They are all planned for approximately fifty to sixty thousand persons and are supposed to be self-supporting and complete with their own industries and educational, commercial, and social facilities. In their way they carry out many of the ideals of the true garden city.

The history of Italian architecture illuminates the differences between the industrial north and the agricultural and traditional south. The art movement called Futurism, with its stress on the dynamic, on struggle rather than repose, on force and motion, was an Italian movement, and one of its heroes was the architect Antonio di Sant' Elia, killed in the First World War. His architectural designs, obviously influenced by American skyscrapers, made enormous use of steel, concrete, and glass. The enthusiasm which they aroused—especially in Milan—made the architects of northern Italy quite susceptible to the ideals of the International Style, and during the 1920's and 1930's International School designs dominated the architectural picture of Milan, Turin, and the north generally. But Rome remained a center of classic and Baroque tradition. Roman architects consistently refused to accept the basic theories of the International School, although little by little they absorbed some of its mannerisms. Eventually these two forces—the classic tradition of Rome and the dynamic modernism of the north—tended to coalesce, and the best work of the Fascist era in Italy owes its vitality to this fruitful marriage. The post office at Naples, by Vaccaro & Franzi, and a whole series of railroad stations—notably those at Florence and Siena (now destroyed)—are typical, and some of the new towns built on reclaimed marshland, like Sabaudia, show how effective even the simplest constructions can be made when local traditions discipline the general picture and the logic of modern design controls the actual building. Since the Second World War the older schisms between the two schools have tended to fade away. The general modern vocabulary is accepted but used again and again in compositions in which classic dignity, Baroque drama, and Italian elegance are combined—as in the new railroad station at Rome, by Calini, Castellazzi, Fadigati, Montuori, Pintonello & Vitellozzi—and in which the fullest possible advantage is taken of those lovely marbles which are so important a part of Italy's architectural alphabet. Excellent apartment houses in Rome by Luccichenti and in Milan by Figini & Pallini show the vitality of the resurrection of Italian architecture since the Second World War. The development of the minor arts has been even more astonishing, and Italian furniture and decorative objects are among the most original and elegant of the mid-century; here the classic background of Italy has joined the impetus of world-wide change to produce new creations of the highest quality. There has also been, since the war, an extremely important development in all types of concrete construction, with a daring inventiveness and freedom known almost nowhere else. This is not the rectangular concrete of the Perrets but design in which the plastic nature of concrete is expressed in curves of all kinds and its structural possibilities are developed in ingenious unit-type and rigid-frame systems. Especially interesting are P. L. Nervi's stadiums at Florence and Turin, bold in their superb handling of cantilevered concrete, and, from the post-war period, the same architect's exhibition hall in Turin, with a magnificent skylighted vaulted interior ingeniously constructed of pre-cast units. That is the medium in which Italy today is making its greatest contribution to the architecture of the world.

It was in the Netherlands that the precursors of modern architecture had achieved outstanding success; the coming of modern architecture therefore was less of a revolution here perhaps than anywhere else in Europe. The interesting and sometimes eccentric brickwork of the housing built during and immediately after the First World War reveals the exuberance of Netherlands taste, as the amount of this housing and the charm achieved in working-class areas and in little suburbs reveal its fundamental humanism of approach. The International Style brought the necessary discipline to that exuberance. The work of Oud, with its precise elegance and its imaginative use of the simplest forms, is outstanding, and the housing which he did at Rotterdam, the Hook of Holland, and the Weissenhof exposition ranks among the great monuments of the period. Other designers followed his lead, and during the 1930's there was an efflorescence of work in the International Style vein in all the Dutch cities, climaxed perhaps by the Van Nelle factory in Rotterdam, by Brinkman & Van der Vlugt. Yet at the same time the other tradition of free, rather Baroque design persisted, and it was not until the mid-1930's that the two movements began to merge in a freer approach on the part of the strict modernists and a more disciplined design on the part of the traditionalists. Through this entire era the figure of Dudok stands out as separate from any school and yet as one of the great creative influences on the development of modern architecture. As city architect in Hilversum and more recently as city planner for the reconstruction of The Hague he has produced work in which his ideals may readily be seen. He is essentially, like Wright, a designer first and foremost. A master of geomet rical composition, he loves richness of color and form. His complex orchestration of vertical against horizontal, of projecting slab against rising tower, and of mass that comes forward against mass that retreats has a marked musical quality. The most characteristic of his works are found in two fields: the schools he did in Hilversum, which in school design set a new note of intimate beauty of the kind that children love—a standard that has been an inspiration to modern school architects the world over—and the Hilversum town hall, one of the most successful attempts to express the dignity of city government and the humanity of community organization in forms that owe nothing to the past. Dudok in his search for beautiful and expressive architectural form is a free creator to whom structure and style are but means to the ends he seeks. Since the Second World War the amount of reconstruction in destroyed Rotterdam and elsewhere in Holland has been enormous, and in it there is great variety as little by little the influences of the International School, of the traditional brick designers, and of free creators like Dudok have become harmonized in varying proportions. J. F. Stahl's new Bourse at Rotterdam, for example, with its colonnaded entrance, its polychrome brick and tile, and its lavish interiors, is typical of the imaginative character of the new work. The Municipal Theater at Utrecht, by Dudok, shows many of the same qualities and reveals as well that, just as the work of many other Netherlands architects has become looser and freer and more imaginative, his has become more disciplined and simpler. Nevertheless, since a love of color, an immaculate use of brick, and great glass surfaces are everywhere to be found, as they have been found in all Dutch architecture since the Renaissance, there is a basic harmony of old and new such as exists almost nowhere else.

Russian architecture since the Revolution has passed through several phases. At first it took the most extreme types of the International Style of Western Europe as its ideal, and many factories, workers' clubs, and housing groups were built in this vein; moreover, distinguished European architects were invited to Russia, including Lurçat, Ernst May, and Le Corbusier, who designed for Moscow the glass, steel, and red granite Light Industries Department building. To this movement the Russians added at times their own native brand of constructivism, producing dynamic and sometimes eccentric designs as though buildings were pieces of constructivist sculpture. Then suddenly, in the early 1930's, there was a complete *volte-face;* the Soviet government officially adopted a kind of neo-classicism as its ideal, claiming that this was the real expression of popular taste and hence the only fit architecture of social realism. Colonnades proliferated, sculpture was used with more lavishness than control, and vast city planning schemes were developed with great avenues and public squares. At the same time, local and regional traditions were brought in again as controlling concepts. The Second World War, with its unprecedented destruction in Russia, put an end to most of the great schemes, but since its close much large-scale construction has been done, especially in Moscow. In this the classic inspiration still controls, though now overlaid with a kind of fantasy of pinnacles and broken lines, somewhat as the Byzantine forms had been fantastically embroidered and broken up in the Russian Baroque of the seventeenth century.

To the Scandinavian countries the International Style came as an importation. They already had a living neo-romantic school of architecture, not archaeological in its nature although aiming at the continuation of all sorts of general local form traditions, and vitalized by a long history of extraordinarily skillful craftsmanship in the minor arts; the town hall at Stockholm, by Ragnar Ostberg, is typical. There was also a school of elegant neo-classicism that controlled much important work. These trends were too vital to be extinguished by any imported style no matter how logical the arguments in its favor. Little by little the ideals of hand craftsmanship were taken over into mechanized industry, and a fastidious perfection in detail softened and ripened the imported austerity, as the native tradition for elegance added a certain richness of color and detail. Thus in the monumental crematorium at Stockholm one of the chief early supporters of the International Style, E. G. Asplund, the designer of the Swedish Exposition of 1930, produced a superb example of this blend and one of the great architectural works of the later 1930's. The Municipal Theater at Malmö of the next decade, by Lallerstedt, Lewerentz & Helldén, shows this integration carried even further; a spread-out yet logical plan, simple structural elements, but a great richness of sculpture and decorative adjuncts make it one of the most distinguished theaters of the century. A creative use of wood has dominated much country work in Norway, Sweden, and Finland, whereas in Denmark it has been the traditional material, brick, that has continued to be fruitful and creative. The roof of gentle slope is more usual in Scandinavia than elsewhere, since under the climatic conditions existing it has for so long proved its essential usefulness. The work of Sven Markelius in Sweden and of Alvar Aalto in Finland is especially significant, and such buildings as schools, housing of all kinds, country houses, and the smaller churches are perhaps the most successful. Notable examples are the Ribershus apartments at Malmö, by Persson and by Helldén; the Stockholm housing at Gärdet, by Sture Frolén, and at Gröndal by Backström & Reinius; the Kollektivhus, a co-operative apartment in Stockholm by Markelius; and housing in Gentöfte and Herlev in Denmark, the first by Arne Jacobsen and the second by Eske Kristensen. Among educational buildings the University of Aarhus, Denmark, by Arne Jacobsen, the Technical School of Oslo, Norway, by Blakstad & Munthe, and in Stockholm, Sweden, the Kungsholmen Girls' School by Paul Hedquist and other schools by Ahrbom & Zundal express the customary high quality. Distinguished modern buildings of other classes include the Luma factory by the Swedish Co-operative Society architects, the great bus garage for Stockholm by Eskil Sundahl, and in Finland the superb concrete sanatorium at Paimo and the cellulose factory and housing at Sunila, both by Aalto, and houses and apartments by Erik Brugman.

The exuberance and impulsiveness, the passion and the variety of the South American peoples have welcomed the novelty of modern architectural forms, and of the staid and austere theories of the International School they have made a playground for their vivid imaginations. The old pseudo-Colonialism of South American eclecticism has everywhere yielded to this new and vital force; but, just as the countries of Hispanic America vary tremendously, so their architecture is varied, each country selecting or developing forms harmonious with its own life. In Chile and Colombia the work is perhaps more European, more disciplined, sometimes more stark, and both German and American influences have been marked. In Uruguay it is a sort of Italian version of modern architecture that seems to have been the chief inspiration, and much of that kind of vitality which one finds in the best Italian work occurs in the best work of Uruguay. Something of this same character distinguishes the work of Argentina. But it is perhaps in Brazil that the most original contributions to modern architecture have been created. The influence of Le Corbusier has been great, yet on this foundation architects like Oscar Niemeyer have developed an architecture in concrete which is imaginative, vivid, at times eccentric, but almost always exciting. The Department of Education building in Rio de Janeiro, of which Le Corbusier was consulting architect, shows Niemeyer in his most quiet vein, just as the Pampulha chapel and the casino and club at Belo Horizonte show him at his most inventive and original. The same exuberance, combined with imaginative concrete construction and excellent planning, characterizes the government housing by A. E. Reidy, the schools in Niteroi by Alvaro Vital-Brazil, the housing by Ferreira, Leal & Torres, and much other work at São Paulo and around the rapidly growing capital. The Cidade dos Motores is a new industrial town, planned by Wiener & Sert, in which local traditions of town form are brilliantly combined with the most modern architectural concepts. The same kind of variety, at times amounting almost to incoherence, distinguishes much modern work in Mexico City. Typical of the better work is the President Aleman housing group in Mexico City by Mario Pani, the parabolically vaulted church at Monterey by Enrique del Mora, and the design for University City in Mexico by Carlos Lazo and Mario Pani, Enrique del Mora and Gustavo Travesi. Latin America is a land of contrasts; it is a land of beginnings rather than of completions, and the abounding vitality of modern architectural work over the entire region gives great promise for the future.

Switzerland, neutral in both world wars, prospered, and a large amount of building was the result. In it influences from Germany, France, and Italy often commingled in a sort of gay insouciance, and the cantonal and linguistic differences in the country—German, French, and Italian—added each its own local variations. Yet over all there is evident a power of social purpose—seen in the number of universities, schools, hospitals, public bathing establishments, and meeting halls—as well as an almost universal desire to produce in modern forms vitality, expressiveness, serenity, and grace. The Zurich neighborhood is generally more German and more "severe"; the Geneva region is full of French elegance. Sculpture and mural painting are used more freely and with less self-consciousness than in most of the rest of the modern world, and the Swiss modern buildings in general have a markedly lived-in feeling—they are obviously built to be enjoyed. The University of Fribourg, for instance, uses a Perret type of concrete design with a plan of Le Corbusier freedom and treats it all with imaginative richness. The churches of Karl Moser (now dead) and his son W. M. Moser are distinguished examples of church design; St. Antoninus at Basel, by the elder, and the Protestant Church at Zurich-Altstetten, by the younger, are typical. The Basel University extension by R. Rohn, with a continuous ground-level colonnade, is characteristically quiet and serene; so is the somewhat similar Bleichenhof office building at Zurich, by O. Salvisberg. Among buildings for public gatherings and recreation, the Congress Hall in Zurich by Haefeli, Moser & Steiger and the freely planned and beautiful Lido at Lausanne, by M. Picard, are outstanding.

The development of modern architecture followed a more confused course in the United States than anywhere else save perhaps in England. Not only had the later eclectic architecture in the United States evolved many regional trends based at least in part upon a deep recognition of regional conditions, but also there was a vivid tradition of creativeness which in sections of the country was producing at the beginning of the century work of true originality. The inspiration of Louis Sullivan was vital, and Frank Lloyd Wright's non-historical and organic houses were winning wide architectural acclaim and were paralleled by inventive work by many other architects in the Chicago area, among them Griffin, Spencer, and Purcell & Elmslie. On the Pacific Coast such architects as Willis Polk, Greene & Greene, and Bernard Maybeck were producing charming houses completely creative in design, with a most expressive use of materials, especially wood. Even in New York, considered the fountainhead of conservatism, the work of men like Robert D. Kohn and Harvey Corbett was pointing, in business build-ings, along ways that were bound to lead eventually to revolutionary design. Later, Raymond Hood carried the movement even further, and in the late 1920's and early 1930's such work as the Daily News Building by Howells & Hood and the first buildings of Rockefeller Center by Reinhard & Hof-meister, Corbett, Harrison & MacMurray, and Hood & Fouilhoux were definitely "modern," although they bore but slight resemblance to con-temporary modern work in Europe.

Indeed, the whole set of problems developed by modern industry, modern business, modern medicine, and congested city life were forcing new forms on architects willy-nilly. Factories, in the mere search for efficiency, were developing shapes and uses of glass and steel which bore no similarity to the past—as, for example, in Harrison & Abramovitz's Corning Glass Center at Corning, New York, or in the General Motors Technical Center in Detroit, by Saarinen, Saarinen & Associates, in both of which glass and metals are used with a new bravura and lavish color adds to the interest—just as innovations in steel and concrete and the perfecting of the high-speed elevator made attempts to frost skyscrapers with eclectic ornament increas-ingly absurd. Similarly hotels, department stores, and even apartment houses—all the results of congested city living—were assuming forms on which eclectic ornament sat with less and less grace. The great hospitals were also forcing their designers to use creative imagination; many hospitals thus became object lessons of the fact that handsome and expressive build-ings could result from the closest and most logical following out of pro-grams without the aid of classic columns or Georgian cornices. Even in indigenous and country building there was still alive a certain independence of mind, a certain creativeness, which had not been entirely submerged in the flood of sentimental Colonialism.

The first enthusiasm of America for the kind of revolutionary modernism that had grown up since the First World War came as a matter of mere fashion and was limited largely to the decorative arts. Following the trend set by the Paris Exposition of Decorative Arts in 1925 and the graceful, smart, though superficial designs produced by craft organizations like the Wiener Werkstaette, the real revolutionary attitude of the International School came therefore not entirely as a surprise, but it was nevertheless definitely an importation, supported at first by only a few enthusiastic partisans. Its similarities in basic drive to the revolutionary architecture of Wright and his followers were minimized, although Wright himself had been one of the great inspirations behind the early International School. In the early 1930's, to these few International Style architects and their supporters, modern architecture became an almost religious dogma from which no deviations were permitted. The basic differences between the traditions and conditions of America and those of Germany and France were forgotten or denied. The result, of course, was unnecessary controversy, lost motion, cliquism, and personal antagonisms which had nothing to do with the real problems of architecture.

Yet the forces for change on the part of all the controversialists were irresistible. The great depression of 1929-32 forced drastic re-examination of many of the bases of American life, and public building and public art—which were introduced as two means of combating it—gave new opportunities to younger minds and fresh talents. They brought new vitality into the entire art world as well as into the world of architecture. And, although much of the building produced was undistinguished, some of it—like occasional schools and especially the dams and powerhouses of the Tennessee Valley Authority, of much of which Roland Wank was chief architect—were extraordinary manifestations of the new ideals. It was rapidly seen that pure importations of the flat roofs, the stuccoed surfaces, and the cubical forms of Europe fitted neither American life nor American tastes and conditions; equally it was apparent that native American creative design needed a much closer discipline and a much more sympathetic acceptance of the new materials and new structural systems which American industry and science were producing. Moreover, under conditions in which the costs of both labor and materials were soaring, it became obvious that the construction to be used in any case should be dictated not by any doctrinaire theories of new versus old but, instead, by conditions of availability and actual cost.

By the mid-1930's the earlier controversies were dying down. On the one hand, the original International School group of architects were using brick, timber, and stone and were designing with a much greater freedom, even trying in many cases to reflect some at least of the local traditions, as was true of some of the work of Gropius and Breuer. This process of Americanization took place in the work of all the architects who had fled Germany and come to this country, as well as in that of other foreign-born architects. Thus Eric Mendelsohn's superb and imaginative work in synagogue and hospital design is certainly today as American as it is German; it has the universality of a poetic understanding of both people and problems. And the later work of the Saarinens—Eliel, now dead, and his son Eero—in its freedom from clichés and its beautiful use of simple materials is characteristic of the very best in American architecture. On the other hand, the free designers were making ever greater use of creatively inspired reinforced concrete, all kinds of glass products, and the new light metal alloys, as can be seen in the stunning concrete cantilevers of Wright's house Falling Water or in the work of Pietro Belluschi in all materials, especially metals and timber. Even the use of ornament began to occupy the minds of architects and architectural critics, and at least lip service was paid to the concept of sculpture and mural painting as appropriate elements in modern building.

The Second World War brought a flood of new building problems, chiefly industrial but including also the erection of new communities for industrial workers. The result was not the paralysis of architecture which the war brought to many European countries but, rather, a new challenge which produced extraordinary results, especially in factory design and in community planning. It came to be realized that not only were houses needed in a community but also shopping centers, schools, and community facilities for social life and recreation—a lesson that had been learned in the early depression housing projects and then forgotten under real estate pressure. And the best of this new war housing, especially on the Pacific coast, contained the seeds of magnificent further development; this promise, however, has since been but seldom fulfilled. Indeed, the government housing movement in the United States since the period immediately after the war has retrogressed and, under the hostile political pressures of real estate groups and an unimaginative Congress, has been reduced to the building of dull, almost standardized high apartment houses in slum areas—houses which, by reason of the high population-to-land-area ratio and the often dreary and uninspired architecture, tend to bring the whole movement into undeserved disrepute. In 1949, however, the passage of the Urban Redevelopment Act made it possible for cities with imaginative leadership to re-attack the slum problem in larger ways, and some bold plans—in construction in 1953—have resulted; especially noteworthy are the plans for Philadelphia and some of those for San Francisco.

Meanwhile an entirely new generation of architects had come to the fore—either men educated in schools now completely devoted to various phases of the modern ideal or else an older group who were still young enough to absorb the ideals of both the International School and of Wright and to give a creative expression to this new integration. It is these two groups who are responsible for the best post-war architecture.

Since the Second World War, American architecture has thus achieved a new balance. To the architects of the 1950's much of the architectural criticism of twenty years earlier seems almost meaningless and the old controversies, so bitter then, appear unexplainable or merely quaint. This new balance has not meant unification; quite the reverse: it has given sanction to the greatest possible variety of individual and regional expression. There are still designers who tend to think in forms closely related to those developed by the International Style designers, although handled now with much greater ease and less doctrinaire strictness; there are designers who think basically in romantic or emotionally expressive terms; there are those who think primarily in terms of structure; and there are those who still design with an innate sense of classic proportion and classic elegance. Yet each of these four classes has a new understanding of the logic of structure, the logic of materials, and the logic of plan. All unite in feeling that inspiration must come first from the problem itself and second from hopes for future developments, rather than from any turning back to past styles. The greatness of Wright has become more and more apparent; his complete independence from the earlier controversies and his refusal to be moved by slogans and accepted dogmas have been seen to be a primary source of his strength, and the brilliant tour de force of his use of concrete and of glass —as, for instance, in the buildings for the Johnson Wax Company at Racine—has proved him to be still a creative genius comparable only to the greatest figures of the past. Yet this universal appreciation has not meant discipleship in the sense that American architects attempt to design like Wright; it is rather that with the example of his independence, his sense of plan, and his feeling for materials and their creative use American architects attempt to design like themselves.

The greatest achievements in the architecture of the United States since the Second World War have been in four fields: business buildings, hospitals, houses, and schools.

Among office buildings, that for the Secretariat of the United Nations, with its long façades all in glass, reveals the power of simple geometry and some of the possibilities in the use of light wall surfaces of glass and metal to be discussed in more detail later; but the climax in this type of building thus far has come in Lever House in New York, by Skidmore, Owings & Merrill, where the geometry is both more complex and yet more refined and the glass walls are handled with a simpler directness. These two structures, coupled with Pietro Belluschi's Equitable Building in Portland, in which all structural members are surfaced in shining metal, represent almost the ultimate developments in their field.

A new concept of medical care, with a tremendous emphasis on out-patient and clinic services, has given new directions to hospital design and, where space is ample, has led to compositions in which frequently a tall ward building is tied to and surrounded by lower structures for service and out-patient departments. The great danger in these buildings is the loss of human scale and an emphasis on the mechanics of healing rather than on the emotional ease of the patient. But newer developments in psychosomatic medicine are tending to correct this imbalance, and the best hospitals strive always to humanize their gigantic scale with refined detail and appropriate color. Especially interesting advances in this humanizing trend are apparent in much of the work of Isadore Rosenfield, as, for example, in the medical center of Puerto Rico.

In the residential field the effect of what has sometimes been termed the San Francisco Bay style—because it is based largely on the conditions existing in that area—has been great, particularly in such matters as relationship to site, the creative use of wood, and general informality of treatment. During the later 1940's, however, another influence appeared: the development of what is known as post-and-plank construction, in which the structure becomes basically a classic repetition of rhythmically spaced wooden posts supporting roofs and floors of heavy planks, with a minimum of beams; walls and partitions, often of plywood and glass, are filled in between as necessary. In a sense this is a sort of wooden analogy to the concrete design of Perret. So numerous are the excellent examples of country house design that any listing is bound to be arbitrary, but Wright himself, Mies van der Rohe, Marcel Breuer, Neutra, Harwell Harris, Belluschi, Carl Koch, Edward D. Stone, George Nelson, Twitchell & Rudolph, Schweiker & Elting, and Harris Armstrong may perhaps be singled out as leaders in this varied field.

But it is perhaps in school architecture the country over that the most constructive and the most revolutionary achievements have been made. Now at last the lessons of decentralization and of child scale which Dudok had first set forth in Hilversum schools have been almost universally accepted, and, except in a few large cities where congestion still forces the erection of enormous buildings of impersonal type, schools—especially elementary schools—tend to be spread out, one-story structures, with classrooms informally arranged, often with movable furniture, and with lighting designed not on the old unilateral principle (which was useful only with fixed desks, and even then hard on left-handed children) but with the desire of equalizing the illumination and producing a pleasant general light everywhere by means of windows on both sides of the room or by artfully arranged skylights and clerestories. Here again, as in the case of house design, particularization is difficult, but in this field the pioneering of William Lescaze, Richard Neutra, and Perkins & Will deserves special notice. Among buildings for higher education, the brilliant concrete buildings of the University of Miami at Coral Gables, Florida, by Robert Law Weed and associates, the Saarinens' new buildings for Drake University in Des Moines, Iowa, and the little library of Carroll College at Waukesha, Wisconsin, by Van der Gracht & Kilham, all show the beautiful possibilities of true twentieth-century architecture in the college field. The new group for Goucher College, near Baltimore, by Moore & Hutchins, is distinguished by its plan and its stylistic simplicity, but generally in college and university buildings conservative inertia still holds sway.

In all the domestic and school work, even the strict limitations on materials imposed as a defense measure have sometimes served as additional stimuli to fresh design, and wood has been treated with ever growing freedom and originality. To make a minimum construction of wood which shall at the same time be beautiful demands not only a sound structural sense but a great aesthetic imagination, and the simple expression of a well-designed structure has brought a new kind of direct charm into many recent buildings. When limitations are lifted, this new pleasure in expressed structure will probably remain.

It is hazardous to predict what future developments will be, for in the mid-1950's American life is generally in a state of confusion and perplexity and many conflicting ideals are being vociferously upheld. Since these ideals will inevitably affect the forms, the techniques, and the ideals behind American buildings, the future of American architecture today lies less in the hands of architects than in the hands of the population at large.

Five major expositions have afforded us an opportunity to evaluate the achievements of modern architecture.

NEW YORK, LEVER HOUSE. Skidmore, Owings & Merrill, architects; Gordon Bunshaft in charge. (Courtesy Lever Brothers.)

DETROIT, GENERAL MOTORS CORPORATION, RESEARCH LABORATORIES. Saarinen, Saarinen and Associates, architects. (Ezra Stoller.)

Plate 89

PARIS, MUSEUM OF PUBLIC WORKS. Auguste Perret, architect. (*Construction Moderne.*)

PAMPULHA, BRAZIL, CHAPEL. Oscar Niemeyer, architect. (Courtesy Museum of Modern Art.)

Plate 90

PORTLAND, ORE., ZION LUTHERAN CHURCH. Pietro Belluschi, architect. (Roger Sturtevant.)

ST. LOUIS, B'NAI AMOONA SYNAGOGUE; MODEL. Eric Mendelsohn, architect. (Courtesy Eric Mendelsohn.)

Plate 91

RIO DE JANEIRO, ISTITUTO VITAL-BRAZIL. Alvaro Vital-Brazil, architect. (Courtesy *Progressive Architecture* and Alvaro Vital-Brazil.)

LONDON, FINSBURY HEALTH CENTER. Barthold Lubetkin and Tecton, architects. (Courtesy British Information Services.)

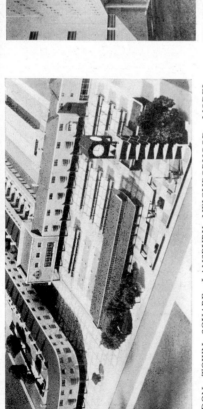

LONDON, TOWN SQUARE, LANSBURY NEIGHBORHOOD; MODEL. Frederick Gibberd, architect. (Courtesy British Information Services.)

LONDON, TRINITY CONGREGATIONAL CHURCH, LANSBURY NEIGHBORHOOD. C. C. Handisyde and D. Rogers Stark, architects. (Courtesy British Information Services.)

Plate 92

STOCKHOLM, PUBLIC SCHOOL. E. G. Asplund, architect. (Courtesy American Swedish News Exchange.)

LONDON, SUSAN LAWRENCE SCHOOL, LANSBURY NEIGHBORHOOD. Yorke, Rosenburg & Mardall, architects. (Courtesy British Information Services.)

LAKELAND, FLA., FLORIDA SOUTHERN COLLEGE, ADMINISTRATION BUILDING. Frank Lloyd Wright, architect. (Courtesy Florida Southern College.)

RIVERSIDE, ILL., BLYTHE PARK SCHOOL. Perkins & Will, architects. (Hedrich-Blessing.)

Plate 93

WESTBURY, LONG ISLAND, CONGER GOODYEAR HOUSE. Edward D. Stone, architect. (Ezra Stoller.)

VENICE, FLA., SIEGRIST HOUSE. Twitchell & Rudolph, architects. (Ezra Stoller.)

Plate 94

LOS ANGELES, JOHNSON HOUSE. Harwell H. Harris, architect. (Maynard Parker.)

MONTECITO, CALIF., TREMAINE HOUSE. Richard Neutra, architect. (Julius Shulman.)

EXETER, CALIF., UNION HIGH SCHOOL. Franklin & Kump, architects. (Courtesy Ernest J. Kump.)

CARMEL, CALIF., WAYFARERS' CHAPEL. Lloyd Wright, architect. (Julius Shulman.)

Plate 95

MILBURN, N. J., SYNAGOGUE. Percival Goodman, architect; Herbert Ferber, sculptor. (Alexandre Georges.)

SAN FRANCISCO, MORRIS JEWELRY STORE; INTERIOR. Frank Lloyd Wright, architect. (Maynard Parker.)

UNIVERSITY OF MEXICO, LIBRARY. Carlos Lazo, Tomas O'Gorman and Associates, architects. (Courtesy Carlos Lazo and University of Mexico.)

Plate 96

The first, only local, was the Weissenhof housing exposition of 1927, already referred to, in which modern architecture received its first great chance to display its possibilities and in which works by Oud, Mies van der Rohe, and others were remarkably prophetic of what was to come. The importance of this exposition has been increasingly realized.

The second was the Chicago Century of Progress Exposition of 1933. Here for the first time American modern architects faced problems of major significance in design; yet, just as the architectural world of the early 1930's was confused, so the Chicago exposition was in important elements confused and the general plan incoherent. Nevertheless its effect was great, because hundreds of thousands of people had an opportunity to see a number of buildings which in their design made no concessions to past tradition and a few in which the use of glass and metal brought new visions of building possibilities.

The third was the Paris Exposition of 1937, characterized by a remarkable general plan, a superb use of the site, and buildings almost all of which were distinguished expressions of various phases of the modern movement, from the neo-monumentalism of the new buildings of the Trocadero site and the art museums which were permanent to the International Style "tent" designed by Le Corbusier for L'Esprit Nouveau. The national buildings were also of surpassing interest because they so clearly expressed the dominant ideals of the participating nations, from the heavy neo-classic of the German building, through the stark power of the Russian, the quiet suavity of the Belgian, and the mechanized beauty of the Czechoslovakian, to the delicate woodwork of the Finnish.

The fourth was the New York World's Fair of 1939-40—Gargantuan in plan, dynamic in spirit, with occasional buildings of great beauty, and with its enormous trylon and perisphere to show the power of pure geometry.

The last was the Festival of Britain in 1950, in London crowded in general plan, with its structurally impressive Dome of Discovery by Ralph Tubbs and its large permanent concert hall by Matthew & Martin. Here it was details which were of especial interest, and the importance given to sculpture was expressive of a new feeling toward the minor arts and their connection with architecture. Significantly, the most effective portion of the exposition was the sample housing group, a permanent development: the Lansbury Neighborhood, where a charming town square by Frederick Gibberd and a new gaiety of color showed the possibilities of modern architecture in making an attractive human community.

Another excellent weathervane to show the direction that international architecture is taking was the design and erection of the buildings for the United Nations in New York. These also simply express the variety of ideals current at mid-century. A board of architects was appointed, with representatives from all the major countries, and to them was given the responsibility of developing a scheme for the site donated by the Rockefellers. This board included many of the most brilliant architects of the time, but their ideals varied all the way from neo-classicism to the strictest International School thinking. The result was bound to be a compromise, but the scheme finally adopted was supposed to be basically functional yet expressively monumental. Large geometric masses were disposed with a kind of formal informality. The Secretariat building was conceived as an office building pure and simple; hence it was made into a vertical skyscraper—a choice open to serious criticism because of the social as well as the purely executive functions of the Secretariat members. The Assembly building was planned as a sort of trumpet-shaped auditorium, obviously based distantly on Le Corbusier's design for the League of Nations buildings. This scheme was then given to an executive committee, under the leadership of Harrison & Abramovitz, for execution. Various changes in program, such as the alteration of the trumpet-shaped auditorium into a fundamentally circular domed room with galleries projecting from one side, were forced into the original scheme; the result is that frequently the exteriors and interiors have little mutual relationship, there are enormous amounts of waste circulation space, and sequences in plan often seem both contorted and meaningless. The execution in details was brilliant but more and more became an exercise in almost purely a priori concepts rather than a simple expression of the requirements. The treatment of the site was hardly convincing; the brilliance of the great parallelepiped of the Secretariat building is undeniable, but the connections between the various parts are loose and the whole, elegant and beautifully detailed as it is, is hardly expressive of the inspiring ideals on which the United Nations was founded.

Modern architecture as of the mid-twentieth century is not a style. It is rather, perhaps, a general constellation of attitudes toward structure and use and materials. It has many unsolved problems, and its achievements thus far have by no means fulfilled all the architectural needs of the day. The two chief questions are those of expression and the related concept of monumentality. Popular protests against wholesale acceptance of modern architecture here and there continue, almost always based on its failure to satisfy some of the deepest urges of mankind—the urge toward a pure, almost non-functional beauty, the urge toward personal expression, and the desire for buildings which shall minister to the spirit as much as to the body.

What, in other words, is the place of pure aesthetics in modern architecture? There has been talk of what some critics call a "new aesthetic," an aesthetic built on the temporary and the exciting rather than on balance and serenity, on emotional stress rather than on emotional satisfaction. Yet people demand serenity and repose, perhaps even more today than ever before. Shall architecture, then, in its search for an expression of excitement and stress, for the "dynamic," leave these thirsts of humanity unfulfilled? This is a basic problem that affects architecture all over the world and today continues to divide architects. But the very existence of the controversy reveals a change in the attitude of even the most radical thinkers; for yesterday they would not have admitted that the problem even existed, nor would they have felt it necessary to erect a theory of a new aesthetic to support their International Style position. All the conditions of modern life, they claim, are transitory; change is of the essence of growth; power and the expression of power are characteristic of modern industry and modern science; science reveals to us a universe no longer static; why, then, should buildings be other than powerful, dynamic, and expressive of the basic stress of nature? Yet those who demand an architecture of a different type—an architecture of restraint, balance, ease, serenity—argue that despite science, despite industry, and despite the achievement of atomic power (the most characteristic product of which thus far has been the bomb) the human, creative soul is above and beyond these things and demands for its environment buildings which shall themselves transcend the disturbances and the stresses, the destructiveness and the temporary quality of modern life. They claim that this attitude is not escapism but transcendence; it is putting the one great reality we have—the individual human consciousness—at the peak, where it belongs, and liberating it from its slavery to time and confusion.

The same controversy surrounds the concept of the monumental. What is monumentality? Is it not the quality in buildings which is greater than the merely personal on the one hand or the merely temporal on the other? It is the expression of mankind rather than of a single individual, an expression of the community of interests, the fellowship of many minds and many hands devoted to the creation of something greater than any one single effort could produce. And, furthermore, it is the effort of man, millennia-old, to transcend the limitations of time. Monumentality and permanence are not the same, but they have close relationships. Today we read the history of the past in its buildings; we learn the dreams and the ideals which it fostered through the buildings that have stood, even in ruin, to fire our imaginations. In these, we feel, man has proved his greatness; here before us is the evidence. Shall we be less great than these people of the past? Shall we be more timorous before the wheel of time, more slavish to its inexorable revolution? Many persons refuse to make this abnegation. It may well be that certain buildings, designed merely to satisfy temporary needs, should be impermanent and should be replaced periodically, so that mankind may always have elbowroom to do his daily work. But there are other types of buildings of which perhaps this is not true—buildings that express the ideals or aims, religious or social or even individual, which have seemed to remain constant throughout the history of Western civilization. In such buildings, some claim, mankind should build for permanence and for enduring inspiration as well as for temporary efficiency. And to guarantee permanence perhaps pure aesthetic quality is the greatest and most efficient means, for somehow time itself and the stress of war and human destruction appear automatically to avoid disturbing or to disturb as little as possible those buildings in which the aesthetic quality has been recognized as supreme.

These, then, are the two great questions which divide architects today all over the world, and in these architectural controversies lies a significant guide to the great controversies that trouble human life as a whole. Are we to seek for a society based on standardization, on mere physical efficiency— a society in which the person is a cog in a great machine and in which the production of anything, irrespective almost of its usefulness, is one of the two great aims and the creation of unlimited power, even for destructive purposes, the other? Or is the rich development of the individual to be the end? Is what the individual feels, loves, or rejects really the most important product of living? Is the aim of life to make people love one another or hate one another? In other words, is life to become the beehive and the anthill, or a stimulus to creativity and fellow feeling—where co-operation is voluntary and variety is as commendable as uniformity? To these problems architects naturally can give no final answer; what they build is what their clients want and need. They can help direct and suggest; but the future of architecture, like the future of the human race, lies in the hands of the people as a whole.

INDEX

INDEX